MW01249197

THE PRESIDENTIAL FAMILIES

By the same author:
Presidential Quiz Book

THE PRESIDENTIAL FAMILIES

E. H. Gwynne-Thomas

HIPPOCRENE BOOKS
New York

Permission to print excerpts from the following works is gratefully acknowledged:

Harper and Row: Jerry Ford, *A Time to Heal*; Eleanor Roosevelt, *This I Remember*; Leach and Brown, *The Garfield Orbit*; Lester David, *The Lonely Lady of San Clemente*

W.W. Norton: William McFeely, *Grant*

Greenwood Press: Ishbel Ross, *An American Family*

Houghton Mifflin: Rosalynn Carter, *First Lady from Plains*

Sunday School Board of the Southern Baptist Convention: Jimmy Carter, *Why Not the Best*

Dresser, Chapman and Grimes: Phyllis Robins, *Robert A. Taft*

Ayer Publishers: Elizabeth Keckley, *Behind the Scenes*

Macmillan: Margaret Truman, *Bess W. Truman*

Putnam: Elliott Roosevelt, *Mother R*

Stern and Day: Madeleine Edmondson and Alden Cohen, *Women of Watergate*

Doubleday: Rose Kennedy, *Times to Remember*

American Heritage: Francis Russell, *An American Dynasty*

Berkley Publishing Group: James Roosevelt, *My Parents*

For information, address: Hippocrene Books, Inc.,
171 Madison Avenue, New York, NY 10016.

Library of Congress Cataloging-in-Publication Data
Gwynne-Thomas, E. H.
   The presidential families / E.H. Gwynne-Thomas.
   Bibliography
   Includes index.
   ISBN 0-87052-590-5
   1. Presidents—United States—Family. 2. United States-
-Biography. I. Title.
E176.1.G89 1989
973'.09'92—dc19
Printed in the United States of America.   8921807

To
I.V.B.
and
E.F.G-T

Contents

Preface

This work offers an informal overview of some of the many problems, pressures and pleasures encountered by White House parents in the upbringing of their children. Only one president (James Buchanan) remained a bachelor for his entire life. Four others had no children of their own, but of these, three (Washington, Madison, Jackson) were directly involved in the rearing and supervision of the activities of step-children and/or nieces and nephews; the fourth (Polk) was married for twenty-five years but he and his wife were without either natural or adopted children. A few presidents were alleged to have fathered children out of wedlock, but Grover Cleveland alone openly acknowledged his transgression and, in consequence, a charitable and compassionate electorate duly voted him in as chief executive of his country. The extra-marital escapades of Warren Harding were not revealed until after his death.

A total of 143 children (85 boys and 58 girls) were born to 33 presidents and their wives, and, of this total, no fewer than 25 children were fathered by just two successive presidents: William Henry Harrison (10) and John Tyler (15, by two wives). It is highly unlikely that this impressive achievement will be surpassed in the foreseeable future, if ever.

A review of White House family affairs provides ample evidence that in no way do the parents escape the troubles, trials and tribulations endured by average American fathers and mothers. Status confers no privilege, and what clearly emerges is that, for the most part, children remain entirely unimpressed by their high-ranking identities as sons or daughters of Presidents of the United States. Furthermore, not merely do the children appear unimpressed, but, in many instances, they have overtly displayed, in no uncertain manner, resentment and anger against the White House goldfish bowl existence, by which every minor character idiosyncrasy or irrelevant behavior is accorded nationwide scrutiny, exposure and publicity, to the embarrassment and humiliation of children and parents alike.

To their credit, presidents and their wives have usually reacted in a positive and forthright manner, combining a commendable degree of stiff upper-lip fortitude with perhaps a sad note of resignation and regret, but almost always with unbending familial loyalty and support for what they explain away as the irrepressible urge for independence along with the natural exuberance of youth.

It was probably the one and only Teddy Roosevelt, who ultimately epitomized the on-going White House dilemma: when privately reprimanded for not better controlling the boisterous behavior-in-public of his mercurial daughter, the famous Alice, Roosevelt tersely responded that he could either be President of the United States *or* he could manage Alice; in no way could he do both at one and the same time.

George Washington

(1788–1796)

It would appear to be the inevitable fate of all persons who either seek power or have power thrust upon them to be subject to relentless and unending scrutiny and probing regarding their public and personal lives. Those who indulge in these investigative exercises offer justification in the alleged insatiable appetite of the man-in-the-street for information concerning the credit-worthiness of the individual elected or appointed to serve in a position of dignity, trust, and responsibility.

No difficulties arise when facts can be verified, documented, or authenticated, but when these fall into dispute or are obscured by rumor and innuendo, then much of the truth may dissolve into myth, legend and silence—most often the silence of the grave whence comes neither confutation nor confirmation. All that remains is the nebulous penumbra of belief, and the greater the uncertainty, the more powerful are the emotions generated on the one hand by protagonists, who assert that those who dispute the virtue of a revered leader are motivated by base impulse, and on the other hand by antagonists who aver that there can be

1

no smoke without fire and, for that reason, allegations of misconduct or impropriety must have some firm basis in fact.

It is a matter of no little astonishment that of all presidents of the United States, the first, George Washington, probably suffered most from the hands of his detractors. As a public man not only was he accused of cherishing ambitions of establishing himself as a new monarch surrounded by the embellishments of a regal court, but he was also made to suffer acutely from disreputable allegations of his misdeeds in high office emanating from the poison-tipped barbs of Benjamin Franklin Bache, the grandson of Benjamin Franklin.[1] Bache was editor of the Philadelphia newspaper, *Aurora,* and he never passed by the opportunity of subjecting Washington to great pain and distress, since the latter had limited access for redressing and refuting the calumnies.

Defending the integrity of his public image was not an exercise unique to Washington, since all political personalities have at some time or other been subject to defamatory statements and allegations. But what is, perhaps, unique is the degree to which particulars of Washington's personal life fell under scrutiny both during his lifetime and well into the nineteenth century, providing historians with a lavish field of inquiry, whose conclusions remain open or closed, according to the whims of the individual reader.

There exists an oft-quoted statement to the effect that God gave Washington no children so that his country might call him Father, a generally accepted conclusion down the ages, except that, according to the *National Dictionary of American Biography,* during his own lifetime a certain "Thomas Posey is said to have been the natural son of George Washington."[2] And who was Thomas Posey? He was presumably named after his father, Captain Thomas Posey, who owned Rover's Delight, a small farm located near Mount Vernon. Both Captain Posey and Washington had participated in the Forbes campaign of the Indian and French Wars. Having retired from military service Posey settled down, was twice married and had four children, named Lawrence, Thomas, Price, and Milly, respectively. He proved to be a most incompetent farmer, whose property was eventually purchased by Washington at a bankruptcy sale. Nevertheless, Posey and his family were not only made hospitable at Mount Vernon, but the daugher, Milly, moved into the home to become the playmate of Patsy Custis for several years, and her dancing lessons were paid for by Washington, who also financed her brother, Lawrence, through school. Price, another brother, attached himself to Jacky, Martha's son, and gouged him for money, while Thomas, the third brother, was guided by Washington as to his future career.

The question arises as to why Washington should have been so generous to such a pathetic and impoverished neighbor family. Rumor has it that Lawrence Posey was born while eighteen-year-old George Washington was in Barbados where his much adored half-brother, Lawrence, had taken him because George had gotten a local girl with child. The elder Posey had married the girl, and brought the child up as his own, but, in return for silence, had demanded monetary aid from the natural father for the remainder of his life.

From here on, even the rumors are confused: in the early 1900's a letter[3] presumably written by George Washington to Lawrence Posey was discovered, with the salutation "My dear *Son*." But the last word was so indistinct that it might well have been "My dear *Sir*." The letter, however, contained nothing of a personal nature.

Returning to the *National Dictionary of American Biography* and Thomas Posey, the latter was born on July 9, 1750, of Thomas Posey and Elizabeth Lloyd, "of a family of high social standing." In 1773, he married Martha Matthews, daugher of Sampson Matthews of Augusta City, Virginia, but she died; and in 1784 he married Mary, daughter of John Alexander (founder of Alexandria, Virginia) and widow of Major George Thornton. During the Revolutionary War he was commissioned Captain and served with the Seventh Virginia Regiment. Posey participated in the surrender of the British general, Burgoyne, was with Lafayette at the Battle of Monmouth, and with Washington at the final British surrender at Yorktown. He later served with Anthony Wayne in the Indian campaigns in the Northwest Territories. He settled in Kentucky after resigning from the army in 1794, and was elected state senator in 1805–6. He rejoined the army during the War of 1812, but for a brief period only, since in 1813, he was appointed as (last) governor of Indiana Territory. He served for three years in that capacity until the state of Indiana was created and admitted to the Union in 1816. Posey died at Shawneetown, Illinois, on March 18, 1818.

Yet another rumor associated Washington with Alexander Hamilton, his Secretary of the Treasury, of illegitimate birth but of whom he is said to have often referred to as "my son." In this instance, it has been alleged that while Washington was in Barbados in 1751 (attempting to escape from the consequences of his having fathered Thomas Lawrence George Posey) he became involved with a married woman by whom he fathered Alexander Hamilton. Hamilton's birth was actually registered in Nevis (St. Croix) in 1755, a discrepancy easily set aside by the rumor-mongers as having arisen from the deliberate falsification of records. Hamilton's mother left her husband and went to live with James Hamilton, a Scot, who claimed to be Alexander's father.

Long after Washington's death, there occurred in Providence, Rhode Island, a case of litigation, Bowen v. Chase (1872) which once again must have tickled the palate of all those fascinated by the alleged foibles and misdeeds of the aristocracy. The plaintiff, George Washington Bowen, aged 78, claimed he was the son of Eliza Jumel, a shameless lady of easy virtue (and herself the daughter of Phebe Kelley, a well-known prostitute of the day). At the time of his birth in 1794, Eliza was known as Betsy Bowen, and one version of the story alleges that she was actually George Washington's daughter by Phebe Kelley, so that George Washington Bowen was not Washington's son, but his grandson.

In due course, Betsy Bowen married Stephen Jumel and became known as Eliza Jumel. Her husband died, and she became intimate with Aaron Burr but they soon divorced, and she resumed the name of Eliza Jumel. The court case of 1872 related to her will in which she bequeathed her estate to her niece, and it was this provision which was contested by George Washington Bowen. The case reached the Supreme Court which disallowed his claim, but throughout the more than twelve years of the protracted proceedings, he never failed to make public his blood affinity to the Founding Father.

Yet one further alleged episode related to Washington and Airy Carter, a slave girl at Mount Vernon, by whom he is supposed to have fathered a daughter, Maria, but this legendary postscript has been modified so as to implicate George Washington Parke Custis (Martha's grandson) as being the actual villain in the affair. Maria eventually married Charles Syphax and bore him ten children "whose many descendants have contributed largely to the George Washington Custis lineage."[4]

Were all of the foregoing love-life exploits of the nation's first President to be believed and verified, it might have been expected that such a sexually precocious youth should have been capable of fathering a prodigious progeny as a married man. After all, he himself was the product of a potent, quiver-full father, Augustine Washington, twice married, first to Jane Butler by whom he had four children, and then to Mary Ball, by whom he had six.[5] Of the four children of Augustine's first marriage, only Lawrence lived to reach maturity, and he and George Washington had a very close, endearing relationship. Lawrence joined the British navy and was promoted captain under Admiral Vernon.[6] Had it not been for the objections of Mary Ball, George would eagerly have accepted the offer of serving as midshipman under his half-brother's command, but this was not to be, so George remained a land-lubber—obviously a fortuitous event for the emerging new nation-state.

Lawrence had married Anne Fairfax (daughter of Colonel William Fairfax, a wealthy landowner in Virginia) by whom he had four children, all of whom died at an early age. In 1751 Lawrence fell sick of tuberculosis and went on a voyage for his health to Barbados, accompanied by his half-brother, George, a voyage embellished by all the subsequent rumors of the latter's sexual escapades, but it did nothing for Lawrence's health, and he died in 1752. Some years later, with the death of Anne, wife of Lawrence, George Washington inherited the substantial estate of Mount Vernon, which initially consisted of 2,700 acres but was eventually expanded to at least 8,000.

By marriage, Lawrence Washington was brother-in-law of George William Fairfax, who had, in 1748, married Sally Cary, a vivacious and charming girl of 18. The Fairfax and Washington families were neighbors and were drawn into frequent and close social contact. George, at age 16, had been employed by the Fairfax family as assistant surveyor of their extensive estates. Introspective and withdrawn by nature, and two years younger than Sally, he was no doubt at first reluctant to participate in the dancing and theatrical productions which she initiated, but flattered by her attention and coquetry, he became completely captivated by her. Yet, recognizing the impossibilities of the situation, he did not lose his head. Well known to his many biographers were several young ladies with whom his name was to be associated over the next decade, including Betsy Fauntleroy and Lucy Grymes, both Tidewater belles who rejected his advances, as did Jane Souther and Mary Cary (Sally's sister).

Washington's military activities during the 1750's no doubt helped to alleviate his lack of success in the world of love, and perhaps helped sober his ignited passions. In 1758, he laid down his command and retired to the life of a gentleman-farmer at Mount Vernon, and was elected to the Virginia House of Burgesses. In the same year, at the home of Major and Mrs. Richard Chamberlayne, he had been introduced to an attractive twenty-six-year-old widow of seven months, Martha Dandridge Custis. A quick courtship followed, and they were married in January, 1759. The Fairfax family remained their neighbors until the cumulative events of the Revolution made them take the irrevocable step of returning to England in 1773. George Washington never saw Sally again. Her husband died in 1787, and she lived on in reduced circumstances until 1810. The young Sally remained in Washington's mind as the ideal, pedestalled image of unrequited love untarnished by the ravages of age and time, and it was she who was the recipient of a sad and poignant letter written by Washington one year before his death when he was 66 and she 68. In it, he recalled some of the memorable events of his life, none of which, he wrote, "have been able to eradicate from my mind the recollections of those happy moments—the happiest of my life—which I have enjoyed in your company. . . ." What must have passed through each of their minds at this time can only be conjectured, but, most obviously, time had only partly healed for Washington the wounds of separation over the past quarter century which had elapsed since he had last seen Sally. Yet there was never anything in his forty-year marriage with Martha which even gave reason to suspect that he was anything but faithful, kind, and solicitious, and she, in turn, was an affectionate, efficient, domesticated wife. She ran a well-regulated household and all was serene except for the unexplained absence of children. Washington was childless and that fact must have galled him, considering that his father had produced ten, and that most of his surviving siblings had also reared families, with his favorite sister, Betty (Lewis), being the mother of no fewer than eleven children.

Martha, herself, was the oldest of the eight children of thrice-married John Dandridge. She was 17 when, in 1749, she married Daniel Custis, a prosperous plantation owner by whom she had four children of whom two sons had died in infancy. Custis had died in August, 1757, leaving her with a son Jacky (aged 4) and a daughter, Patsy (aged 2), but well endowed with a large estate and an ample income. It was not the custom of the day for young widows to pine in perpetuity over the death of a husband no matter how beloved, and Martha was no exception. Obviously, care was needed in the selection of an appropriate partner who was no mere ambitious or unscrupulous fortune-seeker—of such the colonies had no lack. When she met Washington she was at least assured that he was certainly not to be classified in the foregoing category: he was a wealthy and eligible young bachelor of excellent repute and integrity. In his case, her main concern lay rather in the question as to whether he would accept her two young children as his own, and would bear no resentment or animosity towards them in the event children were born of his marriage to Martha.

The incredible fact is that, while Washington may indeed have harbored inner regrets for the remainder of his life regarding his impotency, he was to prove a remarkably indulgent stepfather, adoptive father, foster father (or whatever other term be employed for surrogate fathers), not merely to Jacky and Patsy, but to a host of offspring of his immediate relatives. In due course, Mount Vernon (as well as the presidential mansions in New York and Philadelphia, respectively) literally came to be inundated by all manner of young (as well as old) relatives, and Washington, far from resenting their intrusion upon his personal privacy and the resulting strain upon his financial resources,[7] came to expect and welcome their lively and ebullient contribution to what otherwise might have been an isolated, lonely, albeit serene establishment, fossilized in the expectancy of inevitable death.

Washington set out to please his new bride in every way, and all the evidence indicates that he had no scruples about overindulging her young children. His record of personal expenditures on their behalf reveal that, in the year of his marriage, he ordered from London for Master Custis a suit of summer clothes "to be made of something light and thin," four pairs each of "strong shoes," "handsome silver knee and shoe buckles," "six little books for children beginning to read," and "ten shillings worth of toys." Orders dispatched to England took the best part of a year to arrive, and eventually listed among the toys were: a bird on a bellows, a grocer's shop, a Prussian dragoon, and "a man smoking."

Likewise, for Patsy, were sent orders to London for: eight yards of fine printed linen; eight pairs of kid mitts; two pairs of silk shoes; a piece of flowered dimity, two fans, two bonnets, two necklaces, "a fashionably dressed baby" (doll), and "one Stiffened Coat of Fashl. Silk made to Packthread Stays."[8]

At Mount Vernon each child had a personal house servant: Jacky had a boy named Joe, and Patsy a maid named Rose, both servants being under the supervision of Molly, their nurse. As they developed in age, the education of the children was initiated by Walter Magowan who was brought in as a resident member of the household, while included in their social advancement activities were dancing classes held in each of the large Tidewater mansions in turn, to which the children were transported in coaches along with either their parents or nursemaids.

When Magowan, in due course, announced his intention of returning to England to become an ordained clergyman, it became necessary to find some alternative form of education for Jacky. It had become obvious for some time to Washington that what Jacky needed most was a strong dose of discipline, which he himself had tried to apply but desisted through the intervention of the overindulgent Martha. Jacky had developed into a charming, but somewhat irresponsible, obstinate, and perverse-willed boy who urgently needed to be taken out of the home and placed in association and competition with his peer group. He had taken every advantage of his mother and had set her up against the concerned stepfather who had his own definite opinions as to the discipline of a wayward youth, but was yet hesitant to apply his methods for fear of offending his much-loved wife.

Magowan's departure came as a heaven-sent opportunity to resolve the dilemma. Washington decided to place Jacky in the care of a certain Mr. Boucher, who had come from England with his sister, Jinny, and had set up school on a small plantation in Caroline County, Virginia. Since the only alternative appeared to be that of sending Jacky to England[9] for his education, Martha's reluctance to part with Jacky was quite probably overcome as being the lesser of two necessary evils. So it was that Jacky, at age 15, left home and, during the course of the succeeding two years, his conduct and exploits occasioned appreciable correspondence between Washington and Boucher. The latter having some two dozen other boys in his care was little disposed to tolerate all of Jacky's little idiosyncrasies, and life for the young lad was infinitely more spartan in terms of overall comfort and food than that at Mount Vernon. Moreover, Washington believed that the focusing of more of Jacky's attention upon his studies would measurably assist in keeping him out of mischief. Washington wrote to Boucher:

> His mind is a good deal released from study and more than ever turned to dogs and horses and guns; indeed upon dress and equipment, which till of late he has discovered little inclination of giving in to. I must beg the favor of you, therefore, to keep him closer to those useful branches of learning which he ought now to be acquainted with, and as much as possible under your own eye. Without these I fear he will too soon think himself above control, and be not much the better for the extraordinary expenses attending his living in Annapolis.

For his part, Boucher concurred with Washington, replying that he had noted that Jacky was indolent and showed "a love of pleasure of a kind exceedingly uncommon at his years."

Jacky appeared to suffer from colic attacks, concerning which Boucher wrote, "He is fond of fruit and what is worse for him, he is fond of cucumbers, and to these, I doubt not in a great measure he owes his bilious complaints." Of more immediate importance to Washington was his concern that Jacky be inoculated for smallpox, since he himself had contracted the fever on his visit to Barbados with his half-brother, Lawrence, in 1751, and had nearly died. The problem was Martha who envisioned the worst of consequences at every step. But Washington was determined yet knowing well the risks he was taking, so, in secrecy, he had Jacky inoculated, and though he developed mild fevers, the undertaking was successful, Martha being informed only when the matter was finally concluded.

Boucher had in mind the Grand Tour of Europe for Jacky, but, in this instance, both Martha and George agreed it was entirely out of the question, though for different reasons: Martha, because of her vivid imagination as to the accidents, perils, and mishappenings that could occur to her only son and heir during such a prolonged absence; George, on his part, took the more practical, down-to-earth viewpoint that the cost of financing both Jacky and Boucher on what he believed was nothing more than a fabulous joyride at his expense would be prohibitive. There was no Grand Tour.

In due course, Boucher married and, being attentive to his new wife, he apparently became somewhat lax in school discipline and supervision. Boucher had already reported that Jacky's good looks and charming manners had resulted in many social invitations, but "he seldom goes about without learning something I could have wished him not to have learned." One of these invitations had involved Jacky with a certain Miss Galloway, sister of one of the students at the school. Boucher had frowned upon this association and had ventured his opinion that the Galloway family were indulging in fortune-hunting, and that any advances on their part should be strongly discouraged. Washington gave him full credit for prudence in this matter, but he was far less pleased with respect to Jacky's next amorous adventure, which involved the Calvert family of Mount Airy, Maryland. Benjamin Calvert had ten children, and, while at Annapolis, Jacky had been invited to social gatherings at the home and at the race course. A close friendship had developed between Eleanor (Nelly), the eldest Calvert girl and with little prior indication to Martha and George, there suddenly came a letter from Jacky announcing his engagement to Nelly (who was not yet 16). Washington, caught completely by surprise, roundly berated Boucher for his laxity, but recognizing that the damage had been done and that it was now his, and not Boucher's, responsibility with respect to further action, he decided to write directly to Benjamin Calvert commenting on Jacky as follows:

> His youth, inexperience and unriped Education is, and will be insuperable obstacles, in my eye, to the completion of the marriage—If the Affection which they have vowed for each other is fixed upon a Solid Basis, it will receive no diminution in the course of two or three years—If unfortunately there should be an abatement of Affection on either side, or both, it had better precede, than follow after, Marriage—

Furious with Boucher, and determined to isolate the lovers, Washington decided to withdraw Jacky from the school and send him to King's College, New York, where he could pursue studies in estate management to better equip him for his future responsibilities.[10] So, in May, 1773, Jacky was enrolled at the college, and Washington had every reason to believe that he had successfully negotiated the crisis to his own satisfaction. He was wrong, for in June, tragedy struck the family at Mount Vernon.

Some years earlier, Jacky's sister, young Patsy, at age 12 had suffered a bad fall resulting from a fit of epilepsy. She had since been subjected to all manner of primitive medical remedies, including the wearing of an iron ring, and treatment at the baths at Berkeley Springs in the mountains, all to no good effect, but Washington never ceased to explore possible alleged new "cures." Despite all her sufferings and afflictions Patsy remained a very sweet and much-loved daughter, but on June 8th, as described by Washington, "She arose from Dinner about four o'clock— soon after which she was seized with one of her usual fitts, and expired in it, in less than two minutes, without uttering a word."

The household was devastated. In the months that followed, Martha in her loneliness, deprived of the company of both her children, was not to be consoled. Washington, a military commander, used to having all his orders obeyed, found himself helpless in a family situation where he was aligned against the combined forces of his wife and Jacky. He held out as long as he could, but in a poignant letter of December 1773, to President Miles Cooper of King's College he wrote regarding Jacky:

> At length I have yielded, contrary to my judgment and much against my wishes to his quitting college in order that he may enter into a new scene of life which I think he would be much better for some years hence. But having his own inclination, the desire of his mother, and the acquiescence of almost all his relatives to encounter, I did not care, as he is the last of his family, to push my opposition too far; and I have therefore submitted to a kind of necessity.

Next year, in February, 1774, Jacky came home permanently to marry his bride of 16, and in time, set up on his estate of Abingdon on the Potomac. Martha remained too grief-stricken to attend the wedding after Patsy's death, but she did write her new daughter-in-law a very moving letter:

> My dear Nelly, God took from me a daughter when June roses were blooming. He has given me another daughter about her age

when Winter winds are blowing to warm my Heart again—Pray accept my Benediction and a wish that you may long live the Loving wife of my happy Son, and a Loving Daughter,

Your Affectionate Mother,

M. Washington.

Nellie lost a baby in 1775, but, in May, 1776, a daughter, Eliza, was born to her at her parent's home at Mount Airy, and Jacky wrote home to his mother:

I cannot pretend to say who the child is like. It is much like Dr. Rumney as anybody else, she has a double chin or something like it, in point of fatness, with fine black hair and eyes. Upon the whole, I think it is as pretty and fine a babe as ever I saw. This is not my opinion also, but the opinion of all who have seen her. . . .

A second daughter, Martha ("Patty") was born in December, 1777, during which year Jacky won election to the Virginia Assembly, as the representative from New Kent County. Yet a third daughter, Eleanor, (Nelly) was born in March 1779, but her mother remained in such a poor state of health that the baby was brought to Mount Vernon for nursing, not so much by Martha, (who had regularly been spending her time with George at the varied winter headquarters of the Continental Army),[11] but by the wife of the recently married Lund Washington.[12] It was not long after that a raiding party from the British Army reached Mount Vernon where Lund is reported to have received them with cold courtesy. Other than doing some small damage and taking away some slaves, they departed leaving the estate unscathed.

Great was the joy in the Custis household when, in 1780, their first son was born, to be christened George Washington Parke Custis in honor of his grandfather. Just as much joy was occasioned in the following year when, after an absence from Mount Vernon of six weary years, the grandfather himself appeared. The tide of war was now turning in favor of the Americans, and the British were being maneuvered into an impossible situation in the Yorktown peninsula. Poised for the final advance, Washington had moved swiftly south with his army, accompanied by a number of French officers in resplendent uniforms. Jacky and his wife came over to Mount Vernon to see Washiangton during his visit, a visit, though brief, that was long enough to dazzle Jacky by the colorful accoutrements of war. He immediately declared his intention to join up with Washington as a volunteer aide, and he left with the army first to Williamsburg and then to Yorktown. Jacky soon learned that the life of a military man was far more than that of a mere peacock parading in

Tidewater mansion parlors. Cornwallis had hoped against hope for British naval reinforcements to break the blockade set up by Admiral de Grasse of the French fleet. He held out for six weeks, during which time the weather had begun to deteriorate. Jacky was completely unaccustomed to camp conditions with its indifferent food and poor sanitation. He caught cold which developed into a fever. Too weak to mount a horse, he watched the surrender ceremony of October 19, 1781, from a carriage. He was then conveyed to Martha's sister's home at Eltham[13] near Williamsburg. Jacky's wife, Nelly, and Martha came over to nurse him but all in vain and Jacky died on November 5th. Washington was present at the last.

Martha was prostrated with grief. Her only son, so alive and well when she had last seen him only two months earlier, with himself and his family so close and comforting to her during the prolonged absences of Washington on military duties, had been taken away as a needless sacrifice of the Revolutionary War. Washington himself showed less emotion. He was well aware of Jacky's motives for enlisting, and was completely unimpressed by his belated support of the colonial war effort. Nevertheless, he did feel responsible for having accepted Jacky into his service, and he immediately volunteered to take Nellie's two youngest children[14] to Mount Vernon to be reared by Martha and himself, so that, instead of being grandparents in their fifties, they were once more the parents of young Nellie Custis, aged two years, and her brother, George Washington Parke Custis (Little Wash), who was barely six months old.

Washington eventually returned to Mount Vernon in 1783 and settled down to help Martha rear their new family, which was to include a tutor for the two children, Tobias Lear, a Harvard graduate, as well as Martha's motherless niece, daughter of her deceased sister, Nancy. This was Fanny Bassett, an endearing young girl of 17, who was in Martha's heart to take the place of her own daughter, Patsy, who had expired at that same age.[15] For a period of six years Mount Vernon was a busy homestead as Washington coped with all repairs and rehabilitation of the estate buildings occasioned by his long absence in the military service of his country. But soon his country called upon him again, and he was drawn into its political service as its first President in 1789. This necessitated an uprooting of the family to New York, then the capital of the United States and the seat of Congress.

Washington went ahead to prepare for his inauguration. Martha followed at a more leisurely pace with the children, escorted by Robert Lewis, (21-year-old son of Washington's sister, Betty), who set down for posterity some details of the somewhat hectic journey. They called at

Abingdon to stay overnight with Nelly and David Stuart, and Nelly's four children were united for this brief period. Next morning there were highly emotional scenes upon departure with "the children a-bawling, and everything in the most lamentable situation." The little group was continually feted en route and were so delayed that they missed the inaugural ceremony, but they did participate in the great presidential parade which, according to Martha, left "Little Wash" in a daze.

The bustling life pattern of New York proved to be far more distracting and unsettling than that at Mount Vernon for the upbringing of children. Martha was devoted to her grandchildren, and having herself taught Nelly to play the harpischord, and because so few copies of music were available in New York, Martha laboriously copied out sheets of music, of all types—songs, dances, marches, and favorite items from the classical composers. Washington loved being entertained by Nelly, who was an exuberant and attractive girl, although, according to Martha, she was "a wild creature, and spends her time at the window looking at carriages, etc. passing by, which is new to her and very common to do." The time had obviously arrived for more formal education,[16] so Nelly was placed in a day school to be taught the female accomplishments of drawing, sewing, japanning, with daily exercises in French.

But no sooner had they settled down in New York than the capital was moved to Philadelphia, where Washington rented a home from Robert Morris, the famous banker. They all enjoyed the social life and amenities of the city with its theaters, circuses, and well-stocked shops, and it was in Philadelphia that Nelly, aged 12 years, began a life-long friendship with Elizabeth Bordley, 14, with whom she maintained contact by letters which preserved many intimate details of the family household routines and activities from daybreak to nightfall.

Then two tragedies struck quickly. George Augustine, employed by Washington as his estate agent at Mount Vernon, died in 1793 leaving his widow Fanny with three young children. Washington provided her with a house in Alexandria. About the same time, Tobias Lear's new wife, Polly, died of yellow fever, leaving him a widower with a young son. As events unfolded, widow and widower met, fell in love, and married, but tragedy again struck when Fanny died in 1796, leaving Tobias with four young children under ten. He was eventually to return to a small farm on the Mount Vernon estate.

In the meantime, Nelly was slowly maturing into an attractive young beauty and was described by Benjamin Latrobe, the famed architect of his day, as having "more perfection of form, of expression, of color, of softness, and of firmness of mind that I have seen before or conceived consistent with mortality. . . ." Firmness of mind she certainly possessed: she was bridesmaid at the weddings of both her elder sisters,[17] but she appeared unimpressed by the succession of prospective suitors of Philadelphia, and, upon leaving that city at the end of Washington's second term of office in March, 1797, she remained unattached.

The change of pace at Mount Vernon was welcomed by both George and Martha. Nelly could report that her Grandpa was "very well and much pleased with being once more Farmer Washington," while Martha herself wrote, "I am again fairly settled down to the pleasant duties of an old-fashioned Virginia housekeeper, steady as a clock, busy as a bee, and cheerful as a cricket." Washington, after the death of George Augustine, was now in need of a new estate manager, and once again he found the solution by employing yet another of his sister Betty's ample brood: this time, her son, Lawrence, now a childless widower aged 30. By mutual agreement, Washington paid him no salary but promised to provide (apart from his upkeep at Mount Vernon) "plenty of time for reading and private study." To everyone's surprise, a romantic relationship suddenly developed between Lawrence and Nelly, who, in 1798, wrote to her pen friend Betsy Bordley:

> Cupid, a small mischievous urchin who has been trying some time to humble my pride, took me by surprise, when I thought of nothing less than him, and in the very moment that I had (after mature consideration) made the sage and prudent resolve of passing through life as a prim starched spinster . . . he slyly called in Lawrence Lewis to his aid and transfixed me with a dart before I knew where I was . . . and at last was obliged to submit and bind myself to becoming that old-fashioned thing called a wife. . . .

They were married on Washington's last birthday, February 22, 1799, and he gave Nelly as a personal present a thousand-dollar harpsichord ordered from London, and to the happy couple he made out a joint inheritance of two thousand acres. They remained at Mount Vernon until the new home, "Woodlawn," visible from Mount Vernon, on their estate was completed. Their first child, Francis Parke Lewis, was born at Mount Vernon on November 27th, a joyful event, sadly clouded over in just two weeks by the death of Washington on December 12th, 1799. The Lewises remained on at Mount Vernon to keep Martha company until her death in 1802, but before relating their subsequent history, it is time to consider events in the life of Jacky Custis's youngest child and only son, George Washington Parke Custis.

Little Wash, as he was known to the family, was first labeled "Tub," a fat, spoilt child who was to prove as much a torment, and occasion as much anxiety to Washington as had his father, Jacky. Their incredible parallel story in fact could hardly be rivalled in fiction, and Washington must often at night in the last moments before the blissful relief of sleep would come upon him, and sigh many a sigh of sheer unbelief that all he had experienced in the upbringing of Jacky could once again befall him a full generation later.

Little Wash was only six months old when adopted in 1781 by the Washingtons. Obviously much indulged by Martha, his doting grandmother, he was in due time subjected to the supervision of Tobias Lear, until the family moved first to New York and thence to Philadelphia, when he attended school. Just as Washington was completing his second term of office, Little Wash was sent to the College of New Jersey at Princeton, and, in a letter to Dr. Smith, the President, Washington virtually poured all out his frustrations concerning his grandson's upbringing in a single paragraph:

> From his infancy I have discovered an almost unconquerable disposition to indolence in everything that did not tend to his amusements; and have exhorted him in the most parental friendly manner, to devote his time to useful pursuits.

Little Wash received from his grandfather constant reprimands relating to his behavior and repeated exhortations regarding the need to devote himself to his studies, to all of which the boy responded with aplomb and in a style remarkable for his age. In June, 1797, he wrote to Washington:

> Your letter fraught with what reason, prudence and affection can dictate, is engraven on my mind, and, has taken root in a soil which I shall cultivate and which, I hope, may become fruitful; and dear Sir, while I look up to that Providence which has preserved me in my late contest with my passions, and enabled me to act in a way which will redound to my honor, permit me to make this humble confession—that if in any way I depart from your direction and guardianship, I may suffer as such imprudence shall deserve. . . .

In one epistle, Washington wrote:

> You are now extending into that stage of life when good or bad habits are formed, when the mind will be turned to things useful and praiseworthy or to dissipation and vice. Fix on whichever it may, it will stick by you; for you know it has been said, and truly, "that as the twig is bent, so it will grow". . . . This admonition proceeds from affection for you; but I do not mean by it that you

are to become a stoic, or deprive yourself in the intervals of study of any recreations or manly exercise which reason approves. . . .

Princeton failed to cope with Little Wash, and Washington in despair sent him packing to his mother and David Stuart at their home in Hope Park, stating:

> I can, and I believe I do, keep him in his room a certain portion of the 24 hours but it will be impossible for me to make him attend to his books if inclination, on his part, is wanting; nor while I am out, if he chooses to be so too, is it in my power to prevent it. What is to be done with him I know not! I have little doubt of his meaning well, but he has not resolution, or exertion enough to act well. . . .

Not too long after, it was decided to send Little Wash to St. John's College Annapolis, where Dr. Stuart supervised his admission and domicile. But once more problems arose. Washington paid for all the expenses and had expected his grandson to write home once every two weeks, but it appeared not unusual for Little Wash to delay writing for five or six weeks, a procedure much calculated to raise his grandfather's ire. Above all this came the incidental news that Little Wash had become involved in some amorous episode which resulted in a letter from Washington:

> I have with much surprise been informed of your devoting much time, and paying much attention to a certain young lady of that place. . . . Recollect again the saying of the wise man, "There is a time for all things" and I am sure that this is not the time for a boy of your age to enter into engagements which might end in sorrow and repentance. . . .

On this occasion, nothing untoward eventuated, and Washington must have inwardly given very much thanks that Martha at least had supported him in this instance, whereas, more than twenty years earlier, events relating to the family had caused him with much reluctance to bring Jacky home from college.

In July, 1798, Little Wash wrote home to the effect that, having completed the six books of Euclid, he considered himself educated and his college education at an end. Washington was furious and he replied:

> Your letter of the 28th was received last night. The question "I would thank you to inform me whether I leave here entirely, or not, so that I may pack up accordingly" really astonished me!. . . . Did I not, before you went to that seminary, and since by letter, endeavor to fix indelibly in your mind that the object for which you were

sent there was to finish a course of education which you yourself were to derive the benefits of hereafter, and for pressing which upon you, you would be the first to thank your friends so soon as reason has its proper sway in the direction of your thoughts?. . . .

At this time also Washington wrote to Dr. Stuart:

If you, or Mrs. Stuart, could by indirect means discover the state of Washington Custis's mind, it would be to be wished. He appears to me to be moped and stupid, says nothing, and is always in some hole or corner excluded from the company. . . .

By September, 1798, Washington had to confess he was defeated and he wrote to the principal of Annapolis that the unwillingness of Little Wash to return "was too apparent to afford any hope that good would result from it in the prosecution of his studies." So Little Wash had his way and stayed home. Next year, with the threat of war with France and the prospect that Washington might yet again be called from retirement, the latter suggested that his grandson be recommended for enlistment in a troop of Light Dragoons. But war did not materialize, with Little Wash exhibiting as much enthusiasm for life with the military as he had for collegiate existence.

Washington died a year later and the contents of his will left Little Wash devastated. Washington bequeathed his estate to his nephew, Judge Bushrod Washington, the childless son of Washington's brother, John Augustine. He was not without an inheritance, however, since he was part heir to his father's estates, including over a thousand acres along the Potomac near Alexandria.[18] It was here that he decided to build a new home, which proved an expensive undertaking and was initially dubbed "Custis's Folly." It was this house which Little Wash named Arlington, and it was there upon his marriage in 1804 to Mary Lee Fitzhugh, aged 16, that he brought his bride. Of their four children only a daughter, Mary Ann Randolph Custis, survived infancy.

Despite the seeming lack of any propensity towards effort and work which so plagued his grandfather, Little Wash (a sobriquet which was now abandoned in favor of Parke Custis), perhaps sobered by the deaths of both George and Martha, as well as by the demands of sustaining his new family, settled down and matured into a very respected and creative member of society. He developed a marked interest in farming and he proposed that a national Board of Agriculture be established to coordinate and encourage the work of landowners everywhere. He became especially interested in sheep rearing, and not only organized an annual shearing competition on his estate, but also set aside part of his property as an experimental station for the breeding of merinos famed for the quality of their wool.

He became well known as a playwright, and among his works, which were widely performed along the East Coast, were *Pocahontas* (or *The Settlers of Virginia*), *The Indian Prophecy* (which related to an incident involving Washington), and *The Railroad* (which for the first time ever brought on stage a real steam engine).

He was also a talented amateur artist particularly interested in depicting historical events to which he appended descriptive notes in his own inimitable style, the best known of which was his

> Equestrian Painting of Washington resting on a white charger and contemplating the cannonade at Trenton at sunset, previous to the ever memorable Battle of Princeton the ensuing day.

He added that it was "the work of a purely self-taught artist and the first human figure or horse he ever attempted and it is the work of the last male survivor of Washington's domestic family." This last fact was perfectly correct, and in 1825 he had begun to publish his memoirs in the *Alexandria Gazette,* commencing with his "Conversations with Lafayette," the latter having visited him the previous year. In due course his daughter Mary assisted him to compile his writings into a single volume which were published posthumously as the *Recollections and Private Memoirs of Washington by his adopted son (1860).* To his credit, he made no effort to gloss over the many tribulations which he had occasioned the great man, and it is even possible that he was even proud of them. The memoirs certainly add much to a knowledge of the personal and home life of the first President.

At Arlington itself Parke Custis became enmeshed in the financial problems of completing an elaborately designed home. His daughter Mary, in 1831, married a one-time-childhood playmate, Robert Edward Lee, son of the gallant "Lighthorse Harry" Lee of Revolutionary fame. Lee's military duties dispatched him to different parts of the United States and Mexico, yet it was his efforts which finally completed the decorations and furnishings at Arlington, and six of his seven children were born to Mary at the home. Lee served as superintendent of West Point from 1852 to 1855 and it was during this time that Mary, wife of Parke Custis, died (1853) and was buried in the grounds. When Parke Custis himself died he was buried beside her in 1857. Lee lived on at Arlington until the outbreak of the Civil War when he made his fateful decision to support the Confederacy.

Before the occupation of the home by the Federal army, Mrs. Mary

Lee had evacuated it with most of the Washingtons' treasures, including the famous bedstead (now in Mount Vernon). In 1864 the estate was designated as the national cemetery of the United States.[19]

Parke Custis's sister, Nelly, married to Lawrence Lewis on Washington's birthday 1799, was destined to a far less satisfying and accomplished life than that of her sister. The initial exuberance of her romantic association with Lewis and its promise of the prolonged continuation of the lively social life at Mount Vernon appeared to have rapidly dissipated. Of the eight children born of the marriage only three (two daughters and one son) survived to become themselves parents. In contrast to the happy family life which she had enjoyed at Mount Vernon and elsewhere, she now found life with Lawrence endlessly boring and devoid of interest. Sadly, at age 26, she wrote to Elizabeth Bordley "I shall never know happiness again," and she didn't. The Lewis farm barely prospered and the family could not afford visits to participate in the gay and animated societies of Philadelphia or Washington.

In due course, her three daughers, Frances Parke ("My darling Parke"), Agnes, and Angela attended a boarding school at Philadelphia, where Elizabeth Bordley provided them with loving care in their out-of-class free time. But then Agnes suddenly contracted a fever and died at the age of 15 in 1820. Some years later Frances, to her mother's chagrin, fell in love and married (1826) a military officer, Edward George Washington Butler, which condemned her to the peripatetic life of the army, and deprived Nelly of her company. Butler eventually resigned and decided to settle near New Orleans where he purchased a plantation. It was here, while on a family visit by Nelly, Lawrence, and Angela, that the latter met a Virginia lawyer, Charles Magill Conrad. A romance developed between the young couple, but they had been married for only four years (1839) when Angela died, leaving her husband with two young boys.

Nelly's son, Lorenzo, born in 1803, was happily married to Esther Coxe of Philadelphia, and set up home at his Audley estate in the Shenandoah Valley. Then, after rearing a family of sons, Lorenzo died a young man of only 33 in the year 1839, a year in which Nelly herself became widowed. Since Parke was hundreds of miles away in Louisiana during the last years of her life, Nelly was cared for by Lorenzo's widow at Audley, and it was here that she died in 1852.

Of all Washington's siblings, it was his next younger brother, Samuel (1734–1781), who was to give him most concern. Samuel was four times a widower and five times married. In all, he had five surviving children, four of whom were born to his fourth wife, Anne Steptoe. Samuel died in 1781, and his fifth wife died two years later, but leaving the estate in such considerable debt as led George Washington to write, "In God's name how did my brother Samuel contrive to get himself so enormously in debt?"[20]

The responsibility for the upbringing of the destitute children fell to George Washington, and of these, Thornton, the eldest son, had married early and died early (1787). The next in age, Ferdinand, had died in 1788. The three remaining children were George Steptoe, Lawrence Augustine, and Harriot (Herriot). Of these, George and Lawrence proved as troublesome as had Jacky and his son, Little Wash. They had initially enrolled at Georgetown Academy whence they were moved to Alexandria, where they were lodged with a certain Colonel Hanson. While under his supervision in 1788, they were involved in some fracas or other, whereupon, just as Lawrence (aged 13) was about to be punished physically, his brother, George (aged 15), set upon the Colonel to rescue his brother and both ran away. George Washington, in desperation, reproved the brothers but also reproved the Colonel declaring that he would have hoped the latter could have established a mature relationship with his nephews "than as mere school-boys."

Later, they were apprenticed to law firms at Philadelphia, thus adding appreciably to Washington's expenses and, while in the city, they were boarded with a Mrs. Payne who had two daughters to support. The elder daughter, Dolley, had married but was early widowed, and she was in due course to become the wife of James Madison. The younger daughter, Lucy, at age 15, eloped to marry George Steptoe in 1793 and settled at the neglected Harewood estate of Samuel Washington. Lawrence married Mary Wood and left a son, also named Lawrence, who moved to Texas.

Harriot, the youngest, went to live at Mount Vernon with George Augustine and his wife Fanny (Bassett). She was a pathetic little creature who seemed to have been aware only too well of her charity status, and her position was made all the more difficult by the fact that George Augustine was an increasingly sick man,[21] and Fanny was not in the best of health with three young children to look after. To relieve the situation, George Washington asked his sister Betty to take Harriot over the winter of 1792 to which she answered:

> I shall have no objection to her being with me if she comes well clothed or provided to get them . . . I am sorry it will not be in my power to advance any (money) having at this time three of my grandchildren to support, and God knows, from every account but I may expect as many more shortly. . . .

In reply George Washington wrote:

I shall continue to do for her what I have already done for seven years past; and that is to furnish her with such reasonable and proper necessaries as she may stand in need of[22] . . . Harriot has sense enough, but no disposition to industry, nor to be careful with her clothes. Your example and admonition with proper restraints may overcome the last two; and to that end I wish you would examine her clothes and direct her in their use and application of them, (for without this they will be, I am told, dabbed about in every hole and corner and her best things always in use . . .), but she is young, and with good advice may yet make a fine woman. . . .

Before Betty's death in 1797 she did indeed succeed in becoming this. Harriot eventually married Edward Parks and moved to West Virginia. It would appear that her later years were far happier and serene than were those of her castaway childhood.

John Adams

(1797–1801)

The second President experienced remarkably few of the tribulations and travails of his predecessor in office concerning alleged scandals relating to his personal life. Indeed, he has always been regarded as the very paragon, albeit staid and stolid, of New England fatherhood, even though for years he was away from home serving his country. He resided in Paris for a long period, and while there he abhorred the immoral and dissolute climate of the Bourbon royal court, and was never even tempted to be maritally unfaithful, apparently in direct contrast to his worthy colleague, Benjamin Franklin, whose amorous interludes were the talk of the town. It is a matter for conjecture as to how far his pure life habits contributed to his status as being the longest-lived[1] of all presidents, since skeptics tend to point out that the epicurean Franklin himself enjoyed, and lived to an age only six years less than did Adams.[2]

John Adams was the eldest of three sons[3] born to John Adams, a farmer-shoemaker of Braintree, Massachusetts, and his wife, Susanna Boylston Adams, niece of Dr. Zabaliel Boylston, who had pioneered smallpox inoculation in Massachusetts. John the younger attended Boston Latin Grammar School (where one of his teachers was John Hancock) and entered Harvard at age 15, but finding little there to his liking he decided to return home. This unilateral decision greatly annoyed John the elder, who forthwith set him to the chores of mending fences and digging ditches, tasks which soon prompted a change of mind and John returned to Harvard. He was a conscientious student, but participated little in the social life of the college, recording in his memoirs that "students indulged in gambling, rioting and all kinds of dissipation. Many entertained their friends in their quarters and served them punch. . . . Many even indulged in the practice of addressing the female sex."

Graduating in 1755, he first found occupation as a Latin teacher at Worcester, Massachusetts, in what he called "a school of affliction" where he said he ran the risk of becoming "a base weed and ignoble shrub" from instructing "a large number of runtlings just capable of lisping ABC." He soon resolved that schoolmastering was not for him, and he opted for the law, being admitted to the bar in 1758 and being described by one unfriendly observer as resembling "a short, thick Archbishop of Canterbury."

Adams proved himself to be a successful, ambitious lawyer, and in due course he met and fell in love with Abigail Smith of Weymouth, daughter of Parson William Smith and his wife, Elizabeth Quincy. Abigail had been a very delicate child, who, according to one writer,[4] was extremely fortunate to "have survived the perils of her New England childhood, at a time when infants died almost as fast as they were born from a multitude of ailments, including 'bladders in the windpipe'. . . . If she had 'collick'—which seems inevitable—they gave her ghastly concoctions of senna and rhubarb, mithridate ingredients, and Venice Treacle, consisting . . . of opium, white wine and vipers. For rickets she would have imbibed quantities of Daffy's Elixir; and if she had fits or worms . . . there was nothing but . . . Snail Water." This latter was an incredibly obnoxious recipe of garden snails, earthworms, rosemary, agrimony, dock roots, sorrel, rue, saffron, hartshorne, and the strongest ale and beer.

Abigail never had a day's schooling in her life because she was always sick, but she was assiduously cared for not only by a loving father, but even more so by two doting maternal grandparents who lived at Mount Wollaston where she spent much of her time. Grandfather Quincy had a fine library where Abigail roamed and browsed for hours on end among books and battledores, primers and spelling books, penmanship texts and books on "Arithmetick," setting out the "Rule of False and the Backer Rule of Thirds, and of the accumulations of anchors, tierces and Kilderkins, of pottles, cooms, weys and lasts."[5]

Then there were other books which purported to give:

> The Exact Account of the Conversion, Holy and Exemplary Lives and Joyful Deaths of Several Young Children . . . to which is added a Token for the Children of New England, or some Examples of Children in whom the Fear of God was remarkably Budding before they died.[6]

Grandmother Quincy in turn took painstaking care to groom Abigail in all the desirable attributes considered appropriate for a young lady being reared in Massachusetts. Abigail learned to spin, weave, sew, paint on velvet, bake, brew, preserve, and to make cordials and syrups of "clove, gillyflower, borage, marjoram, poppy water, elecampane root, usquebarb and hypocras."[7]

When Abigail grew she had many close friends whom she addressed in her letters,[8] as "Myra," "Aspasia," and "Aurelia" (adopting the classical pseudonyms of her time), and in which she designated herself as "Diana."

When she met John Adams, the young lawyer, she changed her penname to "Portia," in honor of his profession, while he himself adopted the name of "Lysander." In his correspondence to her John was distantly affectionate, and had no reservations in expressing critical comments upon her observed behavior and deportment. In one of his letters he categorically listed her "faults, imperfections, defects, or whatever you please to call them," including her habit of sitting with her legs crossed, which "ruins the figure and the Air and injures the Health." Most obviously peeved, Abigail tartly replied: "I think that a gentleman has no business to concern himself about the Leggs of a lady."

Her family was much dismayed by her association with a member of the legal profession, regarded by many reputable New England families of the day as the last resort of dishonest and corrupt personalities. Only Abigail's father, Parson Smith, withheld unfavorable comment, and in a delightfully mischievous mood combining a gracious benevolence towards the young couple and discomfiting reproval of the prevailing family hostility towards the groom, he deliberately chose as his text at the wedding ceremony on October 25th, 1764: "John came neither eating bread nor drinking wine, yet ye say, 'He hath a devil'." The Parson's generous instinct predicating a successful union proved correct. John and Abigail enjoyed a blissful marriage relationship of over 54 years, terminated only by the death of Abigail in 1818, at age 74. They were blessed with five children within the first eight years of marriage: three boys and two girls, one of whom, Susanna, died within a year of her birth.

The first to be born was Abigail Amelia (Little Abby, or Nabby) in 1765 at Braintree, and then came John Quincy[9] in 1767, also at Braintree. Since John Adams' legal practice prospered, the family moved to Boston the following year into lodgings in a large building known as the White House in Brattle Square. It was also in this year that he wrote his *Dissertation on the Canon and Feudal Law,* published in England. In Boston he probably fell under the influence of his radical cousin, Sam Adams, thirteen years his senior, who had organized the Sons of Liberty at the time of the Stamp Act of 1765.

The year 1770 was one of mixed family tragedy and joy as well as of political crisis. Abigail's second daughter, Susanna, had been born in Boston, but died scarcely one year old. However, there was some compensation in the birth of a second son, Charles, during that same year. On March 5th there had occurred the Boston Massacre, leaving five citizens dead and six wounded. A friend of Thomas Preston, captain of the British Redcoats, implored Adams to represent the accused officer and soldiers at their trial for murder. In an act of incredible courage, Adams consented, thereby mortgaging his entire future professional and political career with only his personal integrity and adherance to moral precepts as collateral. His staunch advocacy of legal principles as opposed to emotional hysteria secured the acquittal of all the accused with the exception of two found guilty of manslaughter and sentenced to be branded on the hand as punishment.

It is to the credit of the colonial community within which he lived that it bore no lasting resentment toward Adams for performing his duty in the foregoing affair; indeed, the contrary appears to be true since within a few years of the trial he was elected by the Massachusetts General Court as one of the delegates to the First Continental Congress in Philadelphia (1774). This was the beginning of a prolonged and painful period for Abigail, since she was separated from John for no less than ten out of the next twenty years, once for nearly four consecutive years. A third son, Thomas Boylston, had been born in 1772, so that the burden of rearing three boys and a daughter during the highly impressionable and formative years of their lives fell almost entirely upon Abigail.

Already, while Adams had been away from home on his circuit rounds, Abigail had, herself, begun the formal education (which included the study of French) of her two eldest children, Little Abby and John Quincy (Johnny). The latter was subsequently tutored in Latin by Mr.

Thaxter, a former pupil of John Adams, and, while his father was in Philadelphia, Johnny was to write him such remarkably precocious letters as to merit the conclusion of some biographers that John Quincy was never young. At age eight, for instance he wrote:

> Sir, I have been trying ever since you went away to learn to write you a letter. I shall make poor work of it, but, sir, Mamma says you will accept my endeavors, and that my duty to you may be expressed in poor writing as well as good. . . . We all long to see you. I am, sir, your dutiful son, John Quincy Adams.

Some time later, he ended a letter with the following postscript:

> Sir, if you will be so good as to favour me with a Blank book, I will transcribe the most remarkable occurances I meet with my reading, which will serve to fix them upon my mind. . . .

Already, at this tender age, John Quincy had in mind to keep a journal, a journal which in due course was to develop into the most comprehensive and famous of all presidential diaries. He acquired a sophisticated taste in reading which included *The Arabian Nights,* Shakespeare's *Plays* and John Milton, although the latter's *Paradise Lost* proved to be too much for him: "To ease his way through that formidable epic he took to smoking as he read, acquiring a permanent taste for tobacco, though none for Milton."[10]

Abigail and the children moved back to Braintree while John Adams was attending Congress meetings at Philadelphia, and his work there never prevented him from writing endless admonitions to Abigail regarding the virtuous upbringing of their offspring, and that she "habituate them to industry, activity and spirit; make them consider every vice as shameful and unmanly; fire them with ambition to be useful. . . . For God's sake, make your children hardy, active and industrous."[11]

And now political tensions accelerated rapidly: on April 19, 1775, there occurred the traumatic revolutionary episodes at Lexington and Concord which initiated the outbreak of hostilities between the colonists and England. Within two months the Battle of Bunker (Breed) Hill was fought (June 17).

Abigail's home at Braintree lay at the foot of Penn's Hill, and when she heard the great thundering of artillery fire she took little Johnny and ran up to the top of the hill; there they both watched the great blaze from the burning of Charlestown amid the incessant explosion and roar of cannons and guns. It was a night which Johnny was ever to remember; neither did he forget the reactions of his grief-sricken mother when she heard, soon after, that Dr. Joseph Warren, a close friend of the family, had died in the battle.

Abigail kept John Adams well informed of all the exciting and momentous events in Boston, resuming, by way of signature, her time-honored sobriquet of "Portia." She described how she had patriotically donated her pewter spoons to the Minutemen for smelting down into bullets, and how she had also knitted "comfy coats" for the soldiers. At the same time she took the opportunity of reminding her husband that "all men would be tyrants if they could. . . . If particular care and attention is not paid to the ladies we are determined to foment a rebellion, and will not hold ourselves bound by any laws in which we have no voice or representation."[12]

In March, 1776, Admiral Howe decided upon the evacuation of the British fleet from Boston, and once again Abigail took Johnny, as well as little Nabby this time, to the top of Penn Hill to witness the dramatic departure of ships from the city.

The little family now fell victim to a sequence of ill-health problems. A plague of dysentery had caused the death of Elihu, brother of John Adams, as well as of Patty, Abigail's servant, and, culminating her afflictions, Abigail suffered the loss of her mother at a time when both she and Tommy Boylston were slowly recovering from a severe attack of the epidemic.

Fears of smallpox led Abigail to take the children for inoculation, and it was while she was in Boston that she heard the Declaration of Independence publicly proclaimed by Colonel Crofts, an event which impelled her to write at length to John Adams on the matter of education:

> The poorer sorts of children are wholly neglected and are left to range the streets, without schools, without business, given up to all evil. . . . If you complain of the neglect of education in sons, what shall I say with regards to the education of my own children, I find myself soon out of my depth, destitute and deficient in every part of education. . . . I most sincerely wish that some more liberal plan might be laid and executed for the benefit of the rising generation.[13]

Abigail, indeed, could have found little opportunity to give much formal teaching instruction to her children during those months of political and health crises: little Nabby was a long time recovering from the intermittent fevers occasioned by the inoculation, while Charles fared even worse since he had to be moved in to Boston several times because the inoculation had not "taken" and he was a long time sick after all others in the family had fully recovered.

Amidst all these tribulations, John Quincy proved himself to be a little hero. At nine years old and already an accomplished horseman, he served as a first class mailrider, bringing news regularly from Boston to Braintree and vice-versa, including the good news in January, 1777, that not only had Washington, less than a month earlier, crossed the Delaware River and captured nearly a thousand Hessian troops at Trenton, but that he had also conducted a successful military engagement (January 3, 1777) against the British forces under Cornwallis at Princeton.

In November, 1777, John Adams reluctantly accepted an appointment to serve as American commissioner to France, replacing Silas Deane, and, in February, 1778, he embarked upon the frigate *Boston* taking with him the ten year old John Quincy, and Joseph Stevens, a servant. The dreary voyage across the Atlantic lasted nearly six weeks, the only compensation being, perhaps, the abundant provisions which Abigail had had dispatched on board ship. They included:

> six chickens, two fat sheep, fresh meat, fourteen dozen eggs, five bushels corn, a barrel of apples, thirty pounds of sugar, two pounds of tea and chocolate, 2 bottles of mustard, a box of wafers, pepper, a 10 gallon keg of rum, 6 dozen small barrels of cider, 3 dozen bottles of Madeira, 30 bottles of port, two pounds of tobacco, a dozen clay pipes and 25 quills for his pen.[14]

They disembarked at Bordeaux, and eventually reached Paris safely where Adams was completely dismayed by the profligate, immoral society of the royal court. He roundly castigated Franklin, who had been in Paris since early 1777, for the ease with which he had readily involved himself among the city's courtesans, along with his "continual dissipation," commenting that

> by far the greater part (of Franklin's visitors) were women and children, come to have the honour to see the great Franklin and to have the pleasure of telling Stories about his Simplicity, his bald head and scattering strait hairs among their Acquaintances. . . . Mr. Franklin kept a horn book always in his Pockett in which he minuted all his invitations to dinner and Mr. Lee said it was the only thing in which he was punctual.[15]

Yet, to the intense annoyance and displeasure of John Adams, Franklin had successfully concluded (on February 6, 1778) a treaty of defense and commerce between the American Colonies and the French government, a fait accompli which now made Adams' presence entirely unnecessary and so he returned home.

He occupied himself in drafting the State constitution for Massachusetts, but, in 1779 he was appointed Minister Plenipotentiary and was directed to return to France to assist Franklin and John Jay in negotiating a peace treaty with England. On this occasion Adams took along with him not only John Quincy but also his brother, Charles, as well as Mr. Thaxter as tutor. They had the traumatic experience of having their ship, the frigate *Sensible,* spring a leak, so that they were forced to land at Ferrol in the remote northwest corner of Spain, whence they painfully journeyed by mule all the way to Paris, a distance of eight hundred miles.

The long drawn out negotiations on a peace treaty was to lead to a painful separation for Abigail lasting more than three years. In May, 1781, she sadly recounted the fact that a period of more than eight months had elapsed since she had received any communication relating to the health and welfare of her husband and two sons.

The latter had been enrolled in a school in Paris, but Adams had come to be disillusioned with its standard of education, so he had both boys removed, and, instead, sent to the classical school in Amsterdam to learn Latin and Greek. The academic regimen here proved to be far more rigorous, but John Quincy appeared to have flourished and survived to the degree that, in 1781, he successfully matriculated and entered Leyden University. His brother, Charles, was far less comfortable, and complained so bitterly about being homesick that John Adams found himself with no alternative but to send him back to his mother.

Abigail's distress can hardly be even imagined when, after long months of silence from Paris, she next received note that poor Charles, still a young lad aged only eleven years, instead of being safely on board ship headed for home, had been shipwrecked and was all the while stranded in Balboa, Spain. Her devastating agony could only prompt a brief note to the effect that "I must resign him to the kind protecting hand of the Being who has hitherto preserved him." Providence did intercede, since an American traveling in Balboa befriended Charles, who had been placed on board ship to Boston where, in due course, he landed safely, and was restored to the welcoming arms of the much relieved Abigail.

As though this single traumatic experience were not enough for any anxious, overwrought mother, Abigail was yet to undergo still a further ordeal when she received a letter with the news that John Quincy, aged only 14, was to accompany Francis Dana to Moscow, where the latter had been appointed envoy of the United States. Since French functioned as the diplomatic language of the Russian Court of Catherine the Great, John Quincy's linguistic fluency would be of inestimable value to Dana in

his efforts to persuade Catherine to give official recognition to the new
"United States," still fighting for its independence.

Dana and John Quincy left Paris for St. Petersburg the summer of
1781, where they remained for well over a year, with no tangible results
for the "United States" but with agonizing consequences for Abigail,
who never once received any news from her son. The distraught mother
wrote to John Adams in Paris:

> Alas my dear, I am much afflicted with a disorder called heartache,
> nor can any remedy be found in America. It must be collected from
> Holland, Petersburg, and Balboa. . . . Two years my dearest
> friend, have passed since you left your native land. . . .

John Quincy was a lonely young boy in Russia. He did not attend any
school, but did have tutors, who, according to John Adams, charged far
too much in fees. John Quincy was always at home in adult company, of
which he had a surfeit in St. Petersburg, but he missed the gaiety and
more relaxed atmosphere of Paris and its bizarre customs. He was later to
write to his mother, understandably shocked by his bland pre-
cociousness, that when Marie Antoinette had given birth to her son, the
Duke of Normandy, the mob had exercised its right to witness the royal
event. In John Quincy's words:

> For a few minutes before she is delivered, the doors of the apart-
> ment are always opened and everybody that pleases is admitted to
> see the child come into the world, and, if there had been time
> enough, all Paris would have gone pour accoucher la Reine.

Whether John Adams had anticipated information of such an intimate
event as a legitimate dimension of his son's education is not recorded, but
he had once written to Abigail of the need for his offspring to cultivate
knowledge along the broadest possible spectrum:

> I must study Politicks and War, that my sons may have liberty to
> study Mathematicks, and Philosophy. My sons ought to study
> Mathematics and Philosophy, Geography, Natural History, and
> naval Architecture, navigation, Commerce and Agriculture, in
> order to give their children a right to study Painting, Poetry,
> Musick, Architecture, Statuary, Tapestry and Porcelaine.

In due course, John Quincy returned to Paris and to The Hague. He
resumed his studies of the classics, but, once again, these were interrupted, since he was called upon to serve as secretary, this time to his
father, during the peace negotiations of 1783. When these were suc-

cessfully concluded,[16] preparations were made for Abigail and Nabby to sail the Atlantic to join father and son in Europe. Abigail was as meticulous in her provisions for the arduous thirty-day voyage as she had been for those for John and John Quincy. She even had a cow brought on board for fresh milk, but, unfortunately, it did not survive the journey. They sailed on the *Active* in June, 1784, and disembarked safely in London, where they were comfortably lodged at Osborn's Adelphi Family Hotel, to await the arrival of the long-separated male members of the family.

First to arrive was John Quincy, a grown-up and sophisticated young man of 17 whom his mother hardly recognized, not having seen him since his departure from Boston as a lad of only 12. The family reunion was joyfully completed with the arrival of John Adams himself, and then, the entire group left for Paris, where they were to enjoy the company of Benjamin Franklin and Thomas Jefferson, albeit not divorced from critical comments by John Adams.

The Adams family took residence in a large house at Auteuil, in which Little Abby had a delightfully compact boudoir with mirrors entirely lining the walls. She was thrilled with it, but Mother Abigail was not so enchanted: in a letter to her niece, Betsey, she wrote, "Why, my dear, you cannot turn yourself in it without being multiplied twenty times; now that I do not like, for being rather clumsy and by no means an elegant figure, I hate to have it so often repeated to me. . . ."

The other disadvantage of the house for Abigail was that the floors were all tiled, without a single carpet, and that a servant had to be specially employed to regularly polish the tiles. The latter, (the *frotteur*), performed the task by wearing waxed brushes strapped to his feet, and simply danced around each room and corridor from wall to wall.

In November, 1784, Thomas Jefferson received the sad news from Virginia of the death of his youngest daughter, Lucy. Abigail and Little Abby gave him (and his daughter Patsy) as much comfort as was possible under the circumstances, Little Abby herself being extremely unhappy at this time due to the disapproval of John Adams of her friendship with Royall Tyler, a handsome young lawyer. Abigail had seen no reason to end the friendship but her pleas on behalf of her daughter fell upon the deaf ears of her adamant husband. Only in part did the warm welcome of the Marquis and Marquise de Lafayette compensate for Little Abby's despondent mood, diplomatically described by the Marquise as being "grave" but not "triste." The Marquis and his wife had two children named, respectively, in honor of their American Revolutionary experience, Virginia and George, and the Adams household was frequently entertained by them, and, in turn, they themselves entertained the Lafayette family.

In 1785, John Adams received the news that he had been appointed as the United States' Minister to the Court of St. James, London, an appointment received with great trepidation by himself, and with fearful agony by Abigail, whose sudden emergence into the blinding limelight of critical scrutiny by the disdainful and friendless ladies of the English Court was a matter for acute dismay and sleepless nights.

But she nobly survived the initial ordeals of the pretentious court mannerisms and, though never completely relaxed, she came, in due course, to accept and even relish the elegant formalities of the diplomatic scene, to the extent that, with remarkable aplomb, she consented to the suggestion that Little Abby, now a grown-up daughter of 21, be married in the summer of 1786 by none other than the Archbishop of Canterbury, assisted by the Bishop of St. Asaph.

To the great relief of the family, Abby, with great resilience, had not only quickly recovered from her disappointment over the broken Parisian love episode, but had, in London, become emotionally attached to William Stephen Smith, appointed secretary at the U.S. legation in London in 1785. The whirlwind romance and marriage was followed by a continental tour including visits to Prussia, France, Spain and Portugal. Smith's diplomatic service in London terminated in 1788, and the young couple returned to the United States.

The subsequent history of the marriage was one of turmoil, confusion, and disillusion. Born in 1755, Smith later graduated from the College of New Jersey (Princeton), had joined the Revolutionary Army, was promoted to the rank of lieutenant-colonel, and was designated as aide to George Washington during the battle of Yorktown. After his three-year tour of consular duty in London he embarked upon an indeterminate career at home, involving land speculation, and was appointed, in turn, to a variety of offices including that of federal marshal, supervisor of the revenue, and surveyor of the Port of New York, none of which appeared to give him any satisfaction. When a war was threatened with France in 1798, Adams nominated him as adjutant-general but the Senate rejected the nomination.

Smith's restlessness climaxed in 1806 when he was prosecuted for participating in the preparations for a filibustering expedition to South America led by Francisco Miranda,[17] whom Smith met in Europe twenty years earlier while touring the Continent. Smith was acquitted of the charge of complicity, but his political career was temporarily jeopardized, and he returned to farming in Lebanon, New York.

John Adams, not unexpectedly, found much to criticize in his son-in-law, most of all, perhaps, because of his ostentatious display of wealth—insisting that Abby was always to be seen in public in her coach-and-four, that the home furnishings be of the best quality, and that Abby be adorned in the latest of styles and be the focal attraction at all parties. Smith, himself, was a flamboyant extrovert, fond of gaiety and company, living for the moment with little thought for the morrow, so that, inevitably, the family's financial resources were drained, hence the move out of city life to that of a small farm in New York State.

Abby's health slowly deteriorated under the strains of an unstable husband and his uncertain future. In 1813 she died, just as Smith's fortunes began to change somewhat for the better, since he had been elected to Congress and took office in that same year. There he served until 1816, when he, too, succumbed to illness, and died at age 61.

They had three children: William Steuben Smith,[18] John Adams Smith, and Caroline Adams Smith. John Adams Smith, known to all as Johnny Smith, was at one and the same time the pride and bane of his grandfather whom Johnny dominated with "a diminutive finger of iron . . . solid, stolid John Adams . . . in harness indeed, pulling a chair and a boy round the suffering drawingroom carpet, and being slashed unmercifully with a willow-switch if he was not going fast enough. And delighting in it, too."[19]

Young Caroline, in due course, was to become one of Abigail's dearest confidentes, and with devoted friends with whom she corresponded regularly and at length, their letters revealed great insight and observation, delightfully interlaced with sparking touches of humor. They shared with each other the remarkable gift of being able to enjoy laughing at their own foibles.

After serving as U.S. ambassador to England, John Adams was elected Vice President of the United Sates,[20] and, after two terms he was in 1796 elected President, but was defeated in his bid for re-election in 1800. He was the first President to occupy the (still uncompleted) White House, but only for the last four months of his tenure in office. They were dreary winter months of misery, with little fuel for fires, no bells to summon servants, (of whom there were thirty, all paid out of John Adams' salary), no fences to prevent curious visitors from wandering in and out of the mansion as they pleased, no facilities for drying the laundry, so Abigail hung it up in the East Room. Never was a person so relieved to quit Washington and return home to Massachusetts as was Abigail on March 4, 1801, when Thomas Jefferson assumed office as the new President.

The four months of discomfort were compounded by family tragedy:

the death of Charles, the younger son. Following those hectic European adventures as a young lad, he had returned home but had never enjoyed good health. He had a warm relationship with his father, who, anxious for his son's advancement, had even permitted him to study law under Alexander Hamilton, a man whom John Adams disliked intensely, but recognized his legal talents. Charles had set up a promising practice in New York City, and, in 1795, had married Sarah Smith, sister of William Stephen Smith and, in due course, she gave birth to several children. But then Charles became involved in some rash financial enterprise which virtually destroyed his career. He took to drinking heavily, and abandoned his wife and family, an action which caused his father so much pain and distress that he renounced Charles as his son.

On her way to the presidential mansion in November, 1800, Abigail had stopped in New York to visit Charles and was appalled to find him sick and mired in his poverty. Unlike John Adams, she never abandoned her son, and was still in hope for redemption. Probably that was true of John likewise, so that the news of Charles' sudden death came a grievous shock to both. John was to lament: "Oh! that I had died for him, if that would have relieved him from his faults as well as his disease." After their return to Braintree, John and Abigail took in Charles' widow and children to live with them permanently.

Sadly for the Adams family there were moments of despair also related to the activities of their youngest son, Thomas Boylston. A talented young man, he took to the law like his father and experienced a very successful career, rising eventually to become State Supreme Court judge in Massachusetts. He married Ann Hood in 1805, and reared a family of at least six children, five of them boys. He entertained political ambitions, but unlike those either of his father or of his brother, John Quincy, they were never realized, a galling hiatus in his career which appeared to be an important contribution which led him, as had his brother Charles, to seek solace in the bottle, from which he derived such satisfaction that some of his drunken orgies lasted for days. Upon his return to reality he would remain in such an ugly mood as to physically abuse his wife and children, who grew to hate him.

Apparently, the entire blame for his excesses did not rest solely upon his shoulders, since contemporary observers have commented that the shrewish disposition of his wife may have, in large part, contributed to his erratic behavior.

With all the seemingly unending cumulative misfortunes which befell the children of John and Abigail, it would appear that the career of their eldest son, John Quincy, was destined to function as a worthy and redeeming consolation designed to compensate for all the worries and heartaches occasioned by his siblings.

Following his hectic adventures in France, Holland, and Russia, John Quincy had been sent home to pursue his studies. He enrolled in the law school of Harvard, and was later apprenticed in the law office of Theophilus Parsons at Newburyport. It was a matter of great pride both to himself and his parents that, when George Washington visited the town in 1789, it was John Quincy who was asked to compose the address of welcome. He was awarded his master's degree in 1790 and then set up a law practice on his own. He found it disappointingly slow and boring, and so, for relaxation, he turned his mind to politics, and under the nom-de-plume of "Publicola" he wrote a series of articles in answer to "The Rights of Man" by Thomas Paine. They were so cogently written that the public first attributed their authorship to his illustrious father but as more articles appeared under such varied sobriquets as "Barnevelt," "Columbus," "Marcellus" and "Meander," the true identity of the writer became known to the prominent politicians at the country's helm, such that when, at age 27, he was nominated by George Washington as Minister Resident at The Hague, his nomination was unanimously confirmed by the Senate.[21]

John Quincy took along with him his brother, Thomas Boylston, aged 23, also a Harvard law graduate, to serve as his diplomatic secretary, and they arrived at their destination in 1794, just as the French Army had entered the country. John Quincy's diplomatic duties were very light and he took the opportunity to travel. While visiting London in 1795, he met Louisa Catherine Johnson, daughter of Joshua Johnson the American consul. By strange coincidence it was not by any means the first meeting between John Quincy and Louisa, though it is highly improbable that either ever recalled the initial contacts. That occurred many years earlier when John Adams first went to France taking John Quincy with him. Joshua Johnson had been the London partner of an American tobacco firm who had found it expedient to move to France at the outbreak of the Revolutionary War. There, Congress had bestowed upon him the duty of checking upon the financial accounts of Americans on official service in France and who were handling public funds. John Adams fell into the latter category, and, as such, both he and John Quincy had reason to visit the Johnson home on a number of occasions, but at that time, Louisa was but 4 years old and most certainly ignored by John Quincy, already the mature young adult aged 12.

Johnson had transferred back to London at the end of hostilities, and by the 1790's he was the father of no fewer than eight children, seven of them daughters, whose parents no doubt were anxious to see married. It was Abigail, back in America, who fully appreciated the circumstances, and, as a mother and a woman, she was thoroughly alarmed by the news of John Quincy's infatuation with a girl (in so large a family) whom she had never met, and whom she considered from the very outset as being no commendable match for her son, whose father was soon destined to be no less than President of the United States. John Adams, also, may have been somewhat concerned, but his anxieties lay more in the matter of protocol. John Quincy was recognized by most persons in the United States as being an exceptionally gifted young man, and was, at the time of John Adams's election as President, serving as U. S. Minister to Holland appointed by George Washington.

In 1797 John Adams now thought fit to recall him home lest he be accused of nepotism. Abigail had already written to John Quincy warning him that he should not expect advancement in office just because his father was to become President, an admonition to which her dutiful son had replied that . . . "I hope my dear and honored Mother . . . that I shall never give him (i.e. John Adams) any trouble by solicitation for office of any kind."

Before making his final decision John Adams had decided to consult Washington, who thereupon replied:

If my wishes would be of any avail they should go to you in a strong hope that you will not withhold merited promotion from Mr. John Adams because he is your son. For without intending to compliment the father and the mother, or to censure any others, I give it as my decided opinion that Mr. Adams is the most valuable public character we have abroad—and that he will prove himself to be the ablest of all our diplomatic corps. If he was not to be brought into that line or into any other public walk, I could not, upon the principle which has regulated my own conduct, disapprove a caution which is hinted at in the letter. But he is already entered; the public more and more, as he is known, are appreciating his talents and work; and his country would sustain a loss if these are checked by over delicacies on your part.

So it was, and with considerable relief and satisfaction at Washington's support, that, in April, 1797, John Adams assigned John Quincy to be his country's Minister in Portugal. In the following July, John Quincy was married to Louisa, in All Hallows Church, near the Tower of London, but in place of going to Portugal he was reassigned to be Minister to Prussia in Berlin.

As the only son of a President to succeed to that office, his subsequent career as a family man will be pursued in his own right in a later section relating to the sixth President of the United States.

Thomas Jefferson

(1801–1809)

Thomas Jefferson, possibly the only red-haired president of the United States, was born in 1743 in Shadwell,[1] Virginia, and was the third of (at least) ten children, all of whom he survived, born to Peter[2] and Jane Randolph Jefferson. Thomas, the eldest son, was only 14 when his father died, and so at an early age he was forced into the status of being male head of the family.

In 1760, he enrolled at William and Mary College, where one of his professors, Dr. William Small of Scotland, was a true man of the Enlightenment, teaching mathematics, philosophy, rhetoric and Belles Lettres; and to him, Jefferson, in later years, often declared his profound and lasting indebtedness for his clarity of presentation and his intellectual inspiration. Jefferson studied also the classics, and later pursued a five-year course in law.

While still a student at Williamsburg Jefferson became attached to a certain Rebecca Burwell, but, apparently, he delayed a proposal of marriage because of some vague intention to go abroad.[3] The young lady, understandably piqued, accepted an alternative proposal, and the prospective groom promptly invited the possibly embarrassed—yet relieved—Jefferson to be best man at the wedding in 1764.[4]

In 1767, Jefferson was admitted to the bar and two years later was elected to the Virginia House of Burgesses. Peter Jefferson had left his family reasonably well endowed, and Thomas, as the eldest son, had inherited a property of over 2,000 acres (with 50 slaves), which, in due course he extended by judicious purchase. He now drew up plans for a new home, to be named Monticello, and over the next decades he was to lovingly design and supervise the installation of the many innovations to be introduced: the dumbwaiter, the mechanically opening doors, the spiral stairways, the alcove beds. All the bricks were made on the premises, and all the wood was cut and trimmed on the plantation. Even the nails used in the building were made in a special little "factory" set up in one of the barns.

Jefferson became friendly with a lawyer colleague, John Wayles, originally from Lancaster, England. He had been thrice married, and had four daughters, one, Martha, by his first wife, and three by his second wife. Martha, at age 17, had married Bathurst Skelton, but within six years of marriage she lost both her infant son and her husband. She returned to live in her father's home and it was here, during Jefferson's visits, that he played the violin and sang while she accompanied him on the harpsichord. Their friendship ripened into love, and they were married on the first day of January, 1772, he being 29, and she 23. Their homecoming to Monticello was disastrous: they ran into a blinding snowstorm, and were consequently so late that the servants had given up expecting them and had resorted to their own homes, so that there were no fires, no prepared meals, and Jefferson records that they quickly disposed of half a bottle of wine and retired to bed.

Martha had been a wealthy young widow, and she came to inherit still more property after the death of her father in 1773, by which date the Jefferson estate consisted of at least 10,000 acres of land and 135 slaves.[5]

Within eleven years of the marriage Martha had given birth to six children: five daughters and a son. The first child, Martha Washington (Patsy), born on September 27, 1772, was also the strongest baby, and she was the only member of the family to outlive her father. The second, Jane Randolph, born in April, 1774, lived only eighteen months, while an unnamed only son, born in 1777, survived only six weeks. Of the remaining three daughters, only Mary (Marie, Polly) was to live beyond childhood: The last two daughters were both named Lucy Elizabeth; the first, born in 1781, died within six months, the second, born in May

1782, so weakened her mother that Martha died in the following September, while Lucy herself died at age 2. Jefferson was devastated at the death of his young wife and could only write in his diary of September 6: "My dear wife died this day at 11:45 A.M."[6] In time he chose an epitaph for her from the Iliad:

If in the melancholy shades below
The flames of friends and lovers cease to glow
Yet mine shall sacred last; mine undecayed
Burn on through death and animate my shade.

It is alleged that on her deathbed she gained from Jefferson the promise that her children would never have a step-mother: certainly it is true that he never remarried.

Between the time of his marriage and that of the death of his wife, Jefferson had led a very active political life. In 1776, he was preoccupied in Philadelphia writing the Declaration of Independence, while his wife (and daughter, Martha) were domiciled with her half-sister Elizabeth ("Aunty Eppes"), and her husband Francis Eppes. The family had re-united in Williamsburg while Jefferson served for three years in the Virginia House of Delegates, and then, in 1779, they moved into the Governor's Palace, still in Williamsburg, when Jefferson was elected Governor.

Martha, by now continually ailing, had again to move in the spring of 1780 when the government was forced to evacuate Williamsburg for Richmond, and it was there, in the following November, and in a house rented from Thomas Turpin, Martha's uncle, that the fourth child, the first Lucy Elizabeth, was born. But, once more, when Richmond itself was threatened by British occupation, the family again moved to safety in bitter wintry weather and poor, frail Lucy died in April, 1781. The second Lucy, born in May, 1782, contributed to the death of her mother in September, 1782.

In 1783, Jefferson was elected to represent Virginia in the Congress located at Philadelphia, and now began the father-separation problems which were to plague the surviving children for the rest of their young lives; but, unless it was John Adams, there never was such a (future) President who so meticulously set out to supervise the almost daily routines of his children. John Adams was far more fortunate than Jefferson in that his wife, Abigail, was always there to care for the children during his frequent absences from home, and that he could communicate directly with her with respect to his sentiments regarding their upbringing. Jefferson had no such advantage, and, for most of their formative years his daughters were farmed out to relatives, friends, or to boarding schools.

At the first breakup of the little entourage, Jefferson took with him to Philadelphia his daughter Patsy (Martha) now 10, along with Shadwell, the family parrot.[7] But, even in Philadelphia, Jefferson was away from home so often on formal business that it became necessary to place Patsy in the care of Mrs. Thomas Hopkinson, mother of Francis Hopkinson, a co-signatory of the Declaration of Independence. At Mrs. Hopkinson's home she was in the company of other girl boarders, who, for the most part, she found to be gossipy and lightheaded. Moreover, Patsy most probably, unlike her fellow boarders, had in some ways to conform with the detailed precepts of study and behavior set out by her father in his letters:

> The acquirements which I hope you will make under the tutors I have provided for will render you more worthy of my love . . . with respect to the distribution of your time, the following is what I should approve: 8–10, practice music; 10–1, dance one day and draw another; 1–2, draw on the day you dance, and write a letter the next day; 3–4, read French; 4–5, exercise yourself in music till bedtime, read English, write, etc. Communicate this plan to Mrs. Hopkinson . . . Inform me what books you read, what tunes you learn, and inclose me your best copy of every lesson in drawing. . . . Take care you never spell a word wrong . . . If you do not remember it, turn to a dictionary. It produces great praise to a lady to spell well.

But for Jefferson, appropriateness in a lady's apparel (even at 10) was far more important than spelling:

> Above all, and at all times, let your clothes be clean, whole and properly put on . . . Some ladies think that they may be loose and negligent of their dress in the morning. But be you from the moment you arise till you go to bed as clearly and properly dressed as at the hours of dinner and tea. A lady who has been seen as a sloven or slut in the morning, will never efface the impression she had made . . . Nothing is so disgusting to our sex as a want of cleanliness or delicacy in yours. I hope, therefore, the moment you arise, your first work will be to dress yourself in such style that you may be seen by any gentleman without his being able to discover a pin amiss.

Jefferson demanded that Patsy's time in Philadelphia be "chiefly occupied in acquiring a little taste and execution in such of the fine arts as she could not prosecute to equal advantage in a more retired station." She should also become familiar with the "graver sciences" and with such accomplishments as music, dancing, drawing, and belles lettres, inasmuch as "the chance that in marriage she will draw a blockhead I calculate at about fourteen to one," and that, accordingly, "the education of her family will probably rest on her."

Patsy was to write one letter home each week in turn to her Aunts Carr, Eppes, and Skipwith, and each letter was first to be sent to Jefferson for inspection. However, her genial temperament was such that Patsy never seemed resentful of her father's endless stream of instructions. She appeared to have an incomparable capacity for inner serenity which permitted her a remarkable precocity to appreciate her father's concern on her behalf, and yet to modify its mature demands to those more appropriate for her age level.

In 1784, Jefferson was appointed as first Minister of the United States to France, where he was also to assist Franklin and John Adams in the negotiation of commercial treaties with European countries. He took Patsy and the parrot, Shadwell, along with him when he sailed in July of that year. When he had departed from Monticello to Philadelphia, he had left his two younger daughters, Polly (Maria) and Lucy Elizabeth in the care of a maternal aunt, Mrs. Francis Eppes of Eppington. But in November, 1784, the news arrived in Paris of the death of Lucy from a severe attack of whooping cough; Mrs. Eppes' own daughter, Lucy, had also died from the same complaint. Polly had been very ill, but she had recovered and upon hearing the news of Lucy's death, Jefferson resolved to be united with his two daughters in Paris.

But Polly had other ideas. She loved her Aunt and Uncle Eppes, and was extremely loath to part from them. Jefferson was most solicitous in attempting to ensure a safe journey across the Atlantic for Polly. In August, 1785, he wrote to Francis Eppes:

> The vessel should have performed one voyage at least, but not be more than four or five years old . . . I think it would be found that all the vessels which are lost are either on their first voyage or after they are five years old . . . with respect to the person to whose care she should be trusted I must leave it to yourself and Mrs. Eppes altogether. Some good lady passing from America to France, or even England, would be most eligible, but a careful gentleman who would be so kind as to superintend her would do. In this case some woman who has had small pox must attend her. A careful negro woman, as Isabel[8] for instance, if she has had the small pox would suffice under the patronage of a gentleman.

Almost two more years were to elapse before Jefferson's requirements were to be adequately satisfied, and, in the meantime, Polly's reluctance to leave America had appreciated considerably, to the degree that, in a last resort, she had to be grossly deceived and was literally "shanghaied" to Paris: a passage was arranged for her on the ship *Arundel* under Captain Ramsey, a friend of Jefferson. She was enticed on board accompanied by the Eppes family and Ramsey regaled them with adventure stories of the sea, during the course of which Polly fell asleep, the Eppes family was put ashore, so that when she woke up, the ship was well under way to London, its destination. It is not known what her reaction was to this cruel ruse, but at least Captain Ramsey was a close friend, and she had with her Sally Hemings, her personal maid.

While awaiting transfer of ship from London, Polly was befriended by Abigail, wife of John Adams, who had been appointed as the first ambassador of the United States to Great Britain. Abigail, who had already served as a good friend to Patsy in Paris, now proved a lovable companion to Polly,[9] who was once again reduced to a very tearful farewell when the arrangements were complete for her to join her father and sister in Paris.

Polly's reunion with her family was not a happy one. She had been separated from her father for three years, she lacked a mother substitute, while her sister, Patsy, now 14, seemed almost too grown up and sophisticated. At this critical juncture, Jefferson again received invaluable assistance from Adrienne, wife of the Marquis de Lafayette, whom he (Jefferson) had entertained at Monticello years previously. Lafayette had three children: Anastasie (10), George Washington (5), and Marie Antoinette Virginia (6), and the household,[10] already a second home for Patsy, now served in the same capacity for Polly.

The Marquis had earlier been responsible for the sponsorship of Patsy's admission into the select convent shcool, the Abbaye Royale de Panthemont, whose enrollment consisted only of some forty young ladies, and which had, as its principal, Mother Louise-Therese; and now, this was also the school which Polly was to attend.

Patsy's experiences at the convent had already been nothing short of traumatic. She had been plunged immediately into a thoroughly French environment, without knowledge of a word of the French language. Jefferson made daily visits to her until such time as she had gained passing proficiency in the language, which enabled her to converse and communicate with her friends at school.

The convent routine was rigorous: the girls would get up, wash, and dress for Mass at 6:30 A.M., followed by breakfast at 7:00 A.M. There were four hours of classes in the morning, and three further hours in the afternoon. Supper was at 6:00 P.M., followed by study hour between 7:00 and 8:00, then at 8:30 P.M., all lamps and candles were extinguished. The girls were expected to eat their meals in silence, and to leave no food scraps on their plates. Patsy was highly amused that the school uniform included a chemise de bain, to be worn in the bathtub: the convent Sisters were not permitted to gaze upon nudity, and the chemise would permit the scrubbing of the back of a student by placing a hand underneath the robe without the tending Sister being embarrassed with having to observe any other part of the body. The convent was unheated in winter, so that students were obliged to wear layers of clothing underneath the uniform.

Jefferson was ever mindful of Patsy's school progress. She had admitted to him her difficulties in Latin: "Titus Livius makes no sense to me. I flounder and stumble about in his history of Rome," to which her father responded:

> We are always equal to what we undertake with resolution. A little degree of this will enable you to decipher your Livy as an exercise in the habit of surmounting difficulties; a habit which will be necessary to you in the country where you are to live, and without which you will be thought a very helpless animal, and less esteemed.

He continued:

> Music, drawing, books will be so many resources to you against ennui . . . in the country life of America, there are many moments when a woman can have recourse to nothing but her needle for employment. In a dull company and in dull weather, it is ill manners to read; it is ill manners to leave them; no card playing there among genteel people. The needle then is a valuable resource. Besides, without knowing how to use it herself, how can the mistress of a family direct the work of her servants?

There were occasions when Jefferson was away from Paris weeks at a time, as, for instance, during the spring months of 1786 when John Adams requested him to come to London in an effort to negotiate a trade treaty with England. In the following September he had the great misfortune to slip and break his right wrist. The bones never set properly so that not only did Jefferson never again have the enjoyment of playing his violin, but he also had to learn to write with his left hand.[11] That he did this with reasonable and quick success is evidenced by the fact that, in October, he wrote the longest letter (4,000 words) of his life to his close

friend, Maria Cosway, a letter which has always since been identified as a
"Dialogue between Thomas Jefferson's Head and his Heart."

In the spring of 1787, again, Jefferson made an extended tour of
almost four months to the south of France and Northern Italy. Patsy
complained of the long absences without receiving word from her father,
lapses of which he excused himself since he was "almost constantly on
the road."[12] Patsy was often piqued that, instead of describing some of
the interesting places which he was visiting, along with his impressions
of the people whom he met, Jefferson would resort to sermonizing and
pontificating upon her work and duties at the convent, and of his high
expectations of her in terms of becoming a sophisticated young lady, not
the least of those attributes being the necessity to learn "the rule which I
wish to see you governed by, through your whole life, of never buying
anything which you have not money in your pocket to pay for."

He again wrote:

> Of all cankers of human happiness none corrodes with so silent, yet
> so baneful an influence, as indolence. Body and mind both unem-
> ployed, our being becomes a burden, and every object about as
> loathsome, even the dearest . . . No laborious person was ever yet
> hysterical. . . . Exercise and application produce order in our af-
> fairs, health of body and cheerfulness of mind . . . while we are
> young that the habit of industry is formed. If not then, it never is
> afterwards. The fortune of our lives, therefore, depends on employ-
> ing well the short period of youth. . . .

Fortunately for Patsy she was possessed of an incomparably serene
disposition, and to Jefferson's long letter she expressed her gratitude, but
yet she found room to reproach him that "it would have been more so
without so wide a margin."

With Polly's arrival later in 1787, Patsy had more companionship,
although, sadly, Polly[13] was never to enjoy the robust, good health of her
sister. The Lafayette family was always to be a second, possibly a first
home, in Paris at least, for the Jefferson daughters.

A not-so-minor crisis arose in 1788. One of Patsy's favorite childhood
companions had been Thomas Mann Randolph, Jr., son of widowed
Colonel Thomas Mann Randolph ("Cousin Dolph"), a relative of her
mother, Martha. At age 17, Tom had been sent by his father to the
University of Edinburgh. Both Patsy and her father had corresponded
with him, although Jefferson was by no means supportive of his having
been sent abroad to be educated, since in another context, he had once
written:

If he goes to England, he learns drinking, horseracing, and boxing. There are the peculiarities of English education . . . He acquires a fondness for European luxury and dissipation, and a contempt for the simplicity of his own country . . . The consequences of foreign education are alarming to me, as an American, I sin, therefore, through zeal, whenever I enter on the subject.

Tom, indeed, proved not too studious away from home, but eventually he did settle down, although much to Patsy's consternation, the warmth of correspondence between them began to cool and taper off so suddenly that she wrote, reminding him of their tree-climbing fantasies at Monticello: "Whatever may be wrong with His Lordship, Sir Tom Of Tree Top Towers; could he not see fit to take his favorite councilor into his confidence?"

"Sir Tom" indeed, at this time, had every good reason to feel at odds with the world. He had just learned that his widowed father had expressed his intention to remarry a young lady,[14] hardly of Tom's own age, and to redraft his will endowing her with all his worldy possessions. In this way, Tom was likely to be completely disinherited. In this understandably sour mood he had curtly written a brusque note to Patsy: "I am through with the flabby spoon bread of Virginia and the tinkling notes of a pianoforte. I am cultivating a taste for Scottish thistles and shrill bagpipes."

Jefferson, too, was concerned, and made an effort to persuade Tom to come to study in Paris, an offer which was abruptly rejected, but Tom did, in due course, consent to pass by the city en route home to America. As far as Patsy was concerned the visit was a disaster: she herself was in process of recovering from an attack of scarlet fever; she was weak and pale, and, in an effort to minimize the effect of the illness, she had over-rouged herself so that her face appeared as a repulsive mask. She had not seen Tom for five years and they were as strangers, hardly recognizing one another, let alone being capable of sharing experiences of such long separation. Tom remained sullen and indifferent and it was upon such a sad note that they parted.

In this mood it was little wonder that, not long after, Jefferson received a letter from Patsy stating her intention, with his permission, to spend the remainder of her life as a nun in the convent. Jefferson was aghast and reacted with alacrity. He removed both daughters from the convent, and set about introducing Patsy into the social life of French society.

His ruse was successful: Patsy quickly came to enjoy and revel in her new status as her father's hostess. Her great occasion was Jefferson's party for all Americans in Paris on July 4, 1789, celebrating the occasion of the election of George Washington as first president of the new United States. Only ten days later came the fall of the Bastille, and with it the French Revolution. Paris was the scene of mass rioting and chaos, and Jefferson promptly requested leave of absence to safeguard the journey home of his family. They eventually sailed in October, 1789, with 86 packing cases, a new dog, "a chienne berger, big with pup," but without Shadwell, the parrot, who had been left with the nuns, and whose subsequent fate remains unrecorded.

Upon his return to the United States, Jefferson was informed that he had been appointed Secretary of State, so that there was no question of his return to Europe, a fact which led to great rejoicing within the family: there was the joyful union of Patsy with Tom Randolph, and of Maria with the Eppes's family.

Tom had much repented of his boorish behavior towards Patsy and, upon his return to America, he had written her a letter asking for her hand in marriage. She was ecstatic, Jefferson was delighted, and within two months of her arrival, Patsy and Tom were married on February 23, 1790. As dowry, Patsy was given the title of the Edgehill estate and a small home with which the young couple was enchanted.

The day immediately after the marriage, Jefferson set off to New York, the temporary capital and seat of Congress of the United States, and Tom was asked to supervise Monticello in his absence. In February, 1791, Patsy gave birth to the first of her twelve children, a daughter named Anne Cary Randolph, an event which gave Jefferson "the greatest pleasure of any I have ever received from you," but, at the same time, he directed Patsy to "be out in time to begin your garden than which nothing will tend more to give you health and strength."

Maria, now 12, had been placed once more in the care of her favorite Aunt Eppes. Jefferson, always the overconcerned father, was most anxious to prescribe for her well-being, and to have Maria respond in positive fashion to his inquiries, as for example, in a letter dated April 11, 1790:

> Tell me whether you see the sun rise every day? How many pages you read every day in Don Quixote? How far are you advanced in him? Whether you repeat a grammar lesson every day? What else do you read? How many hours a day do you sew? Whether you have any opportunity of continuing your music? Whether you know how to make a pudding yet, to cut a beefsteak, to sow spinach, or to set a ham?

Moreover, Jefferson expected her to keep informed as to when the swallows and martins first appeared, and when she enjoyed the first strawberries and peas of the season.

Poor Maria, as sickly as her mother, did her best to conform to her father's well-intentioned wishes, but most passed over her head. She replied: "I have not been able in Don Quixote every day, as I have been travelling ever since I saw you last, and the dictionary is too large to go in the pocket of the chariot, nor have I had the opportunity yet of continuing my music."

Dissatisfied with the foregoing reply, Jefferson curtly answered, "Your last (letter) told me what you were not doing . . . I hope your next will tell me what you are doing. . . ."

On several occasions, Maria had been remiss in her replies and, in desperation, her father resorted not only to petitioning Aunt Eppes that "as soon as you receive a letter, to make you go without your dinner till you have answered it," but also: "I enjoin as a penalty that the next letter be written in French."

After 1791, when the seat of government was moved from New York to Philadelphia, Jefferson took Maria with him and installed her at a school run by a Mrs. Pines; but six months later the lady left for England and Maria was moved to Mrs. Brodeau's, which, according to Jefferson, was a better school "but much more distant from me. It will in fact cut off the daily visits which she (Maria) is able to make me from Mrs. Pine's."

At this time, in school in Philadelphia, was John (Jack) Wayles Eppes, Jefferson's nephew in marriage,[15] to whom he was closely attached and whose studies he supervised very closely. His work entailed a heavy daily load of four hours of science plus four hours of law, and Jefferson set aside certain hours during each week for tutoring. Jack connived that those hours should coincide with the time when Maria would be home. They had known each other since childhood, and that early friendship now began to mature into love.

Jack was a very conscientious young man, and, in 1793, Jefferson recommended that he accompany a government delegation to attend a great council of Indians to be held during the spring months of that year near Lake Erie. Jack's parents were understandably very concerned about his safety but Jefferson wrote to his brother-in-law, Francis Eppes:

> It is really important that those who come into public life should know more of these people than we generally do . . . I know no reason against his going, but that Mrs. Eppes will be thinking of his scalp. However, he may safely trust his where the commissioners will trust theirs.

Jack survived, and in 1794 he was admitted to the bar and was employed in Richmond. Maria by this time was blossoming into a beautiful, though frail, young lady. As described by Abigail Adams, with great perspicacity:

> Slighter in person than her sister, she (Maria) already gave indications of superior beauty. It was that exquisite beauty possessed by her—that beauty which the experienced learn to look upon with dread, because it betrays a physical organization too delicately fine to withstand the rough shocks of the world.

In October, 1797, Jack and Maria were married. Jefferson's gift was a gray coach pulled by four matched Kentucky horses, along with an inevitable written prescription for conjugal felicity:

> Harmony in the married state is the very first object to be aimed at. Nothing can preserve affections uninterrupted but a firm resolution never to differ in will, and a determination in each to consider the love of the other as of more value than any object whatever on which a wish had been fixed.

The young couple settled at Eppington, but, already by 1798, Maria had become too ill to travel to Monticello. In January, 1800, she gave birth to her first child, which, however, died within a month. Jefferson wrote: "How deeply I feel it. . . . I shall not say, only observe as a source of hope to us all, that you are young, and will not fail to possess enough of these dear pledges which bind us to one another and to life itself."

Maria had a second baby, Francis, following which she seemed to recover and, to Jefferson's great delight, both Maria and Martha were able to be with him in his lonely White House existence during the winter months of 1802–3.

Anticipating their visit, Martha had, in October, 1802, written to her father with the request that he order wigs for them both, "the color of the hair[16] enclosed and of the most fashionable shapes" so that they could compete favorably with those worn by the ladies of Washington. Martha added: "They are universally worn and will relieve us as to the necessity of dressing our own hair, a business in which neither of us are adept."

Maria again sickened during the fall of 1803 when she was expecting another baby. Jefferson wrote to her: "Take care of yourself, my dearest Maria, and know that courage is essential to triumph in your case, as in that of a soldier. Keep us all therefore in your heart, by being so yourself. I live in your love only and that of your sister." In December, he wrote: "Not knowing the time destined for your expected indisposition, I am anxious on your account. You are prepared to meet it with courage, I hope" adding, somewhat callously, but perhaps with the intention of lessening Maria's fears: "Some female friend of your mama's used to say that is no more than a jog of the elbow. . . ."

Two months later, Maria gave birth to her third child, but she was now so ill that she weakened rapidly and died in April, 1804; her youngest baby followed her to the grave within the year.[17]

Before her death, Maria, as well as her sister, Martha, had undergone an intensely embarrassing and traumatic experience: the public scandal which erupted during the year 1802, associating Jefferson with Sally Hemings, and alleging his paternity of no fewer than five of her children. The allegations originated with one James Thomson Callender, a Scotsman who had fled Britain to escape indictment for sedition. Unable to curb a proclivity for vilification, vituperation, and scurrility, upon arrival in the United States he directed his misplaced talents against such political leaders as Washington, Hamilton, and John Adams, in consequence of which he was imprisoned under the Alien and Sedition Acts of 1798.

Jefferson had, misguidedly, and clandestinely, initially provided Callender with some support, but he had then given Callender cause for resentment, by withdrawing such support and by refusing to compensate him with the postmastership of Richmond, for which Callender had petitioned. In revenge, Callender turned upon Jefferson by publishing the libellous attacks relating to Sally Hemings.

Jefferson's father-in-law, John Wayles, had been three times widowed.[18] According to report and rumor, he had then resorted for (non) conjugal comfort to a mulatto slave, Elizabeth (Betty) Hemings, already mother of six children by a slave father, and she bore Wayles six more. Upon his death in 1773, Martha inherited 135 slaves, including Betty Hemings and her children, and all these were brought to Monticello after her marriage to Jefferson. Betty's son, Martin, was employed by Jefferson as a personal valet, while her son, James, was taken by Jefferson to Paris to train and serve as a French chef.

Upon the death of his youngest daughter, Lucy, Jefferson had sent home for Polly, and, as described earlier, she, in due course joined Jefferson and Martha (Patsy) in Paris, accompanied by her slave, Sally Hemings, daughter of Betty and John Wayles. Sally was the half-sister of both Patsy and Polly, and, since what subsequently and allegedly occurred between Jefferson and Sally was never once referred to by Jefferson,[19] everything relating to the affair is based on circumstantial evidence and conjectural supposition.

Jefferson returned from Paris with his two daughters in October, 1789, and it is presumed that Sally's first child, Tom, was born soon after. As described by Callender: "(He) is said to bear a striking, though sable, resemblance to the President himself," while Sally, "the African Venus is said to officiate as a housekeeper at Monticello." Jefferson resided at Monticello between January, 1794, and February, 1797, (when he took office as vice-president to John Adams), and, during this period, according to some reports, she bore two daughters who did not survive, as well as a son, Beverly, born in 1798.

It was in 1802 that Callender viciously set out to destroy Jefferson's prestige and career as President. His allegations led to a spate of spiteful verses in the Federalist press, as for example:

> When pressed by load of State affairs
> I seek to sport and dally
> The sweetest solace of my cares
> Is in the lap of Sally.

And again:

> Oh Sally! hearken to my vows!
> Yield up thy sooty charm
> My best beloved! My more than spouse
> Oh! Take me to thy arms.

Greatly to Jefferson's relief, Callender, increasingly alcoholic and depraved, was found drowned in the James River in July, 1803. Surprisingly little was heard of the Hemings affair during the presidential campaign of 1804 and Jefferson was re-elected. During his second term as President there was a brief revival of the scandal, when, after Jefferson had incurred the displeasure of the British Minister, Anthony Merry, and his wife, the young Irish poet, Thomas Moore, who had come to Washington with them wrote:

> The Patriot, fresh from Freedom's councils come
> Now pleased retired to lash his slaves at home
> Or woo, perhaps some black Aspasia's charm
> And dream of freedom in his bondsmaids arms.

In 1805, Sally had borne another son, Madison, and, three years later, her last child, Eston, was born.

Despite her many ongoing problems with her husband, Tom, Patsy, (henceforth called Martha) continued to bear him children. When Jefferson began his second term of office in 1805, Martha was already mother of six surviving children: Anne Cary Randolph (b. 1791), Thomas Jefferson Randolph (b. 1792), Ellen Wayles Randolph[20] (b. 1795), Cornelia Jefferson Randolph (b. 1797), Virginia Randolph (b. 1800), and Mary Jefferson Randolph (b. 1803).

Martha joined her father in the presidential mansion and it was here, on January 17, 1806, that her son James Madison Randolph was born: the first child ever to be born in what later came to be known as the White House.

Jefferson took great delight in his grandchildren: Anne, the eldest, followed him everywhere, and, as might be expected, he taught her all the delights of nature and the garden, the names and methods of planting of all his flowers and plants, and the recognition by song and coloring of all the resident and visiting birds.[21] But, already, in 1805, and hardly fourteen, she had become romantically involved with a certain Charles Bankhead, considered to be an upstart by the family, and whose widowed father, a doctor by profession, owned a peanut plantation in North Carolina. Jefferson had found it necessary to ask Bankhead not to call at the Randolph home at Edgehill, and had written to his granddaughter: "Do try to understand, Anne Cary, that romance is like a colt. It must be broken before it is safe to ride." But the romance continued such that the Randolphs found themselves faced with the painful alternatives either of having to reluctantly consent to the couple's marriage, or of probably having to confront the dilemma of elopement. With heavy heart, they agreed to the marriage, which took place in early 1809, and Jefferson, generously, had a farmhouse on his Tufton plantation remodeled as their future home. Bankhead went on to study law, but with no success, so that his flamboyant ambitions came to naught. He resorted to heavy drinking and ill-treatment of his wife, although she retained the warm support of his disillusioned parents.

Martha's second-born and eldest son, Thomas Jefferson Randolph, ("Jeff"), was a physically strong boy who was to develop into a giant of a man like his great-grandfather, Peter, father of Thomas Jefferson. Apparently, although big for his age he was frail as a baby, and his mother decided to counteract his physical weakness by raising him in a Spartan environment. He was deprived of all sweet and fancy foods and even spent a whole winter in an outer closet with only a blanket for his bed. Martha's treatment of her son appeared to have borne good results since she later recorded that Jeff was "much mended in appearance, strength and spirits. . . ."

Jeff's grandfather, likewise, was greatly concerned with the boy's development, emphasizing the need for "manly sports," and suggested sending Jeff into the forest alone with a gun to make him self-reliant. It is reported that Jeff did just this, and, once, at the age of 12, he walked four miles in a heavy snowstorm to shoot turkeys. Jeff was educated at home by his mother who taught him French and Latin, as well as at school, where one of his teachers described him as "a boy of uncommon industry and application." He was later sent to college at Philadelphia, the entire cost of his education being paid for by Jefferson. Jeff was told to call by at the President's house en route to Philadelphia so that his grandfather could inspect his trunk: Jefferson found it inadequate so they went out shopping together for a new supply of clothing and basic necessities. Jeff was sent to live in Philadelphia with Charles Wilson Peale, the artist and long-time friend of Jefferson. Peale operated a museum of natural history, which must have been a source of great fascination for Jeff, who shared a room with Peale's son, Reubens. Peale was later to paint a portrait of Jeff.

As might be expected, Jefferson, solicitous as ever with respect to the welfare of his children and grandchildren, and always generous with advice, admonitions, and exhortations, would write at length to Jeff, whom he always formally addressed as "My dear Jefferson." Not long after his arrival in Philadelphia, his grandfather wrote him a homily on "good-humor as one of the preservatives of our peace and tranquility," quoting Benjamin Franklin "the most amiable of men in society," as an excellent model. Jeff was charged to avoid becoming involved with two classes of disputants:

> The first is one of young students, just entered the threshold of science, with a first view of its outlines, not yet filled up with the details and modifications which a further progress would bring to their knowledge. The other consists of the ill-tempered and rude men in society who have taken up a passion for politics . . . Consider yourself, when among them as among the patients of Bedlam, needing medical more than moral counsel. Be a listener only, keep within yourself, and endeavor to establish with yourself the habit of silence, especially in politics. . . .

Jefferson concluded this memorable letter with the more intimate prescription to "be very select in the society you attach yourself to; avoid taverns, drinkers, smokers, idlers and dissipated persons generally; for it is with such that broils and contentions arise. . . ."

As regards his studies, Jeff was recommended to commit to writing every evening the substance of the lectures of the day, and then, "if once a week you will in a letter to me state a synopsis or summary view of the heads of the lectures of the preceding week, it will give me great satisfaction to attend to your progress. . . ."

To his credit, Jeff did his utmost to follow the precepts set by his grandfather. In 1809, he was rewarded by being accorded the privilege of riding beside Jefferson at the Inaugural Ceremony of James Madison, fourth President of the United States.

At this time also, Jefferson was corresponding to Jeff's sister Cornelia, aged 11, to whom he wrote:

> I congratulate you, my dear Cornelia, on having acquired the valuable art of writing. How delightful to be enabled by it to converse with an absent friend as if present! To this, we are indebted for all our reading: because it must be written before we can read it. To this we are indebted for the Iliad, the Aeneid, the Columbiad, Henriad, Dunciad, and now, for the most glorious poem of all, the Terrapiniad, which I now enclose you. . . . I rejoice that you have learnt to write for another reason; for as that is done with a goose-quill, you now know the value of a goose, and of course you will assist Ellen in taking care of the half-dozen very fine gray geese which I shall send by Davy. . . .

Jefferson had, a little earlier in the same year, 1808, enclosed four lines of verse to her in a letter which:

> as you are learning to write, they will be a good lesson to convince you of the importance of minding your stops in writing. I will allow you a day to find out yourself how to read these lines, so as to make them true. If you cannot do it in that time, you may call in assistance. At the same time, I will give you four other lines which I learnt when I was but a little older than you, and I still remember:
> I've seen the sea all in a blaze of fire
> I've seen a house high as the moon and higher
> I've seen the sun at twelve o'clock at night
> I've seen the man who saw this wondrous sight
> All this is true, whatever you may think of it at first reading.

In 1809 Jefferson, at 66, finally returned from politics to Monticello, and his daughter, Martha, accompanied him thence and made it her permanent home. Her husband, Tom, was a business failure and soon filed for bankruptcy, so that the support of his large family fell upon Jefferson, a family which continued to increase, since, in 1809, Martha gave birth to Benjamin Franklin Randolph, in 1812 to Meriwether Lewis Randolph,[22] in 1814 to Septimia Anna Randolph, and, finally, in 1818 to George Wythe Randolph.[23] She had named all her sons after prominent

Americans, and she was most fortunate in raising such a healthy brood: in 1820, Jefferson recorded with pride that eleven of her twelve children were all alive and well at Monticello. Jefferson enjoyed teaching them gardening and they responded with delight, with each one competing with the other to be the first to tell their grandfather of a new spring blossom. Even as President, he had always set aside time to spend with his grandchildren and they went on picnics together:

> His cheerful conversation, so agreeable and instructive, his singing as we journeyed along, made the time pass pleasantly . . . Our cold dinner was always put up by his own hands; a pleasant spot by the roadside chosen to eat it, and he was the carver and helped us to our cold fowl and ham, and mixed the wine and water to drink with it.

But life at Monticello became increasingly more complex, not least because of Jefferson's hospitality to all his kith and kin as well as to visitors, and Martha, upon occasion, would find herself having to cope with as many as fifty persons staying overnight. Jefferson, himself, had the reputation of being an acknowledged epicure and gourmet: apparently, his bills for best quality wines alone in 1804 amounted to $3,000. He is credited with having introduced to the United States the art of French cooking, the use of finger bowls, "and other fashions which had met with his approval in Paris." He is also said to have been the first to serve at the table waffles from Holland, macaroni from Italy, and vanilla ice cream from France (served in little balls enclosed in shells of warm pastry).

In addition to his regard for Martha and her children, Jefferson had special concern for Francis Eppes, the only surviving child of his other daughter, Maria. Francis had, since his mother's death in 1804, lived with his father, Jack Eppes, at Eppington, but they had often spent months at a time at Monticello. Jefferson once wrote young Francis a little homily, this time on the importance of good humor:

> Whenever you feel a warmth of temper rising, check it at once and suppress it, recollecting it would make you happy within yourself and disliked by others. Nothing gives one person so great an advantage over another under all circumstances. Think of these things, practice them, and you will be rewarded by the love and confidence of the world.

Also at Monticello was Mrs. Elizabeth Trist from Philadelphia, at whose home Martha had been boarded, and from whom she had received much love and kindness as a lonely little girl. She had since fallen upon evil days, and Jefferson had invited her to stay, along with her grandson, Nicholas Philip Trist, whom Jefferson employed as his private secretary. In due course, (1824), Nicholas was to marry Virginia Randolph.

Still another permanent resident was Monsieur Louis Leschot and his wife, Madame Sophie. He was, by profession, an expert Swiss watchmaker, whose travel expenses to the United States had been covered by Jefferson, who then suggested that the Leschots stay as long as they pleased, and this they proceeded to do quite contentedly.

It was unfortunate for the otherwise reasonably happy household that Martha's husband, Tom Randolph, was ever a source of difficulty. Even when they all resided at the presidential mansion, Tom, in a fit of jealousy, had more or less accused Jefferson of preferring Jack Eppes to himself, a fact not unlikely since Tom's recurrent fits of depression and anger made him at times a most unpleasant personality. Adamant in his belief, he had moved away from the family into a boarding house. He had also become a sick man, and his years as a Congressman were without distinction of any sort. In despair, he planned to settle in Mississippi to develop a cotton plantation, a project against which Jefferson firmly set his own mind, and was eventually successful in persuading his errant son-in-law to do likewise. Not that Tom was a bad farmer—on the contrary, when the family returned home from Washington, he practiced a most efficient form of contour ploughing to reduce soil erosion, but when it came to operating his estate as a sound financial enterprise he appeared incapable of managing his affairs, and Jefferson was literally obliged to bale him out of his money troubles on a regular basis.

Dogged by his knowledge of constant failure and an increasing sense of inferiority, he welcomed an opportunity of participating in the War of 1812. He had already been in a bad busines deal as a result of the British blockade, and so he sought vindication in honorable active service as a lieutenant-colonel in the Second Regiment of the Virginia Militia. The possible consequences of his death or disablement upon Martha and her large family did not deter him: he assumed that his father-in-law would more than adequately cope with that emergency. Fortunately or not, Tom was only to participate in a minor skirmish with the British during an attack upon Ontario, and, later, president madison granted him a commission as Collector of Revenues at a salary of $4,000.

During the British attack upon Washington in August, 1814, the presidential mansion as well as the Congress buildings suffered severe damage, including the loss of a small collection of books. Jefferson, pressed for money, seized upon the opportunity to relieve his own financial pressures, and offered his own sufficient library of over 10,000 volumes at Monticello to the mansion for $23,950. Congress accepted, but, since $15,000 was immediately sequestered to pay debts, Jefferson was left with less than $10,000 and this soon disappeared.

Now over 70 years of age, Jefferson sought some relief from the burden of administrating his large yet seemingly insolvent estate, and in 1816–17 he made Jeff, his favorite grandson, farm manager. Young Jeff had become infatuated with Jane Hollis Nicholas, daughter of Wilson Cary Nicholas, Governor of Virginia. The bride's family had approved of the betrothal, but Martha had not, probably because of intense dislike of Margaret (Peggy), the bride-to-be's very outspoken mother. Nevertheless, the couple were married[24] in March, 1815, and they lived for the first two years at Monticello, where their first daughter was born. They then moved some four miles distant, but Jefferson, desirous of employing Jeff as his farm manager had them relocated at Tufton, just one mile away.

That his son, Jeff, be favored in this manner intensely irritated his father, Tom, who regarded the appointment as a reflection upon his personal capacities as an estate administrator, his feelings being exacerbated by his ever-increasing debts. Fortunately, in 1819, he was elected into the Virginia House of Delegates which, in turn, elected him Governor of Virginia and he served in this capacity until 1822. Tom had, at least, achieved one pinnacle of ambition—to be a recognized and acclaimed personality in his own right.

In April, 1823, he was elected to the Virginia House of Delegates, but, in comparison with his previous status, he never regarded his new office as being worthy of his abilities. His irritations and quarrels with his colleagues increased, and he transferred them all upon his helpless family.

Apart from trouble with his father, Jeff ran into problems with his sister Anne's husband, Charles Bankhead, who had developed an ugly temperament due to his drunken orgies. He had even refused to provide for his family and Jefferson appealed to Bankhead's father to intervene in an effort to check his son's abominable behavior. Jeff, likewise, was incensed, and, in 1819, he became involved in a physical encounter with Bankhead, who struck Jeff with a knife and injured him so badly that his life was in danger for several days.[25]

Also in 1819 came the news that Jeff's father-in-law, Wilson Cary Nicholas, had failed in business, and Jefferson assumed responsibility for debts of over $20,000. Jeff, deeply grateful to his grandfather for his sympathetic and timely aid, more than doubled his energies to produce a greater profit on the estates.

As though the preceding decade of the 1810's had not brought suffi-cient problems to the Jefferson household, the succeeding decade of the 1820's was cumulatively one of disaster and tragedy, with but little of positive impact to compensate for the all-encompassing gloom and de-spair. In September, 1823, there occurred the death of Jack Eppes whose health had progressively deteriorated since 1819 when he had resigned from Congress because of physical disabilities. Then, Tom Randolph's debts, which had accumulated to more than $30,000, now forced him to sell first his Varina estate, and then Edgehill, into which he had invested over thirty years hard work. It was Jeff, again, who attempted to rescue the situation by assuming some of his father's debts, action which was rewarded by Tom with disdain and anger, and not with gratitude. In 1827, Tom obtained a brief appointment as Commissioner for the United States to establish a permanent boundary between the state of Georgia and the newly acquired (1819) territory of Florida. It did little to enhance the family's financial status, and, in 1828, Tom returned to Monticello but in such bad mood that he set himself up in a room where he completely isolated himself from his family, even to the extent of doing his own cooking. During that same year he was out riding in cold weather, and, it is stated that, in generous mood, he gave his cloak to a ragged beggar; he caught a chill and died.

But there were two happy events to record during the decade: In 1824, Virginia Randolph married Nicholas Philip Trist, and, in 1825, her sister Ellen married Joseph Coolidge, Jr., of Boston. Ellen lived to be a great letter writer, and she once wrote of the generosity of her grandfather: "My Bible came from him, my Shakespeare, my first writing-table, my first handsome writing desk, my first Leghorn hat, my first silk dress. . . ."

In February, 1826, Jefferson's eldest grandchild, Anne Cary (Ran-dolph), died at Monticello, and it was Jeff's wife, Jane, who, already mother of seven children, took into her care Anne's now motherless four children: a sad irony of fate since it was Anne (along with her mother, Martha) who had provided most of the original objections to Jane's marriage to Jeff in 1815.

Jefferson himself, now over 80 years of age,[26] found himself in a morass of debt which amounted to over $107,000. He had made a desperate attempt to relieve his family by applying to the Virginia legis-lature for permission to sell his lands by lottery, the proceeds of which might well have cancelled the debt, but the legislature refused. Upon the celebration of the fiftieth anniversary of the Declaration of Independence, and aware of his financial predicaments, certain cities, notably New

York, Philadelphia, and Baltimore, organized collections on Jefferson's behalf, a sum total which, however, amounted to only $16,500. Cities in Virginia, itself, contributed nothing.

On July 4, 1826, Jefferson died in Monticello, within hours of the death on the same day as John Adams (which left Charles Carroll of Maryland as the sole surviving signatory of the Declaration of Independence). His youngest grandson, George Wythe Randolph, aged 8, was present in the final parting, and his grandfather, still conscious, noted his bewilderment and said "George does not understand what all this means."[27] Jefferson had made a will leaving Monticello to Martha and her children, as well as some provision for Maria's son, Francis Eppes. Jeff had been made one of the executors, (a fact which once again incensed his father, Tom), but, sadly, the sole result was to place upon him the intolerable burden of having to seek an impossible solution to the overwhelming financial problem. Assets from the sale of the estate proved inadequate to liquidate the debts and Jeff nobly paid the large sum outstanding, amounting to $40,000, from his own funds.[28]

Slowly, Monticello fell into disrepair. In 1831, the entire estate was placed upon auction and was sold to a druggist in Charlottesville.[29] Martha lived at Edgehill until she went to Washington to the home of Virginia and Nicholas Trist;[30] but Nicholas proved to have a personality almost as perverse as that of her deceased husband, Tom, so she moved out into a small home of her own. The states of Louisiana and South Carolina, learning of her money problems, had each generously voted to grant her $10,000 and she donated this money in the form of an investment to the University of Virginia, which in turn provided her with a modest income.

In 1833 came the news of the death of her son-in-law, Charles Bankhead, who, in his final inebriated days, had been in the care of Martha's son Dr. Benjamin Franklin Randolph. She made one final appearance in Washington before her death in October, 1836. The occasion was the first state dinner of Martin Van Buren, Secretary of State under Andrew Jackson's administration. Van Buren was a widower and he was at a loss to find a hostess among the wives of his colleagues who were hopelessly at odds because of the Peggy Eaton scandal. Martha just happened to be in Washington at this precise moment, and she accepted Van Buren's invitation to be hostess and so resolve his dilemma. The function, as noted by Van Buren in his autobiography, was a great success.

Under the terms of his will, Jefferson freed all the Hemings children, except for Sally herself, whom he left for Martha to finally release from bondage, possibly to avoid embarrassment for Martha had he, himself, declared manumission. The scandals were revived after Jefferson's death. In the 1830's, Alexander Ross from Kentucky stated that, after Jefferson's death, two of his daughters by an octoroon slave were sold on the block in New Orleans: "Both those unfortunate children by the author of the Declaration of Independence were quite white, their eyes blue and their hair long, soft, and auburn in color . . . Both were highly accomplished. The youngest daughter escaped from her master and committed suicide by drowning herself."

The foregoing episode was incorporated in a popular epic written by William Wells Brown in 1853, and entitled "Clotel, or The President's Daughter," while, only a little later, Frederick Douglass, the famed friend of Lincoln, asserted, on a lecture of England, that a granddaughter of Jefferson was among the liberated slaves who colonized Liberia.

Then, in 1873, Madison Hemings, interviewed by a newspaperman, claimed he was the son of Jefferson and that his mother, Sally, had become Jefferson's mistress while they were in Paris. In France, she was a free woman but she had consented to return to America after Jefferson had promised that he would free any child born to her at the age of 21. Hemings stated that his older brother, Beverly, and his sister, Harriet, had both passed for white persons and had each married whites, but that he (Madison) and his younger brother, Eston, chose to remain in the black community, and had each married black women. Madison Hemings died in 1877.[31]

James Madison

(1809–1817)

Despite the many contemporary adverse comments upon his physical appearance, (including that of Washington Irving who described him as nothing but "a withered little apple-John!"), James Madison, fourth president of the United States, succeeded in being accepted in marriage by possibly the most celebrated, attractive, and vicacious woman ever to serve in the capacity of First Lady: Dolley Madison. At the time of their marriage, Madison was 43, and Dolley, a widow with a young son, was 26. Their union was ineffably happy in all respects but one: it was not blessed with children, a fact most galling to Madison, who, himself, was the eldest of a family of twelve born to James Madison, Sr., and his wife, Eleanor (Nelly) Rose Conway Madison. It was James Madison, Sr., who built Montpelier, the family home in Virginia, after his marriage in 1749.[1] Again, William and Francis, two of Madison's brothers, sired large families, with Francis dying at 43, leaving nine children, all minors.

Dolley was one of at least eight children born to John Payne and his wife, Mary, (first cousin to Patrick Henry). The family had originally lived in North Carolina, but John had come so to abhor slavery, that, having freed those in his possession, he moved to Philadelphia in 1783 and joined the Society of Friends. He opened his own business but this failed financially, and he died in 1792, so Mary Payne set up the home as a boarding house for congressmen.

In 1790, Dolley married John Todd, a Quaker lawyer: their first son, John Payne Todd, was born on Leap Year's Day, 1792. Tragedy struck eighteen months later when a plague of yellow fever overwhelmed the city. Among the first to succumb were both of John Todd's parents, and then, on October 24, 1783, there occurred on the very same day the death not only of John Todd himself, but also of his second son, William Temple Todd, who was less than one year old. Dolley was devastated with grief, and went to live in her mother's boarding house along with her one and only son, upon whom for the rest of her life she lavished her devoted and undiscriminating love and attention; sentiments which were, in due course, to result in unremitting trouble, vexation, and embarrassment for Madison.

One of the frequent visitors to the Payne boarding establishment was New York Senator Aaron Burr, and, in 1794, Dolley wrote in great excitement to her dear friend and confidante, Eliza Collins: "Thou must come to me, Aaron Burr says 'the great[2] little Madison' has asked to be brought to see me this evening."

Madison, now in his forties, had on at least two known previous occasions been disappointed in love. Ten years earlier, he had become engaged to sixteen-year-old Catherine (Kitty) Floyd, one of the three motherless daughters of the widowed congressman, William Floyd, of New York, signatory of the Declaration of Independence, and an intimate friend of Thomas Jefferson. The wedding was to have taken place in November, 1783, but, four months earlier, Kitty had broken off the engagement, apparently having decided instead to bestow her favors upon a nineteen-year-old medical student, William Clarkson, who had "hung around her at the harpsichord." Her letter of rejection to Madison was sealed with a lump of rye dough. Madison had also been attached to an intelligent lady, Mrs. Henrietta Maria Colden, a widow with two sons, but details of the relationship are vague except that it did not result in marriage.

In contrast, Madison's courtship of Dolley proceeded without negative incident, and the couple were married on December 15, 1794, although, during that same month, a series of traumatic events were, in some degree, to mar the happy event: Temple, Dolley's favorite brother and a navy ensign, died suddenly of an illness while living with his brother Isaac, a somewhat disreputable character, who soon afterwards, was likewise to die, this time of a gunshot wound inflicted by a man whom he had offended. Then, on the day after Christmas, Dolley was expelled from the Society of Friends for having married Madison, an Episcopalian. Doubtless Dolley had fully anticipated the latter action, since, only a year or so earlier, her sister Lucy had been expelled from the Society for having, at age 15, eloped and married George Steptoe Washington,[3] aged 17, who, like Madison, was of a non-Quaker faith.

Dolley was ecstatic in her renewed state of married bliss, but Madison probably had less reason to be so, since young Payne Todd proved to be a problem from the outset. Since his father's death, Payne had come to sleep in his mother's bed, and, after the marriage, he insisted that he continue to do so, and Madison's objections were obviously overruled by Dolley. Their close friends, the Hites,[4] were to comment in a letter: "Then there was *that child,* who would have nothing else but to sleep in their bed with them, as he had every night since they had been man and wife." They considered that Dolley must have been singularly obtuse and insensitive to have allowed the situation to persist, while Madison, likewise, was condemned for being so incredibly passive and masochistically indulgent.[5]

Yet Madison came to acquire an unusual fondness for Payne, doubtless to please Dolley. The family was extended by the addition of Anna Payne, Dolley's 16-year-old sister who came to live with them after the marriage,[6] together with Nelly Conway Madison, daughter of Madison's brother, Ambrose, and his wife, Frances, (who had died in 1798).

In 1801, Thomas Jefferson appointed Madison as his Secretary of State, and the family moved from Montpelier to Washington. Madison took good care to provide for personal tuition for the ten-year-old Payne, who was by no means an academically inclined student, and was, as often as not, to be found in the presidential stables or wandering in the streets of Washington rather than applying himself to book studies in his room. For these reasons, it was probably to Madison's great relief that he successfully persuaded Dolley that Payne's education would now be best pursued at Alexandria Academy, to which George Washington had bequeathed $1,000 in his will, and where Washington had seen fit to enroll not only his own stepson but also two of his nephews.

The relief of having Payne away from home was, to some extent, shared by Dolley, (although her heartstrings were no doubt at least partially ruptured by the strain of parting from her only son), since she was now free to participate in the social affairs of the capital city. The situation was immediately seized upon by Jefferson, a widower, who persuaded Dolley not merely to function as his hostess at the many presidential ceremonies, but also to act as surrogate mother to his two daughters, Martha and Maria, when they appeared in Washington. Dolley, in her element, responded genially, graciously, and generously, and Jefferson was ever grateful for her readily contributed services.

Payne was next sent to St. Mary's Seminary in Baltimore, an institution founded in 1802 by Bishop John Carroll. Its principal was Father Louis Dubourg[7] of the Sulpician Order, who ran a well-organized and well-disciplined school which was recognized as such by so many prominent non-Catholics that Madison had few qualms about sending Payne there to be taught and disciplined. It is reported that Payne did, indeed, benefit from his schooling there, and that he became quite proficient in French.

While he was at Baltimore, he fell under the affectionate supervision of Elizabeth (Betsy) Patterson, whom Dolley had met at one of Jefferson's social functions at the presidential mansion. Betsy (17) had met Jerome Bonaparte (18), youngest brother of Napoleon. They had fallen in love and were married on Christmas Eve, 1803. They spent their honeymoon in Washington where the Madisons entertained them as guests. But then tragedy befell the young couple: Napoleon, imperially ambitious and interested only in dynastic marriages for members of the family, declared the marriage illegal on the grounds that it had been solemnized in a foreign land, and without the consent of Napoleon as head of family. In spite of this mandate, Jerome took her to France, but Betsy was forbidden to land. She was forced to return to the United States without her husband. Jerome was later installed by his brother as King of Westphalia, and was forced into marriage with a woman selected by Napoleon. For her own part, Betsy never remarried, and remained a tragic and pathetic figure hovering on the fringe of society until her death, although always addressed as Madame Bonaparte.

Dolley did not enjoy the best of health while she was in Washington at this time. In 1805, she was obliged to spend three months at Philadelphia undergoing treatment for a painful knee ailment, and she also began to suffer acutely from a persistent and irritating eye disorder which she endured for the rest of her life. She also became depressed after the death of her mother in 1807, and of her youngest sister, Mary, in 1808.

On March 4, 1809, James Madison was inaugurated as fourth president of the United States, the ceremony being attended by Payne Todd, now 17, who had been granted special leave of absence from school. During Madison's term of office, the presidential mansion came to be shared by a variety of relatives including Dolley's sister, Anna, and her husband, Congressman Richard Cutts (from the Massachusetts district of Maine) with, initially, their three children, a number doubled by 1816. Cutts was a Harvard lawyer who served in Congress from 1801 to 1813, first as a Representative and then as Senator. He was appointed Superintendent General of Military Supplies during the War of 1812, but much of the family's business property was lost as a result of the cessation of trade between New England and Britain. He later occupied the position of Second Comptroller of the Treasury.

Dolley's sister, Lucy, had married George Steptoe Washington, who was never a healthy man. He died at age 36, after vainly seeking cures in spa after spa. Lucy was left a widow with three sons, Samuel, William, and George, and she and the family were accommodated by the Madisons at the presidential home. Lucy lost a great deal of her natural gaiety after the death of her husband, but then was courted by Supreme Court Justice Thomas Todd of Kentucky, a widower with five grown children. Lucy at first rejected his proposal of marriage, but, no doubt exercising a feminine privilege to change her mind at will, no sooner had Todd departed for home than she decided to accept his offer, and sent a courier posthaste to inform him of his belated good fortune. The consequence for the happy couple was a privileged niche in the annals of the (yet to be named) White House, since they were the first ever to be married in the presidential mansion, and the occasion was attended by all eight children of their respective first marriages.

Dolley's third sister, Mary, had married Congressman S. G. Jackson,[8] but she had died in 1808. They had one surviving daughter, Mary, who after Jackson's decision to remarry, came to live with the Madisons. Still, one more family member, Dolley's youngest brother, John Payne, also came to Washington to live with her. In turn, Madison brought in his two nephews, Robert and Alfred, so that all in all, the President, socially if not politically, was encompassed by a host of kinship allegiances.

In 1812, Payne Todd graduated from St. Mary's, Baltimore, wearing, according to one commentator, one of the new young blood "lizards"— green jackets with long pointed tails, matched with skin-tight trousers tucked into yellow boots. Upon his return to Washington, he apparently moved at ease in society, charming all with his handsome appearance, and his gracious, suave, and affable mannerisms. Madison appointed him as his personal secretary, while Dolley, ever in mind of her maternal duties, imported to the presidential mansion the lovely, young Phoebe Morris as matrimonial bait for her son. However, Payne did not bite, ignoring her at every opportunity, and, when thrown into her company, treating her with such cruel disrespect and disdain, that Dolley mercifully had Phoebe returned to her father's home.[9]

In 1813, Payne attained his majority. He now inherited all the property and money set aside on his behalf, and he promptly initiated for himself a fanciful way of living, by way of an elegant wardrobe, female companionship, and especially gambling—all extravagances which were to remain with him for the rest of his life. It was possibly to offset Payne's all-too-ready spendthrift impulses that Madison appointed him as attaché to Albert Gallatin, Secretary to the Treasury, who was being dispatched on a mission to St. Petersburg to explore the feasibility of Russian mediation in the War of 1812. Payne demonstrated great reluctance to leave home, and Madison was forced to compromise by consenting to a generous allowance to cover expenses.

The mission sailed in early summer, 1813, and after a perilous voyage of six weeks they reached Gothenburg, Sweden, relaxed in Denmark, and finally arrived in St. Petersburg towards the end of July. Czar Alexander was away in his war with France, but, later, the American party attended the varied celebrations commemorating the allied victory over Napoleon at the battle of Leipzig (October, 1813). Payne, as the son of the American head of state, revelled in the attention paid to him, and the whole of his stay appeared to have consisted of one never-ending round of parties, balls, feasts and lavish entertainment, during which Payne endeavored to match the Russians in heavy drinking. He had also, in his brief stay, contrived to fall in love with a certain Countess Olga of the Royal Court, but, apparently, she was "mysteriously abducted" and he never heard of her again—a sad episode which is offered in explanation of his sudden departure from Russia, in November—two months ahead of Gallatin.[10]

Payne went to Paris, where, again, he spent a further three months in prolonged dissipation. Gallatin, now in Amsterdam, had become thoroughly dismayed and alarmed by Payne's behavior, doubtless knowing that he would be held responsible by the Madisons upon his return to the United States.[11] He had booked passage for Payne on the *John Adams* but Payne had rejected the mandate, replying from Paris that he was awaiting word of presentation at the Court of the new French king, Louis XVIII.

During his sojourn in the French capital Payne dallied with Madame de Stael, whom he had originally met in St. Petersburg during her enforced exile from France decreed by Napoleon. Her second husband, Rosco, was less than half her age and Payne found in him a kindred spirit for drinking and gambling. Thus it was that Payne's originally allotted span of six months duty in Europe was extended to two years of high-style living, freed of any obligation to be of service to his country. Likewise, his original allowance of $1,000 had now accumulated into a debt of $10,000, although he did spend a substantial proportion of the latter upon objets d'art, which he brought home to the Madisons, who apparently were well pleased with his purchases.

Payne possessed considerable talent which, however, was misdirected and channeled into self-indulgence in the torrid atmosphere of Parisian high society. He spoke excellent French, wore the latest in French fashion, enjoyed French cuisine to the degree that he was as loathe to leave France in 1815 as he had been to leave Washington in 1813, particularly since he was aware that, upon his return to the United States, Madison had planned for him to enroll at Princeton to renew his academic studies.

Payne was not entirely idle: he had, indeed, been granted a patent by the French government for his invention of a gun-priming fluid whose ingredients included spring water and eau-de-cologne, while John Quincy Adams, who met Payne in Paris remarked of him, "It's surprising! He has sufficient talent to succeed in anything he undertakes."

While Payne had been abroad, the British had, in August, 1814, attacked Washington and had burned the presidential mansion.[12] Madison was obliged to find alternative accommodation in the Octagon House, Washington, for his remaining years of office, but it was during this period that Dolley was instrumental in introducing a unique innovation: upon his return in 1815, Payne had, in casual conversation with his mother, remarked upon an interesting custom in Egypt, about which he had heard while traveling in Europe, where children at festival time were wont to roll gaily decorated, hard-boiled eggs against the base of the pyramids at Giza. Intrigued by this odd fact and with knowledge of the fine lawns fringing the Capitol Building, Dolley decided, upon her own initiative, to have hundreds of hard-boiled eggs dyed in varied colors, and, thereupon, invited the children of Washington to participate in an egg-rolling ceremony on Easter Monday, an event which was so enthusiastically attended that it developed as an annual traditional event.

Returning to the United States, Payne was much less than happy. Madison found him temporary employment as private secretary to James Monroe upon the latter's elevation as President in 1817, but the work proved irksome, and Payne resigned. Since Madison had retired to Montpelier with a very much reduced income it became imperative for Payne, now 25, to find some activity to provide for his own financial support. He did derive a small personal income from real estate in Philadelphia, but the costs of his extravagant way of living far outreached the income provided by his property. Moreover, Madison was most concerned that, as sole heir to Montpelier, it was necessary that Payne be, in some way, adequately trained in the essentials of estate management. Payne himself provided part solution to the dilemma since, in 1818, he purchased Todd(e)sberth,[13] a small estate of 104 acres with boundaries quaintly demarcated as follows: "to wit, beginning at a white oak and gum bush on the east side of Mallory's road . . . thence south . . . to three pines . . . thence south (west) . . . to two white oaks and one hickory sprout. . . ." In such manner, Payne acquired the status of being a Virginia landowner, eligible to vote and run for office.

While in Europe, Payne had visited the Lyons district of southeast France, and had become fascinated by the processes involved in the manufacture of silk. He now determined to set up a small factory on his new estate, and, probably aided by his mother, he financed the cost of importing silk workers to advise him concerning the planting of mulberry trees to provide leaves for the silkworms, as well as upon the details of installation of the sericulture equipment.

The project failed, possibly due to climatic conditions, and Payne now became a dissolute wanderer, to the despair of his mother and Madison, who found himself, like Jefferson, not only having to host a multitude of relatives and guests at Montpelier, but also having to cope with the seemingly never-ending financial problems of his stepson. Furthermore, Madison's family worries were compounded by the problems of Richard Cutts, husband of Dolley's sister, Anna. Cutts had already suffered substantial money losses during the War of 1812, and his efforts at self-rehabilitation had time and time again ended in failure, culminating in imprisonment for debt, with Madison once more spending appreciable sums of money to maintain some semblance of security for Anna and her children.

During the decade of the 1820's, Madison was closely associated with Jefferson in the development of the University of Virginia, which opened in 1825. After Jefferson's death, one year later, Madison was appointed to succeed him as Rector, an honor accompanied by the irony of the sad recognition that, in this capacity, he was actively assisting in the education of hundreds of young students, and thus preparing them for active and worthy careers, he was almost entirely helpless and incapable of directing the energies of one single stepson into any satisfying and creditable occupation.

Both Madison and Dolley implored Payne to return home, where, perhaps, they might exercise better control over his excesses, but Payne continued to ignore all their entreaties, and would leave them for months on end without news of his whereabouts. In April, 1823, Dolley had written:

> I am impatient to hear from you, my dearest Payne, had I known where to direct I should have written you before this; not that I had anything to communicate, but for the pleasure of repeating how much I love you, and to hear of your happiness. . . .

And again in December, 1824:

> I have received yours my dearest Payne, of the 23 and 24 November and I was impatient to answer them. . . . Mr. Clay with two members of Congress left us yesterday . . . (and he) inquired affectionately after you . . . but my dear son it seems to be the wonder of them all that you'd stay so long from us! and now I am ashamed to tell when asked how long my only child has been absent from the home of the Mother! Papa and myself entreat you to come to us—to arrange your business with those concerned to return to them when necessary and let us see you here as soon as possible with your interest and convenience. . . . I recently paid Holoway 100 dollars on your note with interest for 2 years. . . . (The) "occurrence" you allude to, I hope, is propicious and if it were for your good we might rejoice in your immediate action, provided it brought you speedily to our arms, who love with inexpressible tenderness and constancy.

Dolley's pleas were completely disregarded, and Payne's financial situation continued ever to deteriorate. In February 1827, Madison confided in a letter to Edward Coles some of the extent to which he had assumed Payne's debts:[14] $600 to an unknown person; $1,000 to a son of Judge Peters of Philadelphia; $700 to someone in New York; and $1,300 to a Mr. Nicholls of Georgetown. Madison wrote that he had "endeavored in vain to sell land, a part even of the tract I live on" but had failed "because of the scarcity of money." He added:

> His career must soon be fatal to everything dear to him in life; and you will know how to press on him the misery he is inflicting on his parents, with all the concealments and alleviations I have been able to effect, his mother has known enough to make her wretched the whole time of his strange absence and mysterious silence; and it is no longer possible to keep from her the results now threatened.

The sequential story of family distress appeared unending. In 1829, Madison grieved at the death, at age 97, of his mother, Nelly Conway Madison. In the same year, President Jackson dismissed Richard Cutts from his post as Second Comptroller of the Treasury, and Madison had to arrange to assume the $150 monthly mortgage payments on Cutts' Washington home in order to ensure a roof over the heads of Anna and her children. At this very moment, he heard that Payne was incarcerated for debt in Prune Street Prison in Philadelphia, so he hastily procured the necessary money to provide for his release, only to be informed not long afterwards that Payne had been returned to the same prison for some further unpaid debts, and, once again, Madison made a desperate effort to negotiate for his release.

Madison, at 78, was physically aging and was crippled by rheumatism, yet he remained mentally agile and had no reservations in accepting an invitation to function as delegate to the Richmond Convention which had been charged with the task of revising the Constitution of Virginia. He revelled in the intellectual challenge as well, no doubt, as in the renewed opportunity to immerse himself in a political and social milieu which removed him, temporarily at least, from the ceaseless burdens and chores of family problems.

In 1830, Payne, to the great joy and delight of his mother, came home at long last. Fortunately, for Dolley at least, a matter of local interest gained his attention by way of the discovery on his property of a large granite outcrop, which fired his imagination with the possibility of developing a lucrative quarry for building-stone. In 1832, the site was examined by Mr. Featherstonehaugh, a London geologist, who declared that a quarrying enterprise might be a profitable venture. It might, indeed, have been such had Payne possessed the managerial acumen to bring the project into fruition, but this he did not have, and the project never materialized.

Payne next became absorbed with the fantasy of building a new structure on his estate, an architectural project over which he spent years and years, presumably with the ultimate objective of providing Dolley with a home wherein to spend the latter period of her life in relaxation and comfort. The centerpiece was "a large round tower-like building called the ballroom," where Dolley, according to Payne, would be able to entertain on the grand scale to which she was accustomed. He built private rooms for her, all on the ground floor, so that she could avoid having to climb stairs. There were many planned conveniences for her comfort which, sadly, Dolley was never to see, although she occasionally sent thoughtful financial contributions to help Payne with his "folly," contributions which were far too insignificant to cope with extravagances about which Dolley could only make comment: "My poor boy, forgive his eccentricities—his heart is right."

Madison's health continued to deteriorate. He spent most of the year 1832 wrapped up in bed as a very sick man. He later recovered sufficiently to be able to walk around his estate, but he was increasingly troubled by deafness and impaired eyesight. On June 28, 1836, while being served breakfast in bed, he appeared to have difficulty in swallowing his food, and, when asked what the matter was, he replied, "Nothing, but a change of mind." Those were his last words.

Madison had made a will bequeathing almost everything to Dolley, but the fact was she was never, during his lifetime, ever fully informed of the profligate behavior of her son, particularly as regards the extent to which Madison had made himself financially responsible for Payne's extravagances. Before his death, Madison had requested Dolley's brother, John C. Payne, to read a letter and to examine the contents of a package which he (John C. Payne) was then to seal and to retain in safekeeping until the death of Madison, whereupon he was to hand the entire package to Dolley. After Dolley's death, John C. Payne notified his nephew, J. Madison Cutts, of the existence of the package:

> Among the papers of my sister will be found, if not improperly destroyed, a package containing vouchers to the amount of about twenty thousand dollars for the payment of the debts of her son, J. P. Todd, by Mr. Madison! They were examined by me at his request, then sealed up and placed in my hands with the directions to show them to my sister after his death as an evidence of the sacrifice he had made to endure her tranquility by concealing from her the ruinous extravagance of her son. This trust I executed by the delivery to her of the package. Mr. Madison assured me these payments were exclusive of those he had made with her knowledge and of the remittances he had made and furnished her the means of making. The sum thus appropriated probably equalled the same amount. Besides the sums thus furnished by Mr. Madison, a constant drain was kept up by Payne on his mother's purse which she supplied unknown to her husband, from every source she could command, even the limited means I possessed.

In actual fact, the total sum of moneys expended by Madison in behalf of his stepson amounted to at least forty thousand dollars.

In his will, Madison did leave to his stepson a case of medallions from Napoleon, along with a handsome gold and ivory-headed walking stick. He had long hesitated as to whether his bequest to Payne should have been more substantial, but he felt that, in paying so many of Payne's debts, the latter had long past received an ample legacy, and that, in any case, Madison had little doubt that Dolley would amply provide for her son as need arose.

Not long after his death, Montpelier suffered a disastrous fire making it virtually uninhabitable, so Dolley made a permanent move to Washington, D. C., to the former home of the Cutts family. With her was her niece, Anna (the third daughter of her brother, John C. Payne), who was to be her inseparable companion until Dolley's death in 1849.

While in Washington, Dolley entered with zest into a new lease on life. Her expenses were financed from the sale to Congress of Madison's "Notes on the Debates of the Constitutional Convention" which were saved from the fire. Congress voted her the sum of $30,000 for these invaluable papers, the sole record of the convention proceedings (although Madison himself had considered them worth $50,000), and had placed the money in a trust fund, so that the capital was placed out of reach to prevent her impoverishment by any overgenerous impulses on her part to repay any more of Payne's debts. Yet, after payment of the many liabilities upon Madison's estate, only $9,000 remained of the original $30,000.

In 1844, Dolley was left with no option but to sell Montpelier, but the transaction was accompanied by so many complications that the final sale was not completed until 1848. In this same year, Congress agreed to purchase Madison's correspondence for $25,000, although, of this sum, $20,000 was placed in trust, so that apart from $5,000, Dolley had access only to the interest. The correspondence consisted of many thousands of letters. Before Dolley was aware of what was happening, Payne, once more deeply in debt, abstracted a substantial number of these letters before they were delivered to Congress, and gave them to James C. McGuire, who held them as collateral security for Payne's financial deficits.[15]

Payne, now in his fifties, had never held any position for any length of time, but, hearing of a vacancy for the American Consulship at Liverpool, England, he persuaded Dolley to intercede with President Tyler on his behalf, only to be informed that "Mr. Todd is not fitted for the office."

Payne remained an unrepentant profligate. Taking advantage of the knowledge that John Jacob Astor, the millionaire fur trader, had often attributed much of his financial success to Madison's political measures, Payne went to New York and brazenly requested a loan from Astor, and even offered his mother's home in Washington as security. Astor obliged with the sum of $3,000, a matter which, when it came to Dolley's ears, virtually prostrated her with embarrassment and humiliation, and she made haste to repay Astor from her personal capital.

In 1849, just one month before her death, Dolley drew up two wills, the first in June, when, at the instigation of Payne, she was persuaded to make him sole heir of her property. But then she had second thoughts, remembering the loyal service and companionship of her "adopted" niece, Anne, who had served her so well during her residence in Washington. Just three days before her death on July 12, 1849, she made a second will providing for a bequest of $10,000 to Anne.

Incensed by her action, Payne took the matter to court, which decided against him, and the litigation costs seriously diminished the eventual sum accruing both to Anne and to himself. Payne did not long survive his mother. He was badly injured by a fall from which he made only slow recovery; he contracted typhoid and he died on January 16, 1852.

He made a will, which was little more than a statement of good intentions, since it provided for the freedom of all his slaves, along with the sum of $200 each. The balance of the estate was to pass to the Colonization Society. In actual fact, all his worldly possessions passed into the hands of his creditors, so that even his funeral expenses were paid by his relatives. As Dr. James Causten (who married Anne in 1850), remarked: "It proves the cranky character of the man to the last."

James Monroe

(1817–1825)

James Monroe was the eldest of a family of four boys and a girl. Born in 1758, he was the third of the first five presidents to die on Independence Day—in his case, July 4, 1831. His father, Spence Monroe, was a Virginia landowner and circuit judge, who saw to it that James was well educated, sending him first to an academy at Campbelltown, and then to the College of William and Mary in 1774. But it was in this year that Spence Monroe died, so that the responsibilities of managing the family affairs fell upon James, then only a lad of 16.

Spence Monroe had married Elizabeth Jones, daughter of a Welsh immigrant, and it was James' good fortune that her brother, Judge Joseph Jones, had been appointed as executor of the estate. Judge Jones was a talented attorney, educated at the Inns of Court, London, and was a member of the Virginia House of Burgesses. He was later to serve as a member of the Virginia delegation to the Continental Congress, while, following Indpedendence, he was appointed to the Virginia State Supreme Court. He had twice married, but still found time to devote

himself to assuring the welfare of his sister Elizabeth's children, and
James Monroe found in him a willing mentor, ready to promote the well-
being and comfort of the family.

James remained at William and Mary for two years, but then left to
join the Continental Army as a commissioned lieutenant in the Third
Virginia Regiment. He saw action at Brandywine, Germantown, and
Monmouth, and was wounded at the Battle of Trenton. He returned to
William and Mary in 1780 and studied law. In 1783, having served three
years as an officer, he was fortunate in being awarded a land bounty of
over 5,000 acres in Kentucky, and, in that same year, he was elected to
represent Virginia in the Confederation Congress meeting at New York.
There he met his future wife, Elizabeth Kortright, whom he married in
1786, he being 27, and she 17.[1] By all accounts it was a genuine love
match, since Elizabeth brought next to nothing by way of a dowry to the
marriage. Her father, Lawrence Kortright, was a one-time wealthy merchant trading in the West Indies, but the Revolutionary War had brought
him ruin. During that war, he had served with the British and had held
an army commission. Following Independence, he had decided to become a citizen of the new United States, and appeared to have suffered no
penalties resulting from his former allegiance to King George III of
England.[2] He had married Hannah Aspinwall, and the couple were
blessed with four good-looking daughters, all of whom, except Elizabeth, appeared to have made successful and wealthy marriages: one sister
married into the prosperous Knox family of New York; another became
a member of the affluent Gouverneur merchant household, while the
third married a Danish diplomat. In contrast, Monroe found himself
having to cope for his entire lifetime with the needs of his impecunious
brothers and their respective families. Not long after his marriage,
Monroe wrote to his friend Thomas Jefferson:

> A considerable part of my property has consisted of debts and to
> command any part of it hath been no easy matter. Mrs. Monroe
> hath added a daughter[3] to our society who, though noisy, contrib-
> utes greatly to its amusement. . . .

It was at the time of his marriage that Monroe's uncle, Judge Joseph
Jones, proved himself a genuine friend by offering the young couple a
house in Fredericksburg, which enabled Monroe to return to Virginia
and set up his law practice. Earlier, when he had learned of Monroe's
engagement, Uncle Jones had set down on paper what he considered to
be the essential virtues of an ideal female marriage partner:

> sensibility and kindness of heart—good nature without levity—a

modest share of good sense with some portions of domestic experience and economy will generally, if united in the female character, produce that happiness and benefit which results from the married state. . . .

To her everlasting credit and advantage, Elizabeth Kortright appeared to have fully met the foregoing requirements and was consequently accorded the enthusiastic approval of her uncle-in-law.

In 1790, Monroe was elected U.S. Senator, and the family moved to Philadelphia, the temporary capital of the nation. He was able to return to his law practice in Virginia when Congress was not in session, but, at this time, he was more than irritated by the fact that his younger brother, Joseph, for whom he had provided funds to study at the University of Edinburgh, had not only wasted his time in Scotland, but had done likewise upon his return to the United States while supposedly studying law in Virginia, and had then capped his dissolute way of life with an ill-judged marriage.

In 1794, Monroe was offered the post of Minister to France (replacing Governor Morris) by George Washington, and, in June of that year, the family sailed on the *Cincinnatus,* accompanied by Joseph Jones, Jr., son of Uncle Jones, who was being sent to France to complete his education.

Monroe remained in Europe for just three years, during which time he was involved in two episodes, one of which gained him notoriety while the other (because of his wife's courage) gained him great acclaim back in the United States.

The first episode related to his action in helping to secure the release of Tom Paine, who had been nine months imprisoned by the Revolutionary French Government. He was a very sick man and Monroe allowed him to remain at his home for well over a year until he had adequately recovered his good health; but Paine abused his generosity by never ceasing to criticize George Washington, a matter which resulted in much pain and embarrassment for Monroe, who was greatly relieved by the eventual departure of his now much-unwelcomed guest.

The second episode related to the treatment by the French Government of the French-American hero, the Marquis de Lafayette, and his family. Lafayette had been in command of one of the several French armies which had fared disastrously against the Austrians in 1792. Known for his monarchist sympathies, he had been relieved of his command, and then, anticipating trial and execution, he fled the country hoping to obtain passage for America, but he was captured and imprisoned by the Austrians.

By the time the Monroes had arrived in Paris, Madame Lafayette (and her two daughters) lay in La Force Prison fearing the same fate as her sister, mother, and grandmother, all of whom had already died by the guillotine. Elizabeth Monroe, with incredible audacity and sangfroid, brazened her way into the prison and, virtually single-handed, secured the release of the little family, who were then permitted to leave France to join the Marquis.

Almost as dramatic was the story of Mme. Campan,[4] who administered a fashionable girls' academy in Paris, in which the Monroes had enrolled their daughter, Eliza, now 8 years old. Mme. Campan had formerly been a lady-in-waiting in the Court of Marie Antoinette, and she had been with the Queen at the Tuileries up to the last moment of her tragic departure to her execution on August 10, 1792. For the moment, Mme. Campan had, by good fortune, escaped indictment since many of the new proletarian leaders of the Revolution had desired a good bourgeois education for their daughters, and so her school for young ladies survived to become a highly commended and patronized academy. The young ladies in attendance came to be instructed in the manners and etiquette of the ancien regime, and it was to this institution that Napoleon Bonaparte sent his stepdaughter, Hortense de Beauharnais, a decision which made the academy an immediately acceptable and desirable place of enrollment for whoever might be termed the Daughters of the French Revolution. Hortense, who was later to become wife of Louis Bonaparte (installed by Napoleon as King of Holland), was a close friend of Eliza's, and the latter, following upon her return to the United States, never failed to remark upon her association with European royalty, a habit, accompanied by the airs and affectations developed at the school, which seldom endeared her to her contemporaries.

Within two years of his arrival home in 1797, Monroe was elected as Governor of Virginia, but the family suffered tragedy when a son born in May, 1799 died in the following September;[5] there was some consolation with the birth of a second daughter, Maria Hester, in 1803. This was the year when Monroe was again sent to Paris, this time by Jefferson, to assist Robert Livingstone in negotiating the purchase, initially, of New Orleans, and, eventually, of the entire French territory of Louisiana. Monroe then spent some time in Madrid and London before returning to the United States in 1807, and the following year saw the marriage of Eliza to George Hay, twenty years her senior and a widower with two children. Hay, son of the innkeeper[6] of the Raleigh Tavern, Williamsburg, became a distinguished Virginia lawyer, and was one of the prosecutors in the trial of Aaron Burr. He was a talented writer and was to be employed as a publicist and adviser by his father-in-law upon his election as President. In the meantime, Hay continued with a law practice in Richmond, and the newlyweds occupied Ashfield, a small estate donated to them as a wedding gift by Monroe. In 1809, Eliza gave birth to Hortensia Hay, proudly exhibited as the Monroes' first grandchild.

However, prior to this time, the limelight had already fallen upon Maria Hestor, who upon the return of the Monroes from France had been dressed by her mother in the latest French dress fashion for children: a short frock under which she wore a pair of loose pantaloons (or pantalettes), and, as described by St. George Tucker: "The little monkey did not fail to evince the advantages of her dress. She had a small Spaniel dog with whom she was constantly engaged in a trial of skill, and the general opinion seemed to be that she turned and twisted about more than the Spaniel. . . ."

In 1811, Monroe accepted Jefferson's invitation to be Secretary of State, and, between that year and 1816, when he was elected President, Monroe was a very harassed man, since during the War of 1812 he was obliged for a while to serve also as Secretary of War and even as Secretary of the Treasury, it being recorded that, at one time, "he did not undress himself for ten days and nights." His problems of State were compounded by complications within the family domain: his brothers, Joseph and Andrew, appeared always to be enmeshed in financial problems which Monroe was expected to solve. Joseph, a widower, abandoned his daughters, and Monroe, with his own wife, Elizabeth, increasingly an invalid, felt he could not burden her with looking after more children so he offered to pay for their support if cared for either by his brother, Andrew, or his sister, Elizabeth.

In 1816, Monore was elected President and, in 1817, he and his wife became the first occupants of the renovated White House, and they were soon to be joined by the Hays family. The President and Mrs. Monroe had the mansion tastefully furnished and decorated with many items they had either brought or ordered from France, and, in this matter, certain difficulties were encountered with Congress since the costs involved exceeded the initial appropriations.

On New Year's Day, 1818, the White House was placed on display for the public to visit, but, thereafter, Mrs. Monroe exasperated Washington society not only by her extreme reluctance to entertain—in direct contrast to her colorful predecessor, Dolley Madison—but she also flouted precedent by assuming the protocol she had learned in France of not making "the first call." Prior to Elizabeth Monroe, all First Ladies traditionally had made their respective rounds of society to drop their "calling cards" to announce when they would be "at home" for eligible visitors, and it was this practice which she refused to follow. Adding still more fuel to the smoldering fire of society resentment, Eliza Hay, often substituting as official hostess for her ailing mother, extended further the newly adopted practice by refusing to make "the first call" upon the wives of the diplomatic corps in Washington. Eliza had developed into an insufferable, haughty grande-dame, typical of the French ancien regime, and her imperious attitude so incensed society that a virtual boycott followed of all White House receptions. John Quincy Adams, appointed by Monroe as his Secretary of State, described Eliza as an "obstinate little firebrand,"[7] and was furious with her since he was reluctantly but inevitably drawn into the "war of etiquette" by having to convey to members of the diplomatic corps the petty particulars of announcements, messages, and directives relating to White House receptions, which, understandably, became fewer, drearier, and more pathetic, consequences which appeared to give neither the First Lady nor her daughter the slightest concern or misgiving.

In March, 1820, there took place the first time wedding of a President's daughter at the White House, when Maria Hester (17) was married to her cousin, Samuel Lawrence Gouverneur, of New York, who had functioned as one of her father's secretaries. The arrangements were entirely in the hands of Eliza Hay, who decided that the ceremony was to be limited to the presence of a few invited guests, and she, moreover, informed the entire diplomatic corps that they were not expected to take any notice of the affair by way of gifts and presents. Of all White House weddings, this was to be the least publicized and least celebrated, yet the union itself proved enduring.[8]

The social scene remained little changed during Monroe's second term of office. The bitter presidential campaign of 1824, resulting in the election of John Quincy Adams over Andrew Jackson, left Monroe relatively untouched and unmoved. The Monroes held a final reception at the White House during February, 1825, in which Mrs. Monroe, always adorned in the latest and most expensive fashion, was described as wearing a dress "of superb black velvet," with her "neck and arms bare and beautifully formed, her hair in puffs and dressed high on the head, and ornamented with white ostrich plumes; round her neck an elegant pearl necklace." But then her health deteriorated so rapidly that John Quincy Adams was unable to occupy the White House for some time after his inauguration in order to allow her time to recuperate and to move to retirement at the Monroe Oak Hill estate in London County, Virginia.

Unfortunately, those retirement years were beset by financial woes, to the extent that Monroe's debts were estimated to be in the vicinity of $75,000. Monroe's firm belief was this could be appreciably reduced were Congress to reimburse him for his innumerable expenses dating back for more than thirty years, the time of his first mission to France. Congress came to recognize the validity of at least part of his claims, and, in 1825, it enacted a bill of reimbursement for $15,900, a sum which, one year later, was increased to almost $30,000; but even the latter, in Monroe's eyes, represented little more than one half of the money owed to him by his country for legitimate services abroad. Political events were not in his favor since Monroe had given support to John Quincy Adams (as his former Secretary of State) in the election campaign of 1828, during which year he had actually been considered as Adams' Vice-President although he had rejected the offer. Since Andrew Jackson was overwhelmingly elected as President, it is understandable that he gave scant support to any motion relating to monetary reimbursements to Monroe, although the latter did receive, five months before his death in 1831, an additional sum of money.

By this date, however, the former President had been beset by so much tragedy that he was virtually indifferent to any further blows of fate. Both his sons-in-law had problems in supporting their respective families, and Monroe was very relieved when John Quincy Adams had appointed George Hay to a federal judgeship, while Samuel L. Gouverneur became postmaster for New York. In 1829, fears were aroused regarding the security of the foregoing appointments when Charles Hay, (George Hay's son by his first marriage), was removed by Jackson from his long-held position as chief clerk in the Navy Department, but it would appear that Monroe's friendship with Vice-President Calhoun spared the family from further economic disaster.

At his home in Oak Hill, where he had established a library of over 3,000 volumes, Monroe set about occupying himself with writing a political history to which he gave the cumbersome title: *The People, the Sovereigns, Being a Comparison of the Government of the United States with those of the Republics which have existed before, with the causes of their Decadence and Fall*. When, in 1829, it was virtually complete, he gave the manuscript to George Hay for comment, but the latter reviewed it so unfavorably that Monroe abandoned the work in favor of Hay's suggestion that he write an autobiography. He pursued the latter project with enthusiasm, but appeared to have ignored Hay's intention that he should incorporate his personal assessment, impressions, and reactions, with the result that the work did little more than simply record the major events of his lifetime, and was therefore of little value to posterity.

George Hay's health had been steadily deteriorating and he died on September 21, 1830. Only two days later, there occurred the death of Monroe's wife, Elizabeth. The double tragedy prostrated Monroe and his daughter, Eliza. Oak Hill was abandoned and offered for sale, and they were both persuaded to go to New York to live with Maria Gouverneur and her husband, Samuel. Monroe, however, became increasingly incapacitated, and died on July 4, 1831. He had made a will committing the care of his papers to his son-in-law, Samuel, but the latter, not being a literary person, never succeeded in completing the task, and, in the end, his problem was only solved by the offer of Congress itself to purchase the papers.[9]

Eliza, after the death of her father, left the United States for Paris, where she died and was buried in 1835. Her sister, Maria, died in 1850.

John Quincy Adams

(1825–1929)

As mentioned earlier, John Quincy Adams was married to Louisa Catherine Johnson[1] in London in July, 1797, and soon afterwards was sent to Berlin as his country's first Minister to the Prussian Court of King Frederick William II.[2] The latter was too ill to receive them and died soon afterwards; later John Quincy presented his credentials to King Frederick William III.

The almost four-year span of duty in Berlin was far from being a felicitous one. Within a month of arrival Louisa suffered her first miscarriage, and with almost regular monotony she was to undergo a similar experience every six months or so until on April 12, 1801, her first child, a son, was born. John Quincy wrote in his diary: "Long expected, ardently desired, painfully born and only child." George Washington, much admired by John Quincy, had died in December, 1799, and, in his honor, the proud father named his firstborn, George Washington Adams.[3]

John Quincy was beset by a host of financial problems, though none of his own doing. His father-in-law, Joshua Johnson, had involved himself in ill-conceived transactions and, even before John Quincy had left London,[4] Johnson's debtors were demanding restitution from him as the son-in-law. Louisa's embarrassments were permanent—she was all too conscious of being accused of beguiling an eligible young man into marriage and immediately depriving him of the benefits of an anticipated substantial dowry. She was aware of Abigail's opposition to the marriage, and she sensed that her mother-in-law would now feel fully vindicated in her objections.

John Quincy's troubles were compounded when, having entrusted his brother, Charles, with care of his investments in the U.S. the latter, (along with the family's financial adviser, Dr. Thomas Welsh), misused the funds, became alcoholic, and died destitute in November, 1800.[5] John Quincy gave the remaining small sum left from his investments to William Stephens Smith, husband of his sister Abby, who had likewise run heavily into debt.

John Quincy strongly disliked the social obligations of his work, and did all in his power to avoid as many as possible of the balls and banquets which he would normally have been expected to attend. Louise, deprived of the company of her family for the first time ever, would indeed have been a very lonely and depressed woman had it not been for Thomas Boylston, whom John Quincy had brought to Berlin as Secretary of the Legation. The two brothers had been together when John Quincy was at The Hague, and, while they were of opposite temperaments, nevertheless, they appeared to function well together both at home and at work. Thomas had a pleasant, light-hearted disposition, and he often had John Quincy's approval to accompany Louisa, much to her delight, to formal dance and dinner functions, even to the extent of participating in the somewhat eccentric Frederick William's favorite game of blind man's bluff. Unfortunately, Thomas did not enjoy the best of health and, to the mutual chagrin of both Louisa and John Quincy, he returned to the U.S. within a year of his arrival in Berlin.

John Adams lost his bid for re-election as President in 1800, and, in consequence, he thought fit to recall John Quincy home to the U.S. The latter had, one year earlier, successfully negotiated a treaty with Prussia which was signed on his 32nd birthday, July 11, 1799. He had met the challenge of his diplomatic duties with distinction, and now, understandably, he was distressed with the boring prospect of having to return to a dull law practice in Boston. Louisa, in contrast, was thrilled with all the expectations not only of visiting a wonderful country which she, although one of its citizens, had never seen in all the twenty-five years of her life, but also of being reunited once more with her family, now resident in Washington, D.C., the new Federal capital. She arrived home only just in time: within six months her father, Joshua, passed away.

In the meantime, she had to undergo what was possibly the most unpleasant experience of her life to date: the scrutiny of her acknowledged critically disposed in-laws: John and Abigail. John she charmed,[6] but Abigail remained unrepentantly unimpressed. She considered Louisa too frail and too "English" for what Abigail regarded as the "American Way of Life." She had no doubt listed the many occasions upon which Louisa had suffered miscarriages in Berlin, and she remained adamant that John Quincy, her favored offspring, had made a rash choice of a marriage partner.

In 1802, John Quincy became a Massachusetts State Senator and, one year later, he was asked to fill a vacant seat as U.S. Senator for Massachusetts, so the family moved to Washington, where they boarded with Louisa's sister, Nancy Hellen, and her husband, Walter. Life now became more hectic, since Louisa preferred Washington and her family, while John Quincy, apart from his senatorial activities, preferred life in Massachusetts with his family. Separations became inevitable. Louisa had given birth in Boston in July, 1804, to her second son, named after his grandfather, John Adams. But there were complaints that, since John Quincy spent so much of his free time away from Louisa, his young son, John, had resorted to calling everyone around him, "Papa," much to his mother's embarrassment. There were other occasions when the over-conscientious Senator from Massachusetts found his paternal duties too distracting, and he arranged that both his young sons be left home in Massachusetts after vacation so that he be not bothered with them in Washington. Louisa found his attitude inhuman, but that did not deter the immutable John Quincy, so that for several winters she was deprived of the company of her two sons. In 1806, she gave birth to a stillborn baby in Washington. That summer, John Quincy had accepted the position as first Boylston professor of rhetoric and oratory at Harvard,[7] so the family moved to Boston, but then, during the winter, John was back in the Senate, and Louisa spent most of a long, cold winter alone in Boston. She was still there in August, 1807, when she gave birth to her third son, Charles Francis.[8]

In 1807, there occurred the "Chesapeake Incident" when a British frigate, the *Leonard*, forcibly boarded the U.S. vessel *Chesapeake* and removed four alleged deserters from the British navy. This prompted Jefferson to force an Embargo Act through Congress, an act which prohibited the export of any goods from the United States. Jefferson was supported by the South and West, but not by New England, where ships rotted at their moorings. John Quincy, obstinate and independent as ever, gave his support to Jefferson, but predictably lost the support of his home state and, in 1808, was forced to resign his seat in the U.S. Senate.

In 1809, to Louisa's great consternation and dismay, John Quincy accepted the offer of President Madison for appointment as first Minister Plenipotentiary to Russia, without a word of consultation with her. Even worse was the knowledge still to come that the two older boys were to be left at home with Abigail. So, what was left of the family, i.e. John Quincy, Charles Francis, and Louisa, sailed for St. Petersburg from Boston on the *Horace,* accompanied by Catherine, (sister to Louisa), William Steuben Smith (John Quincy's nephew[9] and private secretary), Martha Godfrey (Louisa's chambermaid), and Nelson, the family's black (freedman) servant. They arrived in October, 1809, little knowing at that time it would be six years before they would ever see their two sons again.

Other than to satisfy an insatiable political ambition, it is difficult to understand why John Quincy ever accepted the appointment as Russian envoy. His experience at Berlin had only too well familiarized him with the fatiguing, endless succession of social engagements and ceremonies in which he and Louisa would be expected to participate. He was to write: "It is a life of such irregularity and dissipation as I cannot and will not continue to lead," but he had already written about his life in Berlin in precisely the same vein. Moreover, his official salary was far from adequate, and he was obliged to draw upon his savings in the United States. Upon arrival, the family had taken up residence in an apartment in Nevsky Prospect, and their first shock was to discover that protocol demanded that they employ a steward, cook, porter, coachman, postilion, valet, personal maid, two scullions, two footmen, and a muzhik to make the fires, and that they would have to find accommodation and feed the families of the entire retinue.

The Adams family never succeeded in all their five years in St. Petersburg in finding comfortable and affordable accommodation. John Quincy described one home as being "so full of rats that they would drag the braid from the table by my bedside." In 1810, Louisa suffered yet another miscarriage, but the next year she was to give birth to her fourth child and first daughter, named Louisa Catherine (after Louisa's mother). Born in August, sadly she did not long survive the following bitter Russian winter.[10] John Quincy described her as being "lovely as a seraph," but she was not to be the only cause of deep family bereavement during their stay in Russia, for news came somewhat later of the deaths of Louisa's mother, of a brother-in-law, and of her favorite Aunt and Uncle Cranch, while, in 1813, John Quincy's dear sister, Abby, succumbed to a long, debilitating illness.

While Louisa sank into prolonged depths of melancholy, John Quincy occupied himself with his diplomatic duties, and while out walking, met often and conversed at length (in French) with the Czar. Like his father, John Adams, before him, he set out to instruct his elder sons by mail. He admonished them that "each of you consider yourself as placed here to act a part. That is, to have some single great end or object to accomplish, to which to all the views and the labours of your existence should steadily be directed." Both boys were to write to tell him "what books you are reading and what you have learned from them." They were to improve upon their writing, be respectful and obedient to their elders, "make only good boys your friends, and learn faster than they do."

His ambitions for George were such that he was expected to be the leading Adams of the next generation: at age 11, George was exhorted to study Latin and Greek "until you write them correctly, and read Homer, Demosthenes, and Thucydides, Lucretius, Horace, Livy, Tacitus, and all Cicero with almost as much ease and readiness as if they were written in English."

George had been under the supervision of Aunt and Uncle Cranch until 1811, when they both died suddenly within a day of each other. For a short while he had then attended school in Quincy, whence he was sent to Atkinson, New Hampshire, to live with Abigail's sister, Aunt Elizabeth Smith Peabody, the wife of the Rev. Stephen Peabody. While he found life with the Peabody family more congenial and less demanding academically than that with the Cranch family, he was not to stay there long and he was transferred to a school in Hingham, this being his fourth transfer in four years. He was not a studious boy in terms of John Quincy's academic concepts: rather did he indulge in the romance and fantasies of the imagination. His favorite writer was Shakespeare, and, in the light of his future career, perhaps it was just as well that John Quincy was not omnipresent to supervise every moment of his young life.

In St. Petersburg, young Charles, although deprived of the company of an American peer group, did have the advantage of being reared by his parents, and by simple exposure to the culture of the Russian court, he became almost as competent a linguist as his father, speaking French, German, and Russian.

Without doubt, those who came to enjoy and benefit most from the extended stay in Russia were Catherine (Louisa's sister), and William Steuben Smith, who fell in love and were married in St. Petersburg.

Then, there was also Nelson, the black servant of the Adams family, who undertook the extraordinary experience of becoming a member of the Russian Orthodox Church in a magnificent ceremony of pomp and circumstance witnessed by a vast congregation, following which he accepted an invitation to enter the Imperial household.

While resident in St. Petersburg, the Adams family experienced history at first hand: they were there when French troops entered Moscow in September, 1812, and St. Petersburg itself was within the sound of enemy cannon just before Napoleon ordered retreat in October. John Quincy and Louisa attended the impressive celebrations at the Kazan Cathedral for the deliverance of Moscow from French domination.

Two years later, John Quincy was appointed chairman of the American peace commission which was to meet with the British delegation at Ghent to discuss settlement of the War of 1812.[11] After protracted negotiations, a treaty was concluded on Christmas Eve, 1814, thereupon John Quincy sent message to Louisa to join him in Paris.

There followed the most nightmarish adventure ever undertaken by a (future) First Lady in the entire history of the United States. The Baltic was frozen so that sea transport was entirely ruled out. Louisa, obedient to her husband's instructions, was now to demonstrate that she was not, as portrayed by her mother-in-law, Abigail, a weak, frail, brittle personality, but that, on the contrary, she was possessed of an indomitable spirit and a fearless courage determined to complete and achieve whatever purpose and goal to which she had set her mind.

All arrangements for departure in the middle of the bleak Russian midwinter had to be made by herself. The home furniture had all to be sold and, in a letter to John Quincy, she wrote, "I fear I shall be much imposed. This is a heavy trial, but I must get through with it at all risks, and if you receive me with the conviction that I have done my best, I shall be amply rewarded. . . ."

In the carriage, which, at the outset, was equipped with runners because of the snow, she had a bed made up for Charles (now aged 6), and she traveled with a new French maid, Mme. Babet, along with two men riding behind to guard the coach. They left St. Petersburg on her birthday, February 12, 1815, and she was, thirty years later, to write up an account[12] of the entire journey to Paris, which took 41 days.

They coped with all manner of difficulties: the bitter cold which even froze the wine, the crossing of iced-over rivers, swamps and mud, in which the coach became mired, the dislodging of the wheels necessitating delays for repairs, and indifferent overnight hostelries. A valuable silver cup belonging to Charles was stolen and was never recovered.

Louisa believed that the culprit was one of their own personal guards who was a French soldier taken prisoner during Napoleon's campaign and released to protect the group back to France.

At Berlin, they paused to rest for further coach repairs, and here Louisa had the pleasure of meeting with some old friends of her previous stay some fifteen years earlier. It was here, also, that they heard the news of Napoleon's escape from Elba and of his enthusiastic welcome through France as he recruited a new army. Now the journey became more perilous since the coach was easily identified as being Russian, but the fluent French of all persons on the coach, including Charles, was of inestimable value in escaping molestation, as also was subtle bribery where appropriate.

On March 21, 1815, Napoleon's troops reached Paris, and two days later, so did Louisa, where, at the Hotel du Nord, she was met by a greatly relieved John Quincy, who acknowledged he was "prefectly astonished at her adventures." The Adams family now witnessed the tumultuous excitement and ferment of the One Hundred Days of Napoleon's final reign. The Battle of Waterloo was fought on June 18th of the same year, and the seemingly never-ending European war of more than twenty years was, at last, over.

John Quincy's next appointment was as U.S. Minister to England, a position which his father had held thirty years earlier. Louisa was overjoyed to be "home" in London where she had been born, and which she had not seen for eighteen years. But her ecstasy was boundless when, at long last, the two older boys arrived from America to reunite the family after six years of separation. They took up residence at Ealing where the boys went to a school run by Dr. George Nicholas, an Oxford graduate, whom George considered as "the best master I ever knew" for he gave an interest to the studies which made them agreeable as well as useful. George, now 14, was delegated by John Quincy as the official writer of the family's weekly letter home to John and Abigail, but his procrastinations soon made it necessary for John Quincy to assume this duty once more. A major excuse offered by George was that his schoolmaster had apparently told him that his handwriting might suffer if he were to exercise it too much. John Quincy was understandably skeptical, but submitted to being outrageously victimized. George, already a lover of Shakespeare's plays, came to revel in London's theatreland. He also traveled to France where, again, he became fascinated by the drama offerings of Paris.

John Quincy supervised the studies of all three sons, none of whom, however, displayed either talent or interest in the classics, and he expressed his disappointment to Abigail that he would have to resign himself to seeing his sons grow up "like other men": he had hoped for "something more flattering than all this." In order to broaden their interest, John Quincy bought a telescope, and they spent many hours exploring the marvels of the universe; he also hired a fencing master to introduce them to the skills of swordsmanship.

In 1817, James Monroe succeeded Madison as President, and John Quincy was elated by his appointment as Secretary of State in the new cabinet. Unfortunately, reunion with John and John Quincy was, of necessity, limited in duration since John Quincy and Louisa had to proceed to Washington to find accommodation. Yet brief as it was, it was propitious and providential: Abigail's respect for Louisa's fortitude and courage brought a long overdue reconciliation between mother and daughter-in-law, and this achievement came only just in time, for Abigail's health was rapidly deteriorating and she died at the age of seventy-four in October, 1818.

John Quincy's appointment to Washington entailed yet another heart-breaking disruption of family life since the boys remained in Boston for their education. George was placed in residence with Samuel Gilman, mathematics tutor at Harvard, who prepared him for the Harvard entrance examination, which he passed in 1818 despite his dislike of most subjects. Nevertheless, he forced himself to study and finally graduated in 1821. His great achievement was to defeat Ralph Waldo Emerson for the Boylston Prize in his junior year, but his father withheld his congratulations, choosing to brood over and resent George's involvement in a student romp instead of devoting himself to study. In due course George went on to study law in the office of Daniel Webster.

John and Charles were enrolled in the Boston Latin School. Charles, in particular, thought himself abandoned since this was the first time for him ever to be separated from his parents. He also missed the exhilaration of life in Europe, be it in St. Petersburg, Paris, or London, and he had come to accept French rather than English as his mother tongue. He enrolled at Harvard at 14, participating fully in the convivial social life of the college, but without too much censure from his father since he was the favored son of the family. He graduated in 1825, and proceeded to Washington to study law under John Quincy's supervision.

John was the unfortunate one at Harvard, and more so even than George was he to experience the displeasure and wrath of his father. Complaining of the amount of hard work and small allowance, John received an answer: "Are you so much of a baby that you must be taxed to spell your letters by sugar plums? Or are you such an independent gentleman that you can brook no control and must have everything you ask for? If so, I desire you not to write for anything to me."

John Quincy was even more infuriated when, in his junior year, John was ranked 45th in a class of 85, such that he was refused permission to return home for Christmas, and was instead directed to remain in Cambridge to study. His father wrote: "I take no satisfaction in seeing you, I could feel nothing but sorrow and shame in your presence." He later indicated to his son that he had no intention of attending his commencement unless he graduated in the top five of his class. This latter threat proved to be of mere historic interest since, in 1823, John and the entire senior class at Harvard were expelled for participating in a student riot which came to be known as "The Great Rebellion," and not until 1873 did the college finally relent and grant (mainly posthumous) degrees to members of the class.[13]

In the very controversial election of November, 1823, John Quincy was eventually declared President of the United States, to the pride of his father, John Adams, who lived yet a further two years, himself to die at the age of 90 as the oldest of all Presidents and ex-Presidents of his country.

When he moved into the presidential mansion, John Quincy was accompanied not only by all his three sons in residence but also by the three orphaned children of Louisa's sister, Nancy Johnson Hellen.[14] Of these children, the elder son, Johnson Hellen, one year older than his cousin George, was to attend Princeton and become a lawyer, but he had secretly supported Andrew Jackson rather than John Quincy, his foster father. The second son, Thomas Hellen, very much a wayward youth, was expelled from Harvard in 1827 for "licentiousness." Mary Catherine Hellen, the only daughter but the oldest of the children, caused John Quincy and Louisa much inner discord by her flagrant flirtations with the Adams' sons, first George, and then John, who functioned as his father's secretary. John Quincy was confused and distracted at these events under his very own roof, but helpless under the circumstances, he finally gave his consent first to the engagement, and finally to the marriage of John and Mary which took place in the Oval Room of the presidential mansion in 1828.[15] His first grandchild, a girl, was born in December, 1828, only the second child ever to be born in the mansion.

As President, John Quincy was both a political and social failure. Charles described him as "the only man I ever saw whose feelings I could not penetrate . . . He makes enemies by perpetually wearing the Iron Mask." Louisa, obviously sensing this failure, became more and more depressed, such that John Quincy came to regard her as a hypochondriac.

She relapsed into undisguised and unrelenting self-indulgency, raising silkworms on the one hand and gorging on chocolate on the other. She spent most of her time relaxing in the comfort of her bed, and lost all her natural teeth through sugared decay. To relieve her sheer boredom, she began, in 1825, to pen her eventually published autobiography: *The Record of My Life,* or *My Story.* She was to write to her son George:

> There is something in this great unsocial house which depresses my spirits beyond expression and makes it impossible for me to feel at home or to fancy that I have a home anymore.

For his own part, Goerge, instead of being exhilarated by the fact of his father's ascendancy to the highest office of the land, and being privileged to share in the reflected prestigious glory of the achievement, also became inexorably depressed. He read law in the office of Daniel Webster, and then opened his own law office in Boston. John Quincy, in an effort to finance his son, placed him in charge of the family's accounts, but George proved dilatory and indolent. Reprimanded by his father to keep a regular and accountable diary, (as had John Quincy himself), George maintained such a document for precisely 23 days. He lost all interest in his law practice, and, unlike his brothers, reacted very sensitively to all his father's incessant reproaches.

When John Adams died in 1826, it was George who most felt the loss of his grandfather, to whom he had been very close in spirit. The old man had left his estate in reasonable order, but final settlement still demanded detailed accounts together with the payment of a debt of $12,000. It fell to the task of George to present the inventory, but his procrastinations, excused by himself as sickness, aroused from John Quincy the comment that there were "no desponding fits which you cannot completely cure by going to bed at nine and rising at five o'clock . . ." and that a good night's sleep and useful occupation during the day were "specific and infallible remedies for all the blues."

In 1826, George had actually won election to the Massachusetts State Legislature, upon which John Quincy had offered him his congratulations, as well as, characteristically, his admonitions: "Consider the station to which you are called as a post of danger and of duty, and think as little as you possibly can of it as a post of honour."

George did not give the office all the obligations which it deserved, and resorted to drinking, smoking and napping, to such degree that he was not re-elected in 1828. He became ill, and it was Louisa who went north to nurse him back to health. She described him, sympathetically, as being "surely one of Shakespeare's fools for though full of capacity and intellect, he is constantly acting like one divested of understanding."

It is difficult, at this distance removed in time, to assess whether Louisa was too sympathetic whereas John Quincy was too harsh in their respective judgments upon their son. George was certainly guilty of a number of grievous faults—he had fallen into debt when such an offense was punishable with imprisonment, and the concerned John Quincy had offered to buy his books for $2,000 in an effort to provide him with funds. Furthermore, it became known that George had seduced Eliza Dolph, a young chambermaid in service at the home of Dr. Thomas Welsh, a close friend of the Adams' family, and a child was born in December, 1828.

By this time, George was in a state of despair, and John Quincy appealed to him to come to Washington. After long consideration, George agreed, and took passage on a boat from Boston in April, 1829. Overnight, after turbulent scenes with some of the passengers whom he had accused of deriding and of spying upon him, he disappeared off the boat. The family was in a state of shock and disbelief. Not until June was his body washed ashore, identified by a watch and notebook still intact in his clothes. He was buried in Quincy, alongside his sister (N)Abby in the family tomb.

It was left to Charles to cope with the problems of Eliza Dolph and her child. She had resorted to blackmail, but Charles refused to be intimidated and he negotiated a settlement. Reviewing all the sad events, he was to write: "George's fate was melancholy, but on the whole, I have been forced to the unpleasant conclusion that it was not untimely."

It was John who appeared to have been most upset by his brother's death. Following his expulsion from Harvard in 1823, he was employed at the Columbian Wheat and Flour mills along Rock Creek in Washington, which his father had purchased from Louisa's cousin, George Johnson, as a commercial investment to provide financial security in his later years. Unfortunately, it did nothing of the kind. John, aware of what the enterprise meant for his father, worked hard to make it succeed, but in his frustrations and disappointments, he resorted more and more to the bottle, which came to cloud his judgment.

He functioned as his father's private secretary when John Quincy was President, but, during the election campaign of 1828, caused embarrassment to his father by his intemperate remarks in public. It has been documented by historians that the foregoing campaign was by far one of the most vicious ever fought between two presidential candidates. On the one hand, John Quincy's supporters revelled in accusations of Andrew Jackson's alleged adulterous premarital association with his wife, Rachel, and the intense shock which the latter experienced upon accidentally hearing the scurrilous gossip concerning herself and her husband resulted in her death in December, 1828, within two months of Jackson's election victory. On the other hand, Jackson's supporters, ever mindful of what they considered to be the "corrupt bargain" between Henry Clay and Adams which enabled the latter to win the 1824 election, likewise raised issues deliberately intended to arouse public opinion against Adams. There was, for example, the matter of the billiard table in the White House: John Quincy had purchased one for the "exercise and amusement" of himself and his two sons, John and Charles, and the latter pair had made good use of it. Unfortunately, John had inadvertently included it in an inventory of furniture bought for the White House out of a congressional appropriation of $14,000. The opposition press seized upon the item with unmitigated glee, titillating and provoking the public with highly imaginative descriptions of male indulgence with cigars, strong drink, and salacious stories.

Still worse was the libellous attack by Congressman Russell Jarvis, who alleged that John Quincy, when minister to Russia, had, in order to gain favor with Czar Alexander I, facilitated the latter's lustful desires towards Martha Godfrey, Louisa's nursemaid. Louisa was forced, during the campaign, to issue a public denial of any such association. Jarvis, tactlessly, appeared at a White House reception, upon which John in loud voice declared, "There is a man who, if he had any idea of propriety in the conduct of a gentleman, ought not to show his face in the house." Upon hearing this remark, Jarvis left, but a few days later he saw and attacked John in the Capital building, an episode which led to a congressional investigation, but with no vote of censure upon Jarvis.

John Quincy lost the election of 1828. The disappointment was, in part, mitigated by the birth in the White House to John and Mary, married early in 1828, of John Quincy's first grandchild, Mary Louisa Adams, on December 2, 1828. A second grandchild was born within two years and christened Georgiana Frances Adams. Louisa had never really approved of Mary, considering her to be unworthy of her son, but following the birth of the children, she slowly became reconciled to her daughter-in-law as mother of her grandchildren.

John returned to his work in the mill in 1829, but pressure of work without compensatory financial gain drove him further into depression. He drank more heavily, his health deteriorated, and on October 23, 1834, he died, mourned by his parents and his widow[16] but apparently not by his brother, Charles, who wrote in his diary: "I cannot regret the loss of either of my brothers as a calamity either to their families or to themselves."

As mentioned earlier, Charles, the youngest of the three brothers, had entered Harvard at age 14, and, in due course, had graduated in 1825. His college career was quite undistinguished, and his grades were so low that he was excluded from participation in the final academic exercises. He had continually pestered his father for permission to drop out from college, but his requests were steadfastly rejected by John Quincy. On one occasion, the latter had written to his son: "If I must give up all expectation of success or distinction for you in this life, preserve me from the harrowing thought of your perdition in the next."

Charles, with his brothers, came to live in the White House when his father was elected President. He cared little for his law studies and still less for politics, since all it appeared to do was to vilify the family name, and create great unhappiness for his mother. He wrote that the family had become "exceedingly disjointed and uncomfortable. Indeed, I never saw a family which has so little of the associating disposition."

Unsettled in Washington, Charles often spent time in New York carousing with some of his Harvard colleagues, and it was on one of these visits that he met his future wife, Abigail Brown Brooks,[17] of Medford, Massachusetts, daughter of Peter Chardon Brooks, one of the wealthiest men in the state. The couple had immediately fallen in love, but both were only 19, and Abigail's father was reluctant to allow a formal engagement, since Charles appeared so unresolved about any career. In contrast, John Quincy, presumably eager to dispose of at least one of his sons, waxed enthusiastic, and in over-adulatory terms he described Charles in a letter to Brooks as being "sedate and considerate—his disposition studious and somewhat reserved—his sense of honour high and delicate, his habits domestic and regular, and his temper generous and benevolent. An early marriage is more congenial to a person thus constituted, than to youths of more ardent passions, and of more tardy self-control."

Charles may have hardly recognized himself as the subject of the foregoing encomium, but he was much indebted to John Quincy for his felicitous intervention on his behalf. Peter Brooks was persuaded to permit an engagement, but delayed the actual date of marriage for two years. In 1827, Charles wrote in his diary,[18] "Ever since my engagement, I have been preparing for a close of my licentious intrigues, and this evening I cut the last chord which bound me. What a pity that experience is always to be learnt over and over by each succeeding generation."

Charles was now in Boston studying law under Daniel Webster, and the admonitory correspondence between himself and his father was once more resumed. John Quincy did not want his son to miss out on the opportunity of a good and financially sound marriage,[19] and so the many letters he wrote to Charles were replete with such aphorisms as "Genius is the soil of toil," and such exhortatory verses as:

Six hours to Sleep and Six to Law
      And four devote to prayer;
Let two suffice to fill the Maw
      And six the Muses share.

Charles, always the spoilt and favored child of the family, never took his father's letters seriously, complaining ever that they were mere "sermons"; yet he was increasingly mindful that, through any of his own rash indiscretions and irresponsible misbehaviors, he could well lose a "jewel without reproach." He was, with no small relief, either to his family or himself, finally admitted to the bar in January, 1829. He set up his shingle in a small law office which, to save expenses, had no heating in the depth of winter. As he wrote to his mother: ". . . the toughness of the experiment rather tries me," and it was unpleasant to attempt to pour out a tumbler of water and have it come out ice.

Charles being Charles, with all his fantastic European experience, was nothing if not a "survivor." His reward came just nine months later when, on September 3, 1829, he was married to his Abby at the Brooks home in Medford. Louisa was too sick to travel, but John Quincy was present at the wedding, and, following the ceremony and honeymoon, the young couple moved into a comfortable home in Boston provided by the father of the bride.

In 1831, Abby gave birth to her first daughter, named Louisa Catherine, after the grandmother, and, in 1833, she gave birth to her first son, (John Quincy's first grandson), named John Quincy Adams, the Second. Upon the latter's christening, John Quincy gave Charles the seal that his father, John Adams, had affixed to the peace treaties with Britain. After John Quincy's death, Charles himself gave the seal to his son, in memory of his illustrious grandfather.

His marriage immeasurably changed Charles' attitude to life: he developed as a serious, hard-working young man of literary bent, and completed an edition of his grandmother Abigail's letters for publication in 1840, in the same year that he accepted nomination, and was elected for the Massachusetts legislature, where he served for three annual terms as Representative, and for a further two years as Senator.

In the meantime, young Abby produced offspring with monotonous regularity every two or three years. Charles Francis Adams, Jr., was born in 1835, and Henry Brooks Adams in 1838. Both were to have distinguished careers: Charles Francis, Jr., first as railroad executive, serving as president of the Union Pacific Railroad (1884–90), and later as historian, being elected president of the American History Society in 1901. He wrote biographies of both his father and grandfather (J.Q.A.), as well as his own autobiography, published after his death in 1915. Henry Brooks Adams was to become a history professor at Harvard, an indefatigable traveler in Western Europe, Central America, and Japan, and was author of the classic, brilliant semi-autobiographical study, *The Education of Henry Adams,* in 1906. He died in 1918.

Charles had built a new home for his family near the old house, so that they could be near the aging but still unquenchable John Quincy, who had been elected U.S. Representative in 1830, and held his seat until his death eighteen years later. John Quincy and Louisa adored their grandchildren, and the latter, in turn, adored their grandparents, John Quincy always being addressed as the President and Louisa as Madame.

There was ever present that strange bond of warm communication and understanding, unique to the relationship between grandparents and grandchildren. It is recorded that, on one occasion, young Henry was vociferously protesting his mother's insistence that he should go to school. Overhearing the altercation, John Quincy appeared in the room, and, without uttering a word, took Henry by the hand, walked him to the school a mile away, saw him seated at his desk, and then returned home, all without the exchange of a single word.

Abby, often depressed and worn out by recurrent pregnancies and the endless chores of safeguarding her young brood of children, was finally persuaded in 1843 to take a break from them all and travel with Charles and her father on a leisurely round trip north to Canada and west into New York State. Unfortunately, at the last moment, John Quincy, now an energetic, irrepressible, restless 76-year-old man, decided to accompany them, and the meant-to-be relaxing holiday turned out to be nothing less than an animated and exuberant victory parade. Everywhere they went, there were receptions, demonstrations, cavalcades, processions, to such extent that Abby wrote "I am so cross I can't speak to him."[20] She did eventually part from the group to visit Saratoga Springs, but the fatigues of the journey may well have contributed to a miscarriage in November, 1843.

Within the next decade, event succeeded event with such precipitous pace as to virtually exhaust the family's spiritual resources, since the whole era appeared to have vanished. In 1846, their youngest son Arthur, only 6, passed away; in 1848, John Quincy, at 80, collapsed and died in Congress. The mourning and grief was great, and he was buried in the family vault at Quincy. Joy returned to the family in June of the same year when Brooks, their last son, was born. He was to become a distinguished historian and published several seminal works, of which the most significant was to be *The Law of Civilization and Decay* (1895). He died in 1927.[21]

Charles re-entered the arena of national politics as vice-presidential candidate (with Van Buren) in the election of 1848, won by Zachary Taylor. Abby's father, Peter Brooks, died in 1849, leaving Abby part heiress to an estate valued at more than a half of a million dollars. In 1853, four years after the death of her husband, Louisa died, the last member of the famed husband-wife presidential dynasty of John and John Quincy Adams.

Charles was by no means dismayed by his lack of success in national politics. Financially secure through his wife's inheritance, he devoted himself to the completion of a monumental 10-volume publication of *The Works of John Adams* (1856).[22] He re-entered politics in 1858, being elected to his father's Republican congressional seat, and was re-elected in 1860, but then, in 1861, was appointed by Lincoln as U.S. Minister to Great Britain, a difficult assignment since a Confederate delegation had already arrived in London and had been accorded belligerent rights. Charles, undeterred, arrived in England accompanied by Abby, their daughter Mary (born in 1845), their youngest son, Brooks, and Henry, now 22, who was to serve as secretary to his father. Still uncertain of his reception,[23] Charles, instead of taking a long-term lease of residence, decided upon a month-by-month rental, yet, to his immense surprise and relief, he was to remain in London until 1868, during which period he successfully negotiated settlement of the *Trent* dispute, which at one time threatened to erupt into active hostilities between Britain and the United States.

Charles and the family finally returned to Quincy. In 1870, their first-born daughter, Louisa Catherine, died in Italy as a result of a carriage accident. In 1871, he sailed to Geneva as U.S. representative on the international commission set up to arbitrate the *Alabama* claims issue, in which the U.S. was finally awarded the sum of $15 million in damages.

Upon his return, he narrowly missed being nominated by the Republicans for President in 1872, while later, in 1876, he was unsuccessful in his bid for the office of governor of Massachusetts. For the remaining last decade of his life he devoted himself to literary pursuits and became Vice-President of the Historical Society. He died in 1886.

Andrew Jackson

(1829–1837)

Andrew Jackson and his wife, Rachel, were the first presidential couple not to have children of their own, but they did rear children, for which reason they deserve honorable mention. Also, unlike their predecessors, both Jackson and Rachel experienced lives of harsh reality, and were made only too familiar with the cruel shafts of fate and the bitter folly of expecting justice in a world where it seldom existed.

Jackson was fortunate even to have qualified as a candidate for the presidency, since his father had emigrated from Ireland only two years prior to Jackson's birth in 1767, and had actually died a few days before his son's birth in Waxhaw.[1] Jackson, when only 13, served as a mounted orderly during the Revolutionary War. He was taken prisoner, and suffered a permanent gash on his head as a result of a sword cut inflicted by a vindictive British officer whose boots Jackson had refused to polish. Two of his brothers were killed in the war, while his mother died in 1780, leaving Jackson in the care of sympathetic relatives. Though pursuing a dissipated lifestyle involving gambling and drinking, he made some

effort to becoming qualified in the law, and in due course was admitted to
the bar of North Carolina in 1787. One year later, he proceeded to
Nashville where he practiced as a criminal lawyer, but, whatever success
he experienced in that capacity was to be completely nullified by his
inexcusable culpability and laxity with respect to the complicated legal
problems of his own marriage to Rachel Donelson.

Rachel was a member of a respected family,[2] and was the youngest of
four daughters.[3] At age 17, she had married Lewis Robards, ten years her
senior, and had gone to live in Kentucky. Robards, a jealous and impetuous husband, later accused her of infidelity and forced her to return to
Nashville. A reconciliation was attempted, and Rachel again went to live
in Kentucky, but her stay was brief. The couple quarrelled incessantly
and, fearing physical harm to her daughter, Rachel's mother asked Jackson to undertake the journey to Kentucky and escort her home, which he
did (1790). Thereupon, the sad legal confusion which was to bring so
much heartbreak was set in motion. Robards applied to the Virginia
General Assembly for permission to publicly present in court his allegations against Rachel so as to obtain divorce. However, having been
granted the foresaid permission, he did not, for some reason, proceed
with the divorce action.

It was now that Jackson, without any confirmatory documentary
evidence, made the fatal assumption that Robards had actually gone
ahead and obtained his divorce. He had fallen deeply in love with Rachel,
and had asked for her hand in marriage. She accepted, and, trusting her
intended husband in legal matters, the lovers were married in 1791. For
two years they enjoyed marital bliss and happiness, only to learn, in 1793,
that only now was Robards initiating divorce proceedings on the newly
procured evidence that his wife was living in adulterous association with
Jackson. Rachel was prostrated with shock, and the shame of the event
endured within her for the rest of her life. Jackson never forgave himself
for bringing such calamity into the life of the woman he so dearly loved.
He did all he could to seek amends, first by remarrying Rachel legit-
imately in 1794, after the divorce was finalized, and then, ten years later
he challenged to a duel a young man, Charlie Dickinson, who had made
an offensive remark concerning Rachel. Dickinson was killed, and, presumably, Rachel's honor was vindicated.

Yet Jackson proved incredibly insensitive to his wife's feelings and
emotions: had he been satisfied with a small town existence, Rachel,
surrounded by sympathetic and supportive friends and relatives, might
well have recovered some of her social poise and equanimity, and might

have had restored to her part of the original joy and security which she had felt upon her initial marriage to Jackson.

But Jackson was an ambitious man. Dissatisfied with parochial politics and impelled by the belief that success would silence all scandal, in 1796 he accepted nomination as first Representative to the U.S. Congress of the new state of Tennessee, while, in 1798, he was appointed State Supreme Court Judge. At every election, innuendos of his adulterous association were widely publicized. While he ignored them, some of the unkind comments must inevitably have reached Rachel's ears, but, still, they did not deter him from seeking prominence in public office.

In 1804, Jackson found himself in financial difficulties, and he moved home to occupy a small plantation outside Nashville, which he renamed the Hermitage; and here, Rachel found contentment for many years. Yet, they were no little distressed that their marital union had not been blessed with children. Sadly, Rachel came to regard the situation as punishment by the Almighty for her sin of adultery. Not that the Jackson family was without children for company, since they appeared destined to be guardian angels for the unending progeny of innumerable friends and relatives. First in time, about 1805, were the four children of Edward Butler: two boys, Edward George Washington, and Anthony Wayne, respectively; and two girls, Caroline and Eliza. Edward Butler was the brother of Jackson's military colleague, Colonel Thomas Butler, who had originally requested that Jackson take care of his brother's children, and, subsequently, on his deathbed, had implored Jackson to likewise function as foster father to his own four children, consisting of three sons and a daughter: Thomas, Jr., 20, already a practicing lawyer at the time of his father's death in 1805; Robert, who was to marry Rachel Hays, the favorite niece of Rachel Jackson, and become Jackson's adjutant during the War of 1812; William Edward, who became a doctor and married Martha Hays; and Lydia, who married Stockley Donelson Hays.

After the Butlers, there were the sons of Samuel Donelson: John Samuel and Andrew Jackson. Samuel Donelson had become engaged to Mary Smith, a great favorite of Jackson's. When parental objection had been raised to the marriage, Jackson had, earlier, actively connived in the elopement of the lovers by providing Mary with a grapevine ladder wherewith to escape from her second-story bedroom. Mary's parents were enraged at Jackson's conduct, although the birth of grandchildren did eventually mellow their anger. Andrew Jackson Donelson was in due course to become a close associate of Jackson.

A still further addition was William Smith, a virtually abandoned child of an unhappy neighbor's family. Then the Jacksons undertook the formal legal adoption of one of twin boys born on December 22, 1809, to Severn Donelson (Rachel's next younger brother) and his wife, Elizabeth Rucker. The latter was a very sick woman who could not possibly have nursed two children, so permission was readily granted for Rachel to return with him to the Hermitage, and he was duly christened Andrew Jackson, Jr.

When, in the War of 1812, Jackson left the plantation to assume command of soldiers in the South, he once wrote to Rachel:

> . . . The sensibility of our beloved son has charmed me. I have no doubt from the sweetness of his disposition, from his good sense as evidenced from his age, he will take care of us both in our declining years. From our fondness toward him, his return of affection to us, I have every hope, if he should be spared to manhood, that he will with a careful education, realize all our wishes. . . .

While these fond aspirations were not to come to pass, he did bring great joy and companionship to his adopted mother during Jackson's many prolonged absences from home.

During the war, Jackson first gained prominence by his successful suppression of a Creek uprising in Mississippi Territory in 1813. Under the instigation of Tecumseh, a Shawnee Indian, the Creeks massacred over 400 white settlers at Fort Mims, Alabama. In an expedition of ruthless revenge, Jackson directed his troops in a wholesale slaughter which effectively ended all resistance. After one battle, a dead Indian mother was found still clutching her infant son. Failing to have the child accepted by any of the surviving Indian women, Jackson made the totally unexpected decision to take the boy home to the Hermitage. He was named Lincoyer, and became a playmate of Andrew Jackson, Jr. Presumably, he was never too happy in a white man's home, and attempted to run away to join his people on several occasions. But Jackson provided him with an education, and suggested vocational training as a saddler, but, unfortunately, before he reached the age of seventeen Lincoyer contracted tuberculosis and died.

Jackson's reputation was, for all time, established by his victory over the British at the Battle of New Orleans in January, 1815. It made no difference to the American public that it was fought after the War of 1812 had ended, and therefore played no part in the final peace negotiations. What did matter was that the country now had a new hero, "Old Hickory," tough, resolute, and determined, who had gained the affection of his troops, along with the particular gratitude of the citizens of New

Orleans. Rachel brought Andrew Jackson, Jr., south to the city to share in the acclamations and honors accorded her husband. For herself, she was appalled by what she called the "Babylon-on-the-Mississippi," given over to all manner of dissipation: "Oh, the wickedness, the idolatry of this place! unspeakable the riches and splendor." Yet, even Rachel and her husband relaxed occasionally, and a contemporary eyewitness recorded for posterity one fascinating scene:

> To see there two figures, the General, a long haggard man, with limbs like a skeleton, and Madame la Generale, a short, fat dump-ling, bobbing opposite each other like half-drunken Indians, to the wild melody of "Po-sum up de Gum Tree," and endeavoring to make a spring into the air, was very remarkable and far more edifying a spectacle than any European ballet could possibly have furnished.[4]

An even less kindly comment coupled Rachel to an old French adage that she showed "how far the skin can be stretched."

Yet, even though stout and "homely," and feeling very much out of place in the sophisticated, Creole society of New Orleans, Rachel gained many friends by reason of her undoubted sincerity, good-heartedness, and warmth of personality.

The return home to Nashville was one long glorious journey, since in town after town, the Jacksons were accorded a tumultuous welcome, culminating in a grand banquet at Nashville in May, 1815, where the General was presented with a beautiful ornate sword donated by the Mississippi legislature.

Possibly the only person disconcerted by the celebrations was young Andrew. Spoilt by his adopted father, who remembered only too well the misery of his own childhood days, the boy was presented with a virtually impossible model to emulate. Jackson, accustomed to obedience, very much modified his military stance in the presence of his son, yet could not help but promote the ideal virtues of a soldier, against which Andrew, in due course, internally began to object, and outwardly increasingly displayed signs of resentment at being expected to conform to such impossibly high and moral standards.

For the next few years, the whole family relaxed peacefully at the Hermitage. The plantation, at this time, had but one brick building and a Presbyterian church, which Jackson had had built for Rachel when she joined that faith. Now he resolved upon the erection of a more substantial residence, and, in 1819, there began the building of the first stately Hermitage mansion.[5]

In the meantime, yet another permanent resident had been added to the household. An itinerant portrait painter, Ralph E. W. Earl, had wandered into the district and had found favor with Rachel. In due course, he met, and was attracted to, Jane Caffery, one of Rachel's nieces, and the couple married with the full approval of the General and his wife. But not long afterwards, Jane died, whereupon Rachel insisted that Earl take up residence at the Hermitage. The net result was a series of portraits of Jackson, mostly of mediocre quality, but yet conveying much of the intrinsic qualities of the man—a lean, angular, rugged pioneer of the newly acquired trans-Applachian territories of the United States.[6] Jackson paid Earl fifty dollars for each of his paintings, and, in later years, Jackson seldom traveled anywhere without Earl as companion.

In 1819, Jackson accepted the responsibility of becoming guardian of yet another ward: Andrew Jackson Hutchings, the six-year-old orphan of John Hutchings, who had been Jackson's junior partner in the firm of Jackson and Hutchings, a trading store and early enterprise which both had established in the Cumberland River Valley at Clover Bottom. Hutchings was one of Rachel's nephews. The project had failed and Hutchings had moved south to Alabama, and it was there he died. Jackson adhered to a promise to take care of the family, and the young lad was brought back to the Hermitage.

Retirement at the plantation appeared acceptable to everyone except Jackson. Becoming restless, he accepted an army commission to command an expeditionary force against predatory Seminole Indian incursions into Georgia from Spanish-controlled Florida territory. The net result of his actions led to the secession of Florida to the United States in 1819 and Jackson was appointed as first Governor of the newly acquired lands, with immediate responsibility for concluding the peaceful transfer negotiations between Spain and the United States. With this purpose and duty in mind, Jackson sailed down to New Orleans in April, 1821, with Rachel, Andrew Jackson, Jr., and Andrew Jackson Donelson. From New Orleans they journeyed to Pensacola, the administrative capital of Florida territory. There then ensued weeks of exasperation for Jackson while the Spanish procrastinated in submitting the documents to be signed confirming transfer. Such was Jackson's frustration that it led him on one occasion to completely ignore protocol and direct the imprisonment of Colonel Calleva, the Spanish Governor, and many of his staff. So many were the protests against Jackson sent to John Quincy Adams, Secretary of State in Washington, that Adams was quoted as having stated that he came to fear opening his morning mail.

Jackson's problems were not merely political: Rachel had, a few years earlier, expressed her abhorrence for society life in New Orleans. There, she was helpless to achieve any change, but now, as the Governor's wife in Pensacola, the whole situation changed. She was concerned particularly with observation of the Sabbath, a day in Pensacola "profanely kept, a great deal of noise and swearing in the streets, shops kept open, trade going on, I think, more than on any other day." So, she persuaded Jackson to alter the situation by decree: Sabbath-breakers were to be fined $200 along with the posting of a $500 good behavior bond. Rachel was ecstatic by the reformation achieved:

> What, what had been done in one week! Great order was observed; the doors kept shut; the gambling houses demolished; fiddling and dancing not heard any more on the Lord's day; cursing not to be heard.

But everything in Pensacola—the climate, the food, the people— proved distasteful to Jackson and Rachel. After the transfer of territory was finally concluded on July 17, 1821, Jackson remained as official Governor for less than three months. He had actually returned to Nashville before submitting his formal letter of resignation to President Monroe in November, 1821, yet, despite the sinful pleasures of the South, the Jacksons returned home with not a few of its delectable comforts: new French beds and mattresses, cases and barrels of brandy, porter, whiskey, madeira and claret, while Rachel, always soothed by a pipe of tobacco, had since acquired a taste for Cuban cigars.

Had she been entertaining hopes that her husband had tired of public life, Rachel was soon to be disillusioned. In 1823, Jackson was elected as U.S. Senator, and was then nominated as presidential candidate one year later. The election was bitterly contested, with Jackson receiving a plurality of the popular vote, but John Quincy Adams obtained a majority of the electoral votes. Jackson returned to the Hermitage in the firm belief that he had been cheated of victory by an alleged "corrupt bargain" between Adams and Henry Clay, and he resolved to renew his campaign at the next election.

Jackson was fortunate at this juncture in his career to have the support of his very competent ward, Andrew Jackson Donelson, who had been admitted to the bar in 1823. Donelson, an extremely conscientious young man, had always been highly appreciative of Jackson's financial support in providing him with educational opportunities, first at the University of Nashville, and then at the U. S. Military Academy at West Point. At the latter institution, he had become involved in a fracas when he and other cadets had risen in protest against the physical abuse to which they felt they were being unjustly subjected in the name of military discipline. He had offered to resign rather than embarrass Jackson, but the episode was smoothed over, and Donelson graduated second in the class of 1820. Commissioned as second lieutenant, he served as aide-de-camp to Jackson in Florida, following which he entered Transylvania University of Lexington, Kentucky, to study law.

While he was away at college, he and Jackson corresponded regularly, although occasionally Donelson was guilty of laxity, as evidenced in one of the General's letters:

> Your aunt and myself . . . were fearful from your long silence that you were sick . . . You can attend to nothing more beneficial than writing. It expands the mind, and will give you . . . an easy habit of communicating your thoughts . . . when you know the pleasure it gives me to read your letters why not amuse yourself by writing to me. Choose your own subject—and handle it in any way your judgt may direct . . . This will give you confidence in yourself, which to be great, you must acquire, keeping your mind allways open to reason . . . but never yielding your opinion until the Judgt is convinced. Independence of mind and action is the noblest attribute of man . . .

Upon another occasion, Jackson sought to give his ward sound advice:

> Amuse yourself occasionally with history amonghst which if to be had I would recommend to you the history of the Scottish Chiefs. I have always thought that Sir William Wallauce . . . was the best model for a young man. In him we find a stubborn virtue . . . too pure for corruption . . . always ready to brave any danger for the relief of his country or his friend.

In 1824, Donelson married his first cousin, Emily, daughter of Captain John Donelson, and granddaughter of Colonel John Donelson, father of Rachel. The young married couple settled at Tulip Grove, a neighboring estate to the Hermitage.

The relationships between Jackson and the other wards of his household were not as harmonious as those relating to Donelson. Andrew Jackson Hutchings had been expelled from Cumberland College; Anthony Wayne Butler, attending Yale, had well overspent his allowances; while Andrew Jackson, Jr., the adopted son, at only 16, was already living at an extravagant level and, in six months, had incurred a debt of more than $300 at a fashionable clothing establishment in Nashville. Writing to Rachel from Washington in 1823, Jackson implored her to:

Tell my son how anxious I am that . . . he may become the (worthy) possessor of those things that a grateful country has bestowed upon his papa—Tell him . . . (to) read and learn his Book . . . (because) his happiness thro life depends upon his procuring an education now; and . . . on all occasions to adhere to truth . . . Never to make a promise unless on due consideration, and, when made, to be sure to comply with it . . . having experienced so much inconvenience from the want of a perfect education myself makes me so solicitous. . . .

The venom and viciousness released in the presidential campaign of 1824 was many times intensified as the two same candidates appeared for the 1828 election. Nothing was spared by way of distortion, rumor, and innuendo calculated to vilify the character of one or other of the contestants. Jackson was easily the most vulnerable, by reason of the tragic sequence of events relating to his marriage to Rachel. He was spared nothing, and the following statement was typical of his opponents' attack:

Anyone approving of Andrew Jackson must therefore declare in favor of the philosophy that any man wanting anyone else's pretty wife has nothing to do but take his pistol in one hand and a horsewhip in another, and possess her.

Yet, obviously, the public was not persuaded, and Jackson won an impressive victory as the nation's first elected President outside Virginia and Massachusetts. Tragically, his triumph was shortlived. During the months preceding the election, Rachel had remained at the Hermitage and had blissfully been preserved from all knowledge of the spiteful and merciless allegations hurled at her husband. When she heard of his success she stated, "Well, for Mr. Jackson's sake I am glad; for my own part I never wished it . . . I assure you I would rather be a doorkeeper in the house of my God rather than to dwell in that palace in Washington."

She was to be granted her wish: firmly established legend has it that while shopping for new clothes at Nashville, she overheard a conversation whereby she was abruptly and rudely made aware of all the vituperative abuse, tattle, and gossip of the campaign. Her inconsolable grief killed her. She died on December 22, 1828, and she was buried on Christmas Eve in the grounds of her beloved Hermitage. Her intended white inaugural costume was her shroud, and, standing at her graveside, Jackson stated, "In the presence of this dear saint I can and do forgive my enemies. But those vile wretches who slandered her must look to God for mercy."

Jackson entered the White House as a sad and lonely man; not that he was without company, for with him were Andrew Jackson Donelson, whom he had appointed as his private secretary, and Andrew Jackson, Jr., his adopted son. It was Donelson's wife, Emily, who, for Jackson's eight-year term of office, mainly functioned as his very charming hostess. Four of their children were born in the White House, and, for the most part, they remained a very happy family—except for the social and political embarrassments of the Eaton affair which devastated Washington during the first two years of Jackson's presidency. The President had appointed his close friend, Major John H. Eaton, as his Secretary of War, but, just prior to the appointment, Major Eaton had, in January, 1829, married Peggy Margaret Timberlake (nee O'Neil), daughter of an Irish tavernkeeper in Washington. Peggy, a pretty and vivacious girl, was well known to many congressmen, (including Jackson, himself), who frequented or resided at the tavern when Congress was in session. Peggy eventually married John Bowie Timberlake, a purser in the navy who was away on duty from home for long periods, during which time Peggy's name came to be linked with that of Major Eaton. It was, presumably, on account of these rumors that Timberlake, in 1828, suicided on board the frigate *Constitution*. Major Eaton's marriage to Peggy convulsed Washington, and the city was divided into two camps: on the one hand, Eaton's defenders, who included Jackson, and on the other hand, his many detractors, whose wives refused to include Peggy Eaton among their guests. Foremost among the latter was Jackson's own Vice-President, John C. Calhoun, and, what was worse, his own White House wards, Andrew Jackson Donelson and his wife, Emily.

Jackson was deeply offended. Emily made an attempt to compromise by agreeing to receive Peggy in the White House as Jackson's guest, but she adamantly refused invitations to the Eaton household. The consequence was that Jackson ordered the Donelsons back to Tennessee, stating, "I was willing to yield to my family everything but the government of my House and the abandonment of my friend without cause." The break distressed Jackson so much that he even accompanied the Donelsons back to Tennessee in June, 1830, leaving in charge of the White House, Major William Berkeley Lewis,[7] with his daughter, Mary Ann, as hostess, (whom Emily could not abide).

The household rupture did not last too long. Jackson found he could not manage without his competent secretary, so Donelson returned to the White House on his own, but, even there, the situation remained so tense that days would pass without any conversation taking place between the two men, and they resorted to the writing of notes to each other.

Only in April, 1831, was the crisis finally resolved by Martin Van Buren, Jackson's Secretary of State, who, by his offer to resign, caused other cabinet members (including Major Eaton) also to resign.[8] In 1834, Major Eaton was appointed Governor of Florida, and Peggy found Pensacola society much more to her liking than had Rachel Jackson. In 1836, Eaton became U.S. Minister to Spain, where Peggy became a great favorite at the Royal Court. After her husband's death in 1856, Peggy married an Italian dancing master, who promptly robbed her of her jewelry and money, and then eloped with her granddaughter.

Emily returned to the White House in September, 1831, along with her cousin, Mary Eastin, who had become a great favorite of the President. A lively and flirtatious girl,[9] Mary surrounded herself with a bevy of equally sprightly young maidens, who found easy and ready companionship with the several young blades from Tennessee who were frequent residents at the White House. Among the latter were Daniel Donelson, brother of the President's private secretary, and who later married Margaret Branch, (daughter of John Branch, Secretary of the Navy); Andrew Jackson Hutchings, who seemed destined to be expelled from college at Jackson's expense;[10] Samuel Jackson Hays, who ran up a haberdasher's bill of nearly $300, which the President paid; and then there was Andrew Jackson, Jr.[11]

The latter's unhappy love affairs came to occupy no little of the President's time and attention. There was first, in 1830, the episode with a certain Miss Flora, who lived at the home of Col. Edward Ward of Nashville, and who did not return Andrew's affections. Hearing of the outcome, Jackson wrote:

> I expected the result you name . . . Flora is a fine little girl . . . but as I told you she has given herself to coquetry . . . I assure you I am happy at the result, as I seldom saw a coquett make a good wife, and I wish you to marry a lady who will make you a good wife and I a good daughter, as my happiness depends much upon the prudence of your choice . . . I have councilled you through life to make no promises or engagements and I trust you will keep so until you advise with your father on this interesting subject.

Next, while at the White House, Andrew became involved with Mary Smith, one of Mary Eastin's friends. Overeagerness in his amorous pursuit led him to put aside etiquette, and the President was obliged to apologize for his behavior in a letter to her father, Major Francis Smith:

> . . . He has erred in attempting to address your daughter without first making known to you and your lady his honorable intentions

and obtaining your approbation. Admonished of this impropriety, he now awaits upon you to confess it. I find his affections are fixed upon her, and if they reciprocated, with your approbation, he looks upon the step which would follow as the greatest assurance of his happiness. Mine, since the loss of my dear wife, has almost vanished except that which flows from his prosperity. He is the only hope for the continuation of my name; and has a fortune ample enough with prudence and economy . . . with these prospects he presents himself again to your daughter.

Not that the letter made any difference, since Andrew was once more rejected. But, finally, he met with success, with his love for Sarah Yorke, an orphan girl of Quaker origin from Philadelphia, being fully reciprocated. Jackson was delighted with her,[12] and, after their marriage on November 24, 1831, he showed confidence in the young couple by appointing Andrew as estate manager of the Hermitage plantation. Jackson helped them appreciably by virtually completely furnishing their new home with furniture purchased by himself. When their first child, a daughter, was born, (November 1, 1832) they named it Rachel.[13]

Unfortunately, Andrew proved to be an inefficient manager. A costly fire at the Hermitage in 1834 had already involved Jackson in considerable renovation expenses, and Andrew's financial obligations measurably increased the president's indebtedness to his creditors. Jackson could have invoked the new bankruptcy law on behalf of his son, but, instead, personal honor prevailed, and not only did he sell some of his lands to redeem the debts, but he went and purchased for Andrew the 1000-acre Halcyon plantation on the Mississippi River at a cost of $23,700 in the hope that his son would profit from his experiences.

A very bitter blow to Jackson during his last winter at the White House was the death on December 20, 1836, of Emily Donelson, only 28 years old, who had developed tuberculosis and had returned to Tennessee. After his own retirement as President, there appeared little comfort in his final years at the Hermitage. He lost money during the 1837 Depression, and Andrew's extravagances and incompetencies plunged him deeper and deeper into debt, forcing Jackson to the humiliating position of having to borrow considerable sums of money from close friends.

In September, 1838, he suffered the loss of his near and long-time associate, the portrait painter Ralph Earl, of whom Jackson had said, "He was my constant companion when I travelled. Had I a wish I have now no one to go with me." Earl did leave for posterity a remarkable legacy of portraits of members of the Hermitage family, including those of Jackson and Rachel, of Andrew Jackson, Jr., and his wife, Sarah, of Andrew Jackson Donelson and his wife, Emily, and of Andrew Jackson Hutchings and his wife, Mary.

Although in constant pain through seemingly never-ending chills and fevers, Jackson made the effort to travel to New Orleans in 1840 to participate in the city's celebration of the twenty-fifth anniversary of his military victory. The journey was a nightmare, but no doubt compensated for by the exhilaration of standing on the battle site and reliving the thrills of triumph. As he said on a later occasion, "I am like a taper. When nearly exhausted (it) will sometimes have the appearance of going out, but will blaze up again for a time."

During his 75th year there occurred the opportunity for some distraction from physical suffering and financial worries, when it was suggested that one of his nephews, James A. Laughlin, should come to the Hermitage to help sort out the massive pile of confidential and political documents, and to record in writing the personal recollections of the General of some of the important events of his colorful life history. *Harper's Magazine* published seven installments, but, unfortunately, the project was never completed. In 1843, Jackson decided to rewrite his will:

> . . . Whereas since executing my will of the 30th of September 1833 my Estate has become greatly involved by my liabilities for the debts of my well-beloved and adopted Son, Andrew Jackson, Jr., which makes it necessary to alter the same, Therefore. . . .

A revised document was necessary. While the entire Hermitage estate was bequeathed to Andrew Jackson, Jr., "and his heirs forever," Jackson inserted the provision that the substantial loans made by his two friends, General J. B. Plauché of New Orleans, and Frank Blair of Washington, be repaid.[14] To his "beloved grandson, Andrew Jackson, son of Andrew Jackson, Jr., and Sarah, his wife,"[15] the General bequeathed the sword presented to him by the citizens of Philadelphia, while "to my well-beloved nephew, Andrew J. Donelson,[16] son of Samuel Donelson, deceased," he bequeathed "the elegant sword presented to me by the State of Tennessee, with this injunction that he fail not to use it when necessary in support and protection of our glorious Union. . . ." Jackson was destined to be plagued to his deathbed with financial worries relating to his son's debts. In 1844, the Halcyon plantation suffered a major disaster through flooding by the Mississippi River, to the extent that no income could be derived from the estate for the succeeding two years. The severe loss could have been alleviated had not Andrew, Jr., mismanaged the timber resources of the land. In these desperate moments of despair, Jackson was reduced to tears when, in March, 1845, he received a letter from his friend Frank Blair of Washington authorizing him "to draw upon us[17] at one day's sight for any sum between one and one hundred thousand dollars and his draft shall be honored. . . ." Fortunately, the General found it necessary to draw upon only a few thousand dollars.

Jackson died on June 8, 1845. Only hours later Sam Houston arrived from Texas—Houston, the former Nashville lawyer who had promoted Jackson's first bid for presidency, who had led the pallbearers at Rachel's funeral, and who, as President of the independent Republic of Texas, had finally negotiated with Andrew Jackson Donelson admission into the Union. Too late to have words with his former military chief, Houston, who had brought with him his young heir, said to him, "My son, try to remember that you have looked on the face of Andrew Jackson."

Andrew Jackson, Jr., fared no better after the General's death than he had prior to it. His debts so mounted that, in 1856, he sold the Hermitage plantation to the state of Tennessee for $48,000. He was permitted to occupy the house as "tenant at will" and there he died in 1856 as the result of a gun accident. Likewise, Sarah was permitted to reside at the mansion where she, too, died twenty-three years later, in 1888.

Martin Van Buren

(1837–1841)

Of the first seven Presidents of the United States only two (John Adams and his son, John Quincy Adams, respectively) failed to serve for two terms of office, but of the next ten Presidents not a single person served for eight years. This represented the time span from the accession of Martin Van Buren in 1837 to that of Ulysses S. Grant in 1869. Van Buren claimed to be the first President not to be born a British subject, although his birth, in 1782, occurred before final recognition of the independence of the United States by Britain under the Treaty of Paris, 1783.

Van Buren and his future wife, **Hannah Hoes**, who was also his cousin, had grown up together in the predominantly Dutch-speaking community of Kinderhook, situated on the east bank of the Hudson River in New York State, where his father, Abraham, kept the local tavern.[1]

Martin attended Kinderhook Academy, and then, at age 14, had entered the law office of Francis Sylvester, where he spent the next six years until his departure to New York, where he spent one more year in the law office of William Van Ness. Returning to Kinderhook in 1803, he set up law practice with his half brother, James Van Alen.

Martin married Hannah in 1807 and, in the twelve years of their marriage, she bore him five children: four sons and a non-surviving daughter. Abraham, the first son was born in 1807 at Kinderhook, but then the family moved to the small township of Hudson (30 miles south of Albany), where Hannah gave birth to John, Martin Jr., and her still-born daughter.

Van Buren, at age 30, had become a politically ambitious young man, serving as a New York State Senator (1812–20), and as State Attorney-General (1815–19). This had entailed a family move to Albany, the capital of New York State, a move which very much distressed Hannah, who had deteriorated in both physical and mental health following the death of her daughter. So, at the time when she needed so much the support of her own parents and relatives, she was deprived of them. At Kinderhook, the Van Buren family had been members of the Dutch Reformed Church, but no such Protestant persuasion existed at Hudson, so Hannah had become a member of a Presbyterian church, whose minister was the Rev. John Chester. Subsequently, the latter had moved to Albany, so that when the Van Burens moved to that city, Hannah found at least one old friend in whom she could confide.

Unfortunately, the association did little to alleviate her unending moods of depression and, by now, her quickly declining health. In 1817, she gave birth to her fourth son, Smith Thompson, but, within two years, she died on February 5, 1819, at age 36, and was first to be buried in the newly consecrated cemetery of the Second Presbyterian Church of Albany, but her remains were later disinterred and reburied in Kinderhook, where the inscription on her gravestone reads: "She was a sincere Christian, a dutiful child, tender mother, affectionate wife. Precious shall be the memories of her virtues."

Van Buren never remarried, and was a widower for 43 years until his death in 1862. Yet, left with four sons to raise, the youngest being less than two years of age, Van Buren immersed himself still deeper into political waters becoming U.S. Senator, 1821–28, and Governor of New York in January, 1829, but resigning less than two months later to accept appointment as Secretary of State in Jackson's Cabinet. He gained his President's life-long gratitude for his assistance in resolving the irritating Peggy Eaton affair, when the wives of Jackson's Cabinet members had socially ostracized the wife of Major John H. Eaton, his Secretary of War. Van Buren, being a widower, had nothing to lose by giving Jackson strong support by entertaining the Eatons, and, by finally offering to resign, an action which automatically led to the resignation of the entire Cabinet, thus ending the crisis.

In 1831, Jackson appointed Van Buren as Minister to the Court of St. James in London, where, after six months residence, he was to learn that the U.S. Senate had failed to confirm his appointment. With him in England was his son, John, the most talented of all his sons, who had already displayed his rhetorical gifts while a student at Yale. He had qualified as a lawyer, but his father, who was proud of him, yet had frequent occasion to reprimand him for his extravagances by way of drinking, gambling, and female flirtations, especially when reports of his indulgences were exaggerated by the newspapers and became a source of on-going family embarrassment.

Both father and son were handsomely feted on the London social scene, being received by King William and Queen Adelaide, and their brief stay in England appeared to have been one long round of gracious living by way of attendances at feasts, balls, and aristocratic functions.[2] In addition, they enjoyed a conducted tour of the English countryside over the Christmas holidays of 1831 under the guidance of Washington Irving, who was, at the time of their visit, serving as an attaché at the U.S. Legation in London, to which he had been appointed after living in Liverpool for a number of years attending to his family's hardware business.

During February, 1832, Van Buren received, virtually simultaneously, two items of news affecting his career: the one announcing the rejection by the Senate of his London appointment; the other offering him nomination as Vice-President to Jackson if re-elected in November. Jackson was re-elected, and, for the next four years, Van Buren worked assiduously to justify his expected nomination as successor to Jackson. His expectations came to pass, and, in 1837, Van Buren was inaugurated as President in the White House, where, initially, he was joined by all four of his bachelor sons.

Abraham, the eldest, after attending West Point, had made the army his career and had attained the rank of major before resigning to become his father's private secretary. At that time, Congress made no paid provision for such a post, so Van Buren appointed him as second auditor in the Treasury Department (replacing Major William B. Lewis who had performed similar duties for President Jackson). Since Van Buren was a widower, he did little public entertaining for his first eighteen months of office, so that social life in Washington was at a low ebb. However, the intrigues of Dolley Madison radically changed the situation: she brought to Washington a young relative, Angelica Singleton, who had just gradu-

ated from Madame Garland's fashionable ladies' seminary in Philadelphia. Dolley cared little as to which of the four sons in the White
House would be captivated by Angelica's beauty, and it just happened
that she caught the eye of Abraham at a White House dinner in March,
1838. There ensued a whirlwind courtship, and Abraham and Angelica
were married in November of the same year at her father's plantation in
South Carolina: Dolley's scheme had worked to perfection.

Angelica was true to her name: she was a lovely girl who charmed
everyone with whom she came into contact. Now called upon to be
official hostess at the White House, she performed her new duties with
unqualified grace and elegance. During the spring of 1839 she and her
husband traveled to Europe, but spent most time in London where they
met John.[3] Their meeting was an extraordinary one, since Abraham and
Angelica had both retired to bed when suddenly John appeared at the
bedroom doorway. Ignoring Angelica's modesty and embarrassment, the
two brothers, separated for two years, proceeded to carry on an animated
and vivacious conversation, with Abraham remaining in bed, and John
standing in the darkened bedroom entrance. Eventually, John withdrew
and went off to his exclusive London club, where he dined, drank, and
gambled, recording the episode, for his father's information and, no less,
for his consternation:

> went to Almack—all the world there, Ladies F. Cowper, W.
> Stanhope; presented to the latter, don't like her now I know her, she
> is insipid. Found old Lord Powerscourt dinner party there; Grand
> Duke and Prince William there. I danced with Breadalbane's sister
> . . . wound up at Crockford's.

Angelica's uncle, Andrew Stevenson, was the American minister in
London at the time of her visit, and he was instrumental in having the
young couple formally presented to Queen Victoria.

Upon their return to the United States it appeared that Angelica had
taken it upon herself to affect some of the mannerisms of the English
Royal Court, since, during receptions at the White House, she elected to
remain seated to receive her guests, a startling innovation in protocol for
which, at one and the same time, she was roundly criticized, yet quickly
forgiven since Washington society was quick to recall that virtually ten
years had elapsed since the White House had been graced by the presence
of a First Lady, and, in consequence, the social scene had been dreary and
barren.[4] Sadly for the young couple, their first child, a baby girl, Rebecca, born at the White House in March, 1840, died within a few
months of birth. A second child, a boy, Singleton, was born in May,

1841, in South Carolina, and the proud father wrote later, "He is not large by any means, but in perfect health." The couple were in due course to be blessed by a second son, named Martin after his grandfather.

During the almost two years which the White House had been without a First Lady, Van Buren found himself embroiled in yet one more "affair" which had arisen to trouble Washington society. He had already given Jackson immeasurable support, first in his defense of Rachel during the scurrilous campaigns of 1824 and 1828, and, again, in the matter of Peggy Eaton's non-acceptance by Cabinet members. Now, in 1837, being still a non-remarried widower, he found himself saddled with a Vice-President who had fathered two illegitimate daughters by a colored slave girl. This was Richard Mentor Johnson[5] and his mistress was Julia Chinn, who died when the girls were still very young. Johnson, a courageous army officer (who is accredited with having killed Tecumseh at the Battle of the Thames in 1813) lost none of his military morale when he entered the political arena, so that when he became Vice-President he openly acknowledged being the father of his two colored daughters, and attempted to introduce them into Washington society. He was snubbed by everyone—except Van Buren, who was unencumbered by any female family protests, until the advent of Angelica, who slowly but methodically reduced the social contact with the Johnson family to a minimum. The Democratic party, to relieve itself of future embarrassment,[6] made certain of its refusal to renominate Johnson as Vice-President in its convention of 1840.

Assisting Abraham as his father's private secretary in the White House was Martin, Jr., who seemed to have inherited the sickly ill-health of his mother and early deceased sister rather than the robust, good health of any of his brothers. He was kept busily bored with having to sort and file the mass of documents and correspondence with which the President was daily inundated.

In contrast, his exuberant brother, John, never lost a moment in what, eventually, was to destroy his health through his inordinate capacity for self-indulgence. He enjoyed to the utmost what he considered to be the "good life," as defined by his father[7]—gracious living, in terms of eating and drinking, together with John's incremental specialties of gambling and love of the fair sex, in which the press never failed to take malicious delight and political advantage. The one episode which received most adverse comment, appearing as it did in James Gordon Bennett's scandal-packed *New York Herald,* was that relating to Maria Ameriga Vespucci, an Italian lady of questionable character, who claimed descent from the explorer. She had apparently come to the United States in the hope of obtaining money from Congress to pursue research on studies concerning her ancestor, but, failing in her endeavors, she made overtures to John, mistakenly presuming that her favors would persuade him to assist her in her quest for dollars, but, again, to no financial avail.

Fond as he was of his son, and always grateful for his political support, Van Buren never failed to reprimand him for his indiscretions as well as for his lack of control in money management due to his insatiable love of pleasure. Without doubt, John was an indefatigable worker, as indeed he had to be to remain solvent. His law practice in Albany prospered, his partner John McKeon being an ambitious politician serving in the New York legislature. Van Buren's hope was that his son would marry, and that marriage responsibilities would serve to slow down John's zest for high living.

In good time, but not until after Van Buren's term of office had expired, John did marry. Earlier, he had worked in the office of Judge James Vanderpoel in Albany, and there he had met his daughter, Elizabeth. Their friendship developed into affection, and they were married in June, 1841. John, in considerable debt at this time, said to Van Buren:

> So you see, for a young gentleman about committing matrimony I am as badly off as my worst enemy could desire. One thing is certain, Miss Elizabeth won't marry me for my money.

In 1842, Van Buren was delighted with news of another granddaughter, the daughter of John and Elizabeth. John wrote: "She weighed nine and half pounds at birth which is considered a light child, has dark blue eyes, regular features, and a very fine forehead . . . we all agree to name it after my mother—was her name Anna or Hannah?" The daughter was named Anna. But Elizabeth died only two years later, and John's subsequent history was identical to that of his father following the death of Hannah Van Buren in 1819: both plunged themselves into the maelstrom of state and national politics, ostensibly as the antidote to and distraction from intense grief.[8]

Van Buren's youngest son, Smith Thompson (named after the Chief Justice of the New York State Supreme Court) was said to be closest in physical resemblance to his father. He (and Martin Jr.) had virtually been reared first by his aunt, Maria, in Albany, and then by various relatives and friends. In 1833, he had traveled to Europe with Edward Livingstone, a prominent lawyer and Senator from Louisiana. Livingstone, a Southern gentleman who spoke French fluently, had succeeded Van Buren as Secretary of State under Jackson, and had then been appointed as Minister to France, and it was upon this occasion that young Smith was privileged to accompany the Livingstone family.

After Van Buren's election as President, the White House became, at least temporarily, Smith's first permanent residence with all the family sharing accommodation under the same roof. Van Buren had obviously expected a great deal of work from all of them, but then John, wishing to further his own law practice, returned to Albany, and Smith decided to go with him, and later enrolled in school in Pittsfield, Massachusetts. Unlike John, however, Smith appeared to have limited ambitions, a trait which gave Van Buren no little concern. Smith did, however, qualify for the bar in 1841, and for two years practiced law in New York City. It was during this period that he met and married Ellen King James,[9] the very eligible daughter of William James, a rich Albany merchant.

After his non-re-election as President in 1840, Van Buren enjoyed a relaxed period of semi-retirement, only to re-enter the political arena with increased vigor for the 1844 election. He lost the Democratic nomination even though he had received the majority (but not two-thirds majority) of the delegation votes at the party convention. The successful candidate was the first presidential "dark horse," James K. Polk, who went ahead to victory in the November election.

Again, in 1848, when the expansion of slavery had become the major political issue, the Democratic party split, one of the factions terming itself the Free Soil party which nominated Van Buren as its presidential candidate, with Charles Francis Adams (son of John Quincy Adams) as the vice-presidential nominee. The main elements of the Democratic party presented Lewis Cass as their nominee, but the split gave victory to Zachary Taylor, the Whig candidate.

At the outbreak of war with Mexico in 1846, Abraham rejoined the army and, in recognition of "gallant and meritorious conduct at Contreras and Churubusco" he was promoted to the rank of lieutenant-colonel. He remained in the army until 1845.

Most active politically during this period was Van Buren's son, John. His wife, Elizabeth, had died in 1844, and, in 1845, he won the office of Attorney General of New York State, having served as congressman in the U.S. House of Representatives since 1841. He was influential in organizing the "Barnburners" in the same state, a group which was hostile to any expansion of slavery. He was a gifted, enthusiastic orator, who spared himself nothing in support of his father's candidacy. In 1848, Van Buren wrote and published the first comprehensive statement of the Free Soil position, a document which John helped to edit and publicize.

After the election, however, John, unhappy with the consequences of the divisiveness within the Democratic party, returned to the fold, and gave his support to the compromise measures of 1850. Smith, likewise, had been active on his father's behalf, and had been very critical of Polk when the latter had appreciably weakened the Democratic position in New York by ignoring the patronage privileges claimed by the vigorous "Barnburner" faction in that state.

After his marriage, which now provided him with ample financial security, Smith abandoned his law practice to live a life of leisure. He was once described as a person who was

> afraid himself lest he may disappoint expectations . . . he must by repeated efforts learn to shake off modesty and divers sort of hypercritical anxieties which will embarrass his thoughts and stiffen, if not stifle him. . . .

After the election of 1848, Van Buren retired permanently to Lindenwald, and, anxious for company, he suggested to Smith that, if the latter were to bring his family to reside with him, Smith would be made heir of the estate. Since he had always disliked city life, Smith agreed, but only on condition that the house be completely remodeled. Van Buren was greatly dismayed at what he considered to be unnecessary work and needless expense, but yet he had to acknowledge that he, himself, had already been guilty of similar action. He wrote:

> What curious creatures we are. Old Mr. Van Ness built as fine a home here as any reasonable man could. Its stability unsurpassed and its taste of what was then deemed to be the best. William P. Van Ness had disfigured everything his father had done. I succeed him and pull down without a single exception any erection he had made and with evident advantage. Now comes Smith and pulls down many things I had put up and made the alterations without stint . . . what nonsense.

Van Buren, finding himself with no option, eventually agreed to the renovations, but stipulated that Smith would have to assume part of the burden of cost. Smith promptly engaged the services of Richard Upjohn, a British-born architect, who not only enlarged the building to almost forty rooms but completely transformed the exterior into a hybrid structure of Renaissance, Gothic revival, and Italian palazzo styles. Tragically, no sooner was it completed than Smith suffered the loss of his wife, thus leaving him a widower with three children.

Van Buren now embarked upon the writing of his memoirs along

with other historical materials, work in which he employed both Smith
and Martin Jr. Unfortunately, the latter was in an advanced stage of
tuberculosis, and, having exhausted all the typical remedies available in
the United States, Van Buren decided to take his son to Europe in 1853 in
search of possible cure there. Martin Jr. underwent treatment by physi-
cians in both London and Paris, and recovered sufficiently to join a family
reunion at Vevey on L. Leman in Switzerland, where Van Buren and
Martin Jr. were joyously greeted by Abraham and his family along with
John and his daughter, Anna. Martin then returned to London, while Van
Buren, the first ex-President to visit Europe, was everywhere feted by the
heads of state.[10] In Rome he was granted audience by the Pope and then,
having been lavishly hosted by King Ferdinand of Naples (whose petty
tyranny Van Buren chose to completely ignore) he settled in the Villa
Farangola in Sorrento to write his autobiography.

In 1855, it became evident that Martin was now dying and Van Buren
hurried back to Paris. He wrote:

We have . . . the best of servants and troops of obliging friends by
which the painfulness of our situation is as much as possible
lessened, but the last result is constantly before my eyes and cannot
be disguised and I fear much longer delayed.

Martin died in March, 1855, and, in July, Van Buren sailed home with
the body.

While at Sorrento, Van Buren had been delighted to hear the news of
Smith's remarriage to Henrietta Irving, a great-niece of his friend, Washington Irving. Van Buren wrote of them at the time: "He, of course,
thinks her perfect and she is certainly of a good head, 25 years old."
Smith had brought his wife to live at Lindenwald, and Van Buren greatly
enjoyed their company as well as Smith's assistance in sorting and arranging documentary materials. Smith spent a considerable amount of time
editing Van Buren's major historical work, eventually to be published in
1867 under the title: *Inquiry into the Origin and Course of Political Parties in
the United States.*

In 1858, Van Buren was extremely disappointed when Smith decided
to move from Lindenwald to be nearer his wife's family, thus leaving Van
Buren in relative isolation until his death in July, 1862.[11] Lindenwald and
all its contents were put up for auction, and the proceeds were distributed
among the surviving members of the family.

William Henry Harrison

(1841)

Van Buren lost his bid for re-election in 1840 for a variety of reasons, not least among which was the use by his opponent's supporters of effective campaign slogans. This was probably the first occasion for catchword propaganda to play so significant a role in a presidential election, although, in 1828, the affectionate sobriquet "Old Hickory" was employed to good effect by Jackson's supporters.

Van Buren's ostentatious displays of gracious living at the White House had offended many Americans who compared him unfavorably with his homespun predecessor in office, and they now seized upon the opportunity of again comparing him unfavorably with a possible successor, William Henry Harrison. A Harrison-Tyler ticket had opposed that of Van Buren-Johnson in 1836, but the latter were Jackson's nominees, and his popularity was too great a barrier to be overcome at this juncture; moreover, the campaign slogan of the day: "Whole Hog for Harrison," held minimal appeal for the electorate.[1]

The defeated candidates refused to be despondent: on the contrary,

120

they redoubled their efforts, as did their supporters who came up with two slogans which quickly caught on during the campaign. The first stressed the military record of the candidate, and just as Jackson had been "The Hero of New Orleans" so Harrison was now publicized as "The Hero of Tippecanoe" ("and Tyler too"). The second, equally effective, (and certainly a marked improvement upon that of 1836), sought to recapture the popular pioneer quality of Jackson, with its focus upon Harrison's "log cabin and hard cider" image, in direct contrast to the "wine and golden spoons" stereotype projected by Van Buren:

Old Tip he wears a homespun shirt
He has no ruffled shirt-wirt-wirt
But Mat he has the golden plate
And he's a little squirt-wirt-wirt

It is true that Harrison did once live in a log cabin,[2] but he was born in 1773 in a pleasant country mansion in Charles City County, Virginia. His father, Colonel Benjamin Harrison, had been a prosperous planter and prominent politician who had been a signatory of the Declaration of Independence. His mother, Elizabeth Bassett, was a niece of George Washington's sister, and she had borne at least seven children, of whom William was the youngest. The Harrison estate had been plundered by Benedict Arnold's raiders and while, in time, it did recover, the family's finances had fallen to low ebb at the time of Benjamin Harrison's death in 1791.

William had been tutored at home during his early years, and, at 14, he was enrolled at Hampden-Sydney College whence, upon graduation, he entered Pennsylvania Medical School at Philadelphia. His father's death resulted in a change of plans: he abandoned his ideas about becoming a physician and, instead, enlisted in the United States Infantry. Promoted to lieutenant, he served as aide to General "Mad Anthony" Wayne, and then, as captain, he was given command of Fort Washington near Cincinnati.

It was here that he met and fell in love with Anna Tuthill Symmes,[3] daughter of Colonel John Cleves Symmes, a judge in the Northwest Territory. The judge approved of their friendship but not of the romance, and he insisted that the relationship be terminated; but Anna was a headstrong girl whose mother had died soon after her birth. Anna was then reared by her grandparents[4] who had let her have very much of her own way. So, when the judge was away on business during the month of November, 1795, William appeared at the home to claim his bride, and they were married by Dr. Stephen Wood, a sympathetic justice of the peace. Symmes, upon his return, was predictably furious, and he refused to have anything to do with his disobedient daughter and son-in-law. Only when the grandchildren began to appear did he relent and mellow his attitude—with perhaps the added incentive, although unbeknownst to him at the time, that he was to gain fame as being grandfather of the largest brood of children ever born to one President with one wife: William and Anna had ten children in less than twenty years.

After marriage, Harrison built for his bride a log cabin which, in the course of time, was very much enlarged and extended, but, forty-five years later, the original structure still remained, in the eyes of Whig beholders, the symbol of the unpretentious pioneer spirit which was to win them the 1840 election.[5]

In 1798, Harrison resigned from the army to devote more time to his lands, as well as to the economic and political affairs of the Northwest territory, and he was appointed as its first representative to Congress in 1799. He was instrumental in securing passage of a bill which divided the Territory into two smaller divisions, Indiana and Ohio, respectively, and, from 1800–1812, he served as Governor of Indiana territory, with headquarters at Vincennes where six of his children were to be born, and where he designed a new mansion named Grousland.

His first child, Elizabeth (Betsy) Bassett, saw daylight at Fort Washington in 1796, and, two years later, his eldest son, John Cleves Symmes, was born at Vincennes. A second daughter, Lucy Singleton, was born in 1800 in Richmond, Virginia, at the time when her mother was visiting relatives. The next five children were all given birth at the governor's mansion in Vincennes: William Henry Harrison, Jr. (1802), John Scott (1804), Benjamin (1806), Mary Symmes (1809), and Carter Bassett (1811).

In 1802, Harrison received instruction from Jefferson to obtain as much land from the Indians as possible. This he did so successfully, and at bargain prices, until he found himself opposed by two Shawnee brothers, Tecumseh and Tenskwatawa, (known as the Prophet), who attempted to unite the Indians against the sale of their territory. Resistance came to a head when Tecumseh refused to recognize the Treaty of Fort Wayne of 1809, whereby Harrison had negotiated with the Miami Indians for transfer of two and a half million acres of land to the United States. In November, 1811, Harrison's forces routed the Indians at a point where the Tippecanoe River empties into the Wabash, and so secured Indiana for American settlement. Within a year, Tecumseh himself was killed at the Battle of the Thames River, near Detroit, and, in 1814,

Harrison retired from the army, and returned to farm at North Bend, where his wife had inherited 3,000 acres of land from her father.

In 1813, the Harrisons' ninth child, Anna Tuthill, was born in Cincinnati, and, in 1814, James Findlay was born at North Bend, but died in infancy at the age of three.

With a large family[6] to support, Harrison made every effort to supplement his farming income by engaging in a variety of business ventures, none of which were successful, so that he was obliged to mortgage some of his lands. It was now also that he embarked upon a career in politics, serving as U.S. Congressman (1816–19), and Ohio State Senator (1825–28). Since these duties kept him away from home for substantial periods of time, much of the work of farm supervision, as well as the task of rearing the children, fell to the lot of Anna. Her child-bearing functions did not end until 1814, when six of her brood were below the age of 10. It was in this year that her eldest daughter, Betsy, married her cousin, John Cleves Scott. Their only child, a baby girl, died in 1816. Two more of Harrison's children married in 1819: the eldest son, John Cleves Symmes, to Clarissa Pike, and Lucy Singleton to David K. Este, a Cincinnati lawyer; but, tragically, both were to die at an early age, Lucy in 1826, and John in 1830.

John's wife, Clarissa, was the daughter of General Zebulon M. Pike, immortalized by the mountain named after him: Pike's Peak. John had been appointed by President Monroe as receiver of the Vincennes land office and he took up residence at Grousland, the mansion built by his father. He was a respected member of the local society, serving as chairman of the borough board of trustees, and as supervisor of the library which was housed at Grousland. In the late 1820's, he was unfortunate to become involved in a financial transaction which led to his ruin: he cashed a $5,000 draft on the United States Treasury for Captain William Prince, a former associate of his father. But Prince defaulted and John Cleves was held responsible for this debt, as well as for certain disputed land office claims, which amounted to a total liability of $12,000. When Jackson was made aware of the situation in 1829, he authorized John Cleves' dismissal from office. One year later, the latter contracted typhoid and died, leaving a widow and six children, a blow described by Harrison as "the most severe affliction I have ever experienced."

Harrison had, in 1828, accepted John Quincy Adams' offer of appointment as U.S. Minister to Colombia, but, while in that country, he was less than discreet and voiced his support of political factions opposed to

Simon Bolivar. This resulted in his quick recall by Jackson, who thus, in one and the same year, acted less than generously towards his political adversary, William Harrison, the father, as well as towards John Cleves, the son.

Anna chose to remain home while Harrison was in Colombia, so the latter took along with him, as attache, his youngest surviving son, Carter Bassett, now a maturing youth of 17, who enjoyed every moment of the brief adventure in a foreign land. Upon his return home, he brought back a brightly colored macaw for his youngest sister, Anna, and plants for his mother.[7]

Harrison led a life of semi-retirement from politics for several years after 1829. His financial affairs were now in a sorry state, not only because of the failure of an iron foundry enterprise with which he had become involved, but also because of problems involving the creditors of his deceased son, John Cleves, as well as those of his fourth son, his namesake, William Harrison, Jr.

William Jr. had been educated at Transylvania College, Kentucky, and had later qualified in the law. Of all members of the family, he was to occasion his father most concern because he had, early on, developed a more than ordinary taste and reputation for a convivial way of life. Harrison had once written to him:

> . . . I must again exhort you to abandon the lounging and pro-
> crastinating mode of life which for some time you have followed.
> In the morning, go to your office and stay there until dinner and if
> you have no other business read professional books and never open
> any other book in those hours devoted to business. . . .

William Jr.'s marriage in 1824 to Jane Findlay Irwin had raised fond hopes that his newly acquired responsibilities would appreciably help to foster a much desired sobriety of habits and attitudes, but his pledges of reform were of no avail. He abandoned his law practice in Cincinnati and moved to North Bend, Indiana, where his father had donated him a farm as a marriage gift. His debts appeared without end, and, despite Harrison's sale of his own lands to help solvency, William Jr.'s farm had to be leased out since the son proved no better at the business of farming than he had at the profession of law. He was without redemption, and, in many ways, his premature death in 1838 at age 36, "intemperate to the last," was a happy release both for himself and certainly for the family.

Only two years later, yet another of Harrison's sons died: this was Benjamin; born at Vincennes in 1806, dead at age 33. His was a life of adventure, perhaps emulating that of his father, since, at first, he had enrolled in medical school, but had then favored the more adventurous occupation of soldiering. He had participated in the Texas War of Independence, but had been captured by the Mexicans. In honor of his father's reputation, the Mexicans had released him, even to the extent of providing him with a horse, arms, and a guide to reach the Texas lines. His return with such privileges so disconcerted the Texans that they concluded he had been bribed to function as a Mexican spy, and they promptly placed him in prison. Only after a military court hearing was Benjamin released and, thereupon, sent home. He was twice married, first to Louise Bonner, and then to Mary Raney. His death in 1840 made him the sixth of Harrison's ten children to die before his father's inauguration as President in March, 1841.

Without doubt, the son who gave most satisfaction was John Scott.[8] Like his father, he had initially contemplated pursuing a medical career, but, after graduating from Cincinnati College in 1824, he married Lucretia Knapp Johnson, and thereupon turned to farming at which he proved quite successful. Lucretia gave birth to three children: two girls and a boy, who was named after his grandfather, but did not survive infancy. Their family happiness ended with the death of Lucretia in 1829. John Scott was remarried in 1831 to Elizabeth Ramsey Irwin, and it was the second son, Benjamin, of this second marriage who was destined to become the 23rd President of the United States (1889–1893).[9]

It was John Scott who took over the responsibilities of managing Harrison's farming affairs while the latter was away campaigning, but, again, like his father, John Scott, in due course, also concerned himself with the well-being of the community and he served for many years as a local magistrate and justice of the peace.

In the presidential campaign of 1836, the Harrison-Tyler combination proved inadequate to defeat Van Buren, the nominee of outgoing President Jackson, but, in 1840, the same combination was overwhelmingly victorious, but, for Harrison himself, it was tragically short-lived. In February, 1841, his wife, Anna, had been too ill to accompany him for the inauguration ceremony on March 4th. At the age of 68, he rode his favorite horse, "Old Whitey," down Pennsylvania Avenue and then, the oldest President to date, he also gave the longest inaugural address ever. It lasted 105 minutes, and on the chilly March day Harrison wore neither hat, gloves, nor topcoat. He caught a chill which developed into pneumonia and died on April 4. He was the first President to die in office and to lie in state in the White House.

For the brief period of his presidency, Harrison's acting First Lady had been Jane Findlay Harrison, the widow of William Henry, Jr., (who had died in 1838), and she had been assisted by Harrison's youngest daughter, Anna Tuthill.[10]

Back in Ohio, John Scott cared for his widowed mother until her death in 1864, aged 89.[11] Congress granted her $25,000, or a full year's presidential salary, and this precedent was followed for all presidential widows until a regular pension system was adopted. John Scott emerged on the national political scene for the brief period of four years, 1853–57, when he served as the Whig representative from Ohio in the 34th and 35th Congresses. He spent the remaining years of his life on his Indiana farming estate where he died in 1878, aged 74.

Thereupon there occurred what is probably the most bizarre event ever to befall any son (or daughter) of a President of the United States. The day following the funeral, John Scott's son, John Harrison (brother of Benjamin Harrison), went with friends to locate the body of a young relative which had been taken from the cemetery a few days earlier. These were the days of the "body snatchers" who were paid by medical schools to supply cadavers for dissection. John visited one such school without result, and then, at the Ohio Medical School in Cincinnati, he discovered a body suspended from its neck in a shaft adjoining the dissection room. The body was taken down and, upon removal of the sheet in which it was wrapped, John found to his horror that the corpse was that of his own father, buried only the previous day. The episode created sensational headline news across the country, but apparently left medical authorities unimpressed and unapologetic, since they claimed, that without bodies upon which to experiment, students could not receive adequate training.

John Tyler

(1841–1845)

At the time of their joint inauguration on March 4, 1841, President Harrison had fathered ten children and Vice-President John Tyler had fathered eight, a total of 18 children, which has yet to be surpassed by any subsequent combination of President-Vice-President. John Tyler was elevated to the office of President upon the death of Harrison on April 4, 1841. His wife, Letitia, died in 1842, and Tyler married Julia Gardiner in 1844. In due course, Julia gave birth to seven children, so that the grand total of children fathered by Harrison[1] and Tyler amounted to no fewer than 25, a figure hardly likely ever to be equalled, yet alone exceeded by two successive chief executives.[2]

John Tyler, born in 1790, was the sixth in a family of eight children born to John Tyler, Sr., a judge in the General Court of Virginia, and his wife, Mary, who died when John Jr. was only seven years old.

As a young boy, John was described as having "a slender frame" and "a very prominent thin Roman nose": the nose remained a distinctive feature of his countenance.[3]

While attending elementary school, John participated in a melee resulting from a schoolboy rebellion against a zealous Scottish teacher, Mr. McMurdo by name, who overindulged in the use of the birch. The latter was overwhelmed by a group of the boys who tied him up and left him alone in the classroom. He was eventually freed by a passerby who heard his cries for help, but upon complaining to Judge Tyler about the conduct of his boys, John and William, the judge, who had no liking for brutal schoolmasters, quoted him Virginia's state motto: SIC SEMPER TYRANNIS!

John proceeded to the grammar school of the College of William and Mary, where, like his father, he revelled in the study of ancient history and literature, although the judge had reason to reprimand him concerning one aspect of his work:

> . . . I can't help telling you how much I am mortified to find no improvement in your handwriting; neither do you conduct your lines straight, which makes your letters look too abominable. . . .

Later correspondence between father and son provide evidence that improvement did take place in due course.

John graduated in 1807, and the judge suggested that he select "Education" as a theme for his graduation address; John accepted the suggestion but modified the title to "Female Education." One year later, the judge was elected Governor of Virginia, an office which he held until 1811, when he resigned to accept appointment as judge of the U.S. District Court for Virginia. However, he died in January 1813, leaving John a small farm estate called Mons-Sacer.

John, already a qualified lawyer, had, in the meantime, been elected to the Virginia House of Delegates, and had fallen in love with a young lady of the name of Letitia Christian, whose family only reluctantly consented to the courtship, which lasted five years since Tyler was simply a struggling young lawyer of little financial means. Years later, Tyler's courtship was described as being very much of a formal affair:

> He was seldom alone with her before marriage and . . . never mustered up courage enough to kiss his sweetheart's hand until three weeks before the wedding . . . When he visited her . . . he was entertained in the parlor where the members of the family were assembled. . . .[4]

The young couple settled in at Mons-Sacer as their first home in March, 1813, and the death of both Letitia's parents not long after provided them a legacy which proved most helpful in the early years of marriage. Since Judge Tyler's estate at Greenway had become available after his death, John Tyler later decided to purchase his boyhood home.

His first child, Mary, was born in 1815, and his first son, Robert, in 1816, the year in which Tyler was elected to the U.S. House of Representatives, where he served until 1821, when a combination of ill health and a failing law practice forced him to resign. Letitia gave birth to John Jr., in 1819, and to Letitia Jr., in 1821. For the next two years Tyler devoted himself to his family and the building up of his law practice, but he again became immersed in politics, and, in quick succession, he was elected to the Virginia House of Delegates (1823), to the office of Governor of Virginia (1825), and then as U.S. Senator (1827). By this latter date, three more children had been born: Elizabeth (1823), Anne Contesse (1825, but who died in the same year),[5] and Alice (1827). The eighth and last child was Tazewell (1830), named after Senator Tazewell of Virginia, a close friend of John Tyler.

His occupation with political affairs kept Tyler away from home for prolonged periods of time, and he followed in the footsteps of George Washington, John Adams, and Thomas Jefferson, in the matter of writing lengthy epistles to several of his children, epistles containing, on the one hand, shrewd political commentaries relating to events of the day, and, on the other hand, advice, admonishments and homilies concerning the need for the advancement of academic study, or for the curtailment of aberrant behavior.

His two eldest children, Mary and Robert, respectively, appeared to have been the main recipients of letters from their father. On the day after Christmas, 1827, he wrote to Mary (12):

> You should write to me frequently—every week would not, in fact, be too often, since it would tend to improve your hand and style. A young lady should take particular pains to write well and neatly, since a female cannot be excused for slovenliness in any respect. You should never feel cramped in writing. Write as you would converse, and give your mind free play . . . The history of Greece is the book you should now read; and when you open it, do so with the resolution to understand it. . . .[6]

Tyler not only required of his daughter that she write often, but also that she write accurately:

> I must point out to you two errors into which you have fallen. The river *Rhone* is spelt with an *h*, but not so with James *Roane*. You turned him into a river by your mode of spelling his name. And you say that "this is a great letter to be sent a 150 miles." Thus you

conclude your letter. Now the *a* is out of place, and cannot be the antecedent to *miles*. You would say *a mile* but not *a miles*. I mention this to make you more attentive to your grammar. The mistake occurring with me makes no odds, but if you had been writing to any one else it would be terrible.[7]

There followed a reprimand in a subsequent letter: "You sometimes make a blot which a young lady should carefully avoid. She should be neat in everything."[8]

Soon after celebrating her thirteenth birthday, Mary received a letter which included the following comment:

As to the reason which Mr. (John Quincy) Adams gave "Ebony and Topaz" for a toast, no one can say, unless indeed it was to show his learning. The story which you have read is an excellent moral tale, and one you should always recollect. There are, according to it, two genii who always attend upon us—the one good, the other evil. The first Voltaire calls Topaz; the last Ebony. The first is evermore resisting the last. The last is constantly tempting us from the path of virtue and morality, and in order to do so, spreads before us the most captivating illusions. . . . Ebony speaks the language of the passions, Topaz that of reason. . . . [We should be] always asking ourselves before we commit any action, is it right, is it proper, is it virtuous, is it honorable? This I fondly hope my children will do through life, and Ebony, or the spirit of darkness, will exercise no power over them.

The intellectual expectations of Tyler of his daughter were nothing if not prodigious. When Mary was only 16, he wrote:

I saw today a full set, consisting of fifty odd volumes, of Voltaire's works, in French, and was strongly tempted to buy them for you, but believed that the translation of them might impose upon you too severe a task. If I should meet with them in English, and be able to get them cheap I think I shall buy them. . . .[10]

He continued:

Seek assiduously to improve your mind. The next twelve months are an important period to you and you should devote yourself almost exclusively to the acquisition of knowledge. Should it be your fate in an after day to enter the theatre of the world in an elevated rank of society, you will be to adorn it as it should be; or should you be destined to live in a more retired sphere, you will have resources within yourself which will enliven all around you and contribute to your own happiness.

To the foregoing letter, he added as postscript:

Misses Letty and Lizzie: If you do not learn your books and be obedient and good girls, I shall not love you. You, Miss Letty, do what is right, and Lizzie will follow your example; but if she is a bad girl, don't do, Miss Lizzie, as she does, but do what is right and becoming. Father thinks mighty often of little Alice, and hopes that she does not cry much now.[11]

Just about this time Letty wrote to her father, which led him to comment that he had received from her "a very clever letter, in which she says that Alice is the fattest thing, and the sweetest, and the worst that I ever saw."[12]

Among his other children, his eldest son Robert was destined to be the recipient of most letters from his father, written regularly as they were from the time of Robert's adolescence until Tyler's death. As might be anticipated from the nature of the correspondence which had already passed between Tyler and his daughter, Mary, many of the earlier letters between father and son related to the latter's need to apply himself to his studies; and to attend to the virtue of neatness. When Robert was 14, Tyler complained (December 24, 1830) that he had just received from him a letter

more awkwardly folded and worse written than anything you ever saw. He gives me the *important* information that himself and John dance every night, and the *wonderful intelligence* that John actually dances in time. . . .[13]

One year later he wrote at length to Robert:

My son: Your last letter gives me further evidence of your application to your studies and therefore affords me much pleasure. To witness your advance in knowledge and that of your sisters and brothers, will constitute the charm of my future life and so far I have much reason to be satisfied. Your admiration of the style of Hume is every way just, for undoubtedly few writers have ever equalled him . . . Do not halt . . . because the writer may be somewhat dull or prolix, but encounter him with resolution, resolving to get from him, for the labor he imposes, all he can give you. I would have you form your own style upon the chaste and pure model of Swift, Addison and Hume; but these are rarae aves in terra—all admire, while few attain their excellence. . . .[14]

Like his father before him, Robert attended William and Mary College where, according to Tyler, "The professors advise me that he has never appeared at lecture unprepared," and the "philosophy, metaphysics, chemistry, mathematics, all are alike embraced by him," although at one stage Robert appeared to have run into some difficulties, which impelled his father to comment: "I am sorry that mathematics should puzzle you; but adopt my motto, PERSEVERANDO, and all difficulties will vanish." Tyler also felt that Robert was raising too much of an issue over the fact that he was to be the only graduating senior of his class in 1835, in consequence of which he would be the sole speaker at the graduation ceremony. Tyler reprimanded him: "For this to produce any difficulty is what I had not anticipated. The very circumstance of your being the only graduate, and yours the only speech to be delivered, should be a circumstance rather of gratification than otherwise. . . ."

The "ordeal" was safely negotiated, and Robert then entered upon his studies of the law. To sustain him along the path of a new career, Tyler once more was led to remind his son of the more successful precepts of the work ethic:

> You should set in regularly to work, and prepare yourself for the active concerns of life, so that if anything should befall me, you may be ready to take my place. You are too regardless of small affairs, and overlook the thrifty maxims of life; rely upon it that a knowledge of the minutest circumstances connected with the every-day business of life is essentially necessary to success. System, order and arrangement are better with ordinary talent than the highest intellectual endowment without them . . . You have intellect enough; add to it method and system, and all will be well. I would have you also change your manners somewhat. You should practice a courteous deportment towards all, and regard no inconvenience to yourself in trifling matters in order to gratify others. Destined to the profession of the law, the acquisition of popularity is important. You should, therefore, by gentleness and courtesy to all, win golden opinions from all. Never give way to bad temper; restrain it, and keep it in subjection. "When mad, count ten before you speak; when very mad, count one hundred," so says Mr. Jefferson, one of the greatest and wisest of men. . . .[15]

In 1835, Mary married Henry Lightfoot Jones, and not long afterwards she received a letter from her father relating to Robert, which recapitulated his direct exhortation to his son:

> . . . He should read Lord Chesterfield; half the success in life depends on manners, and the first and highest conquest is for him to obtain a mastery over his passions. I have no fear of him if he will study to be polite to all, learn to sacrifice his own wishes to the

wishes of others, and restrain his temper. His talents ensure him success with these pre-requisites; without them his life will most probably be unhappy. . . .[16]

Tyler always regarded himself to be the best judge of any political issue, and, for that reason, had never considered himself bound to the Whig doctrinaire party approach. Elected to the U.S. Senate in 1827 he had, after Jackson's election, sometimes given the President his support, as in the matter of the lowering of tariffs, but had strongly opposed the President when the latter sought to restrict rights of the individual states. Tyler was nothing if not consistent and honest, and when, therefore, in 1836, he was confronted by party opportunistic cynicism, he decided to resign from the Senate rather than compromise his position. In strange measure, and in the very same year, he was nominated as Vice-President to Harrison, in opposition to the candidacy of Van Buren and Johnson. The election was lost and, for two years, he returned home to spend the time with his family, but the call to return to politics remained too strong, and, by 1838, he was back in the Virginia Legislature, and, in 1840, Harrison and himself were again nominated for the chief executive positions. This time, they were successful.

As Vice-President, Tyler had expected to live a life of comparative leisure as he attended to his law practice in Williamsburg, a life only to be occasionally interrupted by the chore of traveling to Washington to attend sessions of Congress. These expectations were rudely shattered when, on April 5, 1841, just one month after his inauguration as Vice-President, Tyler was informed of the news of Harrison's death by Daniel Webster's son, chief clerk of the Senate, who had ridden down from Washington.

A generally accepted version of the event relates that the two dispatch-bearers from the capital discovered Tyler down on his knees playing marbles with his sons in the driveway outside his home. Tyler loved the company of his children, and, the very next day, he took Robert and John with him to Washington for the swearing-in ceremony as President.

Tyler, only one week earlier, had celebrated his 51st birthday, so that he was the youngest President to assume office up to this time. But whatever exhilaration he may have experienced at assuming the most exalted office in the land was sorely tempered by the fact that his wife, Letitia, had a few years earlier suffered a stroke which left her paralyzed. The functions of First Lady fell upon Tyler's daughters, Letitia (Lettie) and Elizabeth (Lizzie). On January 31, 1842, Elizabeth became the first daughter of a President to marry[17] in the White House, and this also marked the first occasion for Tyler's wife, Letitia, to appear downstairs at

the mansion. Her health continued to deteriorate and she died the following September.

After her wedding, Elizabeth moved to Williamsburg to be with her
husband, and Lettie now shared the duties as First Lady with Priscilla
Cooper Tyler, whom Robert had married in 1839. Priscilla was the lovely
daughter of the British tragedian, Thomas A. Cooper, who had married
a New York society belle, Mary Fairlie. He had been a popular matinee
idol in America, and, after her mother's death, Priscilla had toured on
stage with her father. It was while she played the role of Desdemona at
Richmond, Virginia, that she was seen by Robert, who immediately fell
in love with her.

Since Elizabeth, as well as Lettie, had been so often occupied in
attending to their invalid mother, many of the duties of First Lady fell to
Priscilla, who once complained that she had to spend three hours a day
three times a week simply returning calls to visitors at the White House.

On one occasion, Priscilla gave rise to acute embarrassment by faint-
ing away at a reception. She herself described the incident to one of her
sisters:

> . . . at the moment the ices were being put on the table, everybody
> in good humor, and all going merry as a marriage-bell what should
> I do, but grow deathly pale, and, for the first time in my life, fall
> back in a fainting fit! Mr. (Daniel) Webster . . . picked me up . . . in
> his arms . . . and Mr. (Robert) Tyler, with his usual impetuousity,
> deluged us with ice-water, ruining my lovely new dress, and, I am
> afraid, producing a decided coolness between himself and the Sec-
> retary of State.[18]

Priscilla's first daughter, Mary Fairlie, named after one grandmother,
was given a brilliant costume party in 1843 in order to help enlighten the
gloom cast over the entire White House by the death of the President's
wife. Priscilla owed much to Dolley Madison in matters pertaining to
etiquette and protocol, and, in appreciation for all her assistance, she
invited Dolley, who was 75 but still always charming to children, to be
the sole adult participating at the party, which was one great success. As
Priscilla stated later: "It is so easy to entertain at other peoples expense."
Priscilla's second daughter, Letitia Christian, named after Robert's
mother, was the first girl to be born (1842) in the White House.

Also resident at the presidential mansion was Tyler's son, John, along
with his wife, Martha Rochelle, whom·he had married in 1838. Alice
(14), and Tazewell (11), the President's youngest children, made up the
remainder of Tyler's large family retinue in Washington.[19]

The year 1843 opened a new chapter in Tyler's life, since during the social season of that winter he had met Julia Gardiner. She was the attractive daughter of former Senator David Gardiner, a wealthy citizen of New York who had introduced his children to high society both in Europe and in the United States.[20] She was thirty years younger than Tyler, being only 23 at the time of their first meeting,[21] which made her younger than three of his oldest children, Mary, Robert, and John.

On February 28, 1844, Tyler invited Julia and her father to be among his guests on board the U.S.S. *Princeton* for a day's cruise on the Potomac. The *Princeton* carried a new gun, the "Peacemaker," which had been successfully fired earlier that day, but when fired the second time, in salute as they passed Mount Vernon, the gun exploded, killing eight persons including Tyler's Secretary of State, his Secretary of the Navy, and David Gardiner. When Tyler had, prior to the tragedy, proposed marriage to Julia, she had refused, but when, after the death of her father, Tyler had again offered marriage, she consented, and the private ceremony took place on June 26, 1844, at the Church of the Ascension in New York City, Tyler being the first President to be married in office.

His children were very much opposed to this second marriage, but their objections remained private and muted, and only many years later was any resentment voiced either in print or in public.

Julia proved to be a highly spirited First Lady, and her eight months of service in that capacity represented a period of lavish entertainment at the White House, during which she was often assisted by her sister, Margaret. It was Julia who set the precedent for the Marine Corps Band to play "Hail to the Chief" upon the appearance of the President on formal occasions, the first being the ball held in February, 1845, to celebrate the entry of Texas into the Union.[22] She was very fond of fashionable clothing, and Tyler spared no expense in pleasing his wife in this respect, although he did occasionally express concern at being "desperately bare of cash" in letters to Robert, who had moved out of the White House to pursue his law practice in Philadelphia.

Upon retirement from the presidency, Tyler moved into a new home, "Sherwood Forest," on a substantial estate which he had purchased adjoining "Greenway," his place of birth, and it was here that he was to spend the remaining years of his life. The original house was a small one, and Tyler proceeded to extend it in stages until the distance from front to back doors was over one hundred yards. It was at Sherwood Forest that Julia gave birth to all but one of seven children, the exception being her first, David Gardiner (Gardie), born in 1846 in Charles City County, Virginia. Thereafter, at almost regular intervals, there followed John

Alexander (1848), Julia (1849), Lachlan (1851), Lyon Gardiner (1853), Robert Fitzwalter (1856) and, finally, Pearl, who was only two when her father died at the age of 72 in 1862; she herself lived until 1947.

Tyler was saddened by the lack of fraternization between the children of his first and second marriages, although, since Robert had become increasingly involved in politics, Tyler maintained a steady correspondence with his son. In April, 1846, Tyler wrote:

> I very much rejoice in your success in the last greeting of the Democratic party. . . . You should not go into Congress at least I think, not unless you come to a determined resolution to bear or to be indifferent to everything that shall be said of me. . . .[23]

Three years later, in a letter, again to Robert, he gave forthright expression of his opposition to all forms of tyranny, in this instance, that of the Austrians in their ruthless suppression of Hungarian attempts at independence:

> . . . We are interested in seeing that the rules which civilization has prescribed for the conduct of war shall be observed by nations at war. When Austria subjects to the scourge women of worth and character—thus trampling civilization in the dust, and reverting to days of worse than Gothic darkness and barbarity—it becomes our duty, as it is that of every civilized State, to protest against such proceedings; and, if our protest is unavailing, to manifest our displeasure by withdrawing all diplomatic intercourse. The United States should not be left in a doubtful position. . . .[24]

In one of the few extant letters making reference to the children of his second marriage, Tyler wrote to Robert in October, 1856, since his heart was filled wth gratitude to his Maker for "the rescue of my noble boy, Gardiner, from an untimely grave." The latter had suffered an acute bilious attack lasting over a week:

> He was frantic and wild beyond anything I ever knew and opiates had to be freely administered. On Friday morning he was cupped freely in the temples—fell away into a profound slumber from which he had not thoroughly awakened until this morning. So great has been his improvement that today he has been setting up reading newspapers and amusing himself with cards. . . .[25]

Robert advanced himself in politics to the extent of being elected chairman of the State Democratic Central Committee in Pennsylvania, and his party efforts had been much appreciated by Presidents Pierce and Buchanan. But such efforts had apparently not advanced his financial security, and, in the late 1850's, he had been concerned whether or not to apply for a position as paymaster, regarding which Tyler had written:

> Give up politics, by which no man profits other than a knave; retrench, as far as retrenchment be practicable, and wait for political preferment to reach you at its own gait. I estimate you unjustly if it do not come at some day or other. . . .[26]

Tyler himself expressed regret that he hadn't been able to financially assist either Robert or any other members of his family: he had not been too successful as a farmer—he wrote in 1860, for example, that his wheat crop had failed in two successive years, and further commented:

> It is a shame to the country that an ex-President who is obliged to keep an open house, should not receive a pension, when every man who has but shouldered a musket in war is pensioned. He is commander-in-chief (of the Army and Navy). . . .[27]

Tyler was a slaveholder,[28] and he considered the anti-slave and Free-Soil movements as a threat to the Union. With Lincoln's election in November, 1860, events moved quickly: South Carolina seceded, followed by Florida, Mississippi, and Alabama, so, as a desperate measure, the Border States quickly convened a Peace Convention at Washington in February, 1861. John Tyler was named by the Virginia Legislature as one of its five delegates, and, at the opening meeting, he was appointed President of the convention, but it failed in its mission, and the Civil War hostilities began on April 12, 1861.

Tyler now cast in his lot with the Confederacy, and in the fall of 1861 he was selected to represent his Virginia congressional district in the permanent Congress of the Confederate States, but before he could take his seat he collapsed and died on January 18, 1862, at the Exchange Hotel, Richmond. His wife, Julia, and his son, Robert, were present at his deathbed.

In consequence of their Confederate sympathies, the Tyler family suffered severely as a result of the war. Tyler's home, Sherwood Forest, was devastated by Union soldiers, and after the war, the house was converted into a school. Julia and her children succeeded in joining her mother in New York, but her deceased husband's action made life very difficult for her.

No fewer than five of Tyler's sons were to serve the South in one capacity or another. Robert, who was 44 at the outbreak of the Civil War, was literally hounded out of Philadelphia by a hostile mob well aware of his Confederate viewpoints. After reaching Richmond, he was appointed

Register of the Southern Confederacy by Jefferson Davis. He also served in what came to be known as the "Treasury Regiment" in General Custis Lee's Brigade, which had been specifically established for the defense of Richmond.[29] After the war, Robert and his family moved to Alabama, and he had great difficulty in re-establishing his career. Hearing of his plight, ex-President Buchanan wrote to him in August, 1865, from his home in Wheatland, Pennsylvania:

> My Dear Sir: I have learned through our old friends that you now need the assistance of your friends, and I hasten to send you a check for $1,000 on the Chemical Bank of NY. Please to acknowledge its receipt.
>
> Though I could not approve your course in favor of the secessionists, yet I have never doubted the sincerity of your belief and the purity of your motives. Thank God! the war is over, and the Union has not been beaten. May His infinite mercy preserve it for ages to come. . . .

Robert was most appreciative of this magnanimous gesture, but could not bring himself to accept the money. In due course, he again became active in politics, serving as chairman of the Democratic State Central Committee of Alabama, and as editor of the *Montgomery Mail and Advertiser,* one of the leading newspapers of the region. He resided in Montgomery until his death in 1878.

Robert's brother, John Tyler Jr., served as a clerk in the Confederate War Department at Montgomery, and eventually was promoted to the rank of major. His daughter, Letitia, married General William Shands. Tyler's two eldest sons of his second marriage, David Gardiner (Gardie) and John Alexander (Alex), both enlisted as privates in the Confederate Army at ages 16 and 15, respectively. Both, also, spent some time as students in Germany after the Civil War, with Alex even serving as Uhlan in the German Army during the Franco-Prussian War of 1870, and he was awarded a badge of honor by the Emperor for his services. He later qualified as an engineer and died in New Mexico in 1883. David Gardiner was to be elected State Senator in 1891, and as U.S. Congressman in 1893–97. He died in 1927.

Tyler had found little opportunity during his own lifetime to arrange his papers for publication, and he had hoped that his eldest sons could perform the task for him, but the chaos of the Civil War prevented this from happening.

It was left to Lyon Gardiner, Julia's fifth child (and fourth son) to edit the materials, and, in 1884, he completed the first volume of the *Letters and Times of the Tylers.* The two subsequent volumes were published in 1885 and 1896, respectively. He was nationally recognized as a distinguished historian, and from 1888 to 1919 he served as President of the College of William and Mary.

Tyler's widow, Julia, suffered considerable financial hardship after her husband's death. The Virginia estate was in ruins, and she was left with seven children of ages two to sixteen to rear. In 1879, she petitioned Congress for a pension as a presidential widow. One year later, she received a grant of $100 a month, but as the widow of a veteran of the War of 1812.[30] She died in 1889 at the age of 61, in the same hotel in Richmond where her husband had passed away 27 years earlier.

James Polk

(1845–1849)

The Polks were a childless couple. James Polk, the eldest son in a family of six boys and four girls, had received a good education, was admitted to the bar, and elected to the Tennessee Legislature. In 1824, he married Sarah Childress, who had graduated from the Moravian Institute at Salem, North Carolina, and she gave her husband every possible encouragement to advance politically. Polk served for 14 years as U.S. Congressman, then served for two years as Governor of Tennessee; yet he was comparatively unknown nationally when Jackson had supported his nomination in 1844.[1] His tenure as President was eventful since, just as Jefferson had presided over the extension of U.S. territory from the Mississippi to the Rocky Mountains, so Polk, a firm believer in Manifest Destiny, presided over the acquisition of the entire Pacific region of the United States, thus extending his country's borders from "sea to shining sea."

Sarah (Sally), free of family responsibilities, served efficiently as Polk's secretary when she was First Lady. Her strict religious upbringing resulted in the prohibition at the White House of all card playing, dancing, and the use of alcohol, yet presidential functions and receptions were popular and well-attended.

Two events of social interest occurred in 1848: Polk became the first President ever to have his photograph taken;[2] he also became the first President to enjoy gas illumination in the White House.

Polk was an indefatigable worker. He was 53 upon completion of his term of office, but he died only three months later. Sarah survived him for 42 years, and died in 1891, in her 88th year, at the home, Polk Place, in Nashville, Tennessee, which her husband had purchased for his intended retirement years.

Zachary Taylor

(1849–1850)

Zachary Taylor was the first professional soldier to be elected President of the United States, and the second President to die in office. Born in 1784, he lived the life of a typical frontier and career army man until his inauguration as President in March, 1849. He was the third son (in a family of nine children) of Colonel Richard Taylor and his wife, Sarah, who had moved west from Virginia to Kentucky. After some cursory schooling, Zachary had accepted a commission as a first lieutenant in the army; then, in 1810, he married Margaret (Peggy) Mackall Smith, daughter of a planter, and one of the most remarkable women ever to become First Lady. She had been born in Calvert County, Maryland, in 1788, but her father, a major in the Revolutionary War, had died when she was only 12, and she was sent to live with an older married sister, Mrs. Samuel Chew, of Harrods Wood Creek in Kentucky, and it was there that she met Zachary. Thenceforth, she shared the crude, uncomfortable, peripatetic garrison existence of her husband, living for decades in barracks, forts, log cabins, or tents with never a permanent home she could call her own.[1] Nevertheless, she was determined to remain with her husband irrespective of the innumerable discomforts, and remain she did. The Taylor's first child, a daughter named Ann Mackall, was born in 1811 at Jefferson City, Kentucky.

During the War of 1812, Taylor ably defended Fort Harrison in Indiana territory against an overwhelming attack by Indians led by Tecumseh, and for this action he was promoted to major. He was later in command of Fort Knox, and his second daughter, Sarah Knox, born in Vincennes in 1814, was, in part, named in recognition of his service there.[2]

After the war, he resigned from the army with the intention of settling down to the relatively peaceful[3] and sedentary life of a corn and tobacco planter on land which he had received from his father as a wedding present.

The farming venture lasted less than a year; in 1816, he rejoined the army, was commissioned as major, and was sent to Fort Howard, Green Bay, Wisconsin. Margaret remained behind until the birth of her third daughter, Octavia Pannill, after which she went north to join her husband. He was then transferred, first to Louisville, and then to Bayou Sara, Louisiana, where tragedy struck the family, all of whom fell sick of swamp fever: in July, 1820, Octavia died, and four months later she was followed to the grave by the Taylors' fourth child and fourth daughter, Margaret Smith, born in 1819.

Their fifth child and fifth daughter, Mary Elizabeth (Betty), was born in 1824, and finally their sixth child and only son, Richard (Dick), was born in 1826.

With four surviving children to rear, Margaret was faced always with the dilemma, either of being with her husband in one post after another, or of providing the children with a stable upbringing and some semblance of the schooling of which both parents had been deprived.[4] Hence, while the children were often with their parents, they were seldom together as a complete family, but spent time with friends or relatives or were boarded in private schools. In 1828, Taylor was in command of Fort Snelling in Minnesota territory. Margaret and Ann, (now 17), were with him, and it was here that Ann met and fell in love with Dr. Robert Crooke Wood, a young army assistant surgeon: they were married in September, 1829, and were to rear four children, two boys and two girls.[5] Wood was later to become surgeon-general of the United States Army.

During the 1830's, Taylor saw action in the Black Hawk War in the Upper Mississippi, and then in the campaign against the Seminole Indians under Osceola in Florida: it was after his victory against the Indians

at Lake Okeechobee on December 25, 1837, that he acquired the nickname of "Old Rough and Ready." After promotion as brigadier-general
in command of Florida, Taylor was, in 1841, placed in charge of the First
Military Department which covered the entire southeast region of the
United States. His headquarters were at Baton Rouge, and this gave
Margaret a life-long opportunity to purchase and renovate a small house
which she felt she could really call "home," with a vegetable and flower
garden near the river, where she could sit, relax, and watch the ships and
the world go by.

In addition to the upsetting transfers of command, the Taylors had
faced a severe emotional trauma during the decade of the 1830's. Their
lovely and vivacious daughter, Sarah Knox, had been educated privately
while Taylor was at the frontier, first under Thomas Elliott in Jefferson
County, and then at the Pickett School in Cincinnati. She had rejoined
her parents in 1831 at Louisville, and went with them to Fort Crawford,
Michigan, to which Taylor had been transferred. It was here that she met
Jefferson Davis.

Davis had been born in Kentucky, and was the fifth son and last child
of Samuel Emory Davis, a planter and horse breeder. Although a Baptist
by religious persuasion, Davis sent his son, Jefferson, to a Dominican
Academy in order that he receive the best available education in the
region. Jefferson then entered Transylvania University at Lexington,
Kentucky, and at 16 was accepted into West Point. After graduation in
1828 his tour of duties took him to outposts in Wisconsin and Iowa, and
then, in 1831, to Fort Crawford at Prairie du Chien, headquarters of the
First United States Infantry. In 1832, Colonel Zachary Taylor succeeded
Colonel Willoughby Moran in command of the Fort. Sarah's attachment
to Davis was virtually an inevitable one, since there were few eligible
women for unmarried officers stationed for years on frontier posts. The
couple declared their intention of marriage, subject to Taylor's approval,
which, however, he refused. Taylor was understandably concerned about
his daughter's future happiness. He was only too well aware of what his
own military career had meant to his wife: isolation from civilized
society, deprivation from a stable home life, and suffering separation
from her children sent to relatives and boarding schools in order to gain
some minimal standards of education.[6] Yet he admitted to having already
consented to his eldest daughter's marriage to a career army officer, and
the immediate obstacle to an identical marriage by Sarah Knox appeared
to have arisen out of a trivial incident relating to court martial protocol:

Four officers, Taylor, Davis, "Tom" Smith, and another whose name is not known, were detailed as a court martial. Taylor and Smith disliked each other exceedingly. The fourth officer had been ordered up to Fort Crawford from Jefferson Barracks and had lost or left behind his full dress uniform which it was the custom to wear when serving on court martial duty. So he asked the other members to excuse him from wearing uniform. Taylor voted not to excuse him, Smith voted, therefore, to excuse him, and Davis voted with Smith. This enraged "Old Rough and Ready" who after further irritation swore, it is said, that no man who voted with "Tom" Smith should ever marry his daughter. Davis was ordered to cease his attention to Miss Taylor and to come no more to her father's quarters.[7]

There remain doubts as to whether the foregoing episode represents the "whole truth" of the affair, but whatever did happen did nothing to diminish the love which existed between Sarah and Davis. In 1833, the latter left Fort Crawford to join a new Dragoon Regiment at Fort Gibson in Indian territory and the lovers were separated for two years. In one of the few extant letters of their mutual correspondence during this prolonged absence Jefferson wrote, on December 16, 1834:[8]

. . . . Sarah, whatever I may be hereafter, neglected by you I should have been worse than nothing, and if the few good qualities I possess shall, under your smiles yield fruit, it shall be yours, as the grain is the husbandman's.

. . . . Shall we not meet soon, Sarah, to part no more? Oh I long to lay my head upon that breast which beats in unison with my own, to turn from the sickening sights of worldy duplicity and look in these eyes, so eloquent of purity and love. . . .

Write to me immediately, my dear Sarah, my betrothed; no formality between us. Adieu ma chere, tres chere amie.

Jeff.

In June, 1835, Davis was granted leave of absence from his regiment. About the same time Sarah left her family to visit relatives in Kentucky, near Louisville, where the couple were reunited and unknown to her father, and possibly her mother, Sarah married Davis on June 17, at Beechland, the home of her aunt Elizabeth, Taylor's eldest sister. Also present at the ceremony were Taylor's eldest brother, Hancock, and his wife, and Sarah's sister, Ann, and her husband Dr. Wood.

Sarah wrote to her mother on the morning of her wedding day:[9]

You will be surprised, no doubt, my dear mother, to hear of being married so soon . . . I am very gratified that sister Ann is here. At

this time having one member of the family present, I shall not feel
so entirely destitute of friends. But you, my dearest mother I know
will still retain some feelings of affection for a child who has been
so unfortunate as to form a connection without the sanction of her
parents, but who will always feel the deepest affection for them
whatever may be their feelings toward her. Say to my dear father I
have received his kind and affectionate letter, and thank him for the
liberal supply of money sent me. Sister will tell you all that you
wish to know about me . . .

Believe me, always, your affectionate daughter.

Knox

The wedding ceremony itself was thus described by Anna Magill
(aged 11), daughter of Hancock Taylor:

My Cousin Knox Taylor was very beautiful, slight, and not very
tall, with brown wavy hair and clear gray eyes, very lovely and
lovable and a young woman of decided spirit. She was dressed in a
dark travelling dress with a small hat to match. Lieutenant Davis
was dressed, in a long-tail cutaway coat, brocaded waistcoat,
breeches tight-fitting and held under the instep, and a high
stovepipe hat. He was of slender build, had polished manners, and
was of a quiet, intellectual countenance. [10]

She also remembered that "after the service everybody cried but
Davis, and the Taylor children thought this most peculiar."

Davis and his bride left for Mississippi, where Joseph Emory Davis,
his oldest brother and a wealthy planter, had given them Brierfield, a
small estate, along with fourteen slaves sold on credit; the intention was
to develop it as a cotton plantation, but, tragically, within three months
both succumbed to malaria, and Sarah died on September 15. Davis,
prostrated with grief, remained in seclusion at Brierfield for the next ten
years.

There then occurred a quick succession of events: In February, 1845,
Davis married Varina Howell, a local beauty from Natchez, Mississippi,[11] while, in the following December, he was elected to the U.S.
House of Representatives.[12] In June, 1846, he resigned his seat to take
charge of a volunteer regiment, the "Mississippi Rifles," and to participate in the war with Mexico.

During that war, Taylor was in command of U.S. forces on the
Mexican border and although greatly outnumbered, he won victories at
Palo Alto, Monterey, and Buena Vista. He was ably assisted by Jefferson
Davis (whom Taylor had appointed as one of the commissioners to

negotiate the surrender of Monterey). In 1847, Davis returned to Mississippi, and served as U.S. Senator from 1848 to 1851.

As a result of his victory at Buena Vista, Taylor was acclaimed a war hero, whom the Whig party seized upon as a prospective winning presidential candidate in the 1848 election.[13] They were correct, and in March, 1849, Taylor was inaugurated as the twelfth President of the United States.

Taylor's entry into national politics was contrary to all the wishes of his wife. She had lived the life of the truly pioneer woman, knowledgeable in the simple and honest virtues, and she desired nothing more than to settle down to a homely, domestic existence with her husband. In 1848, she had prayed regularly for someone other than her husband to be elected to succeed President Polk, but her prayers went unanswered, and, in 1849, she found herself as a very reluctant First Lady in Washington, D.C.

Her only compensation was that her youngest daughter, Mary Elizabeth (Betty), had, in December, 1848, married Captain William Wallace Smith Bliss, known familiarly to all members of the Taylor family as "Perfect Bliss." He had served as Taylor's aide-de-camp for a number of years, and was an exceptionally gifted personality. He was well educated, had a mastery of at least six languages, and, while at Fort Smith, he had spent most of his leisure time translating articles on philosophy written in German, which he then forwarded to a close friend, Major Ethan Allen Hitchcock, with whom he kept up an invigorating, intellectaul correspondence relating to philosophical issues and dilemmas. Upon Taylor's election as President, Bliss was appointed as his personal secretary at the White House, where his wife, Betty, functioned as hostess for much of the time of Taylor's tenure, since her mother now suffered from ill-health and fatigue accruing from her additional chores. While Jefferson Davis was Senator, he and his wife were frequent guests at the White House, and the friendship between the families was maintained after Taylor's death.[14]

From time to time, Taylor's daughter Ann, her husband, Dr. Wood, and their children visited the presidential mansion: the eldest, John Taylor, was a navy midshipman, while his brother, Robert (Bob), variously described as a "high-spirited rascal" and "harum-scarum lad." had been accepted into West Point. Ann's two daughters, Blandina, (known as "Puss" or "Nina"), and Sarah Knox, (whom "Zach" called "Dumple"), were great favorites of the President and his wife, and on their visits they served as companions to Rebecca, (daughter of Taylor's brother, Joseph,) who spent much of her vacation time at the White House while attending school in Georgetown. Among other youthful visitors always welcomed by the President were the children of his eldest sister, Elizabeth Lee, (who had married her cousin, John Gibson Taylor).

Taylor had seen to it that his one and only son, Richard (Dick), had received the best possible education: he had attended an exclusive preparatory school in Lancaster, Massachusetts, and had then visited England, Scotland, and France. His father had failed to obtain his admission as a cadet into West Point, so Richard went first to Harvard, but transferred to Yale, and graduated in 1845.

Richard developed as an intellectually minded man, a competent linguist in both French and Spanish, and a welcome guest at social functions because of his ready wit and conversation. Yet, by the end of the Mexican War, which he had sat out, (by reason of indifferent health), with his sister, Betty, at Baton Rouge, he had remained undecided as to a future career. So, Taylor decided to place him in charge, first of his cotton plantation, which failed, and then of a sugar plantation named Fashion in Louisiana, which prospered, and, in 1851, Richard married Louisa Marie Myrthe Bringier of New Orleans.

Taylor's death was sudden and unexpected. His brief term of office had been a turbulent one: his support of the Wilmot Proviso's exclusion of slavery from new territories lost him support in the South, as did his approval of the admission into the Union of California and New Mexico as free states. On July 4, 1850, a hot and sultry day, he had attended ceremonies relating to the laying of the cornerstone of the Washington Monument. Legend has it that, to cool off, the President ate a copious quantity of strawberries and cold milk. He quickly developed an acute form of gastroenteritis, or possibly cholera, and died on July 9.

His wife, Margaret, went south to live with her son, Richard, and it was at his home that she died two years later in August, 1852.[15] Richard then became interested in politics and he served as State Senator, 1856–1861. At the outbreak of the Civil War he was appointed colonel of the Ninth Louisiana Infantry Regiment. He saw considerable action, for a time serving under Stonewall Jackson, and was successively promoted to brigadier-general, major-general, and finally to lieutenant-general, in which capacity on May 4, 1865, he surrendered the last Confederate army east of the Mississippi.

The effect of the Civil War upon his family was disastrous. His sugar plantation was confiscated, while two of his five children had died of scarlet fever during the years of conflict. He undertook a visit to Europe and was well received by statesmen in England, France, and Germany.

He served as trustee of the Peabody Education Fund, which had been established to promote education in the South. In 1879, he completed writing his reminiscences in a work entitled *Destruction and Reconstruction* and he died the same year at the home of a New York friend, Colonel S. L. M. Barlow.

Millard Fillmore

(1850–1853)

Millard Fillmore, the nation's second "accidental" President, appears to have suffered the misfortune, not only (as had James Polk) of being virtually unknown when Taylor's death precipitated him into the office of chief executive, but also of having remained unknown ever since. Moreover, possibly more than to any other First Lady, full credit should be given to his wife, Abigail, for having facilitated his advancement and encouraged his ambitions in terms of his career, first in law, and then in politics.

Fillmore was born in 1800 in Locke, New York, the second of nine children of Nathaniel and Phoebe Millard Fillmore. As a boy, Fillmore worked on his father's farm and was then apprenticed to a wool-carder, but he had higher aspirations and decided to enroll at the local village school to learn the three R's. By good fortune, his teacher was Abigail Powers, the daughter of the Rev. Lemuel Powers, an itinerant Baptist minister of New York who had died while Abigail was still young. His death left the family bereft of income, so his widow moved up-country in New York State where she believed the cost of living would be less. To support her mother, Abigail, then 16, took up teaching, and it was three years later that Fillmore (17) asked whether he could attend classes at her school. She agreed and gave him individual instruction. He was a ready learner and the warm friendship which developed between them ripened into love: as Fillmore described it, Abigail was "eight years my sweetheart, twenty-seven my wife."

They were married in 1826, by which time Fillmore had struggled hard with strong support from Abigail, to become a lawyer, as well as to build a home for his intended bride at East Aurora near Buffalo. Here, their first child, Millard Powers, was born in 1828. Abigail continued to teach after Fillmore was elected to the New York State Assembly in which he served from 1829 to 1831. In 1832, Abigail gave birth to a daughter, Mary Abigail, soon after which time Fillmore's political ambitions had earned him a seat in the U.S. House of Representatives from 1833 to 1835, and again from 1837 to 1843.

The education of their young children was left very much to Abigail, who, not only taught them the conventional subjects, but also French and music, which she herself had acquired almost entirely on her own initiative, and she became both a competent pianist and harpist.

In 1844, Fillmore was a candidate for the Whig vice-presidential nomination, as well as the Whig candidate for the position of Governor of New York, but he lost on both occasions. However, in 1848, success came with his nomination as Vice-President to Zachary Taylor.

By this date, his son, Powers, had graduated from Harvard and had selected a career in law. Young Abigail (Abby) had attended a well-known private school, that of Mrs. Sedwick, at Lennox, Massachusetts,[1] and then, aspiring to be a teacher like her mother, had enrolled at, then graduated from, the State Normal School of New York. She proceeded thence to teach in a public school in Buffalo, acquired linguistic proficiencies in French, Spanish, and German, and, even after her father had succeeded to the presidency after Taylor's death in July, 1850, she continued her school work as usual.

But, by 1850, the health of her mother had deteriorated quickly, and young Abigail was forced to abandon her teaching career to function as substitute White House hostess. She was only 18, but she performed her duties with grace and elegance. Edward Everett, appointed Secretary of State in 1852, wrote of her at one function:

I had the honor to take in Miss Fillmore, a pretty, modest, un-

effected girl of about 20, as much at ease at the head of the
presidential table as if she had been a princess.[2]

Young Abigail and her mother, (when she felt well enough), performed together to sing and play the piano and harp to entertain guests at
the White House. Powers also came to live at the White House to serve as
his father's private secretary.

Although very much incapacitated, Fillmore's wife effected two significant innovations: as a former school teacher, she deplored the absence
of books in the presidential mansion, and she so goaded her husband that
he successfully pressured Congress into granting an appropriation for the
first library in the White House. She was further instrumental in having
installed water pipes and the first (zinc) bathtub, as well as the first iron
range for the kitchen (to replace open fire cooking) which was so modern
a contraption that Fillmore was obliged to pay a visit to the Patent Office
to see how it worked. He then had the additional problem of having
himself to train the unwilling White House cook to operate the new
gadget. It was little wonder that Fillmore came to label the White House
as "his temple of inconvenience."

Fillmore had stated on the day that he took the oath of office as
President that he would not seek re-election. His was a controversial term
when division between North and South, especially on the issue of
slavery, was perceptibly widening, with less and less opportunities being
presented for compromise. He had been persuaded to submit his name
for renomination at the 1852 Whig party convention, but he lost to
General Winfield Scott, who, in turn, lost the presidential election in
November of the same year to Franklin Pierce.

On the eve of the latter's inauguration, his only son died, and Pierce's
wife was unable to be present. Abigail Fillmore volunteered to stand in
her place: the day was bitterly cold, and she caught chill. Within less than
four weeks she died (March 30, 1853) at the Willard Hotel, Washington.
Fifteen months later, in July, 1853, young Abigail died suddenly of
cholera in her twenty-second year. Fillmore had returned to live in
Buffalo where he was to spend the remaining years of his life. He and his
son, Powers, undertook several journeys together within the United
States, and then, in 1855, Fillmore himself spent almost a year in Europe
meeting with most of the prominent political heads of state.[3]

Upon his return home, Fillmore, misguidedly, accepted nomination in
1856 as presidential candidate of the American or Know-Nothing party, a
chauvinistic group very much opposed to foreign immigrants. He carried only one state, Maryland, in the election, and, thereafter, retired

from national politics to attend to his private law practice in Buffalo. In 1858, he remarried a wealthy widow, Caroline Carmichael McIntosh.[4] There were no children of her first marriage nor of that to Fillmore, who died in 1874.

Powers Fillmore never married, and, after pursuing a private law practice, he obtained an appointment in the federal court system, and eventually became a U.S. commissioner. As a wealthy bachelor, with a private income derived from his father's estate, he lived a life of ease, and, at one time, was a close associate in Buffalo of Grover Cleveland, who, likewise, was a financially well-endowed bachelor.

Fillmore's second wife, Caroline, appeared to have developed strange eccentricities after his death, including the writing of an elaborate will, which she hopelessly complicated by juggling the names of the beneficiaries, all of whom were her own kin, with Powers Fillmore being completely ignored. After her death in 1881, Powers contested those provisions of the will which, in his view, related to the disposal of his parents' personal belongings, including books, household silverware, and, in particular, a large cask of madeira wine which Commodore Perry had brought back from Japan in 1854 when Fillmore was President. The latter had paid the customs duties on the cask, which, however, had remained unopened, so that its value had appreciated considerably. After the court had ruled in his favor, Powers then sold most of the items which had passed to him.

He died in November, 1889, at the age of 61, but his will directed his executors "to burn or otherwise effectively destroy all correspondence or letters to or from my father, mother, or me." In due course this was done, except that many papers were preserved by Charles D. Marshall, a lawyer and one of the executors. The papers were stored away and forgotten and they did not re-emerge until 1969, when a tally revealed the existence of over 10,000 documents whose contents have yet to be revealed and published.

Franklin Pierce

(1853–1857)

In terms of the anticipated joys to be derived from the birth and rearing of a happy brood of children, Franklin Pierce and his wife were, of all presidential families, to be the most cruelly deprived and emotionally devastated; it is nothing short of a miracle that Pierce endured and survived one single term of office.

His father, Benjamin Pierce, a general in the Revolutionary War, was twice married, with one child, a daughter, of his first marriage, but with seven children of a second marriage; Franklin, born in 1804, was the fifth child (and fourth son) of that union. Franklin enjoyed and relished all the pleasures and delights of a close-knit sibling relationship, and at the same time, he was made aware of the existence of a much wider, less stable world involving the subtleties and nuances of politics, economics, and society after his father had been elected Governor of New Hampshire.

Pierce received a good education, attending academies at Hancock and Francestown in New Hampshire, then proceeding to Bowdoin College in Brunswick, Maine, where one of his classmates was Nathaniel

154

Hawthorne. It was while he was at college that he became acquainted with Jane (Jeanie) Means Appleton, daughter of the Rev. Jesse Appleton[1] (former president of Bowdoin), and sister-in-law of one of Pierce's instructors at the college.

Pierce and Jane were a most ill-assorted and mismatched couple: like his father, Pierce was an outgoing, jovial, and convivial personality, easily diverted from his work to attend student tavern revels, and in later years, relishing the challenges of political argument and confrontation. Jane, on the contrary, aged 20 when she met Pierce, and already in delicate health, was studious, shy, and sought to avoid all society outside her immediate family contacts as much as possible.

Pierce graduated from Bowdoin in 1824, was admitted to the bar in 1827, and, two years later, was elected to the lower house of the state legislature. In 1833, he was elected to the U.S. House of Representatives, and in the following year he married Jane. At the time of their marriage he was 31 and she 28. Their long engagement had apparently been due to her family's doubts and uncertainties as to Pierce's eligibility as an approved suitor.

Jane, likewise, had many doubts concerning marriage to a prominent politician. She made every effort, but to no avail, to dissuade him from seeking public office. Following his admission to the bar, Pierce had set up a law practice at his hometown, assisted by Albert Baker, a graduate of Dartmouth College, and whose sister Mary (Baker Eddy), was eventually to found the Christian Science Movement in the United States. But, once in politics, Pierce left most of the office duties to Baker in order to focus upon state and national affairs.

In 1836, while Pierce was in Washington, the first tragedy struck the family: their first born, named after his father, saw light of day on February 2, only to die three days later. In 1837, Pierce was elected U.S. Senator. During all her husband's time in Washington, Jane remained in New Hampshire, where at Concord in 1839, she gave birth to her second child, again a son: Frank Robert. In 1841, a third child, and third son, Benjamin, was also born at Concord.

By this time, Jane's health had very much deteriorated and, in 1842, Pierce resigned his seat in the Senate and returned home to resume his law practice. Tragedy again struck when, in November, 1843, Frank Robert, their second son, died of typhus fever at age 4. Jane succumbed to feelings of guilt and self-reproach, condemning herself for having devoted too much time to her children: that she "should have lived for God and left the dear ones to the care of Him who is alone able to take care of them and us." Now, with but one child, she proceeded to lavish all her love and attention upon him. She reared him in an atmosphere of strict religious practices including the observances of family worship each morning and family prayers each evening.

In 1845, Pierce enlisted in the ranks to participate in the Mexican War, was soon commissioned as brigadier-general, and served under Winfield Scott in the advance on Mexico City. Upon his return home in 1848, he refused nomination as State Governor, but his strong inclination towards politics did not abate, and culminated in his nomination as one of several presidential candidates in the 1852 convention. Fully aware of his wife's disapproval, he affected to show little enthusiasm, yet he did not openly disavow his nomination. The consequence was that his supporters won the nomination for him as a compromise candidate on the forty-ninth ballot. When the news reached her, Jane Pierce fell into a faint, and, soon afterwards her eleven-year-old son, little Bennie, wrote her: ". . . the news from Boston is that Father is a candidate for the Presidency. I hope he won't be elected for I should not like to be in Washington and I know you would not either."

In the presidential campaign, Pierce came to be labeled as "Young Hickory" from the Granite Hills, and he received support from his college friend, Washington Irving, who wrote a biography of him as a document of political propaganda. Irving wrote:

> I have come seriously to the conclusion that he has in him many of the chief elements of a great ruler. His talents are administrative, he has a subtle faculty of making affairs roll onward according to his will, and of influencing their course without showing any trace of his action. . . . He is deep, deep, deep.

Pierce's opponent in the 1852 election was his former commander, General Winfield Scott, and, in terms of the electoral vote, Pierce scored handsomely with 254 votes as compared with only 42 for Scott, (although his margin of victory in the popular vote was little over 200,000 with over three million votes cast).

Pierce had sincerely believed that in pursuing his political ambitions he was measurably advancing the opportunities for his only son to attain some (reflected) recognition in society, and, thereby, derive considerable benefit from his father's status on the national scene. He had, likewise, fondly hoped that with his emergence as chief executive of the United States, his wife would derive inner satisfaction and substantial pride from his great achievement.

Both his aspirations were to be cruelly crushed when yet a third major tragedy overwhelmed the family. After enjoying hospitality of friends in

Boston, the Pierces boarded a train for Concord, New Hampshire (on January 6, 1853), where they were to make their final preparations for departure to Washington. The train had proceeded hardly a mile from the station at Boston when an axle caused the railroad car, in which the Pierce family were travelling, to be derailed. It rolled off the embankment, and, while Pierce and his wife escaped except for minor injury, they suffered the excruciating agony and horror of seeing young Bennie killed before their eyes: he was the sole immediate fatality of the accident. The parents were understandably stupified by grief and shock. Bennie was laid to rest at Concord, and twelve of his former schoolmates served as pallbearers.

In the days which followed, Jane Pierce indulged in morbid self-probing sessions in a vain effort to seek tangible reason for having such punishment inflicted upon herself and her husband by the Almighty. She remained distraught and inconsolable, but appeared, in time, to have reached the conclusion that her only surviving son had been removed from earth so that her husband would not be distracted from his ambition to achieve high political office: his son's sacrifice was the price he had to pay.

Pierce was completely unsettled, and this at a time when momentous decisions at national level would demand careful consideration and concentration in a reasonably calm and stable atmosphere. Worse was to follow: Jane Pierce had felt too ill to attend the inauguration and had gone to stay with relatives in Baltimore, and it was there she learned[2] with dismay that, contrary to what Pierce had told her with regard to his reluctance to be nominated, he had actively solicited the position as candidate, and, in that way, his political ambitions had been directly promoted at the expense of his family's happiness and comfort.

Pierce visited her on March 2, and a bitter confrontation ensued, a confrontation which, had he had any compensatory satisfaction with anticipation of the impending honor to be bestowed upon him, not only removed the last vestiges of personal pride but replaced it with an overwhelming sense of guilt. No President was ever to experience such a burden of futile honor upon his inauguration day. A further tragedy was yet to come: since Jane was not present at the ceremony on March 4, Abigail Fillmore, the outgoing President's wife, volunteered as stand-in on her behalf, with the sad consequence referred to in the last chapter: she caught a chill which developed into pneumonia and died on March 30.

During this chaotic period of sequential traumatic events, Pierce was further handicapped by the absence of his Vice-President, Rufus King. The latter, already a sick man at the time of his election, had gone to

Cuba in a vain search for a more congenial climate that might restore him to health. Too ill to return to Washington in time for his inauguration, the oath of office was administered to him in Cuba. He then made an effort to return to the capital, but in mid-April he died in Alabama.[3]

Until Jane Pierce finally and reluctantly consented to come to Washington, Pierce himself lived virtually alone and friendless at the White House. Any sense of exhilaration at being chief executive in the land had long since been dissipated. When she arrived at the end of March, she was in a deep melancholy mood, obviously unwilling as well as incapable of functioning as a creditable and gracious First Lady. The duties of that office fell upon Mrs. Abby Kent Means, a girlhood friend from Amherst, Massachusetts, and a lady of appreciable wealth possessed of the social graces.[4]

The whole atmosphere at the presidential mansion was inhibiting.[5] Pierce, who enjoyed festive occasions, attended concerts and social gatherings without his wife. It was not until New Year's Day, 1855, that she made her first appearance as White House hostess, and then in black.[6]

Pierce had little success as President. He favored slavery, and became recognized as "The Northern man with Southern principles." Losing the support of the North, and regarded only with suspicion in the South, Pierce failed in his bid for renomination in 1856. In that year, both he and his wife lost, through death, their valuable companion, Mrs. Means, so that the remaining months of office relapsed into a dreary waiting routine, as depressing as that of the first months of tenure.

Possibly more in search of his own mental well-being than that of his wife's, who could seldom be aroused out of her persistent mood of melancholy, Pierce went with her on an extended tour of Europe, from which they did not return until 1859. All the while, Jane carried with her little Bennie's Bible, along with a small box (given to her by Mrs. Means) in which she had carefully placed the locks of hair of her "treasured dead": those of her three boys, her mother, and her sister.

Franklin and his wife retired to live in Concord, New Hampshire, and there Jane Pierce died in December, 1863. Franklin Pierce died nearly six years later in October, 1869.

James Buchanan

(1857–1861)

James Buchanan is the only President of the United States to have remained a bachelor throughout his entire life, a unique status apparently traceable to a tragic incident which occurred during his late twenties.

Born in 1791, and the second child of a large family of eleven of Scotch-Irish immigrants, he received a good education and eventually qualified as a lawyer, although it seems that he was expelled from one college for excessive drinking. He enlisted during the War of 1812, and was elected to the state legislature of Pennsylvania, 1814–1816. In 1819, he met and fell in love with Anne Coleman of Lancaster County, daughter of one of America's first millionaires. All the facts relating to their engagement have not been disclosed, but malicious gossip alleged that Buchanan was more interested in his fiancee's fortune than in Anne herself. The latter broke off the engagement, then died suddenly a few months later. Her parents forbade Buchanan's presence at the funeral, and he apparently resolved to honor her memory with a vow never to marry.

Thereby freed of emotional entanglements, he re-entered the political arena, and he served as U.S. Congressman, (1821–31), U.S. Minister to Russia (1832–3), U.S. Senator (1834–45), Secretary of State (1845–49) in Polk's administration, and Minister to Great Britain (1853–56) during Pierce's tenure of office.

Buchanan took along with him, to London, Harriet Lane, his young and vivacious niece, for whom he had acted as guardian after the death of her mother (Buchanan's sister, Jane) and father, leaving Harriet an orphan at age 9.[1] Buchanan had seen to it that Harriet received a good education in a fashionable school in Charles Town (Virginia), as well as at a convent in Georgetown, D.C. She was a very attractive young girl of 20 when she went to London, and she reveled in all the social functions and activities at which Buchanan's official presence was demanded. She was presented at Court and Queen Victoria was most gracious to her.

Since Buchanan had been out of the country during the highly controversial issue of the status of Kansas as a slave or non-slave state, he proved more acceptable than the incumbent President James Pierce as the Democratic nominee, and, in the presidential election of 1856, he defeated Republican John C. Fremont and "Know-Nothing" Millard Fillmore.

During his four years of office, Buchanan, an irresolute leader and "a man of conciliation," failed to stem the rising tide of anger and hostility between North and South; but if he failed politically as President he was a great success socially, due to his niece, Harriet, whom he brought with him to the White House as acting First Lady.[2] His sumptuous Inaugural Ball set the stage and opened a new festive era for Washington society, which was only too eager to dispel the long gloom cast by a decade of glum, unsocial Presidents and their wives.

Buchanan was a wealthy man, and he spared no cost in entertaining the five thousand or more revelers who attended the ball: according to the records, the caterers supplied 125 tons of chicken salad, 400 gallons of oysters, 500 quarts of jellies, 300 gallons of ice cream, together with mounds of hams, tongues and venison, flowing streams of wine, and a four-foot high cake featuring the 31 states of the union.

Harriet was in her element as hostess—she loved the many opportunities which came her way to supervise the lavish feasts for which the presidential mansion became renowned. She persuaded her uncle to extend the old conservatory[3] at the White House to ensure an appropriate seasonal supply of flowers for the dining tables, reception halls, and private rooms.

The climax of Harriet's tenure as acting First Lady came in 1860 with the first visit of a member of British royalty since the Revolutionary War. This was the nineteen-year-old Edward Albert, Prince of Wales, traveling incognito as Baron Renfrew. There were no guest facilities at the White House, so Buchanan, cavalier as always, gave up his own room to the Prince, and slept on a couch in his office. Harriet acted as the Prince's mentor on his several tours to places of interest in and around the capital, including a visit to Mount Vernon, where he placed a wreath at the tomb of George Washington, and to the gymnasium of a young ladies' school, where he played ten-pins to promote an appetite for evening dinner. The national press recorded all the events and activities in detail and with gusto, presumably in the fond hope of promoting a romance between the young couple. Upon the Prince's return to London, his mother, Queen Victoria, sent a letter of warm gratitude to Buchanan and Harriet, along with an engraved etching of the royal family.

Buchanan refused to allow his name to be put forward for nomination as Democratic candidate in the election of 1860. When the Lincolns moved into the White House, Harriet, recalling her own chilly reception at the mansion four years earlier, prepared for them a welcoming repast as a housewarming gesture.

Buchanan retired to "Wheatland," his home in Pennsylvania. Just before resigning as President, he almost recanted upon his non-marriage vow: he had met a certain Mrs. Bass, a widow with three children, and he took them all for a holiday to Bedford Springs, Pennsylvania. There, the lady's black servant girl was persuaded to run away with some abolitionists, an episode which so upset Buchanan that it ruined the vacation as well as the romance.

Harriet herself, at age 33, married Henry Elliott Johnson, a Baltimore businessman. Two children were born of the marriage, but, tragically, within a few years she lost her husband, her children, and her uncle, James. The latter died in June, 1868, leaving a large fortune of $300,000, mostly to Harriet. In his will, he gave instructions that his love letters to Anne Coleman, which he had preserved for nearly half a century, were to be destroyed unread, and his wishes were observed.

During her thirty or so years of widowhood,[4] Harriet traveled extensively in Europe, and spent much of her fortune accumulating a valuable collection of paintings which she was to bequeath to the Smithsonian Institution, where it became the nucleus of its National Collection of Fine Arts. She also donated the sum of $100,000 for the erection of a monument in honor of her uncle, but the largest proportion of her substantial fortune was left to John Hopkins Hospital in Baltimore for the purpose of founding a wing in memory of her two sons, and which was dedicated to the treatment of all children regardless of race, creed, or finance.

Abraham Lincoln

(1861–1865)

Abraham Lincoln, probably the most honored and most beloved of all Presidents of the United States, was born in a log cabin near Hodgenville, Kentucky, on February 12, 1809, only seven months earlier and in the same state as his Civil War counterpart, Jefferson Davis. Both families soon left Kentucky, that of Lincoln to Indiana, and that of Davis to Mississippi.

Lincoln was the second child of Thomas Lincoln and Nancy Hanks. The first child, Nancy (Sarah), lived only until she was twenty-one,[1] while the third (and last) child, Thomas, was but two years old when he died. In 1818, Lincoln's mother passed away, and one year later his father married Sarah (Sally) Bush Johnston, a widow with three children.

Both Lincoln and his sister had attended local schools sporadically, and the former was considerably influenced by one of his teachers named Swazey. Lincoln's stepmother, likewise, gave him every encouragement to pursue his fondness of books and reading. He was a strong, lanky youth who loved the outdoor life of the western pioneer family, and earned his living as a railsplitter, as well as on a flatboat carrying goods down the Mississippi to New Orleans. He was later offered the job as a clerk in a general store at New Salem, a settlement founded just west of Springfield, Illinois. After brief service in the Black Hawk War of 1832, he returned to assume duties, first as postmaster of New Salem, then as a surveyor, and it was there also that he met his first love, Ann Rutledge, daughter of James Rutledge, a tavern keeper, although how much of the story of the romance is fact, and how much is fiction remains a matter of conjecture and opinion. Most of what is known was written up at a later date by William H. Herndon who was, at one time, Lincoln's law partner.[2] Herndon was much disliked by Lincoln's wife, Mary Todd. The dislike proved mutual, and it was after Lincoln's death that Herndon, who had conducted extensive research on the President's life and ancestors, wrote the account of his courtship with Ann in an attempt to embarrass Mary Todd. But, whatever developed between Lincoln and Ann, whether it was a close love or merely a close friendship, was abruptly terminated by Ann's death from typhoid in 1835.

Lincoln next cultivated an attachment for Mary Owens who had, in 1833, come to New Salem from Kentucky to visit her aunt, Mrs. Bennett Abell. She did not respond to his advances, and rejected his proposals for marriage. At a later date she said of him that "he was deficient in those little links which make up the great chain of woman's happiness. . . ."

In 1834, he had sought and won an election for a seat in the Illinois House of Representatives and, in the fall of that year, he moved to the state capital, Vandalia, which was later moved to Springfield, where Lincoln settled in 1837, having being admitted to the bar in the same year.

As a prominent legislator and successful lawyer, Lincoln found acceptance by the social circles of Springfield and, in 1839, he met Mary Todd, aged 22, daughter of a bank president, Robert S. Todd, and his first wife, Elizabeth Parker, of Lexington, Kentucky.

Mary was one of six children of her father's first marriage. Her mother died when she was but 7, and her father had remarried and reared eight more children by his second wife, so that Mary was much relieved to be given the opportunity of moving to Springfield to live at the home of her married sister, Mrs. Ninian Wirt Edwards, daughter-in-law of the Governor of Illinois.

Mary had been reared very much as a young aristocrat: she had, for four years, attended the select boarding school for young ladies of Madame Victorie Charlotte Leclerc Mentelle, where she had learnt to speak French reasonably well; she wore the most fashionable of dresses, and had assumed the most superior of affected airs, possessing as well a temper which was both quick and unmindful of consequences.

Lincoln, at age 30, had become much attracted to this high-spirited creature; he proposed marriage and was accepted.[3] The ceremony was scheduled for January 1, 1841, but the only verifiable fact as to what exactly happened on that date is that Lincoln did not appear for the ceremony. Some biographers claim that he suddenly panicked at the thought of finally committing himself to marriage; others aver that, feeling inadequate to his partner, he had given her due notice that he could not go through with the ceremony. What is again certain is that he spent the next eighteen months in a mood of black despair and despondency. He did, in time, recover, he became reconciled to Mary, and they were finally united in wedlock on November 4, 1842.[4]

The subsequent story of Lincoln's marriage was that of a sturdy vessel cast loose on a tempestuous sea. He and Mary were a devoted couple, but her many uncontrollable outbursts and unpredictable behaviors gave rise to frequent embarrassments in public. Yet Lincoln, possessed of incredible patience and inner serenity, seldom failed to respond with anything but a reassuring calmness of temperament, which immeasurably served to restore harmony and equilibrium within the household.

Their first child, Robert Lincoln, named after Mary's father,[5] was born on August 1, 1843, in one of the rooms they had rented at the Globe Tavern, Springfield. Not long after Robert's birth, Lincoln bought the house at the corner of Jackson and 8th Street, which subsequently became known as the Lincoln Homestead. It had been previously owned by the rector who had officiated at their wedding, and the purchase price was $1,500. The home was to be the birthplace of their three other sons: Edward Baker, born in 1846 (but who died in 1850); William Wallace (Willie), born in 1850; and Thomas (Tad), born in 1853.

Lincoln was often away on circuit duty, so that much of the work of rearing the children fell upon Mary's shoulders. When he was at home, he proved to be an overindulgent father, believing that "it is my pleasure that my children are free, happy, and unrestrained by parental tyranny. Love is the chain whereby to bind a child to its parents." Lincoln's law partner, William Herndon, disagreed intensely with this method of the upbringing of children, complaining that, when the latter were brought to the law office, they would create chaos by the scattering of papers, pulling books from the shelves, and spilling ink. He later wrote that he often "wanted to wring the necks of these brats and pitch them out of the windows."

On one occasion, the Lincoln family traveled to Lexington to visit

Mary Todd's relatives. By coincidence, one passenger on the train happened to be Mary's nephew, Joseph Humphreys. He had never met the Lincolns and was completely unaware of whom he was talking when, having arrived home, he blurted out, "Aunt Betsy, I was never so glad to get off a train in my life. There were two lively youngsters on board who kept the whole train in a turmoil, and their long-legged father, instead of spanking the brats, looked pleased as punch and aided and abetted the older one in mischief." To Joseph's great consternation, the long-legged father and those very same brats walked in to occupy his own home a few minutes later. His subsequent reaction to the "invaders" remains, sadly, unrecorded, although it may well be imagined.

Lincoln was apparently not the most efficient of babysitters. He undertook to take care of his youngsters while Mary went to church. One story relates that, while pulling a little wagon with his children in it up and down the street before the home, Lincoln became too deeply absorbed in a book which he held in one hand, and failed to notice that one of his sons had fallen out. He even failed to hear the boy's persistent cries for help, until he found himself soundly berated and publicly reprimanded by none other than Mary who unexpectedly appeared on the scene.

It was about this time that, in a letter to a friend, he described his own son, Robert:

> Bob is "short and low" and I expect always will be. He talks very plainly—almost as plainly as anybody. He is quite smart enough. I sometimes fear he is one of the little rare-ripe sort, that are smarter at about five than ever after. He has a great deal of that sort of mischief that is the offspring of much animal spirits.

One other person described Bob as a "bright boy" but "seemed to have his own way."

The happy Lincoln family encountered its first tragedy with the death of young Eddie (Edward Baker) in February, 1850, but the grief and loss was at least to some degree assuaged by the birth, ten months later in the same year, of a third son, William Wallace,[6] who entered this life just four days before Christmas.

Mary was again pregnant in 1852, and the Lincolns had fond hopes that their fourth child might be a daughter. It was not to be: Thomas Lincoln was born on April 4, 1853. Lincoln's father had died in 1851, so the latest born was given his grandfather's name. His head appeared to be unduly large for his body so his father nicknamed him "Tadpole" or "Tad" for short, a name by which he became universally recognized. He

had been born with a cleft palate, which left him with a speech impediment for the rest of his life, but which also made him the special subject
of endearment of both his parents.

In 1846, Lincoln had been elected to the U.S. House of Representatives, but he served for one term only (by prearrangement with his three
political associates in Illinois, each of whom was also to serve only one
term). He settled back in Springfield, devoting himself to his family and
law practice until the issues raised by the Kansas-Nebraska Act of 1854
propelled him back into the political arena. Fearing the extension of
slavery into the North, Lincoln vigorously campaigned against the bill,
and he joined the newly formed (1856) Republican party. In the election
of 1858, he was selected as a candidate in opposition to the Democratic
Senator for Illinois, Stephen A. Douglas (who had been instrumental in
proposing the measures incorporated into the Kansas-Nebraska Act).
This led to the famous Lincoln-Douglas debates, and, although Lincoln
lost the election to Douglas,[7] the publicity engendered by the confrontation brought him national recognition which gained him his nomination
as Republican Presidential candidate in 1860.

It was by reason of an incident which occurred in the course of the
ensuing election campaign that the nation was confronted with its first
bearded President. In mid-October, 1860, he received a letter from Westfield, Chautauqua County, New York, which read as follows:

Hon. A.B. Lincoln

Dear Sir,

I am a little girl 11 years old, but want that you should be President
of the United States very much so I hope you wont think me very
bold to write to such a great man as you are.

Have you any little girls about as large as I am if so give them my
love and tell her to write me if you cannot answer this letter. I have
got four brothers and part of them will vote for you any way and if
you will let your whiskers grow I will try to get the rest of them to
vote for you. You would look a great deal better for your face is so
thin. All the ladies like whiskers and they would tease their hus-
bands to vote for you and then you would be President.

                                        Grace Bedell.

Lincoln replied in a letter from Springfield dated October 19, 1860:

Miss Grace Bedell
Westfield N.Y.

My dear Little Miss:

Your very agreeable letter of the 15th is received. I regret the necessity of saying I have no daughters. I have three sons, one seventeen, one nine, and one seven years of age. They, with their mother, constitute my whole family. As to the whiskers, having never worn any, do you not think people would call it a piece of silly affectation if I were to begin it now?

Your very sincere well-wisher

A. Lincoln.

But Lincoln did grow a beard, and, on the way to his Inauguration, he had his train stop at Westfield, where he met and kissed his little correspondent, saying to the assembled crowd, "She wrote me that she thought I'd look better if I wore whiskers."[8]

It was Lincoln's victory[9] in November, 1860, which precipitated first, the secession of the Southern states, and then the outbreak of civil war in April, 1861.[10] Within the first year of hostilities Lincoln suffered the personal tragedy of the loss of his son, little Willie, aged 12, at the White House in February, 1862. Mary was inconsolable and distraught with grief. Her reaction was upon occasion so overwhelming that Lincoln, in sheer despair for her state of mind, once took her to a window and, pointing to the insane asylum said, "Mother, do you see that large white building yonder? Unless you control your grief I am afraid we shall have to send you there."

Apart from the gloom and despondency cast upon the White House by the death of Willie, the presidential mansion was no place to find solace or comfort. Soldiers were regularly encamped in several of the rooms and corridors reducing privacy to its minimum. In order that Mary should have some company, Lincoln sent for her sister, Elizabeth Grimsley, who had been bridesmaid at their wedding. Mary did have also a regular daily visitor in the person of sixteen-year-old Julia, daughter of Judge and Mrs. Horatio Taft. She was a delightful girl who captivated Lincoln by her youthful charm. He described her as a "flibbertigibbet," which he promptly went on to define as "a small slim thing with curls and a white dress and a blue sash who flies instead of walking."

It was part of Julia's duties to bring along her two younger brothers, "Bud" and "Holly" to play with Willie and Tad, and to supervise their play activities, but the boisterous quartet made this an almost superhuman task. In despair, Mary hired tutors, presumably to further the boys' education, but doubtless also to restrict their movements to one place, at least, temporarily. However, what eventuated was that tutors "came and went, like the changes of the moon."

Lincoln, as usual, paid no attention to law and order in the White House, and Julia once described seeing him on his back, grinning broadly as the four boys vainly tried to pin him down to the floor, each boy desperately holding on to one of the President's arms or legs.

On Sundays, all the boys went to Julia's church:

> Its special attraction lay in the fact that when the preacher prayed for the President of the United States, the "seceshes," as Tad called them, would get up and leave in a marked manner banging the pew doors behind them. This entertaining performance ceased abruptly when an order was issued for the arrest of anyone leaving before the service was over. Tad was frankly disappointed that no spirited "secesh" looking for trouble challenged this order. [11]

Tad once asked his father, "Pa, why do the preachers always pray so long for you?" and Lincoln replied, "I suppose it's because the preachers think I need it;" he paused, then added "and I guess I do."

Because of his son's physical infirmities, Lincoln always held a special place for Tad. He said of him: "Let him run, there's time enough yet for him to learn his letters and get poky. Bob was just such a rascal and now he is a very decent boy." Mary called him a "troublesome little sunshine," while her sister, Elizabeth, considered Tad to be the child closest in resemblance to his mother:

> a gay, gladsome, merry, spontaneous fellow, bubbling over with innocent fun, whose laugh rang through the house, when not moved to tears. Quick in mind, and impulse, like his mother, with his naturally sunny temperament, he was the life, as also the worry of the household! [12]

The White House attic, remote from the affairs of state, was a veritable paradise for all the boys. Here, using wooden logs as cannons, they set up a "military post" in defense of the mansion. They formed themselves into "Mrs. Lincoln's Zouaves," with Willie as colonel, Bud as major, Holly as captain, and Tad as drum major. The company was reviewed by President Lincoln and his wife, who formally presented them with a flag, along with acknowledgment for their meritorious service to their country.

While he was yet alive, Willie took good care of his younger brother. One of their favorite cooperative antics was their "circus on the roof" when Willie would love to dress up in his mother's old clothes, and Tad would blacken his own face. They would charge their parents an admission fee of five cents, for which, Lincoln commented, they "got out of it a gold coin's worth in laughs."

Mary dressed both of them in very practical clothes, with Tad once being described as "rather a grotesque looking little fellow in his gray, trapdoor pants made in true country style to button to a waist. . .," while Willie was equally baggy, but "there was a flow of intelligence and feeling on his face which made him peculiarly interesting and caused strangers to speak of him as a fine little fellow." Julia Taft called Willie "the most lovable boy I ever knew, bright, sensible, sweet-tempered, and gentle-mannered." He was a studious boy and, just before his death he wrote, at the age of ten, quite a remarkable poem upon the passing of Colonel Edward Baker,[13] whom he had known before his death on the battlefield:

> There was no patriot like Baker,
> So noble and so true;
> He fell as a soldier on the field,
> His face to the sky of blue.
>
> His Country has her part to pay
> To'rds those he has left behind;
> His widow and his children all,
> She must always keep in mind.
>
> His voice is silent in the hall
> Which oft his presence graced;
> No more he'll hear the loud acclaim
> Which rang from place to place.
>
> No squeamish notions filled his breast,
> "The Union" was his theme;
> "No surrender and no compromise,"
> His day-thought and night's dream.[14]

After Willie's death, Mary never once entered the bedroom where he had died nor the Green Room where he had been embalmed.

While in the White House, Mary, of all First Ladies, suffered most since there was nothing which she could do right. At the time of Willie's illness, she had been informed by her doctors that he would recover, and so she went ahead with the planning of a great ball for Washington society, considering it her duty to do so as the President's wife. She was roundly castigated for her extravagance, and a six-stanza poem entitled

"The Lady President's Ball," written by Eleanor G. Donnelly, was given wide publicity. It purported to be the reaction of a wounded soldier lying in a nearby hospital hearing the sounds of revelry from the White House:

Hundreds ay! hundreds of thousands
    In satins, jewels, and wine,
French dishes for dainty stomachs
    (while the black broth sickens mine!)
And jellies, and fruits, and cold ices
    And fountains that flash as they fall.
O God! for a cup of cold water
    From the Lady-President's Ball[15]

Willie's death, only four days after the publication of the foregoing poem, brought her not sympathy, but instead, reprimands for her apparent callousness for conducting festivities on the threshold of death. It became increasingly obvious to Mary that she was in the White House solely to be persecuted. Lincoln's secretary, William O. Stoddard, was to write, "There is one tide . . . which never turns, and that is the tide of criticism and advice which sets toward and into the White House."

Unfortunately, much of it stemmed from the simple fact that so many members of her immediate family were serving in the Confederate army: they included one brother, three half-brothers, and three brothers-in-law, and of these, Samuel Briggs Todd was killed at Shiloh, David H. Todd at Vicksburg, and Alexander H. Todd at Baton Rouge; when she received the calamitous news of their deaths, in no way could she be seen to express her grief in public.

Her sister, Emilie, had married a close friend of the family, Ben Hardin Helm, to whom Lincoln had, at outbreak of war, offered the position as paymaster in the U.S. Army with the rank of major. Helm had refused the offer and joined the Confederate Army, greatly to Lincoln's disappointment. In September, 1863, he was killed at Chickamauga, Georgia. Emilie, now left with three young children, sought to pass through the Union lines to join her mother in Kentucky. It was Lincoln who gave her his personal permission to come north and, on her way home, she stayed at the White House in December, 1863, an episode which a hostile press in Washington widely publicized.[16]

Washington seethed with rumors that Mary Todd was a Confederate spy. There are conflicting reports as to Lincoln's reaction to these allegations, but one version has it that he appeared before a committee on the conduct of the war and made the following statement:

I, Abraham Lincoln, President of the United States, appear of my volition before this committee of the Senate, to say I, of my own knowledge, know that it is untrue that any of my family hold treasonable relations with the enemy.[17]

During all these years of national and personal tribulations, Lincoln probably found most solace in his relationship with Tad. The latter had often been allowed to sleep in his father's bed, and Lincoln occasionally permitted him (most inappropriately according to several members), to attend important cabinet meetings; when Tad became sleepy, he would climb upon his father's knee and go to sleep. As described by one observer:

> As the long bony hand spread over the dark hair, and the thin face above rested the sharp chin upon it, it was a pleasant sight. The head of a great and powerful nation . . . soothing with loving care the little restless creature so much dearer than all the power he wields. . . .[18]

Tad's antics never ceased to amuse his father. One day he took it upon himself to go to the War Department, where Secretary Stanton decided to humor him by having him commissioned as a lieutenant. Upon his return to the White House, Tad dismissed the regular guard, and, having drilled the servants and given them guns, he set them up on duty to replace the discharged men. Lincoln treated the affair as one huge joke and, after Tad was safely in bed and fast asleep, he restored things back to their normal order.

Upon another occasion, Tad, having discovered the system of operating the White House bells, contrived to have them all ring at once, to the consternation of the entire staff and occupants of the building. His pets, particularly the goats, were a special menace: not only were they permitted to tear through the mansion, irrespective of its guests, but one goat, Nanny, was singled out for special attention. During August, 1863, while Mary and Tad were away, Lincoln had occasion to write him a letter:

> The day you left, Nanny was found resting herself and chewing her little cud, on the middle of Tad's bed. But now she's gone! The gardener kept complaining that she destroyed the flowers, till it was concluded to bring her down to the White House. This was done, but the second day she had disappeared, and has not been heard of since. . . .

Suspicion fell on the gardener, but that was all. Tad had once eaten all the specially forced strawberries for a state dinner, a deed which earned him the sobriquet of "The Madame's wildcat."[19] When Lincoln proclaimed a "fast day," Tad stocked up food in the White House larder; when his action was reported to his father, the latter remarked with obvious relish: "If he grows to be a man, Tad will be what the women all dote on—a good provider."

Despite his innumerable pranks,[20] Tad was as warmhearted and as generous as his father. At his last Christmas in the White House, he brought in all the waifs and strays of Washington whom he could find and fed them in the White House kitchen. At the annual White House egg-rolling functions, he shared his Easter eggs with handicapped children. He was a great source of comfort (and worry) to his mother, who, after the death of Willie, appeared constantly dejected and inconsolable.

Mary had resorted to spiritualism, and had encouraged quack practitioners to hold seances at the White House when it was claimed that messages were being received from Willie. After much effort, Lincoln finally succeeded in having the deceptions exposed.[21] Mary continued to remain depressed and increasingly extravagant concerning clothes, but the amount of debt into which she entered remained unknown to her husband.

She became more moody and erratic in her behavior, causing Lincoln considerable public embarrassment, perhaps the most widely publicized incident being that which occurred in March, 1865, shortly after the second inauguration ceremony. Lincoln had taken his family to visit General Grant at the latter's headquarters at City Point, Virginia. While Mary had accompanied Mrs. Grant in a horse-drawn carriage, Lincoln had ridden horseback to review his troops with Mrs. Ord, the attractive wife of Major-General Edward Ord, at his side. When she observed what was happening, Mary's anger erupted into an unprecedented outburst of invective directed against both her busband and Mrs. Ord. Lincoln's attempts to calm her rage were unavailing; he could but lead her away in shame.

Mary's tragedies appeared to have had no bounds; with the war ending on Palm Sunday, April 9th, 1865, she had every reason to anticipate that her husband's second term of office would bring more relaxation and serenity to the White House. But only five days later, on Good Friday, Lincoln was assassinated, and Mary entered into yet another world of chaos and embitterment.

Five weeks elapsed before she was in a fit state to leave Washington. During this period, her eldest son, Robert, gave her invaluable support, though in all years prior to the assassination his contribution to the family welfare had been at best nondescript and neutral in character. He had always been something of a problem child, alternately described as being withdrawn or bumptious, traits possibly attributed to his displacement on the family eldest-son pinnacle, as his three younger brothers were each, in turn, accorded attention and affection which Robert had perforce to share and not monopolize. According to Herndon, Robert was cross-eyed as a young child, a handicap which he apparently overcame by peeping through keyholes, although in school he was nicknamed "Cockeye."

No one ever described Robert as a happy, outgoing boy, and he had, on several occasions, attempted to run away from home. He had received the best of education, attending first Phillips Exeter Academy, and, in 1859, entering Harvard, where, at the time of his admission he presented to the college president a letter of introduction from Stephen A. Douglas which described him as the son of his friend "with whom I have lately been canvassing the State of Illinois." Robert had expressed to his father a wish to study law, but, fully conversant with his son's apparent inability to enjoy life, Lincoln had responded: "If you do, you should learn more than I ever did, but you will never have so good a time."

At the outbreak of the Civil War, Robert had been eager to enlist in the Union Army, but Lincoln had hesitated to grant him permission lest political complications arise from his possible capture by the Confederates. Having also witnessed Mary's reaction to the death of Willie in 1862, Lincoln was fearful of her sanity in the event of any further immediate tragedy within the family.[22]

However, having graduated in 1864, Robert virtually demanded of his father that he now be permitted to enlist. Accordingly, in a letter to General Grant dated January 19, 1865, Lincoln wrote:

> I do not wish to put him in the ranks, nor yet to give him a commission, to which those who have already served long are better entitled, and better qualified to hold. Could he, without embarrassment to you, or detriment to the service, go into your military family with some minimal rank, I, and not the public, furnishing his necessary means?

Grant readily agreed, and, in February, 1865, Robert was given appointment as aide to the General, with the rank of captain. He saw little or no action, but he was present at the surrender proceedings at Appomattox, and he accompanied Grant when the latter returned to Washington to report to Lincoln on the morning of April 14, 1865. On that very evening, Lincoln was assassinated at Ford's Theatre, and Robert was present when his father died the morning of the next day.

At the age of 21, he was immediately forced into the situation of having to function as a mature adult responsible for a grievously distressed mother, along with a handicapped brother who was only 12. To his great credit, Robert rose nobly to the occasion.

After Lincoln's burial at Springfield on May 4, 1865, Mary, still confined within the White House, finally decided to live, not in the family house in Springfield, which held too many sad memories for her, but in Chicago; and it was here that she found herself having to cope with an entirely new and endless series of tribulations.

For the rest of her life, despite all that was done to dissuade her otherwise, Mary was obsessed by her conviction that she was a poor widow. The facts were that the Lincoln estate had been valued at $83,000, a sum which had increased to $110,000 by the time of the final settlement in 1868. Lincoln had left no will, so the latter sum of money was divided equally between Mary and her two sons. Public subscriptions on her behalf had raised $10,000, while Congress voted to grant her the remaining part of Lincoln's annual presidential salary, which amounted to $22,000.[23] Mary used most of the latter to purchase and furnish a modest house at 375 West Washington Street, Chicago.

Mary had been an exorbitantly extravagant wife,[24] and Lincoln, always lax about his domestic financial affairs, must have known little of, or had consciously ignored, the eccentricities of his wife in this direction, and he must also have assumed that Mary received much of her clothing gratuitously, by way of free advertisement, from her couturiers. After Lincoln's death, whatever the nature of the credit earlier accorded her by the clothing stores, it ceased abruptly. Mary Lincoln, ex-First Lady, was no longer an asset, and the demands of the creditors now poured in to overwhelm her. Her biographers vary widely in their estimates of Mary's total indebtedness, which range from a still substantial sum of $25,000 to that of a possibly exaggerated amount of $70,000.[25] Still, especially to Robert, who was suddenly confronted by a host of Mary's debtors, the outstanding debt for clothes was outrageously high, and he himself, as a young struggling lawyer,[26] was financially helpless to assist his mother.

It was at this stage that there occurred what the newspapers publicized as "The Old Clothes Scandal." In September, 1867, Mary went to New York with a trunk full of clothing and jewelry which she proposed to sell for as much money as possible. She registered at the St. Denis Hotel under the assumed name of "Mrs. Clarke," and she solicited the assistance of her former black seamstress· at the White House, Elizabeth (Lizzie) Keckley. Unfortunately, the commission brokers, whom Mary had employed to sell her possessions, discovered her identity, and they proceeded to exploit the situation with a view to their utmost financial advantage. Mary had indiscreetly written letters indicting the Republican party leaders for allowing her, as widow of a President, renowned Victor of the Civil War, to be reduced to such humiliating financial circumstances as to have to resort to the sale of her personal clothing,[27] and these letters came to be published in the *New York World,* a newspaper notorious for its anti-Republican viewpoints.

Robert was understandably furious. He had become engaged to Mary, daughter of Senator Harlan of Iowa, but had delayed his marriage until such time that his mother and Tad were reasonably accommodated in a stable home. But there appeared to be no end to the scandals which had suddenly erupted. Elizabeth Keckley herself (aided by a ghost writer) had published what she considered to be an account favorable to Mary Lincoln, of her association with the First Lady, both during and after the White House period.

Her book was published in 1868 under the title of *Behind the Scenes— Thirty Years a Slave and Four Years in the White House.* Robert took quick action to suppress the work, and he prevailed upon the publishers to withdraw it, in consequence of which, Lizzie Keckley, who died in 1907, received nothing by way of royalties from the sale of the book.[28] Mary never forgave the authoress.

Along with her problems relating to debts and her obsession with poverty came the cruel embarrassment of having to face the malicious and uncharitable attacks made upon her by Lincoln's former law partner, William Herndon. In November, 1866, the latter gave a public lecture at Springfield asserting that Lincoln's only true love had been Ann Rutledge. He claimed that Mary Todd had been fortunate to "catch" Lincoln on the rebound, so to speak, and that the ex-President had never really been in love with her, as witnessed by the fiasco of the first wedding ceremony. Mary Todd, who apparently had never even heard of Ann Rutledge, was appalled and shocked, as were Robert and the immediate relatives, even more so since there was no possible way in which the spiteful allegations could be refuted. Herndon relished the publicity, and ignored all of Robert's appeals to desist from the offensive scandal. In due course, and in collaboration with Jesse Weik, Herndon published his *Life of Lincoln* (1889), in which he expanded upon his unsavory theme.

The climax of the attack upon Mary Todd was probably the poem written by Edgar Lee Masters which appears on the tombstone of Ann Rutledge. One verse reads:

I am Ann Rutledge who sleep beneath these weeds

Beloved of Abraham Lincoln,
Wedded to him, not through union
But through separation.
Bloom forever, O Republic,
From the dust of my bosom.

Ruth Randall appends a parody of the verse which, she asserts, provides the greater truth.[29]

This is Ann Rutledge who sleeps beneath these weeds
Beloved and betrothed to John McNamar.
Lincoln, the friend of both, grieved when she died;
That tells the story; but the legend blooms forever
Out of the quirks and hate in Herndon's bosom.

In 1867, Mary, concerned with Tad's education, visited a school in Racine, Wisconsin, with a view to enrolling him there, but she said of it: "there was an air of restraint which I did not exactly like." So, the proposal to send him there was dropped. Tad then attended an Academy School in Chicago, where slowly his speech improved, and he even became one of the editors of the school newspaper. Nevertheless, he remained very much an academically handicapped boy.

By the summer of 1868, weary of the reproachful and unsympathetic social climate of the United States, Mary decided to go abroad. Robert, having long delayed his marriage, was finally united in wedlock in September of that year and, on October 1st, Mary and Tad sailed to Europe on the *City of Baltimore*.

They spent three years abroad, visiting England, Scotland, France and Germany, travelling incognito and living in the cheapest apartments.[30] At Frankfurt-on-Main, where Tad had been placed in the "Institute" of Dr. Hohagen "with a number of well-behaved German and English boys," Mary was paid a visit by her friend, Mrs. James H. Orne, who thus described the occasion:

I followed the waiter to the fourth story and the back part of it too—and there in a small cheerless, desolate-looking room with but one window—two chairs and a wooden table with a solitary candle—I found the wife, the petted indulged wife, of my noble-hearted, just, good, murdered President Abraham Lincoln. . . .shame on my countrymen. . .she lives alone. I never knew what the word Alone meant before.[31]

In 1870, with the outbreak of the Franco-Prussian War, Mary and Tad fled to England, and here she found a tutor for Tad, and then had him enrolled in a boarding school to improve his English education while she sojourned in Italy for her health. At this very same time she had been relieved to hear the good news from the United States that, in July, 1870, Congress had finally approved for her a presidential widow's pension of $3,000.

Mary and Tad returned to the United States in the late spring of 1871. Tad was thus described in the *New York Tribune:* "He had grown up a tall, fine-looking lad of 18 who bears but a faint resemblance to the tricksy little sprite whom visitors to the White House remember"; another friend said of him that he "was a very lovable boy, quiet, gentle-mannered, and good-natured, nothing loud or boisterous about him. . . ."

Mother and son went back to live in Chicago, but shortly after their return, Tad became severely ill and died on July 15, 1871.[32] He was buried in Springfield alongside his father and two brothers. Once more, Mary lay in a state of collapse: she had now suffered the loss of a husband and three sons, and was not to be comforted. She had deserted the family home in Springfield because of its sad memories of life with her husband. Now, she decided to vacate the Chicago home because of its association with Tad, and she took to endlessly roaming around the country in a desperate effort to avoid facing reality. Robert failed to prevent her, although he did succeed in having Mary travel with a lady companion.

She was in Florida during the winter months of 1874–5 and, while there, she developed hallucinations of the impending death both of herself as well as that of Robert. She hurried back to Chicago carrying over fifty thousand dollars worth of securities in her purse, and on the train she created a scene by alleging her coffee had been poisoned.

In despair, and seeking to protect her from herself, Robert felt compelled to apply to the Cook County Court for a declaration that his mother was legally insane. In May, 1875, she was committed to the State Hospital where she attempted suicide and thereupon was removed to a private mental institution at Batavia, Illinois. There, the relaxed atmosphere restored her mind to a more stable condition, and she persuaded her sister, Elizabeth Edwards, to seek means for her release, which she achieved in May, 1876.

Temporarily assigned into the custody of her sister, she again made plans to get away from her relatives believing that, in their hearts, they all regarded her "as a lunatic." So, in 1877, and escorted by Edward Lewis Baker, Jr., one of her sister's grandsons (who was very kind to her and reminded her of Tad), she traveled to New York and took ship for Europe.

She settled in Pau in Southern France as her base for the next three years. She traveled to various parts of Western Europe until, in December, 1879, she suffered a spinal injury through falling off a stepladder. She sailed home on the *Amerique* and arrived in New York in October, 1880.[33] She was met by Lewis Baker and not by Robert, who wished to avoid any unpleasant scenes—Mary had never forgiven him his action in having her declared insane and, while abroad, she never wrote him a single letter.[34] She returned with Lewis to her sister's home in Springfield, and it was there in May, 1881, that Robert and his wife came to visit and present her with their youngest daughter saying, "we have brought to you your granddaughter and namesake, Mary Lincoln." There was immediate reconciliation and forgiveness. Two years later, after considerable suffering due to her back injuries, Mary died on July 16, 1882, age 63. Before burial, she lay in the same room as that in which she had been married forty years earlier.

Mary's estate included $6,000 in cash and $75,000 in government bonds, representing substantial assets which could hardly be reconciled with her endless and wearisome protestations of poverty. Found in her home were dozens of boxes of clothing which, as a compulsive spender, she had ordered, but had never even opened nor possibly ever intended to. Once before, in 1875, when she had been committed to the mental institution, Robert had been confronted with the task of returning countless cartons of unused clothing to Chicago stores, and now, after her death, he was again saddled with the identical chore.

Robert had progressed in his career as a competent lawyer and he was charter member (1874) of the Chicago Bar Association. He had developed an interest in politics, and was a delegate at the Republican Convention of 1880 and, upon Garfield's election as President, Robert was appointed Secretary of War, a position which he retained under Chester Arthur's administration following Garfield's assassination in 1882.[35]

Robert was meticulous in his efforts to avoid being accused of capitalizing upon his father's name and fame.[36] He abandoned politics to resume his law practice but then, in 1889, he accepted Benjamin Harrison's offer to appoint him as U.S. Minister to London. The appointment was marred by tragedy. Robert's only son, Abraham Lincoln II, accompanied the family to England and was then sent to France so that he could learn the language fluently before proceeding to Harvard. But, in March, 1890, he contracted blood poisoning and died aged 16.[37]

Robert returned to the United States in 1893 to resume his lucrative law career with the Pullman Car Company, of which he eventually (1897) attained the status of president. As one of the senior executives of the company at the time of the famous Pullman Strike of 1894, he was roundly castigated for his role in allegedly defending the company at the expense of the workers. Insidious negative comparisons were drawn between his stance and that which might have been expected of his father as a "Man of the People." Robert rejected the diatribes and criticisms, asserting that his detractors might have better profited by focusing upon the role of leadership in effective labor-management relationships: Abraham Lincoln was an effective political leader; he, Robert, was a leader in the field of industry, and in his own view, equally effective.[38]

For reasons not entirely understood, Robert destroyed most of the correspondence between his mother and father, thus following the precedent set by the son of Millard Fillmore.[39] Nicholas Murray Butler, president of Columbia University was appalled, when, on a chance visit, he discovered Robert in the process of destroying invaluable historical documents, but even he was able only to retrieve a small fraction of the papers.[40]

In 1911, Robert resigned from the presidency of the Pullman Company and, thereafter, spent his retirement between winters in Washington and summers at "Hildene," his home in Manchester, Vermont.

A controversy arose in 1917 over the matter of a statue of Lincoln: it had been commissioned by Charles and Annie Taft of sculptor George Grey Barnard for Lytle Park, Cincinnati. Robert was appalled at the result: he could not prevent the unveiling of the statue at Cincinnati, but he took immediate measures to prevent the export overseas of what he considered to be a grotesque and unnatural image of his illustrious father. Originally, replicas were to be sent to London and Paris, but they ended up in Louisville, Kentucky, and Manchester, England, respectively.[41]

In Manchester, Vermont, Robert spent his last years in tranquility, playing golf by day and observing the stars by night.[42] He passed away peacefully, July 25, 1926, and was survived by his wife and two daughters: Mary Lincoln, who had married Charles Isham of New York, brother of Samuel Isham, the artist; (they had one son, Lincoln Isham); and Jessie Harlan Lincoln, who was twice married: to Warren Beckwith by whom she had two children, Mary and Robert Lincoln,[43] and Frank Edward Johnson of Norwich Town, Connecticut.

Andrew Johnson

(1865–1869)

Andrew Johnson, the first and only American President to be subjected to the ordeal of impeachment,[1] owed as much, if not more, of his advancement in his political career to his wife, as had James Polk.

His early life was one of unrelieved poverty, his father, Jacob Johnson, being simply a handyman at a local tavern, Casso's Inn, in Raleigh, North Carolina, who died aged 33 when Andrew but three years old.[2] In due course, the latter was put to work as a tailor's apprentice, and, since it was customary for someone to read to the apprentices as they cut, measured and sewed, Andrew himself became interested in learning to read and in acquiring more education. It was recorded that both Andrew (Andy) and his elder brother, William (Bill), ran away from the apprentice workshop,[3] with what consequences it remains uncertain, except that, two years later, in 1826, Andrew was known to have set up his own tailor's shop in Greeneville, Tennessee.

It was here that he met Eliza McCardle (15), the orphan daughter of a shoemaker. She had received some elementary school education, and, at his request, she proceeded to teach him the elements of writing and arithmetic. Andrew was a skilled craftsman, his business prospered, and, remembering what he owed to the reading-aloud sessions at the apprentices' workshop, he now employed a man, a good reader, to recite to him passages from history, politics, and, particularly, the U.S. Constitution, much of which Andrew came to memorize by heart.

In 1827, when he was 18,[4] he married Eliza, aged 16, and their first child, a daughter, Martha, was born in 1828, the year Johnson entered politics, first being elected alderman and then (1830) mayor of Greeneville, at age 22. It was also in 1830 that their first son, Charles, was born, to be followed in 1832 by a second daughter, Mary, and in 1834 by a second son, Robert. The third son, Andrew Jr., was not born until eighteen years later, in 1852.

In 1835, Johnson was elected as member of his state's lower house; then, in 1841, as State Senator, and in 1843 as U.S. Congressman in Washington for ten years, resigning thence to become Governor of Tennessee for four years. From 1857 until 1862, he was U.S. Senator.

After the Civil War had broken out, Tennessee seceded in June, 1861, yet Johnson insisted on retaining his seat in Congress since he did not believe in the dissolution of the Union. He was the only Southern Senator to remain loyal, and this created problems for his family. Eliza had returned from Washington to Greeneville in 1860, and she was there when the Confederate Army moved in to confiscate the home and convert it into a hospital and barracks. She had received no news of her husband for some time, and rumors had circulated that he had been captured and hanged. She had been ordered to leave the home, but, fortunately, under an agreement concluded between the Union and the Confederacy for the exchange of prisoners and refugees, she and the children were placed on a wagon and given safe conduct northwards to Nashville through the Southern lines by Confederate General Nathan Bedford Forrest.

In 1862, Lincoln had appointed Johnson as military governor of Tennessee with headquarters at Nashville, and it was there, with indescribable relief, that the family was reunited in a tearful but joyful homecoming in October, 1862. In the following year, their happiness was marred by the news that their oldest son, Charles, (who had trained as a doctor and pharmacist and had joined the Union Army[5]) had died as the result of injuries sustained in a riding accident. Later, they also received the tragic news that their son-in-law, Daniel Stover, (who had married the Johnsons' second daughter, Mary, in 1852) had died of exposure. Stover, a Colonel in the Union Army, had led a group of guerrilla fighters called the "Bridge Burners," who had harassed the Confederates by disrupting their communication lines in the rear. While she was still resident in the south, in Confederate territory, Eliza, with incredible courage, had maintained contact with the raiders as long as she could, and had assisted them by making available hidden supplies of food.

In 1864, Johnson was selected as Lincoln's running mate, and he was inaugurated as Vice-President on March 4, 1865. His behavior at the inauguration ceremony occasioned him considerable humiliation: recovering from the effects of typhoid fever, he overdosed himself with liquor, and it was obvious to all present that he was intoxicated as he made a pathetic acceptance speech. However, his lapse was forgiven him since it was known that he was not a drinking man. With Lincoln's death, Johnson was again inaugurated, this time as President, on April 15, 1865, upon which occasion he was described as being "as sober as a judge."

When Johnson moved into the White House, the mansion lay in a very neglected state due partly to conditions resulting from the Civil War, since soldiers had trampled over the carpets, slept on sofas, and the furniture had become worn, soiled, and never replaced; and partly from the fact that Mary Todd Lincoln had not been the most efficient of housekeepers. The new President was accompanied by the family of his eldest daughter, Martha, who, in 1855, had married Senator David Trotter Patterson of Tennessee, and it was upon her shoulders that there fell the duties as officiating First Lady, since her mother, Eliza, (who joined them in June), was very much an invalid. Martha received assistance from her widowed sister, Mary Stover.

Martha Patterson was a sheer blessing in fact, not in disguise. Appalled at the condition of the presidential mansion, she spared no physical effort in organizing the complete renovation of both private and public rooms. She was a gracious and candid hostess, and she is recorded as having stated to a reporter: "We are a plain people from the mountains of Tennessee and we do not propose to put on airs because we have the fortune to occupy this place for a little while." She added, "I trust too much will not be expected of us." She had two Jersey cows brought in to pasture on the White House lawn; she milked them herself to provide the family with a daily supply of fresh milk and butter. In 1867, a fire in the conservatory did considerable damage; however, an appropriation of $30,000 by Congress measurably helped to finance the noble and indefatigable exertions of Martha Patterson to restore the mansion to that tasteful elegance and beauty which, as the nation's reception hall, it deserved to be. Eliza, although confined to her private room for most of the time, carefully supervised activities within the White House, while also enjoying the company of her extended family, which included five grandchildren, along with her own youngest son, Andrew Jr. (Frank), who was only 12 when his father became President.

The family problem was the second son, Robert. Trained as a lawyer, he had been appointed private secretary to his father, prior to which he had served as a colonel in the Union Army. He and his regiment had undergone considerable hardships, but his men remained loyal and devoted to him. Unfortunately, the rigors of combat had resulted in his becoming addicted to alcohol, and, after moving into the White House, he became a source of acute embarrassment to the President and his family. Apart from his several drunken escapades, there were widespread rumors in Washington that he was consorting regularly with prostitutes even to the extent of entertaining them at the White House. Among the foregoing "lady friends" was a certain notorious Mrs. Cobb, whose name came to the fore when General Baker, (wartime head of the Secret Service, seeking to embarrass the President because of his dismissal), published in 1867 an account of the trial of Mrs. Cobb. The account purported to establish that Johnson himself was closely implicated in a prostitution ring focused upon the White House. The allegations were considered as having such significance as to lead to the appointment of a congressional investigating committee, which completely exonerated Johnson of the scandalous innuendoes, but left questions unanswered as to the immoral activities of his son, Robert.

One year later, Johnson, having sought to implement Lincoln's policy of reconciliation with the South, incurred the displeasure of his party colleagues, who introduced articles of impeachment against him. On May 16, 1868, the motion, which required a two-thirds majority, was defeated by only one vote, 35 to 19.[6] Understandably, Johnson was not nominated for a second term.

On a political issue relating to the constitutional powers of a President versus those of Congress, Johnson had felt much aggrieved by the action of General Grant, who, having accepted appointment as Secretary of War in 1867, suddenly resigned in 1868 when Congress questioned the legitimacy of his appointment by the President. Johnson's resentment was such that he refused to attend Grant's inauguration on March 4, 1869, and he and his family left for Tennessee the night before.

Johnson had held one last reception prior to departure, and the estimate was that more than five thousand persons attended to bid him farewell. Martha Patterson was hostess, and she was described as being a handsome, though not tall lady, of very pleasing manners and appearance. She wore a black velvet dress trimmed with bands of satin and black lace, and she had a shawl of white lace over her shoulder. One paper reported that "when some of the bare-armed, bare-necked would-be-dowagers were presented to her, the contrast was entirely in favor of the President's daughter.[7]

In 1875, Johnson was elected to the U.S. Senate from Tennessee, the only ex-President ever to have been so honored. He served only one session. Stricken with apoplexy at the home of his daughter, Mary, he died in July, 1875. A few years earlier he had stated, "When I die I desire no better winding sheet than the Stars and Stripes, and no softer pillow than the Constitution of my country." His wishes were observed: his body was wrapped in the 37-star flag of the United States and, underneath his head, was placed his own much-fingered and worn copy of the Constitution.[8]

Eliza survived him only six months: she died on January 15, 1876. Of their children, Robert had died in Greeneville just over one month after Johnson's term of office had expired in 1869. Andrew Jr., who had married Bessie May Rumbough, and who had opted for a career in journalism, becoming editor of the *Greeneville Intelligencer,* died in March, 1879. Mary, remarried to William R. Brown, died in Bluff City, Tennessee, in April, 1883, while Martha, the first born, was last to die in July, 1901, at Greeneville.

Ulysses Simpson Grant

(1869–1877)

During the last months of the Civil War, Lincoln had taken his wife, Mary Todd, on a brief tour of some of the battlefields. On one of their visits, Mary had been accompanied by Julia Grant, wife of the General. It happened that Lincoln, quite innocently, had given Mary cause to feel offended, and, as was her customary wont, she had given way to sudden anger, and vented her spleen upon the nearest unfortunate human being, in this case, Mrs. Grant, saying "I suppose you think your husband should be President, but it's mine who is." Little did she realize that in less than four months, Lincoln would be dead, while in less than four years, Grant would have been elected President, and that, while Julia occupied the White House, she (Mary) would be confined to a mental institution.

Julia was, in fact, a gentle, genial, plump creature, said in her later years to have resembled Queen Victoria. She was the nation's only cross-eyed First Lady.[1] But this affliction had never made the slightest difference to Grant's deep love and affection for her, and, when it was once

185

suggested that she undergo an operation, he adamantly refused to consent to it, and the proposed surgery was never performed.

Her brother, Fred, had been a classmate of Grant's at West Point, and it was he who introduced the latter to the Dent family home at White Haven near Jefferson Barracks, St. Louis. Fred had been named after his father, a plantation owner of strong Southern loyalties, and as such he had bestowed upon himself the honorific title of "Colonel" Frederick Dent. Initially, he had little regard for Grant, but then, when the latter, during the Mexican War of 1845–48, had been instrumental in saving Fred's life, he had grudgingly acknowledged his gratitude, and had even, with much reluctance, consented to the marriage at the Dent home of his daughter, Julia, to Grant on August 22, 1848. At the time of the wedding, Grant was 26, and Julia 22, and for the next twenty years they had no permanent home. They were separated on one occasion for several years, and they drifted from one military camp to another, with no place in which they could really settle down and feel secure. Perhaps, under these trying circumstances, it was little short of incredible that the marriage endured, but endure it did, given its basic essential of permanency: the solid bond of love and loyalty of the two partners.

During the Mexican War, Grant had risen to the rank of brevet captain, but, in the reduced peacetime army he retained only the status of first lieutenant, and was assigned to an army post in Detroit, whence Julia accompanied him, but she returned to the family home in St. Louis for the birth of their first child, Frederick Dent Grant, born on May 30, 1850. Then, there followed two years of disaster: Grant was transferred to the northwest Pacific coast in 1852, and he was unable to see Julia for two years. The California gold rush was in full swing, hundreds died from outbreaks of cholera and other fevers, prices for all basic commodities soared, and Grant's plans for bringing Julia out to the West slowly dissolved into the vaguest of dreams. He tried desperately to raise the travel money by resorting to truck farming, timber logging, and even raising chickens, cattle and hogs to ship to San Francisco, but most of them seemed to have died on the voyage.[2]

Depressed by the constant damp climate, the failure of his financial efforts, and the unending monotony and loneliness of the dreary outpost,[3] Grant apparently took to the bottle in such manner as to be threatened by disciplinary action, to avoid which he chose to resign.

He returned to St. Louis where he received an overwhelming welcome from Julia, but only a cool reception from her father. The latter had given his daughter sixty acres of undeveloped land as a wedding present, and, with no other prospect in sight, Grant found himself with no alternative but to make an effort at farming. He built a log cabin for his wife and two children—soon to be three, with the birth of Ellen (Nellie) on July 4, 1855. With grim humor, reflecting back-breaking tasks, he named his new home Hardscrabble.

After four tedious, unprofitable years of farming, Grant, at 35, appeared exhausted; he sold the property and moved into St. Louis, where he worked in a real estate office with a rental collection agency. But Grant was neither an astute salesman nor a ruthless demander of money, and he again quit his job, now with yet a fourth child to rear, Jesse Root Grant having been born in February, 1858.

He returned to the family home in Galena, Illinois, to become a clerk in his father's leather store, work which he hated intensely; but within little more than a year of his taking up residence, his fortunes changed dramatically.

On April 12, 1861, Fort Sumter was attacked by Confederate forces, an event which precipitated the Civil War. Grant immediately became active by recruiting a volunteer (Galena) company, and within two months, he was appointed Colonel of the 7th District Regiment of Illinois volunteers. In a strategic move in September, his forces occupied Paducah on the Ohio River, which was a key position commanding movements southwards along the Tennessee and Cumberland valleys into the heart of Kentucky and Tennessee. His temporary headquarters were at Cairo, Illinois; here he was joined by Julia and the four children, and, for the duration of the war, Julia made every effort to be as near as possible to her husband despite the many hardships and dangers involved.

When the campaign moved south, Grant took his son, Fred, aged 12, with him, but then wrote to Julia: "We may have some fighting to do, and he is too young to have the exposure of camp life," but Julia protested: "Do not send him home, Alexander was not older when he accompanied Philip. Do keep him with you." Her letter, however, arrived too late, and Fred was already on his way home, covering the last seventeen miles alone on foot. Grant later relented, and Fred was with his father during the Vicksburg campaign, when, at the battle of Port Gibson, he received a slight bullet wound, and contracted a near-fatal fever. Fred was with Tuttle's division in the assault upon Jackson, Mississippi, and in the confusion of battle, he wandered into the town in advance of the Federal forces while it was still occupied by the Confederacy. His capture could have led to acute embarrassment for Grant and the Union cause, but in later years, Fred always joked about his singlehanded capture of Jackson.

Grant's first efforts to subdue Vicksburg in 1862 had failed, partly due to a great raid by the Confederacy upon the Federal supply depot at Holly Springs. Julia had brought young Jesse Root (aged 4) with her to the small town, where she had been billetted at the home of the wife of a Confederate officer. While she was there, other Confederate wives assembled to promote the rebel cause, and to sing Confederate songs, without in any way attempting to be offensive to Julia. It was an experience which she never forgot, not only by reason of the "southern hospitality" which was accorded her, but also because of the fact that a sudden raid upon the town by Van Doorn forced the rapid evacuation of herself and Jesse, who later described it:

> . . . I remember now, as though it were yesterday, the young officer coming to tell us that the enemy was close upon the town, and the confusion of our hurried departure, at night, in a box car. I can see the dim, shadowy interior of the empty box car, with mother sitting quietly upon a chair, while I huddled fearfully upon a hastily improved bed upon the floor. . . .[4]

During the Vicksburg campaign, Grant gave Jesse a pony which he called Rebbie, and they were inseparable until the animal died of old age in 1883.

After his successful assault upon Vicksburg, Grant was promoted first as major-general, then as lieutenant-general, and was given command of the Army of the Potomac, leading to the final victory of the Union forces by the surrender of Robert E. Lee at Appomattox on April 9, 1865. He then went to Washington to see Lincoln. On the morning of April 14, he was at the White House, and the President invited Grant and his wife to accompany him to Ford's Theater that same evening. Grant would probably have accepted, but Julia dissuaded him, being anxious to continue to Burlington, New Jersey, where two of their children had been placed in boarding school since the preceding summer. They had only reached Philadelphia by train when news came of the assassination attempt upon Lincoln. After ensuring Julia's safe conduct to Burlington, Grant immediately returned to Washington to be of assistance as required.

At the end of the Civil War, Grant received many gifts from the grateful people of the North; these included at least fourteen horses, houses in New York, Washington, Philadelphia, as well as in Galena[5] (his home town in Illinois), and a substantial collection of books valued at $5,000 from the city of Boston.[6]

After the strenuous years of military service he sought to relax, but events dictated otherwise. President Andrew Johnson's moderate policies relating to Reconstruction in the South had irritated, incensed, and isolated so many members of his party that they subjected him, in 1868, to the ignominy of impeachment proceedings, from which he was absolved by the margin of only one vote. His party members did not wish to lose the presidential election of the same year: they had in mind previous occasions when the successful nominee had been a military hero, regardless as to what political principles he may have held. Washington, Jackson, Tyler, and Taylor provided ample precedents, so that Grant was inevitably drawn into the maelstrom. His blunder in temporarily accepting appointment as Johnson's Secretary of War to replace Stanton was forgiven him, and, nominated as Republican presidential candidate, he went on in November, 1868, to carry 26 of the 34 states, with a popular majority of more than 300,000.

Grant proved to be one of the most inept of all the Presidents of the United States, since he had little or no conception as to what was involved in the political machinations in Washington. His cabinet appointments were made honestly, by reason of the fact that he was, by nature, an honest man, but he was despicably betrayed by colleagues, friends, and relatives. Incredible as it may seem, despite the ongoing scandals which marred his term of office, Grant remained a symbol of integrity, which not only earned him the only presidential second term of office since that of Jackson in 1832, but also, had he insisted, might have earned him an unprecedented third term of office in 1876. Julia, given the choice, would certainly have so insisted: White House occupation for no less than eight years had given her the opportunity to establish herself at long last in a home which she made her own for the first time in her marriage. She had revelled in every moment of her status as First Lady; she had at all times functioned as a gracious hostess, and she saw no reason, voluntarily, to abandon this delectable position.

Between the close of the Civil War in 1865 and the end of the second presidential term of office in 1877, much had happened to the Grants' four children. Fred, the eldest, had expressed a wish to emulate his father in a military career, and, in 1866, had been enrolled at West Point, whence he graduated in 1871. His progress there was hardly what could be considered as a credit either to himself or to his distinguished father since his final record indicated that, in the graduating class of 41 cadets, he ranked 37th in academic standing and 41st in discipline. Moreover, much to his discredit, he was known to have prominently participated in the constant harassment of James Webster Smith of South Carolina, the first black cadet ever to have enrolled at West Point (1870). As the son of the President he was in a position to have influenced his cadet colleagues to promote a conciliatory role of acceptance, but, instead, he openly proclaimed his opposition, and he once declared to his father: "No damned nigger will ever graduate from West Point." There is no evidence that Grant himself voiced any opposition to his son's views on the matter. The net result was that Smith eventually withdrew from West Point without graduating.[7]

In 1871, General Philip Sherman visited Western and Eastern Europe and Fred, commissioned as lieutenant-colonel, was appointed as one of his aides. At times, the occasion proved to be an acute embarrassment to both, since several European and Middle Eastern dignitaries appeared to have assumed that the American party was a delegation from the U.S. President, who was being represented by his son, with General Sherman serving merely as one of his (Fred's) aides. In Turkey, for example, upon being presented to the Sultan, Fred was compelled to take precedence over his commanding officer, and to receive the greetings and speech of welcome to which he was obliged to respond. Running out of words, Fred, in desperation, pleaded in low tones with U.S. Minister George H. Boker, standing at his side, as to what else he could say. Boker replied "Ask him who made his trousers." With a smile Fred did so, and the Sultan responded amicably so that the tension was broken to the relief of all concerned.[8] The party was lavishly entertained during a brief cruise of the Black Sea, at the termination of which it was General Sherman, and not Fred, who was presented by one of the Sultan's officers with a bill for $600. Sherman paid.

Upon his return to the United States, Fred rejoined his regiment, the Fourth Infantry, and participated in its activities in the Yellowstone region in 1873, and in the Black Hills of Dakota in 1874, along with Custer. In October, 1874, he married Ida M. Honoré, daughter of Henry Hamilton Honoré of Chicago.[9] A reporter of the *Chicago Daily Tribune* described the bride, "the new Mrs. Grant," as being:

> . . . . smaller than the medium size; a lithe, girlish form, with drooping shoulders so much admired, and with a round beau-tifully-modeled bust that leads to the symmetrical proportion of a tiny waist, that small and loving hands might span. . . .[10]

In June, 1876, Ida's first daughter, Julia, named after Fred's mother, was born at the White House.[11]

Much abuse was directed against Grant during his second term of office because of the corrupt practices of many of his cabinet officers and their financial cronies. One particular publication, *The Capitol*, edited by Don Piatt, made it a practice of attacking Grant as well as members of his family. These were usually ignored, but when Piatt proceeded to demean Fred's wife, Ida, because of her alleged "plebian" origins, Fred went directly to the editor's office, gave Piatt a sound thrashing for which in court he was fined $100, which he apparently paid with great satisfaction as being money well spent.

Grant's second son, Ulysses II,[12] born when Grant was away on service duty on the Pacific coast, narrowly escaped being named Telemachus (son of Ulysses and Penelope in Homer's *Odyssey*). Instead, he was always known as "Buck" since he had been born at Grant's family home, Bethel, Ohio (the Buckeye State). In due course he received the best education of any of his siblings; after attending (Philips) Exeter Academy, he went on to Harvard, and Columbia Law School, as well as spending a year in Hanover learning German. When his father's private secretary, Orville Babcock, became enmeshed in the St. Louis Whiskey Ring scandal, Grant replaced him with Buck, who proved conscientious and devoted. The Grant's third child, Nellie, christened Ellen Wrenshall after his grandmother, has sadly been described as one of the unhappiest of all White House children:

> She was handed over from one empty world to another. She was the daughter of two people so dangerously innocent that they did not comprehend their own vulnerability, or that of their children. Julia and Ulysses were the owners of an unusual property; Nellie was sold at a low price—it took only a dashing young man with an English name and beginnings of a splendid life to fetch her. The young girl was barely allowed to have any life at all. . .She was seen as the president's princess daughter, while she was, in fact, a nice teen-age girl.[13]

Nellie was only thirteen when she moved with her parents into the White House. Earlier, she had proved eager to go to a girls' boarding school in Connecticut. Her parents had accompanied her, and had left there, presumably happy and secure, to spend a night at a New York hotel on their way home. But at the hotel, there awaited them three telegrams the text of each of which read "I shall die if I must stay here." Grant immediately despatched one of his aides to the school to escort her back, and she was reunited with her parents the next day.

The White House had been bereft of young girls since the Tylers had evacuated the premises in 1845, so that newspapers lost no opportunity of presenting her to the American public as the Princess Charming of Washington. She had already, many years earlier, in 1864, received wide publicity from a photograph of her being dressed up wearing spectacles as the "Old Lady who lived in a (papier-mache) Shoe" at a sanitary-commission fair in St. Louis. She was again photographed in 1869, wearing a tartan cloak, by the famed Civil War photographer Matthew Brady.

Widely sought by Washington society, she attended a host of functions, reluctantly chaperoned by her brother, Jesse, who sought in vain to be relieved of what he considered to be tediously boring and irksome duties.

Fearing that she was being completely spoilt by these never-ending social invitations, Grant and Julia seized the opportunity of having Nellie accompany Adolph Borie and his wife on a visit to Europe.[14] As Grant expressed it:

> She's so young yet, hardly through playing dolls, but she's been getting offers—we thought it better to get her out of harm's way.[15]

Nellie was as much an attraction in Europe as she had been in Washington. She was received by Queen Victoria, and the round of balls, receptions, and entertainment was without end—until her return voyage home in 1872, when she fell hopelessly in love with Algernon Charles Frederick Sartoris, a vain, attractive, self-seeking Englishman, who traded upon the fact that his mother, Adelaide Kemble, was the sister of the celebrated actress, Fanny Kemble. Grant and Julia themselves were dazzled by the association with English celebrity: they quickly gave their consent to the marriage, which was celebrated on May 21, 1874, in the East Room of the White House. Nellie was but 18, and she left immediately for England with her husband. In 1875, she returned to the United States and, while staying with her parents at Long Branch, she gave birth to their first grandchild, Grant Greville Sartoris, who, however, died one year later.

She paid her parents another visit in 1877 just as they were about to evacuate the White House after Grant's second term of office, and, only two weeks later, on March 17, 1877, at the home of Hamilton Fish, Grant's former Secretary of State, Nellie's second child, Algernon Edward Urban Sartoris, was born. She returned to England soon after.

Jesse Root was the Grant's fourth and last child, and, in many ways, he was the spoilt child of the family. As previously mentioned, he was with his mother at the famous Civil War incident at Holly Springs, Mississippi, when they were almost captured by Confederate troops. Some time later, he recalled being at City Point, Virginia, when his father was visited by Lincoln and his son, Tad. Jesse's horse bolted, and both Grant and Lincoln rode in pursuit until the horse was finally brought under control.

To some degree he was inadvertently responsible for Grant's rejection of Lincoln's invitation to attend the performance of "Our American Cousin" at Ford's Theater on the fatal evening of April 14, 1865. Julia had been anxious to join the older children who were at school in Burlington, New Jersey, but she had also been concerned that Jesse, who was with the family, appeared to have lost his appetite: she thought that he might be developing a sickness—until it came to light that he had, before their meal, already eaten two helpings of hard-boiled eggs and ice cream.

Jesse was later to be the author of a book entitled *In the Days of My Father, General Grant,* and, in it, he recalls that all he remembered of the first inauguration of 1869 was "that a man of very considerable weight stepped upon my foot." Jesse could identify the exact place where it happened: "I am certain that I could put my foot now, fifty-four years after that event, on the same spot, and in the same position."

When his sister, Nellie, returned home after spending only one night at a boarding school, Jesse had been loud-voiced in deriding her, and declared that he would never have done such a thing. But when, a few years later, it was his turn to be sent away to school,[16] he came to regret his boast. No sooner was he at the school then he wrote home to his mother: "I do not believe I am making satisfactory progress here." His mother replied, "It is too soon to determine this. When you have been there longer you will take it better." The resourceful Jesse tried another tactic and complained of ongoing headaches.[17] Julia then agreed to his return, fearing that he might be contracting typhoid, thus terminating his early formal schooling which lasted only two months. Grant commented at the time: "Jesse's so smart. Learns like lightning when he wants to, so doesn't see much sense in going to school every day. Doesn't like being away from us, either."

Jesse enjoyed the company of two playmates at the White House, his cousin, Blain Dent (son of Julia's brother, Louis), and Willoughby Cole, (son of Senator Cornelius Cole of California). Julia furnished a pleasant playroom for their use, and one of their main diversions was to play at being firemen. Jesse had a toy fire-engine and, whenever they heard the clanging of a real engine, they would immediately don their uniforms and drag Jesse's machine to the scene of the conflagration.

They had a number of pets with which to amuse themselves, including Jesse's pony, "Rebbie," his favorite dog, "Faithful" (a fine New-foundland specimen), a parrot, and some gamecocks. Jesse would like to have had some pigeons, but these were taboo: Lincoln had allowed his son, Tad, to own pigeons, and their descendants were a major nuisance among the public buildings of Washington.

In his biography, Jesse later recalled an amusing incident relating to his newfound hobby of stamp collecting. He sent $5.00 to a Boston dealer but received no reply. He informed his father who suggested that Jesse present his case at a formal meeting of the presidential cabinet. Here, both the Secretary of State and the Secretary of War vied for the "honor" of demanding satisfaction from the stamp dealer. In the end, the cabinet voted that Kelley, the Capitol policeman, should be delegated the responsibility of writing, on executive mansion notepaper, to Boston. Kelley wrote in no uncertain terms:

> I am the Capitol Policeman. I can arrest anybody, anywhere, at any time, for anything. I want you to send those stamps to Jesse Grant right at once.
>
>   Signed, Kelley,
>   Capitol Policeman

The stamps were delivered.[18]

Jesse and his friends formed a secret society known as the K.F.R., its only secret, apparently, being the meaning of its name. Grant speculated that it was the Kick, Fight, and Run Society, but there was never confirmation nor denial. It began on Christmas Day, 1871, with 6 members and Jesse as its first President. Its meeting place was the gardener's toolhouse on the White House grounds. A formal constitution was drawn up, including the statement that:

> The objects of this society were, are, and ever shall be, to improve its members individually and collectively in mental and moral culture and to encourage them in their attempts towards literary and mental success.

The members set up a circulating library, a debating club, and a magazine entitled "The K.F.R. Journal," whose first editorial (December, 1872) declared that "The want of some vent for our extraordinary literary genius has long been felt and hence the origin of this design." The magazine contained boyish stories, made occasional reference to national affairs, and included a White House advertisement announcing President Grant's office hours.

Elections were held to fill membership vacancies since families came to and left Washington, and a system of honorary membership was begun in 1872 and continued until 1883, when the last active member was elected; thereafter all became honoraries. When President Grant finally left the White House in March, 1877, the society took up new quarters on the third floor of 1427 F Street, and members maintained contact with each other for decades.[19]

At age 16, Jesse left the White House and enrolled in the engineering school at Cornell. His progress there was described as "uneventful," but he did have, as his roommate, his bosom friend, Willoughby Cole.

Upon vacating the White House in 1877, Grant was at a loose end as to what to do with his time, and he promptly decided to travel abroad. Within three months, he, Julia and Jesse were on board the *Indiana* en route from Philadelphia to Liverpool, England. For the ex-President and his wife, there followed over two years of continuous receptions, fetes, and feasting, of which both never seemed to tire. In England, they received a great welcome, and were so constantly in demand that they were able to spend only one week with Nellie at her home on the south coast.[20]

The Grants were the invited guests of Queen Victoria at Windsor Castle. They were accompanied by Adam Badeau, the American consul-general in London, who had been a member of the General's staff during the Civil War. At Windsor, the party was informed that only Grant and Julia were being invited to dine with the Queen, and that Jesse and Badeau were to have meals with the Queen's household, all of whom, they were informed, were members of the nobility. Jesse took umbrage, and immediately declared his intention of returning to London. According to reports, the Queen's first reaction was the statement, "Well, let him go," but she later relented and Jesse was seated at dinner between his mother and Lady Derby to avoid further trouble. Victoria later commented that Jesse was simply "a very ill-mannered young Yankee," but that Julia was "civil and complimentary, in her funny American way."

After six months, Jesse, tired of endless traveling, decided to go home to enter Columbia Law School. He was replaced by Fred for the remainer of the Grants' tour eastwards around the world. Having visited Egypt,[21] they passed through the Red Sea[22] en route to India.[23] They went on to China and Japan, and finally docked at San Francisco on September 20, 1879. Here they were welcomed ashore by Jesse and Buck, who were immediately taken aside by Julia and warned: "If your father asks if there is anything peculiar about his articulation, pretend not to notice it." She went on to explain that Grant's Japanese servant had accidentally thrown overboard his plate with two front teeth attached, and, that, ever since, he frequently whistled in his speech.

Despite his long absence aboard, Grant had remained a favorite contender for his party's presidential nomination in 1880, and his supporters would have preferred a six months (at least) delay in his return so as to maintain the exuberance of his welcome home. At the 1880 Republican Convention, Grant consistently received a majority of the delegate votes, yet not sufficient for an absolute majority.[24] The result was that James Garfield was eventually nominated on the 36th ballot as a compromise candidate.

Grant was not unduly disappointed, but Julia was, since the eight year stability of "home life" at the White House had appealed to her immensely;[25] and now, again, after more than two years of world-wandering, she had sought to renew social life as First Lady, but it was not to be. The Grants took up residence at Long Branch, New Jersey.

It was now that Grant became involved in a disastrous financial enterprise. His investments had been managed by Buck who had, in November, 1880, married Fannie Josephine Chaffee, daughter of a successful land and mining speculator, who, at the time of the marriage, was president of the First National Bank of Denver. In 1881, Buck, with the loan of $100,000 obtained from his father-in-law, had entered into partnership with Ferdinand Ward, considered by many to be a financial wizard, and had set up the new Wall Street brokerage firm of Grant and Ward. By 1883, Buck was a near-millionaire, and he offered his father the opportunity to invest in his company. Grant obliged, and placed $100,000 of his savings for investment. But, by May, 1884, Ward's true character as a rash speculator was exposed, and the Grant family suffered ruin. Grant received generous aid from Vanderbilt, who gave him a promissory note for $150,000 to cover emergencies.

In a desperate effort to regain his financial independence, Grant responded to a suggestion that he should write his memoirs. Greatly encouraged by Mark Twain (who was major partner in the publishing firm of C. L. Webster Company of Hartford), he eventually completed his monumental *Memoirs,* despite great suffering and agony from cancer of the mouth.[26] Only two weeks before his death on July 23, 1885, he had implored Julia:

> Look after our dear children and direct them in the paths of rectitude. It would distress me far more to think that one of them could depart from an honorable, upright and virtuous life than it would to know that they were prostrated on a bed of sickness from which they were never to arise again. They have never given us any cause for alarm on their account, and I earnestly pray they never will. . . .

Julia was to receive a first check of $200,000 for royalties from her husband's book; in due course, she was to receive yet another identical sum of money, so that she was ensured of financial security in her widowhood.

The subsequent story of the lives of his four children was that of many vicissitudes of fortune, but not one brought dishonor to their father's name, although certain of their activities did not pass without criticism. The *New York World*, for example, commented that:

> . . . .the Grant sons, but for the accident of their father's presidency might have been respectable dry-goods clerks in Galena. They have no qualifications as successful speculators. How much better for his sons if they had remained clerks or shopkeepers in a quiet Western town.[27]

Fred, who had given his father considerable assistance in the detailed research and laborious copying of the manuscript of the *Memoirs,* had, after his return from the world trip, resigned from the army to enter business.[28] By 1886, he had so prospered that he became president of the American Wood Working Company, while a year later, the Republican party gave serious consideration to Fred's nomination as presidential candidate, with Robert Todd Lincoln as his running mate for the 1888 election, but the initial enthusiasm for their candidacy waned and the project was dropped.

In 1889, President Harrison appointed him as envoy extraordinary and minister plenipotentiary to the Austro-Hungarian monarchy. He served in that capacity in Vienna until 1893, and he was commended for his efforts to further the exchange of trade products between his own country and the central European empire.

He served as one of the commissioners of police of New York City from 1895 to 1897, and, one year later, at the outbreak of the Spanish-American War, he rejoined the army as colonel of the 14th New York Infantry. In 1899, he commanded a brigade against guerrillas in the Philippines, and was later responsible for establishing civil government in certain of the occupied islands.

Upon his return to the United States he was promoted to the rank of major-general, and assumed territorial commands in Texas, the Midwest, and the Northeast. He died in New York in April, 1912, and was buried at West Point.

Grant's second son, Buck, suffered considerable loss from the collapse of his brokerage firm, but, with the aid of the Chaffee money, he recovered and resorted to the life of a country gentleman at leisure in New York State. He and his wife, Fannie, had five children, and when her health began to deterioriate, they decided to move to San Diego. There Buck practiced law and became interested in the hotel business, investing more than a million dollars in the U.S. Grant Hotel which, at one time, was managed by his brother, Jesse.

Buck maintained an active interest in politics, and was twice a delegate to the Republican National Conventions. He had, at one time, sought nomination to the U.S. Senate, but the only public office he ever held was as assistant to the U.S. district attorney.

In 1909, his wife, Fannie, died, and four years later, Buck, now 60, secretly married America Workman Wills, a widow aged 36.[29] He completely alienated his children when, upon making public the fact of the marriage, he also announced that his new bride would inherit two-thirds of his estate, valued at three million dollars. Years passed before any reconciliation was effected. Buck died in 1929.

At the time of her parents' visit to Europe in 1877–78, Nellie was the mother of two children. In 1879, she gave birth to her third child, Vivian May, and, in 1880, to her fourth and last child, Rosemary Alice. But her husband's extramarital philanderings caused her to become increasingly disconsolate and depressed since she was completely out of touch with her husband's family and their social activities. She came to America for a brief visit to be with her father at the time of his death in 1885.

In England she had been visited by Henry James, who was much impressed by the brilliant conversation of Nellie's mother-in-law, Adelaide Sartoris. But he wrote:

> . . . Poor little Nellie Grant sits speechless on the sofa, understanding neither head nor tail of such high discourse and exciting one's compassion for her incongruous lot in life. She is as sweet and amiable (and almost as pretty) as she is uncultivated—which is saying an immense deal. Mrs. Sartoris . . . thinks very highly indeed of her natural aptitudes of every kind, and cannot sufficiently deplore the barbarous conduct of her mother leaving such excellent soil so perfectly untilled.[30]

In due course, disillusioned with her life in England, Nellie returned permanently with her children to the United States and, in 1895, she moved in to live with her mother, now in Washington. Nellie and her youngest child, Rosemary, were with Julia when the latter died in December, 1902.[31]

In 1912, Nellie married Frank Hatch Jones of Chicago, and she spent the last years of her life before her death in 1922 as an invalid in her home on Lake Shore Drive.

Jesse was the last born and was the last surviving child of Grant and Julia. He died in June, 1934, and, in his obituary notice, he was described in the *New York Times* as a "mining engineer and a wanderer." Upon his return from Europe at the time of Grant's world tour, Jesse had entered Columbia Law School but had failed to qualify. From that time onwards he was literally a "wanderer" seeking rewarding occupations and investments such as those achieved by his two brothers, but their success appeared to elude him.

In 1884, Governor Leland Stanford of California happened to have dined with the Sultan of Turkey, who, fully aware of Stanford's railroad interests, offered him a franchise of constructing a line from Constantinople to the Persian Gulf. Stanford, at first, expressed much interest in the project and set up his son as president of a newly formed company. But then his son died, and Stanford offered the franchise to Jesse, who eagerly set about accumulating capital, and even persuaded Mark Twain to invest: the subsequent history of the ill-fated venture might well have provided Twain with, at least, the title of his (unrelated) work, "Innocents Abroad."[32]

In 1897, Jesse was involved in negotiations to set up a gambling institution in Tijuana, Mexico, just across the U.S. border of California, and, as mentioned earlier, he, at one time, managed the U.S. Grant Hotel in San Diego.

Always the maverick, and Queen Victoria's spoilt "young Yankee," Jesse asserted his political independence by rejecting the Republican tenets of his family, and, in 1908, he announced his intention of seeking nomination as Democratic candidate in the presidential election of that year. He was, however, defeated by Williams Jennings Bryan, who, in turn, lost to the Republican, William Howard Taft. In view of his father's popularity in China at the time of his visit there in 1879, Jesse was considered by President Wilson as an eligible U.S. Minister to China, but the proposal was not pursued.

Jesse had married Elizabeth Chapman in 1880, by whom he had two children, but they separated in 1902, when it was revealed that it was Jesse's mother who had paid the wedding expenses and had, moreover, bestowed her son with a monthly allowance of $250. In 1914, Jesse petitioned for divorce, but it was contested; however, four years later, Elizabeth relented, and the divorce became final, upon which Jesse married Lillian Burns Wilkins, twenty years his junior. She died of cancer in 1924, and Jesse died in 1934.

Rutherford Birchard Hayes

(1877–1881)

Rutherford Hayes married his fiancee, Lucy Ware Webb, in December, 1852. Their first five children were male, a fact which, on one occasion, prompted Hayes' humorous remark that he and Lucy were in "the boy business." The sixth child was Fannie, their only daughter, and she was followed by yet two more boys. Three of the boys died in infancy, so that when Hayes succeeded to the office of President,[1] he was accompanied by his wife, their daughter, and four sons.

Hayes was the last of five children born to his parents, but three of his siblings had died either before or soon after his birth, while his father had died three months before Hayes was born in October, 1822. However, a wealthy bachelor uncle, Sardis Birchard, appeared to have filled the role as surrogate father, and he was generous in financial aid so that Hayes received a good education and graduated from Harvard Law School.

Lucy, likewise, lost her father, Dr. James Webb, a physician: she was only two when he had departed home in Chillicothe (then capital of Ohio) for Lexington, Kentucky, on the philanthropic mission of arranging for slaves whom he had set free to be sent to Liberia. He contracted cholera on the journey, and Lucy and her two brothers were left fatherless. But Lucy's mother, Maria Cook Webb, was determined that her three children should be well educated, and she moved her family to Delaware, Ohio, where, in due course, Lucy's two brothers were enrolled at Ohio Wesleyan University and where she, at first, attended a private school (where she was the only girl), and then entered the Wesleyan Female College in Cincinnati, whence she graduated at age 19 in 1852.[2]

Hayes was a promising young lawyer when he met and married Lucy. Their first child and son, born in November, 1853, was first christened "Birchard" only, and was called by members of his family, "Birch," or 'Birchie," or (less often) "Birtie." Later, when he became aware that his benevolent uncle's name was Sardis, Birch added that name to his own, but, since it proved unpopular, he decided to drop it. His father then suggested that he select one of the family ancestral names, which included those of Austin, Cook, Russell, and Scott. Birch chose the first (the maiden name of one of his great grandmothers), and henceforth was recognized as Birchard Austin Hayes.

As the firstborn son, Birch was the apple of his father's eye, and in his *Diary* Hayes wrote on November 6, 1853, (two days after Birch was born):

> For the "lad" my feeling has yet to grow a great deal. I prize him and rejoice to have him and when I take him in my arms begin to feel a father's love and interest, hope and pride, and enough to know what the feeling *will* be if not what it *is*. . . .[3]

Some time later, Hayes described him a being "handsome, plump, fat, and saucy." He recorded that Birch's first spoken word was "up," while the second was "charcoal" (which he caught from the street crier). When Birch was little more than two, Hayes noted of him: "He talks a good deal. Would not try to say "Washington" without a good deal of coaxing, but now makes a queer stagger at it."

Hayes' second son, born in March, 1856, also appeared to have had some name changes. He was christened James Webb Hayes, but then it was decided to drop "James" and add "Cook" as a middle name:[4] thus he was always identified as Webb C. Hayes. His father described him as being "healthy, stout, short, and noisy."

The third son, born in June, 1858, was named Rutherford Platt, or "Ruddy" for short, and so it was that, when the Civil War broke out, Hayes had a family of a wife and three sons, whom he had to leave behind

when he enlisted in the Union Army with the rank of major in the Ohio
23rd Volunteers. Eventually promoted as brigadier-general, he saw appreciable action, and was wounded no less than five times.

Two more sons born to Lucy during the period of the Civil War:
Joseph Thompson, who saw light of day in December, 1861, but who
lived only eighteen months; and George Cook, born in September, 1864,
who likewise lived less than two years. Of Joseph, known as Little Jody,
Hayes wrote:

> His brain was excessively developed and it is probable that his early
> death has prevented greater suffering. He was the most excitable
> nervous child I ever saw. . . .[5]

Whenever possible, Hayes arranged for Lucy and the boys to visit his
army camp, and he encouraged his sons to participate in outdoor activities such as riding, rowing, and fishing. He once commented:

> I am in no hurry about having my boys learn to write. I would
> much prefer that they would lay up a stock of health by knocking
> about the country than to hear that they were the best scholars of
> their age in Ohio.[6]

While still in the army, Hayes was nominated for Congress. He
continued to serve after his election victory, and did not take his seat until
the war had ended. In 1867, he was elected Governor of Ohio (serving
two terms of office), and it was in this year that his sixth child, but first
and only daughter, Fanny, was born. In his final year as Governor, Lucy
gave birth to Scott Russell (1871), and when Hayes was defeated in his
bid for re-election to Congress in 1872, he moved his family to "Spiegel
Grove," a beautiful estate at Fremont, Ohio, which his uncle, Sardis
Birchard, had built and developed. It was here, in August, 1873, that
Manning, his eighth and last child, was born. Hayes described him
briefly in his *Diary:* "Weight nine pounds. Eyes called black, fat and
healthy." In the following January he wrote: "He is growing well, and is a
great favorite. No better baby, no merrier; and few prettier are to be
found." In August, 1874, there were two poignant (and somewhat con-
tradictory) entires in the *Diary:*

> *August 13* Little Manning is a fine dark-eyed little fellow. Lively and
> promising. A year old on the first. No stick he.

> *August 28* (Recording the death of his son soon after midnight,
> Hayes added): He has not seemed altogether healthy at any time.

He was a lively, beautiful child. His eyes were very dark, large, mild and sweet.

Manning was buried on the next day and the Nineteenth Psalm was read at the funeral service.

In 1875, Hayes won a third-term re-election as Governor of Ohio, and one year later he was eventually declared victor of the 1876 presidential election, announcing at the same time that he intended to serve but one term as chief executive, a promise which he duly observed.

All of Hayes' four surviving sons were to graduate from Cornell University. Birch, the eldest, had been accepted in September, 1870. His weak background in Greek had proved inadequate for admission into the Classical course, and so he had pursued French and German as part of the language requirements; his deficiencies in Latin were made up during his first year of attendance. He successfully graduated in 1874, and at this time Hayes observed in his *Diary:*

> He is an accurate, thorough student, not fond of books as I was, with an unusual fondness for statistics, especially for the preparation of tabular information.[7]

Birch proceeded to Harvard Law School, and in due course entered into law practice at Toledo, Ohio.

Hayes was very uncertain about Webb's career and remained in some doubt as to whether he would be accepted by Cornell, but he was, to his father's great relief. On September 28, 1872, Hayes wrote:

> I was glad to get your first letter from Cornell today. . . . It was a genuine freshman's letter. A page or two of rushes and the like and few lines about studies. But that is what I want. Letters that show me just what you are thinking of and what you enjoy.

But, just one month later, Hayes penned an admonitory epistle to his son:

> I need not urge you to give solid and honest work to your studies. Whatever the line of business you pursue in life, training that hard study will give you will be of service to you. Try to understand fully whatever you go over. Thoroughness is the vital thing. More important than study, however, is honesty, truthfulness, and sincerity. Resolve to abide by these under all circumstances and keep the resolution. . . .[8]

In 1874, he was to note that: "Webb is not scholarly. He will not graduate. A special course is the most he will attempt."[9] Hayes's conclusions were only partly realized: Webb was not scholarly, in an academic sense, but he did graduate and entered the world of business. As his father later remarked: "He is honest, cheerful, very sensible, and full of social and friendly qualities with good habits and principles . . . ," all of which virtues were presumably to assist him immeasurably in his destined career.[10]

Hayes' third son, Rutherford Platt, known to all the family as Ruddy, did not enjoy the best of health. His father wrote of him: "Ruddy is our invalid. Tall and slender at sixteen, he is unfit for hard work or hard study. A bright, handsome, jovial boy—we now are talking of trying a manual-labor agricultural college."[11]

Six months later, Hayes recorded the fact that:

> Rud and I go to Lansing to deposit him in the freshman class of the Michigan Agricultural College. His weak eyes and delicate health have prevented him from entering . . . Yale or Harvard. He is scholarly enough, but health and eyes interfere.[12]

Yet, Ruddy did do well at the college, but left to enter Cornell, like his brothers, whence he graduated in 1880, probably greatly to the surprise and delight of his disbelieving father. Ruddy did yet one further year of postgraduate study at the Polytechnic Institute in Boston.

When Hayes entered the White House in March, 1877, his two youngest surviving children, Fanny and Scott Russell, were only 10 and 6 years old, respectively. In 1872, Fanny had very narrowly escaped serious injury when, in an accident with her horse, she was dragged for some distance on the ground, with one foot in the stirrup. She was unconscious for several hours but, in time, made a miraculous recovery to the immense relief of all her family. Hayes wrote in 1874 that "she has made small progress as a scholar. She is healthy, very bright and happy, well-looking and a treasure." In the same year, his father described Scott as:

> . . . our handsomest. Interesting, too honest to joke, or to comprehend a joke readily.[13] He talks with some hesitation when excited, and has many pretty ways. He says many queer things. He and Fanny naturally run together. . . .

As First Lady, Lucy was very diligent as hostess,[14] but she also took good care to see to the education of her two youngest children, as well as to their social well-being, and she planned many parties[15] for young people in the executive mansion. When Congress banned the traditional Easter Monday egg-rolling festivities[16] on the grounds of the Capitol Building, Lucy Hayes promptly invited the children of Washington to participate in identical festivities transferred by her directive to the White House lawn where they have been held ever since.

On December 30, 1877, the Hayes celebrated their silver wedding anniversary, and, at the same time, they took the opportunity of having Fanny and Scott Russell baptized into the Methodist Church.

Hayes served only one term of office, and, after graduating from Cornell, his son, Webb, worked in the White House as his father's unofficial private secretary.[17]

In 1881, Hayes retired to Spiegel Grove, and, not long afterwards, the home nest, while not entirely vacated, became relatively empty when Fanny was dispatched to Cleveland in 1882 to attend the school of Miss Mittleberger, and one year later, Scott was sent to Green Spring to attend the academy of the Reverend R. B. Moore, although since it was not too far away, he returned home for weekends.

Scott's education was uneventful and Hayes records that, upon his departure for Cornell in September, 1888, "my talk to him was, in substance":

> Be a good scholar if you can, but in any event be a gentlemen in the best sense of the word—truthful, honorable, polite, and kind, with the Golden rule as your guide. Do nothing that would give pain to your mother if she knew it.[18]

In 1890, Scott left Cornell to enter the world of business, a move which later prompted a letter from his father:

> I want you to think with a purpose on the question of how to use your spare time, especially your evenings. At all times have on hand some solid reading. Either history, biography, or natural science connected with *your present business*. Do not fail to learn all you can on your interesting department of natural science. Watch all workmen, learn all facts, be practical as well as a man of theories. . . .[19]

Hayes appeared to have been more expansive in his correspondence with Fanny than with any of his other children, possibly because she was his only daughter. No sooner had she been sent to school in Cleveland than Hayes was in communication with the principal on the matter of homework: He wrote to Miss Mittleberger:

> Too much is required of young girls at all of the schools with which I am acquainted. It is a great evil. Health and life are sacrificed cruelly. One half the study's work should be dispensed with. I shall never find fault with a school because too little is attempted. A few studies and thorough work is the true aim.[20]

He always welcomed letters from Fanny, and in his replies he sometimes took advantage of the opportunity to assist and remind her of some
of the principles and rules of letter writing:

> Your letter is well written. You do not always use periods at the end
> of a sentence and you sometimes begin a sentence without a capital
> letter. . . . But your letter is so good and has so few faults that on
> the whole I must compliment you on its excellence.[21]

Towards the end of her first year in school Fanny seemed to have
become involved in a school episode, details of which are not available
but, whatever happened, gave concern to her father and prompted him to
write as follows:

> I am made a little weary—not seriously, however—by the myste-
> rious intimation of your last letter to your mother. You must curb
> your rebellious spirit. You inherit, I know, enterprise and daring
> from a long line of Scotch borderers—the Scotts, the Rutherfords,
> and the Hayeses. There are, I must tell you, a basketful of reasons
> why a demure and subdued line of conduct is most becoming in
> you. Your immediate ancestors, maternal especially, have a place in
> the good opinion of good people not to be imperilled by their
> children's wild oats without misgiving and perhaps tears. Think of
> it, darling, and make us all happy by your considerate and discreet
> conduct. . . .[22]

Since there was no later reference to the episode the problem was,
presumably, amicably resolved.

Hayes remained ever solicitous concerning Fanny's academic career.
During her second year at Cleveland he commented on one of her school
reports:

> I am glad to hear you are practicing bookkeeping. To keep accurate
> accounts promotes economy and you know what economy is the
> road to—if not to heaven, at least to peace of mind. . . . The
> scholarship of the report was altogether satisfactory. "Deportment
> 83"—that is fair. But I want it to go up. Can't you make it *one
> hundred!* Try it.[23]

In his (extant) letters to Fanny, her father remained in a didactic mood,
as, when he suggested: "When you hear a good lecture I would like to
have you give me a brief abstract of it. To do this fastens it in your
memory and enables you to make it part of your mental equipment."[24]

Again, in answer to one of her letters, he had this to state:

> . . . You write a charming little letter. Try to enlarge a little. Be

discursive, give wings to your imagination. Indulge in a few long sentences. Tell us in a poetical way, or a humorous way, or an impressive way, some of the facts—some of the secrets of your environment. . . .[25]

In 1885, Fanny began her first of two years' study at a young ladies college at Farmington, New York, where, once more, the question of her curriculum arose, prompting Hayes to comment:

As to your studies, I agree with you. There are too many of them. The only question is which to drop. My decided preference is that you drop either Grecian history, physics, or astronomy. You will have another year at Farmington, I hope. I don't know what "harmony" means. You may drop *that* if you prefer. Music, you know, is the *pet* of both your mother and father. But if you can't manage it, why, do as you suggest. . . .[26]

As to the possible dilemma of what Fanny should be doing upon completion of her college career, Hayes was ready with a solution:

. . . We want you here with us. I am already planning the *oceans of reading* together. What do you think of that? The old father for a teacher? I have some fears that it will be dull for you in the old home. I recall as the doleful period of my life the first year out of college. The loss of companionship—the lonely, dull days with no bright young fellows around me. But I survived, and I hope you will. The secret of happy life is *congenial occupation*. That we can contrive for ourselves, after a few months of longing.[27]

During the fall of 1887, Fanny accompanied a friend of the family, General Hastings and his wife, to Bermuda, where they were to spend a prolonged vacation lasting more than six months. While she was there, Hayes sent his daughter some religious journals, including the *Advocate* and *Zion's Herald* "to keep up your Methodism," as he put it. However, in one of the accompanying notes he added: "On reflection, I fear the *Zion Herald* will give too much sectarian news for one week, and I therefore send you the *Cincinnati Gazette* to furnish a dish of politics and agriculture. . . ."[28]

Fanny returned home safely in May, 1888,[29] but, just one year later, the family suffered a great tragedy when Lucy died suddenly at the age of 57. Less than four years later, after a visit to her grave, Hayes wrote in his diary: "My feeling was one of longing to be quietly resting in a grave by her side." His wish was granted in just nine days.[30]

Fanny was the longest-lived of the entire family, and was 82 when she died in 1950. In 1897, she married Harry Eaton Smith of Fremont, Ohio. Their son, Dalton, served in World War I, and was wounded in the Argonne Forest just one month before the Armistice. He recovered, but unlike all his uncles he went on to graduate at Princeton, not Cornell.

Birchard, the eldest son, and a respected lawyer in Toledo, married Mary Sherman, (a distant relative of the General), a sister of one of Birch's college mates at Cornell. In 1887, Mary gave birth to the Hayes' first grandson and first grandchild, whom they named Sherman. Other sons followed, and no fewer than four saw service in World War I. During the latter conflict, Scott Russell, the youngest born of the Hayes' family, was sent on a mission to Russia in 1915, and later served as a submarine officer in the U.S. Navy. He died of a brain tumor in 1923, and, at the time of his decease, he was vice-president of the New York Airbrake Company, prior to which he had been connected with the Railroad Springs Company of New York.

Webb, who had entered the hardware business in Cleveland, suffered considerable financial setback when his factory, of which he was secretary and treasurer, was burned down during the winter of 1886. A year later, he was employed in the National Carbon Company, also in Cleveland, and was able slowly to retrieve some of his losses.[31]

After the death of Hayes, his children agreed to bequeath Spiegel Grove to the Ohio Archaeological and Historical society, on condition that the latter raise the sum of $25,000, the income from which was to be devoted to the care and preservation of the ex-President's home. The society failed to raise the money, so that in 1899 the property passed to Webb, who was now a colonel in the U.S. Army during the war against Spain.[32] He saw service in Cuba, Puerto Rico, and the Philippines, where he was awarded the Congressional Medal of Honor for distinguished gallantry in action. In 1900, he accompanied the U.S. Relief Expedition to China during the Boxer Rebellion, while four years later, at the time of the Russo-Japanese conflict, he functioned as a U.S. military observer both with the Japanese Army in Korea as well with the Russian Army in Manchuria.

In 1910, Webb made the decision to bequeath Spiegel Grove to the State of Ohio with the understanding first that the home itself be preserved and maintained as a typical American residence of the late nineteenth century, and second, that the state finance a building to house the many books, papers, and memorabilia of the ex-President. The state fulfilled its obligation, and, in 1916, the dedication ceremony took place of the completed Hayes Memorial Library and Museum erected in the Spiegel Grove State Park.

In 1912, Webb had married Mary Otis Miller, and she accompanied him to Europe at the outbreak of World War I. Before the United States entered the war, Webb served as a dispatch bearer between the American ambassadors in Paris, London, Berlin, and Brussels, and while he was away on duty, Mary occupied herself as a Red Cross worker, first in Paris, and, later in Rome. During the war, Webb served as Regional Commissioner with the American Expeditionary Force in France and North Africa, and, in 1918, he was decorated by General Lyautey, the French Resident General in Morocco.[33] He and his wife returned home together after the Armistice, along with Fanny's wounded son, Sergeant Dalton Hayes Smith. Webb, now 62, then retired to Fremont, Ohio, where he died in 1934.

After his unexpected success at college, Rutherford (Ruddy), had returned to Fremont, and entered banking, a career which he pursued until his retirement. He developed a marked interest in the Birchard Library, founded by Sardis Birchard, his bachelor great-uncle, and set out to make its facilities available for children as well as for adults. He pioneered one of the first children's reading rooms in the United States, and had it furnished with appropriate-sized small desks and chairs, along with a substantial collection of suitable books. In addition, seeking to make full use of the library's ample resources, Rutherford arranged to have boxes of books dispatched to local townships, whose citizens could thereby take advantage of what came to be, in effect, a traveling library.

He was one of the founder members (1895) of the Ohio Library Association, and was instrumental in the establishment of the State Library Commission, on which he himself served for six years. He was later secretary of the American Library Association, as well as its vice-president and acting president.

In 1894, he married Lucy Platt, granddaughter of Judge Joseph R. Swan, a famous lawyer of the period. He moved his family to Asheville, North Carolina, where he associated himself with real estate projects and progressive farming techniques, and was president of the Western North Carolina Fair for several years. In 1920 he moved again, this time to Clearwater, Florida, and maintained his varied interests in cultural and practical affairs until his death in 1927 at the age of 70.

James Abram Garfield

(1881)

James Garfield served only four months in office before he was shot on July 2, 1881, by Charles Guiteau, a discontented office seeker. The President died of his wounds on September 19. He was mourned by his wife, Lucretia, ("Crete") and five of his eight children. Of the three deceased children, Eliza, his first born and eldest daughter, had survived only three years, (1860–63); his fifth child had been stillborn (1868); while Edward, the last son, had died in 1876, at the age of two.

Garfield had been named after his maternal grandfather, James Ballou, gifted mathematician and astronomer-astrologer, who cast horoscopes and was accredited by some with second sight. He had died suddenly in 1808, whereupon his wife, Mehitabel, moved first from New Hampshire to Worcester, New York, and thence to Ohio. It was there that Eliza, one of her daughters, married Abram Garfield in 1820. They were blessed with five children of whom James, born in 1831, was the last; he was but one year old when his father died.

The Garfields were a sturdy, pioneer family living in a log cabin in which James was born. His mother, Eliza, was a woman of indomitable spirit and of an independent disposition, who now, as a widow, was determined to be beholden to none. She had four children to rear, (one having died in 1829 at age three), and, after having been obliged to sell part of her landholding, she steadfastly set her mind against having to part with any more, and set to work as a seamstress.

Having survived ten years of widowhood, Eliza, in 1842, decided to remarry, but much confusion prevails as to precise details of events which occurred in the immediate subsequent years. All that can be confirmed is that, in 1848, her second husband, Alfred Belding, petitioned for divorce, claiming that Eliza had left him after one year of marriage, and had ignored all his appeals to be reunited. The divorce was granted in 1850, but thereafter, Eliza was addressed by all as the Widow Garfield.

The whole episode must have been extremely disquieting to James. He had attempted to "run away to sea," but, after six weeks on a canal boat, he lost his love for "life on the ocean wave" and returned home.[1] His mother desired that he should receive a good education and sent him away to Geauga Seminary, a college sponsored by the Free Will Baptists. Here, one of his classmates was Lucretia Randolph, and it was she whom he married in 1858. Meanwhile, Garfield had attended Williams College (as well as the Western Reserve Eclectic Institute), had developed considerable self-confidence, as well as such public recognition as a good teacher and competent debater, that, in 1859, he was elected as a member of the Ohio Legislature.

Lucretia's first child was born in 1860, and was named Eliza Arabella, in honor of the two grandmothers,[2] but was always called "Trot" by Garfield, with vague allusion to Betsy Trotwood in Dicken's novel *David Copperfield*. When the Civil War broke out, Garfield was appointed colonel of the 42nd Ohio Volunteer Regiment, so Lucretia and Trot went home to live with her parents.

The second child, a boy, Harry Augustus, was born in October, 1863, but Garfield and Lucretia's joy was shortlived on account of the death, through diphtheria, of their beloved Trot less than two months later.

In 1862, Garfield had been elected to the U.S. House of Representatives, but did not take his seat until December, 1863. He was now away in Washington, and, in the summer of 1862, Lucretia poignantly reminded him that, for the past four years and nine months, they had only lived together for 20 weeks. Garfield, conscience-stricken at his thoughtlessness and indifference to Lucretia's welfare, now determined that they would be separated no more, so thereafter, he rented rooms, or houses, in Washington during the winter-month sessions, so that the family could be together.

Their first two children, Eliza and Harry, had been born in Hiram, Ohio, as was their third, James Rudolph, in 1865. The fourth, Mary (Mollie), was the first to be born in Washington, and (following the stillborn death of their fifth), Irvin McDowell (1870), and Edward (1874),[3] were both born in Hiram, Ohio, while Abram (1872, the eighth), saw light of day in Washington.

To accommodate his growing family, as well as to offset the high cost of rental, Garfield resolved in 1869 to build a three-story house in Washington and, upon its completion, it became the family home in the capital until 1880. Garfield's mother, Eliza, was with the family for much of the time both for summers in Ohio, and for winters in Washington, so Lucretia had the problem of adjusting her ways to her mother-in-law, which she did quite well, although Mollie, who later took to writing a diary,[4] wrote of her grandmother: "My! I don't wonder she nearly worried the life out of Papa and Mamma—such a woman as she is, I just can't stand."

The home in Washington was, according to all reports, a very lively one. One visitor, after dining there, wrote to his wife that "there was lots of trouble to keep the little shavers straight. Miss Mary and Master Jim had to be sent away from the table for being bad."[5] Jim, apparently, was the least controllable of all the family, and Garfield was once led to give him a sound thrashing back on Mentor Farm despite "some doubts about this business of pounding goodness into a child."

Lucretia often found the chores of childrearing to be almost unbearable, and she wrote: "To be half civilized with some aspirations for enlightenment, and obliged to spend the largest part of the time the victim of young barbarians keeps one in a perpetual ferment." And of young Irv and Abe she commented: "They are passing through that dreaded period of boyhood when the chief joy in living seems to be measured by the discomfort they can occasion to everybody else."[6]

Garfield was concerned that his children should be well educated, and the two older boys Harry (Hal) and Jim were enrolled in a public school but not for long. Not only were both boys averse to learning, but Garfield himself had become disillusioned with the system:

> My faith in our public schools is steadily diminishing. The course
> of study is unnatural and the children are too overcrowded for solid
> healthy growth and that ought to be the chief business of children,
> and study must not interfere with it too much.[7]

The two boys were later sent to a private school, but after the death of Edward in 1876, all five children were taught at home with a governess employed to supervise the youngest members of the family. The process was described by Lucretia:

Miss Mays, a young English woman whom we all love very much, is with us and is teaching Mollie, Irvin and Abram. . . . Hal and Jim are reading the first book of Caesar's Commentaries. They are shut up for two hours each morning to learn their lesson in Latin Grammar and read a lesson in Caesar. I then spend between two and three hours hearing each one recite alone the whole lesson, spell and read. It is their regular work and my chief purpose is to try to get them into habits of thorough careful study without help. In the evening or at dinner Papa reviews them in their Caesar and each Friday he requires of each one some literary exercise, either a declamation or composition. We are all very happy in our winter's work, and I believe are making more progress than ever before.[8]

Whenever possible, the children were taken to the theater in Washington, especially to performances of the plays of Shakespeare, among which they attended *Macbeth, Othello,* and *Henry V.* In 1876, Garfield and Lucretia took the three older children to Philadelphia to visit the Centennial Exhibition, and they took the opportunity as well to acquaint their offspring with the several national historic sites and buildings of the city.

Both Garfield and his wife stressed the importance of letter writing as a means of reducing the strain of family separations. In 1875, Garfield embarked on an extended visit of the West Coast and, at the beginning of his tour, he wrote to his children:

I am going to write you letters every few days while I am gone, to let you know where I am, and also to help you in your knowledge of the Geography of your own country. I will try to write so plainly that Harry, Jimmie, and Molly can read what I write, and so can improve in learning to read writing. I want you to take the large atlas, and trace my journey, and then recite to Mamma, so as to be able to tell her the places I pass through and tell her what states they are in, and what rivers I cross.[9]

The family normally spent summers in Ohio at the home base in Hiram, until it was sold in 1872. After four years of uncertainty as to where they could next locate, Garfield bought a farm of over a hundred acres, "the old Dickey place" in Mentor. The buildings, as purchased, were in an extremely dilapidated condition. Garfield wrote: "As a finan-

cial investment I do not think it very wise; but as a means of securing a
summer home, and teaching my boys to do farm work, I feel well about
it." He invested a considerable sum of money in the property, including
the construction of a new three-story house[10] and farm buildings, equipment, and stock. While they may not have learnt much farming, the boys
reveled in the freedom of the outdoor life, and the entire family benefit-
ted from the opportunities afforded them for constant exercise either
demanded by farm chores or in the enjoyment of walking and horse-
riding,[11] and boating (since Lake Erie was but two miles distant.)

In 1879, Harry and Jim were sent to a well-known college-preparatory
school, St. Paul's, in Concord, New Hampshire. It had been founded in
1855 by Dr. George Cheyne Shattuck, Jr., with an initial enrollment of
exactly three boys, but by dint of hard work, enthusiasm, and growing
reputation, it had increased to 227 when the two boys entered the school.
Its director was, at this date, Dr. Henry A. Coit, an Episcopalian clergyman, of whom Garfield did not have a favorable impression upon the
first meeting, and he noted "I shall watch the further development with
anxious interest."

The dislike may have stemmed from religious differences, since Epis-
copalians valued their rites and rituals whereas Garfield was a member of
the Disciples of Christ, followers of the teachings of Alexander Camp-
bell, who had sought to emphasize prayer and preaching, and eliminate
all elaborate and needless formalities.

The boys were committed to a strict regime of work at the school,
with studies being conducted in the mornings and evenings, while the
afternoons were free for outdoor games and activities. Jim found the
academic challenges relatively easy, and his grades were so good that
Garfield found it necessary to write to Dr. Coit as to whether any boy
could get such good marks without ruining his health.[12] Harry found
more difficulty with his studies, but he did succeed in passing all his
examinations at the end of the first Christmas term with the exception of
Greek, and he went on to receive a prize at the end of the year for the best
"English Declamation."

Harry, by nature, a friendly outgoing personality, was initially dismayed by the somewhat aloof attitude of the students at the school. He
wrote:

> My first term at St. Paul's was rather unsuccessful as regards
> making friends, for, as I afterwards learned, a new fellow who is
> "cheeky" is disliked, and I had an idea that the way to get along
> with fellows at a boarding school was to be familiar with them and
> go in for everything.[13]

But in time he settled down, and he and his brother were eventually to form a life-long friendship with two of their schoolmates, Don Rockwell and Bentley Warren.

In January, 1880, Garfield was elected by the Ohio Legislature to the U.S. Senate for the term commencing March 4, 1881, but he was never to take his seat in the Upper House. At the June Republican Convention in Chicago, Ulysses S. Grant was seeking an unprecedented third term as President of the United States, but, although he consistently led the field, he never succeeded in gaining an absolute majority over his rivals. After thirty-three ballots, the stalemate persisted, with Garfield receiving only one vote as compared with 309 for Grant, 276 for Blaine, and 110 for Sherman. Then came the deluge: on the 34th ballot, Garfield received 17 votes, on the 35th ballot 50, and finally, on the 36th ballot, he was nominated with 399 votes. Completely surprised and stunned by the sudden turn of events, Garfield's only immediate comment was "I don't know whether I am glad or not."[14]

In an astonishingly prophetic comment written during his succeeding fall term at St. Paul's, Harry wrote:

I managed to keep pretty cool during the campaign concerning politics, but then I thought of the risks of health and peace of mind, the latter of which would certainly be sacrificed should the fight end in favor of the Republicans, and the former be in great danger. Then came the end. The end of what? Was it to be the end of home life or the end of a clean record of unsought nominations, followed by glorious victories. . . . While this was being decided, I ran on the hare and hounds to give my feelings a vent. When I got back a telegram was put in my hands saying that home life must be sacrificed, and that victory was complete and grand. I was thankful that my father had not been defeated since he was nominated, but I was sorry he had been nominated.[15]

Within a year, "the end" was to come, in a manner as sudden and unexpected as the beginning.

One year after the boys had left for Concord, Mollie, now 14, was sent to Cleveland to the young ladies' school of Miss Augusta Mittleberger. She lived during the week at the home of her cousins, the Masons, but she was able to ride the train back to Mentor for weekends since Cleveland was little more than twenty miles away.

In the presidential election of 1880, Garfield received a comfortable majority of electoral votes over his opponent, General Winfield Hancock, although in terms of the popular vote, his majority was less than ten thousand in the total electorate of over nine million Americans. With the election over, Harry and Jim persuaded their father to allow them to leave St. Paul's at the end of the Christmas term and to study under a tutor in Washington. Garfield had readily consented to the change since growing doubts had arisen in his mind concerning the religious influence of the school. It was Episcopalian in persuasion, and it was his intention that the boys, in due course, be enrolled in Williams, a strictly Congregational institution. Moreover, he had heard from Harry that the Rector of St. Paul's had invited him to attend his next confirmation class with the object that Harry might become an Episcopalian. Garfield was quick to respond, and in a letter dated November 26, 1880, he had written at length:

> . . . Now Hal, on the subject of your confirmation, I say again you must be perfectly free to decide for yourself in all matters relating to religion. . . . Do not permit yourself to be persuaded or influenced to act hastily. I greatly prefer that you take no preliminary step, or binding obligation until after the holidays, for I have some suggestions to make which I think will aid you. Remember that all the influences now around you are in one direction, and you may be a broader man, for having looked on all sides before acting. Please do not forget that the ministers of almost every church are drumming up recruits for their own sect. I do not mean this in a bad sense; but I do mean, that it often amounts to undue influence. I have never asked you to join my church, and I don't want any other man to take away your liberty. . . .[16]

Upon the recommendation of a former classmate of his, Garfield arranged for the hire of Dr. William H. Hawkes from Montana Territory to teach his own boys as well as their friend Don Rockwell, at the latter's home. In due course, the tutorial venue was moved to the White House.

Garfield's inauguration was a particularly happy one since it was an occasion when one Ohio resident was in process of succeeding another as President. It also happened that the two presidential daughters, Mollie Garfield and Fanny Hayes, both 14, were the only girls in their families and each had four brothers. In these respects, therefore, they shared much in common and they held hands during the inaugural ceremony, which was also attended by Eliza Garfield, who at 80 was the first mother of a President to attend her son's inauguration.

Life at the White House was reasonably quiet, and mealtimes provided the occasion for the President to enjoy the company of his wife and children. He would take the opportunity of questioning the boys about their daily work, and, if their tutor ever complained, Garfield would have their assignments sent directly to him for grading. This action usually brought the anticipated results, and the complaints would cease. Garfield often relaxed in a game of billiards with the boys, while the whole family would play a variety of card games together.

Mollie attended Mme. Burr's school on New York Avenue, where one of her classmates was Lulu Rockwell, of whom Harry had become very fond, and he confided with his father who was led to note in his journal:

> I have never known such frankness in any lad of his age. He feels powerless to draw back from the passion which involves him. It is a most innocent and intense passion—which, of course, at his age cannot last.[17]

The summer of 1881 was, as usual, hot in Washington and both Eliza and Lucretia became sick. The family spent some time at the ocean resort of Elberon, New Jersey, and then, for July, Garfield planned to attend the commencement exercises at Williams[18] with his two older boys whom he intended to enroll at the college for the session commencing in the fall.

On July 2, Garfield set off in a good mood[19] for Washington Station with himself and Secretary of State, James Blaine, in the first carriage, and with Harry and James following in a second carriage. By the time the two boys had alighted at the station Garfield had been shot twice by Charles Guiteau, a frustrated office seeker. Despite the terrible shock of finding their father lying wounded on the floor, the boys did not panic and accompanied the wounded President back to the White House.

The bullets in his body were never recovered until the autopsy after his death eighty days later at Elberon, where he had been moved at his own request in the hope that the sea air would help him recover.[20] He died on September 19, and his body was eventually buried in Lake View Cemetery, Cleveland.

Lucretia survived her husband by thirty-seven years. She was 49 when he died, and, one year later, Congress awarded her $50,000 in addition to an annual pension of $5,000. She kept the family together until the children were grown up, and then, finding the Ohio winters too bleak, she spent those months either in Florida or in California, and it was in Pasadena that she died in her eighty-sixth year in 1918. She did all in her power to see that the name of Garfield was held in high honor by her children, and Garfield himself would have been proud of her efforts.

His one and only daughter, Mollie, had formed a liking for his secretary, her "cool" Mr. Joseph Brown. The friendship had ripened into love, and had been encouraged by Lucretia, but with two stipulations:

first, that he change his family name to Stanley-Brown, and second, that he graduate from college.

With respect to the change of surname, Joseph Brown's paternal grandfather's family name was Stanley. Involved in a legal tangle in Scotland, he had sought refuge in the U.S. and, at the same time, changed his name to Brown. Lucretia deemed it a pity to sacrifice ancestral tradition, and so persuaded Joseph to assume the name of Stanley-Brown.

Lucretia had also recognized that Joseph possessed unique talent and ability. He was a self-taught stenographer, who had obtained the post as secretary to John Wesley Powell, director of the Survey of the Rocky Mountain region. Powell, a friend of Garfield, had been instrumental in persuading the latter, in 1879, to support consolidation of the various separate topographic divisions into the U.S. Geological Survey, and when Garfield had mentioned his need of a competent secretary, Powell had suggested Joseph Brown.

In due course, Joseph accepted Lucretia's offer to pay for his college expenses and, in 1888, after graduating from Sheffield Scientific School of Yale University, he found employment with the U.S. Geologic Survey, and in the same year, married Mollie Garfield, now 21.

Joseph fully justified Lucretia's confidence in him, since his subsequent career was an exceptionally productive one. Having examined and re-ported upon the conditions which led to the Bering Sea controversy with Great Britain in 1891-93, he was asked to serve as one of his country's representatives during arbitration of the dispute in Paris. Although sub-sequently entering the world of business, first as secretary to several railroad companies, and then as an investment banker, he maintained his interests in geology, and for years edited the proceedings of the National Geological Society. He also served as chairman of the finance committee of the National Academy of Sciences.

In accordance with their father's wishes, both Harry and Jim had entered Williams College in September, 1881. They had departed from Washington in the full belief that Garfield was on the way to recovery, so that the shock of his death within two weeks must have been extremely upsetting to both sons. They both graduated in 1885, the acme of their college career being the senior course taught by their father's revered mentor, Mark Hopkins, still intellectually vigorous and active at age 83. Both boys proceeded to Columbia Law School and, after qualifying, they set up practice together in Cleveland in 1888.[21] This was also the year when, in a double marriage ceremony at the Memorial Library, (dedi-cated to Garfield, and erected on the Mentor Farm estate), Mollie was married to Joseph Stanley-Brown, and immediately afterwards, Harry and Belle Hartford Mason[22] took their vows. Eighteen months later, Jim married Helen Newell, daughter of a Chicago railroad president.

The married families always contrived to spend some time together during the summer at Mentor, and also made a special effort to spend Christmas there with Lucretia, although, as she became older she preferred to spend her winters in the warmer South. The last Garfield family Christmas at the old home was in 1898, when Lucretia was hostess to all her family, including ten of her grandchildren.

After three years of their joint law practice, the divergent interests of Harry and Jim led to separation. In 1891, the former accepted a position as Professor of Contracts at Western Reserve Law School and, in 1903, he responded to an invitation from Woodrow Wilson to become Professor of Politics at Princeton, thereby replacing Grover Cleveland, who had presented lectures in the same domain, but had decided to retire. In 1908, Harry moved on to become president of Williams College, and it was here that he spent the remainder of his active career until his retirement in 1933, except during World War I,[23] having served under Herbert Hoover as chairman of the price-fixing committee of the Food Administration office, he was then appointed as U.S. Fuel Administrator by President Wilson, for which services he was in due course awarded the Distinguished Service Medal.

Upon his return to Williams after the war, Harry gained an international reputation for the college by establishing there first an Institute of Politics, and then, an Institute of Public Relations, to which prominent scholars and statesmen were invited to speak. He more than tripled the endowment funds of the college, but, without any doubt, what gave him enduring satisfaction was his appointment as president of the very college which his father so dearly loved, and, had he lived, might well have been appointed to the very same position.

Following his retirement in 1934, Harry and Belle went on a world tour, during which they were delighted to meet up with many of the prior participants of the Williams International Institute of Politics. Upon his return, Harry recorded his impressions in a book entitled *Lost Visions,* in which he propounded his theories relating to the fall of great nations. He died at age 79 on December 12, 1942, at Williamstown.[24]

Jim had become interested in politics, and was the only one of the Garfield sons to follow in his father's footsteps. He served in the Ohio State Senate from 1896–99 and, during Theodore Roosevelt's presidency, Jim was appointed, in 1902 as chairman of the Federal Civil Service Commission, in 1903 as Commissioner of Corporations in the Department of Commerce and Labor, while, from 1907 to 1909, he was Secretary of the Interior and a member of T.R.'s "lawn tennis" cabinet. He was a firm supporter of his President's "trust-busting" activities, but, later as a "Bull Moose" candidate he was defeated in his bid for election as Governor of Ohio, following which he lost interest in politics for a number of years.

During World War I, he served for some fifteen months as divisional manager of the American Red Cross in the states of Ohio, Indiana, and Kentucky, and following the cessation of hostilities, he returned to his law practice.

In 1929, he was appointed by President Hoover as chairman of the Commission on Conservation and the Public Domain, while, in 1932, he headed the Republican platform committee. He was strongly opposed to many of the actions and measures of Franklin D. Roosevelt, and, in 1940, he presented a report to the American Bar Association "attacking the usurpation of judicial functions by Federal administrative tribunals."[25]

In Cleveland, where he had lived and worked for over sixty years, he engaged in philanthropical activities, and was particularly involved with the Cleveland Hearing and Speech Center of which he was president of the board of trustees. His wife, Helen Newell of Chicago, whom he had married in 1890, was killed in an auto accident in 1930, and, for the last years of his life, until his death in 1950, Jim lived with his brother, Abram.

Garfield's two younger sons, Irvin and Abram, also attended Williams College, whence they both graduated in 1893. It was Irvin who, during the family's brief occupation of the White House, had given Colonel Crook, one of the senior ushers, such palpitations when, while walking near the grand staircase, he heard a shout of warning and, he, himself, describes the incident:

> I sprang to one side, and as I did so quickly glanced upward. And there, perched on one of the old-fashioned bicycles with a high wheel was President Garfield's young son, Irvin, coasting down that staircase like lightning. In an instant he had reached the foot of it, zipped across the broad corridor, and turned into the East Room, the flashing steel spokes of his wheel vanishing like the tail of a comet. . . .[26]

Crook had pursued him, fully expecting serious accident to have occurred, but Irvin was in full control then, as well as later, when he would bring in some friends and hold bicycle races in the East Room, always when his parents were away from home.

In 1896, he graduated from Harvard Law School and pursued a law career for the remainder of his professional life, which he spent in Boston where he died at the age of 80. He maintained close contact with his alma mater and was at one time president of the Williams College Alumni Association.

The interests of Abram, the youngest son, were widely divergent from those of his brothers. He decided upon the career of that of an architect, and, graduating from the Massachusetts Institute of Technology in 1896, he traveled widely in Europe absorbed with the great variety of building styles in the cities of that continent. He set up practice in Cleveland where he designed several new colleges and many residences.[27] In 1909, he was appointed by Theodore Roosevelt to the National Council of Fine Arts, and in 1925, President Coolidge assigned him as a member of the National Fine Arts Commission.

Abram was instrumental in the creation of a school for architecture in Cleveland, which he headed for fifteen years before it was incorporated as a school within Western Reserve University. He was also president of the Cleveland City Planning Commission for twelve years. He was the longest-lived of the family, and died in 1958, just one month short of his 86th birthday.

Chester Alan Arthur

(1881–1885)

When Arthur became President following the death of Garfield, he was appalled at the condition of the White House, which he termed "a badly kept barracks." He had permitted Garfield's widow time to recover from her grief, but then he refused to take occupation of the mansion until he had arranged for a wholesale clearance of its contents. He auctioned off more than 20 wagonloads of furniture and used clothing (which included a pair of Lincoln's trousers), and then engaged Louis Comfort Tiffany, the famed artist and interior decorator of the day, to renovate the whole house on the grand scale. Tiffany readily responded to Arthur's love of lavish decor, and, in addition to wall and ceiling adornments and expensive furniture, he arranged for the installation of two new bathrooms and an elevator.

Known as the "Dude President," Arthur, in every way, enjoyed elegant living, although he had certainly not been reared in luxury. He was born the fifth child and the eldest son in a family of nine, and while the records indicate that he was born in the year 1829, a quirk of vanity made him change the date to 1830 to appear younger. His father, William Arthur, was a Baptist clergyman, and, at the time of Chester's birth, he was living in a log cabin awaiting the completion of a new manse.[1] The Arthur family knew very little of stable home life since, by reason of his occupation, William Arthur was obliged to move from one parish to another, the average length of stay in any one parsonage over a period of thirty years being little more than three years.

William Arthur was a genuine intellectual with antiquarian interests, and he made every effort to ensure that his son, Chester, should derive every benefit from a good education. Chester graduated from Union College, Schenectady[2] and subsequently became principal of an academy at Cohoes, where, at the same time, he began a study of law. He eventually qualified and took up law practice in the state of New York.

In 1859 he married Virginia-born Ellen Lewis Herndon, the only child of Commander William Lewis Herndon, a Latin American explorer, who went down with his ship in 1857 during a storm off the coast near Cape Hatteras. Their first child, William Lewis Herndon, was born in 1860, but died in 1863. A second son, born in 1864, was named after his father as Chester Alan Arthur, II.

During the Civil War, Arthur was quartermaster general of the state of New York, and, coming into contact with many prominent persons, there was aroused in him such an interest in politics that, by 1868, he was chairman of the state Republican executive committee. On the very same day as the birth of his third child and only daughter, Ellen Herndon Arthur, on November 21, 1871, he was appointed as collector of customs for the Port of New York, a position which controlled the enormous political spoils system of the city. When the Democrats assumed power of New York State in 1874, reforms were instituted, and Arthur was removed in 1878.[3] Whatever the allegations of corruption directed against him, they seemed to have had little effect upon his political career, and, in 1880, he was nominated as vice-presidential candidate on the Garfield platform.[4] After the latter's death, Arthur took the presidential oath of office on September 19, 1881.

He was the third widower to enter the White House. His wife, Ellen (Nell), had died in January, 1880. She was a very talented woman, with a fine contralto voice, and, being interested in philanthropic activities, she often sang for charity. It was as the result of singing at one such event that she caught a chill which developed into pneumonia, and she died at the early age of 42. Arthur kept a portrait of his wife in his White House bedroom, and had fresh flowers placed before it daily. He also donated in her memory a stained glass window to the church which they both attended.

Arthur never remarried, and, instead, persuaded his youngest sister, Mary (Mrs. John McElroy), to function as White House hostess for four months of the year, and to act as surrogate mother to his two children, Alan, aged 17, and Nell, aged 11. Mary brought along with her to the White House her own two daughters, May and Jessie, who shared the services of Nell's French governess. She proved to be an excellent and gracious hostess, and Arthur, always the "Dude President," provided the most epicurean of entertainment with an abundance of colorful decorative plants and flowers.[5] Always fastidiously dressed,[6] he also insisted that his son, Alan, be likewise appropriately attired, and there is little doubt that, when they appeared together at White House functions, Arthur, at six-foot-two, and Alan, at six-foot-four, furnished an unforgettable impression upon the assembled guests.

In 1881, Alan had been enrolled as a Columbia College freshman, and, upon hearing of the death of Garfield, he returned quickly to Washington, where he drove up just in time to be present for his father's inaugural ceremony. Alan later entered Princeton, where he did not allow his studies to interfere with his many diversions relating to female friendships, sport, and gambling. He would often avoid classes to travel by train to Washington for some entertainment or other, and would often surprise his father by appearing unexpectedly at breakfast next morning. Arthur could hardly have been unduly startled or taken unawares by this behavior since his son was simply emulating much of his father's recognized lifestyle.

Alan did graduate from college in 1885, at age 21, with no set career in mind, and then, only one year later, the death of his father provided him with a substantial income from one-half of the estate, the remainder of which was to accrue to him at the age of 30. Thus, ensured of financial security for the rest of his life, Alan became nothing more than a playboy, readily identifiable as a lover of fast living, fast women, and fast horses. Free of all responsibilities, he roamed and traveled within and beyond the boundaries of the United States, and it was in Europe in the year 1900, that he met and married (at Montreaux, Switzerland) a California heiress, Myra Townsend Fithian Andrews. There were no children of the marriage, and the couple separated in 1916, but it was not until 1927 that the wife sued for divorce, charging desertion, in Santa Barbara, California.

Alan, after living in New York and Philadelphia, among other places, finally settled upon Colorado Springs as a place of residence. Here, he was simply recognized as a competent polo player and as a gentleman of leisure and connoisseur of art, possessed of a fine stable of horses and elegant carriages.

In 1934, he was remarried to Miss Rowena Dashwood Graves of Colorado Springs. In the press reports of the wedding she was described as being "prominent in society," and "engaged in the real estate and insurance business," as well as being active in civic affairs.

Alan died at age 72, within three years of his second marriage. In several of the obituary notices prominence was given to both his past and current club memberships and activities, including those of the Racquet and Knickerbocker Clubs of New York, the Travelers Club of Paris, the Cheyenne Mountain Country Club, the El Para Club, as well as a number of like-association groups within the vicinity of Colorado Springs.

Chester Arthur made every effort to preserve privacy for his family. He was once quoted as having remarked "I may be president of the United States, but my private life is nobody's business." He made this principle particularly applicable to his daughter, Nell, who was not quite 10 when he assumed the office of the presidency, and was but 15 when he died in 1886. She had been given piano and singing lessons by her mother, and had remained on in New York with a governess for fully a year after her father had become President. Arthur was most strict about not having photographs taken of his daughter, and very few currently exist. She attended a boarding school in Farmington, Connecticut, and there she made friends with both Fanny Hayes and Mollie Garfield who were students at the same time. When she returned to the White House for holidays, Arthur permitted her appearance at occasional afternoon receptions, and she accompanied her father on drives around the city and into the country. Whenever possible and convenient, the White House entourage would take a trip along the Potomac, or even travel by boat to New York. Nell's one major annual public appearance was as president of the Washington children's Christmas Club, whose function it was to provide dinners along with a Christmas tree and presents for the "children of the deserving poor" in the capital city.

After the death of her father, both she and Alan traveled to Europe together where they spent a number of years. In due course, she married Charles Pinkerton of New York, and she lived an uneventful life until her death in 1915, at age 44.

Grover Cleveland

(1886–1889; 1893–1897)

Grover Cleveland remains as the only President of the United States to serve two nonconsecutive terms of office. The issues of the day related to tariffs and currency, and, in the election of 1884, he defeated the Republican candidate, James G. Blaine, was himself defeated by Benjamin Harrison in 1888, (although he received a majority of the popular vote), but regained office in a victory over Harrison in 1892. He was the only Democratic President between 1861 and 1913.

The very fact of his first election was in itself remarkable. He was a bachelor, qualified in law and had practiced in Buffalo, New York. A stubborn, rather humorless but honest man, he was sequentially elected as sheriff of Erie County, Mayor of Buffalo, and Governor of New York. Then, selected as the Democratic party's presidential nominee at the Chicago Convention of July, 1884, he became the subject of a vicious campaign of vilification. He was labeled as the Hangman of Buffalo since, as mayor of the city, he had personally supervised and, on occasion, had pulled the lever for the hanging of a criminal.

It was also reported that, a decade earlier, he had fathered an illegitimate child by an attractive widow, Maria Crofts Halpin, who had arrived in Buffalo from Pennsylvania. Mrs. Halpin had charged Cleveland with the paternity of the child, who had been named Oscar Folsom Cleveland.[1] The real identity of the father was unknown, since she had associated with a number of men, mostly married, in Buffalo. It was, apparently, to protect his friends that Cleveland, unmarried, accepted responsibility and agreed to provide financial support for the boy. Later, Cleveland considered her to be an inadequate mother and arranged for the boy to be removed from her care to an orphan institution. The mother made public her protestations, and the scandal reached nationwide proportions at the time of election, with the Republican jingle:

Ma! Ma! Where's my Pa?
Gone to the White House. Ha! Ha! Ha!

Cleveland responded with his now famous remark: "Tell the truth."

His opponent, James Blaine, fared little better since the fact was uncovered that, while he was married in March, 1851, a son had been born to him in the following June. Blaine was also charged with corruption, and all-in-all, the American voters were presented with the dilemma of having to select between two nominees each with distasteful reputations. Blaine defended himself of the shotgun wedding accusation by declaring that he had gone through a wedding ceremony in June, 1850, and that only a legal technicality had made that ceremony invalid; the union had been formally legalized in March, 1851.

A Chicago citizen offered the American voter the following suggestion:

We are told that Mr. Blaine has been delinquent in office but blameless in private life, while Mr. Cleveland has been a model of official integrity, but culpable in his personal relations. We shall therefore elect Mr. Cleveland to the public office which he is so well qualified to fill, and remand Mr. Blaine to the private station which he is admirably fitted to adorn.[2]

His advice was obviously followed and Cleveland won the election. His delighted followers now composed their own victory jingle:

Hurrah for Maria
Hurrah for the kid[3]
I voted for Cleveland
and I'm so glad I did

Cleveland's hostess at the White House was his youngest sister, Rose Elizabeth, whom he always called "Libbie" within the family circle. Rose was in her forties, and had been a teacher in private schools for girls. She was very much a feminist and prohibitionist, but her brother vetoed her proposal to make the White House "dry" in conformity with the precedent set by Rutherford and Lucy Hayes.

To while away her time at the White House she wrote a book on the poetry of George Eliot, and, during formal receptions, which demanded tedious hours of handshaking, Rose relieved her boredom by silently conjugating Greek verbs. She may also have been subsequently consoled by the fact that her span of duty lasted little more than a year.

At Buffalo, Cleveland's law partner, Francis Folsom, had been involved in an accident when he was thrown out of his carriage and instantly killed. Cleveland had undertaken responsibility for the welfare of his partner's widow and her child. The latter was named Frances, and was only eleven years old at the time of her father's death. Cleveland became known to her as her "Uncle Cleve," and she to him as "Frank." She would often visit his office where he would assign her legal documents to copy, and he bought her numerous gifts and presents including a horse and buggy. Cleveland's name had often been linked, in terms of possible marriage, with that of the widow, but that was not to be.

Frances went away to Wells College in Aurora, New York, and, when Cleveland became Governor, both Frances and her mother frequently attended as guests at the Governor's mansion in Albany. After his victory in the presidential election of 1884, they were both invited to the inaugural ceremony in Washington.

Frances graduated from college in 1885 and, upon Cleveland's suggestion, she and her mother went to Europe to "complete Frank's education." In the meantime, she had become secretly engaged to her "Uncle Cleve," but it was not a secret too well kept, since, when he went to New York to meet the boat upon her return, the bank struck up "He's going to marry Yum-Yum" and followed it with the Wedding March. Cleveland decided upon a ceremony in the Blue Room of the White House, and it took place in the presence of a limited number of guests on June 2, 1886, under a huge wedding bell of white roses.[4] At the time of the wedding, Frances was 21, and Cleveland, 49. He was the first President and she was the first First Lady to be married at the White House.

They spent their honeymoon at Deer Park in Maryland, where the President expressed considerable annoyance with the antics of press reporters and photographers who constantly intruded upon the privacy of the newly wedded couple.

As President, his demands for tariff reduction resulted in the mobilization against him of influential industrial and business interests, and, while he received more popular votes than Harrison in the 1888 presidential election, he lost with respect to the electoral vote.

After his defeat he returned to his law practice in New York, and it was here, in October, 1891, that his first child, his daughter, Ruth, was born, upon the occasion of which he wrote to his former law partner, Wilson S. Bissell, (who had married in 1889, and was himself expecting the birth of his first child):

> . . . . I, who have just entered the real world, and see in a small child more of value than I have ever called my own before; who puts aside, as hardly worth a thought, all that has gone before—fame, honor, place, everything—reach out my hand to you and fervently express the wish . . . that in safety and in joy you may soon reach my estate.[5]

In 1892, Cleveland was re-elected,[6] and Baby Ruth became the focus of nationwide attraction. The White House grounds were open to the public, so that, whenever the child and her mother went outside, they were immediately followed by a host of curious onlookers. On one occasion Ruth had been taken out by her nursemaid, and Frances, looking out of the window, suddenly lost sight of both; rushing out, she found them in the middle of a crowd of women, who were passing Ruth around one to the other, smothering her with kisses in the process. Frances was horrified, and demanded that her husband close off a section of the grounds so that the family could stroll around unmolested. Her action led to all manner of gossip imputing that Ruth was either deaf and dumb, or had only partly formed ears, or was half-witted.

Easily the most auspicious social event of Cleveland's second term of office was the birth of his second daughter, Esther, in September, 1893, the first child of a President ever to have been born in the White House.[7] Cleveland commented that "Ruth, thus far, seems to think the newcomer's advent as a great joke," and, in a letter written within a week of Esther's birth, he elaborated upon the problem of naming his new daughter:

> It may be very disappointing to those still alive whose names are passed by, but I have determined to ignore mother, grandmothers, and great grandmothers and avoid all jealousy by going back to biblical times. I mean to call the little child Esther. It is a favorite name with me and associated in a pleasant way with things I remember besides the hanging of Haman.[8]

Now the mother of two young children, Frances was limited in the amount of hostess entertaining, and, always the considerate husband,[9] Cleveland purchased a small farmhouse on the outskirts of the city where the family could enjoy greater freedom from White House cares and chores. Because of its red roof the home became popularly known as "Red Top."

During his last years of office, Cleveland was confronted with major problems of labor unrest, which included the march upon Washington of unemployed citizens led the Popular leader Jacob S. Coxey, and the Chicago Pullman Strike sponsored by the American Railway Union of Eugene V. Debs. In the Democratic Convention of 1896, William Jennings Bryan, with his "Cross of Gold" speech, received the nomination of the party, and Cleveland was eliminated. His major consolation during the political convulsions was the birth, in July, 1895, at his summer home in Buzzard's Bay, Massachusetts, of yet a third daughter, named Marion. When public regret appeared to have been expressed at the birth of three successive daughters to the President, Frances made her delightful comment as rebuttal that "little girls were exceedingly nice."

Upon relinquishment of his office in March, 1897, Cleveland moved his home to Princeton, New Jersey, where he purchased a house, which he named "Westland" in honor of his friend, Professor West. On October 28 that same year, the Clevelands rejoiced in the birth of their first son, as did the entire college, on the bulletin board of which was posted the notice:

> Grover Cleveland arrived today at 12 o'clock; will enter Princeton with the class of 1916; and will play center rush on the championship football teams of '16, '17, '18, and '19.[10]

The announcement was premature in that Cleveland did not name his son after him. As he explained in a letter dated November 11 to his friend, Richard Olney:

> I wish I could write something satisfactory to the ladies of your household touching our new boy. This I cannot do on my own responsibility, for I agree with you that when they count but two weeks as the period of earthly experience, all babies are very much alike, both as regards their looks and conduct. As sort of secondhand information, however, I venture to say that the female members of our household declare that this particular child looks like his father, that he has blue eyes, a finely shaped head, and bids fair to be a very handsome and a very distinguished man. I have no doubt this is all true, because a neighbor lady who was today

admitted to a private inspection of the specimen told me he was the "loveliest thing" she ever saw. We have named him Richard Folsom—my father's first name and my wife's father's last name. Some good friends thought we ought to call him Grover Jr.; but so many people have been bothered by the name Grover, and it has been so knocked about, that I thought it ought to have a rest.[11]

Cleveland had accepted an honorary degree from the university in 1897, and three years later, following the foundation of the Henry Stafford Little Lectureship on Public Affairs, he gave his first two lectures on campus. In 1901, he became a trustee of the university, and was later president of the Board of Trustees. He and Frances relished the campus intellectual and social life, and when his home developed as the terminal point of all student demonstrations, Cleveland himself participated vociferously in all the college yells, commenting that "I feel like a locomotive hitched to a boy's express wagon."

In July, 1903, the happiness of the Cleveland family appeared unbounded since a fifth child, and their second son, was born to them on the 18th day of the month, while they were on a vacation at their summer home in Buzzard's Bay, Mass. Cleveland wrote to the wife of the president of Princeton on the same day:

I sent you a telegram this morning that a tramp boy had trespassed upon our premises. He was first seen and heard at 10 o'clock A.M. (I hear him now). . . . The shameless naked little scoundrel weighed over nine pounds. Richard was very much tickled as long as he thought it was something in the doll line, and was quite overcome with laughter when he found it was "a real baby." He and I have been planning for the amusement of the newcomer when he shall arrive at Richard's present age. He denies with considerable warmth any intention of taking him by the hair and throwing him down. In point of fact we have agreed upon no particular line of conduct, except an engagement on Richard's part to teach the young brother to swim if all goes well.[12]

Sadly, the rejoicing over the birth of a second son, who was named Francis Grover, was short-lived, since within six months, the family was prostrated by grief over the sudden and unexpected death through diphtheria of the eldest daughter, Ruth, in January, 1904, at the age of 12. Cleveland died only four years later on June 24, 1908. His widow, Frances, remarried in 1913, and was the first former First Lady to do so. Her second husband was Thomas J. Preston, Jr., a professor of archaeology at Princeton. She lived to be 83, and died in October, 1947.

Esther, the oldest of the four surviving children, became interested in nursing and worked in a hospital in London during World War I. While traveling in Europe before the outbreak of war she had become friendly with William Sydney Bence Bosanquet, an Englishman on holiday in Switzerland. By the strange quirk of coincidence, they next met in London, where as a captain in the Coldstream Guards, he had returned from the battlefield to receive treatment for wounds. Their friendship ripened into love, and they were married in Westminster Abbey. After the war, they went to live in Yorkshire where Bosanquet died in 1966.

Marion, the younger sister, after graduating from Westover School, New York, in 1914, attended Columbia University Teachers' College, and then married William Stanley Dell of Princeton. In 1926, she was remarried to John Harlan Amen, a New York attorney, who, during the decade of the 1930's established himself nationally for his "racket-busting" activities within the city. He had been educated at Phillips Exeter Academy (where his father had been headmaster), and then at Princeton and Harvard Law School. It was after his appointment in 1928 as special assistant to the U.S. Attorney General, Homer S. Cummings, in connection with antitrust violations, that Amen achieved fame as a eminently successful prosecutor. His four-year-long investigation (1938–42) of official corruption in Brooklyn, New York, is acknowledged as being "the longest and most sweeping study of municipal misconduct in the country.[13] The investigation was estimated as having cost a million dollars, but it was evidently worthwhile financially as well as socially, since the revenue from fines and penalties amounted to more than two million dollars.

Amen had served in the Marine Corps during World War I, and he rejoined the army in World War II, when he was promoted to the rank of colonel, and in due course, received decorations from the governments of Norway and Czechoslovakia for his services. He was appointed as member of the Federal Loyalty Review Board during the Truman administration in which capacity he served for seven years. He died in March, 1960.

Marion devoted a great deal of her time to service with the Girl Scouts of America as community relations officer in New York. She was also very active in women's clubs in the same city. She passed away at her home there in June, 1977.[14]

Richard Folsom, fourth child and first son of the ex-President, was "good copy" for the local press at Princeton where he was born, and, at the age of 6 was described as "a sturdy fellow, wears Russian blouse suits and has his hair cut square across the back. He is a great chum of his father."[15]

He was later sent to Phillips Exeter Academy, where he participated in student activities, being editor of the school monthly, member of the student council, and president of the Christian Association. At the age of 15, he entered Princeton, and, as the college bulletin at the time of his birth had announced, he did play center for the college team, but only in his freshman year.

At the outbreak of World War I, he enlisted with the Marine Corps, and was then sent to China where he served for six months as military attaché to the American Legation in Peking. Returning to Princeton, he graduated in 1919,[16] and obtained his Master's degree in 1921. While on a visit to Europe, he met and fell in love with Ellen Douglass Gailor, an English teacher, and a graduate of Vassar and Columbia.[17] They were married in June, 1923, in Memphis, Tennessee, at which time Richard had enrolled in Harvard Law School, whence he graduated in 1924.

Richard joined a law firm in Baltimore, Maryland, and remained with it until his retirement in 1969. In the meantime, he was active in state politics first as a Democrat, but later he openly expressed dissatisfaction with the Franklin D. Roosevelt administration, and gave his support to the Republican party presidential candidacies of Alfred Landon and Wendell Wilkie.

In the domain of social welfare, Richard was much concerned with the problem of juvenile delinquency, and he served as chairman of a commission appointed to consider possible measures of coping with adolescent crime. He also became interested in the survival of St. John's College, Annapolis, which had initiated the controversial Great Books curriculum, sponsored by Robert Hutchings, and he gave full support to the efforts of the innovative educational pioneers.

Richard's first marriage ended in divorce, and in 1943 he married Jessie Maxwell Black. He died in January, 1974, at the age of 76.

Francis, the youngest child of the family, was only five at the time of his father's death. Like his brother, he was sent to Phillips Exeter Academy, whence he proceeded to Harvard, not Princeton, although he does not appear to have graduated with his class. Instead, he took time away from college to marry Alice Erdman, daughter of the Reverend and Mrs. Charles R. Erdman. The bride's father was a member of the faculty of Princeton Theological Seminary and Pastor of the First Presbyterian Church, where the couple were married in June 1925. Francis' brother, Richard, was the best man.

Francis returned to Harvard and became interested in the stage, although, after graduating, he taught for some years at the Browne and Nichols School in Cambridge. In due course, he pursued an acting career, although few notices of his activities were ever published.[18]

Benjamin Harrison

(1889–1893)

After continuous occupancy of the White House for twenty-four years, Republicans underwent a traumatic shock when Democrate Grover Cleveland triumphed over James Blaine in 1884. They explored a variety of strategies in seeking to redress the situation, among which was that of "the great names" approach: Lincoln and Grant had been the only Presidents who had sought and gained re-election since the days of Andrew Jackson, and, to the initial delight of protagonists of the scheme, both Presidents each had a son who appeared to be eminently eligible as presidential timber, and what better arrangement could there be than to present them together on the Republican ticket as President and Vice-President nominees, respectively. The proposed names were those of Robert Todd Lincoln and Frederick Dent Grant.

But Robert Todd had already made his position unequivocally clear:

As to being a candidate for the Presidency, I regret the use of my name in connection with any public office whatever. It seems difficult for the average American to understand that it is possible for anyone not to desire the Presidency, but I most certainly do not. I have seen enough of the inside of Washington official life to have lost all interest for it.[1]

Fred Grant had had the problem of rehabilitating the family name after the financial crash of the firm of Ward and Grant, but certain Republicans still believed that the prestige of the father could yet counterbalance the negative effects of the disaster. The matter was put to the test in 1887, when Fred was nominated as candidate for the office of Secretary of State by the Republicans of New York. He was defeated.

In despair, the Republicans renewed their efforts to seek a great name, and they were rewarded by that of Benjamin Harrison, grandson of President William Henry Harrison, and great-grandson of Benjamin Harrison, one of the signatories of the Declaration of Independence.[2] Harrison's selection as presidential nominee was not one of universal Republican acclaim since, at the Chicago convention of 1888, he was not finally nominated until the eighth ballot. Harrison's son, Russell, and his son-in-law, Robert McKee, were both at the convention, and the latter was led to comment:

> If any fellow can make heads or tails out of the grand hub-bub of claims, counter-claims, lies and a few truths that slap him on every side he is more level headed than I am.[3]

and again in a letter home to his wife (on June 17, 1888), he wrote:

> . . . the whole race seems to be like a lot of horses on a track. One runs to the front awhile, then another lays on the whip and forges ahead, but the horses cannot hold the gait clear around the track— so another lays on the whip in turn and comes to the front for a moment and so it goes. . . .[4]

Harrison's father, John Scott Harrison, had served in the U.S. House of Representatives, while Harrison himself had already served in the U.S. Senate during the period 1881–87. In the course of the presidential campaign, appropriate publicity was given to his illustrious ancestors as well as to his own public service more especially in a biography compiled by his close friend General Lew Wallace, of whom one wit remarked: "He did so well on *Ben-Hur* that we can trust him with *Ben-Him.*"

In the 1888 presidential election, Harrison, while receiving less popular votes than Cleveland, gained a substantial majority of the Electoral College votes, and was thereby declared President.[5]

Upon entry into the White House, Harrison had been married for over thirty-five years to Caroline (Carrie) Lavinia Scott, daughter of Dr. John Witherspoon Scott, principal of the Oxford (Ohio) Female Seminary. Young Benjamin had been a student at nearby Miami University, and, after graduation, had studied law, and had then moved to Indianapolis. He and Carrie had married in 1853, and their first child (and only son), Russell Benjamin Harrison,[6] had been born in 1854, while their second child, a daughter named Mary Scott, (Mamie),[7] was born in 1858. A third child, also a daughter, died at birth in 1861.

During the Civil War, Harrison became Colonel of the 70th Indiana Volunteers which he had helped to recruit. His son, Russell, occasionally visited his father's headquarters and later commented:

> I was too young to know the causes which led up to the war, and the great forces which were factors in the intellectual struggle which preceded it, but I was with the Army for a time, and I know what it all meant.[8]

Apart from furloughs, Harrison saw little of his children during the war, but he was a regular correspondent to his family with advice as to their behavior and activities, and with promising predictions as to home life when the war was over. In a letter dated March 31, 1865, he told his children:

> . . . to help Ma fix up the yard, and keep . . . all nice and clean. The grape vines will need to be tied up and trimmed and the strawberry bed weeded and thinned. . . . You know that I am to come home from the army to stay at home with you . . . and I want to see our little house and everything about it as neat and trim as an old maid. What a good time we will have when we all get together again at home, and Pa does not have to go away to war any more. We will make everything about the dear cottage shine like a new dollar, and will try to keep things as bright inside the house as they are outside. We will have the stable fixed up and bring our horse . . . home and maybe get a nice little buggy to ride. . . .[9]

Harrison, however, was not in the best physical condition after the Civil War: first, he contracted scarlet fever, and then he exhausted himself by overwork in his law practice. He was wise enough to recognize the dangers, and eased up on his work schedule. He feared that Russell was being adversely influenced by the several women in the household, and so he was enrolled as a cadet at the Pennsylvania Military Academy at Chester, whence he proceeded to Lafayette College, Easton, Pennsylvania. In June 1877, he graduated with a degree in Mechanical Engineering, his final thesis being a "Review of the Exploitation of Coal, Empire

Shaft Colliery, Wilkes Barre, Pa."[10] He obtained employment, first as an engineer with a gas-light company in Indianapolis, then as assistant assayer of the United States Mint at New Orleans, whence, in 1880, he obtained a transfer as assayer of the U.S. Mint at Helena, Montana.

In 1881, Harrison was elected U.S. Senator, and Russell spent several of his vacations with the family in the capital city. It was on one such visit that he was introduced to and fell in love with Mary Angeline, the only daughter of his father's Senate colleague Alvin Saunders from Omaha, Nebraska. They were married in 1884.[11] Russell's mother, Carrie, was too ill to travel to Montana, having recently undergone surgery, but both Harrison and his daughter were present at the ceremony. According to one press report, Russell's voice was "audible and firm," while his bride answered "in a low yet earnest voice."[12] After the wedding the bride and groom spent a six-week honeymoon traveling in the luxurious railroad car loaned them by the director of the Union Pacific.

Later in the same year, in the month of November, Mamie was married to James Robert (Bob) McKee of Indianapolis. Mamie had always been a favorite of her father, who had acquiesced to all her whims except one, that of dancing. But Carrie, recognizing the social necessity of acquiring some skill and proficiency in the art, resorted to intrigue with some of her woman friends, and Mamie received lessons at one or other of their homes. Presumably, because he was supposed to be ignorant of the matter, Harrison made no comment as to whether he knew or not.[13]

Elected to the U.S. Senate in 1881, Harrison was active in politics, but he became increasingly concerned with the financial speculations of Russell in Montana. The latter, only in his early thirties, had not only invested in mining, but had broadened the scope of his activities to include cattle. He became manager of the Montana Cattle Company, as well as part owner of the *Montana Livestock Journal*, but rash statements published in the latter led to libel suits. On May 28, 1886, Russell received the following letter from his father:

> I am greatly troubled that you should be so much troubled. If you could get your matters into a shape that would enable you to sit down at home to some regular business that would give you a comfortable support I should be more pleased than you can know, as much excitement and care is not good for you—wealth cannot compensate either you or me for such a strain & so much risk. You have shown an amount of industry and enterprise that has won the admiration of your friends and your Ma and I have felt great pride in you. I have often given you a father's most affectionate counsel

upon this subject. But it is not profitable to talk of the past. I want to help you now and would make any money sacrifice that was not unjust to your Mother and Sister to do so and they no doubt would be as glad as I to make any sacrifice in your interest.[14]

But Russell was obstinate, and had even gone to New York to risk losing not only his own capital, but also that of the family, as well as that of his company's stockholders. Harrison was appalled, and again wrote, (August 20, 1886):

> . . . all my investments for six years have been in Montana and all of them now stand in your name—the Townsend Ranch—the Gulch property and the cattle stock. I do not know whether any of them could be sold or used in any way to help you. Here I have only our home, the Wash. St. property and the Penn. St. property. I have given the little 1st St. property to Robert and Mamie & they are going to put up a little house on it. Indianapolis real estate is low and hard to sell. But I can help you and will to the extent of my ability, if I can only see you and you will go over all your affairs with me fully and frankly.[15]

But it was not his father's words which caused Russell to hesitate; rather was it the fact that the several financiers with whom he had been in negotiation now expressed considerable reluctance to proceed further with Russell's schemes. He found himself with no alternative but to withdraw, and, to Harrison's inestimable relief, he returned to Helena.

However, Russell's speculative urges had yet not been entirely quenched, and one year later, (August 8, 1887), Harrison found it again necessary to pen some fatherly advice to his son:

> There is nothing for you except to meet your difficulties bravely and squarely. You had too much courage in going into debt—and must not lose your pluck when it is needed. As a lawyer I have so often seen men under pressure do things that affected their standing and character that I am anxious for you. You may lose everything you have in the way of property but if no man can say that you have done a tricky or dishonorable thing, you have still a chance to recover. Do not let any pressure of seeming necessity draw you one inch away from the line of honor and duty. You will then retain the confidence of everyone—even if they have lost money by you.[16]

Despite the ongoing mental suffering occasioned by Russell's imprudence and impetuosity in financial matters, the Harrison household was the scene of unbounded joy, when on March 15, 1887, Mamie gave birth to her parents' first grandchild, whom she named after the proud grandfather, Benjamin Harrison McKee. Harrison wrote to his cousin Mag (Margaret Peltz) on March 15:

> Mamie continues to get along nicely—no trouble of any sort. As to the baby, I told his mother to say to him that if he would be patient until the snow is gone, we would all move out on the roof and give him the house.[17]

No doubt many of Russell's sins were forgiven him when, less than a year later, on January 18, 1888, there was born to his wife, Mary, the second Harrison grandchild, this time a daughter named Marthena. There was still more bliss to come when, on the Fourth of July, 1888, Mamie gave birth to her second child, a daughter, Mary Lodge McKee.

When the Harrisons moved into the White House following the inaugural ceremonies of March, 1889, they brought along with them not only the McKees and their two children, but also Carrie's father, Dr. John W. Scott, aged 90. In due course, the family was joined by Russell's wife, Mary, and their daughter, Marthena, while Russell himself divided his time between Montana, New York, and Washington, until 1890, when his father appointed him as his secretary.

Carrie, who was not in the best of health, greatly appreciated the assistance of her daughter and daughter-in-law, but since, as mothers, they had the care of young children, one further member of the family moved in: this was Carrie's older sister, Lizzie (Mrs. Russell Lord),[18] who brought along her widowed daughter, Mrs. Mary Scott Lord Dimmick, who functioned as Carrie's secretary.

Harrison was overwhelmed by his Hoosier friends and supporters no sooner had he reached the White House. He had indiscreetly invited any visitors from his home state to call on him, and hundreds took up his suggestion; he claimed he had shaken hands with no fewer than 8,000 on the day following the inauguration, and he was grateful for the fact that his son-in-law, Bob McKee, was present to assist him by acting as guide on tours of the public rooms.

However, it was Bob McKee's infant son, Benjamin, who, as "Baby McKee," became the center of attraction of the national press during Harrison's administration. Young children at the White House had been a virtual rarity for decades, and newsmen now took advantage of every opportunity offered them to report upon the activities, antics, and exploits of young Ben, as well as of his cousin, Marthena.[19] Both received countless gifts and toys, and were forever being photographed. Ben had a pet dog named Dash, as well as a tame billy goat which was hitched to a little red wagon in which both he, Marthena, and his sister, Mary, would ride. One day when Ben was driving alone, the goat was seen by the President to be careening out of control on to the street. Harrison gave chase and, after an exhausting run, he succeeded in bringing the goat to a halt, with his grandson in an undisguised state of glee over the entire escapade. The goat's days were, however, numbered after he attacked Willis, the White House coachman, who, thereupon, presented the President with an ultimatum to the effect that either he or the goat would have to go: it was the goat which went, or at least was confined to much more restricted quarters. Harrison adored his grandchildren, and at his first Christmas in the White House, he set up the first Christmas tree ever to be placed within the mansion.

When Mrs. Cleveland had vacated the White House in March, 1889, she is reputed to have told one of the servants, "Take good care of all the furniture and ornaments in the house for I want to find everything just as it was when we come back again, four years from today." Frances Cleveland's prediction was incredibly accurate, but she did not find the White House in the same condition as she had left it.

Carrie Harrison had her own ideas of redecoration and, through her husband, she presented Congress with a plan for complete remodeling, but it proved far too ambitious, though the sum of $35,000 was voted for limited renovations.[20] Carrie was a very sensitive and artistic person. She adored flowers and the greenhouses were extended to such a degree that they could furnish, for a formal party, several thousand azaleas, hundreds of carnations, and countless orchids.

The First Lady was skilled in china painting and she herself designed the Harrison presidential china set. Finding many miscellaneous pieces of china stored in closets, it was she who initiated the White House China Collection with representative items of china from previous administrations.[21] She was active in social events at Washington and, when the organization of the Daughters of the American Revolution was being initiated, she became the first president-general of the society.

Not long after moving into the White House, Carrie slowly succumbed to tuberculosis, and died on October 25, 1892, at the age of 60. She was therefore not to know of her husband's defeat at the presidential election of November of the same year,[22] although she was sufficiently conversant with the political climate of the day to have expressed some nonsanguine expectations of his success.

Harrison's re-election campaign of the fall of 1892 had been complicated by acute differences of opinion with his former Secretary of State, James G. Blaine, who had also sought the presidential nomination. Harrison's son, Russell, had made indiscreet references to Blaine's mental and physical health, and, in turn, had been attacked in the opposition press for his unaccounted-for prosperity following his appointment as his father's secretary. There were reports of substantial gifts of stock from companies seeking government contracts, along with comments relating to his wife's fashionable mode of dress.

Harrison lost the election of 1892 to Grover Cleveland, and he confided to a colleague:

> The result is more surprising to the victor than to me. For me there is no sting in it. Indeed, after the heavy blow the death of my wife dealt me, I do not think I could have stood the strain a re-election would have brought.[23]

Be that as it may, it had, meanwhile, become evident within the family that Harrison was forming a very strong attachment to his deceased wife's niece, Mary Lord Dimmick, who had accompanied the party on the election campaign West Coast rail trip. This upset Russell so much that, after his mother's death and the election defeat, he and his wife left the White House, leaving the McKees to attend to ceremonial functions during Harrison's last months in office. It was the McKees, likewise, who accompanied Harrison back to Indianapolis in 1893 where he resumed his law practice.[24]

Russell continued to be engaged in a variety of pursuits, including involvement in the Frank Leslie publishing business in New York (where he worked on two journals: "Leslie's Weekly" and "Judge"), and in a street car system in Terre Haute, Indiana, where he became president of the transport company. In 1894, there had been rumors of a breakup in his marriage but this had been denied by his wife, who explained that she had left the marriage home temporarily only, so that she could accompany her young daughter to Hot Springs, South Dakota, for treatment of a complaint which appeared to resist normal medical remedies.

Meanwhile, Harrison made serious and definite plans for remarriage, and his proposal resulted in increasing estrangement from both his two children, Russell and Mary. On December 3, 1895, Harrison felt himself obliged to write to Russell:

> It is natural that a man's former children should not be pleased ordinarily, with a second marriage. It would not have been possible for me to marry one I did not very highly respect and very warmly love. But my life now and much more as I grow older, is and will be a very lonely one and I cannot go on as now. A home is life's essential to me and it must be the old home. Neither of my children

live here—nor are they likely to do so, and I am sure they will not wish me to live the years that remain to me in solitude.[25]

His sentiments appeared to have made no impression upon Russell, and neither he nor his sister were present at their father's second marriage ceremony on April 6, 1896, at St. Thomas's Episcopal Church in New York City; their conspicuous absence received the normal expected publicity by the press.

The newlyweds established residence at Indianapolis, and, upon observing his newly found bliss, there arose speculations as to whether Harrison might not consider presidential candidacy at the 1896 election. Harrison rejected out of hand all such suggestions, commenting: "Few of the newspaper writers seem to get on to the fact that a poor ass that is carrying three loads cannot expect to be as frisky as a led colt," and again, "I do not see anything but labor and worry and distress in another campaign, or in another term in the White House."[26]

His reference to "three loads" was opportune, since on February 21, 1897, a daughter, Elizabeth, was born to the Harrisons, he being 63, and his wife, Mary, 38. At the time of her birth, Elizabeth was younger than all four of Harrison's grandchildren.[27]

Harrison pursued an active law career, selecting only those cases which appealed to his interest, among the most important of which was his representation of Venezuela in its territorial dispute over British Guiana with Great Britain in 1899. The new Mrs. Harrison accompanied her husband to Paris where he presented the Venezuelan case before a tribunal, and although Harrison lost the decision, the couple enjoyed a relaxed six months in Europe. After their return, Harrison continued to enjoy excellent health, but then a brief illness developed into pneumonia, and he died on March 13, 1901. His two children (of the first marriage) attended the funeral service, but neither sat in the same pew as their stepmother.

One month before his death, Harrison drew up his last will and testament. He set up a trust fund of $125,000 for his second wife and her child, but he also, in the hope of effecting reconciliation, made provision for the two children of his first marriage, although one clause subsequently provoked humorous comment in the press. It read:

> If another child shall be born to me by my present wife, I give and bequeath to such child the sum of $10,000. If a boy shall be born to me he shall bear my name, and my sword and sash shall be given him instead of to my son Russell.[28]

Since no son was born, the sword and sash remained in Russell's possession.[29] The second Mrs. Harrison survived her husband by 47 years, and died on January 5, 1948, in New York City.[30]

During the Spanish-American War, Russell saw service in Cuba as well as in Puerto Rico. He was commissioned major in the inspector general's department of the U.S. Army, and, while in service, he took up the study of law and, following his discharge, he was admitted to the Indiana bar. He joined the legal firm in Indianapolis of which his father had been a member, and remained associated with it until his retirement.

Russell was consul to Mexico for almost twenty years, and he served in the Indiana State Legislature, first in the House of Representatives (1921–23), and then in the State Senate (1924–27). He mobilized support for the Spanish War veterans, an organization which he personally helped to promote, and, in 1927, he became involved in a dispute, wherein he claimed that money for veterans had been misspent for the purchase of medals. His accusations brought him before a veterans' court-martial, but Russell was vindicated.[31] He died, aged 82, at Indianapolis in December, 1936. His widow, Mary, died in November, 1944, aged 84.

Harrison's younger daughter, Elizabeth, attended Westover School in Middlebury, Connecticut. She was a very talented young lady in whom her father, had he lived to see her achievements, would have taken immense pride. She obtained a science degree from New York University, following which she enrolled in law school and eventually obtained a doctorate of Jurisprudence. In 1921 she married James Blaine Walker, a great-nephew of James G. Blaine, the occasion being described in the press as a "marked alliance of two distinguished Republican families."

Elizabeth developed interests relating to women and banking and, apart from her many public, radio, and television engagements and appearances, she was the "founder, publisher, and editor of 'Cues on the News,' a monthly news service for women investors that was distributed by banks throughout the country."[32] She died on Christmas Day, 1955.

"Baby" McKee, the idol of the White House during his grandfather's administration, also became involved in banking, in which profession he carved out for himself a very successful career. He was employed by the National City Bank of New York and he served for several years in the company's Paris office. He died in Nice in 1958.

William McKinley
and Theodore Roosevelt

(1887–1901)   (1901–1909)

There can be little doubt that the wildest, most ebullient, least inhibited family ever to occupy the White House was that of Theodore Roosevelt, his wife and six children (of two marriages). They could never have experienced a dull moment, and the individual who most enjoyed and reveled in the ongoing circus was Roosevelt himself.

The hilarious routine typical of the White House during Roosevelt's two terms of office contrasted markedly with the lugubrious atmosphere associated with its previous tenants: William and Ida McKinley.

William McKinley, Jr., was born the seventh of nine children at Niles, Ohio, in January, 1843. His father was anxious that his children should have a good education so he moved his family to Poland, Ohio, where there was an academy. McKinley went on to Allegheny College in Meadville, Pennsylvania, but was obliged to withdraw by reason of illness and lack of money.

During the Civil War, he served under Major Rutherford B. Hayes, following which he took up the study of law, and, in 1867, was admitted to the Ohio bar. He set up practice in Canton, Ohio, and it was here that he met and fell in love with Ida Saxton, the daughter of a prominent banker. They were married in January, 1871. There was great rejoicing when their first daughter, Katherine (Katie), was born on Christmas Day of the same year. A second daughter, Ida, was born on April 1, 1873, but family joy was subdued, since shortly before the birth, Ida McKinley's mother, Mrs. Saxton, passed away, and the grief became cumulative with the death of baby Ida on August 22. Worse was to follow with the death of Katie on June 25, 1875, at the age of only three years and six months. Ida McKinley never recovered from this quick succession of calamities, being thereafter physically handicapped through phlebitis, walking only with the aid of a cane, as well as being mentally depressed, and suffering from frequent attacks of petit mal which caused her to faint in public. She never regarded these attacks as being anything of an embarrassment, and never allowed them to interfere with family social engagements. McKinley adored her, and his devotion remained unabated during the remaining years of their lives together.

He found solace in politics, and was first elected as Congressman in 1876. He temporarily lost his seat in 1884, but was soon re-elected, while in 1892 he became Governor of Ohio until 1896 when he was nominated as Republican presidential candidate. He defeated William Jennings Bryan in the election of that year as well as in that of 1900.

In Washington, Ida was virtually confined to her room, but she had, as her companions, her sister, Pina Barber, and her niece, Mary Barber. To occupy her time, Ida resorted to the making of bedroom slippers and it is estimated that she completed no fewer than five thousand of them, most of which were donated to charity, along with gifts to friends and relatives.

As his Vice-President in 1896, McKinley had selected Garrett A. Hobart, a distinguished lawyer and businessman who brought great credit and prestige to his office. His wife, Jennie, was a pillar of support to Ida with regard to both her official and unofficial duties. But Hobart died in November, 1899. Had he lived, it is more than probable that McKinley would again have selected him as running mate for his second term of office—in which case Theodore Roosevelt would never have become President of the United States.[1]

During his early youth, Roosevelt had been a weak, asthmatic, short-sighted boy, whose physical handicaps had caused him to be a reticent and withdrawn personality. After suffering a beating from some street bullies, he vowed he would not allow that to happen to him ever again, and it did not. He undertook vigorous physical exercises in a small gymnasium set up in the home by his father to help his son overcome his body frailties, and, possibly by reason of overcompensation, he pursued physically demanding activities, such as arduous horse-tracking, cavalry training, and wildlife safaris, for the remainder of his life.[2]

Theodore had one brother, Elliott, and two sisters, Anna (Bamie) and Corinne. Elliott turned out to be a highly embarrassing individual to the Roosevelts since he was an alcoholic, and there was undoubtedly great relief when he died at the age of only 34.[3] Bamie had a congenital spinal defect which resulted in a stooping gait, but she had inestimable charm and was a godsend to the Theodore Roosevelt family since she was so often available for "baby-sitting" activities, even after her unexpected marriage in 1895, at the age of 40, to Lieutenant William Sheffield Cowles, naval attaché to the U.S. Embassy in London.

Corinne was three years younger than Theodore and, when the family lived in New York, her closest friend had been Edith Carow, who lived nearby. In April, 1865, Theodore, Elliott, Corinne, and Edith had together watched from a window of the Roosevelt home the long, sad, historic procession of Lincoln's funeral moving up Broadway, New York.

Theodore ("Teedie") was then nearly 7, and Edith not quite 4, and they remained playmates for years. The Roosevelts had a summer home at Oyster Bay where Edith was a regular guest, and Theodore, in time, became Edith's idol. Teedie entered Harvard in 1876, and Edith was several times invited to participate in some of the college revelries. But two years later, Teedie's father died, and for reasons never clearly understood Roosevelt formed a new attachment, this time for Alice Hathaway Lee, and they were married on his twenty-second birthday, October 27, 1880.

The shock to Edith must have been devastating: to be so flagrantly abandoned after at least fifteen years of close association. In 1882, there came another rupture in friendship with the marriage of her long-time companion, Theodore's sister, Corinne, who, in that year, married Douglas Robinson and moved out to New Jersey.

In the meantime, Theodore was advancing in his political career. After graduating from Columbia Law School, he had been elected (1881) to the New York State Assembly, but then tragedy struck twice. On St. Valentine's Day, 1884, his mother died at 3 A.M. at her New York home. At 2 P.M. on the same day, his wife, Alice, died, just two days after giving birth to their one and only child, named Alice after her mother. Theodore had been present at the death of each person, having simply passed from one bedroom to another in the same house. The overwhelming catastrophe could well have unhinged the mental stability of a less balanced personality. As it was, Theodore was beside himself in grief for a considerable period. In an attempt to escape the scene of the tragedies and yet to become reconciled with the painful events, he left Baby Alice with Bamie and went west to his Dakota ranch to seek communion with nature, and, during the winter of 1884–85, he wrote a book entitled *Hunting Trips of a Ranchman.* During the year, 1885, he renewed contact with Edith, and this time the friendship ripened into love. Seeking to avoid all publicity, Edith went to London, where she was later joined by Theodore and, on December 2, 1886, they were quietly married at St. George's Church, Hanover Square. Theodore was 28, and Edith 25. They spent a honeymoon on the French and Italian Rivieras, returning to New York at the end of March, 1887.

Thereupon, there arose the problem of the custody of Alice, now three years old. Bamie loved her young niece and would have gladly continued the task of her upbringing.[4] Theodore was, likewise, of the same opinion, but Edith was not, and she was adamant that Alice should be in the care of her father, and raised within a family; her decision was final. The result could hardly be called predictable: Theodore insisted that no reference should be made to her mother, and never once did he or his daughter ever mention her either in confidences together, or in open conversation within the family. Young Alice herself, apparently, believed for years that Edith was simply Theodore's sister and not his wife, and the overall spiritual and emotional detachment between daughter and father persisted to the end of their respective lives.

Alice came to believe that her father held her directly or indirectly responsible for her mother's death, and, years later, she sadly confided to herself in a diary that he loved his other five children far more than he did her. At the same time, she acknowledged that her stepmother had done all in her power to provide a mother's warmth and care and, for that, she (Alice) was ever grateful to her.

On September 13, 1887, Edith gave birth to her first child, a son named Theodore Jr., after his proud father; he was ever, thereafter, known as Ted. Alice described him as a "howling polly parrot." Edith had a miscarriage almost one year later, and was pregnant again during the summer of 1889. Always at this time of the year Roosevelt was away on his annual trip to the western mountains, where he spent weeks outdoors, camping, hunting, riding and fishing. Edith wrote to him from their home on Oyster Bay on one occasion:

> . . . You have been away so much I am accustomed to not seeing
> you in the house, but it has been a hopeless kind of summer to look
> back on, and all I can think of are the times you have been here. . . .
> I am trying to make Alice more of a companion. I am afraid I do
> not do rightly in not adapting myself more to her. . . . I wish I
> were gayer for the children's sake. Alice needs someone to laugh
> and romp with her instead of a sober and staid person like me. . . .[5]

Her second child and second son, Kermit, was born in October, and
this time it was young Ted who expressed an opinion: "Baby bruvver
Kermit miaows."[6]

Roosevelt had now received appointment by President Benjamin Harrison as a Civil Service commissioner[7] so that in January, 1890, he moved
the family to Washington, which pleased Edith immensely since she
could participate in the lively social activities of the capital. The year
passed quickly and pleasantly because she was taken out by Theodore to
his Elkhorn ranch in Dakota as well as to Yellowstone Park.

By the spring of 1891, Edith was again pregnant, an event which led
one of her "friends" to comment to Henry Adams that she appeared

> disgustingly pleased. . . . When I think of their very moderate
> income, and the recklessness with which she brings children into
> the world without the means either to educate them or provide for
> them I am quite worked up. . . . She will have a round dozen I am
> sure. . . . It is a shame.[8]

Edith's third child was her first daughter, Ethel, who was such a
stocky, sturdy child that Theodore, promptly but rather cruelly dubbed
her "Elephant Johnny." She was described as a "jolly, naughty, whacky
baby," packed with energy and ready to wrestle with her brothers or her
mother to get her own way.

Ted was somewhat of a delicate child, and almost died of pneumonia
contracted during his third year. He developed a squint by reason of
weakness of the eye muscles, and suffered from headaches from having to
wear spectacles. His doctors recommended an eye operation, but Edith
adamantly refused to agree. His father was very proud of his eldest son
and considered him as

> the most loving, warm-hearted gallant little fellow who ever
> breathed. . . . I often show him and Alice books; the great, illus-
> trated Milton, the *Nibelungenlied,* or hunting books; and Ted knows
> any amount of poetry from Scott to Longfellow. I tell them how I
> hunted the game whose heads are on the wall; or of Washington
> crossing the Delaware, or of Lincoln or Farragut. We have most

entrancing plays in the old barn, and climbing trees in the orchard, and go to Cooper's Bluff; Ted usually having to come back part of the way piggy-back. He wears big spectacles, which only make him look more like a brownie than ever; and delights in carrying a tin sword, at present, even in his romps. It is an awe-inspiring sight to see him, when Alice has made a nice nest in a corn-stack, take a reckless header in after her, with sword and spectacles, showing a fine disregard both of her life and his own.[9]

Kermit was a much quieter boy than Ted, and enjoyed sitting and talking peacefully to his mother. Edith became quite concerned when, at the age of four, not only did Kermit develop knee trouble necessitating a steel brace, but then Alice developed ankle weakness, likewise necessitating braces which she wore for years. Edith came to the conclusion that Roosevelt bones were congenitally impaired, since, in addition to the problems in his immediate family, Theodore's sister, Bamie, as well as his brother, Elliott's, daughter, Eleanor,[10] both suffered from spinal weaknesses.

Theodore was probably as much concerned as Edith, and his remedy was that which he had long followed for himself: ample vigorous outdoor exercise. Whether at Oyster Bay for the long summers, or at Rock Creek Park, Washington, for the rest of the year, Theodore's motto was "Over and through, never around" for his "point-to-point" excursions, and all obstacles had to be overcome head-on, irrespective of difficulty, whether they were fences, haystacks, ravines, or steep rock faces and cliffs. He taught all his children to swim at Oyster Bay by the simple process of pushing them off the pier into deep water; none of them resisted, since they were more terrified of his reprimands than of drowning—yet not one drowned, either.

Both Theodore and Edith were great readers and tellers of stories. Theodore, particularly, would rant and roar his way through the Indian wars, the Civil and Revolutionary Wars, the Viking sagas, and the newest stories by Kipling. Even though he considered Dickens to be an "ill-natured selfish cad and boor," he admired his novels and advised his children to "skip the bosh and twaddle and vulgarity, and get the benefit out of him."[11] Theodore loved to act out his stories and what the children enjoyed most was when, reminiscing about his experiences in the Wild West, he would resort to the use of a heated hatpin to brand the toy, hide-covered horses and cattle which they possessed.

Edith held Sunday school lessons for the children, and she read and re-read to them all their favorite stories. Alice was given her own special copy of the Bible, and was encouraged to study on her own one chapter a day until she had perused the entire book from Genesis through Revelation.[12] Alice was especially privileged since the Lees, her maternal relatives, provided her with a more than adequate clothing allowance. Edith expressed no objection: on the contrary, she went out of her way to buy the most expensive apparel for her stepdaughter stating: "Mrs. Lee wishes it, and I am glad as Alice is a child who needs good clothes, and would look quite as forlorn as Eleanor in makeshifts," this in reference to the daughter of Theodore's brother, Elliott.

In April, 1894, Edith gave birth to her third son, Archibald Bullock, named in honor of Theodore's maternal great-grandparent, who was President of Revolutionary Georgia. Then, one year later, Theodore resigned from the Civil Service Commission to accept an appointment as one of the four New York City police commissioners. This involved uprooting the family once again, and back they all went to New York. Nostalgic memories of former city life were revived for both Edith and Theodore, since among their children's new tutors was their own dear Mr. Dodsworth, the dancing master, who had given them many years earlier their basic instructions on the dance floor.

Theodore continued to find relief from his work as police commissioner among his children. He wrote to Bamie:

> I wish you could see [the boys'] costumes, especially Kermit's; he wears the blue overalls, which are perhaps the finest triumph of Edith's genius, and which are precisely like those of our hired man, with a cap like that of a of second-rate French cook, a pair of shabby tennis shoes, and, as his hands are poisoned [from ivy], a pair of exceedingly dirty kid gloves. When, in this costume, turning somersaults on the manure heap, he is indeed a joy forever.[13]

His son, Ted, now nine, was the first of the children to attend a public school, in his case, Cove Neck School, where he settled in quite comfortably and happily. Archie was considered to be the "prettiest of the family," while Ethel, still robust and plump, loved horseriding wearing bloomers "which did double duty as a place to store vast quantities of apples." Theodore described young Archie as having "lots of character, all of it bad."[14]

Becoming disillusioned with his work as commissioner, Roosevelt once again sought new pastures. While he expressed little private respect for McKinley,[15] nevertheless Roosevelt gave him public support during the election campaign of 1896, and, in due course, he received his due reward by being appointed as Assistant Secretary of the Navy, which entailed a move back to Washington. No sooner was this accomplished than Edith gave birth in November, 1897, to her fifth (and last) child, her fourth son, Quentin, named in honor of her grandfather, Isaac Quentin Carow. She told Henry Cabot Lodge, "Now I have five boys," (to include her husband), but Lodge was scarcely impressed and he, only with "gloomy reluctance," attended Quentin's christening ceremony for it was "against his principle to sanction anything so antimalthusian as a sixth child."[16]

1898 proved an eventful year for the family since, in March, Edith underwent an operation for an abdominal abscess. Alice, now a rambunctious 14 year old, and, being in "the habit of running the streets uncontrolled with every boy in town" was sent to Bamie in New York.[17] She complained that living with Bamie, a strict disciplinarian, was worse than being in a boarding school, and Edith tersely replied that that was precisely why she had been sent there.[18]

On February 15, 1898, the U.S. battleship *Maine* had blown up in Havana harbor. Theodore resigned from the navy department, organized his "Rough Riders," and rode up San Juan (Kettle) Hill on July 1. No sooner had he returned home in August than he was nominated for Governor of New York and was duly elected in the November election, an event which once more entailed a family move, this time to Albany.

Here, the Governor's mansion was a large spacious building to which the children immediately brought their pets from Oyster Bay. These included rabbits, hamsters, and guinea pigs, the latter being provided with the names of real people, such as Admiral Dewey, Fighting Bob Evans, Bishop Doane, and Father O'Grady. There was also Alice's bear, named Jonathan Edwards (after Edith's ancestor), since, according to Theodore, it showed "a distinctly Calvinistic turn of mind."[19] She later owned a macaw bird, dubbed Elihu (Eli) Yale "with a bill that could bite through a dinner plate."

The spaciousness of the mansion not only pleased the children, but the new Governor as well. Hitherto, town houses in Washington and New York had been small and restrictive, but the new residence virtually offered the same advantages as Oyster Bay, and Roosevelt promptly resorted to the wild frolicking activities characteristic of the summer home. On one occasion, a visitor was astonished to see the Governor lowering his children by rope to the ground, one by one, from a second-story window. The explanation turned out to be that an "attack" upon the mansion by Indians on the warpath made it essential for the occupants to escape in a hurry.

As Governor, Roosevelt emerged as a most controversial personality, and succeeded in irritating almost everyone within range, most of all the members of his own Republican party. Its leader, Senator Thomas Platt, encapsulated their sentiments in his open declaration: "I want to get rid of the bastard. I don't want him raising hell in my state any more." So it was, that, at the Republican Convention of 1900 held in Philadelphia, Platt maneuvered the strongest possible support for Roosevelt as Vice-President on the McKinley ticket.

Republicans, generally, were confused by having to weigh the advantages of having an exuberant, volatile, nationally recognized personality on the party ticket, against the disadvantages succinctly compressed in Mark Hanna's[20] rhetorical question: "Don't any of you realize there's only one life between this madman and the White House?"

His remark proved prophetic: that "one life" was terminated by the bullets of the self-proclaimed anarchist, Leon Czolgosz, on September 6, 1901, at the Buffalo Exposition. McKinley died on September 14,[21] and on that day Theodore Roosevelt took the oath of office as twenty-sixth President of the United States.[22]

Roosevelt, at age 42, was the nation's youngest President to date. He brought with him to the White House his second wife and their five children, along with Alice, the child of his first marriage. The ages of his children ranged from 3 to 17 years, and, judging from their behavior it is much less than certain that any of them, eight years later, when Roosevelt relinquished his office, had the slightest idea that, for those memorable years, they were in any way privileged to have resided in the nation's most prestigious home, or that their father occupied their country's most honored status.

Roosevelt's fmaily was the largest to live at the White House since the days of Garfield's brief residence thirty years earlier. The exploits and escapades of the President's children were to provide more than ample "copy" for the nation's press during Roosevelt's two terms of office, and all this, in addition to the reporting of the pyrotechnic activities of the most irrepressible, impetuous, and boisterous personality ever to occupy the office of President of the United States.

Some indication of what lay in the future was provided on the very day of Roosevelt's first inauguration, when Quentin, aged 3, flatly refused to go to hear his father "pray at the Senate," and declared that, if forced to attend, he would talk loudly throughout the ceremony. Edith had the good sense to capitulate and leave him at home. Ted, the eldest son who was 14, literally wore a three-piece suit, each piece belonging to a different suit, while later on the same day he drank several glasses of champagne in mistake for fizz-drink, but apparently without any noticeable ill-effect—which prompted Edith to remark that the incident "spoke

volumes either for Ted's head or the President's champagne."[23] It is little
wonder that Ike Hoover, the White House usher, was later led to comment that the advent of the Roosevelts marked the "wildest scramble in
history."

Upon occupation of the presidential mansion, the whole menagerie of
animals from Oyster Bay and Albany was transferred in. The White
House had served for countless years as a residence for the varied pets of
the children of Presidents, but its past functions in this respect were
nothing compared to what may only be described as the Barnum and
Bailey circus atmosphere which prevailed during the entire period of the
Roosevelt regime. Apart from the usual range of white mice, hamsters
and dogs, there were several cats, the best known of which was Tom
Quartz, whose most famous exploit was to lie in wait on the grand
staircase and pounce upon the ankles of Mr. Cannon, Speaker of the
House, "an exceedingly solemn elderly gentleman with chin whiskers."
Describing the episode to Kermit, his father wrote that Tom

> jumped to the conclusion that he was a playmate escaping and raced
> after him, suddenly grasping him by the leg . . . then loosening his
> hold he tore downstairs ahead of Mr. Cannon who eyed him with
> iron calm and not one particle of surprise.[24]

An equally famous episode was that relating to Archie's pint-size
pony, Algonquin. When Archie succumbed to measles and was confined
to his bedroom, the children succeeded in smuggling the animal into the
White House, and transported him via the elevator into Archie's room to
his immense comfort, delight, and quick recovery. Then there was Alice's
snake, named Emily Spinach, whom she kept in a handbag for the
specific purpose of releasing it among a crowd of respectable but unsuspecting visitors. In his turn, Kermit had a Kangaroo rat as his special
pet, which he kept in his pocket. He was wont to release it on to the
dining table when guests were present, and the overall consensus of
opinion was that meals at the White House were very little removed from
the March Hare's tea party.

With such demands made upon her to subdue and control her unpredictable progeny, it was Edith who first engaged a social secretary to the
First Lady. Then, by dint of persistent persuasion (via her husband) she
succeeded in persuading Congress to allocate a substantial sum of money
for much-needed renovations and additional space at the White House.
The conservatories and greenhouses were removed to provide for new
executive rooms, thus permitting the former offices to be used for the
family. The only problem lay in the fact that Roosevelt insisted that the

project be completed within a limited time,[25] in consequence of which, less than half a century later, the mansion as in a state of collapse, and, during Truman's administration, it was completely restructured internally.

For the children, the White House and its precincts were nothing short of paradise. They cycled and roller-skated both inside as well as outside. They stilt-walked along the corridors and, when tired of routine games, they invented a new one which consisted of climbing the lampposts along Pennsylvania Avenue and putting out the gaslights almost as soon as the lamplighter had passed by.

The family had some relief when Ted and Kermit were sent to Groton, and Ethel was enrolled as a Monday-to-Friday boarder at the Cathedral School in Woodley Street, Washington. The intention was also that Alice should be sent away to school, but, if her parents persisted, she threatened to do something drastic, drastic enough to put herself in gaol, she said. Well aware that Alice was indeed fully capable of such action, she was permitted by her father and stepmother to remain at home.[26]

The event of the year 1902 was the coming-out reception for Alice, almost eighteen, a few days after the President's first New Year's reception (when Roosevelt claimed he shook 8,000 hands). She was the first daughter of a President to be privileged with a debut in the executive mansion; she was now the White House Belle, and she revelled in all the attention and publicity accorded her in the press.[27] In 1903, she received an invitation (brought by Prince Henry of Prussia) from the German Emperor to christen his new yacht, which was being completed at Shooter's Island, New York. She accepted, named the yacht, "Meteor," and was duly presented with a diamond bracelet, a gift from the Kaiser, by his brother. Speculation became rife as to whether or not a marriage proposal by Prince Henry was to be anticipated, but, while the public may have been disappointed at the negative outcome, the event led to the "christening" of the President's daughter herself as "Princess Alice."

The euphoric atmosphere engendered by the endless gaiety, pomp, and array, was somewhat rudely dampened by the President himself, when Alice, having received an invitation from the U.S. Ambassador in London to attend the coronation of Edward VII, was refused permission to do so. She was understandably furious, but her father was adamant, sensing the adverse publicity that might accrue to the family were it to be over-associated with European royalty.[28]

With his two sons away at school, Roosevelt now found it necessary to keep in touch with each of them by letter. While, with all his energetic activities, it might have been concluded that he would stress the need for physical prowess and achievement upon his offspring, such was not the case. Writing to Kermit in October, 1903, he stated:

I would rather have a boy of mine stand high in his studies than high in athletics, but I would a great deal rather have him show true manliness of character than show either intellectual or physical prowess.[29]

And, soon after, he wrote this to Ted:

Athletic proficiency is a mighty good servant, and like so many other good servants, a mighty bad master. Did you ever read Pliny's letter to Trajan, in which he speaks of its being advisable to keep the Greeks absorbed in athletics, because it distracted their minds from all serious pursuits, including soldiering, and prevented their ever being dangerous to the Romans.[30]

Surprisingly enough, also, Roosevelt, never one to place in low key the spectacular deeds of himself and his Rough Riders at San Juan (Kettle) Hill, expressed concern over Ted's aspirations to embark upon a military career. He virtually accused his son of wishing to enlist because "you would then have a definite and settled career in life and hope to go on steadily without any great hope of failure," adding that this "may betray lack of confidence," and that, on the contrary, "I have great confidence in you. . . . I believe you have the ability, and above all, the energy, the perseverance, and the common sense, to win out in civil life."[31]

In lighter vein, Roosevelt would often recount incidents which occurred during some of his vigorous physical exercises at the White House, as, for example, playing "single stick" with General Leonard Wood[32] resulting in a bruised eye and swollen wrist; or undergoing bouts with two Japanese wrestlers three times a week:

. . . My throat is a little sore because once when one of them had a stranglehold I also got hold of his windpipe and thought I could perhaps choke him off before he could choke me. However, he got ahead. . . .[33]

Again, he would describe the events of the day including some of the quaint sayings of Quentin: when the latter was asked by a reporter about some of the activities of the President, the boy (aged 7) answered, "Yes, I see him sometimes, but I know nothing of his family life." Quentin's eighth birthday party held on November 19, 1905, proved to be quite a hectic affair, since his brother, Archie, brought along his entire football team, and, as described by Roosevelt:

. . . we had obstacle races, hide and go seek, blind man's buff, and everything else; and there were times when I felt that there was a perfect shoal of small boys bursting in every direction up and down stairs, and through and over every conceivable object.[34]

Roosevelt was elected President in his own right in November, 1904, and the family settled down to four more years of occupancy of the White House.[35] Two social events colored the year 1905, the first being the wedding of Edith's "ugly duckling," Eleanor Roosevelt, to her cousin, Franklin Delano Roosevelt[36] on St. Patrick's Day, March 17. She was given away by her uncle, Theodore, who so dominated the proceedings that Alice was led to comment that her father wanted to be "the bride at every wedding and the corpse at every funeral."

The second event, or more correctly, series of events, concerned Alice herself. One of the newest attractions on the Washington scene was the arrival of the very eligible bachelor Congressman from Cincinnati, Ohio, Nicholas (Nick) Longworth. Longworth, 34, was a Harvard Law School graduate, an accomplished violinist, yet something of a balding, moustached dandy who could drink and play poker all night. One of his lady friends had been Marguerite,[37] who may have come to regret the fact that it was she who introduced him to Alice, since, thereafter, it appeared that he had eyes only for the vivacious twenty-one-year-old daughter of the President.[38]

Roosevelt sent William Howard Taft, his Secretary of War, on an official tour of the Far East.[39] Alice was included in the party, in part to compensate for her father's refusal to allow her to go to the coronation of Edward VII. Also included was Representative Nick Longworth in his capacity as member of the House Foreign Affairs Committee. The press made the most of the entire visit, which was recorded in every detail, including reports that Alice had been invited by the Sultan of Sula to become the seventh wife in his harem; that Alice almost missed the boat at Honolulu, and that she jumped into the deckpool fully clothed, but, despite all the excitement and hilarity, there was no announcement of the fully expected betrothal. When, on several occasions, she was accosted by Taft, "I think I ought to know if you are engaged to Nick," Alice gave the simple answer "More or less, Mr. Secretary, more or less."[40] However, within two months of her arrival home in October, 1905, her engagement to Nick was formally announced, and the wedding set for February 17, 1906. It took place in the East Room of the White House, and Alice was given away by her father.[41] She insisted on having no bridesmaids, so that the focus of attention would be entirely upon her; Nick, however, had no fewer than six groomsmen. There were hundreds of guests, and they included Ellen Grant (Sartoris), who had been a White House bride thirty-two years earlier. The honeymoon was spent first in Cuba and then the couple went to Europe where they were guests of Kings and Queens and Presidents.

They received wedding gifts from all over the world including a priceless Gobelin tapestry from France, and a $25,000 pearl necklace from Cuba. When, within the United States itself, there arose the proposal to raise nearly a million dollars by ten-cent subscriptions, it was immediately vetoed by Roosevelt, an action which considerably incensed Alice, who is reported to have stated: "I'll accept anything but a red-hot stove."[42]

Ethel made her debut on December 28, 1908, when she was 17. The celebration was elaborate, but it drew far less attention than that of Alice's. Ethel enjoyed party-going but, being very much more of a tomboy, preferring games with her brothers, she disliked the chore of dressing up in fashionable costumes. She taught a Sunday school class of colored children at St. Mary's Chapel, Washington, and played the organ at the family church in Oyster Bay.

Ted, the eldest son, after attending Groton, and then studying under a private tutor, had entered Harvard in the fall of 1905 where his indifferent grades caused his father no little concern. He then developed eye trouble which required an operation, but he made a good recovery and returned to graduate. Of all the sons, he most resembled his father in physical appearance, one reporter commenting that

> . . . the only difference is that Teddy, Jr. is older in his ways than Teddy, Sr. There is a popular impression at Oyster Bay that Little Teddy was close to forty years when he was born. He is the philosopher of the Roosevelt family—calm and dignified always.[43]

Having graduated, Ted was uncertain as to what he should do, but then, as Roosevelt wrote in a letter,

> As soon as he left Harvard he had gone into a mill, had worked with blouse and tin dinner pail, exactly like any other workman for a year; and when he graduated from the mill, had gone out for the same firm to San Francisco, where he was selling carpets.[44]

His prospects markedly improved when he married the daughter of the company's president and chief stockholder.

Kermit was an introspective young boy who exhibited little interest in sport although he enjoyed cycling. He did not make friends too readily, and Edith said of him: "Very few outsiders care for him, but if they like him at all they like him very much." He was fond of books as well as of the outdoor life, and, while still at school, he spent a summer camping out with the 13th Cavalry.

Archie followed his brothers to Groton, and, when this happened in the fall of 1907, Quentin, the youngest, was left all alone, although not for long. Roosevelt had once written:

> What a heavenly place a sandbox is for two little boys! Archie and Quentin play industriously in it during most of their spare moments when out in the grounds . . . arranging caverns or mountains with runways for their marbles.[45]

Now that Archie had left home, Quentin imported his school and other friends to the White House to form a gang, one of whom had three uncles who had belonged to the similar group formed thirty-five years earlier by Jesse Grant, while another was Charlie Taft, who had become Quentin's bosom friend.[46] In letters to Archie, Roosevelt described many of the antics of the gang members including one (which he just managed to prevent), which involved Quentin's plan to release sulphuretted hydrogen on the boys when they were asleep in bed. On yet another occasion, the fond father was far from being amused when he found that the boys had flung spitballs at the portrait of Andrew Jackson. He hauled the sleeping Quentin out of bed and did not let him return until he had removed them all from the painting.

Roosevelt wrote in 1908:

> I like to see Quentin practicing baseball. It gives me hopes that one of my boys will not take after his father in this respect, and will prove able to play the national game![47]

He also began to realize that he was not quite as young as he was when he first entered the White House. He joined in the games of the gang but "it made me realize how old I had grown" and that "they had grown so I was not needed in the play."[48]

In due course, Quentin also entered Groton, but before that time he had been enrolled at the age of 9 at the Force School in Washington. Here his teacher, Miss Virginia Arnold, found him more than a handful, and she complained in writing to the President who promptly replied:

> Dear Miss Arnold,
>   I thank you for your note about Quentin. Don't you think it would be well to subject him to stricter discipline? . . . Mrs. Roosevelt and I have no scruples whatever against corporal punishment. . . . I do not think I ought to be called in merely for such

offences as dancing when coming into the classroom, for singing higher than the other boys, or for failure to work as he should at his examples, or for drawing pictures instead of doing his sums. . . . If you find him defying your authority or committing any serious misdeeds let me know and I will whip him. . . .[49]

Quentin's exploits were both legion and legendary, and they provided his father and mother with a fund of stories which they faithfully recorded in their letters and diaries.

Roosevelt would have liked to have served yet one more term of office, but, four years earlier, he had made a statement (which he had come to regret) to the effect that he would not seek re-election. Consequently, his own nominee, William Howard Taft, was elected in November, 1908, and the months remaining before the latter's inauguration were spent by the Roosevelts in packing their accumulated belongings of eight years residence.

At the last Thanksgiving dinner, a pig was supplied by Quentin, who went himself to procure it from the slaughterhouse. The family was together for Christmas and, three days later, an elaborate coming-out ball was held in honor of Ethel.

Roosevelt planned to leave the country immediately after Taft's inauguration. He arranged to go on a year's safari in East Africa accompanied by Kermit. They stayed for the inaugural ceremony itself, when Quentin stood side by side with Charlie Taft, but then left immediately en route, first for Oyster Bay. Alice was very irritated, not only with her father for not seeking re-election, but also with Mrs. Taft. The latter had sent her a ticket for the inaugural ball to ensure her admittance, since she had gone to the railroad station to see her parents off by train. But Alice deplored the fact that *"I* was going to be allowed to have a ticket to permit *me* to enter the White House—*I*—a very large capital *I*—who had wandered in and out for eight happy winters."[50]

On March 23, 1909, Roosevelt and Kermit left Oyster Bay and embarked on the S.S. *Hamburg*. The expedition was exceptionally well prepared, not only with a more than adequate supply of appropriate clothing, weaponry, and ammunition, a library of sixty books in pigskin covers to ensure protection from the weather, but also with experienced big-game hunters from England, and natural science experts from the Smithsonian Institution. *Scribner's Magazine* donated $50,000 in return for exclusive articles by the ex-President.

Landing in Mombasa, Roosevelt hired 240 native porters and gun carriers, and the expedition moved inland to the uplands of Tanganyika and Kenya where its participants slaughtered thousands of animals, birds, and snakes, many of which were preserved for the Smithsonian by its taxidermist, as well as by Roosevelt and Kermit, who were skilled and proficient in the same art.

During the summer of 1909, Edith sailed for Europe accompanied by Ethel, Archie, and Quentin. They stayed in Italy with Emily, Edith's sister, for a short while, and after Archie and Quentin returned in September to attend school, Edith and Ethel toured Italy and Switzerland before they, too, returned home in November.

In March, 1910, Edith and Ethel again set sail, this time for Egypt and the Sudan, where, at Khartoum, they were joined by Roosevelt and Kermit who had traveled downstream on the Nile from East Africa. The family party next proceeded on a tour of Western Europe, when Roosevelt took the opportunity of belatedly collecting his Nobel Prize[51] at Christiana (Oslo), Norway.

In May, 1910, King Edward VII of England died, and Taft requested Roosevelt to represent his country as special ambassador at the funeral. This was attended by no fewer than nine reigning sovereigns, an event which led Roosevelt to remark that "I felt that if I met another monarch I should bite him."[52] Alice, who had been refused permission to attend the deceased King's coronation, came to London to attend his funeral, but her presence passed virtually without comment. The entire Roosevelt entourage finally returned to New York on June 18th, 1910. They were met by Archie and Quentin, as well as by Ted and his fiancee, Eleanor Butler Alexander, who had announced their engagement just before Edith had left for Egypt. Two days later, the young couple were joined in holy matrimony at the Fifth Avenue Presbyterian Church, New York, (where 500 gallery seats had been reserved for Roosevelt's Rough Riders). Ted was still in business, but was rising rapidly up the executive ladder of the Hartford Carpet Company by whom he was employed.

Archie, now 16, had given the family some cause for concern since he had been expelled from Groton for writing a letter highly critical of the headmaster. He had been relocated at a school in Arizona, so Roosevelt, at a loose end, went to see him and together they rode down the Grand Canyon. Roosevelt went on to dedicate the dam named in his honor.

Quentin, growing up quickly, was doing exceptionally well at Groton, and his father described him as "an affectionate, soft-hearted, overgrown puppy kind of boy, absorbed in his wireless and in anything mechanical,"[53] the latter including automobile and motorcycle engines. In time, he also became editor of the school magazine.

Roosevelt had become disillusioned with Taft who, wishing to determine his own destiny, had rejected most of Roosevelt's advisors and their recommendations; these actions prompted Roosevelt to declare political war on Taft for his lack of gratitude, stating "My hat is in the ring, the fight is on, and I am stripped to the buff." He added, "We stand at Armageddon and we battle for the Lord." But he lost the Republican nomination at the Chicago Convention of 1912, and, thereupon, accepted the nomination of the Progressive party, announcing himself as being "as fit as a bullmoose." While campaigning in Milwaukee he was shot at by an assassin, but was saved by his spectacle case which deflected the bullet from his heart. He easily defeated Taft at the presidential election in November, but the split Republican vote permitted Woodrow Wilson's victory. Nick Longworth, a Taft supporter, had found himself in an embarrassing situation, in consequence of which, after five terms as Congressman, he lost his seat, and to the great annoyance of Alice, they were obliged to leave Washington for Ohio.

Ted's marriage in 1910 appeared to have unsettled him somewhat, and he decided to quit his job in San Francisco to seek new opportunities on Wall Street. It was in New York in August, 1911, that his wife, Eleanor, gave birth to a daughter, Grace, the Roosevelts' first grandchild. The young family spent much of their time at Sagamore Hill, and, later Eleanor was to write a hilarious description of life at Oyster Bay:

> Something was going on every minute of the day. The house was always full of people. . . . At first I thought everyone would be tired when the day was over and would go to bed early, but I soon found out nothing of the kind could be expected. The Roosevelt family enjoyed life too much to waste time sleeping. Every night they stayed downstairs until nearly midnight; then, talking at the top of their voices, they trooped up the wide uncarpeted stairs and went to their rooms. For a brief moment all was still, but just as I was going off to sleep for the second time they remembered things they had forgotten to tell one another and ran shouting through the halls. . . . By six the younger ones were up, and by seven I was the only one who was not joyously beginning the day.[54]

With one son returning to the family fold, the Roosevelts now lost one—this time, Kermit, who after graduating from Harvard, had accepted an executive post in South America with the Brazil Railroad Company. Ethel was to have paid him a visit early in 1913, but her mother raised objections, and, instead, Ethel decided to get married to Richard Derby, a New York doctor, who originally hailed from Massachusetts. The wedding took place at Christ Church, Oyster Bay, on April 4, and the married couple left for Europe for their honeymoon.

Not long afterwards, they were joined by Edith, who had received word that her sister, Emily, was to undergo an appendix operation at Lausanne, Switzerland. After Emily's recovery, Edith, Ethel and Dick sailed home together in August.

His election defeat had made Roosevelt more discontented and frustrated than ever, and, as in 1909, he had taken off for Africa after his tenure at President, so, in 1913, he decided upon another adventure expedition, again with Kermit, this time to the Amazon Valley, to explore the course of an unmapped river. Kermit had quit his job with the railroad company to take up a position with a bridge-building firm which had granted him leave of absence. The expedition was far more rigorous and hazardous than father and son had anticipated, but as Roosevelt stated, "I had to go. It was my last chance to be a boy."

Nothing was heard of the party for four months, and, during that time, its members were sick with jungle fever, Roosevelt suffered leg injuries, and lost almost sixty pounds in weight. But they accomplished what they set out to do, and the former "River of Doubt" was renamed "Rio Roosevelt." Kermit described their experiences in a later book entitled *The Happy Hunting Grounds,* while he himself was described by his father in a letter to Edith:

> . . . Kermit is his own mother's son. He is to me a delightful companion, he always has books with him, and he is a tireless worker. He is not only an exceptionally good and hard hunter, but as soon as he comes in he starts at his photographs or else at the skins, working as hard as the two naturalists. . . .[55]

At the outset of their journey, Roosevelt and Kermit had been accompanied on the sea voyage by Edith, and they had proceeded leisurely along the east coast of South America. At Buenos Aires, Kermit was ecstatic upon the receipt of a cable from a young lady, Belle Willard, who therein stated that she agreed to marry him. Belle was one of Ethel's friends, and she had been described by Edith as the "Fair One with Golden Locks." Her father was the American Ambassador to Spain, so that upon Kermit's return to civilization, he immediately embarked for Madrid, followed closely by Roosevelt and Alice who came to attend the wedding which took place on May 30, 1914.

Earlier in the same year, Ethel had given birth to her first child, Richard, while Alice's Grandmother Lee had died in January, leaving Alice with an annual income exceeding ten thousand dollars a year. The Longworths apparent renewal of good fortune was capped by Nick's re-election to Congress in November, so his resentment against his father-in-law's maverick political behavior measurably subsided.

At the outbreak of World War I in Europe, General Leonard Wood set up a military training camp for volunteers at Plattsburg, N.Y., in which Ted, Archie, and Quentin enrolled. At this time, Kermit was in South America working for the City National Bank. His son, also named Kermit (Kim), was born there in 1916. As the involvement of the United States became more imminent, Ted encouraged his wife to raise a battalion of 1200 women who, including Edith, marched in a New York procession headed by an enormous banner, "Independent Patriotic Women of America."

On April 6, 1917, the United States issued a declaration of war against Germany, and Roosevelt immediately requested permission to head a division of troops to Europe, but his request was refused. Ted and Archie[56] sailed to France in June, while Kermit, to avoid camp training delays, volunteered to serve with the British Army, and was despatched to Mesopotamia. Quentin, despite his weak eyesight and a back injury sustained in Arizona when his horse rolled over him, was found a place in the U.S. Air Force through the manipulations of his father, but before leaving for Europe, he had introduced to his parents his girl friend, Flora (Foufie) Payne Whitney, 20-year-old daughter of Harry and Gertrude Vanderbilt Whitney, and heiress to an immense fortune derived from oil, tobacco, and real estate.

In November, 1917, Dick Derby was in Europe with the American Medical Corps, leaving Nick Longworth as the only male member of the extended Roosevelt family not in uniform.

The Roosevelts, isolated in Sagamore Hill, were comforted by their daughters-in-law and, by 1918, their no fewer than eight grandchildren, so they all shared the news of the military activities of their sons and son-in-law. Ted, commissioned first as a major, then lieutenant-colonel, was wounded and gassed at the battle of Soissons. He was awarded the Distinguished Service Medal, the Distinguished Service Cross, and received decorations from both France and Belgium. Archie, a captain, badly wounded in the knee and arm, was awarded the Croix de Guerre, and invalided home in September, 1918.

Kermit received the British Military Cross for gallantry before being transferred from Mesopotamia to France to join the American Expeditionary Force, in which, as captain, he later served under his brother, Ted, a lieutenant-colonel.

Quentin had received assignment as flying instructor at Issoudon, and was piqued at the fact that, while all his brothers had participated in active combat, his role appeared to be that of a passive observer. Edith had suggested that Quentin should ask Flora to go to France where they could marry, a suggestion which very much pleased him, since it clearly indicated that his Mother "had passed the fact that (Flora) was one of the Whitneys and powdered her nose"[57]—a reference to the fact that Edith had, earlier, expressed disapproval for Quentin's association with what she considered to be the fast-living multi-millionaire family. Flora was unable to go since her request for a passport was refused. In June, Quentin was transferred to Orly Airport for active duty, and he wrote to his family that he had been involved in his first "dogfight" on July 5, and had brought down an enemy plane a few days later. But within less than two weeks, news was received that Quentin himself had been shot down over enemy territory. He was buried by the Germans with full military honors, and the shattered propeller and the wheels of his plane were placed upon his grave.

Roosevelt and Edith were prostrated with grief at the loss of their beloved youngest son, yet, true to the Roosevelt tradition, they faced the tragedy with typical stoicism. Edith was forced to recall a much earlier statement of hers that "You cannot bring up boys as eagles and expect them to turn out sparrows," while Theodore, within two days of receiving the news, was on his way to keep a prior commitment to address the Republican State Convention in Saratoga.

On October 27, 1918, Theodore celebrated his sixtieth birthday. He told his sister Corinne, "I have kept a promise that I made to myself when I was 21—that I would work up to the hilt until I was 60, and I have done it." He had campaigned for the Republican party in the election of November, 1918, and the party recorded gains in both the House and Senate. But he was tiring rapidly, much more rapidly than his family had believed, and he, himself, had been warned that he might soon be confined to a wheelchair for the rest of his days. But that was not to be: in the early hours of January 6, 1919, he died peacefully in his sleep. Archie cabled to his two brothers in France the simple but adequate statement: "The Old Lion is Dead."

With the removal from the earthly scene of the patriarch, and the return to the seemingly lesser challenges of peacetime existence, the Roosevelt family appeared to have found life increasingly boring, and actively pursued means to make it less intolerable.

Edith traveled abroad almost annually over the next twenty years, seeking to avoid living so intimately with the many memories of Sagamore Hill. She went to France and arranged for a fountain to be erected at her expense at the village of Chamery, where Quentin lay buried, and later, at Groton, she dedicated in his name a memorial alcove where boys could study.

During the winter months of 1919–20, she accompanied Kermit to South America where he was to serve as representative of the American Ship and Commerce Corporation, while, two years later, she was again with him on a several month voyage around the world.[58]

Her eldest son, Ted, had, upon his return home[59] after the war, decided to enter politics, and in November, 1919, he had been elected as member of the New York State Assembly. In 1921, President Harding appointed him as Assistant Secretary of the Navy, as his father had been before him, but this proved to be an unfortunate assignment. Ted was only 34, and he became unfairly associated with the machinations of his superior officer, Secretary of the Navy Edwin Denby, in the Teapot Dome Scandal. Denby had transferred Navy Oil Reserve leases to the jurisdiction of the Department of the Interior, where Secretary Albert B. Fall had, thereupon, made the leases available for exploitation to private interests,[60] for which services he had received at least $125,000.

In 1924, Ted quit his post and ran for governor against Democrat Al Smith, the incumbent. During the campaign, his cousin, Eleanor, (wife of Franklin D. Roosevelt, now a Democrat)[61] toured the constituencies making speeches against Ted in a specially constructed truck shaped like a tea-pot, and, in one of her speeches, Eleanor declared:

> Of course, Mr. Roosevelt is a young man who is personally honest, he has a fine war record but very little political experience, and his record in the public service shows him willing to listen to his friends and do as he is told.[62]

Ted lost the election, and, during the course of the next five years, he was without a regular position so he traveled extensively in Asia, either on his own initiative, or sponsored by the Chicago Field Museum of Natural History, in company with Kermit. In 1928, they were both in Burma where they succeeded in returning with a giant panda along with several thousand smaller stuffed animals for display in the museum.[63]

A new but brief career opened for Ted in 1929, when President Coolidge appointed him as Governor of Puerto Rico, where his genuinely good intentions to assist in the alleviation of the appalling poverty on the island met growing resistance from the wealthy and influential sections of the community. In January, 1932, President Hoover selected him as Governor-General of the Philippines. Here, even worse conditions prevailed, and Ted became increasingly frustrated. In November of the same year, Franklin D. Roosevelt was elected President and, when Ted was asked by a reporter as to the exact relationship between himself and Franklin, he wittily responded that he was the latter's fifth cousin "about to be removed." He tendered his resignation, which was accepted. Upon his return to the United States, he ventured upon several unsuccessful business projects, but, in due course, he became an executive officer in a book publishing company.[64]

In 1938, Ted and his wife, tiring of living in rented accommodations for over twenty years, decided upon building a home of their own. It had been accepted by the family that the property of Sagamore Hill would be bequeathed to Ted, but Edith, now 77, was still in occupation, so Ted built a new house nearby. A year later, Edith's sister, Emily, died in Italy, and Ted inherited her house, the belongings of which were shared between himself and his sister, Ethel.

Following upon his world travels and expeditions in company either with his mother or his brother, Ted, during the decade of the 1920's, Kermit found increasing difficulty in settling down. He was fond of book learning and he wrote several works including *War in the Garden of Eden, The Happy Hunting Ground,* and *Trailing the Great Panda,* but these brought him little income, and, since he had a wife and four children to support, he was obliged to find more remunerative work.

Employment with a shipping company permitted him to travel, but he became depressed, was never in good health,[65] and he began drinking heavily as well as associating with women "outside his own class" for the most part (one was a masseuse)—much as his Uncle Elliott had done.[66] He underwent several treatments for alcoholism, but none were permanent cures. He was somewhat of a further embarrassment to his family since he was its only member to associate with F D.R., and Kermit and Belle were often guests of the President on fishing cruises.[67]

Archie, like Ted, had been involved with the Sinclair Oil Company, and Edith had accompanied him to Europe in 1922 on one of his business trips. He was associated with several other companies, but he suffered considerable financial losses during the Depression years. With four children to support, he and his wife, Grace, decided upon opening a small private school for children, aged 10 to 16, in the garage adjoining his home. While he supervised the entire undertaking, Grace functioned as its principal. It was a successful venture in more respects than one, since Archie educated all three of his daughters in the little institution.[68]

By 1920, Ethel had given birth to three children, Richard, Edie, and Sarah Alden, but, two years later, Richard, always a delicate child, died of tuberculosis at the age of 8. In the meantime, Dick Derby had accepted a position on the staff of the Long Island Insane Asylum, and the family had moved to the "Old Adam House" which they proceeded to renovate, and which was located only four miles away from Sagamore and Edith, whom they visited regularly.

The death of her father in 1919 in no way diminished Alice's zest for political commentary. She detested Wilson, and gave loud-voiced support for Republicans who were determined not to ratify the Versailles Peace Treaty. One group became known as the Battalion of Death, and, since Alice made her home its welcome base for activities in Washington, she became known as the Colonel of Death.[69]

At their national convention of 1920, the Democrats selected James M. Cox as their presidential nominee, with Franklin D. Roosevelt as his running mate. The Oyster Bay Roosevelts now openly declared F D.R. to be a traitor to the family political tradition, and they campaigned vigorously for Harding, who was elected Republican President in November of the same year. Alice's husband, Nick, was re-elected, and the Longworths were ensured of a further term of enjoyment of Washington society, which, *inter alia,* flagrantly ignored the precepts of the Eighteenth Amendment: the White House set the precedent, with alcoholic drinks being made freely available on most occasions. The Longworths brewed their own beer, distilled their own gin, and fermented their own grapes— all on the premises, whenever external sources were in short supply.

By 1924, Alice's ambitions were such that she entertained fond hopes that Nick might be the Republican presidential nominee, but the incumbent, Coolidge, had no difficulty in receiving his party's acclaim, and thereby was immortalized by Alice's famed comment that he appeared "to have been weaned on a pickle."

Alice, always ready to surprise her adoring public, certainly succeeded in astounding it when, on St. Valentine's Day, 1925, at the age of 40, she gave birth to her only child and daughter, Pauline, "in honor of the apostle who preached the virtues of self-denial."[70] Later in 1925, Nick was appointed as Speaker of the House of Representatives, a position which he retained until 1930, when the House attained a Democratic majority of Representatives. Less than a year later, he fell sick and died of pneumonia. His entire fortune of approximately three quarters of a million dollars was bequeathed to Alice, who, thereupon, left Washington to live in the family home in Cincinnati, although she retained a residence in Washington.[71] For a short while, she was commissioned by the *Ladies Home Journal* to write her memoirs in monthly installments as well as (later) to contribute a Washington column. But, by 1935, it was discontinued, Alice apparently having substantially mellowed and seeming no longer capable of providing her typical scintillating and scathing observations upon society. To her chagrin, her column was replaced by the serialized version of Eleanor Roosevelt's autobiography, *This Is My Story.*

On September 1, 1939, German troops invaded Poland, an action which led to the outbreak of World War II. Kermit, still an alcoholic, now found some motivation in life and sailed to England to offer his services to the British Army. He was accepted and commissioned as major in his former World War I Regiment in Mesopotamia, the Middlesex. He fought with the British forces during the Norwegian landing at Narvik, and following their withdrawal, he was sent to Egypt, but fell sick with malaria and dysentery.

The British Army found itself with no alternative but to invalid him out, and, despite a personal appeal to Winston Churchill, he found himself back in the United States in June, 1941. He fell into a deep mood of depression, began drinking heavily, and was once more committed to an alcoholic treatment center, the Hartford Retreat, in Connecticut. He was released for a while but was recommitted, and then, hearing of the family plight, F.D.R. contacted Archie, suggesting that Kermit be commissioned in the U.S. Army and despatched to a noncombat post: Alaska was suggested. Roosevelt's offer was accepted, and Kermit found himself even more bored to death in the dreary, prolonged winter climate of the northwest territory. In sheer despair he took his own life in June, 1943.[72]

When the U.S. entered the war, Ted, promoted to the rank of brigadier-general, returned to his command in World War I: the 26th Infantry First Division. He saw action in North Africa, Italy, and was then sent to England in preparation for the invasion of France.[73]

Ted's youngest son, Quentin, had enlisted under his father's command and, in April, 1944, Ted was best man at Quentin's wedding to Frances Webb, an American Red Cross volunteer from Kansas City.

On D-Day, Ted and Quentin were together on the first wave of invasion. Ted, at 56, was the oldest serving officer of the assault troops, but the strain proved too much, and on July 11 he died peacefully of a heart attack. He was posthumously awarded the Congressional Medal of Honor.

Archie saw service in the Pacific theater of war and was battalion commander with the 162nd Infantry in New Guinea. He was wounded in his left leg, as in World War I, and contracted malaria as well as pneumonia. He was awarded the Silver Star for gallantry in action.

At home, Alice had supported Robert Taft as presidential nominee at the 1944 Republican Convention, but the nomination went to Thomas E.

Dewey. Her daughter, Pauline, had been enrolled at Vassar but left after two years, and then, in August, 1944, she married an author, Alexander McCornick (Sandy) Sturm. He proved unsuccessful in his career, and, instead, set up a firearms company. He suffered from ill health and died of hepatitis, leaving Pauline with a daughter, Joanna. Then, at the tender age of only five years, Joanna herself discovered the body of her mother who had, accidentally or otherwise, taken an overdose of sleeping tablets. Alice, now 73, took Joanna into her own home to live.

Edith had died in September, 1948, at the age of 87, and her estate, valued at over $400,000, was divided equally between Archie, Ethel, Eleanor, and Belle. Since Alice had a substantial personal income, she received only a token gift. In her later years, Alice never lost her caustic wit, but her political views mellowed to the degree that she came to admire and enjoy the company of Democratic Presidents John F Kennedy and Lyndon B. Johnson.[74]

At the age of 83, she attended the unveiling of Paul Manship's bronze statue of her father in Washington, and it was in the capital city that she died in February, 1980, aged 96.

William Howard Taft

(1909–1913)

Robert Alphonso Taft, the eldest son of President Taft, was the only Congressman in the annals of the United States to have been honored by a monument erected on the grounds of the Capitol in Washington, D.C. The monument, the Robert A. Taft Memorial, was presented to Congress on April 14, 1959, by President Eisenhower, and one of the speakers at the dedication ceremony was eighty-four-year-old Herbert Clark Hoover, who, in his concluding remarks, stated:

> Who is great and who is small in a republic? It hardly matters. What does matter is that the essential virtues among men and women which made this country strong, which built great cities and verdant farms out of a wilderness, which stand for moral principles in public life, be preserved by reminders of such men as Robert A. Taft.
>
> Fortunately, in the belfry of this monument there is a magnificent carillon. When these great bells ring out, it will be a summons to integrity and courage.[1]

Why was this man so honored, while his father, not only President of the United States, but also Chief Justice of the U.S. Supreme Court, two of the highest offices in the land, was never accorded such homage? There can be no ready answer, but a review of the story of their respective lives may offer some relevant observations which may, or may not, provide at least a partial response to the foregoing query.

Robert (Bob) Taft was born on September 8, 1889, in Cincinnati, Ohio, to William and Helen (Nellie) Taft, who had been married in June, 1886. He was the first of their three children, the second being Helen, born in August, 1891, and the third, Charles Phelps, born in September, 1897. William was a son of the second marriage of Alphonso Taft, who was not only Secretary of War and Attorney-General under President Grant, but was later U.S. Ambassador in Vienna (1882) and St. Petersburg (1884) under President Arthur.

Thus, even before Robert's birth, the principle of dedicated service in the interest of the national welfare had already been firmly established within the Taft family. William, who was sent to Yale whence he graduated in 1878, and thence proceeded to law school in Cincinnati, practiced law in that city, and, in the year that he married Helen Heron, he was elected to the Supreme Court of Ohio.

William, the heaviest man ever to occupy the office of the presidency of the United States, was weighed at 225 pounds when he graduated at age twenty from Yale. He proceeded to add pound after pound, and, after Robert's birth, Nellie became concerned that the latter, likewise, was becoming overly obese since, like his portly father, he had developed a huge appetite. When Robert was fifteen months old, Nellie wrote:

> We are going to have our hands full with him. . . . How I wish you could see him running at full speed from one end of the parlor to the other, or waving his arms and talking at the top of his voice. . . .[2]

She made an effort to control his appetite by giving him cream and sugar with his first bowl of cereal, milk and sugar with the second bowl, and plain milk with the third. Her approach appeared to have met with success, since Robert never became as corpulent as his father, who, at his maximum, came to weigh as much as 350 pounds, yet, seemingly, with no major outward discomfort nor with any inner ill effects. As an extrovert who enjoyed life to the full, he had no regrets as to being overweight when he died at the age of 72. All his presidential antecedents were leaner and most of them had died at an earlier age.[3]

Robert attended the local public school in Cincinnati. The Taft home

lay directly across the street from the firehouse, and the daily activities at
the latter so fascinated him that, after a year's constant observation, along
with interviews with the firemen, he presented them with a detailed chart
upon which he had carefully recorded all the fire calls, and the location of
the conflagrations, as well as the call boxes, thus demonstrating a capacity for meticulous attention to relevant details which characterized his
activities throughout the rest of his life. He was also enlisted in the
"Buckeye Cadets," a troop of some forty boys in neat uniforms with
spiked muskets, who were drilled by a regular officer of the U.S. Army.

Robert taught himself chess from a book, but he learned to play golf
from his father, who also introduced his young son to the workings of
the law to the degree that Robert, before the age of ten, could recite by
heart the Constitution of the United States.

In 1900, William Taft was appointed by President McKinley to head a
Commission charged with setting up a civil government in the Philippines. Helen Taft almost immediately found herself confronted with all
manner of unexpected family problems: a bubonic plague in Hawaii
almost resulted in the quarantine of the ship on which they were sailing
to Japan. They were fortunate in that no restrictions were imposed upon
their arrival in that country, where, however, both Robert as well as
Charlie's nurse, Bessie, were laid low with diphtheria, so that Taft was
obliged to sail on with members of his commission to the Philippines
without his family.[4] Inwardly, he might have been quite relieved for the
respite since he had written to his elder brother, Charles, about the latter's
namesake, aged 2:

> We call him the "tornado," he creates such a sensation when he
> lands in the midst of the children of the ship. He is very badly in
> need of discipline and yet I cannot very well administer it in a
> crowd.[5]

In Manila, Charlie received the gift of an orangutan which provided
him with endless delight since it was as mischievous as he was. Nellie's
fear was that the animal might well abduct her son into the jungle, with
possibly full acquiescence on his part, and her qualms in this matter were
not finally alleviated until an episode when the animal wrecked a room in
the Governor's mansion, and he was promptly despatched to the local
zoo. Charlie, greatly disappointed but as resilient as ever, found consolation in playing with the gardener's two boys who were a few years older
than himself but about his size. As Nellie recalled:

> He used to order them around in a strange mixture of Spanish,

Tagalog and English, which made me wonder at my wholly American child, but it was an effective combination, since he seemed to have them completely under his thumb, and, as he reveled in his sense of power, he never tired of playing with them.[6]

In Manila, Taft had been pleased to renew acquaintance, after almost thirty years, with President Grant's eldest son, Fred, whom he had first met when he (Taft) had served as attorney-general. Fred, now 50, was brigadier-general of volunteers whose function it was to reduce guerrilla resistance and to set up local government. Fred's headquarters were in North Luzon, and he invited Robert, aged 10, to return with him and serve as aide. Resplendent in a military uniform (made to size) of a cavalry lieutenant, together with his army hat and leggings, Robert set out with Fred and enjoyed the entire experience immensely.

In 1901, the Tafts returned to the United States en route to Rome, where Taft had need to discuss with Pope Leo XIII alternatives for the disposal of church lands in the Philippines. He was obliged to make the journey alone (except for his mother who insisted on accompanying him) since Robert had contracted scarlet fever, and had also undergone an operation for the removal of adenoids as well as of a nasal polyp. Following his recovery, Nellie and the children traveled to Rome to join William. They were accorded an audience with the Pope, and Robert, when asked what was his ambition, dutifully answered (reflecting the probably oft-quoted ambition of his father): "Chief Justice of the Supreme Court."

Taft returned to the Philippines, but the departure of the family was once again delayed because of news of an outbreak there of cholera. Nellie took the opportunity of sightseeing with the children in various countries of Western Europe, and upon their arrival in the United States, she paid a visit to William's brother, Horace, who, eleven years earlier, had decided to open a private school on his own initiative, first at Pelham, New York, and then at Watertown, Connecticut, where he had taken over and converted a former hotel building to accommodate his students.

Nellie was obviously pleased and satisfied with what she observed, but, at that time, Robert was too young to be admitted, so once more they all traveled to join husband and father in Manila. Two years later, arrangements were completed for Robert's admission, and, on August 20, 1903, almost on the eve of his fourteenth birthday, he was placed on board ship in the company of army officers. After reaching San Francisco, he traveled cross-country by train to New York, and thence to Watertown, where he arrived on September 29.

In a lengthy letter to his brother, Horace, William had written (August 19, 1903):

> I do not think Robert has any bad habits; at least I know of none, except that he keeps his mouth open and he is not as particular in cleaning his nails as he ought to be. I hope you will find him readily amenable to discipline. He becomes intensely interested in games and in discussions, and with a nature somewhat highly wrought his tears are pretty near the surface. He has a taste for study, a love of mathematics and a great love of games, cards and chess, and I think he will develop some taste for, and skill at, athletics. He has played at baseball but I do not know how successfully; he plays tennis some. He has grown pretty rapidly but I think is fairly strong.
>
> I am not able to give you with exactness just where he is in his studies except to say, generally, that he is about beginning the second year in the high school. . . . He is reading Caesar and has studied elementary algebra and is now studying geometry. He has studied Spanish, French and German and I should like to have him keep up the French and German at least. I hope you will be able to prepare him in three years for college, for he would then enter in the September of his seventeenth birthday, which I think is a good age for entrance, and would graduate in the class of 1910, which I prophesied on the day of his birth. Though he has more taste for mathematics than for languages, I am exceedingly anxious that his education should not be as defective as mine in the matter of linguistic knowledge, and that he should be able to speak French and German. He has quite a taste for history.[7]

Robert was two weeks late for class and was obliged to work on his own for a while until he "caught up." His Uncle Horace wrote to his father (September 30, 1903):

> . . . I am trying him in the Middle Class. He is fully up to that class in Algebra, I think, though rusty on the subject. He is considerably behind them in Latin and these two weeks behind them in Greek. He has done nothing since he came here but study Greek. I think that by this evening he will be up with the class in that subject. Then he will take all the studies with the Middle Class and do extra work in Latin until he is up with the procession. I shall be very much surprised if he does not lead the class soon. Football clothes have been ordered for him and he is looking forward eagerly to diving into the game. When I find out what he can do, I expect to give him work according to his strength.[8]

But Robert was precocious: as a much younger boy, he had, on his own volition, memorized the entire Constitution of the United States, and now, faced with a new academic challenge, he devoted all his attention to his studies, such that, after one month of schooling, his Uncle again wrote:

> It is Nip and Tuck between him and some others in his algebra as yet and so in one or two other studies, but his average is the highest.[9]

Having firmly established himself as one of the smartest boys in the school, Robert freely participated in all its sports and games, since every afternoon was free from class so that the students could enjoy outdoor activities.[10] In due course, he also became president of the chess club, as well as editor of the Taft Annual and, in one letter, he hastily compressed into one paragraph a listing of all his commitments during one week:

> Must know Colonization Speech by heart. Two weeks later a debate on the Tariff System. Every Monday, Glee Club. Have to sing next Wednesday at the Kettledrum, a kind of church fair. Every Wednesday Chess Club . . . Saturday night a kind of Literary Club. I got on the play and have rehearsals three nights a week. . . .[11]

The Tafts had returned to the United States in December, 1903, since William had accepted an invitation from Theodore Roosevelt to become a member of his cabinet as Secretary of War. They settled in Washington where Helen and Charles were both enrolled in school. Helen suffered from a slight curvature of the spine which, for a while, obliged her to wear a plaster jacket to correct the deformity. She also undertook special physical exercises over a long period of time. She slowly regained strength and confidence, and entered Baldwin School in preparation for entry into Bryn Mawr. She was a reserved and studious girl, though never as brilliant as her elder brother. On one occasion she wrote home apologetically, "You mustn't be disappointed if my marks seem low for they have a way here of marking everybody extremely low."[12]

In 1905, William led a congressional party on a goodwill tour of the Philippines and the Far East, a tour on which the star performer was Alice Roosevelt and her (to be announced) fiancé, Nicholas Longworth. Nellie did not accompany the party, and instead, took the children to Europe, where Robert accompanied his Uncle Charlie on a tour of Norway, Sweden, and Denmark, which so impressed Robert that he wrote, "I feel as if I had seen almost every part of the world."

He was now about to enter upon his final year at the Taft School, and his Uncle wrote to William (January 25, 1906):

Debating is hard for him. He grasps arguments, easily, but has no readiness of speech on his feet, and he will need a great deal of practice in that line before he can be a debater. Of course he is very quick at understanding the force of an argument, but not so apt in giving sharp forceful expression to it.[13]

Whatever his forensic disabilities, Robert had no problems with his written examinations, and he not only gained admission to Yale with ease, but achieved excellent grades in all his subjects at the university. He was also most gratified to be accepted into the Psi Upsilon fraternity to which his father had belonged, as well as to the Skull and Bones secret society, of which his grandfather, Alphonso, had been a founder member, and of which, again, his father was also a member.

During the year 1907, William, Nellie and Charlie (aged 10) went around the world, by boat to the Far East, thence by train through Siberia to Europe. They corresponded regularly with Robert at Yale, and with Helen at the Baldwin School, although what has been preserved of their letters remains prosaically descriptive of sights and scenes and schedules. On one occasion Helen wrote: "I send my report in case it may interest you. It doesn't interest me. . . . Give my respects to the Czar, Kaiser, and King and any other big people you may meet."[14] Helen's grades at this juncture of her career were only mediocre, and her academic talents appeared to be in the chrysalis stage of development.

Upon his return to the United States, William became involved in the presidential campaign of 1908. Roosevelt had nominated him as his successor, and William easily won not only the nomination but also the election in November, 1908. He remained unenthusiastic throughout the entire course of events, and was unimpressed by his political successes.[15] Yet eventually, he did express pride in the fact that he was the first Yale graduate to become President of the United States.

Apart from Nellie, who had been mainly responsible for persuading her reluctant husband to accept the presidential nomination, the other family members exhibited as little enthusiasm as had their father. Charlie, a long-time regular playmate of Quentin Roosevelt's at the White House, was the least impressed of all, and, at the inaugural ceremony on March 4, 1909, he took along with him a copy of *Treasure Island* to read, in the anticipated event of being completely bored by the proceedings in general, and his father's speech in particular. As events turned out, the book remained unread: Charlie actually listened to Taft's presentation, and his father was, later, always to regard it as the finest compliment ever paid him by his younger son.

At the actual time of the inauguration, all the children were away at school—Robert at Yale, Helen at Bryn Mawr, and Charlie at Uncle Horace Taft's School in Connecticut, although all three were present at the ceremony. Nellie broke all precedents when she insisted on riding back to the White House with her husband after the conclusion of events. Since the Roosevelts had left hurriedly, the occasion gave her full opportunity to carry out her wishes, her only immediate problem having been that of the public's impression of her large hat, whose aigret feathers had been badly singed by a gas jet a few days earlier.

Nellie's joy and pleasure at being First Lady was tragically short-lived, since two months after the inauguration she suffered a stroke—on the same day that Charlie had undergone an operation for the removal of adenoids. Nellie's recovery was long and painful, and Helen was brought home from Bryn Mawr for three years to perform duties as her father's hostess. Nellie recovered much of her physical strength,[16] but was to endure permanently a speech impediment.

Helen performed her duties with grace and composure, but the family was made only too well aware of the negative comparisons drawn between life in the White House during the Taft regime compared with that which had prevailed during the time of Roosevelt. An attempt was made by the fashion industry to promote a "Helen Pink" as rival to "Alice Blue," but the effort proved abortive.

While Charlie struggled with his studies at the Taft School,[17] Robert was making excellent progress at Harvard Law School and was to graduate first in his class, going on to qualify with fullest honors in the Ohio state bar examination. By this time he had overcome all reticence in public speaking, and, before leaving Harvard, he had been elected president of the University Debating Society.

During his first years in office, William had upset his presidential sponsor, Theodore Roosevelt, by rejecting many of the latter's proposed nominees as Taft's cabinet ministers. The rift continued to widen, culminating in Roosevelt's bid to seek re-election in 1912. His efforts divided the party, and Woodrow Wilson, while receiving a minority of the popular vote, was easily the victor in the electoral college.[18]

But never was there a President of the United States who was so relieved to quit office. Taft stated: "The people of the United States did not owe me another election," and he went on to consider that his only problem lay in finding, at the age of 55, alternative occupation to that of returning to his great love, the profession of law: he felt that he had appointed so many judges that his appearance as an advocate in any prominent lawsuit could well have prejudiced decisions in his favor. His problem was solved by his sequential appointments, first as professor of

Constitutional Law at Yale, then as chairman of the National War Labor Board during World War I, and finally, in 1921 what, to him, was the acme of aspired ambition, as Chief Justice of the U.S. Supreme Court, a position which he held until his retirement in February, 1930; he died only one month later.[19]

During his final year at Yale, Robert had met and become emotionally attached to Martha Wheaton Bowers, the only daughter of Lloyd Wheaton Bowers, a brilliant lawyer whom Taft had appointed as his solicitor-general. The Bowers family had made a fortune in Minnesota lumber, and among their illustrious ancestors were Timothy Dwight, first president of Yale, and Jonathan Edwards, the fiery evangelist of colonial America.

According to truth or legend, Martha, who enjoyed riding, had borrowed a horse from Robert's sister, Helen, but while out in the street, the animal bolted, and broke its neck upon impact with a street car. Martha was extremely fortunate only to break an arm, but, genuinely concerned for her welfare, Robert took it upon himself to propose marriage and was accepted.

Preparations for the ceremony had commenced in early summer, 1914, and Mrs. Bowers traveled to Paris to purchase a trousseau. She was there in late July as the war clouds were gathering, but she succeeded in returning home just before hostilities actually commenced.

Robert and Martha were married on October 17 at St. John's Church, Washington.[20] Helen was maid of honor, and the best man was George Harrison, a close friend of the groom's, who, although crippled by polio, had graduated from Yale and, later Harvard Law School.

Robert, himself, upon graduating from Harvard Law School, had been offered a position as secretary to Justice Oliver Wendell Holmes, but this he had rejected in favor of practical law experience, and he entered the law firm of Maxwell and Ramsey in Cincinnati. Here, two sons were born to Martha: William Howard (1915), and Robert Jr. (1917).

When the United States declared war on Germany, Robert had attempted to enlist, but was rejected because of his poor eyesight. He was then appointed as assistant counsel in the U.S. Food Administration office headed by Herbert Hoover, and, on Armistice Day, November 11, 1918, Robert was ordered to sail to Europe to serve as Hoover's assistant in the enormous famine relief program undertaken by the United States at the end of the war. He was joined in Paris by Martha,[21] the city being the headquarters for the Relief Administration. Robert traveled widely through the destitute areas of Central Europe, and, for his assistance to

the war-devastated countries, he received decorations from the governments of Belgium, Finland, and Poland.

In the meantime, his brother, Charlie, had successfully graduated in
1913 from the Taft School,[22] and had entered Yale. He enlisted as an army
private in 1917, but before sailing to Europe he married Eleanor Kellog
Chase.[23] In France, he attended an artillery training school at Saumur
and, in due course, was promoted to the rank of first lieutenant. He saw
action at Verdun and, after the Armistice, returned to complete his degree
at Yale.

Charlie's college career was a highly successful one, both in sport
(where he played on the varsity football team, standing 6 feet 1 inch, and
weighing 190 pounds), and in academics: he was awarded the Gordon
Brown Prize for manhood, scholarship, and leadership.

He entered Yale Law School, and in 1922 qualified for the Ohio State
bar following which he set up practice with Robert in the law firm of Taft
and Taft in Cincinnati. The first of Eleanor and Charlie's seven children
was herself named Eleanor, known as Nonie, and was born in September, 1918, while her father was in France. Of the six children to follow,
four were girls and two were boys.[24]

After the Taft family had vacated the White House, Helen returned to
Bryn Mawr to complete her degree. In this, she had the full support of
her mother, who, in an interview concerning higher education for
women, stated:

> I believe in the best and most thorough education for everyone,
> men and women, and it is my proudest boast that all my children
> are studious. My idea about higher culture for women is that it
> makes them great in intellect and soul, develops the lofty con-
> ception of womanhood, not that it makes them a poor imitation of
> a man. I am old-fashioned enough to believe that woman is the
> complement of man, and that what is most feminine about her is
> most attractive to man and therefore of the greatest utility to the
> world.[25]

Helen, intellectual and studious, was awarded several prizes at Bryn
Mawr, and, after graduating in 1915, she enrolled at Yale for a master's
degree, which she completed in 1916. One year later, she returned to
Bryn Mawr as dean of the college, and, in 1919, she was appointed acting
president. In 1920, Helen wrote: "I am going to marry a most unusual
young man on July 15th (probably) in Murray Bay. Unusually poor and
unusually young, but also unusually clever and nice. And most unusually

fond of me."[26] Her father attempted to persuade her to delay marriage until she had completed her Ph.D. degree, but Helen was adamant, and she married Frederick Johnson Manning, a professor at Yale, on July 19. Their first child, a daughter, also named Helen, was born in October, 1921, and the mother, to her father's great pride and satisfaction, completed her Ph.D. in 1924.[27] Her husband was appointed to the history faculty at Swarthmore, and Helen herself returned to Bryn Mawr, where they both resided.[28]

Upon his return to the United States from Europe, Robert was, in 1920, elected as representative to the Ohio State Legislature, and he served there until 1926 when he resumed his law practice.[29] Two more sons were born to the family during this period: Lloyd Bowers (1923), and Horace Dutton (1925). He returned to politics in 1930, when he was elected to the Ohio State Senate and, at the same time, maintained and extended his involvement in the business world as director of a number of companies,[30] while being also actively engaged in philanthropic and cultural organizations in Cincinnati.[31]

In 1932, Robert took his family on a visit to Europe, but it was the election of Franklin D. Roosevelt in the same year, and the subsequent provisions of the New Deal programs, which were so to incense and motivate Robert into adopting a vigorous opposing viewpoint that he emerged on to the national scene as "Mr. Republican"—the apotheosis of conservative political philosophy, particularly after his election to the U.S. Senate in 1938.[32]

But even this distinctive appellation, which he carried so proudly, proved inadequate to propel him forward to fulfill his prime ambition to become presidential nominee upon no fewer than three occasions: in 1940, he lost out to Wendell Wilkie, who, in turn, lost the election to Franklin D. Roosevelt;[33] in 1948, Robert was defeated by Thomas A. Dewey (who lost to Harry S. Truman); while, in 1952, it was Eisenhower who took the nomination from Robert on the very first ballot, and went on to overwhelm Adlai Stevenson in the subsequent presidential election.

Yet, had Robert gained the much-coveted nomination in 1952, along with probable subsequent victory, his elation with, and enjoyment of, savoring the status of having been elevated to the office of his country's supreme executive, would have been tragically short-lived: in April, 1953, he developed cancer in the hip and he was dead in three months.[34]

Whatever his political views, Robert was universally recognized as a man of impeccable honesty and integrity, and as a person whose attention to procedural detail and facts was unrivaled. Congressmen could at all times rest assured that his arguments for or against legislative proposals were based on thorough research whence, according to Robert, certain logical conclusions supporting his personal viewpoint were inevitable.

While he is probably best remembered for his opposition to the New Deal programs, as well as to the Nuremburg Trials of Nazi war criminals,[35] and for his work in promoting the Taft-Hartley Act of 1947 (designed to curb the power of labor unions), Robert gave support to many measures normally associated with more liberal-minded colleagues, such as federal aid for education, public housing, the Marshall Plan, and the United Nations Charter.

All his four sons served in World War II, and, subsequently, the eldest, William Howard, entered the diplomatic corps and was Ambassador to Ireland; Lloyd Bowers became an investment lawyer in New York; Horace Dutton was physics professor at Yale; and Robert Jr. followed his father's footsteps as a lawyer and Congressman in the Ohio State Legislature.

In direct contrast to Robert, his brother, Charlie, became acclaimed as a "national crusader at large." His Uncle Horace of the Taft School had made the astute observation that Charlie appeared to have been inoculated by the virus of reform. While always loyal to the Republican party, he insisted on interpreting its principles and precepts according to his own individual beliefs: *res-publica* means "public affairs," and to Charlie it signified active involvement in attempts to cleanse the affairs of the public of dishonesty, corruption, injustice, and intolerance.

He was Hamilton County prosecutor in 1927 and 1928, and authored a book entitled *City Management*. It was due to his efforts, along with those of a group of like-minded colleagues, that Cincinnati became the first major town to adopt the city-manager form of government.[36] He was outgoing, friendly, with such an infectious smile that "his legal opponents would complain: 'Charlie smiled me out of court.'"

He was a firm believer in international cooperation, and he deplored the fact that the United States had not joined the League of Nations. In 1925, he was elected the youngest president of the International Y.M.C.A. His liberal Republicanism[37] led him to give full support to Wendell Wilkie in his presidential campaign of 1940, and, although opposed to many of the New Deal programs of Franklin D. Roosevelt, the latter recognized Charlie's abilities and brought him to Washington during the war years to serve in a variety of government posts, including those as director of the Division of Health and Welfare for the Federal Security Agency; director of Wartime Economic Affairs, U.S. Department of State; director of Transport and Communications Policy, U.S. Department of State; and member of the President's War Relief Control

Board. In 1945, he was adviser to the American delegation to the San Francisco Conference, whence emerged the United Nations Organization.

He was a prominent member of the Episcopal Church, and, in 1947 and 1948, he served as the first lay president of the Federal Council of Churches of Christ in America, an organization which later became the National Council of the Churches of Christ in the U.S.A.

He was a member of the provisional committee that established the World Council of Churches at a meeting in Amsterdam in 1948. He attended council meetings throughout the world serving for seven years until 1961, as chairman of the committee that directed news and publicity for the council.[38]

In 1945, he was elected to the Cincinnati City Council upon which he served until his retirement in 1977, during which period he was city mayor, 1955–57. In 1952, he was defeated as the Republican candidate for governor of Ohio by Frank Lausche, a Democrat.

Charlie, and his wife Eleanor (who matched her husband's concern in the humanitarian field), were active in the matter of post-World War II refugee resettlement, and they themselves cared for a Latvian family of nine children for five years before a place was found for them in Kentucky. Later, President John F. Kennedy appointed Charlie to his American Food for Peace Council.

Charlie and Eleanor suffered three tragedies within their family of seven children: Rosalyn, the sixth, died of polio in 1941; Lucia, the seventh, a graduate of Vassar suicided in 1955; while Cynthia, the fourth, stricken by paralysis at the time of Rosalyn's death, made slow recovery and overcame her physical handicap to the extent that she not only graduated from Vassar but obtained her Ph.D. degree in Economics from Yale in 1959. Eleanor died in 1961, and Charlie survived until June, 1983, when he died at age 85.

For the first half of the twentieth century the name of Helen Taft Manning will forever be linked with that of Bryn Mawr. After graduating from the college she was, at age 25, appointed as its youngest dean ever, and when she eventually retired in 1957, she had served at least sixteen years in that capacity, along with several years as acting principal; after 1941, she became professor and chairman of the history department.

She reveled in all the faculty theatrical performances, and she authored two works entitled, respectively: *British Government after the American Revolution, 1782–1820*; and *The Revolt of French Canada, 1800–1835*.

Woodrow Wilson

(1913–1921)

With the election of Woodrow Wilson, the era of Presidents with young children at the White House came to an end for many decades. Even Charlie Taft was nearly 12 when his father assumed office, and his most famous exploits belonged rather to the Teddy Roosevelt period. Wilson had three children, all daughters, and when they came to the White House, Eleanor, the youngest, was already 23, while her sisters, Jessie and Margaret were, respectively, 25 and 27. They had all lived as a very close-knit, happy family until they moved into the executive mansion, but then a quick succession of events was to change their entire lifestyle drastically.

The President had been baptized as Thomas Woodrow Wilson, and had been known as Tommy for years. His father, Joseph, was a Presbyterian minister and was recognized as a fine orator, an endowment which he passed on to his son, who received an excellent education, first at Princeton and then at John Hopkins.

Wilson appeared to have been disappointed in an early love match with his cousin, Harriet Woodson, and, it was at this time, that he decided to drop what he considered to be the all-too-plebian "Tommy," and to assume the more dignified "Woodrow" as his first name. He then met the daughter of another Presbyterian minister, and, just before taking up appointment as history instructor at Bryn Mawr, the new Quaker college for women, he married Ellen Louisa (Ellie Lou) Axson in June, 1885.

Ellen was a talented painter who was pursuing art studies in New York when she fell in love with Wilson. Upon their engagement, she surrendered her career to devote her time exclusively to her future husband. She was very nervous at the time of the births of both her first child, Margaret, in April, 1886, and her second, Jessie, in August, 1887, since her mother had died at childbirth. Consequently, she moved back to her home at Gainesville, Georgia, at the time of both confinements so that she could be among her relatives and friends. Presumably, also, an added incentive to go South was her wish that her children should not be born "Yankees," that is, in Pennsylvania, north of the Mason-Dixon line.

Her third child, Eleanor, was not so "blessed." In 1888, Wilson accepted an appointment at Wesleyan University, Middleton, Connecticut, and it was here that Eleanor was born in October, 1889. The family was somewhat disappointed that this third child was not a son. Ellen cried bitterly upon hearing the news, while Wilson's father, Joseph, is recorded as having commented "Oh, it's just another of Woodrow's little annuals!" Years later, Eleanor inadvertently overheard a conversation which made reference to her mother's reaction at her birth, and she is said to have brooded secretly over a long period of time at the apparent lack of family welcome at the time of birth—not that she ever had the slightest reason to complain of any adverse treatment accorded her by either her mother or father.

In 1890, Wilson was appointed a professor at Princeton, and it was here that the family resided for the next twenty years, first in a house rented from one of the professors, then in a new home, the Library Place House, and finally, in 1902, when Wilson was appointed president of the University, the family moved into "Prospect," the official residence of the chief executive of the institution.

To the outside world, Wilson has been invariably portrayed as an austere, humorless, frigid personality, who might well have posed as the original sitter for Grant Wood's famous painting, "American Gothic." Wilson's image was certainly not improved upon by the publication of his *Biography* by William Allen White, who recalled Wilson's first handshake as feeling "like a ten-cent pickled mackerel in brown paper," adding that, when Wilson "tried to be pleasant, he creaked." Certain observers have claimed that Wilson deliberately set out to project this negative image so as to maintain distance between himself and the public, thereby preserving privacy in his home life.

On the family hearth Wilson was the quintessence of the indulgent husband and father. Nell (Eleanor), his youngest daughter, wrote:

> I was conscious of him first as a voice; the limpid clearness of that voice laughing, singing, explaining things stirred a sense of beauty in me, and gave me a vague but warm feeling of protection and security.[1]

He would sing to the children at bedtime to soothe them to sleep, and among the lullabies they always remembered was one that began as follows:

> I have four brothers over the sea,
>   Peri, Meri, Dictum, Domini:
> They each sent a present unto me,
>   Partum, Quartum, Peri, Meri, Centum
> Peri, Meri, Dictum, Domini.

It continued for many stanzas.

He was a gifted raconteur, and reveled in dialect imitation with appropriate facial and physical contortions. The children's favorites were his "Superior Englishman," the "Insufferable Yankee," the "Irishman" with his brogue, and the "Scotsman" with his burr.

He loved limericks, and among two of his favorites were:

> For beauty I am not a star
> There are others more handsome by far,
> But my face—I don't mind it,
> For I am behind it;
> It's the people in front that I jar.

and:

> There was a young monk of Siberia
> Whose existence grew drearier and drearier,
> Till he burst from his cell
> With a hell of a yell
> And eloped with the Mother Superior.[2]

Wilson often used to comment: "I have the silliest memory in the world. I never forget a nonsense rhyme but I don't know one piece of fine poetry by heart."

In the Library Place House, Wilson had a study and, as Nell described it:

> The most important thing in the room was the large roll-top desk that father always closed and locked when he stopped working. The sound of that desk closing made us listen sharply, for if that was followed by a soft whistle and the jingle of keys in a sort of jolly accompaniment, it meant that he had finished and would soon come out and play with us. It was the most important moment of our day.[3]

Apart from his gifts as storyteller and impersonator, Wilson had a splendid singing voice, as did Margaret, and the whole family spent many happy hours harmonizing around the piano with such tunes as "Sweet and Low," "By the Light of the Silvery Moon," "The Kerry Dancers," and "Watchman, What of the Night." He loved the many solos and choruses of the Gilbert and Sullivan operettas, and always fancied himself as the rollicking Duke of Plaza-toro.

Since, at first, there was no conveniently located school at Princeton, the work of providing education for her children fell upon Ellen, a task which she undertook very conscientiously. In teaching the three R's, she exposed them to the great literature of the world and she read to them appropriate passages from Homer or Shakespeare almost as a daily routine. She related the stories of famous historical personages from classical times through to the American Revolution and the Civil War, and the children, thrown upon their own resources would, in their playtime, act out scenes and episodes from the Trojan Wars, King Arthur and his Knights, or Shakespeare. When Grover Cleveland left office in 1897, he retired to the Princeton campus, and gave lectures on government. Like Wilson, he, too, had three young daughters, and they would join in the games of the Wilson children. On one occasion, Wilson happened to pass by, and was told they were playing Shakespeare. When asked what characters they were representing, Esther Cleveland said she was Marc Anthony, Ruth Cleveland was Caesar, and Eleanor Wilson was Brutus. Observing that little Marion Cleveland (who lisped in her speech) was standing some distance away, he enquired as to her role and she answered "Oh, I'm duth the mob."[4]

The girls exercised a considerable amount of imagination in their daily games, one of which consisted of "dividing" things between themselves, as, for example, the rooms of the house, the buildings on the campus, the Greek gods, and even the Universe itself. When Margaret, the eldest, took first choice with the moon and stars, Jessie, the sun and sunset, and

Eleanor, the youngest, would complain that all she could claim was the sunrise and the rainbow. A halt was quickly called to one dimension of the game when, having divided the world among themselves, they ransacked the house for maps, and ruined many books by scribbling their individual names on the places which were their "possessions."[5]

On Sunday, the family would attend the Presbyterian church, where the girls would be bored by the long sermons, while at home, the Day of Rest would be strictly observed. No games were played, and the only book of reading was the Bible, with Ellen conducting her own Sunday school class for the girls.

As the children grew older, it was decided to employ a governess, a certain Fraulein Clara Boehm, who was to teach them German and French. The girls reacted to her very differently, with Margaret taking a dislike to her, possibly because of her strict disciplinarian approach, while Eleanor considered her to be a good teacher, although she, too, took fright on one occasion during a lesson on European history: Eleanor had commented: "Fraulein, if Prussia and America went to war, you wouldn't hurt us would you?," in response to which Fraulein Clara said, "If mein Kaiser ordered me to kill you I would do it at once—like this," and she drew a finger across her throat with an ugly gesture.[6]

The girls had also attended a private school, some three miles away, with a Mrs. Scott in charge. As Eleanor described her, she was "a tall, severe person with a great beak of a nose and a husband who reached to her shoulder, and respectfully called her 'Birdie.' "[7] The school had only one redeeming feature, an aviary "with strange, bright birds" whose colors and antics fascinated the students.

To everyone's relief, a new school was opened by Miss Fine, sister of Professor Henry Fine, a close friend of the Wilsons, and she proved to be a competent and sympathetic teacher, whom all the girls enjoyed.

The latter went through all the traumatic processes accompanying the transition between infancy and girlhood. Eleanor still believed in Santa Claus until she was nine, and when her two sisters callously broke the cherished illusion, she bore "a hot wave of resentment" against them over a long period of time. Eleanor was also unfortunate in that her teeth had to be straightened, so that she had to endure the daily agony of having a cumbersome set of wires and strings tied and untied every morning and evening, respectively. She wrote later:

> I felt like a horse with a curb bit . . . I now crept about praying that no one would look at me. Hair in two long tight braids, long black-stockinged legs, a pinafore over my school dress and a mouthful of "hardware," I must have been a startling apparition.[8]

In addition to his duties as professor at Princeton, Wilson had also coached the football and basketball teams. Mrs. Wilson was bored with team games, but her husband enjoyed them, and made it a practice to take along the girls to see all the home games. In appreciation of his work, for years after, when he was university president, a home win would almost invariably be climaxed with a band parade to his home.

The Wilsons were never short of company. His father, Joseph, was a permanent if somewhat irascible resident, whose eating habits drove Eleanor "frantic": she could never make out why he always put his cake in water, and put salt on his strawberries. When she asked him the reason, he would simply and tersely tell her to mind her own business. He died soon after Wilson became the university president.

Then there were Mrs. Wilson's brothers, Stockton Axson (Uncle Stock), a bachelor, and Ed Axson, (who later married, but he, his wife, and his child were all drowned in a tragic accident related to a runaway horse). Mrs. Wilson's sister, Margaret, was a frequent visitor as were her cousins, Mary, Florence, Margaret and Will Hoyt. Wilson's sister, Annie Howe, her husband, and three children and his two cousins, Marion Brower and Helen Bones, made up the relatively full complement of the immediate family clan.

Annie Howe's husband died, and when she later came to visit, she seemed to Eleanor to be the "perfection of widowhood":

> Her weeds fascinated me and I determined to be a widow when I grew up. The idea appealed to me so much that often, when I was alone, I trailed along with downcast eyes and mournful dignity, drowned in the pleasant despair of the loss of an imaginary husband.[9]

At the time when Wilson moved into the university president's residence, "Prospect," the girls were of age 16, 15, and 13, respectively, and not too long afterwards the concerned father was confronted with the problem of his daughters' "dating" procedures. It would appear that the girls were in growing demand as the years passed by, but what most irritated Wilson was the boy-friend habit of using the telephone, an instrument which, at best, he considered an abominable nuisance, and, at worst, a pure invention of the devil. A telephone inquiry from one of his daughters' current "beaus" as to whether she was at home, would prompt an explosive burst, "Come and find out," greatly to the poor girl's distress. The daughters were under constant pressure to remind their respective boyfriends that their father considered such use of the telephone to be a base intrusion of the family's privacy, and that they should

rather take the trouble of walking over to the house and, "like gentlemen," make their enquiries at the door.

Wilson was likewise apt to make negative observations concerning
certain of the young men, and would mutter to his wife, "What on earth
does she see in that fool?" to which his wife would laughingly respond,
"Is he a fool because he is interested in your daughter?"

Mrs. Wilson had always been a very economical housekeeper, ensuring that the family expenditure was kept within the limitations of a
professor's very moderate salary. But when her husband was appointed
president of the university it became necessary for an outlay on new
clothes to be worn at the inaugural ceremony. The girls were ecstatic: in
the past, the most fortunate among them had been Margaret, since she, at
least, receive new clothes, but then they became the modified "hand-me-
downs," first for Jessie, and then for Eleanor.

The increase in salary also enabled the family to indulge in travel
overseas, although not all together at one and the same time. In 1903,
Wilson and Ellen separated for the first time from their children, and
traveled together, while the girls spent their summer with an aunt in
North Carolina. In the following year, Ellen took Jessie and their cousin,
Mary Hoyt, to Italy, and, while there, Jessie contracted diphtheria, but
fortunately made a good recovery. In the meantime, while their mother
was away, and they were being cared for by their father, both Margaret
and Eleanor contracted measles, a situation which apparently they both
enjoyed. Even Wilson saw its humor and wrote to his wife (April 12,
1904):

> The plot thickens! Margaret has the measles on schedule time . . .
> Isn't it a rum go. And yet I must say that the amusing side of it
> appeals to me strongly. Happily, measles is a disease which we
> cannot take tragically.[10]

In reply, Ellen, in a mood of guilt and self-reproach observed:

> That *all* the children should be ill during practically the whole of
> my absence from home is strange indeed. I am certainly being
> bitterly punished for my selfishness in leaving home. Well, I hope I
> have learnt my lesson by heart at last. . . .[11]

Later, Jessie and Eleanor were given the opportunity to travel to
Europe in the company of the Smiths, two daughters of a Presbyterian
minister with whom the Wilsons had become so friendly that they were
known as Cousin Lucy and Cousin Mary. But, overall, the trip was a
disappointment since the "cousins" were by no means wealthy, and the

party was obliged to stay in a variety of cramped lodgings and low-class hotels, and they virtually nibbled their way from city to city. Moreover, the Smiths were determined to visit all the historic sites and buildings, so that each day proved to be an interminable walking marathon which completely exhausted the girls by evening. Still they survived, and the stories of their many adventures kept the entire family in a hilarious mood for many a bleak winter's evening ever after.

The older girls were now of college age, so both Margaret and Jessie were enrolled at the Women's College in Baltimore while Eleanor, (born in Connecticut), was sent to a school in Raleigh, North Carolina, to develop a Southern accent. She took some time to settle down, but eventually she did, and was even voted by her classmates as being "the most intelligent" student, an honor which gave her great disappointment since she had hoped to be nominated as "the most beautiful." Upon returning home, she suffered the additional chagrin of having her parents (humorously) comment that such an honor bestowed upon Eleanor was a "serious reflection on the intelligence of Southern girls in general."

Wilson, through overwork, now began to suffer deterioration in the sight of his left eye. His physician recommended a complete breakaway from his duties, and so, in 1906, Wilson took his entire family to the Lake District of England. It proved to be a thoroughly enjoyable experience which restored Wilson to full health. Both he and Ellen sat for Fred Yates, the English portrait painter, while Wilson also traveled to Scotland taking Eleanor with him. He was very fond of Scotland, and often said that his Scotch blood was stronger than his Irish: "Whenever the Irish gets too strong in me, the dour Scot sternly reprimands me."

In 1908, Wilson was induced to enter the political arena and he was elected Governor of New Jersey. Since there was no executive mansion, the family was obliged to house in some old-fashioned house in Trenton, the capital. However, the state did provide a summer "mansion" at Sea Girt, and it was here that the family gained the acquaintance of William Gibbs McAdoo, known to virtually everyone as the "Tunnel Man." He was a businessman who had efficiently reorganized the Hudson and Manhattan Railroad Company and, after several unsuccessful efforts by other firms to complete tunnels under the Hudson River, he undertook the projects himself, and, in 1904, completed the first railroad tunnel under the river. By 1909, he constructed three more tunnels, whereby New Jersey became virtually a dormitory suburb of New York.

He was very much a practical idealist, and became attracted to Wilson by reason of the latter's speeches during the gubernatorial campaign of 1908, although he had already met Wilson, since his son, Francis Huger

McAdoo, had been a student at Princeton. Following Wilson's election as Governor, McAdoo went ahead to persuade him that his next office should be that of the President of the United States. His promotion efforts proved successful even though Wilson was not finally nominated at the 1912 Democratic Convention at Baltimore until the 46th ballot.

During Wilson's term as Governor, a parting of the family began with Margaret residing in New York with the intent of pursuing a career in music. Jessie had expressed a keen desire to become a missionary, a project which gave both her parents no little concern, and they, no doubt, felt considerable relief when the selection board concluded that Jessie's physical constitution did not appear robust enough to withstand the strenuous demands which accompanied work in the mission field. She bore the disappointment well, and opted to perform social service at the "Lighthouse" settlement in Philadelphia, where she worked weekdays, and returned to her family at weekends.

Eleanor followed in her mother's footsteps and developed a taste for art. She had wished to enroll in her mother's former college in New York, but she was persuaded to study painting at the Pennsylvania Academy of Fine Arts in Philadelphia, and commuted thence daily from Princeton. While on holiday with friends in Mexico, she became attracted to a young American missionary and the romance lasted, at a distance, for several years. At one stage, it became so serious that her mother's brother, "Uncle Stock," was despatched to Mexico to interview the young man, and he returned with comments highly in favor of the prospective beau. During her stay in Mexico, Eleanor was caught up with the revolution that occurred when President Madero was assassinated at the instigation of the rebel, Huerta. Eleanor's party had a difficult, but to them, exhilarating journey, when making their way back to the U.S. frontier. Their adventure became headline news when they were "lost," and when, at the final stage, they were "rescued" by a carload of reporters, all four car tires blew out, and they drove the last few miles to safety on the wheel rims.[12]

In 1912, McAdoo's wife, Sarah, died, leaving him a widower with six grown children. Being active in Wilson's presidential campaign, he was now a regular visitor to the home, and, gradually, Eleanor became attracted to him. This was made most evident to the family when, after the election, Wilson took them to Bermuda where they stayed at a home kindly lent to him by his friend, Mrs. Mary Allen Peck (later Hulbert). Here, Wilson spent part of his time selecting members of his Cabinet, and from time to time he would discuss names in casual conversation with his wife and daughters. One day, Eleanor came out with the statement, "Well, I don't really care who you choose, as long as you make that *nice* Mr. McAdoo Secretary of the Treasury," an unexpected utterance which provoked Wilson to laugh and comment, "Just imagine; Nell wants me to appoint a man to the Cabinet just because he is attractive to women!"[13]

Wilson took time to relax playing golf, walking, and cycling, but he became increasingly irritated by the ever-present press correspondents. On one occasion, returning back hot and disheveled after a cycle ride with Jessie, they found themselves confronted by a group of trigger-happy photographers, and he appealed to them: "Gentlemen, you can photograph me to your heart's content, I don't care how I look. But I request you not to photograph my daughter. You know how women feel about such things and I myself would rather not have the ladies of my family made to . . ." at which point a photographer aimed his camera at Jessie and snapped her. Wilson is said to have turned "the color of a strawberry" and, clenching his fists, he rushed on the photographer. Realizing what he was doing, he stopped short of blows, but cried "You're no gentleman! I want to give you the worst thrashing you ever had in your life, and what's more, I'm perfectly able to do it." The outburst had its effect, and the family was left in peace, at least temporarily.

After their return home, Ellen's next concern was that her girls should be appropriately dressed for their debut into Washington society in general, and for the inauguration ceremonies in particular. As Eleanor later commented:

> . . . for the first time in our lives we bought what we wanted without having to dwell too carefully on the price . . . one new dress had always been a thrill for me and to choose a complete wardrobe was simply my idea of heaven.[14]

The full expectations of the girls were not initially fulfilled, however, since Wilson decided that an inaugural ball was out of keeping with a democratic society, and so it was dispensed with, to the great disappointment of the capital's society ladies, as well as of his own daughters. Eleanor wrote "I shed some tears; I knew he was right, but wished desperately that he wouldn't be so Jeffersonian."

Ellen recalled that at the time of Wilson's nomination, a news reporter had enquired whether, since neither she nor any of her daughters wore any jewelry, she harbored a dislike for jewels, and she answered that it wasn't a question of dislike, it was simply that she possessed none. This was still the same situation four years later, but this time, not wishing that her daughters suffer embarrassment over the same issue, she made a secret journey to New York and purchased jewelry for each of them, but, for some unaccountable reason, she bought nothing for herself. Whereupon, Wilson went out and bought her a diamond pendant which, thereafter, was always referred to within the family as the "crown jewel." He was able to indulge in this little family extravagance since he had borrowed the sum of five thousand dollars to cover the expenses of moving from Princeton to the White House.

Wilson had once casually remarked to his family that he believed he might have as many as fifty first cousins, but this apparently proved to be a very conservative estimate, since hosts of relatives turned up for the inauguration, and a hasty improvisation was arranged so that they were, respectively, accommodated at either a "Woodrow Lunch," a "Wilson Dinner," or an "Axson-Hoyt Lunch." Most of those who attended were never seen or heard of again.

Like any other presidential family, the Wilsons fell immediately under national scrutiny and attention, much of which came to be considered by Wilson as sheer harassment, and he voiced his objections in no uncertain manner, as he had already done in Bermuda. He was the first President to initiate regular press conferences, and here he took full advantage of the opportunity of expostulating against the irresponsibility of certain of the reporters and their newspapers for publishing all manner of ridiculous assertions relating, particularly, to Margaret's alleged romance(s) with a host of beaus, many of whom she hadn't even met. He deplored this effort at "creating news" and he was led to the outburst:

> I am a public character for the time being, but the ladies of my household are not servants of the government and they are not public characters. I deeply resent the treatment they are receiving at the hands of the newspapers at this time. . . .

He added vehemently:

> . . . . If this continues I shall deal with you, not as President, but as man to man.

It is possible that the girls themselves were less disturbed than their father with the increased publicity accorded them as daughters of the President. Their social calendar was filled with almost nightly invitations to attend dances, balls, and functions, and their only objection appeared to be directed against Ellen's insistence that they appear individually and separately at each of the invitations, so that the presidential "favors" could be more widely distributed among the prominent hostesses of

Washington society. What gave them most irritation was the protocol that no guest could leave any function until the daughter of the President herself left. The girls were young and lively and had the physical capacity to dance all night, but this imposed stresses and strains upon the more elderly guests who were led to quiet remonstrance with the social secretary of the First Lady. While, in good time, the daughters responded, there were several unfortunate lapses for which Ellen had perforce to offer her personal regrets.

The girls found one other practice to be irksome—that of the daily bus tours around the White House precincts, when the mere presence of one of the girls would bring a tour to a halt, and the megaphoned comments of the guide would destroy all privacy and ruin an afternoon's relaxed stroll on the lawn.

So, deciding upon a hilarious retaliation Margaret and Eleanor set out one afternoon, dressed in old clothes, and half-veiled to avoid recognition, to join one such "rubber-neck wagon." At first they were quiet, but their "adventurous spirits" soon took the upper hand and, as they approached the White House, Margaret, in a loud voice, pleaded with the guide, "Oh, mister, can't we go in? I want to see where the Wilson girls sleep. Please take us in . . . Why can't we go in? . . . ." The guide explained that a visit inside the White House itself required a special permit which he would try to obtain for her, but even that would not allow access to the bedrooms. As Eleanor commented: "Weak with laughter, I dragged her (Margaret) off as soon as I could."[15]

Eleanor was approached by a silk company for the purpose of dedicating a new color in her name, which she was invited to select along the lines of "Alice Blue" of Roosevelt fame. The new color was named "Nell Rose" but the gentle flame color selected by Eleanor emerged as a "hideous magenta red," and the project was a disastrous financial failure.[16]

Whatever Wilson thought about the unwarranted intrusions by the press into his daughter's private affairs, the fact remained that romance was in the air. Eleanor was still involved with her American missionary in Mexico, but, slowly, distance failed to lend the necessary enchantment, and the all-too-close proximity of William Gibbs McAdoo gradually gained the upper, as well as his, hand. "Mac" as he came to be known within the family, invited her to play tennis, then was in attendance at dances, where apparently he became very possessive, and would object to anyone "cutting-in" on his partner, growling, "It's not etiquette to cut in on a Cabinet Officer."

Albeit, the first daughter to marry was Jessie. During her settlement work at Philadelphia she had become associated with Francis Bowes Sayre, a graduate of Williams College and Harvard Law School, who had received appointment in the office of the New York Commissioner of Corrections. Sayre had, during summer months, worked with Dr. Wilfred Grenfell of Labrador fame, and contemporary observers remarked upon his startling likeness in physical appearance to Woodrow Wilson himself. On November 25, 1913, Jessie and Francis were married in the East Room of the White House, with Dr. Grenfell as best man. A crisis occurred the evening before the wedding, since the bridesmaids' headdresses, designed by Eleanor and delivered just that day, proved to be a "complete and hideous failure." The girls sat up most of the night to remake them and, by morning, were exhausted, but they had the satisfaction of completing presentable alternatives. Following the ceremony, Jessie contrived to throw the bridal bouquet in Eleanor's direction and she caught it.

Considering it a good omen, and likewise greatly impressed by the quantity and quality of the wedding presents received by her sister, Eleanor lost no time in accepting the latest of McAdoo's persistent offers of marriage, so that, within less than six months, on May 7, 1914, a second wedding was celebrated in the White House, this time in the Blue Room. A humorous commentator of the day suggested that, in the light of events, it would not be inappropriate to appoint a permanent committee of Congress to purchase wedding presents for the President's daughters.

After a honeymoon in Europe where they visited settlements, Francis and Jessie made their home in Williamstown, where Francis had been appointed as instructor in government and as assistant to Williams College President Harry A. Garfield. Jessie returned to the White House for the birth of their first son, Francis Bowes, Jr., who was born in 1915. Sayre received a doctorate from Harvard Law School in 1918, and was a member of the faculty from that date until 1933. Jessie gave birth to two other children, Eleanor Axson, and Woodrow Wilson, respectively.

After her marriage to Mac, Eleanor and her husband took up residence at the White House, where it now became obvious that Ellen was a very sick woman. Tubercular infection of her kidneys had led to rapid deterioration of her health, and her family watched helplessly at her prolonged pain and suffering. When she died on August 6, 1914, their great grief was also accompanied with no little thankfulness that she had been finally relieved of her agony and torment.

Wilson himself was devastated—his much-loved helpmate of twenty-eight years had suddenly been removed, and he felt completely isolated, and all this in his status as the highest executive officer in the land, when the daily public burdens and chores demanded some private relaxation provided by the comfort and warmth of his immediate family contacts. He remained inconsolable and depressed for months. The McAdoos did their best to ease his despondency, as did his close friend, Dr. Gary T. Grayson, Ellen's physician, and Helen Bones, Ellen's social secretary. It happened that Dr. Grayson had fallen in love with a certain young lady, Alice Gertrude Gordon, known as Altrude, who was the ward of a Washington widow, Edith Bolling Galt. The latter's husband, Norman Galt, who had died in 1908, had been a prominent Washington jeweler, while she herself proudly claimed descent from the marriage of John Rolfe and his Indian princess, Pocahontas.

Dr. Grayson introduced his fiancee and Mrs. Galt to Helen Bones, who invited them to tea at the White House. On his part, Grayson often played golf with Wilson in an effort to compel the President to relax by participating in some outdoor physical exercise, although the latter was once quoted as having defined the game as "an ineffectual attempt to put an illusive ball into an obscure hole with implements ill-adapted to the purpose."[17] It was upon the return from one of his games with Grayson, that Wilson was introduced at a tea-session to Mrs. Galt, and, between them, there developed a warm friendship which quickly matured into love, and their marriage took place on December 18, 1915.[18] The honeymoon was spent at Hot Springs, Virginia.[19]

The family appeared to have approved of the romance since it brought Wilson out of his prolonged depression. His immediate political colleagues were less sanguine since they feared the effect of so soon an engagement after Ellen's death upon the presidential election of November, 1916. While the race was close, Wilson emerged as the victor with 277 electoral votes as compared with 254 for Charles Evans Hughes.

Wilson's second term of office proved to be one of toil and tumult, since, in little over one month of his inauguration, the country was at war with Germany. But turbulent as were the years of conflict, the ensuing years of peace were even more so. Ominous political signs were clearly evident from the results of congressional elections held only six days prior to the signing of the Armistice on November 11, 1918: the Democrats lost their majorities in both the Senate and the House.

In December, Wilson and his wife sailed to Europe where the President proposed to participate in treaty negotiations. They landed at Brest, France, where they were met by Wilson's daughter, Margaret. The latter had embarked upon a singing career after the death of her mother. A music critic writing in 1915 stated that her voice had "a sympathetic quality, which is its most commendable attribute," and added that she sang "with intelligence and feeling and without affectation."[20] After a singing tour of the military camps in the United States, Margaret had sailed to Europe to perform similar duties for the American Expeditionary Forces, and, on Christmas Day, 1918, she sang to the troops at Gondercourt in the presence of her father.

While Wilson was fully occupied in Paris, Margaret and her stepmother had undertaken some diversionary trips to various places in Western Europe, including Italy. They enjoyed their visits, some of which were hilarious and were delectably described by Edith in her autobiography, the first such publication by any First Lady. While in Rome, for instance, on a visit to see the illuminations of the Forum, Margaret was hosted by the over six-foot-tall Duchess of Aosta, who made Margaret feel "like the lesser end of Mutt and Jeff." Again, at a state banquet in the Quirinal, Margaret found herself seated next to the very deaf Duke of Genoa. Marconi was a guest at the same function, and Margaret, seeking to make small talk communication with her neighbor, had four times to repeat a comment expressing her admiration for the great scientist, whereupon, finally, the Duke responded: "Yes, there are more tunnels in it than any other in the world between here and Paris, I am told."[21]

On their visit to Belgium, Edith and Margaret were guests with the Queen of Belgium on a tour by motorcade of the devastated towns and villages. The open cars raised considerable dust, and Margaret had pleaded to accompany Edith and the Queen in the first car to avoid being choked. Her Majesty did not take lightly to her request, but finally permitted her to sit on a low, and extremely uncomfortable pull-down seat, whence Margaret proceeded to bounce and fall off at regular intervals. The Queen was even more annoyed and irritated since she had been given bouquets of flowers, to certain of which she was allergic, but, under the circumstances, she could hardly dispose of, so she spent most of the journey red-eyed, weeping, and sneezing.[22]

Despite these diversions, Margaret was exhausted by the time she returned to the United States, when she suffered a nervous breakdown. While recuperating in Asheville, North Carolina, she was asked to sing at a function sponsored by General Pershing. She was unable to respond since her voice had become overstrained, but Pershing publicly voiced his appreciation for her sustained efforts on behalf of the armed services.

Her breakdown almost coincided with that of her father, who had undertaken a strenuous tour of the United States by rail in an effort to gain support for his concept of the League of Nations. While returning from the West, he suffered a mild stroke on September 25, 1919, at Pueblo, Colorado, and yet another on October 2, after his return to Washington. The latter left him partially paralyzed, and, for over six months, Mrs. Wilson functioned as "acting President," making her own decisions as to which documents her husband should see, and which persons he should be seen by.

Despite considerable sympathy for his tragic illness, Congress rejected his appeal on behalf of the League of Nations. The sole remaining topic of interest now lay in the presidential nominations and election of November, 1920. Wilson's son-in-law, William McAdoo, had served him well as Secretary of the Treasury for eight full years, and, during the war, he had successfully promoted the Liberty Loans of 1917 and 1918, and his wife, Eleanor, had ably supported him. During the flu epidemic at the end of the war, she had helped to organize a kitchen-canteen for invalids associated with the Treasury Department, and had personally trained a group of Girl Scouts to render assistance.

McAdoo's abilities were well known and widely recognized by the country, and many Democrats voiced their support of him as a presidential candidate, but before committing themselves, they awaited some tangible evidence that Wilson approved of the nomination. This was not forthcoming, possibly by reason of the President's fear of being accused of nepotism,[23] and so the nomination passed to James M. Cox of Ohio, with Franklin D. Roosevelt as his running mate. They were overwhelmingly defeated by the Republicans, Warren G. Harding and Calvin Coolidge.

Wilson spent the last years of his life at a house on S Street, Washington. He recovered sufficiently to be able to attend Saturday night performances at Keith's Vaudeville House, while at home he enjoyed Hollywood films on a projector given him by Douglas Fairbanks, who also took the trouble to direct a family film of the McAdoo children.

His constant companions were his wife, Helen Bones, and Margaret who, still pursuing her musical career in New York, commuted to Washington on weekends. She was with her father when he died on the third of February, 1924. Three months earlier, Wilson had given a public address over the radio in which he reaffirmed his faith in the League of Nations, but, on his deathbed, Margaret claimed to have heard him say that perhaps it was a good thing that the concept of the League had been rejected, since the country wasn't ready for it. When Margaret made public this admission, Edith Wilson was furious, and she accused Margaret of having betrayed her father.

Under the terms of his will, Wilson left his entire estate to his widow for life, except for $2,500 a year to be paid to Margaret as long as she remained unmarried. At Eleanor's wedding, a decade earlier, Margaret had caught the bridal bouquet, but she never married. She bore a very close resemblance to her father with his jutting chin, his long straight nose, and like him, she even wore rimless pince-nez spectacles. She was a very independent personality, but she appeared rootless after her father's death. For two years she pursued a career in the advertising business, along with speculating in oil stocks, where she lost an appreciable sum of money, and, in 1927, a court judgment of over $10,000 was entered against her. To her credit, she worked hard and succeeded in paying off the debt.

Her subsequent activities excited little comment until 1940, when George Nakashima, an American-born Japanese architect, reported that he had seen and talked with her at a religious colony at Pondicherry, Southern India, where he had been commissioned to design and construct a dormitory. Apparently, Margaret, while living in New York, had happened upon a book written by Sri Aurobindo, an Indian Hindu mystic. She became fascinated with his beliefs and doctrines, and, in 1939, left her homeland forever to live as a white-robed disciple at the asram he had established in Pondicherry.

In 1943, she was interviewed by *New York Times* correspondent Herbert L. Matthews, who described her as being happy and contented, with no wish ever to return to the United States. In the asram she had been given the name of Dishta, a Sanskrit word meaning "leading to the discovery of the divine self in every human being." It was there that she died of uremia on February 12, 1944, at age 57.

While her husband, Francis, was a member of the Harvard law faculty, Jessie, Wilson's second daughter, involved herself politically in the League of Women Voters, in support of the League of Nations, and in the enhancement of the Democratic party image in Massachusetts. In 1929, she was approached for nomination as candidate for the U.S. Senate, but this she declined.

Francis concerned himself with matters relating to international law, and was for a number of years extra-territorial rights consultant to the King of Siam. The Sayre family spent a year in that country in 1923–4. At home, in accordance with his earlier missionary and settlement activities, he was deeply concerned with the problem of juvenile delinquency.

In 1933, Jessie died suddenly following an operation for appendicitis. She was only 45 years old. Four years later, Francis married Elizabeth Evans Graves, widow of Ralph Graves of the National Geographic Society. In the year of Jessie's death he accepted an appointment by

Franklin D. Roosevelt as Assistant Secretary of State in which capacity he served until 1939 when he became High Commissioner to the Philippines,[24] whence he escaped by submarine from Corregidor after the Japanese invasion.

After World War II, Francis continued his distinguished career as U.S. Diplomatic Advisor attached to the U.N. Relief and Rehabilitation Administration, and, from 1947–52, he was U.S. representative on the U.N. Trusteeship Council. On the national front, he was active in the councils of the Episcopal Church, and it gave him no little pride when his elder son, Francis B. Sayre, Jr., was appointed Dean of Washington (Episcopal) Cathedral. Francis Sr. was 86 when he died in March, 1972.[25]

William McAdoo, having failed in his initial bid as presidential candidate in 1920, re-entered the hustings in 1924, where his party opponent was Alfred E. Smith. In an ensuing deadlock, a compromise candidate, John W. Davis, was selected, and he lost to the Republican incumbent President, Calvin Coolidge.

The McAdoos had, in 1923, taken up residence in Los Angeles, where McAdoo set up a law practice. In 1931, he published an autobiography, *Crowded Years,* and returned to the national scene when, at the Democratic Convention of June, 1932, McAdoo was instrumental in switching California's vital 44 votes (pledged to John Nance Garner) in support of Franklin D. Roosevelt at the fourth ballot, thus ensuring the latter's nomination.

In the November election, McAdoo was elected U.S. Senator for California, but then domestic problems interceded. Eleanor found that her health could not stand the oppressive humid climate of the capital and, in 1934, she successfully sued for an uncontested divorce. Eleanor remained unmarried until her death in April, 1967, at Montecito, California.[26]

McAdoo was remarried in 1935 to Doris Cross, a nurse in the U.S. Health Service. At that time, he was 71 and his bride, 26. In 1940, they adopted the son of his elder daughter, Ellen Wilson McAdoo (by Eleanor), who had married Rafael Lopez DeOnate, but had suicided. One year later, McAdoo succumbed of a heart attack in a San Francisco hotel. He was buried in Arlington Cemetery, in honor of his service as a member of Woodrow Wilson's War Cabinet.

Warren Gamaliel Harding

(1921–1923)

The presidential election of November, 1920, was the first in which women were permitted to exercise their right to vote, in accordance with the passage of the 19th Amendment to the Constitution.[1] For the first time also, at least in the twentieth century, the nation's electorate was confronted with the dilemma of having to make a choice between two relatively unknown candidates; unknown, that is, outside Ohio, for it happened that both men were natives of that state. James M. Cox, the Democratic presidential candidate, was a millionaire who had twice been elected Governor of Ohio. It took forty-four ballots before he was nominated, and then he chose as his running mate Franklin D. Roosevelt. Cox's opponent was Warren G. Harding, who had served as lieutenant-governor of Ohio and as a U.S. Senator. The Republican party leaders were confident that the country's electorate would reject the Democratic party's policy of adherence to Wilson's international program involving the United States in a League of Nations, but they were also concerned lest a party split, as in 1912, could nullify their aspirations. Hence, after

protracted negotiations, culminating in a final discussion held in the early
hours of the morning in Room 404, the famous "smoke-filled room," of
the Blackstone Hotel, Chicago, the decision was made to nominate the
noncontroversial, inconspicuous Warren Harding, who went on to defeat
Cox easily by the electoral vote of 404 to 127.

The party caucus members, before finally deciding upon Harding, had
inquired of him as to whether there might be any incident in his past life
which, if given publicity, could embarrass the party during the forthcoming presidential campaign. Harding had given them a simple answer,
"No," whereas the simple answer should have been "Yes."

Harding's wife, Florence (Flossie) Kling, was five years older than her
husband. She was a widow (with a son, Marshall Eugene De Wolfe)[2]
whose husband, Henry De Wolfe, had died after she had divorced him in
1885.[3] Harding married Florence in July, 1891, and she was his very
competent assistant in the running of his newspaper in Marion, Ohio.
There appeared to have been, however, another "assistant" in the newspaper office, at least according to her own account.[4] She was Nan
Britton, a physician's daughter, and a schoolgirl of only 14, who brought
in to the *Marion Star* items relating to high school events and activities.
Harding was thirty years older than Nan, who developed a "crush" for
the handsome editor of the newspaper. She had dozens of his photographs pinned up in her bedroom, so that he would be the last person
she saw at night and the first when she awoke in the morning. She
scandalized the small community where she lived by openly declaring
her love for a married man, and her embarrassed mother made desperate
efforts to "turn her off" by making derogatory remarks concerning
Harding's love of smoking and (still worse) of chewing tobacco.

Her infatuation for him appeared to have passed unnoticed by Harding
at this time, and, in 1915, having been elected U.S. Senator, he moved to
Washington. It was there he received a letter from Nan, now in New
York, pleading for assistance in obtaining employment. In reply, Harding
suggested that they meet in New York upon his next visit to the city.

Nan was now 18, and, as she described their first meeting in, of all
places, the bridal chamber of the Manhattan Hotel in Madison Avenue,
"we had scarcely closed the door behind us when we shared our first
kiss," and "between kisses we found time to discuss my immediate need
for a position."[5] Harding obtained employment for her with the United
States Steel Corporation at a wage of sixteen dollars a week.

They subsequently rendezvoued both in New York as well as in
Washington, sometimes in hotels, and at other times in apartments

(loaned by Harding's cronies) or even in his private office on Capitol Hill. On one occasion they traveled together to Indiana as "uncle and niece."

On October 22, 1919, at Asbury Park, New Jersey, Nan gave birth to a daughter, which her mother named Elizabeth Ann Christian, since she (Nan) and Harding had fabricated a story that Nan was the wife of a certain Lieutenant Christian, serving overseas in the U.S. Army. Nan's mother was said to have objected to the marriage, hence Nan was having her baby away from home. At this date, Harding was 54, and Nan was 23. Harding never once saw his daughter. Nan moved to Chicago to reside with her sister, Elizabeth, after whom the baby was named.[6]

In, June, 1920, the Republican Convention was held in Chicago, and Harding arranged for Nan to work as a clerk at the party's headquarters, while the baby was cared for by Nan's sister. It was at this convention that, (as noted earlier), Harding's name was proposed and accepted in the famous episode of "the smoke-filled room."

After his election as President, Harding met secretly with Nan in the White House, where, in a five-foot-square closet adjoining the Cabinet Room, they made love on a number of occasions.

Upon one of his concert tours of the United States, Enrico Caruso, the famed Italian tenor, who was also a gifted cartoonist, drafted a sketch of Harding to resemble George Washington, and he captioned his drawing, "Harding becomes Father of Country." Upon seeing this, Nan commented in her autobiography that it

> . . . struck a deep longing in my heart, for my yearning was not that he be known as the Father of his Country, but that I might proudly say to the world, "He is the father of my child![7]

Nan had attended Columbia University in New York for a brief period during 1921, and, in the following year, she obtained a post as secretary to the president of Northwestern University, Evanston, Illinois. She again considered returning to academic studies and, in January, 1923, she went to Washington to discuss her future with Harding. This proved to be their last meeting. Later in the year, Nan went with a friend, Helen Anderson, to Europe (at Harding's expense), while the President paid a visit to Alaska and the Pacific coast. He was taken ill suddenly and died at a San Francisco hotel on August 2, 1923. Nan was in France when she heard the news.

Her main source of income having been terminated, she contracted a short-lived marriage with a Swedish ship captain who failed to support her. She then set about to make clandestine inquiries as to whether

Harding had made any provision for the support of herself and her daughter. The results were negative and, Mrs. Harding having died in November, 1924, Nan decided to approach the Harding family directly for financial assistance. Harding's sister, Daisy, proved sympathetic to her plea, and gave her $890, but then the younger brother, Dr. George T. Harding, intervened and forbade any further payments.

The latter conducted a four-hour-long interview with Nan in response to her demand for a trust fund of $50,000 for her daughter, and $2,500 for herself. She produced no letters in support of her claim that Harding had promised to look after herself and her child, and, as a result, Dr. Harding did nothing.

It was in consequence of her inability to obtain a share of the Harding estate that Nan published her autobiography in 1927. Five years later, a second book was published under her name entitled, *Honesty in Politics*. It contained little by way of "new revelations" concerning her affair with Harding, but it did include several photographs of the daughter, who, some readers claimed, bore a close likeness to the alleged father.

In 1931, there appeared a book, *The Strange Death of President Harding* based on material provided by Gaston B. Means, a disreputable character, formerly employed by the Department of Justice, who had been imprisoned for illegally selling liquor permits to bootleggers. Obviously intent upon making money out of the scandal, he claimed that he had gained access to love letters written by Harding to Nan Britton, and that he had showed them to Mrs. Harding. By innuendo, he then proceeded to persuade his readers that her inflamed jealousy had led her to deliberately poison her husband at San Francisco, and that his death was not the simple case of food poisoning, as generally assumed.

One of the irritating mysteries pertaining to the entire story involving Nan Britton is why not a single genuine, original love letter, either to or from Harding, was ever produced and published. Nan Britton claimed that she had destroyed Harding's letters lest they fell into the hands of some unscrupulous person who might then resort to blackmail. Her own letters to Harding appear to have been all destroyed either by the President himself or by the First Lady.

Harding's activities as a womanizer were not confined to Nan Britton; in 1964, there appeared a book entitled *The Shadow of Blooming Grove*, by Francis Russell who, several years earlier, had uncovered a collection of approximately two-hundred-and-fifty love letters written by Harding between 1909 and 1920 to Carrie Phillips, wife of a prominent department store part-owner in Marion, Ohio. According to Hope Ridings Miller,[8] Russell had fully intended to publish a biography of Harding, to include the letters in 1965, the one-hundredth anniversary of the President's birth, but he had been prevented from doing so as the result of a lawsuit filed by Dr. George T. Harding III, one of Harding's nephews.[9]

The Harding and Phillips families were close friends and they had traveled abroad together to the Mediterranean and Egypt, as well as to Bermuda. The illicit relationship between Harding and Mrs. Phillips later became known to the respective spouses of both participants, and the affair terminated before Harding was elected President. To avoid the possibility of disclosure of the affair, Mrs. Phillips was offered the sum of twenty thousand dollars, with an additional monthly allowance for as long as Harding was in office, on condition that she and her husband undertook an expense-paid trip around the world; they agreed, and they remained abroad until Harding's death. Mrs. Phillips lived on until 1960, and it was following her death in that year, that the love letters were made available to Francis Russell.

Harding was fortunate: the scandals relating to his personal life, as well as to his political administration, did not erupt until after his death. To his many admirers he still remains one of the most handsome men who has ever graced the office of chief executive.

Calvin Coolidge

(1923–1929)

Calvin Coolidge was Vice-President during the Harding administration, but his reputation remained unsullied through the long drawn-out investigations and court trials relating to the corrupt practices of so many of the Cabinet officers. To Americans he remains the epitome of honesty in high places and, during his six years of office, it was he, also, who successfully brought to fruition Harding's plea for a "return to normalcy": whatever the crisis, Coolidge presented a calm, serene, and imperturbable image.

In college, he had been nicknamed "Cal the Clam"; as President, he became known to posterity as "Silent Cal", a sobriquet usually accompanied by a host of delightful anecdotes to prove it. As described by the famous Alice (daughter of Theodore Roosevelt), Coolidge appeared as though he had been "weaned on a pickle." If Harding has qualified for consideration as the nation's most handsome President, Coolidge (like Woodrow Wilson) could be regarded as the very original for Grant Wood's painting "American Gothic." He was always portrayed as an unsmiling, indifferent, expressionless individual to the extent that, when Dorothy Parker, the famous columnist, was informed of his death in 1933, her simple comment was, "How could they tell?"

Coolidge was born on July 4, 1872, in Plymouth, Vermont, of John Calvin Coolidge, Sr., (who had been a member of both state legislatures) and his wife, Victoria Josephine (Moor), who had died when Calvin Jr. was only 12, and when the latter's sister, Abigail Gratia, was 9. Both Calvin and Abigail attended school together at Black River Academy, Ludlow, but then Abigail was stricken suddenly with appendicitis and died at age 15 in 1890.

In due course, Coolidge qualified as a lawyer and hung up his shingle in Northampton, Massachusetts, where he met Grace Anna Goodhue, a teacher at the Clarke School for the deaf and dumb, and a graduate of the University of Vermont. They were married in October, 1905. They were blessed with two sons, John, born in 1906, and Calvin Jr., born in 1908. The family never lived in a house of their own at Northampton, where they rented one-half of a two-family dwelling. Coolidge had entered the political arena, first as a member of the Massachusetts Legislature, then as Mayor of Boston, and finally as State Governor. During this period of fifteen years, Coolidge roomed in Boston and spent his weekends at Northampton, leaving Grace with most of the responsibility of rearing their two sons. Fortunately for Coolidge, Grace was an outgoing, charming personality who not only ungrudgingly accepted her home responsibilities, but also gave her husband her dedicated support and encouragement to advancing his political career. She was an active member of the Red Cross and, apart from knitting all the socks for her husband and sons, she made dozens of sweaters for members of the armed forces during the war period of 1917–18.

The two boys were educated in the public schools of Northampton, whence they proceeded to Mercersburg Academy in Pennsylvania. While at the latter institution, they had occasion to write home with a request that Coolidge purchase dressing gowns for them, but his reply was that, since he wore nothing around the house except his night gown, he saw no reason why the boys could not do likewise. It was Grace who, out of her personal allowance, eventually purchased the garments and sent them to her sons.

Academically, Calvin Jr. was not as bright as John, but both boys were popular at school by reason of their sunny dispositions—a trait obviously acquired from their mother rather than from the father. She encouraged them to develop a taste for music, and Calvin learned to play the violin, and John, the mandolin. She participated in all their games, even to helping them lay out a railroad track on the dining room floor, and, to their great delight, she even learnt to throw a fast baseball, and to acquire a lasting love for and interest in the national pasttime—unlike her husband who (much to his disgust when President) found himself having to attend the opening matches of the season in Washington. . . he sat bored to death throughout the games. To the intense joy of Grace and the boys, the local team, the Washington Senators, won the World Series in 1924.

The family had moved to the capital city in 1921 when Coolidge was Vice-President, and they had taken up residence at the Willard Hotel, since Coolidge had concluded that, on a salary of $12,000, he could not afford to rent a house. The boys, particularly, hated the confinement of restricted accommodation and welcomed the long congressional summer recesses when they could return to New England and spend time on the farm estate owned by Coolidge's father in Plymouth, Vermont. It was to this place in the early hours of the morning of August 3, 1923, that the news arrived of Harding's death, and it was here, by the light of a kerosene lamp, that Coolidge was sworn in as President of the United States by his father, in his capacity as a notary public.

At the time that their father became President, John, the elder son, was nearly 17, and his brother, Calvin Jr., was 14. During the summer of 1923, John had enlisted at a citizen's military training camp at Fort Devens, Massachusetts. His father expected him to complete the course before returning to Washington, and he did just that. Cal Jr. had found employment on a tobacco farm at Hatfield, Massachusetts, and, according to the oft-told story, when one of the laborers had said, that, if his father were President of the United States, he wouldn't work in a tobacco field, Cal retorted: "If my father were your father, you would."

Coolidge's salary as President permitted some relaxation in terms of the family's financial pressures, if the President so desired, but his austere New England upbringing led to no overall splurges or over-indulgences. Of all the Presidents known to the White House staff, none had been so economical in terms of upkeep expenditures than Calvin Coolidge. As a legendary tale or not, the President was once asked as to what had been his major disappointment while at the White House; his reply was simple, direct, and typical—that he had never been able to ascertain what happened to the leftovers. He meticulously supervised all the household accounts, and, in this respect, his administration was fortunate, since it was the first to be accorded by Congress an entertainment expense account. The latter carried with it one important proviso: that such entertainment was to be accorded to the leaders of both political parties. Coolidge immediately took advantage of this clause, and one of the major innovations of his administration was that of the "Coolidge Breakfasts" held at 7:45 A.M., which relatively few attended on a regular basis because of its inopportune hour for most Congressmen accustomed to late night society life, but it afforded Coolidge an expense account meal for the entire family.

He tolerated no exception to his rule that all his family should be present at breakfast. On one occasion, Grace's cousin, Marion Pollard Burrows, had been invited to stay at the White House. Thrilled with anticipation, she imagined herself pleasantly dozing in bed after a good night's sleep, to be gently awakened by a solicitous maid bringing her a tray with "iced orange juice, coffee in a little silver pot, and everything else in covered dishes, all gay with flowers."[1] The rude reality was far removed: she was expected to appear fully dressed at the breakfast table like everyone else.

The White House dress code was, in the same way, rigidly maintained at all times. John once remarked that, since he expected to be late arriving home one evening, he would not have time to dress for dinner, to which Coolidge replied: "You will remember you are dining at the table of the President of the United States, and you will present yourself promptly and in proper attire."[2]

Yet Coolidge was not utterly devoid of a sense of humor, as when Calvin Jr., clad in a formal suit, was having difficulty with his tie: his father said, "Son, I know how you fix that. Get a rope and fasten it on the back there. Then tie a flatiron on each end, and put the flatirons in your coat pocket."[3]

Coolidge insisted upon early retirement at 10 P.M. at the White House, and he imposed a number of restrictions upon the activities of his wife: she was not, for example, permitted to bob her hair in the fashion of the day, or learn to drive a car, or even to ride a horse. Her only alternative was to walk, and this she did, regularly and vigorously. The daily exercise may have, at least in part, accounted for the fact that Grace survived her husband by almost 25 years.

Despite any frustrations she may have felt from the many limitations imposed upon her freedom of action, Grace faithfully deferred to her husband in all his wishes. She nobly bore the brunt of his frequent outbursts of irascibility when irritated by a Congress opposed to his proposals, and she summarized her philosophy in the following passage:

> I have scant patience with the man of whom his wife says "he never gave me a cross word in his life." It seems to me he must be a feckless creature. If a man amounts to much in this world, he must encounter many and varied annoyances whose number mounts as

his effectiveness increases. Inevitably comes a point beyond which the human endurance breaks down and an explosion is bound to follow.[4]

Yet, despite his overly authoritarian mannerisms, Coolidge was a humane father and an affectionate husband. He was only too well aware of his own shortcomings as a social success, although that never bothered him, and he remained immune from the darts of adverse public opinion. But he was also aware that he owed Grace an enormous debt by reason of her unfailing charm and affability which more than compensated for his own apparent boorishness towards guests in the White House. He also recognized that Washington society was capable of inflicting considerable pain and humiliation upon the victims of its spleen, so that Coolidge permitted himself to be untypically extravagant with respect to his wife's wardrobe. He insisted that, at all public receptions, Grace should never be attired in anything less than the most fashionable and elegant of clothing. So clad, Grace exuded nothing but ease, confidence, and serenity at all times.

Within less than a year of moving into the White House, the Coolidge family suffered a cruel tragedy. While playing tennis with his brother John, Calvin Jr. accidentally stubbed his toe, and what initially appeared to be a matter of minor concern slowly developed into a severe case of blood poisoning for which the day and age had no antidote. The distraught father and mother watched helplessly as their beloved son suffered increasing pain with no relief. Knowing his son's love of animals,[5] Coolidge caught a rabbit in the White House garden and brought it in to the sick boy's bedroom in an effort to alleviate the agony. It was to no avail and Cal Jr. died on July 7, 1924.

Coolidge, later recording the event in his autobiography, wrote of his son, "When he went, the power and the glory of the Presidency went with him. . . . I don't know why such a price was exacted for occupying the White House."[6] He said to Taft, "I do not mind the loss of the boy so much. My sorrow is occasioned by the belief that he possessed great power for good that would have made itself felt, had he lived."[7]

At the time of his brother's death, John had just graduated from Mercersburg and, in the fall of the same year, he proceeded to Amherst, his father's alma mater.[8] Well aware of the rigid expectations of his father, John was always attentive to his studies, but yet took time out to participate not only in athletics (especially boxing, which earned him the nickname of "Butch"), but also in college theatricals where he excelled in the comic operettas of Gilbert and Sullivan.

The junior class of Amherst published an annual entitled *Olio,* and, in 1928, it made reference to John:

> Coolidge came to college with a second-hand pea jacket, a perfect complexion, and an air of perfect boredom. These possessions he has guarded jealously, and has augmented them in his three years here with a very slight knowledge of the saxophone, a slighter acquaintance with the art of pugilism, some seven thousand scented letters from admiring school girls, and a scrapbook bulging with newspaper clippings arranged alphabetically from "Elopement" to "Secret Service." John is really a darn good gent but so reserved it's hard to get acquainted with him. So saying, the entire college bodies of Amherst, Smith, and Mt. Holyoke excuse themselves to their friends for not spending their vacations in the White House.[9]

Reserved or not, this trait did not prevent John from becoming amorously attached to Florence Trumbull, daughter of the Governor of Connecticut, and they were married on September 28, 1928, only three months following his graduation at Amherst. He decided to pursue a business career, and was employed as an agent by the New York, New Haven, and Hartford Railroad Company.

Earlier in the year 1928, Coolidge had made public his decision not to seek re-election as President in a simply but typically laconic six-word statement, "I do not choose to run."[10] Following the expiry of his term of office he returned to Northampton, Massachusetts, where he devoted himself to the writing of his *Autobiography,* for which he eventually received the sum of $75,000.[11]

On January 5, 1933, Coolidge died suddenly of a heart attack, aged 60.[12] He had bought a new home, "The Beeches," but, after his death, Grace moved into a smaller house, where, in time, she came to love the company of her grandchildren, Cynthia and Lydia, the two daughters of John and Florence. On the anniversary of his father's death John sent flowers annually to his mother, before she, too, died on July 8, 1957. She was buried in the family plot at Plymouth, Vermont, beside her husband and her son, Calvin Jr.

John had resigned in 1941 from his employment with the railroad company to become treasurer and president of a small company manufacturing manifold forms. According to Cavanah (1958), he proposed, after retirement, to return to Plymouth, Vermont, his father's place of birth, to re-open an old cheese factory which his grandfather had been one of the first shareholders.[13]

Herbert Clark Hoover

(1929–1933)

The Hoover family could lay claim to several notable distinctions; in the first place, it was easily the most traveled of all presidential families—the President's first son, Herbert Clark Hoover, Jr., had circumnavigated the world with his parents three times before he was three years old. Herbert Hoover, Sr., was the first President to systematically preserve all his papers and correspondence for posterity.[1]

The future President was a member of the first graduating class of 1895 of the newly founded Leland Stanford Jr. University, Palo Alto, California. He had majored in engineering geology and, for his first major assignment he was sent to the Australian goldfield of Coolgardie, where he literally "struck it rich."[2] Upon returning to the United States he proposed marriage to, and was accepted by, another Stanford geology major, Lou Henry. As soon as the marriage celebrations had been concluded, the couple sailed to China, where, almost immediately, they found themselves involved in the emergency task of having to organize the defense of the Tientsin Legation Compound, besieged for three months by the Chinese during the Boxer Rebellion of 1900.

Hoover's expanding mining interests took the family to London in 1903, and it was here, on August 4, that their first son, Herbert Clark Hoover, Jr., was born. Within two months they were in Australia, this time in Broken Hill, and, after returning to London, they once more found themselves on board ship bound for South Africa and again for Australia before making another stop in London, where on July 17, 1907, Lou Henry gave birth to her second son, Allan Henry Hoover. No sooner had she recuperated than she was preparing for another journey, this time to Burma. She accomplished miracles by way of transporting her two young children, and providing for appropriate food, clothing, and medical necessities, all of which chores she performed with seldom a word of complaint. She loved the physical challenge of outdoor life, for which she had been prepared first by her mother, who had enrolled her for one year at the state normal school in Los Angeles because "it had the best gymnasium west of the Mississippi," and then by her father: the latter was a banker, but once when asked as to what kind of person she might consider getting married to, Lou Henry replied "I want a man who loves the mountains, the rocks, and the ocean, like my father does."[3] She was fortunate in finding her ideal husband in the person of Herbert Hoover.

With a young family to rear and educate, the Hoovers recognized that, while the very nature of the husband's profession made overseas travel virtually imperative, it was necessary to provide a stable home and base for the children. With this in mind, they planned for a residence at Stanford, and it was there in the public schools that both boys received their early education. In 1908, Hoover chose not to renew his contract with his engineering firm, and, instead, expanded upon his own consultancy services. This enabled him to spend more time with his family, although his work still entailed extensive traveling, including journeys to Russia and Siberia. With Stanford as his base, he became involved in the affairs of the university, and he contributed a substantial sum of money towards the construction of a new Stanford Union Building while, in 1912, he was elected a member of the university board of trustees.

Before the outbreak of World War I, the family was again uprooted, this time to London, where the "Red House" in Kensington was to become a well-loved and cherished home. The war itself completely transformed Hoover's career, when he acceded to a request from the U.S. Ambassador that he help organize the repatriation of stranded Americans

in Western Europe. This temporary assignment developed into prolonged involvement with the Belgian refugee problem.

Lou Henry sailed back to the United States in the fall of 1914 with the
two boys. While still on board ship, Herbert Hoover, Jr., sent a
cablegram to his father to the effect that, after undergoing an initial bout
of seasickness, he had celebrated his return to good health by eating no
fewer than seven cream puffs in one day. This strange communication
immediately aroused suspicion that it was a code message involving
some form of espionage, and in consequence of the ensuing hassle, Lou
Henry made certain that no further dispatches were sent to Hoover while
the family was on board ship.

Back at Stanford, the boys re-enrolled in the local public schools, but
not for long, since, within a year, she took her family back to London so
that she could be near her husband. The boys were placed in a private
boarding school while Lou Henry volunteered her services in a hospital
staffed by Americans.

In 1916, there came yet another transfer back to California, this time
based on Lou Henry's humorous pretext that her sons were acquiring too
good an Oxford accent for American boys.[4] With the declaration of war
by the United States on April 6, 1917, Hoover returned home, having
accepted President Wilson's invitation to set up and direct the Office of
American Food administration.

This entailed a transfer of residence from California to Washington,
where Hoover rented the former Adams home on Massachusetts Avenue
in which, subsequently, the family was to entertain some of the most
notable personalities of the period, including Paderewski, Masaryk,
Nansen and Marshall Joffre. The boys were enrolled in a school sponsored by the Society of Friends.[5]

Following the termination of hostilities, Hoover was again in Europe
to serve, first as chairman of the Supreme Economic Conference held in
Paris in 1919, and then as chairman of the European Relief Council in
1920.

Hoping to return to private life after his duties in Europe, Hoover next
proceeded upon the construction of a permanent home on the Stanford
campus in Palo Alto. The house took two years to build, but the family
was never to enjoy its comforts until twelve years after its completion
since, in 1921, Hoover was appointed Secretary of Commerce by Harding, and he was to continue in that office under the Coolidge administration.[6]

Back in Washington, Hoover bought a house on S Street (where the
Woodrow Wilsons were their neighbors), and this was to be the family

home for the next eight years, to be followed by four years' residence at the White House after Hoover defeated Al Smith in the presidential election of 1928.

At the time of Hoover's inauguration in 1929, Herbert Jr. was 25, and Allan Henry, 21. Both boys had grown up in the unique atmosphere of an intellectual home where the parents seldom indulged in petty gossip and, instead, conversed at length on matters relating to engineering projects, mineral resources, historical treatises, and international affairs. It is little wonder that Herbert Jr. developed interest, skill, and dexterity in technology, while Allan, likewise, was to pursue a career first in modern farming, and, later, business.

Herbert Jr. suffered the handicap of impaired hearing (which remained with him for the rest of his life) following a severe attack of influenza in 1918. What is remarkable is that his early interest in the new science of radio drove him to make his own hearing aid which he improved along the years as technology advanced. He enrolled at Stanford University, and no sooner had he graduated than he married Margaret (Peggy) Eva Watson, one of his classmates, in June, 1925. The young couple then went to Massachusetts where Herbert entered the Harvard Graduate School of Business Administration. He next proceeded to merge his ongoing interest in radio with the new technology of air transportation, and, upon graduation from Harvard, he took a $200-a-month job as a radio technician with Western Air Express, one of the pioneer airlines which was later absorbed into TWA. He focused upon the development of ground-to-air communication, and, as the result of his efforts, Western became the first airline to have ground radio communication with all its planes over 15,000 miles of airways. Herbert's most publicized achievement was his nationwide broadcast (over the NBC network) from an airplane (which he had converted into a flying laboratory), describing the landing of the Graf Zeppelin at Los Angeles in 1929.

The following year was one of major setbacks: The U.S. postal administration had been permitted by Congress to offer competitive contracts for airmail service by the newly developed airlines. Western was successful in receiving several contracts, and there immediately arose the accusation of nepotism involving the son of the President. The accusations persisted for years and, in 1934, Franklin D. Roosevelt ordered the suspension of all contracts, and directed the army to arrange for airmail service. However, the new system broke down completely since the military resources for such a service were completely inadequate, and, within a short space of time, Roosevelt was obliged to restore the airmail contracts to the private air companies. A subsequent congressional investigation completely exonerated Herbert Jr. and Western Air Express from charges of corruption or malpractice.

In the fall of 1930, Herbert Jr. was diagnosed as having contracted tuberculosis,and he was sent to a sanitarium in Asheville, N.C., for an extended period of enforced rest. A third child (Herbert Hoover III), was born to his wife at this time, and, while the father was recuperating, she and the three children were accommodated at the White House. The eldest child, Peggy Ann, was a great favorite of the President, perhaps because, in an environment which exuded pomp and circumstance, she was in no way awed by it; on the contrary, she took it upon herself to insist that her grandfather, irrespective of any demanding official duties, should attend family meals on time, and any delay would prompt her expostulation: "I said luncheon was ready; come you lazy man!"[7]

Herbert Jr. made a complete recovery from his illness and, in 1933, he and his family accompanied his father and mother back to California, where they were at last domiciled at their Palo Alto dream home. Herbert Jr. was a versatile engineer. He had taught for a while at the California Institute of Technology and, later in the 1930's, he established his own company, the Consolidated Engineering Company of Pasadena, to manufacture sophisticated seismological equipment for use in oil and mineral exploration. After the outbreak of World War II, the company was under contract to produce Sperry instruments.

The varied pressures of living in the shadow of the White House were also experienced by Herbert Jr.'s younger brother, Allan. He, too, had graduated (in economics) from Stanford, and had obtained his M.B.A. degree from Harvard Business School (1931). After some brief experience with banking, he decided that a desk job was not for him, and he embarked upon a farming career in the San Joaquin Valley in California.

Hoover had been in office little more than six months when, on October 29, 1929, the stock market crash precipitated the country into the Great Depression, when thousands of banks failed, and millions of Americans were unemployed. Hoover was completely confused by the unexpected economic chaos, and, in his firm belief that the free enterprise system would right itself in due course, he was adamantly opposed to the use of federal funds and programs as aids to economic revival. He steadfastly maintained this attitude not only throughout his own administration, but also during that of his successor, Franklin D. Roosevelt.

It was Hoover's opposition to Roosevelt's New Deal in general, and to the Agricultural Adjustment Act in particular that presumably prompted an outburst from Henry A. Wallace, the Secretary of Agriculture, who voiced his cynicism that, while the father was occupied in attacking the administration's farm policy, the son, Allan, was happily pocketing a government subsidy of no less than $20,000 for curtailing crops through his ownership of shares in the Kern County Land Company.

When Hoover read the comments he was enraged, the fact being that, while Allan certainly owned shares in the company, his annual subsidy actually amounted to only $2. The ex-President deplored the secretary's remarks and he labeled Wallace's unsubstantiated calumny as a "pretty immoral attempt to smear me over the shoulder of a decent boy."[8] Hoover was ever mindful of the pecuniary temptations dangled before the offspring of Presidents, and he made every effort to impress upon his own sons that high moral and ethical codes in business did actually reap rewards. It is to their credit that both Herbert Jr. and Allan responded positively to his appeal and the father had every reason to feel proud of their behavior, since neither of them ever brought discredit to the family name.

The talents of the ex-President were completely ignored by Roosevelt, but were recognized by Truman, who not only despatched him in 1946, at age 72,[9] on a global fact-finding mission relating to the post-World War II famine situation, but later appointed him as head of a commission on the Organization of the Executive Branch of the Government. The commission produced two monumental reports, in 1949 and 1954, respectively, which were model prescripts of inestimable value in the assessment of practical alternatives available in the process of administrative reform.

Herbert Jr. maintained his interests in seismological oil exploration, and extended his expertise into the complicated legal domain of international oil contracts. In 1943 he received, and accepted, an invitation from President Medina of Venezuela to assist his country's negotiators in formulating the basic principles of model contracts. The experience proved invaluable when, in 1953, Herbert Jr. was appointed as Under-secretary of State (to John Foster Dulles) in the Eisenhower administration, and his first major assignment related to the resolution of the oil crisis in Iran. There, the petroleum industry had been nationalized in 1951, but the British, whose assets had been confiscated, organized an effective two-year international boycott of Iranian oil products. The deteriorating economic situation resulted in serious political disturbances, and the United States became increasingly concerned that the USSR might take advantage of the situation to provoke a revolution supported by Soviet arms.

Over a ten-month period Herbert Jr. virtually commuted between Washington, London, and Tehran, and his efforts were crowned with success when, in 1954, a compromise agreement was concluded between the opposing parties. In 1955, the New York Board of Trade elected him as recipient of its annual Gold Award for public service. Herbert Jr. was abroad at the time of the presentation, which was thereupon accepted by his father on his behalf. Hoover had been honored with the same award in 1949, and, as a part of his acceptance speech, he said:

> There is nothing that makes a father's heart glow warmer than accomplishment of his sons. It took me seventy-five years to achieve such merit as seemed to warrant the Board of Trade to confer this very medal upon me some five years ago. Herbert Jr. achieved that degree of merit after only fifty-two years. That you recognize that he is better material than his dad was at that age confirms my view of him.[10]

In 1957, Herbert Jr. retired to private life and, twelve years later, at age 65, he died in Pasadena, California. His father had died five years earlier in New York at the age of 90, and of all Presidents and ex-Presidents, only John Adams was older, by 176 days, at the time of death.

Allan, who, in 1937, had married Margaret Coberly, a graduate of the University of California, had retained his interests in farming. His estates were in the Bakersfield area of California, and, despite the vicissitudes of the early Roosevelt days, his efforts prospered and, in 1944, he was able to sell part of his property for almost half a million dollars.

Franklin Delano Roosevelt

(1933–1945)

When Franklin D. Roosevelt took office at age 51 on March 4, 1933, as the nation's 32nd President, three of his five (surviving) children had already married, and one had achieved the dubious distinction as being the first son of a President ever to be divorced. A further likewise dubious distinction was accorded to Roosevelt's one and only daughter, Anna, when she became the first "White House daughter" to be granted a divorce: during his "First One Hundred Days" in office, it fell to Roosevelt to call Anna's husband by phone to inform him of Anna's wish to seek separation and eventual divorce. In fact, a persistent feature relating to the years of Roosevelt's tenure of office (and beyond) was the ongoing pattern of marriage-divorce, remarriage-divorce within the family, such that his five children compiled between them no fewer than seventeen marriages, a record hardly likely to be surpassed. Yet, despite these domestic upheavals and conjugal adventures, there appears to be not the slightest evidence that they in any way affected the President's political career.

Roosevelt had married his cousin, Anna Eleanor Roosevelt, on St. Patrick's Day, 1905. The bride had been given away by her uncle, President Theodore Roosevelt, who literally "stole the show" as the "lion of the afternoon," the young couple being virtually ignored by the guests.[1] At the time of his marriage, Roosevelt was 23, and was working casually as a lawyer but was bored with his work. His father had died when he (Roosevelt) was 18, up to which time he had lived a very sheltered life, being taught by a home tutor until 14. He had then attended Groton, proceeded thence to Harvard and to Columbia Law School. He failed to qualify at the latter institution, but, after sitting an examination, he was admitted to the New York bar.

The dominant personality in his life was his mother, Sara, who had taken him to Europe no fewer than eight times, and whose sole ambition for him was that he simply stay at home on the Hyde Park estate and relax for the remainder of his life as a country squire.

As for his wife, Eleanor, she had survived a most unhappy childhood, her mother having died when she was 8, and her father, much-adored but hopelessly alcoholic, had passed away only two years later. He was Elliott, the brother of Theodore Roosevelt. Her early experiences had caused her to be shy and withdrawn, such that her mother had once introduced her to some friends: "This is my daughter, Eleanor. She's such a funny child—so old-fashioned that we always call her 'Granny.' " Eleanor developed a spinal defect which entailed the wearing of an uncomfortable backbrace for years. She occasionally visited the Sagamore Hill residence of the "Oyster Bay Roosevelts," and it was upon one of these visits that Edith, Theodore's second wife, made her famous comment on Eleanor: "Poor little soul, she is very plain. Her mouth and teeth seem to have no future. But the ugly duckling may turn out to be a swan."

After the death of her mother, Eleanor had been sent to live with her Grandmother Hall, where she spent a very disciplined and lonely existence; but then it became her good fortune to be sent to a boarding school in England, where the experience was to change her whole outlook upon life. The school was Allenswood in Wimbledon, London, run by Mlle. Souvestre, an elderly French lady, who had once taught Anna, (Auntie Bye), Theodore Roosevelt's elder sister, in Paris. Mlle. Souvestre had left France after the Franco-German War of 1870, and she became the first person in Eleanor's life to appreciate the latter's lovely but latent personal attributes, and it was at this school that Eleanor literally "turned out to be a swan." She enjoyed her studies and was, moreover, immensely proud of the fact that she "made" the school field hockey team, although this ultimately proved to be a somewhat empty achievement upon her return to the United States where no one played the game.

What actually brought Franklin and Eleanor together remains a mystery. They had, infrequently, met at parties, but, whereas he was, according to his son, James, an extrovert, something of a ladies' man, "a passion he passed on to his sons, for better or worse,"[2] she remained an introvert. Why, then, did he marry her, when so many other lively, beautiful girls were available? James believed it was because his father had, for over twenty years, felt repressed by Sara, his domineering mother, and that he had no wish to spend the remainder of his life subjugated to another authoritarian, overbearing woman. Eleanor appeared to fit the bill, and, still suppressed, passive, obedient and unromantic, she was to admit later that she had not even asked Franklin to kiss her before they were married.

Because of Sara's objections, the wedding had been delayed for over two years after Franklin's proposal of marriage. Her objections may not have been unreasonable at the time, since Franklin was only 21, and Eleanor 19, and he had no means of supporting a wife, not that he had advanced much more in his capacity to do so two years later, so that after the marriage, the young couple found themselves entirely dependent upon Sara for financial support.

After the marriage, Franklin continued with his law studies, and their first home in New York was a small hotel apartment, whose rent and furnishings were paid for by Sara. Eleanor found herself with next to nothing to do, and with even still less when she went to stay with her mother-in-law at Hyde Park, where the entire work was performed by servants. Franklin and Eleanor spent a delayed honeymoon in Europe, and, upon their return, they discovered that Sara had procured a house for them within a few hundred yards of her own residence in New York City.

In May, 1906, their first child, Anna Eleanor, was born. Eleanor admitted: "I had never had any interest in dolls or in little children, and I knew absolutely nothing about handling or feeding a baby." So she hired a hospital nurse who became "a menace, for she was constantly looking for obscure illnesses and never expected that a well-fed and well-cared-for baby would move along in a normal manner."[3]

She was soon replaced, but, on one occasion, a home crisis arose when guests had been invited to dinner on the nurse's evening off. After feeding Anna, her mother put her to bed, but her complete dependence upon the nurse had made her forget to burp her. Anna howled and howled and in desperation Eleanor phoned her doctor, who immediately diagnosed the situation, and the panic subsided.

In December, 1907, James, their first son, was born, to Eleanor's great relief, since she had only too often been made aware by innuendo that it was her paramount duty to produce an heir. During the next few months, Sara had persuaded Eleanor to "air" Anna and James in a chicken-wire cage hung outside an upper window over the sidewalk of their New York home. But one day Anna, possibly feeling the draught, cried so loudly that a neighbor threatened to report Eleanor to the Society for the Prevention of Cruelty to Children, and the cage was withdrawn. James later recorded:

> I am convinced that I contracted pneumonia in that crazy con-
> traption. After that, I was subject to constant colds and developed
> digestive disorders which led to ulcers. A heart murmur was also
> detected, and I had to have rest periods daily. I hated my bad
> health.[4]

Again, responding to Sara's exhortations for "fresh air," the family rented a cottage one summer at Sea Bright, New Jersey. The house was on stilts, and, one day, Anna, in a contrary mood, pushed James in his carriage off the high, unprotected veranda. Fortunately, James sustained little injury but, in reprisal, he stabbed her in the hand with a pencil, and she bore the mark for the rest of her life. When a storm drove the sea into the front room, the quest for salubrious breezes was abandoned, and was never again sought for on the ocean front of New Jersey.

Since Sara now considered the Roosevelt's home in New York as being too small, she bought a plot of land, and, on it, she arranged for the building of two houses, Nos. 46 and 47, respectively, in E. 65th Street. The Roosevelts were to occupy one house while she, Sara, would reside next door, with intercommunicating rooms. Sara selected and paid for the entire furnishings and decoration of both houses, leaving Eleanor with absolutely no choice in anything, a situation which, on the one hand, appeared to satisfy Eleanor, since for the first ten years of her marriage she was either recovering from the birth of one baby, or about to have another; yet, on the other hand, it sometimes reduced her to tears, since she owned nothing and was responsible for nothing, even in her own home: "I was simply absorbing the personalities of those about me and letting their tastes and interests dominate me."[5]

A third child, and second son, Franklin Jr., was born in March, 1909, and was described by Eleanor as the "biggest and most beautiful of all the babies," but to the family's great distress, he contracted the flu and died in November of the same year.

Anna and James were close playmates, and resorted to all manner of mischievous pranks, such as dropping water bombs out of the upstairs windows of the home onto unsuspecting pedestrians below, or setting off stink bombs inside as guests were assembling for a reception.

In 1910, Eleanor gave birth to Elliott, always known as "Bunny" to the family. This was the year when Roosevelt was elected as Democratic Senator in the New York State Legislature, and it entailed a move to Albany. This pleased Eleanor since she was, at last, free from her mother-in-law, although she was never certain as to what she should do with her newfound independence.

Roosevelt reveled in the political environment, and he was literally "at home" to his colleagues all hours of the day and night to the degree that, one day, the children's nurse complained to Eleanor that they were slowly choking to death in their room because the cigar fumes from below had percolated upwards through the ceiling into the bedroom. The result was not the prohibition of visits and smoking, but the transfer of the bedroom one flight higher.

Sara's home at Hyde Park was always the place which the children most enjoyed, since it offered so many attractions by way of outdoor, rural activities. Moreover, they were certain of being well fed and pampered by their doting grandmother at all times. After the New Jersey "Sea Bright" fiasco, Sara gave thought to an alternative, and it was at this time that she purchased a summer home at Campobello, in New Brunswick, Canada, where all the family could be together to sail, fish, swim, and have picnics on the beach. It was at Campobello in 1914 that a third surviving son was born, and he was given the name of the deceased son born in 1909, Franklin Delano Roosevelt, Jr.

The children's adventures and misadventures continued at Campobello and elsewhere. Elliott suffered from a weak constitution during his early years, and was obliged to wear leg braces. One day he accidentally tripped and fell into the campfire, burning his hands badly as well as part of his legs when hot coals got underneath the braces. It was at Campobello that the nurse of the newborn Franklin Jr., seeking to protect his face from the sun, placed a thin blue veil over his head; but he sucked it into his mouth which became covered with the blue dye, and it was at first feared that he might die of poisoning. A thorough washing and rinsing, however, proved effective, and he appeared none the worse after the episode.

In 1913, Roosevelt had been appointed as Assistant Secretary of the Navy, and this entailed a family move to Washington, D.C. It was here, in 1916, that the last child of the Roosevelts was born: John Aspinall, named after one of his father's uncles. He saw the light of day on March

16, just one day short of his parent's wedding anniversary and of Eleanor's (deceased) mother's birthday. As described later by his brother James,[6] John "began life as the real runt of the family," yet he grew up to be the tallest: six feet, five inches.

It was at Washington that the endless rounds of social entertainment forced upon Eleanor the need to develop and function as an adept hostess. In this new capacity she owed much to Louis Howe, her husband's campaign manager in New York. Described as a sickly "menopause child" who wore a clumsy truss for most of his life, and who smoked incessantly such that his clothes were always smothered with cigarette ash, he was at first much detested by Eleanor, while Sara abhorred him at all times. Yet, he carefully tutored Eleanor out of her shyness, and, in time, she became ever grateful to him for teaching her the rudiments of public speaking and social poise.

It now became necessary for her to employ a part-time social secretary, and, as future events proved, at least where she herself was concerned, she made the ill-fated choice of employing Lucy Page Mercer. Lucy's mother, Minnie Tunis, had been one of the beauties of Washington society, but she had made two unhappy marriages, the second being to Carroll Mercer, one of Theodore Roosevelt's Rough Riders. He proved to be a very plausible, attractive, alcoholic spendthrift, and Lucy's upbringing had been one of pain and penury. Yet, she remained a lovely, capable, young girl, anxious to please, and Eleanor found her pleasant and amenable. Later, the famous Alice (Longworth), Theodore's daughter, was to claim part responsibility for introducing Lucy to the family: "It was good for Franklin. He deserved a good time. He was married to Eleanor."

Certain it is that Eleanor at this time still retained much of her self-deprecating mood, particularly with respect to her appearance. As she herself commented:

> Luckily for them all, the children have inherited their looks from their father's side of the family. . . . I had prominent front teeth, not a very good mouth and chin, but these were not handed down to any of my children.[7]

In addition to her social duties, Eleanor had to cope with an increasingly boisterous handful of children. Even before her last two children had been born she had found it difficult to manage, and, while visiting relatives, she had once written to her husband: "The children have been the wildest things you ever saw and about ready to jump out of their skins. . . ." For the foregoing reasons she had readily accepted

Sara's proposal to employ an "English nanny," an initial concept which extended into a "series of English nannies," since several of the latter were so driven to despair that they resigned within months of appointment.

Of all these "nannies," the best remembered was "Old Battle Axe." According to varied accounts by the children she was nothing less than the apotheosis of tyranny: an obstreperous Anna was subdued by pushing her to the floor and kneeling on her chest; both Elliott and Franklin Jr. were locked in dark closets, Franklin for no less than three hours since the key had broken in the lock. James wrote later that when Franklin Sr. heard of this, it was one of the few occasions when he saw his father's face flushed with livid anger—yet the Old Battle Axe was not dismissed.

James himself appeared to have suffered most: fascinated by her habit of putting vast quantities of mustard on her meat, he continued to stare at the procedure even though reprimanded; so, as punishment, he was given a spoon and directed to consume a whole bottle of mustard, an imposition to which he ever after attributed his many stomach ailments. Again, when he denied the nannie's accusation of not having brushed his teeth, he was sent outside to parade the public sidewalk with a sign on his back, "I AM A LIAR," to his intense chagrin and humiliation.

Old Battle Axe remained in the service of the Roosevelt family until, by chance, Eleanor discovered a cache of empty gin and whisky bottles in her room. This being considered as *the* cardinal sin (in view of the alcoholic tragedies within the family), it resulted, to the immense relief of all the children, in the immediate dismissal of their favorite enemy. However, James records that his "faith in the British Empire" was eventually restored by "Connie," a Scotswoman, who, while exercising a firm discipline over the children, was yet humane and was much beloved.[8]

Roosevelt enjoyed romping around with his children whenever possible, especially at Campobello as well as at Hyde Park, but what most of them treasured best were the memories of Christmas. The Christmas tree would be appropriately decorated, and always illuminated with lighted candles and not with electric bulbs. Roosevelt said that was how his father had lit the tree, and he intended to continue the tradition; in case of fire, he kept nearby a bucket of water along with a large sponge tied to a cane. On Christmas Eve, he would begin the first of a three-night reading of Dickens' *Christmas Carol*. As James recalls:

> As I write this, I can almost hear his clear, confident voice once again, soaring into the higher registers for the part of Tiny Tim,

then shifting to a snarly imitation of mean old Scrooge. How we would thrill as father rolled out that final soaring line, "And so, as Tiny Tim observed, God Bless Us, Every One![9]

On Christmas morning, the children would rush into their father's bedroom, where all the Christmas stockings would have been hung by the fireplace. Afterwards, they would proceed to the library where the presents had been stacked under the tree. The whole family would usually go to church, and then, the culminating event of the day was the lavish Christmas dinner, where Roosevelt loved to display his prowess as a turkey carver—he claimed that his slices of white turkey were so thin that one could almost read through them, not that this pleased everyone since the meat was so quickly eaten that appetites remained unsatiated through the long delays for the second and third helpings.

During the war years, Washington was besieged by many famous overseas personalities, and one memorable event was the visit of Marshall Joffre, hero of the Battle of the Marne. But, at the time of his visit, Anna, James, and Elliott all contracted whooping cough and were despatched to Hyde Park where, as James records it, "we might contaminate our grandmother, but not the rest of the family." Sara herself, ever the stoic grandmother, was less concerned with the consequences to her own health than she was with missing the opportunity for the children to see the famous hero. So, she bundled them all back to New York, where arrangements were made for the Marshall to call upon her, and though, presumably, fully informed of the circumstances, he dutifully kissed all three children, whose main recollection was that of being tickled by his walrus moustache. For his part, Joffre remained immune from the contagious affliction.

The year 1918 proved to be climactic in the annals of the Roosevelt family. Roosevelt had been sent to Europe to report upon the American naval bases, but upon his return he became very sick with double pneumonia, and was confined to bed. In seeking to assist him by unpacking his clothes, Eleanor came across the highly compromising letters written to her husband, while he was abroad, by her former social secretary, Lucy Mercer. At the outbreak of the war in 1917, Lucy had enlisted as a navy yeoman, becoming a member of Roosevelt's staff at the Navy Department, and it was here that they met after hours.

Eleanor was devastated. Unable to think clearly, she first of all considered divorce on the grounds of adultery, but, when Sara came to learn of the affair, the latter adamantly opposed any such action in the interests of the family name. She demanded that her son break off the relationship immediately, or else she would cut off all financial assistance, so that his political career would be in ruins. Eleanor, upon reflection, and with the interests of the children at heart, went along with Sara, and agreed to continue the marriage as a business partnership only, and not as husband and wife.

Roosevelt was left with no option, since he was aware that Lucy, herself a Catholic, could not bring herself to contemplate marriage to a divorced man and father of five children.[10] Upon his next visit to Europe in January, 1919, Roosevelt was accompanied by Eleanor, and they both returned on the same boat as President Wilson and his wife.

In the following year, Roosevelt was selected as running mate to the Democratic presidential nominee, James M. Cox, but, with the Republican victory, Roosevelt reverted to a law practice in New York, whence the family moved back to from Washington. All the children were now receiving some formal education, either with tutors or in school. James had entered Groton in the fall term of 1920, and had been dismayed and disgusted that a straw presidential vote among the students had already forecast the election result, despite the fact that his father was known to be an alumnus of the school.

The "affair" of 1918 was little known, if at all, to the children, but the tragedy which struck the family in 1921 overwhelmed them: Roosevelt, at age 39, was stricken by infantile paralysis, and the father whom they had always recognized and admired as a physically vigorous and energetic man, would never walk again.

Yet, in their many memories of their father, none of the children could ever recall him uttering a single word of self-pity or lament at his misfortune and its effects upon his career. Certainly, there were many expletive expressions of irritation and exasperation as he made constant and desperate efforts to rehabilitate himself. But his courage and pride were indomitable, and it was again at this period that Louis Howe immeasurably sustained Roosevelt's hopes and ambitions, and helped to invigorate his innate confidence in his abilities.

Eleanor, likewise, now forced into a more active and mobile family role, benefited greatly from Howe's advice, and the consequence was that Howe became a permanent resident in the Roosevelt home, a move which infuriated Anna, since she was obliged to vacate her own room for another, one floor above. She accused Howe of stealing her mother's affection, and she never forgave him.

With Roosevelt physically incapacitated, his mother on the one hand, and his wife on the other, now appeared to have entered into a fierce rivalry with respect to the attention and welfare of the children. During the winter months of 1924–5, Sara took Anna and James to Europe, much to Eleanor's chagrin, since she herself had wished to show her children so many of the famous sights and to share with them so many of her personal memories.

Anna and James enjoyed the visit, although, while in Italy, Anna could never understand why her grandmother, at first a Unitarian, and then (after her marriage) an Episcopalian, should seek audience with the Pope, as well as with Mussolini. The visitation with the former dignitary proved to be a great disappointment, since Anna had anticipated an impressive ceremony in a beautiful Renaissance room-like setting. Instead of which, the Roosevelts, in company with a number of other visitors, were led into a very plain room and were directed to kneel; "Then," she wrote to her mother:

> . . . the Pope, looking like a well-fed, flabby, unintelligent (though I've heard he is very intellectual) and totally unnecessary human being, squeaked in in carpet slippers, attended by a sleepy, fat military something or other. He gave everyone his hand so that they could kiss his ring, then he muttered a few words of blessing, and it was over. When his ring came under my nose I tried to get a look at it, instead of kissing it, but that was enough to show him I was an awful heretic, so he moved on before I got a good look. . . .[11]

For her part, Eleanor made an effort to provide some family recreation for the two younger children, Franklin Jr. and Johnny, so she decided to take them for a camping trip through eastern Canada to Campobello, in company with two other boys, and her two colleagues, Nancy Cook and Marion Dickerman.[12] The outdoor adventure was successfully completed, despite the fact that Franklin Jr. cut himself with an axe, the wound taking weeks to heal, while Miss Cook was involved in a hilarious episode with a burro which persisted in lying down and rolling over her.

Since Sara had taken the two older children to Europe, Eleanor, in 1929, decided to take the two younger children with her on an identical tour and again she was accompanied by Miss Cook and Miss Dickerman. This may have been a rash decision, since once they had crossed the Atlantic there was no easy way home, and time and time again Eleanor became exhausted with having to cope with two boisterous, irrepressible sons who seemed never to rest even at night. Eleanor was to make a vow that never again would she make a trip on which she had to be responsible for the young. Apparently, the highlight of the tour was an incident which occurred at Mont Saint-Michel, when Eleanor, exasperated by the squabbling of the boys, went off sightseeing on her own. Upon her return, she found Franklin dangling Johnny by his heels from an upstairs window of the pension, watched by a crowd of people who had assembled in the street below.[13]

While Eleanor was still coping valiantly with the problems of her younger children, the three eldest were slowly loosening the family ties. Under the "enlightenment" ideas of the 1920's, consideration was given to the proposal that Anna, the eldest daughter, should possibly be trained to earn her own living. Anna was not at all in favor of such a proposal, and when, after long discussion, it was decided to send her to Cornell University in the fall semester of 1925 with a view that she might enroll in the Agricultural Department where she could develop skills to enable her to manage the Hyde Park estate, she rebelled.

For weeks after enrollment, she refused to answer her mother's letters, and, in a final decisive act of rebellion, after only one semester at the college, she defiantly announced her intention to get married. She declared: "I did it because I wanted to get out of the life I was leading." As James later commented, this was a poor reason for marriage, "but then the Roosevelt children did not have good reasons for many of the marriages they entered into." He added:

> . . . no matter who or what parents may be, their children can create their own destinies. In our case, our parents being who and what they were, it was harder than it is for most. Our father and mother belonged to the world more than they belonged to us. What they could do for the world was far more important than anything they could do for us.[14]

In June, 1926, Anna married Curtis Dall, at least ten years her senior, a graduate of Princeton, a career stockbroker and securities salesman. He was described as being:

> . . . tall, lean, with a receding hairline, whose chief interests seem bounded on the south by Wall Street and its style of male camaraderie built upon the sport of money; on the west, by class reunions at Princeton football games, and on the north by horsemanship and hunting in Westchester County and the Adirondacks.[15]

Before her marriage, Anna has recalled that

> . . . my mother asked me if there was anything about the "intimacies of marriage" I would like to ask her. My answer was a firm NO: I had learned a little, so very little, as I later discovered, but I

had definitely learned at that particular time what one did and did not talk about with one's parents.[16]

Anna and her husband set up home on a thirty-six acre estate on Sleepy Hollow Road in North Tarrytown, New York. Their first child, born in 1927, a daughter, was christened Anna Eleanor (the third in line of that name), but was always known as Sisty (Sistie). The second child, Curtis (Buzz), was born in 1930, but by that time the marriage was already encountering difficulties. The Dalls had a lovely home with three servants at hand, but this gave Anna little to do and she became bored. Then, her husband suffered considerable losses in the Wall Street crash of 1929, the home was sold, and they were given refuge at the Roosevelt's New York house on 65th Street. They now discovered that they had nothing really in common, and a parting of the ways began, when, while campaigning for her father in the fall of 1932, Anna found a more kindred soul in the person of John Boettiger.

After six years at Groton, where Dr. Peabody had once described him as "a very good chap . . . (he) ought to become a useful man," James was set to enter Harvard, although he would have preferred Williams College. Eager to have his son "prepared for life," Roosevelt arranged for James to work during the summer of 1926 at the Quebec lumber camp of a Canadian paper mill company. James found the physical demands exhausting, since the job entailed a twelve-hour day, at only 18 cents an hour plus keep. James fumed at his father for arranging such slave toil for his son, but he recognized eventually that it had been a worthwhile experience, and, in any case, since the camp was isolated, he had been forced to save his money, so that upon his return he indulged himself by buying a car.

Before James entered Harvard in the fall of 1926, his father had received a request for his own personal assessment of his son from the dean. He penned a long letter in reply, including the following paragraph:

> Concretely in regard to my boy I feel that the following should be the objectives: 1) Better scholarship than passing marks. 2) Athletics to be a secondary not a prime objective. 3) Activity in student activities such as debating, Crimson, etc., to be encouraged. 4) Acquaintance with the average of the class, not the Mt. Auburn St. crowd to be emphasized. 5) Opportunities to earn part of his education.[17]

Before the letter was despatched, James was given an opportunity to comment, which he did, most vociferously, on two counts: first of all, he objected to his father's assumption that he belonged to a pleasure-seeking group; and second, he asserted that, if he were expected to devote his time to study, as well as to participate in normal extra-curricular activities, then part-time work would inevitably interfere with both. Roosevelt's letter was never mailed, but it remains on file at the Hyde Park Memorial Library.

While at Harvard, James joined the same traditional and privileged clubs as his father—Hasty Pudding, the Fly Club, and the Mt. Auburn St. "eating club." James commented, "By now I realized this is what he wanted me to do all along."[18] James joined one other society, the Circulo Italiano Club, which, his father had assumed, related to the study of Italian culture; but again in James's words: "The fact is, it specialized in the study of speakeasies which I visited often."

James was a Harvard sophomore when he "went overboard" upon meeting Betsey Cushing, one of the three daughters of Dr. Harvey Cushing, a famous brain surgeon, of Brookline, Massachusetts. They did not plan to marry for two years and, in 1929, James went to Ireland to spend a vacation with his fiancee at a home which her parents had purchased.

While there, he became fascinated with horses, and, in a rash decision, he spent his home-passage money on a colt, which, he had been persuaded, would earn him thousands of dollars on the racetrack. Explaining the situation to his father, James requested reimbursement for the ticket money, assuring Roosevelt that he could amply repay him from the prize money he expected to win in the Irish Sweepstakes. James received a curtly worded cable in reply: SO HAPPY ABOUT THE HORSE. SUGGEST BOTH OF YOU SWIM HOME.[19] Aware that his father meant it, James wrote immediately to Sara, who, as might be expected, promptly came to his rescue with the necessary funds to return home.

In June, 1930 James married Betsey, with Dr. Peabody, principal of Groton, officiating, as he had at the weddings of Roosevelt and Eleanor, and of Anna and Curtis Dall.

Upon graduating from Harvard, James remained uncertain as to his future career. Now he had a wife to support, and Roosevelt suggested a career in law. In response to his father's suggestion, James duly enrolled in Boston University Law School, but, hating his studies, he left within a year, and accepted a part-time position in an insurance office at fifty dollars a week. It was with this appointment that Roosevelt, while making every effort to permit his sons to make their own decisions, began to find it necessary to issue warnings not to allow unscrupulous business interests to exploit the Roosevelt name.

Like his brother James, Elliott enrolled at Groton, but while James accommodated himself reasonably well to the experience of a boarding school, his brother, more independent, was less of a conformist, and consequently experienced difficulties. He resented what he appeared to have interpreted as James's big brother approach, and, in response to one incident which had been reported to him, his father commented humorously:

> Jimmy says you are in the squad of which he is corporal. Don't try to beat him up while you are a mere private in the ranks—you might get court-martialed and shot![20]

Elliott was a well-built lad, but not very studious. It was Roosevelt's conviction that his son's rapid physical growth at early adolescence had perhaps impaired his intellectual capacities, but that, if some of his energy could be productively channeled into games, the experience of success could be transferred into his studies. In a letter to Dr. Peabody, Roosevelt admitted that he, too, while at Groton, had passed through a similar phase, and

> (I) can readily understand why he can see very little use in the daily grind of Caesar's commentaries, and at learning certain parts of algebra, which seem to him of no possible use in after life.[21]

In due course, Elliott was given ample opportunity of being a school team member in various sports but, in 1927, he was accused of being overstrenuous on the football field and of deliberately kneeling upon a member of the opposing side. Dr. Peabody explained the matter, as he saw it, to Roosevelt, who, however, reacted vehemently, and not only indicted the school for falsely accusing his son of guilt in an unintentional accident, but he went further and accused Peabody and the school authorities for its alleged all-too-ready propensity always to blame and never to praise. He expressed the opinion, in no uncertain terms, that Elliott for three years had been thoroughly discouraged by the attitude of the teaching faculty and that:

> . . . I think that if you could all try the experiment of encouraging him when he does well in studies or sport, patting him on the back occasionally, and if anything goes badly to talk it over with him— give him a chance to explain, instead of assuming that it is an "angry spirit," it might work vastly better. . . .[22]

Elliott did eventually graduate from Groton, but then his school career ended. Not ever of academic bent, he had, probably, been unsettled not only by his adverse experiences at Groton, but also by more positive experiences in the American West. He and James had spent some time together on a ranch in Wyoming during the summer of 1925, and, then, in 1928, following a trip with his father to the Democratic Convention at Houston, he was scheduled to travel north again to a certain ranch in Wyoming. The family remained for two months without a single word relating to his whereabouts. Roosevelt, unperturbed, was only moved to act when Eleanor forced him to do so, and, in due course, Elliott was located in Wyoming but at another ranch. He returned home full of apologies and full of his adventures and love for life of great outdoors. This experience led to his adamant refusal to go to Harvard. At first, he had compromised by suggesting he apply for Princeton, but when he sat the college board examinations, he turned in blank pages. He drifted west, contracted debts which his father paid, and, mindful of his son's difficulties, Roosevelt took Elliott with him to Europe in 1931 to attend to Sara who had become ill in Paris.

In January, 1932, Elliott married Elizabeth Browning Donner, whose father had founded the Donner Steel Company of Pennsylvania. His newfound family responsibilities appeared to have made no impact upon him, since he refused the offer of a job in his father-in-law's steel company. He had worked with a New York advertising agency, but nothing in the East appeared to him attractive enough. In 1933, he received an invitation from Congresswoman Isabella Greenway (who had married one of Theodore Roosevelt's Rough Riders and who lived in Arizona) to stay at her ranch. Elliott eagerly accepted, abandoned his wife, and took off with a friend, Ralph Hitchcock. En route, they ran into money difficulties since this was precisely the time that Roosevelt had been forced to close all the banks. Elliott phoned his father, who couldn't help since he, too, was without ready cash, having apparently only eight dollars in his wallet. Then the news leaked out that the President's son was traveling penniless in the Southwest, and, immediately, the two young men were plied with lavish hospitality at Dallas, Fort Worth, El Paso, until they arrived exhausted, but in excellent spirits, at their destination near Tucson: "Elliott discovered that powerful people courted the sons of kings, and he didn't mind a bit."[23]

En route to the West, he met and fell in love with Ruth Josephine Googins, and he decided to end his marriage, the first son of a President ever to do so. In July, 1933, he and Ruth were married in Burlington, Iowa.

After serving two terms as Governor of New York, Roosevelt received the Democratic presidential nomination at the Chicago Convention of 1932. As part of his campaign strategy he undertook a whistle-stop train tour, taking along with him Eleanor, Anna, and James and his wife, Betsey. Roosevelt often irritated James (24) by introducing him: ". . . and this is my little boy, Jimmy." He would pause, and then add, to the humorous applause of the crowd, ". . . and I have more hair than he has." As mentioned earlier, it was on this train trip that Anna came into close contact with John Boettiger, a reporter with the Republican *Chicago Tribune*. The friendship apparently developed into an affair on board the train, which they both recorded in passionate "first anniversary" letters written on October 10, 1933,[24] but no word reached the public of the breakup of Anna's marriage until after her father had been elected. She obtained a divorce from Curtis Dall at Reno in June, 1934, and was married to Boettiger in January, 1935.

Before her remarriage, Anna moved into the White House with her two children, Sistie and Buzz, whose antics were duly recorded with glee in the national press. On one occasion, just before a formal reception, it was discovered that they had draped the bannister of the grand staircase with toilet paper. They were frequently photographed, and even had their portraits painted, albeit with difficulty. According to the artist, Buzz obeyed instructions and sat quietly, but Sistie was a different matter: "The only way I could get her at all was by making her in little bits. I made sketches of her eyes, nose, and mouth separately. It wasn't that she meant to be unpleasant. It's simply that she had had her picture taken so many times that she did not like to pose."[25]

In the meantime, Boettiger had resigned from the *Chicago Tribune*, and upon the recommendation of Joseph Kennedy, Sr. (who had also made a substantial contribution towards Roosevelt's presidential campaign expenses), he was appointed as executive assistant to Will Hayes, president of the Motion Picture Producers and Distributors of America. He did not remain long at this work since, in 1936, he accepted an offer from William Randolph Hearst of a three-year contract as editor of the *Seattle Post-Intelligencer* at a salary of $30,000 a year. Anna, likewise, accepted the offer of a position as associate editor of the women's page in the same newspaper, with a salary of $10,000 a year.

Hearst was an implacable enemy of Roosevelt, and there is no doubt that he made his offer for the purpose of embarrassing the President. Yet, knowing full well the nature of Hearst's motives, Roosevelt raised no objection to the appointments, and the couple moved their home from New York to Seattle. It was there, in 1939, that their one and only child, John Roosevelt Boettiger, was born.

Roosevelt had established the practice of not providing his sons with allowances after their marriages. Both James and Elliott had married before their father entered the White House and there came the problem of providing for their families, a problem which was to lead to acute embarrassment, since they were both confronted, at a time when neither had developed a maturity of judgment, with lucrative job offers for which they were not qualified, by not too scrupulous businessmen, anxious to profit from the family name.

While still at law school, James had taken a part-time job in insurance, and eventually formed his own company in partnership with John Sargent in Boston. It was a successful venture and James became interested in politics, when politics in Massachusetts was synonymous with the name of Boston Mayor Jim Curley, the "lovable crook."

Roosevelt was much amused by this contact and intimated to James that he was likely to learn much from it. Curley had given Roosevelt active support during the 1932 presidential campaign, and had duly expected to be rewarded for it, by appointment, possibly, as Ambassador to the Vatican, or Secretary of the Navy, so that when he was offered the position as Ambassador to Poland, he was furious, and, in reprisal, dissociated himself entirely from James, whose political ambitions were thereby completely undermined.

Between the time of the November election of 1932, and the inaugural ceremony of March, 1933, there had occurred the death of Calvin Coolidge. Unable himself to be present at the funeral, Roosevelt requested Eleanor and James to represent him. There then occurred an unfortunate incident concerning James' suit. James was traveling in the Midwest when he received the telegram request from his father, and he arranged for appropriate clothing to be sent to Northampton, Massachusetts, where the funeral was to take place. But instead of the striped pants, cutaway and silk hat, he was sent a full dress evening suit with a collapsible opera hat. He went to the funeral hoping to disguise the sartorial error by wearing a heavy top coat, but, to his dismay, he found himself perspiring profusely in the overheated church. The repeated mopping of his brow evoked spasms of giggling from Eleanor, which proved contagious, and, unfortunately, the photographs portrayed them both in hilarious mood, for which the press provided reprimanding headlines.

In 1933, James and Betsey accompanied Joseph and Rose Kennedy on a visit to Europe. Kennedy seldom missed an opportunity to combine pleasure with business, and, on this occasion, anticipating the repeal of prohibition in the United States, he entered into negotiation with several Scottish whiskey distillers by whom the party was lavishly entertained, to establish franchises for the sale of the product in the United States. The deal was eminently successful, and Kennedy profited from it to the extent of millions of dollars. James, with little capital to invest, remained a simple onlooker, probably to the (later) immense relief of his father, since, while still in Massachusetts, he had already been implicated in the accusation of obtaining appointments for his friends as receivers of banks (closed by Roosevelt) from which experienced bankers were excluded.

In 1935, James, at age 28, was appointed president of the National Grain and Yeast Corporation at a salary of $25,000 a year. A press investigation alleged that he had received the appointment solely for the purpose of facilitating the issue of government permits. Also, Henry Morgenthau, Roosevelt's Secretary of the Treasury, had approached the President with the information that Frank Hale, the owner of the company, had for years been illicitly converting the yeast into bootleg alcohol, and that, therefore, public exposure of James's association with this enterprise could render the President infinite harm. To his credit, when James was confronted with this information, he resigned in the year of his appointment.

In 1936, Roosevelt was dealt a severe blow by the death of his long-trusted aide, Louis Howe. Feeling the acute need of having someone near to him whom he could implicitly trust, he asked James to come to the White House as a personal aide. Fearing the accusation of nepotism, Eleanor strongly opposed the appointment, but Roosevelt overrode her objections.

For a while, James exhilarated in the experience of being a power behind the throne, acting as liaison between the President and influential political personalities, possessing the power to select all persons seeking interviews and consultations with his father. But he was soon to discover that one adverse criticism would far outweigh a dozen statements of praise, and to many, he was simply the "Crown Prince" or the "Assistant President."

In the same year, Roosevelt took James along with him to the Pan American Peace Conference held at Buenos Aires. To James it was a memorable occasion since never before had he spent so long a time in his father's company. On the return journey they called at Montevideo, where the President of Uruguay was somewhat nervous, since upon the last visit of a head of state, shots had been fired and the visitor had been wounded. Roosevelt took all this in its stride and laughingly suggested that James should sit in the front seat of the car so as to be the recipient of any bullet.

Upon their return to Washington, James coped as well as he could with his increasing duties, which included those of answering the voluminous mail to the White House, in dealing with which his father had provided him with the practical advice that "two short sentences will generally answer any known letter."

In 1938, James was forced to resign from his White House duties by reason of ill-health, and he underwent surgery for stomach ulcers at the Mayo Clinic, Rochester. At the same time, his marriage with Betsy Cushing was breaking up, greatly to Roosevelt's annoyance. While she was at the White House, Betsy had very much pampered the President, who enjoyed her vitality and vivaciousness, much to Eleanor's disapproval.

After his illness, James went to live in California, where Sam Goldwyn made him his administrative assistant for $25,000 a year. James later went ahead and formed his own independent company to make slot machine films. In the following year, while visiting England for promotion of his films, James was asked by his father to arrange details of the forthcoming visit to the United States of King George VI and Queen Elizabeth.[26]

James' marriage to Betsy was dissolved in 1940, and in 1941 he married Romelle Schneider, who had been his nurse at the time of illness in 1938. Within a week of his marriage he was sent on a round-the-world diplomatic mission by Roosevelt, and visited with a variety of political leaders and heads of state.

After his marriage to Ruth Googins, Elliott found varied employment including work as an aviation editor of the Hearst newspaper, the *Los Angeles Express,* and he soon found himself involved in the controversy over mail contracts by commercial airlines. Because of certain irregularities Roosevelt decided upon the cancellation of all such contracts, and instead, directed that all mail be transported by the U.S. Air Force. The latter was ill-equipped to do so, and the resulting chaos forced the President to return to the original private contract system. In the course of the dispute, Elliott had strongly opposed his father's measures, much to the delight of Hearst.

The latter then employed him as a commentator for the Mutual Radio Network, and Elliott went ahead to organize the Hearst radio system across the country. Feeling confident in his own abilities, he next attempted to set up his own radio network in Texas, but was soon in such financial difficulties that, with reluctance, Roosevelt felt obliged to ask Texas tycoon Jesse Jones to bail him out with a two-million-dollar loan.

Elliott made forthright attacks upon his father's New Deal policies, and was strongly opposed to a third term for the President, suggesting that, instead, John (Jack) Nance Garner of Texas might be the ideal

Democratic candidate. When questioned about Elliott's opinions and activities, Roosevelt remained unperturbed, stating succinctly and clearly:

> Mr. Elliott Roosevelt is an American citizen—free and of adult age. He therefore enjoys, among other things, the right of free speech, and is entitled to the exercise of that right. There is no censorship in this democracy of ours. Those who hear him are entitled to their opinions—to speak or to write them. I do not believe that you would change these fundamental principles of democracy in government.[27]

Ironically, it was not Elliott's opposition to his father which aroused public opinion against him; rather it was his decision in late 1939 to volunteer in the air force reserves with a commission as captain. He was accused of seeking a desk job to escape active duty and, during the presidential campaign of 1940, he received as many as 30,000 malicious letters and cards, mostly unsigned. In consequence, he applied for transfer, and he began training as an air intelligence officer.

Franklin Jr. was still at Groton when his father was elected President. He graduated in June, 1933, and then proceeded to Harvard, where he became notorious for his love of driving fast cars. He wrecked the first, which was given him upon graduation from Groton, and his parents decided to punish him by letting him go without a car for a while. But they reckoned without Sara, who, when informed by Franklin Jr. of his plight, promptly bought him another. Roosevelt and Eleanor were furious—and helpless. As Eleanor wrote, plaintively:

> Five individualists, such as our children, growing up in a family, where the father was deeply immersed in public affairs, and the grandmother, true to her Delano tradition, bent on being the head of the family, did mean that life was never dull for me.[28]

On another occasion, Franklin Jr. was taken to court for speeding, and the magistrate, upon learning of his identity, promptly dismissed the case, and took him home for dinner.

Franklin Jr. graduated from Harvard in 1937, and then planned to enter the University of Virginia Law School. In the interval between the two schools he married Ethel DuPont, the daughter of one of Roosevelt's most outspoken political opponents. The wedding was held on the DuPont estate, and lavish hospitality was provided. Roosevelt was present and enjoyed himself immensely, never ceasing to appreciate the extremely humorous situation, as he saw it, of being an honored guest, as father of the bridegroom, in the home of so bitter an adversary. He continued to support Franklin Jr. through law school, lest the latter be accused of marrying only for money, and, after qualifying, Franklin took up practice in a Wall Street law office.

Following in the footsteps of two of his brothers, John Aspinall, Roosevelt's youngest son, went to Groton and Harvard, whence he graduated in 1938. Comparatively little was heard or written about him until the summer of 1937 when his alleged exploits in France made headline news. According to the reports, he attended the Cannes Festival, became drunk, struck the city mayor over the head with a bouquet of flowers, and then poured a bottle of champagne all over him. John claimed that the press accounts were grossly exaggerated, and his mother believed him, asserting that "he is one of the most dignified of my children." As usual, his father remained unperturbed, and, in jocular vein, commented that he would liked to have sent John a postcard, "Wish I could be there!"

Just as he was graduating from Harvard, John married a Boston North Shore debutante, Anne Lindsay Clark, whose wealthy father was partner in a prominent financial firm. According to his brother, James, John was the least close to his father, made less use of the Roosevelt name than any of the other children, and led "the smoothest, if least exciting, life of all of us."[29] John's wife's family was Republican and he, himself, appeared to have Republican sympathies, which, his brothers claim, originated with a legendary incident which occurred on Inaugural Day, 1933: John, while at Groton, had been granted permission to come to Washington, but, instead of returning to the White House before midnight as directed, he spent much of the night celebrating, and turned up about 3 A.M. He introduced himself to the guard, who, after looking over the old jalopy which John was driving, said, "No son of a President would ever be riding around in a car like that!" John was refused entry and spent the rest of the night in a hotel lobby.

Of an independent frame of mind, he set out to support his wife by earning his own living, and started work at Boston's Filene's department store at a salary of $18.50 a week. His grandmother, Sara, was appalled when she read in a flippant magazine article that her own grandson was contentedly selling women's panties to earn his daily bread.

On a later occasion, while John and Anne took a holiday, they left their firstborn at the White House. When the date approached for their return, John phoned his incredulous father asking him to order six dozen diapers. Having been understandably unnerved by the unexpected request, Roosevelt soon recovered his composure, and repeatedly and delightedly rehearsed the whole procedure of how he would speak to the store assistant on the phone: "This is the President of the United States. I would like to order six dozen diapers to be delivered to the White House as soon as possible, please." To his great disappointment, the pressure of daily business never did permit him the anticipated pleasure of the phone call, which was eventually made by one of the White House assistants.

With the outbreak of World War II, the entire presidential family became mobilized. Elliott was first to enlist, and, in due course, was assigned to the 21st Reconnaissance Squadron stationed in Newfoundland for air patrol duties in the North Atlantic, focusing upon the Nazi submarine threat to Allied shipping. During the summer of 1941, he was in Britain locating possible staging sites for ferrying U.S. fighter planes across the Atlantic.

While in England, he was invited by Churchill to spend a weekend at Chequers, the Prime Minister's country home. He arrived with a minimum of luggage, and had to apologize for having no pajamas, so his host lent him a pair made of Chinese silk. To his embarrassment, Elliott awoke next morning and found that, the pajamas being too small for his six-foot-five frame, he had split them, in his own words, "from stem to stern."

By August 1941, he was back at base in Canada, when he received notice to fly to Argentia harbor, where, to his surprise he encountered his father, and later, Winston Churchill, who were meeting to process the final draft of the "Atlantic Charter." Churchill had arrived on the battleship *Prince of Wales,* which, tragically, was sunk only a few months later at Singapore, when the Japanese launched their Pacific-wide attacks. Franklin Jr., who had joined the navy in June, 1940, was serving on the destroyer *Mayrant,* which was in the North Atlantic at the time, and his ship was directed to Argentia, so that father and two sons were reunited for the historic occasion.

Elliott's next assignment was that of the extensive series of photographic surveys (in unarmed planes) demanded in preparation for Operation Torch, the American invasion of North Africa. In January, 1943, when Roosevelt and Churchill met at Casablanca, Morocco, both Elliott and Franklin Jr. were again present.[30]

Elliott rose in rank to become a brigadier general, in command of more than 5,000 men and 250 planes, and he received the award of the Distinguished Flying Cross for his services, not only in North Africa and Italy, but also in Northern Europe, where he had been sent in preparation for Operation Overlord, the invasion of Normandy in June, 1944. While he was based in England, his mother arrived there, and both were guests of George VI at Buckingham Palace. Elliott also made two visits to Russia, when he accompanied staff officers to Moscow for the purpose of inspection of airfields.

Towards the end of the war, Elliott once again ran into domestic problems, and, in March, 1944, his second wife, Ruth, sued for divorce after a marriage of over eleven years and three children. Elliott next became engaged to Faye Emerson, a divorced film actress and mother of a five-year-old; they were married at the Grand Canyon, Arizona, in December, 1944.

Elliott and his new wife were present at the celebration of Christmas at Hyde Park during the same month. As usual, Roosevelt proceeded with the reading of Dickens' *Christmas Carol,* but, on this occasion, he had unfortunately forgotten to place in position a false tooth in his lower jaw. In the middle of the recital, Chris, Franklin's three-year-old son, suddenly interrupted his grandpa's reading: "Grandpere, you've lost a tooth." Roosevelt went on reading, but Chris again interrupted: "Grandpere, you've lost a tooth; Have you swallowed it?" That concluded the proceedings, and it was also, sadly, the last of all Roosevelt's many readings of the *Christmas Carol.*[31]

Elliott's wife, Faye, returned to her film work in Hollywood, while Elliott went back to England, and, once again, adverse publicity for the Roosevelt family occurred with "L'Affaire Blaze." Elliott had purchased a bull mastiff, "Blaze," in England, and had had it shipped to Washington. Thence, it was to be transported by cargo plane to Los Angeles, Elliott's intention being that it would provide company for his new wife. Unfortunately, an overzealous officer, seeing the name of Roosevelt, assumed the shipment had presidential priority, and a sailor on compassionate leave was "bumped" off the plane. It was immediate headline news, and Elliott had no option but to "ride it out."

Franklin Jr., after seeing action at Casablanca, when the French fleet under Admiral Darlan offered resistance instead of surrender, was sent to the Mediterranean, and his ship, the *Mayrant,* saw action in the invasion of Sicily. He was awarded the Silver Star for carrying a critically wounded sailor to safety under heavy fire. He was known as "Bull Moose" to his men, and he rose to the rank of lieutenant-commander.

Following his round-the-world mission in 1941, James was assigned as intelligence officer to the Fifth Marine Division operating in the Pacific theater of war. There, he served with a famed commando group known as "Carlson's Raiders," and was involved in a surprise attack landed from a submarine upon Makin Island. He was later awarded the Silver Star for bravery, and was promoted from major to colonel. He saw further action at Midway, Guadalcanal, and Okinawa.

John, because of his store experience was, at first, drafted into the Navy Supply Corps, but, seeking a more active role, he was transferred onto the aircraft carrier *Hornet* in the Pacific. In due course, he won the Bronze Star for courageous action, and emerged from the conflict with the rank of lieutenant-commander.

During the first years of the war, Anna and her husband, John Boettiger, remained in Seattle. They came east to spend Christmas 1942 at the White House, and stayed on to await Roosevelt's return from the Casablanca Conference. During the course of conversation with his father-in-law, John expressed a wish to attend another such high-level conference, but Roosevelt stated that it would be impossible since he was not in uniform. John, 43, and beyond the draft age, felt rebuked, and, to Anna's consternation, he set about enlisting. By March, 1943, he was commissioned a captain, as a civil affairs officer with duties relating to the administration of occupied territories. Irked by his noncombat duties, he applied for transfer and, later in the year, he was with the Fifth Army in its assault upon central Italy.

In the meantime, Anna felt desolate and isolated in Seattle, and she was increasingly sensitive to the fact that members of the Hearst press considered her to be overprivileged. In January, 1944, she finally resigned, and came to live in the White House to work, unsalaried, for her father. Here she remained until his death sixteen months later, and she came to exert considerable influence, since she was able to select among which of the many political and other personalities on Capitol Hill she considered eligible to have conference with Roosevelt. During the same year, John Boettiger returned to the United States, having been assigned for duty at the Pentagon, and he took up residence with his wife at the White House.

At his fourth inaugural in January, 1945, it became more and more obvious that Roosevelt was a sick man. No doubt fully aware that this would be the last such ceremony, he insisted on being photographed with all thirteen of his grandchildren: three by Anna (Sistie, Buzz, and John Roosevelt Boettiger); James, two (Kate and Sara); Elliott, four (Elliott Jr., William, Chandler, and David); Franklin Jr., two (Christopher, Franklin D. the 3rd); and John, two (Haven and Anne).

Within a month of the inaugural ceremony he was at Yalta, conferring with Churchill and Stalin, and, on this occasion, he took Anna with him.[32] Upon his return, he found it necessary to sit down when presenting his report to Congress. In April, he went to Warm Springs, Georgia, to relax, and it was here that he died suddenly on the 12th, at the age of 63.

Not long afterwards, Eleanor learnt that Lucy Mercer Rutherfurd had been present in Warm Springs at the time of her husband's death, and that, at the moment of collapse, he had actually been sitting for a portrait which Lucy had commissioned. But the greater shock came when she discovered that Lucy, with Anna's connivance, had actually been entertained at the White House during her (Eleanor's) absences. She felt betrayed and bitter, and years were to elapse before her inner anger at her daughter's actions was to subside.

For her part, Anna justified what she did by claiming that, with the enormous strain placed upon her father during the years of war, he was entitled to some degree of the comfort and warmth of friendship which Eleanor could never give. Her mother was never a good listener, and she occasioned considerable irritation to her husband by constant and tactless interruptions while he was speaking. Lucy, on the other hand, was capable of just listening, and Anna was convinced that she had a most soothing and tranquilizing effect upon her father's frayed nerves and jaded spirits.

With the death of the President and the end of the war within a few months, the life patterns of the entire Roosevelt family changed rapidly, necessitating all manner of adjustments. Strangely enough, perhaps, it was Eleanor who made the best adjustment. In 1941, her mother-in-law, Sara, had died, and Eleanor felt as though a great oppressive weight had been taken off her back. Sara had dominated the family for almost forty years, and Eleanor wrote that, at Sara's funeral, she was completely dry-eyed. In 1945, the responsibilities that she had accepted on behalf of her husband throughout his presidential tenure now passed away, and she was free to pursue her own course of action. A new career opened to her when, in 1946, President Truman asked her to be a delegate to the United Nations Assembly in London, and she now became, in Truman's own words, First Lady of the World. Until the very last year of her life, she was active in all manner of activities relating to human rights on a global scale. She died on November 7, 1962, at the age of 78.

All five children continued to have domestic problems, and, by the 1980's, they had collectively contracted no fewer than seventeen marriages. For her own part, Eleanor made an effort to retain contact with the numerous ex-wives, so that her grandchildren would not feel neglected and ignored.

Anna and John Boettiger decided to embark upon a new venture in Phoenix, Arizona, where they hoped to convert a giveaway advertising weekly into a legitimate newspaper. But they were immediately beset by the financial strain of providing capital for new plant machinery, as well as problems relating to the limited supply of newsprint after the war. The lack of success caused John to relapse into angry depressive moods such that, by the end of 1947, they had separated. Anna also discovered that, without her knowledge, there was another woman in his life, and it was at this moment that Anna probably came nearest to appreciating what her own mother must have experienced first in 1918, and then again in 1945.[33]

Anna remained behind in Phoenix valiantly attempting to run the newspaper on her own, but the task was an impossible one, and the enterprise was losing $30,000 a month. In the summer of 1948, she abandoned it entirely, and moved to Los Angeles. Sistie was married in the same year, and went to live in Portland with her husband. Buzz gave the family major cause for concern when he contracted polio, but to the immense relief of all, he made a complete recovery, and Eleanor took him on holiday to Europe.

In 1949, Anna obtained a divorce from her husband, but a still further crisis developed when it was diagnosed that she had tuberculosis, and would have to consider spending two or three years recuperating at a sanatorium. Young Johnny Boettiger, now 10, was placed in a camp school where he was fortunate to find a capable and sympathetic mentor. A second medical opinion brought relief, in that re-diagnosis established that Anna had noncontagious "valley fever" and not tuberculosis, but it was still necessary for her to move to Berkeley for treatment.

John Boettiger remarried, but failure to find suitable work increased his despondency, and, in October, 1950, he committed suicide by jumping out of the seventh-floor window of a New York apartment hotel. Since he was, physically, the nearest of all the relatives at the time, the grim task of identifying the body, at the request of the police, fell to Elliott.

Not long after, Anna met James Halsted, a doctor with six children, but separated from his wife, and in process of obtaining a divorce. In 1952, they openly set up house together, an arrangement which Eleanor came to accept though not approve of, and, in November of the same year, they were eventually married. They moved from Los Angeles to Syracuse, New York, where James received appointment as director of the Veterans Administration Hospital, and Anna became employed as public relations representative of the State University of the New York College of Medicine.

In 1958, Anna and James went for two years to Shiraz, Iran, where

James was Fulbright Exchange Professor at a local hospital. Eleanor came to visit them in 1959, and brought with her Nina, one of James's daughters from his previous marriage.

Upon their return to the United States, James accepted a post as assistant dean of a new medical school at Lexington, Kentucky, and thence he moved to Detroit as chief of the Department of Medicine at the union-run Metropolitan Hospital and Clinic. He resigned from this position in 1970, and moved to Hillsdale, New York, to begin general practice in the nearby city of Hudson. Since they now lived only thirty miles away from Hyde Park, Anna kept herself occupied with matters relating to the Franklin D. Roosevelt Library and the Eleanor Roosevelt Museum, in addition to which she maintained an interest in a school for emotionally disturbed children, and served on boards of the National Committee on Household Employment.

Her last years were spent with her husband in quiet retirement, but in December 1975, she died of throat cancer at age 69.

After World War II, James Roosevelt returned to California and insurance, and became involved in politics. In 1946, he was elected as Democratic state chairman, but, in 1948, he made a political indiscretion by supporting Eisenhower as a possible contender for the presidential nominee in place of Harry Truman. The latter was intensely displeased, and, when James, in 1950, opposed Earl Warren for the gubernatorial post in California, Truman gave him no support, although he made no adverse comments either.

In 1952, while James gave support to Adlai Stevenson at the Democratic Convention in Chicago, his brother, Franklin, supported Averill Harriman, and this gave rise to some family embarrassments, but was accepted by all as part of the normal independent Roosevelt tradition. James lost a further campaign to become Mayor of Los Angeles, but then succeeded in being elected to the House of Representatives for five consecutive terms, and only resigned in 1965 to accept an appointment to the United Nations as U.S. envoy to the Economic and Social Council. He retained that position for one year, since, in 1966, he was offered a salary of $100,000 to serve on the board of a company named the Investors Overseas Services. Its headquarters were in Switzerland and James records a humorous episode when it was decided to move the headquarters to France, where it was also proposed to establish an international school to be called the "Eleanor Roosevelt School". Approval from President De Gaulle was necessary for the project, and he, recalling a remark by Roosevelt that the latter believed De Gaulle thought himself a "modern Joan of Arc," agreed to the establishment of the school on the condition that the name be changed to "The Joan of Arc School"! Mismanagement of the company led to James' resignation in 1971, when he set up his own consulting company.

James' second marriage to Romell Schneider was dissolved in 1955, partly because she objected to his entering politics, and uprooting his home to Washington. James was remarried to Gladys Irene Owens in 1956. She had led a very unhappy existence, her father having shot himself in her presence, her mother being confined in a mental home, while she herself had entered into several rash marriages. She had worked in James' office, and they had fallen in love. They had no children but, in 1959, they adopted a boy, whom they named Hall Delano Roosevelt.

It was due to the substantial alimony payments to Romelle that James had accepted the position with the Investors Overseas Services, but it had entailed a move to Geneva where Irene was very unhappy. Quarrelling resulted, and during the course of one argument, Irene stabbed James with a knife, an act which ended the marriage.

James's son, Delano (Del) had been taught at the International School at Geneva, where one of his teachers had been Mary Winskill of England, who helped the boy during the marriage breakup. A close relationship developed between James and Mary, who was thirty years younger, and they were married in 1969. A daughter, Rebecca Mary, was born to them in 1971. They returned to California, where Mary obtained a position supervising student teachers at the University of California, Irvine, where James also taught occasional courses in government.

Upon his return to civilian life, Elliott remained very uncertain as to what he should do, and his mother made the suggestion that he should enter into partnership with her to run the estate farm of over a thousand acres at Hyde Park, which he did. But he remained very dissatisfied, since his wife, Faye, who now supplemented her film career with lucrative television appearances, was earning far more money than he was.

He decided to write a series of articles based upon his war experiences, especially those relating to his presence at major conferences involving his father and other war leaders. The articles formed a book entitled, *As He Saw It*. It met criticism concerning Elliott's capacity as an observer, but the publicity helped sell the book, and it proved a financial success.

He was commissioned by *Look* magazine to go to Russia. He took Faye along with him, and he achieved a scoop by being granted an interview with Stalin, whom he had met earlier at Teheran.

Eleanor suggested that Elliott should edit some of the hundreds and thousands of his father's papers and have them classified with an aim to their publication, and he did spend a considerable amount of time and energy in this work.

He became involved in the production of radio programs, with the object of funneling some of the proceeds into assisting his sister, Anna, and her ailing newspaper project. His mother cooperated, as did Anna, herself, but all to no avail where the newspaper itself was concerned.

By 1949, Elliott's marriage to Faye Emerson had failed. She married bandleader Skitch Henderson and Elliott married Minnewa Bell, member of a wealthy California family whose fortunes were founded on oil. They lived at Top Cottage on the Hyde Park estate, but dissension occurred when John and his wife, Anne, also came to live at Hyde Park at Stone Cottage. John and his wife were most definitely Republican in outlook, and, in the 1952 election, John became chairman of Citizens for Eisenhower.

Elliott moved away, and he embarked upon a series of business enterprizes, few of which succeeded. He went to live in Havana for a while, seeking to purchase radio stations with a view to introducing television. But not long after his arrival, Batista emerged as dictator, and made impossible demands upon foreign businesses. Elliott withdrew to Colorado where his wife owned a ranch.

He speculated in a variety of schemes including oil drilling, uranium mining, as well as a project for a luxury mountain vacation retreat for jaded executives. As he himself commented: "Here was another Roosevelt caught up in the quest for Golconda that was almost an obsession among us five."[34]

The net result was the break-up of Elliott's fourth marriage. Minnewa suffered a nervous breakdown, and spent time in a sanatorium. In October, 1960, Elliott married Patricia Peabody Whitehead, whom he had met while negotiating transactions in real estate. Her friends made joking references to her being the "fifth wheel on the wagon," but she herself, when presented to Eleanor, said "I'm Patty. I'm the last one and the best."

Elliott formally adopted all four of Patty's children by previous marriage, and she, herself, gave birth to a son by Elliott. He was named Livingston Delano Roosevelt, but he was a two-month premature baby by Caesarian section, and he died when only five days old.

The Campobello summer home had not been used since the beginning of World War II, and the buildings had deteriorated. Eleanor agreed to its purchase by Elliott for $12,000, but he made little use of it, and could not afford the cost of rehabilitation. He sold the property to Armand and Victor Hammer, who were brothers and oil millionaires. They had it

restored, and then offered it to the governments of the United States and
Canada as a joint memorial to Roosevelt. The gift was accepted in 1962,
but Eleanor had passed away and was not present at the formal ceremony
of dedication.

Eleanor blamed much of her children's marriage problems upon herself. In conversation with Elliott she once said:

> . . . I'm afraid I failed you terribly in your earlier years . . . I spent
> so much time away that you never knew what home could be. It
> was selfishness on my part . . . None of you older children experi-
> enced security. You could never count on the advice of a father and
> a mother. All you could possibly see in me was the disciplinarian,
> and bad-tempered too, at times. . . .[35]

Elliott went to live with Patty in Minneapolis, where he worked for a
while with Howard Hughes. He became involved in a fertilizer business
in Iowa, and then moved to Florida, where he was elected Mayor of
Miami Beach. He served only one term: the community was predominantly Jewish, and Elliott joined the only country club which excluded
Jews. This and other indiscretions prompted his opponents to set up a
Jew at the next election, and Elliott was easily defeated. He moved to
another part of Florida, and set himself up to grow fruit and rear horses.

His business ventures were still not concluded: he attempted ranching
in Portugal, but the left-wing government confiscated his holdings and,
later, he settled for a while in England where he rented an estate owned
by former Prime Minister Harold Macmillan. Meanwhile, he made a
good recovery from an operation for a heart ailment. He collaborated
with James Brough in the writing of three books relating to the Roosevelt
family: *An Untold Story* (1973); *A Rendezvous with Destiny* (1975); and
Mother R (1977). His comments upon the family members were not
always acceptable to them and, meeting Elliott in London, James subsequently wrote that he told Elliott:

> I wouldn't bother to denounce his second book no matter how he
> insulted me. I warned him I might insult him in my book. We
> agreed, however, that blood is thicker than water, and our feelings
> for one another would endure, no matter what we wrote.[36]

Franklin Jr., often described as having the closest resemblance to Roosevelt in looks and mannerisms, joined a law firm in New York after the
war, and lived on an estate at Woodbury, Long Island. Separation from
his wife, Ethel DuPont, during the war apparently took its toll in an
uneasy reconciliation which finally ended in divorce in May, 1949,[37] the

same month as he was named to fill an unexpired term of office in the U.S. House of Representatives. Truman had appointed him in 1946 as member of the President's Committee on Civil Rights, and presidential support enabled him to be re-elected to the House in 1950, and again in 1952. He was remarried in 1949 to Suzanne Perrin, one of his election campaign workers.

His record in Congress, particularly his poor attendance, brought adverse criticisms, and he resigned, and later sought election, first as Governor of New York, and then as Attorney-General, but he failed in both attempts. He campaigned for John F. Kennedy in 1960, and was subsequently rewarded by being appointed as an undersecretary in the Department of Commerce as well as chairman of the President's Civil Rights Commission.

In his career as lawyer, Franklin Jr. had vigorously advocated the cause of the homeless veteran in New York City, and had urged more speedy action on the matter of provision of more adequate housing. Later, however, he had given his mother considerable concern when it became public that included in his legal clientele was General Trujillo, the ruthless dictator of the Dominican Republic, Eleanor was appalled that a Roosevelt could, in any way, appear to give support to a dictator by acting as his legal representative. Franklin ended his association with Trujillo as a direct result of her protests.

Franklin's second marriage ended in divorce and, in 1970, he married Felicia Schiff Warburg Sarnoff, a relative of the *New York Post* publisher, Dorothy Schiff, former wife of RCA's president, Robert Sarnoff. Franklin became interested in the business economics of car imports, and he became distributor for Fiat automobiles. He was so successful that he eventually sold his dealership for a considerable sum of money.

John was the President's only son who never ran for public office, except for a "brief flirtation with the 1967 New York City mayoral race."[38] In 1946, he went to work in Los Angeles for the Grayson-Robinson Stores, which he subsequently left to open and operate his own department store. He became involved in a variety of business enterprises relating to investments, merchandise, and pharmaceutical products, prior to entering the brokerage firm of Bache and Company, (later Bache, Halsey, Stuart, Shields and Company), in which he rose to become senior vice president and a director before his retirement in 1980.

John emerged as the maverick Republican of his family, supporting Eisenhower in 1948, and again in 1952, when he made the seconding speech for Eisenhower at the Republican convention.

The family suffered a grievous tragedy in 1960 when John and Anne's daughter, Sally, only 13, died as the result of a horse-riding accident. Anne never recovered from the shock: she became depressed, and eventually sought a divorce, after which she went to live with Elliott's divorced wife, Faye Emerson, in Majorca.[39]

In 1965, John married Irene Boyd McAlpin. He and his wife set up home in an apartment in New York City, and spent their summers upstate in Tuxedo Park, N.Y., where John enjoyed the life of a country gentleman until his death by heart failure in 1981, aged 65.

Harry S Truman

(1945–1953)

What Mary Margaret Truman best remembers about the year of her birth was that, in 1924, her father lost the only election of the many in which he had been a candidate. She will enter the record book as being the first girl to be the only child of a President Harry Truman was 40, and his wife, 39, when Margaret was born. They had married on June 28, 1919, the day the Treaty of Versailles was signed in Paris.

Truman had been born in 1884 in Lamar, south of Kansas City, Missouri, and was the oldest of three children. The family moved to Independence, but, following the death of the father in 1904, it moved back again to the grandfather's farm in Grandview, adjacent to Lamar. With the involvement of the United States in World War I, Truman enlisted in an artillery unit, of which he became captain, and, after his demobilization, he returned to marry Elizabeth (Bess) Virginia Wallace of Independence, his childhood sweetheart. The young married couple took up residence in the home of Bess's mother, Madge Gates Wallace, a widow, whose father had been a successful flour miller and had built the home in the 1860's.

At the end of the war Truman (35) faced the problem of supporting his wife with little training in any craft or profession other than that of farming. He decided to set up a haberdashery store in downtown Kansas City with his close wartime friend, Eddie Jacobson. The venture failed, the partners owing $20,000 to their creditors, but, instead of declaring bankruptcy, Truman vowed to pay back all the debts, which he did, in fifteen years.

The problem of the future was inadvertently solved by another wartime veteran, Jim Pendergast, who had served in Truman's artillery unit. In the 1920's, Kansas City politics was dominated by Tom Pendergast, a genial but corrupt personality, who eventually ended his days in Leavenworth Federal Penitentiary. Pendergast happened to need a forceful candidate as eastern district county judge,[1] and, in the course of casual conversation with his Uncle Tom, Jim suggested Truman's name. His suggestion was accepted, and Truman was duly elected in 1922, but, because of his too-honest approach to county business, he lost his re-election bid two years later.

However, he was not forgotten, and, in 1926, he was again elected as presiding judge of the county court, but, this time, he had greater acquaintance with legal procedure since he had attended the Kansas City School of Law as a part-time student during the period, 1923–25.

By 1934, he had achieved sufficient prominence in Missouri politics to be elected U.S. Senator, with its resultant impact upon, and disruption of, the hitherto stable family routine. In the early formative years of her life, Margaret had been reared in the lovely old rambling house at 219 N. Delaware St., in Independence. She had attended the local public school, all her friends were close neighbors, while, at home, she was much loved and treasured by both parents: her mother taught her the principles and etiquette of becoming a young lady, while her father, always supportive of the mother, introduced her to one further dimension of living which was subsequently to determine her professional career—a love of music.

Truman, as a boy, had not enjoyed physical health, and, in particular, he suffered severe sight impairment which necessitated the wearing of spectacles. This excluded him from participation in most games, and he became instead, a rabid book-reader, as well as a pianist of no mean talent. He became Margaret's first piano teacher, but the chores of endless practice did not have any particular appeal for her. In the hope of motivating his daughter, Truman, for her Christmas present of 1932, had, with considerable financial sacrifice, purchased, without her knowing, a brand new baby grand piano. On Christmas morning, he led her down to his "great surprise," but to his incredible disappointment, Margaret, instead of throwing her arms around his neck in embrace, suddenly burst into a spasm of inconsolable tears: her Christmas was ruined since it was simply not what she had expected by way of a "great surprise." For several months before Christmas she had constantly dropped hints that what she really wanted was a toy electric train set, and when it did not materialize she was disconsolate beyond words.

Margaret and her playmates later formed a club, the Henhouse Hicks. They met in some outbuildings adjoining the home, and they revelled in the joy of reading film magazines and they collected pictures and reports of the activities of their favorite movie stars. Margaret's love of movies never forsook her and, (as will be seen below), the film privileges afforded to the daughter of a President ranked easily among the foremost advantages of her newly acquired status.

While she was still attending grade school in Independence, an ugly incident occurred which marred the family's happiness. Truman's honesty within the corrupt Democratic organization in Kansas City created him enemies, and, one morning, a certain individual appeared at the school and informed her teacher that he had been requested to take home "Mary Truman, Judge Truman's daughter." By sheer providence, the teacher became alert to the fact that the judge's daughter was never called by her first name. She phoned Margaret's mother, who phoned Truman, who phoned the police, but by the time of their arrival at the school the intruder had disappeared. This stark and genuine threat of kidnapping ever after colored Truman's approach to the safety of his daughter.

Following upon his election as U.S. Senator, the family commuted annually to the capital, usually spending the months of January to June in Washington when Margaret attended Gunston Hall, a private school, and the remainder of the year in Independence, when she attended the local public high schools.

Truman was fond of driving, so they always went by car to and from the capital, and the family's needs were always dictated by what could be packed into the back seat and trunk. Among the "necessities" appeared to be Margaret's substantial collection of Raggedy Ann dolls which had been donated to her over the years by loving aunts and relatives. At first, Truman himself had undertaken the not-unsubstantial chore of carefully packing all the dolls so that Margaret would miss nothing of home comforts while away from Independence. After a few years, however, and when she had reached the age of 14 or 15, he suddenly announced that it was time for her to take responsibility for the assignment. Overnight, her love and devotion for her treasured possessions vanished, and thereafter, the dolls were always left at home in Independence.

Another practice which also suddenly ceased was Margaret's habit of employing what her parents considered to be undesirable slang expressions, which included her regular use of the word, "dearie," when conversing with all and sundry. They decided to impose a ten-cent fine upon each occasion when she was overheard using the objected-to terms, and their solution proved effective.

In 1941, Truman was appointed chairman of the special committee to investigate the National Defense Program, a committee which, ever thereafter, became known simply as the Truman Committee, and it earned the man from Independence, national recognition. But for the family, it meant prolonged periods of separation, when Truman travelled all over the country with his investigative committee, and it began a new era by way of extensive correspondence between the family members. The only problem, normally, was that, while Truman hated the phone but loved to pen his thoughts on paper, Margaret was the reverse. She was often very remiss in replying to her father's regular letters, so that he would resort either to capital-lettered reminders such as: YOU OWE ME TWO LETTERS; or to plain sarcasm: "Is your arm paralysed?"; or yet to the plaintiff plea: "I am lonesome this morning. Thought maybe I might get a letter from my little girl."

As a nonlettered history buff, Truman, while lacking all degrees, was extremely well-read and well-versed in the basic principles of democracy, and, in his correspondence to Margaret, now 17, he made every effort to instill into her that the major purpose of a study of the past was the better understanding of the present, whereby, in turn, mankind might progress into a more secure and agreeable future:

> For instance, if you were listening in on the Senate Committee hearings of your dad, you'd understand why old Diogenes carried a lantern in the daytime in his search for an honest man. Most everybody's fundamentally honest, but when men, or women, are entrusted with public funds or trust estates of other people they find it most difficult to honestly administer them. I can't understand or find out why that is so—but it is.[2]

Occasionally, he would pass on to her an item of interest:

> Buy this month's National Geographic and see how like us Ancient Egypt was. Here's a dollar to buy it with. You can buy soda pop with the change. . . .[3]

On Sunday, December 7, 1941, Margaret was at home in Independence listening to a philharmonic broadcast from New York. She became irritated by constant interruption of the music program by news items relating to the Japanese bombing of Pearl Harbor, which she assumed was some place associated with the Pearl River of China. At last, she went to share her annoyance with her mother who, immediately recognizing the significance of the event, phoned her husband at his hotel in Columbia, Missouri. The whole family at once went to Washington, where, on December 8, Margaret was present at the historic meeting in Congress, when Roosevelt proclaimed December 7, 1941, as the day which would "live in infamy," and proceeded to announce the declaration of war on Japan.

Truman, like all other Congressmen, became increasingly engulfed in the matter of war preparations, yet he was always mindful of his daughter's progress. On the 13th of March, 1942, he wrote to her from San Francisco:

> . . . You have a good mind, a beautiful physique and a possible successful future, but that is now up to you. You are the mistress of your future. All your mother and dad can do is to look on, advise when asked, and wish you a happy one. There'll be troubles and sorrow aplenty but there'll also be happy days and hard work. From a financial standpoint your father has not been a shining success but he has tried to leave you something that (as Mr. Shakespeare says) cannot be stolen—an honorable reputation and a good name. You must continue that heritage and see that it is not spoiled. You're all we have and we both count on you. . . .[4]

On June 2, 1942, Margaret graduated from Gunston Hall, and her proud father gave the commencement address: Margaret, among other honors, was awarded both the English prize and the Spanish prize.

In the following September, she enrolled in George Washington University in D.C. and went on to major in history, although her father expressed regret that it was an emphasis upon English rather than American history, upon which, according to his daughter, her father considered himself an expert.

As an attractive young lady in Washington, Margaret found herself increasingly involved in Washington society, albeit a subdued war-time society. In January, 1944, she was asked to christen the new battleship, *Missouri*, at Brooklyn Shipyard. She did so, and effectively, but in some way the ship was launched so quickly that the champagne bottle upset itself not only over the attending admiral but also over herself, such that her clothes, and especially her fur, reeked of champagne for the rest of the winter.

At a later date, her mother was asked to christen a bomber plane, but, in this instance, someone had forgotten to score the bottle for easy breakage. Bess tried to smash the bottle against the soft aluminum nose of the airplane no fewer than six times before success, a hysterical scene which drew sarcastic comment from Margaret, who was present: "A fine thing for a girl who was her school's shot-put champion!" Bess was, indeed, at one time, a good athlete, and, whenever possible, she seldom missed an opportunity to see the Washington Senators baseball team in action. Moreover, she and Margaret were always the closest of friends, revelling in a relationship which went far beyond that of mother-daughter, and they played all manner of games together, including table-tennis, bowling, and bridge. For his own part, Truman played nothing, but he loved walking, and always claimed he was too young to play golf.

In July, 1944, at the Chicago Democratic Convention, a reluctant Truman accepted nomination as Vice-President, and his attitude was reflected in the fact that he made the shortest vice-presidential speech on record: 92 words. Margaret almost missed the inauguration ceremony on January 20, 1945, because of pressure of mid-year examinations at George Washington University. But she did attend and stood with Mrs. Woodrow Wilson, aged 73, while her father took the oath, and she was later able to assist her parents in welcoming their many relatives and friends who had come specially to Washington to attend the ceremonies. For Margaret, the major difference resulting from her father's new status lay in the fact that she was now privileged to travel to the university in a chauffeur-driven car.

Within three months, the lifestyle of the entire family was transformed. Roosevelt died on April 12, and the Trumans moved into Blair House for three weeks to give Eleanor Roosevelt time to vacate the contents of the White House after twelve years of residence. When they eventually moved into the presidential mansion, Margaret had hoped to relish the luxury of having breakfast served in bed every morning, but greatly to her chagrin this was not to be, since her father insisted upon family meals whenever possible, in order to maintain daily contact with his wife and daughter. He, likewise, insisted that the conversation be kept free of politics: "If you are in these things up to your neck all the time, you don't discuss them when you have a little leisure."[5]

Truman's main problem with the food was that the famous Mrs. Nesbitt, the housekeeper (about whom the Roosevelts found frequent cause to complain), constantly served up brussel sprouts, a vegetable which he loathed. When Bess began sending meal suggestions to the kitchen, Mrs. Nesbitt finally sent in her resignation, but as Margaret commented, the poor lady did have almost insurmountable problems to cope with:

> . . . . the White House kitchens are so enormous that the food is perforce institutional. When there are six to eight cooks with their fingers in the pie it's apt to taste that way. There are cooks for the executive wing who feed the people who work in the offices, and there are cooks for the White House incumbents and guests. There was great rivalry between these two groups. . . .[6]

All in one day, the kitchen staff might have to cope with luncheon for sixty people, tea for over a thousand, and an official reception for several hundred.

The quality of the food was not the only problem encountered by the new residents of the White House: the elevator mechanism had hardly been renovated since the hectic days of the Theodore Roosevelt "gang" and, now, forty years later, it was so enfeebled that "to get it to descend you had to take the button off, stick a pencil in the hole and give it a twist."[7] But this proved to be a very minor inconvenience in the light of what occurred at the time of Truman's election in 1948. The leg of Margaret's piano sank through the floor, and, upon investigation, an official committee condemned the whole interior structure. The Truman family was moved out into Blair House and there they remained for three-and-a-half years, while the White House was completely rebuilt at a cost of over five million dollars.

As daughter of the President, Margaret was now called upon to adorn, by her mere presence, all manner of functions and festivities, in addition to answering the many hundreds of letters from friends and well-wishers, and all the while she was obliged to maintain adequate grades at college, as well as to attend to her music studies. Truman, though expressing doubts as to the feasibility of a music career, gave his approval to his daughter on condition that she first graduate from college, and Margaret faithfully adhered to her father's stipulations.

In common with all the family members of past Presidents, what Margaret found most difficult was accommodating her life and activities to facing up to the fact "that we were living in a goldfish bowl," where every move was subject to scrutiny, comment, criticism, and appraisal. There was even the matter of boy-friends: apart from the inevitable romantically inclined press reports of her engagement to virtually every eligible bachelor in the country, irrespective of the fact that she had not even met most intended fiances, Margaret found all manner of restrictions in the way of even the least innocuous friendship. As she once plaintively commented:

> I ask you to consider the effect of saying good night to a boy at the door of the White House in a blaze of floodlights with a Secret Service man in attendance. There is not much you can do except shake hands and that's no way to get engaged.[8]

Her father recognized all the attendant perplexities of White House existence, and, he wrote later:

> I have sometimes wondered whether a President ought to have any descendants when I see how complicated their lives are made by their connection with the White House. . . . Throughout our history, it has been a very difficult situation for the descendants of Presidents, because so many people insist on regarding them as if they were the offspring of dignitary rulers. I feel that the descendants of Presidents are entitled to be treated just as any citizens. And they ought to have the same chance to make their own way.[9]

However, despite all the negative dimensions, Margaret retained her good-natured affability and lively sense of humor. What she most enjoyed was the privilege accorded the President to request any film for private viewing in the White House. She could now freely indulge in her adolescent fantasies and she enjoyed all her past and present favorites, even to seeing "The Scarlet Pimpernel" no fewer than sixteen times, with "Naughty Marietta" running a close second.

She loved to entertain her college friends, and, one night, she invited two of them to sleep with her in Lincoln's bed. Learning of her intentions, Truman thought of playing a trick by having one of the White House butlers, a lean "cadaverous man like Ole Abe," dress up in white, and appear at the bedroom door at midnight. But the butler, unenthused with the project, either reported sick or arranged for a night off, and the plan fell through. In any event, the bed proved so hard, that the girls talked all night and ended up on the floor.[10]

Both of Margaret's grandmothers came to stay at the White House. Bess's mother, Madge Gates Wallace, died there on July 26, 1947, aged 94. Truman's mother, Martha Ellen Young Truman, whom her son called the "Old Rebel," was a confirmed and unrepentent Confederate supporter, who, over 90 years of age, had too many memories of Northern raids upon her farm in Grandview, Missouri, to forgive easily. When she was brought on a visit to the White House she adamantly refused even to see the Lincoln Room, let alone sleep in the famous bed.

With reference to the trick of Lincoln's "ghost," Truman had this to say about White House apparitions in general:

> . . . I'm sure they're here and I'm not half so alarmed at meeting up with any of them as I am at having to meet the live nuts I have to see every day . . . So I won't lock my doors or bar them either if any of the old coots in the pictures out in the hall want to come out of their frames for a friendly chat.[11]

Margaret graduated from George Washington University in June, 1946, and it was her proud father, the President, appropriately robed in cap and gown, who presented her with her diploma. He at the same ceremony was awarded the honorary degree of Doctor of Laws, and he subsequently teased Margaret that, while she had taken four years to obtain a degree, he had obtained one in four minutes.

Having satisfied the parental proviso that she satisfactorily complete college before embarking upon a musical career, Margaret now proceeded to investigate possibilities relating to her future. Her father appeared to have overheard one of her comments to the effect that she was "after the big money," which provoked him to state:

> Now that I don't approve of. I want you to have artistic perfection—and the money will come of itself.—There are lowbrows who'll never appreciate the good you do who make burlesque singers a success. I don't want you to be burlesque—I want you to be the real thing and I am sure, now, that you can.[12]

He did add a snide remark:

> You know you could make a right good income if you wanted to do a Roosevelt stunt and sell your White House connection by selling records. . . . [13]

He strongly objected to the capitalization of the family name, and at one time he and Margaret seriously considered possible options for a stage name. Truman suggested alternatives "within the family tree," noting such antecedents as Mary Jane Holmes, Harriet Louisa Gregg, Peggy Seton, Susan Shippe, Mary Margaret Gates, and Matilda Middleton. But since these could hardly be considered as appealing to the public as such names as Adelina Patti, or Concita Supervia, and since Margaret herself offered few imaginative alternative sobriquets, her name was left unchanged. Indeed, what concerned her more was one of

Truman's remarks that he would rather have grandchildren in the family
than a prima donna. Margaret had already made a vow that she would
not marry until she had left the White House, and this vow she kept.

One apparent physical handicap gave her some concern but obviously,
not to any great extent since she made light and humorous comments
upon it:

> . . . I used to worry about my nose. It has since been described
> with many strange adjectives even including patrician, but the fact
> is, it's better on one side than the other.[14]

Margaret made her music debut in March, 1947, with the Detroit
Symphony Orchestra on a nationwide radio hookup, but, on the night of
the concert, she developed bronchial pneumonia. However, the concert
was rescheduled, and she made her appearance one week later. The
critics, she commented, "on the whole were very kind." She immediately received an offer from Hollywood to appear for a fee of $10,000 in
a film, *Las Vegas*, but, probably mindful of her father's admonitions
concerning persons eager to reap in the "fast buck" with the family
name, she declined.

1947 was what Margaret came to call the "Year of the Truman Traveling Troupe," when the President, wishing to establish closer relationships
with countries in the Western Hemisphere, visited Mexico, Canada, and
Brazil. Margaret accompanied him to Canada, while the whole family
went to Brazil, flying outwards in the *Independence* (which had replaced
Roosevelt's *Sacred Cow*), and returning leisurely on the U.S.S. *Missouri*.

After an August appearance at the Hollywood Bowl with an orchestra
conducted by Eugene Ormandy, Margaret undertook an extensive two-
month concert tour which began in Pittsburgh in October and concluded
at Constitution Hall, Washington, in December, following which the
family spent its first Christmas in the White House. All previous Christmas celebrations had been at Independence, Missouri.

The following year was that of the presidential election, made memorable by the famous *Chicago Daily Tribune's* premature headline, "Dewey
defeats Truman." The incumbent President had encountered many difficulties during his term of office, such that in April, 1948, a *New York
Times* commentator wrote "At this writing, the President's influence is
weaker than any President's has been in modern history." Within the
Democratic party itself, two factions appeared, led by Henry Wallace and
Strom Thurmond, respectively, and the fall campaign opened in an
atmosphere of Democratic gloom and despondency as compared with
Republican exhilaration and optimism.

Truman responded in typical vein—by action. He set out on two major whistle-stop train journeys all across the United States to convey his campaign message to the people. With him were Bess and Margaret: the former, he introduced to the audience as his "Boss," and the latter as the "Boss's Boss."

On election day, Truman acknowledged defeat as late as midnight, but to his own admitted surprise by 4 A.M. next morning, he found himself the victor.

No sooner was the campaign over than the Trumans were forced to move into Blair House (because of the many necessary renovations to the White House), and here they were to remain until March, 1952.

During the fall of 1949, Margaret again undertook an extensive concert tour, while in June, 1950, she made her first national television appearance on the Ed Sullivan show, "Toast of the Town." During that very same month, national events were suddenly to be eclipsed by the North Korean invasion of South Korea, followed by Truman's dramatic intervention on behalf of the United Nations. On November 1 of the same year, there occurred his attempted assassination at Blair House by Puerto Rican terrorists. Margaret was on her annual fall tour at this time, and was scheduled on December 5 to make, as usual, her final appearance at Constitution Hall, Washington, D.C.

Tragically, on the very day of the concert, Truman's life-long friend, Charlie Ross, died suddenly. The President was very upset, and he debated whether or not to inform Margaret, to whom Ross had always given the warmest encouragement in the pursuit of her chosen career. He decided not to upset her, even knowing full well the risk of her being informed from some other source. Truman always admitted to being nervous when he attended any concert of Margaret's since he was over-anxious for her success, and, in consequence, he usually tore up his program during the performance into smaller and smaller shreds. Legend states, that on this occasion, his anxiety was such that he so tore up several programs that they resembled confetti.

The next day he read the concert review by Paul Hume of the *Washington Post;* the section concerning Margaret read: "She is flat a good deal of the time . . . She cannot sing with any professional finish . . . She communicates almost nothing of the music she presents. . . ."

Truman was livid and he expressed his anger in no uncertain terms in an oft-quoted letter in response to the said review:

I have just read your lousy review buried in the back pages. You sound like a frustrated man that never made a success, an eight-ulcer man on a four-ulcer job, and all four ulcers working. I never met you, but if I do you'll need a new nose and plenty of beefsteak, and perhaps a supporter below. Westbrook Pegler, a guttersnipe, is a gentleman compared to you. You can take that as more of an insult than a reflection on your ancestry.

This was "Give 'em hell, Harry!" at its best, but even General Marshall, commenting on Paul Hume's review, stated that the only thing the latter didn't criticize was the varnish on the piano.

Truman's retort was received with mixed publicity, but it had no adverse effect upon Margaret's career. In 1951 she embarked upon an eminently successful goodwill ambassador trip to Western Europe representing her father, the cost of which was entirely borne from her concert earnings. She was hosted by royalty in England, Holland, and Norway, and elsewhere by heads of state, including Pope Pius XII, for whose audience she was dressed in such funereal black from head to toe that when he saw her photograph in the morning newspaper, one of the President's aides, Bill Hassett, brought it in to Truman declaring, "Here's a picture of the mother superior!"[15]

She again visited Europe in 1952, this time on holiday but it probably occasioned her "most embarrassing moment": at a party for the Queen of England given by the U.S. ambassador, Margaret was proceeding downstairs in the procession of notables, when her petticoat slipped loose and fell to her feet. With superb aplomb, she stepped out of it, picked it up, flung it to one side, and continued as if nothing had happened.[16]

By 1952, Truman had decided that seven years of office were enough, and he made clear his intention not to seek re-election. He had once stated his opinion of the White House: "It is a very nice prison, but a prison, nevertheless. No man in his right mind would want to come here of his own accord. There are a lot of them who are not in their right minds, I'd say."[17]

In the presidential election of that year, the Democratic nominee, Adlai Stevenson, was easily defeated by Republican Dwight Eisenhower. The Truman "lame-duck" interval between November, 1952, and January, 1953, was saddened by the death at the White House, on December 6, 1952, of Bess's mother, Madge Gates Wallace. When the family returned to Independence after the inauguration ceremony of President Eisenhower, they found themselves alone as a discrete unit, and the former President was now "Mr. Citizen." As Margaret recalls it, this was the first time she had ever known her father as plain "Mr. Truman"—hitherto, she had recognized him only as Judge, Senator, Vice-President, and finally, President. While her parents were now able to relax at home,

Margaret pursued her music career and also appeared on radio and television shows. In 1955, she was given the opportunity to substitute for Ed Murrow on the CBS television program, *Person to Person,* when she, in New York, interviewed both her parents in Independence.

It was in November of this same year that she met Clifton Daniel at the home of some mutual friends. Daniel was a world-traveled newsman with the *New York Times,* and, in his memoirs, he noted that their romance began badly since Margaret stood him up on their first date in favor of Maurice Chevalier whom she was to interview on the NBC radio program *Weekday.*[18]

Obviously, however, this initial setback was not permitted to sour their friendship, which matured rapidly to the point that they were married only five months after their first meeting, on April 21, 1956.[19] He was 43 and she 32.

Since Truman's ambition, voiced a decade earlier, was to be a grandfather, the Daniels proceeded to satisfy him not once, but four times, and with all boys, all born within the ten years of the marriage, and all named within the (joint) family hierarchy: Clifton Truman Daniel,[20] William Wallace Daniel, Harrison Gates Daniel, and Thomas Washington Daniel.[21]

Truman was not the type of grandfather who played on the floor. He told and read stories to his grandchildren, he treated them (usually) with dignity, and in turn he (usually) expected reciprocity. Daniel reported that in the earliest stages of grandfatherhood, Truman reacted with little confidence in his new role: when the Daniels brought their firstborn to Independence they set him on grandpa's lap while the father went to the kitchen to see to the milk bottle: "When I came back, the former President of the United States looked like a man with a time bomb and no place to put it."[22]

Yet as time passed, Truman's influence had effect: he kept his grandsons in awe; when he bawled, they obeyed in silence; whereas when their father bawled, they bawled back.[23]

Years later, upon the occasion of the celebration of the centennial of Truman's birth, the two older boys contributed an article to the *Kansas City Star,* recalling fond memories of the house in Independence. To them, Bess was "Gammy" and recognized by all the grandchildren "as a soft touch," always ready with cookies and candies—"in contrast with Grandpa Truman, around whom we learned to tread lightly."[24]

The house itself was sheer paradise for children "cribb'd, cabin'd and confin'd" to apartment living in New York: with its twenty-two rooms inside, colored light streaming in from stained glass windows, dark wood walls and furniture, and lots of spare rooms to hide and play in such that "Our parents could never find us." Its literal apotheosis and zenith was the attic, "a goldmine of junk." The house had been built in the 1860's, with next to nothing discarded for the best part of a century—old clothing, old byegones, old toys, and, as the boys commented, what modern plaything could possibly compare with a teddy bear on wheels? Their own favorites were the hats, and "the individually wrapped bars of soap from Grandfather's haberdashery," which, fortunately, "went unsold long enough to eventually become historical artifacts."

Outside, in summer there was grass, an abundance of grass, again unknown in New York, while, in winter, when it snowed, it really snowed, creating cottonwool-like mounds, glistening in unspoiled, untarnished, pristine beauty, which only the boys, themselves, and not passersby, nor trashmen, nor road clearance vehicles, could ruin, to their hearts' delight.

The saddest regrets of the grandsons lay in the fact, that, when Grandpa Truman died in 1972, the eldest boy at that date was hardly fourteen years of age, so that there was little of the great contribution to the history of their country which he had made which he could have talked to them about. Nevertheless, they were remarkably privileged to be able to converse with their very own mother about the global, disruptive events of the age, of which she was a close participant-observer, domiciled in the home of the premier executive in the land.

Margaret's husband, Clifton, shrewdly yet humorously comments upon the radiant and unblemished harmony of this presidential family:

> Whatever my merits or demerits as a son-in-law, I never felt that I fully penetrated that circle of solidarity formed by the three Trumans. My position as head of my family was scrupulously respected but the Trumans were a breed apart—them against the world.[25]

Truman's widow, Bess, lived to be the oldest of all First Ladies when she died in October, 1982, aged 97. After her death, more than a thousand letters written by her were discovered at the home in Independence. They formed the basis of a new biography of her mother by Margaret, entitled *Bess W. Truman*. She introduced the work with the words:

> This is the most difficult book I have ever written. It is about a woman I thought I knew better than any other person in my life. But I have discovered, as I wrote it, that it is about a woman who

kept her deepest feelings, her most profound sorrows, sealed from my view—from almost everyone's view.[26]

Sixty-seven years after the wedding of Harry and Bess Truman on June 28, 1919, Margaret's oldest son, Clifton Truman Daniel, was married to Polly Bennett on the same date in 1986, at Wilmington, North Carolina. Clifton, 29, was the first of the four brothers to marry. He had attended the University of North Carolina, but had left to study acting in New York. At the time of his marriage he was a reporter for the *Wilmington Morning Star.*

Dwight David Eisenhower

(1953–1961)

(Ike) Eisenhower was the first and only career serviceman to become President of the United States during the twentieth century. He was the third of the seven sons of David Jacob Eisenhower and Ida Elizabeth Stover, and, after graduating from West Point, he was assigned to Fort Sam Houston near San Antonio, Texas. It was here in October, 1915, that he met Mamie (Marie) Doud, the second of four daughters of a wealthy meatpacker, John Sheldon Doud, and his wife, Elivera. Ike and Mamie were married within a year of their meeting at Denver, the home of the Doud family; Ike was 25 and Mamie 19. From the date of their marriage, on July 1, 1916, until the day of Ike's inauguration as President on January 20, 1953, neither of them was to enjoy the blessings and comforts of anything resembling that of a permanent family home. Biographers vary in their estimates, but even the most conservative concur that, within the foregoing 37-year period, Mamie lived in no fewer than 19 army camp residences, and in, at least, another 30 hotels. With each move she tried to maintain her favorite colors of pink for the bedroom and sunshine yellow for the kitchen, although, since she had not learned to cook, she was obliged to leave most of the culinary duties to Ike.

Even though stationed at one particular camp, Ike would be dispatched for occasional assignment elsewhere, and he was not present when their first child, Dwight Doud Eisenhower, was born on September 24, 1917. By this date, the country was at war and, after temporary duties at Fort Oglethorpe, Georgia, Ike became commander of a tank training unit at Camp Cole, near Gettysburg. The unit was still in training when the war ended, and Ike saw no overseas duties.

On Armistice Day, November 11, 1918, the Doud family suffered its second tragedy: Mamie's eldest sister, Eleanor, had died in 1912 at the age of seven, and now, in 1918, another sister, Eda Mae (Buster) died at the age of 17, and was buried on the day the war ended. The very presence of young Dwight Doud, without doubt, helped Mamie to endure the family losses as well as the loneliness of camp life in the absence of her husband, and Ike found great enjoyment and pleasure in attending to and playing with his son and heir: like all children of this age, the latter would wet his pants without warning, and he came to be nicknamed "Icky."

In 1920, Ike, now a major, was assigned to Camp Meade, Maryland, and he set about preparing for the Christmas festivities by having a tree placed in the family living room complete with garlands and decorations. But during the week prior to Christmas Day, Icky became ill. At first it was believed he had merely caught a bad cold, but he developed a high temperature and died on January 2, 1921,[1] by which time his illness had been diagnosed as scarlet fever, for which, at that period in time there were no known antibiotics; only later was it discovered that one of the child's baby-sitters had just recovered from scarlet fever and had remained a carrier.

Ike's grief was intense, and the birth of a second son, John Sheldon Doud Eisenhower, in August, 1922, apparently did little to dispel the inner anger and deep resentment against some Almighty Being which had so abruptly and so cruelly removed from him the ecstasy and joy of his firstborn. He appeared to have inwardly vowed never again to allow himself to be so hurt, and, years later, John recalled that, while his father was ever mindful and caring, he was yet always distant, strict, and stern, demanding obedience and observance of rules: "Dad was a terrifying figure to a small boy."[2]

For her part, Mamie was ever apprehensive of losing her second son. Her own parents had gone through the agony of burying two young daughters, and she knew how they could not be consoled or comforted in their loss. She, therefore, became overanxious and overprotective of her young son, sending him to school so over bundled in jackets and coats and scarves that he became an object of derision among his elementary school classmates.

The round of army camps continued throughout the 1920s, although, in 1928, John, age six, was in Paris with his father, who was serving on the Battle Monuments Commission. John attended the McJanet School for American children, but his father occasionally took him along to visit the trenches, villages, and towns devastated by the fighting during World War I.

Upon their return to Washington, John enrolled in the John Quincy Adams Grade School, but every summer he was sent to Denver to be with his maternal grandparents. John's memories of these visits were not particularly happy ones. The Doud home he found dark and cheerless, while his grandfather ("Pupah") and grandmother ("Nana") never appeared to have recovered from the loss of their two daughters, as well as of the Eisenhower's firstborn son, Dwight Doud. They would visit the Fairmont Cemetery, Denver, every Sunday to place flowers on the three graves, and then "sit silently for what seemed to a small boy an interminable length of time."[3]

Yet, despite his grandfather's normally gloomy disposition, John concluded that Pupah possessed certain positive and redeeming qualities, not the least being his capacity as a vivid raconteur of his varied career as a freight-train hopper and a stockyard entrepreneur at Boone, Iowa, activities which he supplemented with a store of memories and songs of the Civil War. John was further impressed by Pupah's enormous appetite which enabled him to dispose of an entire cherry pie at one sitting. They both enjoyed a game of pool, especially since the basement room was the coolest place in the house.

Perhaps it was due in part to Pupah's influence that Nana often appeared depressed, yet John found her outgoing and friendly, and was captivated by her unexpected love of baseball and her pride in still being able to throw a fastball in her fifties. Her affection for the game she passed on to Mamie.[4]

But, by far the most exciting personality in Denver was John's Aunt Frances ("Mike"), Mamie's youngest sister. She was a lively, irrepressible young lady whose exploits were a constant source of ongoing conversation within and without the family—as for example the time when she and her boyfriend drained Pupah's entire supply of gin during Prohibition days, replacing it in the bottles with plain water. Her marriage was no less dramatic since, in the mid-1920's, she eloped with a wealthy Texan businessman.[5]

Occasionally, John would visit the paternal grandparents resident in Abilene, Kansas, where he came in contact with his several uncles (his father's five brothers), who might also be visiting the parental home, along with their wives and children. All the uncles were successful in their respective careers, so that contact with any one of them was stimulating. Moreover, both Eisenhower grandparents were graduates of Lane University, Lecompton, Kansas, and both had even studied Greek. Yet Grandfather Eisenhower could be as depressing as Grandfather Doud, since, unfortunately, he had been involved in unsuccessful business ventures and, following his financial losses, had become increasingly withdrawn and morose, which made him a less than congenial companion for his grandchildren.

In 1935, Ike was sent to the Philippines[6] to serve as lieutenant-colonel under General MacArthur. By this time, John was in eighth grade at the John Quincy Adams school in Washington, D.C. He was performing well academically, and he was elected president of his class. Ike agreed that he should remain in school until the end of the year, so that John and his mother did not join Ike until 1936, and they were to stay in the Philippines for the next four years, by which time Ike had been promoted to full colonel.

John attended an Episcopalian mission school, the Brent School at Bagnio in Luzon, during the family's stay in the East Indies. At first, there were only a hundred children enrolled in the entire twelve grades, but numbers increased somewhat in 1937 when American military dependents were evacuated from China to the Philippines following the invasion by Japan, along with the Panay "incident," when a U.S. naval vessel was bombed by Japanese airplanes.

While in the Philippines, Ike learned to fly and he obtained a pilot's license[7] while John, for his part, once received lessons from Bill Tilden, the U.S. tennis champion, who was on a visit.

Upon the outbreak of World War II in Europe, Eisenhower returned with his family to the United States. John continued his academic studies at Stadium High School, Tacoma, whence, after graduation, he proceeded to Washington, D.C., where he enrolled at a West Point preparatory school, and he was admitted to West Point itself on July 1, 1941. His career and progress there were unexceptional. He apparently suffered from some form of loose-jointedness, which made him "bounce" when marching, a peculiar abnormality which earned him the nickname of "Tanglefoot Eisenwilly."[8]

Required course work at West Point was reduced from four to three years because of the war situation, and John graduated on June 6, 1944, D-Day in Europe, when the Allied Forces first landed on the Normandy beaches. On the very same evening of his graduation, which was attended by Mamie, John, in company with 15,000 other American soldiers, was on board the *Queen Mary*. Upon arrival in England, he spent his first weeks with his father, who was inspecting the battle zones.[9] John was introduced by his father to Kay Summersby, Eisenhower's controversial English chauffeuse. In July, John and Kay returned together to the U.S. where John introduced her to Mamie and took her to see the Broadway musical show "Oklahoma." The subsequent rumors which alleged intimacy between Kay and Eisenhower so upset Mamie that she refused her husband's invitation to come to Europe in September, 1945, and they may have led her to resort to the bottle for comfort.[10]

John saw no battle action, since the authorities feared that the loss of a second son could be devastating to the Allied Commander-in-Chief. He was assigned to the staff of General Bradley, and he visited Buchenwald concentration camp a few days following its liberation.

In August, 1945, John accompanied his father to Moscow where he met Stalin, and they were still there when news was received of the surrender of Japan. During the post-war occupation period, John was assigned to duties in Vienna, and, in 1946, while on leave in Britain to meet with his father and mother, the family were guests of King George VI and Queen Elizabeth at Balmoral Castle, Scotland. It was here that John met Barbara Jean Thompson, daughter of Colonel Percy W. Thompson of the U.S. Army H.Q. On June 10, 1947, John and Barbara were married at Fort Monroe, Virginia, where the groom was stationed following his return to the United States.[11]

Then John was assigned as instructor in English at West Point and it was here, on March 31, 1948, that their first child, Dwight David Eisenhower II, saw the light of day. Over the next seven years, three more children were born to Barbara and John, all daughters: Barbara Anne (1949), Susan Elaine (1951), and Mary Jean (1955).

After three years in West Point, John was transferred to the Fort Knox Advanced Armored School and, with the invasion of South Korea by North Korean forces in June, 1950, he was assigned to duties in the new theatre of war. At this date, Eisenhower, having served first as Army Chief of Staff from 1945 to 1947, then as president of Columbia University, N.Y., from 1948 to 1949, was named Supreme Commander of

NATO forces, and took up residence in Paris. He had refused nomination as presidential candidate in 1948, but four years later he accepted a Republican invitation and went on to record easy victories over Adlai Stevenson, his Democratic opponent, in the 1952 as well as in the 1956 elections.

Eisenhower had, during the election campaign of 1952, promised to end the war in Korea, and, following his November victory, he visited the beleaguered country in December. John had seen some action, but, as in World War II, he was kept away from the main battle front, since his capture, to say the least, would have compelled his father to withdraw his candidacy, while having been elected, the situation was even more compromising and complicated.

Eisenhower was inaugurated in January, 1953, and John received an order recalling him to attend the ceremony. John protested since he believed that such a favor might well prejudice his opportunities for promotion. Eisenhower, likewise, was most displeased, and on the very day of the inauguration he expressed his concern to Truman, who subsequently recorded the conversation in his autobiography, *Mr. Citizen,* as follows:

> I wonder who is responsible for my son John being ordered to Washington from Korea? I wonder who is trying to embarrass me?
>
> HST: The President of the United States ordered your son to attend your Inauguration. The President thought it was right and proper for your son to witness the swearing-in of his father to the Presidency. If you think somebody was trying to embarrass you by this order, then the President assumes full responsibility.

Truman commented:

> I thought this was a curious reaction by a father to the presence of his son on an occasion so historic for himself and his family. I could only account for it on the grounds that it was a manifestation of hostility towards me.[12]

Eisenhower remained unconvinced by Truman's explanation, and the hostility between them lasted for years.

In 1949, Eisenhower purchased a 189-acre estate at Gettysburg, with the object of providing for himself and Mamie a stable and secure retirement home. But, because of his absence in Paris and his duties as President, the task of remodeling was not completed until 1956.

Meanwhile, John had returned to the United States in September, 1953, following the Korean Armistice, and took up military assignments at Fort Leavenworth, Kansas, and Fort Belvedere, Virginia. He had accompanied his father to the Summit Conference at Geneva in 1955, the year in which his fourth and last child, Mary Jean, was born.

The Eisenhowers were proud grandparents, and Eisenhower doted particularly on his one and only grandson, David, who always called his grandfather, "Ike." In order that they might re-establish family unity, John and Barbara purchased a former one-room schoolhouse on the edge of the Gettysburg estate which they proceeded to convert to domestic use. Eisenhower had a road made between the two residences to maintain easy access.

Eisenhower was very fond of Barbara, his daughter-in-law, and, when he hosted world leaders such as Macmillan, De Gaulle, and Khrushchev, both formally at the White House, and informally at Gettysburg, he would be sure to include John and his wife at the functions. Eisenhower managed to interest David in baseball and basketball, but never in golf or fishing, when the young lad would tend to use his rod like a baseball bat. The grandfather kept a stable of ponies at Gettysburg for the exclusive use of all his grandchildren.[13]

Eisenhower's health began to deteriorate after 1955 when he suffered a mild heart attack, and after 1957, when he suffered a stroke. Yet he made a remarkable recovery from both disabilities, and John was assigned to White House duties, commencing in 1957, to assist his father in the matter of intelligence briefings.

Following upon the visit of Vice-President Nixon to Russia in August, 1959, Khrushchev, his wife and three children, came to the United States in September, and were hosted by Eisenhower. Khrushchev appeared to have enjoyed his conversations with talkative young David, who later wore a red-star pin to school, much to John's disapproval. Khrushchev sent all the children presents for the following Christmas.

During his last year of office, Eisenhower undertook an extensive series of overseas visits, and, since Mamie did not feel capable of undertaking any undue physical stress, Barbara accompanied the President and John as hostess, first on a strenuous two-week visit of eleven countries on a round-the-world tour, which included S.E. Asia, India, Iran, Greece, Italy, and Morocco, and then on a goodwill visit to Brazil, Uruguay, Argentina, and Chile. A summit conference planned at Paris during May, 1960, did take place, but since, only two weeks earlier, the U-2 incident had taken place, nothing was accomplished.

In January, 1961, Eisenhower retired to Gettysburg, which, for the first time in the lives of the ex-President and his wife, became a truly permanent home. John now resigned from the army for the specific purpose of assisting his father in assembling and editing the latter's many thousands of presidential and personal papers.

Eisenhower had, in 1948, already written his memoirs of World War II experiences, published under the title of *Crusade in Europe*. With John's assistance, he produced a further work, the *White House Years*, in two volumes: the first, *Mandate for Change* in 1963, and the second, *Waging Peace*, in 1964.

With the foregoing task brought to a successful conclusion, John, at age 42, was engaged as executive vice-president of Freedoms Foundation at Valley Forge, and, in due course, he himself was commissioned to write a book on the Battle of the Bulge, which was published in 1968 as *The Bitter Woods*. It proved to be a highly successful financial venture.

In this same year, two of John and Barbara's children were married: in November, Barbara Ann to Fernando Echavarria of Bogota, Colombia; and in December, David to Julie Nixon.

The family had expected David to proceed to West Point, like his father and grandfather, after graduation from high school, but instead he had enrolled at Amherst, the same time that Julie Nixon had entered Smith College, just seven miles away. It was Mamie Eisenhower who had suggested that it would be "very nice" if David were to visit Julie, and he did. They fell in love and were married at the Marble Collegiate Church in New York City, three days before Christmas 1968. Neither Eisenhower nor Mamie were able to be present at the ceremony, since it happened that they were both hospitalized at the Walter Reed General Hospital, D.C., but they viewed the proceedings on closed circuit television. Less than three months later, Eisenhower, 78, died on March 28, 1969, at the same hospital. Mamie survived him by ten years and she was 82 when she died on November 1, 1979.

Eisenhower had hoped to retain the Gettysburg estate within the family, but the rising costs of maintenance had made his desires impracticable. In 1967, he decided to donate the estate to the government, with the reservation that he and Mamie could live out their lives at the home. After her husband's death, Mamie, treasuring her independence, did just that and she steadfastly refused to move in with John's now reduced family.

Within two months of his father's death, John, who had been appointed by President Nixon as U.S. Ambassador to Belgium, took up residence in Brussels, where he remained for two years until his resignation in September, 1971. The assignation proved hilarious as well as tumultuous, as when Mamie paid the family a visit: she brought so much baggage that John termed it the Second Invasion of Normandy. The pace

of life in the city was hectic, since Brussels had been honored as the seat
of administration of both NATO and the EEC, and foreign missions
abounded. The round of formal functions and receptions was endless, in
addition to which there were the special celebrations relating to the
twenty-fifth anniversary of the liberation of Belgium by the Allies in
1944, as well as the special visit to Brussels by the astronauts who had
made the first moon landing in July, 1969.

Another happy occasion was the marriage in January, 1971, of John
and Barbara's second daughter, Susan, to Alexander Bradshaw, a barri-
ster by profession, and son of the British consul in Brussels. John later
recorded the amusing circumstance at the ceremony, when, having been
asked to read a passage from the Bible, he inadvertently turned over the
page and, instead of extolling the bliss of matrimony, he read the lesson
which castigated the sin of fornication.[14]

After graduating from Amherst, John's son, David, enlisted in a Naval
Officers Candidate School, but, as hostilities in Vietnam drew to a close,
he enrolled at George Washington University Law School, and was also a
sports columnist with the *Philadelphia Bulletin*. The Watergate crisis
interrupted his studies while he and his wife, Julie, were in the White
House to give support to the family. He finally graduated in 1976.

According to Harry S. Dent, special counsel to Richard Nixon from
1969 to 1973,[15] plans had been advanced to embark David upon a
political career, with the proposal that he become Republican Congressman from Gettysburg, Pennsylvania. But, with Watergate, the
dream vanished.

Since that time, David became increasingly absorbed in research relating to a three-volume biography of his grandfather, the first volume of
which, *Eisenhower at War, 1943–45* was published in 1986. By the latter
date, Julie also, along with her family obligations as mother of three
young children: Jenny (7), Melanie (5), and Alex (2), had seen the light of
publication of a biography of her mother, entitled *Pat Nixon: The Untold
Story*.

John Fitzgerald Kennedy

(1961–1963)

John F. Kennedy was the first President to be born in the twentieth century—on May 29, 1917, the second child and the second son in a family of nine. Only one other President in this century has originated from a larger family: this was William Howard Taft, who was seventh of his father's ten children, albeit from two marriages.

The Kennedy family formed a close-knit prolific clan, governed by an authoritative, millionaire patriarch, Joseph Patrick Kennedy, Jr. The latter died in 1969, and his widow, Rose Fitzgerald Kennedy, published her memoirs, *Times to Remember* (1974), in which she recalls that, at Hyannis Port in 1972, she proudly presided over a gathering of all 28 of her grandchildren, of whom two were the surviving children of John F. Kennedy and his wife, Jacqueline Lee Bouvier Kennedy.

The Kennedys' American ancestors were Catholic immigrants who had left Ireland during the disastrous famine years of the 1840's. They were soon involved in politics: Patrick Joseph Kennedy, Sr., was an early labor leader, and it was he who propounded what came to be firmly recognized as the motivating family maxim: "Come in first; second place is failure." P. J. (as he was known), served in both houses of the Massachusetts Legislature. On the Fitzgerald side, Rose's father, John Francis Fitzgerald, was U.S. Congressman for six years, following which he was elected Mayor of Boston (1906–1908), and he was the first son of foreign parents to achieve this prominent status.

The ancestry of Jacqueline Lee Bouvier, (the first First Lady to be born in the twentieth century) was very different from that of her husband's. The Bouviers were originally from France, and they had come over to serve with Lafayette during the War of Independence, following which some had returned to France, but a few remained to make their home in the new United States of America. Jacqueline's father was third in line of a succession of "John Vernon Bouviers." He was a very handsome, charming man (known to his friends as "Black Jack"), but an ineffective provider, yet of whom Jacqueline was very fond. He was divorced by his wife, Janet Lee Bouvier, a former New York society belle, and the early family life of both Jacqueline and her sister, Lee, was one clouded with unhappiness.[1]

According to his mother, Rose, her son, John F was a "very active, very lively elf" who "thought his own thoughts, did things his own way, and somehow just didn't fit any pattern."[2] Yet she wrote:

> Almost all his life, it seemed, he had to battle against misfortunes of health. Perhaps this gave him another kind of strength that helped him to be the great man he became.[3]

As a young boy, and as a young man, John F contracted, in succession, scarlet fever, appendicitis, and hepatitis (on more than one occasion), such that Rose, later, humorously commented:

> He went along for many years thinking to himself—or at least trying to make others think—that he was a strong, robust, healthy person who just happened to be sick a good deal of the time.[4]

But, apart from his bouts with ill health, John F had one other major on-going problem with which to contend, that of the hero-image of his older brother, Joseph Patrick Kennedy III, two years his senior, and, in the eyes of his father, the heir who could do no wrong, and who was destined to achieve, with the aid of the family fortune, the ultimate goal of the presidency of the United States.

John F's entire early career was in the shadow of his brother. Joe went to Choate Boarding School, where his career appeared to be one of uninterrupted brilliant success—his academic grades were excellent, he was editor of the yearbook, and was a member of an undefeated football team. John F. joined his brother at Choate, but his achievements were nonspectacular, although he was voted "most likely to succeed."

Joe went to the London School of Economics, with Socialist Harold Laski as his tutor;[5] John F. followed suit, but an attack of hepatitis forced him to withdraw and to return to the U.S. Both Joe Sr. and Joe Jr. had attended Harvard and John F. sought, at this point, to break out of the familiar tradition, and he enrolled at Princeton. But, again, an attack of hepatitis caused him to withdraw, and, in the fall of 1936, he resigned himself to enroll at Harvard.

Before graduation in 1940, he had once more been beset by illnesses which curtailed his attempted athletic achievements: he was laid low with influenza at the time of a crucial varsity swimming contest, and he received injuries at football which limited his participation in that sport, also.

In the meantime, his father had, in 1937, been appointed U.S. Ambassador in London by F.D.R. and he encouraged both his sons to be with him and to travel in Europe. Joe Jr. visited Spain at the time of the civil war, while John F. went to Germany and Russia, and it was as the result of his experiences, that, in 1940, he published *Why England Slept,* an astute analysis of the political situation of the immediate pre-World War II period.

Joe Jr. enlisted in the U.S. Air forces at the time of World War II, and was killed in August, 1944. John F. became commander of a naval vessel, P.T. 109, which was rammed and sunk by a Japanese warship. He survived, but sustained a back injury which troubled him for the rest of his life.

After his discharge in early 1945, John F. seemed to have set out to achieve those goals which his father had originally planned for Joe Jr. The goals were political and the initial step was taken in 1946, when, at the age of 29, John F. was elected from Massachusetts to the U.S. House of Representatives: it was at this same election that his future rival, Richard Milhous Nixon, at 33, likewise became a U.S. Congressman from California.

In 1953, John F. entered the U.S. Senate, and he consented to be interviewed by a young, charming, 23-year-old news-photographer from the *Washington Times-Herald:* her name was Jacqueline Lee Bouvier. She was a Vassar graduate, who had later attended the Sorbonne in Paris, and George Washington University in the nation's capital.

John F. (Jack) and Jacqueline (Jacky) immediately formed an attachment. Jacky was sent by her editor to cover the coronation events of

Queen Elizabeth II, and upon her return, Jack and Jacky announced their formal engagement, and they were married on September 12, 1953, at Newport, R.I. Sadly, Black Jack Bouvier, who was to have given his daughter away, was so drunk that he failed to make an appearance at the wedding. Jack Kennedy's brother, Robert (Bobbie), was best man, and Bishop Cushing conducted the ceremony.

Before the wedding, Jacky had, as a matter of course and courtesy, been introduced to the members of the Kennedy family, and she, herself, has furnished her impressions of her first contact with the family at Hyannis Port:

> It was a marvelous weekend. How can I explain those people? They were like carbonated water, and other families might be flat. They'd be talking about so many things with so much enthusiasm. Or they'd be playing games. At dinner or in the livingroom, any- where, everybody would be talking about something. They had so much interest in life—it was so stimulating. . . .[6]

This was in direct contrast to her own lonely, isolated family upbring- ing where she had been expected to occupy herself with so much of her own entertainment, at least until she went to private school and college.

Following a honeymoon in California and Mexico, the young couple took up residence in Washington, D.C., where their first few years were clouded with misfortune. In October, 1954, Jack underwent a spinal operation; in 1955, Jacky suffered a miscarriage; in 1956, Jack lost the Democratic vice-presidential nomination to Estes Kefauver, and shortly thereafter, Jacky suffered yet another miscarriage.[7]

Anticipating a happy event, the Kennedys had already planned a house move where Jacky had prepared a nursery, but now, the whole project had to be abandoned. This, the Hickory Hill estate, was sold to Robert and Ethel Kennedy, who needed the space for their own expanding brood, and, later, following Robert's assassination, Ethel retained it as her home for many years.

The good fortunes of the Kennedys appeared to have been measurably restored by 1957, when, on November 27, Jacky gave birth to Caroline Bouvier Kennedy. It was followed by a house move to a residence in Georgetown, described by Jacky as "leaning slightly to one side and where the stairs creak."

In 1960, Jack won the Democratic party's presidential nomination on the first ballot and he went on to defeat Richard Nixon in the November election.[8] Three weeks later, on November 25 Jacky gave premature birth by Caesarian operation to John Fitzgerald Kennedy, Jr. He weighed only

6 pounds 3 ounces and had to be placed in an incubator for a number of days in order to treat a lung infection. He survived, and became known to his father and all the family as John-John. He was the first child ever to be born to the wife of a President-elect of the United States. [9]

Jacky, very weak upon leaving the hospital, had been invited by Mamie Eisenhower to visit the White House so that she could prepare beforehand her own furnishing and decorative schemes, as is the privilege of all incoming First Ladies. It had been arranged that a wheelchair be available for her, but, in some incredible fashion, upon arrival at the executive mansion, Mamie neither offered its use nor did Jacky request it, so that after over an hour's tour, she was completely exhausted. She was flown to the Kennedy family home in Palm Beach, Florida, where she spent days in bed recovering. In actual fact, it proved to be the worst place ever for recuperation, rest, and relaxation, since Jack was now in the process of forming his Cabinet, and the house at this time, was once described as nothing less than a railroad station or a transient hotel, with its continuous stream of relatives, visitors, colleagues, politicians, and representatives of the media.

The Kennedys returned to Washington for Jack's inauguration on January 20, 1961, [10] but Jacky was able to make only token appearances at the festivities by reason of her physical condition.

The children were truly an event, for never since the time of Theodore Roosevelt had there been young children in the White House, but this made Jacky even more determined to preserve their privacy. There were, first of all, problems relating to play space, both for outdoor as well as for indoor activities. On the White House grounds, Jacky provided for a recreation area to include a treehouse, a swing, a slide, and a barrel tunnel; then there was accommodation for all manner of animals and pets, including Caroline's famous pony, Macaroni; Charlie, a Welsh terrier; Shannon, Jack's favorite dog from Ireland, and Pushinka, a gift of Nikita Khrushchev and direct descendant of one of the Soviet canine astronauts.

Indoors, Jacky was confronted with the dilemma either of having the children's rooms placed adjoining to those of their parents, or of having a convenient family dining room upstairs. She opted for the latter to avoid all food being brought up on trays, or else having to troop the family downstairs for all their meals. Consequently, what was formerly Margaret Truman's bedroom was transformed into a kitchen, and her bathroom was made into a pantry, with cabinets built over the bathtub, and shelves inserted into the clothes closets to provide a storage area for food. There was one other alteration: an old-type radiator was removed from Jacky's bedroom "so that Caroline could have her own exciting place in which to hide."[11]

Apart from actively safeguarding the privacy of her children, Jacky was concerned with ensuring that they be not deprived of contact with their peers. So, she organized a play group at the White House in cooperation with other mothers, which, at first, met usually twice a week. As the group increased in numbers the third floor solarium was converted for the use of the children, and their supervision was undertaken in turn by several of the participating mothers.

As the children grew older, a regular teacher was employed, and, in time, it became possible to reorganize the group into a kindergarten of about ten children, and a first grade class of approximately the same number. This made it necessary to add further qualified assistants. How many of their unusual and exhilarating experiences these children were ever to remember is uncertain, but they were certainly exposed to a world unrivaled by other students of the same age. When famous personalities visited the White House, the children would be taken down and introduced to them in the state rooms. Great musicians in person would play for them, while the President himself would often take time out to appear in the classrooms. Films would be presented at the White House cinema, and regular visits would be made to one or the other of the many museums situated within the precincts of the capital city.

The mothers were immensely loyal to Jacky's request of avoidance of all publicity, and not until the school was closed, following the assassination of the President in November, 1963, did any hint of the regular activities reach the media.[12]

Jacky was once quoted as having stated: "People have too many theories about raising children. I believe simply in love, security, and discipline."[13] At the time of John's birth, she had written an article: "How to bring up children to be happy," in which she encouraged mothers to have their young children gain pleasure by being given praise for such accomplishments as learning simple poems for one or other of their parents' birthdays, or producing cards, with drawings, however crude, or with words, however simple, upon the occasions of some special family anniversary or observance. These ideas Jacky made every effort to put into practice in the White House, and there is little doubt that, with the full cooperation of all her assistants, she succeeded beyond all her initial expectations.

During Jack's first year of office, Joe Sr. paid very few visits to the White House, fearing lest his son be accused of being unduly influenced by his father, although there was obviously nothing to prevent frequent phone calls between father and son. The father, therefore, saw relatively little of his grandchildren, although Rose was more privileged, since she never fell under the same political handicap as did her husband, and she was a frequent visitor. Tragically, the situation changed after December, 1961, when, six days before Christmas, Joe Sr. suffered a severe stroke; his speech was greatly impaired and, for the rest of his life he was confined to a wheelchair. Thereafter, his visits were more frequent, since there were no further innuendos concerning political pressure upon his son.

To comfort his days, Jacky encouraged Caroline to dictate simple letters to her grandfather, which Jacky would write down, and then Caroline would add some drawings of herself, her pets, or of John-John, whom she once described as a "bad squeaky boy who tries to spit in his mother's Coca Cola and who has a very bad temper."[14]

In order to escape the goldfish bowl environment of the White House, Jack rented Glen Ora, a large estate near Middleburg, Virginia. The very size of the house and the estate presented the Secret Service with many problems concerning the security of the First Family: a preliminary search of the house happened to have unearthed a cache of cartridges, stored in the attic but long forgotten by the owner; they might have been rediscovered by the children on some roaming expedition of the house on a boring, rainy day.

Before moving in, Jacky had the interior entirely redecorated at a cost which so staggered her husband that, when the latter was introduced to his "landlady," his opening remark was, 'Your house cost me a lot of money!' She, in turn, felt so insulted by this insensitive comment that she refused to renew the two-year lease.[15]

Jack then bought a smaller estate upon which he built a new home, named Wexford, in honor of the original Kennedy home county in Ireland.[16] The estate was in mountain country, which did not please Jack too much since his preference was for the sea, but such suitable sites within easy reach of the capital were not readily available.

During his term of office, Jack went abroad on several occasions taking Jacky with him, but leaving the children at home. During May and June, 1961, they made a highly successful visit first to France, and then to Austria, when Jacky charmed De Gaulle in Paris and Khrushchev in Vienna. In the following year, Jacky took Caroline with her to Italy where they stayed at the home of her sister, Princess Lee Radziwill.

In June, 1963, Jack visited West Berlin where he uttered his widely acclaimed remark, "Ich bin ein Berliner!" At this time, Jacky was well advanced in pregnancy, and Jack took over several of her engagements, explaining, on one occasion, that he was very happy to do so while his wife "was adding to the gross national product."

The family joy at the birth of a second son, Patrick Bouvier Kennedy, on August 7, was cruelly curtailed. He was over five weeks premature, weighed less than five pounds, and lived only two days. He was buried in the Kennedy family plot in Holyhood Cemetery, Brookline, Massachusetts. [17]

A month later, Jacky went to Europe to recuperate, joining her sister, Lee, on a Mediterranean cruise on a luxury yacht owned by Aristotle Onassis, the Greek shipping magnate. [18]

On November 22, 1963, the President was assassinated in Dallas. At the funeral service in St. Matthew's Cathedral, Caroline, just six years old, sat with her mother, while John-John, a restless three, was at first kept occupied with books at the rear of the church, and then joined his mother and Caroline as they moved out after the service. As his father's body was carried down the steps, Jacky leaned down and whispered in his ear: he promptly sprang to attention, raised his hand to his forehead and gave a smart salute, a tribute to his father which has been captured in an ever-to-be-remembered photograph taken of the event.

Before the family was forced to evacuate the executive mansion, Jacky held a party for both children, each of whose birthdays had fallen within days of the assassination. She had the U.S. Marine Band play its liveliest tunes with great gusto so that the sorrow and mourning could, in part at least, be countered by one last happy memory of the White House.

The Kennedy clan closed its ranks to give full support to the young family in its tragedy, and Robert (Bobbie), in particular, was a tower of strength. After the birth of Caroline, Jack had purchased a house at Hyannis Port to be near other members of the family at vacation time although Jacky had not been too enthusiastic, since she often felt overwhelmed by the host of Kennedys. After Jack's death, however, she came to appreciate the value of the clan, who, in every way, attempted to assist her and, especially the children, to overcame their loss and grief.

The children were all very much attached to their grandparents, and Rose quotes a poem written by Caroline for her Grandpa, Christmas, 1967:

Once there lived a little blue mouse
Who wasn't scared of cats
He lived in a tiny pink house
With his friend the sparrow, Ignatz

They went on long walks and had long talks

In mostly the month of May
They would picnic by a laughing brook
And spend a pleasant day

The only thing they didn't have
For which they used to pray
Was someone as nice as Grandpa
Who they missed more every day.[19]

After a brief respite from tragedy in the middle 1960's, the seemingly now becalmed waters of the Kennedy family relationships were troubled by a renewed series of storms which occurred during the years 1968 and 1969. Bobbie, campaigning for the Democratic presidential nomination, was shot on June 5, 1968, and died one day later. Jacky, having formed a gradual attachment for Aristotle Onassis, a divorced man, and a member of the Greek Orthodox faith, was married to him in October, 1968, in Greece.[20] Her action brought her much criticism both within and outside the family, and several years were to elapse before reconciliation was to occur.

Perhaps such reconciliation came about sooner than expected through the action of Rose: Joe Sr. died on November 18, 1969, and perhaps she, now, became fully aware of what the permanent absence of a loved one could mean in terms of the loneliness of a widow. Soon afterwards, she accepted invitations to stay on the Onassis yacht[21] cruising in the Caribbean, as well as in Greek waters. On the latter occasion, in 1970, she was on the return from Ethiopia, where she and Haile Selassie had celebrated their respective birthdays together in Addis Ababa: hers on July 22 and his on July 23.

Jacky returned to Hyannis Port, at first only occasionally, but then, for the sake of the children, more frequently. As mentioned earlier, by 1972, there were, in all, 28 grandchildren, and they all assembled at Hyannis Port for a unique reunion with Rose, their grandmother. By this date, Caroline (15) and John (12) had attended private elementary schools and had continued into secondary boarding schools. Their permanent residence was now a Fifth Avenue apartment in New York.

In her book *Times to Remember* Rose quotes another poem by Caroline, this time written for her Grandma for Christmas 1971, the topic being her brother, John:

He paints his bathroom walls in the middle of the night,
He comes into my room and unscrews every light,

Swinging on a door smeared with Crazy Foam

Singing to himself, "Consider Yourself at Home,"

At four in the morning you can find him making glue
In the back hall near his guinea pig zoo.

He is trying to grow sea monkeys in his toothbrush glass,
You can see it on his teeth which bear a coating like grass.

He comes spitting in my room jabbing left and right
Shouting, OK, Caroline, ready for a fight.

He is trying to blow us up with his chemistry set,
He has killed all the plants but we've escaped as yet.

He loves my mother's linen sheets and hates his own percale.
He can imitate the sounds of the humpback whale.

I love him not just because I oughter
But also because blood runs thicker than water.[22]

In the same book of memoirs, Rose refers to some "oral histories"
written by her children and grandchildren about herself. An extract from
Caroline's account read:

> Grandmothers don't have to get mad at you for a lot of things
> like mothers do, but Grandma only gets mad at stuff you do that's
> not nice to other people—if you're rude or mean or something.
> Even then she does it nicely. She doesn't get really mad—she just
> says something in a way that you can see that it wasn't nice to
> somebody else.[23]

Young John was more matter of fact:

> She really likes me to learn a lot. And every time you go over
> there she asks you all about math and history and languages, or
> who were the Pilgrims and when they came and asks you who
> everyone is. And like, do you know this and do you know that.
> And she talks about the church and talks about learning things, and
> she tries to teach you things. She talks a lot, but it's interesting what
> she talks about. Sometimes she talks about my father and she'll
> maybe tell a story about how bad he was when he was little, or
> when she was little and some of the bad things she did. She laughs
> and then you laugh. Every time we go she tells a few of the same
> stories. Most of the things are pretty funny.
> She has very good food. She has really good Boston cream pie.
> She has millions of cakes all of the time and she has good custard.
> I'd like to come back here every year. I love it.[24]

Without any doubt, the children were extremely privileged to enjoy the continuity and security of an ongoing close and warm relationship with their grandmother and their clan peer group.

When she began boarding school at Concord Academy, Caroline received a letter from Rose in France suggesting that she

> . . . learn all you can about Concord and New England, the part of the world which your dear father cherished so deeply and to which he referred nostalgically in several of his speeches . . . .
> When you pass the Concord Library, the Concord High School or the Catholic church, think of me almost seventy years ago driving my horse and carriage to the library in the summer, searching the Louisa Alcott books—studying my Latin (The Aeneid) in high school—going to Mass at the Catholic church; and if you are near say a little prayer for me, as I pray for you here in Paris—that all may go well.[25]

In due course, Caroline went on to obtain a fine arts degree from Harvard, and became a research assistant at New York's Metropolitan Museum of Art.

In July, 1986, at the age of 28, she married Edwin Arthur Schlossberg (41), at Our Lady of Victory Roman Catholic Church in Cape Cod, Massachusetts. Caroline was given away by her uncle, Senator Edward Kennedy, while her brother, John, was best man. The marriage service was conducted jointly by a priest and a rabbi, since the groom is Jewish. Schlossberg is the son of a wealthy New York textile manufacturer, and has been described as a renaissance man—a multi-talented personality who has authored a number of books, invented computer games, and heads his own design firm, specializing in museum interiors and exhibitions. But at the time of the wedding, Schlossberg was apparently little known to most friends of the Kennedy family: George Plimpton, the author, commissioned to design fireworks for the reception, with each display "individualized for various members of the family reflecting some aspects of their nature," stated that he had read a recent profile of the bridegroom, "but I still don't know what he does."

> So the fireworks display he has created for Mr. Schlossberg will be "a series of strange fireworks, a whole barrage," including floating flairs, and entitled "What Ed Schlossberg Does."[26]

The honeymoon was spent in Hawaii and Japan.

For his own part, John, having attended Phillips Andover Academy, enrolled at Brown University where he graduated in 1982, with a degree in history. Developing an interest in, and concern with world problems, he spent a summer in Africa while at college, and, in 1984, he studied at the University of Delhi, and traveled widely throughout the country to gain firsthand experience of the varied environments and cultures of the vast subcontinent.

Lyndon Baines Johnson

(1963–1969)

A feature unique to the Johnson family was that all its members carried the same initials, unintentionally, or otherwise. Johnson's father was Sam Early Johnson, and his mother's maiden name was Rebekah Baines. Johnson's future bride was christened Claudia Alta Taylor, but, according to the family tradition, she was described by her nursemaid as being "as purty as a lady-bird," and the name adhered, so that when she was married in 1934, she too, became an L.B.J. In due course, two LBJ daughters were born: Lynda Bird in 1944, and Lucy (later Luci) Baines in 1947. There was even a dog, Little Beagle Johnson.[1] Johnson, himself, once humorously justified the procedure: "It's cheaper that way because we can all use the luggage."

Johnson's antecedents were pre-oil Texan pioneers: one of his grandfathers had driven cattle along the Chisholm Trail to Abilene. The family had settled in the Pedernales river valley, less than a hundred miles from San Antonio, and had given its name to the local community: Johnson

City, which remained so isolated and small that, when Johnson graduated from its high school, there were only 6 students in the senior class.

But Johnson, the eldest of five children, was fortunate in his parents. His father was an active politician serving as state legislator at Austin for twelve years, so that, from an early age, Johnson was made readily aware that a wide and stimulating world lay beckoning outside the seemingly always monotonously hot and dusty landscape of the unbroken Texas plains.

His father's cosmopolitan outlook was rivaled by his mother's intellectual gifts. She was a journalism graduate of Baylor, a college of which her grandfather, a Baptist minister, had been one of the founders. Her keen interest in social affairs made home conversation keen, provocative, and lively. She had poetic insight and, writing about the day when she gave birth to Lyndon, her firstborn, she stated:

> Now the light came in from the east, bringing a deep stillness, a stillness so profound and so pervasive that it seemed as if the earth itself were listening.[2]

Later, she gave Lyndon every encouragement to advance in his studies, and, after leaving high school, he entered the Southwest Teachers' College at San Marcos whence he graduated in 1930 with a major in history and a minor in English. He had no great love of teaching, however, and after brief experience as a schoolmaster in Houston, he sought and obtained the post as secretary to newlyelected Democratic Congressman Richard Kleberg, whose family owned the famous King Ranch in Texas.

As mentioned earlier, in 1934 Johnson married Lady Bird Taylor, who, like his mother, had majored in journalism at the University of Texas, Austin. One year later, he was appointed as Texas state director of the National Youth Administration, and, at 27, he was the youngest such director in the entire country.

His entry into national politics came unexpectedly in 1937: the death of Representative James Paul Buchanan created a vacancy, and Johnson won the special election. He was to serve in the U.S. House of Representatives until 1948 when he was elected U.S. Senator.[3]

In furthering his political ambitions Johnson was given every support by Lady Bird. She used an inheritance from her mother (who had died when Lady Bird was only 6 years old) to buy a debt-ridden radio station in Austin, and, as an astute businesswoman, she eventually transformed it into a million-dollar enterprise, and used it effectively in support of the Democratic platform.

The Johnsons' first child was born ten years after the marriage (during which period Lady Bird suffered four miscarriages): Lynda Bird was born in March, 1944, in Washington, D.C., where her sister Lucy Baines, was likewise born in July, 1947. The two girls were to encounter experiences common to all offspring whose respective fathers and mothers were actively involved in politics, so becoming absentee parents. The girls would often protest at being left alone so often by their mother, and Lynda once said: "Washington is sure meant for the congressmen and their wives, but it is not meant for their children."[4]

Lady Bird was fully aware of the problem of finding sufficient time to spend with her children, and, in her autobiography, she wrote that she was made to realize what it had meant to them at a certain dinner with herself, Luci, and a friend in attendance. As she described it:

> [Luci] was all wound up and talked and talked and talked. I learned a lot about my shortcomings and something about my virtues! She's a very interesting, exciting, perceptive, emotional, high-strung little girl for whom my heart aches. . . .[5]

Johnson, who had taught speech and debating classes during his brief career as a schoolmaster, actively encouraged both his daughters to gain confidence by making them prepare short papers which they then offered for presentation before the family circle. Lucy experienced an eye infection which temporarily resulted in low academic performance at school, but, upon recovery, her grades returned to normal. Her affliction possibly led her to become interested in human ailments, and, at the age of 17, she was working as an optometry assistant to Dr. Robert Kraskin of D.C., and she had expressed the intention of pursuing a career related to nursing. When, on June 1, 1965, she graduated from the National Cathedral School, her father gave the commencement address, in which he first of all commented, to the amusement of his audience, that no matter how much homework he had, as President, Lucy always brought him more; he then expressed his pleasure that she had proposed to follow a profession which sought to aid the afflicted.

Lucy functioned as an excellent public relations aide to her father, since, in his early years in the presidency, she was, *inter alia,* appointed as honorary chairman of the National Symphony Orchestra's annual series of free concerts, "Music for Young Americans," sponsored each spring for high school students visiting the capital city; she launched a ship at New Orleans, and she was crowned, by General Curtis Le May, Queen of the Shenandoah Apple Blossom Festival at Winchester, Virginia. It was upon this occasion that Johnson dispatched a message to the festival officers to be read aloud at the proceedings:[6]

> People of Virginia, Intelligence reports the City of Winchester is in danger of being taken over by a new monarch. I urge all Citizens to be on the alert. I have known this new ruler all her life. She entered the world with a commanding voice, and has been taking over ever since. Beware of her bewitching smile; underneath that kid glove is a strong hand. Past experience indicates the best way of dealing with her is with total attention and love.
>   Lyndon B. Johnson

It was in the fall of 1964 that Lucy made two (for her) momentous decisions: the first was to alter the spelling of her given name, Lucy, to Luci; the second was to announce her intention to become a member of the Roman Catholic Church.

Despite the strong Protestant-Nonconformist traditions of her parents, they both accepted their daughter's decision in their stride, though not without considerable misgivings, due to the unfortunate coincidence of two partially related events.

For almost the entire period of his political activities, one of Johnson's most loyal supporters had been Walter Jenkins. He was from Johnson's home state and had once attended the University of Texas, but he had been forced to withdraw because of lack of funds. He thereupon came to Washington, where he obtained a position as special policeman on Capitol Hill. Here, he had met Johnson, who appointed him as an accountant in his congressional office in Austin. Jenkins served in the armed forces during World War II, and had impressed Johnson by the fact that he had saved no less than five thousand dollars out of his service pay, a feat which led Johnson to appoint him as a permanent member of his Washington staff.

Jenkins, a Protestant, fell in love with Marjorie Whitehill, a Catholic, and he forsook his religious persuasion in order to marry her. A close friendship developed between the Johnson and Jenkins families, and, upon entering the White House on their first day, the Johnsons were entertained at dinner that evening at the Jenkins' home. Jenkins, an efficient administrator, was later appointed as Johnson's chief executive officer in the White House.

Jenkins had a daughter, Beth, who was the same age as Luci, and they had become very close friends. It was Beth who had persuaded Luci to visit with her the Catholic Marquette University in Milwaukee, and it was presumably the cumulative influence of personal friendship and the institutional environment which had led Luci to make a decision to convert to the Catholic faith. It was Beth, also, who had inadvertently changed Luci's career in another significant direction, since it was she who had introduced Luci to her future husband, Pat Nugent.

Out of this seeming whirlwind of activities, there suddenly dropped a thunderbolt. Jenkins, a family man with six children, was, in October, 1964, barely one month before the presidential election, "arrested for disorderly conduct in the basement of the YMCA, which the newspapers blatantly characterized as a hangout for sexual perverts."[7]

The families were devastated. Jenkins was hospitalized, but the damage was done. Political pressure was such that Johnson had no option but with considerable upset and sadness to request his resignation, although, judging from the subsequent election results of November, 1964, the Jenkins affair would have had little impact had it been passed over without action.[8]

While the episode must have had a profound effect upon Luci, it made no difference to her decision to convert, and, on July 2, 1965, her eighteenth birthday, she was baptized into the Catholic Church at St. Matthews Cathedral in a private ceremony attended only by her family and a few invited friends. After the brief ceremony, Luci remained behind for confession, and Lady Bird later commented, "I could not help but think we went in four and came out three."[9]

Luci was nothing if not independent. In many ways she was a blend of irrepressible imp and delightful sprite, who reminded her mother of Christopher Robin:

And the look in his eye,
Seemed to say to the sky
'Now how to amuse them today.[10]

Many previous Presidents have attempted to impose strict limitations and regulations regarding the activities of their children by way of contact with the press and, in modern days, the media. Johnson had no doubt expressed his personal opinions concerning the need for discretion on the part of the children of a President, but, as a liberal-minded man, he had probably gone no further, so that he should not have been surprised when, in January, 1965, while still a girl in high school, Luci had given a personal interview to Erica Vexler, a newswoman from Chile, who had promptly sold it to *Ebony* magazine.[11] Luci, free from inhibition, has responded to all queries in an honest fashion, without perhaps consideration for the consequences upon her family. Johnson, for example, possibly may or may not have winced when he read:

My father is terrible about spending. Anyone in the family who leaves a light burning is fined a dollar. If we needed 800 bulbs burning in a room in order to study better, or read, or do something useful, he wouldn't care, but needless expense annoys him.

She complained about being reared in isolation by political parents, and she openly admitted being frequently angered by these circumstances, and that politics "seemed to me to be the most despicable, lowest and most compromising activity in the world"—until the assassination of John F. Kennedy. This event completely altered her attitude, and, thenceforward, she interpreted the word to signify "a means of personal surrender to a public cause," and she gave her father all her support, since it was also with him that she "got on best."

She did not minimize possible rivalry between herself and her sister, Lynda, but she simply attributed this to the simple fact that "Lynda thinks very different from the way I do."

She made mature comments upon the importance of education which she defined as "training to reason without passion and without prejudice."

All in all, the President's already existing pride in his daughter should have been measurably enhanced by the publication of the interview.

Johnson had suffered a heart attack on Luci's eighth birthday, July 2, 1955, but had made such a remarkable recovery, that it had not affected his political career. However, in October, 1965, he underwent gallbladder surgery at Bethesda Naval Hospital, an event which was taken in its stride by both Johnson and Lady Bird, but not, apparently, by Luci, who, as her mother described her:

> . . . sometimes behaves like a free psychiatrist. Tonight she delivered me a lecture on our reactions—Lyndon and mine—to the approaching operation. She feels we are unduly controlled and unemotional. One thing about Luci, she is very sure of her verdicts. She is opinionated, uncomfortably intuitive, and a joy to have for a daughter.[12]

Perhaps Luci's concerns were not entirely unjustified since only one year later Johnson underwent further surgery for a ventral hernia, as well as for the removal of a nonmalignant vocal cord polyp.

During all the years of the presidency, Lynda Bird had kept the lowest profile. When her father became President, she had already completed high school, and was enrolled at the University of Texas. On the day of Kennedy's assassination she had immediately come to Dallas to be of some assistance and comfort to the family of Governor John Connally, who had been wounded as he rode in the motor cavalcade. She did well in her freshman year at the university, but being the President's daughter, she no longer enjoyed the privacy of a normal student since she now fell under the constant surveillance of the Secret Service, and there had been the problem of where the men should stay.

She had become friendly with a young man, Bernie Rosenbach, but, during the year 1964, the relationship had cooled and the engagement was broken off. Friendships with other men followed, including that with Brent Eastman a year later, with whom she spent a holiday in the Grand Tetons, including a raft trip together down the Snake River. By 1966, she was close friends with the handsome young film actor, George Hamilton, who was present at Lynda's graduation ceremony during that year at the University of Texas, thirty-two years after her mother had graduated from the same institution. There were changes, as Lady Bird noted: "Signs of the times . . . babies crying during the ceremony, young marrieds on the campus—a third or more of them in graduate school. . . ."[13]

Lady Bird was also at times drawn to make comparisons between her two daughters:

> How different those children are about money—Lynda handles hers so carefully, so well aware of what everything costs and can look very nice in a dress three years old. Luci adores clothes, buys so many of them, her money vanishes like snow under the Texas sun. . . . Last year's clothes are never quite right for that butterfly.[14]

Little wonder that when, in 1966, an article in a lady's journal commented unfavorably upon the fashion standards set by the White House ladies, it was Luci who exploded and she blamed it all on Lynda's penchant for bobby socks and sneakers.

Yet, 1966 was, without any doubt, Luci's year: on August 6, she was married to Patrick John Nugent, although, as described by Liz Carpenter in her book *Ruffles and Flourishes,* the wedding appeared to be one prolonged series of crises[15] which exhausted the resources of the White House staff.

First, there was the matter of the engagement: at 11:30 P.M. on Christmas Eve, 1965, the Johnsons received a phone call from Luci in Texas announcing that Pat had just given her an engagement ring. But she was just going to midnight mass and she did not want to remove the ring, so she feared that some prying eye among the ever-observant press corps might notice it and immediately claim a scoop, an event which might seriously embarrass the White House in its efforts to maintain favorable rapport with news reporters. In consequence, hasty communication was immediately established with all the important news agencies, so that Luci's engagement became a page one story in all papers on Christmas Day, 1965.

Liz Carpenter's second crisis related to the matter of the wedding gifts. Inevitable comparisons were drawn with the famed White House wedding of Alice Roosevelt Longworth, who allegedly received fabulous presents from all over the world, although she herself commented: "I only wish I'd gotten all those things they said I got." In Luci's case Johnson made the decision that she and Pat should only accept gifts from their close friends.

The matter of Luci's wedding apparel was the next crisis—fear again that a "leak" would result in a "scoop." This was averted by careful release in "bits and pieces" of the main components—enough to appease curiosity yet stimulate speculation, and thus encourage and maintain circulation of interested journals.

Another crisis—still related to Luci's dress—concerned the matter of union labor. The wedding dress had been designed by Priscilla of Boston, who was a non-union employer but claimed she paid more than basic union wage. This incensed the leaders of the International Ladies Garment Workers Union, and only after compromise was the dispute allowed to subside, with union workers being permitted to "assemble" the dress, while Priscilla's employees supervised and added the trimmings.[16]

At the time of her wedding, Luci was a student of nursing at Georgetown University, and the suggestion had been made that it might be an appropriate gesture for Luci to leave her bouquet at the feet of the patron saint of nursing instead of those of the Virgin Mary. But complications immediately arose when it was discovered that the nursing profession had no acknowledged patron saint—and, in fact, research unearthed seven possible candidates for the honor, of whom four were male. Again they resorted to compromise with the selection of St. Agatha, although only after long search was a suitable representation of her obtained—one which eliminated the horrifying scenes of her martyrdom in Sicily.

The wedding itself took place on the hot sultry day of August 6, 1966. The church was not air conditioned and it would be necessary for the invited guests to sit for several hours in discomfort before and during the ceremony. A solution was suggested by United Airlines, whose airplanes were grounded by reason of a strike, so that the blowers normally used to air-condition planes on the ground would be ideal; the company offered to use the blowers to cool the church overnight. The news reached the ears of the Labor Department who feared its impact upon the labor-management negotiations then in progress, so the project was cancelled, and the guests remained bathed in perspiration. The bride's sister, Lynda, was taken faint during the ceremony, but she recovered sufficiently to last out the proceedings.[17]

At the White House itself, the catering staff was almost completely exhausted by having to prepare not only refreshments for the wedding with its five-foot-high cake, but also for the state visit of the President of Israel. That the combined events were successfully executed is no mean tribute to the efficiency, adaptability, and ingenuity of the members of the staff concerned.

The wedding, naturally, was a national event and hundreds, if not thousands, of newsmen and media reporters had crowded into Washington, and had created a major problem of accommodation. This so affected the press representatives from the groom's home town that they sent a telegram to Lynda, as the "next" White House daughter: "FOR GOD'S SAKE, DON'T MARRY A BOY FROM WAUKEGAN, ILLINOIS."[18]

Pat and Luci spent their honeymoon in Nassau, and on June 21, 1967, they presented Lyndon and Lady Bird with their first grandchild, a boy christened Patrick Lyndon Nugent, to be known as Lyn.

Lynda had become emotionally attached to a member of the White House Color Guard of the Marines, Charles Spittal Robb, known familiarly as Chuck. He was a graduate in Business Administration from the University of Wisconsin, and, among his ancestors was a great grandfather who had served as Secretary of the Treasury of the Confederacy. Their wedding, in the East Room of the White House on December 9, 1967, was the first to take place in the presidential mansion since 1914.[19] The proceedings were far less hectic than those of Luci's wedding, a matter which greatly irked the many social reporters who were driven to seek the slightest tidbit of information so as to create news. A great deal, for example, was made of the fact that two persons turned up at the reception in wheelchairs. They were, respectively, Alice Roosevelt Longworth, who had herself been a White House bride sixty-one years earlier, and the President's brother, Sam Houston Johnson. The latter, recovering from hospitalization, has once been described as a "cheerful rogue . . . who walked in his brother's shadow."[20] Sam held a law degree but had never practiced, and while he had served often as babysitter for both Lynda and Luci in between his several marriages, Johnson tended to keep him virtually under house arrest, or under close Secret Service surveillance, by reason of his erratic behavior, most often brought about by his love of the bottle.[21]

Then there was the matter of the wedding cake—a 250-pound old-fashioned pound cake—and it occurred to one of the famined news reporters to ask at a press conference how many raisins there were in the cake. The news-starved participants took up the item of trivia with irrepressible enthusiasm and Liz Carpenter found herself delegated with the task of assessing the exact number, while the press corps itself held a ten-cent lottery on the outcome. Her count of 1511 raisins[22] was accepted as final and possibly is still retained as a basic figure in the event of a claim for inclusion in the *Guinness Book of Records*.

However, in its relationships with the press, there was even worse to follow, when the White House released the pound cake recipe. It led to a voluminous amount of correspondence, and resulted in ridiculous demands upon the presidential staff to satisfy the many thousands of trivia queries which poured into the mansion.

1968 was the year of crisis. The problems and anxieties relating to the President's deteriorating health were compounded by the mounting criticisms relating to his leadership arising out of the escalation of the country's military involvement in the Vietnam war. Johnson was led to months of agonizing as to whether to seek renomination as candidate for the November presidential election. He discussed the matter at length and openly with his family and on January 15, Lady Bird penned him the following note:

> Luci hopes you won't run. She wants you for herself and for Lyn and all of us. She does not want to give you up. Lynda hopes you *will* run. She told me so this afternoon with a sort of terrible earnestness, because her husband is going to war and she thinks there will be a better chance of getting him back alive and the war settled if you are President. Me—I don't know. I have said it all before. I can't tell you what to do.[23]

It was at first believed that Johnson would have made public his decision in his State of the Union message, but he did not do so, and delayed his announcement until a televised appearance on March 31.

Only one day earlier, on March 30, Chuck Robb had left for duty in Vietnam and Pat Nugent had followed within two weeks. Once again, a President of the United States was faced with the dilemma of having immediate relatives in areas of combat, and having to face the issue of either being accused of favoritism, if they were not sent to the battle front, or being confronted with the possibility of their being captured by the enemy, which was likely to extract the utmost possible advantage from such an eventuality. The prospect of death was a far simpler issue since it would bring the nation's sympathy, and honor would accrue to the family.

In October, 1968, Lynda gave birth to the Johnson's first grand-daughter, Lucinda Desha Robb[24] and in December, Lynda flew to Bangkok where she was joined for his Christmas leave by Chuck.

In January, 1969, just a few days before leaving the White House, the Johnsons were paid a surprise visit by Alice Roosevelt Longworth who brought a gift for Lucinda. As might be expected, Alice, now 85, was as irrepressible as ever, and she appreciably relieved the gloomy atmosphere of the impending departure with her incomparable and irreverent imitations of the past First Ladies Eleanor Roosevelt and Mrs. William Howard Taft.

The other memorable highlight of the departure from the White House was provided by Luci's boy, Lyn. Having some six months earlier, upon the occasion of his first birthday, placed his foot right in the middle of a chocolate cake made by his mother, he, now, on the very last day at the White House, walked straight into the freezing water of the fish pond. His diversionary adventure apparently did him no harm through prompt remedial action by the family members.

The Johnsons retired to the LBJ Ranch, not far from Austin, Texas, and there Johnson planned his presidential library during the years before his death on January 22, 1973.

Both Pat Nugent and Chuck Robb returned safely from Vietnam, and, in due course, Pat and Luci were to raise four children: Lyn, Nicole, Rebekah, and Claudia. Sadly, however, family dissensions led to a divorce in 1979, and, five years later, in March, 1984, Luci was remarried to Ian Turpin (also a one-time married divorcee), a British banker, with one son. Luci, in her own right, became vice-president of the LBJ Company, which is responsible for the family real estate and banking enterprises. Chuck Robb embarked upon a political career in Virginia, and during his campaigns, first in a successful bid to become Lieutenant-Governor and later (in 1981), to be elected Governor, he was given full support not only by his wife, Lynda, but also by his mother-in-law, Lady Bird. When the latter was asked to comment upon her daughter's entry into politics by reason of her husband's ambitions, she "ruefully observed," first of all, that a politician "should be born a foundling and remain a bachelor," and then added that "Lynda will just have to realize that you have to give a lot and postpone personal indulgences to another day, which is sort of a chapter of my life that I'm living right now."[25]

Lynda, herself, is the mother of three daughters, Lucinda, Katherine, and Jennifer.

Richard Milhous Nixon

(1969–1974)

Richard Nixon was only the second President of the United States to be confronted by the threat of impeachment, and, while Andrew Johnson successfully survived the indictment (by a margin of only one vote), Nixon chose to resign before proceedings were set in motion and he remains the sole President to do so.

The effect upon the members of his family was understandably traumatic, but, to their credit, they neither balked nor flinched when the crucial decision was made, possibly because Nixon's political career itself was one of roller-coaster dimensions in which apices and nadirs had come to be accepted as a normal course of life.

As he himself described her, Nixon's mother "was a saint."[1] She was Hannah Milhous, who, in 1906, had graduated from Whittier College and, two years later, had married Francis (Frank) Anthony Nixon. The latter was a man with no fixed occupation and, at various times, had found employment as a streetcar motorman, lemon farmer, and gas station operator. According to Nixon, his father was twice within reach of a fortune: oil was discovered on the lemon farm, and then on the gas station site, but, in each instance, only after the respective properties had been sold by Frank.

Richard was the second son in a family of five boys, and his Grandmother Milhous predicted that, when he was born in January, 1913, he so howled "that he'll be either a lawyer or a preacher."[2] The family moved several times until Frank Nixon finally settled at Whittier, where he ran the gas station and general store.[3] All the boys were expected to contribute to the family well-being by working hard, but then came tragedy, first, when Arthur, the fourth son, developed a sudden fever and died in 1925 at the age of 7; then, five years later, Harold, the oldest, contracted tuberculosis, and his protracted illness, which entailed costly sanitarium expenses in Arizona, seriously depleted the family budget, sadly to no avail, since he, too, died at the early age of 23 in 1933. The youngest member of the family, Edward, was born in 1930.

In the meantime, Richard had proceeded through high school to Whittier College, where he majored in history and where he had gained a reputation as a competent debater. He graduated in 1934, and entered Duke University Law School, completing his professional studies in 1937.

He returned to Whittier, and, having qualified for the California bar, he joined a local law firm, as well as a little theater group. It was while rehearsing a play entitled *The Dark Tower* that he met Pat Ryan.[4] Apparently, he proposed to her on their first date but was rejected. She later relented and they were married on June 21, 1940. When, within eighteen months of their marriage, the Japanese attacked Pearl Harbor, Nixon left Whittier for Washington where he was employed in the Office of Price Administration. In September, 1942, he was commissioned as a navy lieutenant serving in the Pacific, and, in July, 1944, he became a lieutenant commander in the Fleet Air Wing.

The year 1946 was a momentous year for the Nixon family. He had been demobilized in January, and, on February 21, Pat gave birth to their first daughter, Patricia (Tricia). In California, the Republican party had need of a candidate to oppose Democrat Jerry Voorhis, who had represented the Twelfth Congressional District in the U.S. House of Representatives since 1936. Nixon's name had been put forward for consideration as the Republican nominee and it had been accepted, so that both Nixon and Pat were soon on the campaign trail leaving young Tricia in the care of Frank and Hannah.

Voorhis astutely rejected all suggestions that he appear with Nixon in public debate since, while he stood to gain nothing, his opponent, at the

very least, would gain valuable publicity. Nevertheless, he inadvertently
committed a major blunder which led to his political demise. As a
measure of political propaganda, he was in the habit of sending out to all
new parents resident within his congressional district, a government
pamphlet entitled *Baby Care*. Aware of the fact that his opponent had just
become a father, Voorhis innocently wrote on the cover of the copy sent
to the Nixons: "Congratulations! I look forward to meeting you in
public."

Nixon and his Republican committee immediately seized upon the
opportunity of giving fullest publicity to the foregoing note, and Voorhis
found himself committed to five public debates. It proved to be a devastating smear campaign, with Nixon, a war hero on the one hand, and
Voorhis, accused of being supported by the C.I.O. Political Action
Committee, on the other, a committee which, it was prominently alleged
by Nixon, gave unremitting support to the enemies of America. It was
Nixon who was the victor in the November, 1946, election, an achievement whereby he was successfully launched upon a political career.

The family moved to Washington in December, 1946, and, in the
following year, Nixon was appointed as member of the House Un-
American Activities Committee (HUAC). He gained national prominence as a relentless prosecutor in the indictment of Alger Hiss, who was
eventually proved guilty of perjury and sentenced to five years imprisonment.

In 1950, Nixon advanced still further when he scored a victory in a
U.S. Senate election over Helen Gahagan Douglas, in yet another ugly,
smear campaign,[5] which obviously did not affect his career since, in
1952, he was selected by Eisenhower as the latter's Vice-President, and he
served in this capacity for the next eight years.[6]

Since the Eisenhowers attended society functions only with great
reluctance, the Nixons found themselves fully involved as the President's
representatives at the many official Washington dinners, receptions, and
balls. Busy as he was, Nixon would always make an effort to join his two
daughters for daily breakfast before they left for the Horace Mann
Elementary School and (later) the Sidwell Friends School which they
both attended. Moreover, he and Pat rigidly observed Sunday as the
family day when they would all attend the Westmoreland Congregational
Church in the morning, while often during the evening Nixon would
play the piano, and they all enjoyed a family sing-song.[7]

But while Nixon reveled in the thrust and parry confrontations of the
political arena, Pat was never too happy, and she increasingly felt the
strain of attempting to be a devoted mother as well as the obedient wife

of an energetic and ambitious husband. During his term as Vice-President, Nixon, usually accompanied by Pat, made nine major overseas trips to over 50 countries,[8] in several of which, particularly in South America, they were confronted by hostile and violent demonstrations. These received widespread television coverage, some of which was viewed at home by their two young daughters, who were occasioned great distress by the scenes. Subsequently, Pat was led to plead with her husband to quit politics for the sake of the family's well-being, and she succeeded to the extent of gaining from him a written statement: "I promise to Patricia Ryan Nixon that I will not again seek public office" (following the expiry of his second term as Vice-President in 1961).[9] But, presumably, it was too much to expect of him, and, eventually, it was only by virtue of his narrow defeat in the 1960[10] presidential election that Nixon found himself obliged to revert to the status of a private citizen. He returned to a lucrative law practice in the Beverly Hills region of California, and, within a year, he could boast that he had paid more in income tax than he had ever received as salary as Vice-President.[11]

Isolation from the mainstream of politics proved irksome, and, in 1962, he entered the race for the governorship of California, which, however, he lost to Pat Brown. Considerably irritated by adverse newspaper commentaries, Nixon gave way to an untypical bitter series of remarks in his final press conference, which he concluded with the statement, ". . . You won't have Nixon to kick around anymore, because, gentlemen, this is my last press conference. . . ."[12]

Disillusioned with California politics, he once more moved the family, this time to New York, where they took up residence in a Fifth Avenue apartment overlooking Central Park, with Nelson Rockefeller and William Randolph Hearst as neighbors. Nixon's interest in national politics was revived during the 1964 presidential campaign when he vigorously endorsed the policies of Republican candidate Barry Goldwater of Arizona. But with the latter's overwhelming defeat by Lyndon B. Johnson, the Republican party was confronted with the problem of selecting a more viable alternative when, in 1968, Johnson announced his intention of resigning: Nixon became his party's choice when he was easily nominated as presidential candidate on the first ballot at the Republican Convention in August, 1968. In the following November, he was elected President, receiving 301 electoral votes to his Democratic opponent's 191.

While resident in New York, both daughters attended the exclusive Chapin School for girls. After graduation, Tricia went on to Finch College, a liberal arts institution in New York City, whence she graduated in 1968. Julie enrolled at Smith College in Northampton, Massachusetts, where she majored in history, and obtained her B.A. degree in 1970, but, in the meantime, she had fallen in love with David Eisenhower who was at Amherst, nearby.[13] They were married on December 22, 1968,[14] at the Marble Collegiate Church in New York City, and it was Julie's personal decision that the ceremony be held before the family moved into the White House in January, 1969. The bridal bouquet was caught by her sister, Tricia, and it was she who had the White House wedding, when she married Edward Finch Cox, scion of a prominent New York family, on June 12, 1971.[15]

Julie's last two years on campus were those of the political turmoil associated with the Vietnam conflict. Antiwar student demonstrations not only kept Nixon from attending his daughter's graduation ceremony, but even forced Julie herself away from it in 1970, to her intense chagrin.

When David entered the navy, Julie lived at the White House and, to keep herself occupied, she enrolled at the Catholic University in Washington, where, in due course, she qualified as a teacher. In 1971, she moved to Florida where David was stationed, and took up an appointment in an elementary school, but broke her toe on her second day at work. She had encountered criticism alleging favoritism in the matter of the appointment, since she had been assigned to a nonghetto school only a few blocks away from the apartment in which she and David lived, whereas less favored teachers complained they were obliged to travel miles to less desirable institutions.[16] Julie countered the attacks by stating that she had taken up a $6,000-a-year job because she had a genuine interest in the teaching profession, in preference to the many offers of employment, at three or more times that salary, from companies which sought only to exploit the Nixon name. In due course, she obtained work as an editor with the *Saturday Evening Post,* which enabled her to work at home.

When David was demobilized in 1973, he was uncertain as to a future career, and he worked first as a newspaper sports columnist for the *Philadelphia Bulletin,* and then, being advised by her father, he decided to enroll at George Washington University Law School. But it was now that the Watergate scandal began to obtrude upon the private lives of all members of the family.

David and Julie had already endured caustic press criticism for having accepted, at a very low rental, residential occupation of a lovely home in Bethesda, Maryland, owned by Nixon's wealthy friend, Bebe Rebozo. Now, at law school, David everywhere encountered nothing but outspoken indictment of his father-in-law, and he so much felt the ongoing pressure that for a time he considered transfer to another campus, but he recognized that he might again be accused of rank cowardice by running away.

What obviously became unbearable was the fact that David was made increasingly aware, by the very nature of his legal studies, that his father-in-law's actions were grossly in violation of the moral standards expected of the nation's President. Julie, ever loyal and devoted, could see absolutely nothing wrong in any of her father's acts and decisions; on the contrary, she adopted, much to David's embarrassment, a militant and aggressive pose which led her, in 1973 alone, to make almost 150 public appearances in defense of her father,[17] a feat which, in December of that year, led to her inclusion among "the world's ten most admired women," as listed by *Good Housekeeping* journal.[18]

Ignoring all the consequences, Julie persisted, up until the very last moment, in urging her father not to resign, but, when the final moment came on August 9, 1974, she found faith and serenity in her personal religious beliefs, and retained a strong positive attitude in respect of the destinies of her family. Her optimism proved infectious since David himself could state at this time:

> You do not have the kind of background we've had and then be satisfied living the rest of your life lounging around. We want to be in the middle of things, influencing the course of events. . . . Politics is in our blood, Julie and me. It's early in our careers, but we think we have a future there. . . .[19]

Tricia, though less outgoing and aggressively defensive of her father than Julie, was equally loyal.[20] She had represented him on the 1968 campaign trail in various ways, including a four days' attendance at Virginia's Azalea Festival. Following the election she had functioned as a lovely hostess upon the occasion of the visit of Prince Charles and Princess Anne of Great Britain in 1970, as well as for a television tour of the White House by Harry Reasoner and Mike Wallace.

After her wedding in June, 1971, to Edward (Eddie) Cox, she went to live in New York, where her husband had taken up employment with a law firm. Busily occupied, either at school or college before her marriage, Tricia, apparently, was no expert in the domain of the domestic arts, having been once quoted as stating that "bacon is one of the hardest things to learn to cook. To do it just right and not have it greasy is real gourmet cooking."[21] Sheer necessity as a dutiful housewife soon brought about marked improvement in these matters, as it has done in the case of millions of others confronted by the same situation.[22]

Like her sister, Tricia gave unswerving allegiance to her father at the time of Watergate, which she dismissed as a "vicious witchhunt."[23] Both daughters were adamant that their father should not resign since this action could be misconstrued as an acknowledgement of guilt in a trivial affair which bore no significance in the light of his major political achievements, such as ending the conflict in Vietnam, and establishing diplomatic relationships with Communist China.

Yet, when the decision to resign was finally announced, it is more than probable that, after the last painful and traumatic public appearance at the White House, the entire family experienced immense relief from the ongoing tension of the preceding months, and welcomed the hoped-for anonymity of the return to life as private citizens.

After the televised speech of resignation at 10:00 A.M., August 9, 1974, Nixon and his wife, accompanied by Tricia and Edward, left for their home in San Clemente, California, while Julie and David remained in Washington.

Two years later, Pat suffered a stroke which left her partially paralyzed on the left side and slightly affected her speech but, in time, she made good recovery. Her children gave her every support, as they had also done when Nixon, himself, underwent surgery for phlebitis only two months after his resignation in 1974.

In 1977, Julie wrote up her impressions of six famous personalities she had met during her father's presidency in a book entitled *Special People*. Since that time, both she and David have considered writing family biographies, she, of her mother, Pat, and he, of his grandfather, Ike.[24] Their first daughter, Jennie, was born in 1978, and their first son, Alexander, in 1981. A second daughter, Melanie Catherine, was born in 1984.[25]

Tricia's husband, Edward Cox, pursued his law practice with a New York firm until 1981, when he became an attorney in Washington with the Synthetic Fuels Corporation. The corporation, funded by the Reagan administration, was created to advance development of synthetic fuels. Edward and Tricia have one son, Christopher, born in 1979.

Gerald Rudolph Ford

(1974–1977)

Gerald Ford was the first person in the history of the United States ever to become President without being elected by the people. When Spiro Agnew, Vice-President in the Nixon administration, resigned, Ford was nominated Vice-President by Nixon in October, 1973, and his appointment was confirmed by Congress.[1] When, in turn, Nixon resigned on August 9, 1974, Ford succeeded to the presidency.

Ford was born Leslie Lynch King in Omaha, Nebraska, in 1913, but, when still young, his parents had divorced, and his mother, Dorothy King, moved with him to Grand Rapids, Michigan, where she was remarried to Gerald Rudolff Ford, a paint salesman. The latter adopted Leslie and renamed him Gerald Rudolff Ford, Jr.[2] Apparently, not until he was 17 did the boy learn that he was adopted: while still at high school and working part-time in a restaurant, he was approached by a man who said, "Leslie, I'm your father." After a brief conversation the man left, and that was the first and last time that Ford ever met his real father.[3] The latter remarried in 1919, and fathered three children from his second marriage: Margaret (1921), Leslie (1923), and Patricia (1925), who were thus Ford's half-sisters and brother on his father's side. There were also three half-brothers on his mother's side as the result of her second marriage: Thomas Gardner (1918), Richard Addison (1924), and James Francis (1927).

Ford graduated from South High School, Grand Rapids, Michigan, in 1931, and from the University of Michigan in 1935. For the next six years he was at Yale, first as a football and boxing coach, then as student in the law school whence he graduated in 1941.

During the Second World War he served in the navy, and he was discharged with the reserve rank of lieutenant-commander, following which he returned to law practice in Grand Rapids.

The year 1948 was one which brought significant changes into Ford's lifestyle: he was married in October to Elizabeth (Betty) Bloomer Warren, and, three weeks later, he was elected as Republican member to the U.S. House of Representatives.

At the time of his marriage, Ford was a 35-year-old bachelor. His bride, Betty, was 30 and a divorcee; she had married William (Bill) Warren in 1942, but they had divorced in 1947. Warren was a furniture salesman who was away for considerable periods of time, so they enjoyed little home life. In addition, he was a diabetic, whom Betty had to nurse back to health, but then, sensing there was no future for her in a situation of this nature, she sought and obtained a release from the marriage bond. There were no children from the union.[4]

Not long after his successful bid for election to Congress, Ford and his wife moved to Washington, and it was there that all their four children were born: Michael Gerald (1950), John (Jack) Gardner (1952), Steven Meigs (1956), and Susan Elizabeth (1957).

As described by Betty in her autobiography,[5] life in the capital city was never short of domestic adventures, and the Fords moved house several times to as to accommodate their growing family.

After the birth of Michael (Mike), and while she was still in hospital, a visit by Ford's parents almost sent the latter into shock when they observed that the baby's feet were black, and they immediately feared that it was suffering from some incurable fatal disease. Their immense relief could well be imagined when they were informed that all that had happened was that Mike's feet had been blackened for footprints to allow for easy identification.

On the New Year's Eve following Jack's birth in 1952, the Fords had returned home very late after a party to find that Mike had "poured a bottle of Baby Lotion over Jack's head, and had presumably fed him with a whole bottle of teething syrup containing sedative."[6] Ford immediately took Jack to hospital at 7 A.M. on New Year's morning to have the stomach pumped out. The fears of the family were allayed only when nothing harmful was discovered. Mike and Jack had David Eisenhower as a playmate for a while, at a time when the Fords were near neighbors of John and Barbara Eisenhower.

After the birth of Steven in 1956, the Fords decided upon an extended vacation to Europe during the winter months of that year. They left the three boys under the supervision of Clara Powell, their devoted black housekeeper, and they had looked forward to a freedom-from-care holiday. Betty, however, derived less benefit than anticipated since she was not in the best of health; the cause did not become apparent until after her return, when it was found that she was unexpectedly pregnant: Susan, her fourth child and first daughter, was born in July, 1957. As her mother delightfully describes the occasion, Susan saw light of day during the seventh inning of the Yankees versus Washington ballgame, to which Ford had taken Mike and Jack on the evening of her admission to hospital.[7]

Betty seems to have been particularly unfortunate during her lifetime with respect to the peripatetic occupations of her close male relatives. Her father, William Stephenson Bloomer, was a rubber firm traveling salesman; her first husband was, likewise, occupied in the traveling promotion of furniture products, and finally, Ford, having abandoned his law practice for a career in politics, seemed destined to spend more time on the road than ever he did at home—to the extent that daughter Susan was once led to comment: "I love my father, but I didn't know I had a father until I was ten or twelve years old. . . . Everybody was supposed to be home for dinner Sunday night because Daddy always made it a point of being home for Sunday night dinner. Well, it meant nothing to me. Just a man sitting there at the table."[8]

With four children born to her in seven years, and with an absentee husband, Betty was more than fully occupied during the Washington years. The children attended the public schools, and the family had its fair share of childhood incidents and accidents: "If you have four children, you spend a lot of your waking hours in hospitals. When the children get old enough to stop drinking teething syrup, they start breaking bones, and unless you've been through it, you have no idea how many bones there are in the human body . . ."[9] Ford made every effort to share with his wife and children the two major annual vacations, those of summer and Christmas, respectively. The family would go home to Grand Rapids for the summer, where they could enjoy the company of the grandparents.[10] In the earlier days, they also spent Christmas in Michigan, but, as the children grew older and learnt to ski, the Fords ventured westwards to the mountains and made Vail, Colorado, the site of their winter vacations. The family would be together, also, for the regular Republican National Conventions, when Mike and Jack would be kept occupied as platform pages.

In 1965, Ford was appointed Minority Leader in the House of Representatives and the demands upon his time increased measurably, such that he would be away from home for a total number of days amounting to more than eight months in the year. At this time, Betty was suffering from a severe neck ailment, complicated by arthritis, which brought unremitting chronic pain. Her frustrations and loneliness resulted in a prolonged mood of depression which drove her to seek psychiatric care over a period of two years.

After graduating from high school, Mike, the eldest boy, whom his mother called "the tidy one," enrolled at Wake Forest College, North Carolina. Having successfully completed his degree, he remained uncertain as to his future plans, and took time off to consider one or two alternatives: either to enter law school and eventually perhaps to emulate his father as a politician, or to become a minister. He opted for the latter, and he entered the Gordon Conwell Theological Seminary in South Hamilton, Massachusetts.

At Wake Forest College, Mike had met and fallen in love with Gayle Brumbaugh, a young lady with identical interests to his own in religious matters, and who, later, spent a year in Switzerland advancing her studies in that domain. Rather than wait until Mike had completed his degree in theology, the couple decided to get married, and the wedding took place at the home of the bride's parents in Catonsville, Maryland, on July 5, 1974. Ford, now Vice President (since December, 1973, following upon the resignation of Spiro Agnew), served as best man.

The turmoil of Watergate was now reaching its climax, and, at the end of July, the House Judiciary Committee had voted to recommend impeachment of President Nixon on the grounds of obstruction of justice and contempt of Congress. During the first week of August, uncertainty prevailed in Washington as to Nixon's intentions. Mike and Gayle decided to drive back to Massachusetts with a U-Haul trailer filled with wedding presents and the household equipment essential to the setting up of a new home prior to the commencement of the fall semester at the seminary. However, no sooner had they reached their destination than they were met by the Secret Service who provided them with plane tickets back to Washington in time to be present at Ford's swearing-in ceremony as President, shortly after mid-day on Friday, August 9, 1974.

At this very same time, a hectic search by helicopter had to be made for Jack, who, working as a ranger in Yellowstone National Park, was out riding in mountain country. He was eventually located and, like his brother, he arrived just in time for the taking of the presidential oath by his father.

Unlike Mike, Jack was described by his mother as "sloppy," and his room looked "as if a bomb had gone off in a thrift shop."[11] He had grown up to be more restless and perhaps more adventurous than his older brothers, becoming at one time enamored of rock stars and the night life of the capital city, but then breaking away to work his passage across the Atlantic on a freighter. There were also occasions when he would leave home for several weeks without informing his parents of his whereabouts, a habit which, initially, gave them great concern, but which, later, they came to accept with resignation though never without some distress and anxiety. After graduation from high school, he decided to major in forestry at Utah State University, and he spent much of his vacation time fighting fires or studying conservation and management with the National Forestry Service, as well as with the National Park Service.

Steve was the "charmer" of the family, a natural "con-man" from a very early age, according to Betty. Like his two elder brothers, he attended public schools, and, although he received good grades, he looked forward to graduation, after which he expressed an intention to enter dental school. As he himself said: "A dentist can be his own man, set his own hours. I could never shuffle papers eight hours a day."[12] But those plans never matured, not unexpectedly perhaps: Ford had taken him, at the age of 12, to Alaska on a campaign trip. There, he had made friends with whom he spent several subsequent summers reveling in the wilderness life: riding, fishing, camping, hunting. He later worked on a Montana cattle ranch, and having learned bareback bronco-riding, he participated in rodeos.

As the only daughter, Susan often felt left out since her three brothers tended to dominate the family activities. As mentioned earlier, she saw little of her father when she was growing up, and, at the age of 12, she was enrolled at a private high school in Bethesda, Maryland, where she boarded during school days and returned home for weekends. Though subjected to strict discipline at the school, in many ways she preferred to be there: "I was at the age when mothers and daughters don't get along anyway . . . You'd do anything to make your mother mad."[13]

Her fondest memories of youth may well have been those of her summer holidays at Grand Rapids, when she was thoroughly spoiled by her Grandma Ford. The latter had, hitherto, been involved in the up-bringing of boys only: her own four sons, and Susan's three brothers. Unfortunately, these happy times and the great love between grand-mother and granddaughter were abruptly terminated with the sudden death of the former at age 75 in 1967,[14] when Susan was only 10.

Susan also spent some time in summer camps, but only really enjoyed them when there was horse riding. At one camp, the regulations proved so strict that "every time you did anything you were breaking a point." In despair, hoping to be sent home, she deliberately exposed herself to poison ivy, but to no avail: she received the usual medical treatment for the infection, "and spent the rest of the time scratching."[15]

If Susan had, earlier, felt conscious of being left out of family affairs by reason of being the only girl, she found herself, after August, 1974, when her father became President, the focus of national attention, since she was the only one of the four children to reside at the White House for any length of time. There was no way in which she could escape the glare of brash publicity, and, in common with all preceding "White House daughters," she was obliged to endure recurrent rumors, predictions, and reports alleging her romantic attachment to a variety of both known and unknown suitors.[16] She graduated from Holton Arms School in June, 1975, and she enjoyed a hilarious eighteenth birthday party at the White House on July 4. Among the guests was Brian McCartney, one of her ski instructors at Vail, of whom she had become very fond, and with whom she had even contemplated marriage; however, within six months or so the attachment had cooled off considerably, although the couple re-mained friends.

One of Susan's close companions at the White House had been David Kennerly, the official presidential photographer, and there is little doubt that interest in his work prompted her to enroll in a photography work-shop sponsored by Ansel Adams and to undertake employment for six weeks during the summer of 1975 as a news photographer with the *Topeka Capitol Journal*.

In the fall of the same year, Susan enrolled at Mount Vernon, a girls' college in Washington, but during the first month there occurred the traumatic events of the assassination attempts upon her father's life, first, on September 5, at Sacramento, by Lynette Alice ("Squeaky") Fromme (a devotee of the killer, Charles Manson), and then, on September 22, at

San Francisco, by Sara Jane Moore. Ford, fortunately, was uninjured on both occasions.

In December, 1975, Ford made his second trip to China,[17] taking along with him Betty and Susan. The visit came after two political setbacks of the preceding November, the first being Nelson Rockefeller's decision not to seek re-election as Vice-President, and then the announcement by Ronald Reagan that he intended to campaign for the Republican presidential nomination at the summer convention of 1976.

It is possible that each of the foregoing political personalities was, in his own way, sensitive to the growing undercurrent of adverse public opinion directed against Ford engendered by what was considered to be the all-too-precipitate decision of granting Richard Nixon a presidential pardon within two months of his resignation in August, 1974. Ford had hoped that his action would end the turmoil which had so beset the country for the period preceding the resignation, and that the nation could then settle down to concentrate upon the more felicitous anticipation of its bicentennial celebration in 1976. But Ford's assumptions did not come to pass, and the remainder of his term of office was plagued by questions, rumors, and innuendos relating to the pardon. Even his own son, Mike, had been publicly quoted as having expressed the viewpoint that Nixon owed the public a total confession of his part in Watergate, but when asked about Mike's statement, Ford had commented: "All my children have spoken for themselves since they first learned to speak, and not always with my advance approval. I expect that to continue."[18]

It did not help matters that son, Jack, had been caught off-guard by some press reporter who made public his (Jack's) remark that his mother would feel very upset if her husband were to seek re-election in 1976. Upon hearing of this remark, Ford's reply to the press was simply: "*I'm* going to look after his mother and the White House, and *he's* going to look after his bears and tourists in Yellowstone."[19]

To the external observer, Ford's family embarrassments appeared cumulative and, no doubt, to the delight of his political adversaries, these possibly reached their zenith in 1976 when Betty consented to be interviewed by Morley Safer for a CBS "Sixty Minutes" television presentation. Without prior notice, she was suddenly confronted with Safer's question: "What if Susan Ford came to you and said 'Mother, I'm having an affair'?" Betty answered:

> Well, I wouldn't be surprised. I think she's a perfectly normal human being like all young girls. I would certainly counsel her and advise her on the subject, and I'd want to know pretty much about

the young man—whether it was a worthwhile encounter or whether it was going to be one of those. . . .

To further questions posed by Safer, Betty stated that her children had probably tried marijuana, that the decision of the U.S. Supreme Court to permit abortion was "the best thing in the world . . . a great, great decision," and that premarital sex might well lower the divorce rate.[20]

Public reaction was swift and intense, and Betty's remarks met with a spate of negative criticism, which included the comment that the President "had long given up attempting to control his wife."[21] Even Susan found it necessary to express her embarrassment by her mother's remarks: "It put me in a tight spot as far as dating guys. They thought, 'She's easy, her mother'll let her have affairs.'"[22] Betty's other children were no less unfavorably disposed to her public statement that they might have experimented with marijuana, since they all vociferously denied having done any such thing.

While Ford narrowly defeated Ronald Reagan for the Republican presidential nomination in August, 1976,[23] he lost the November presidential election (by an electoral vote of 240–297) to Jimmy Carter. The outcome of the election had remained uncertain until 9 A.M. of the morning of November 5, and the result was a great disappointment to the Ford family, all of whom had campaigned vigorously on behalf of the incumbent. Ford himself recorded his dismay:

> . . . my son, Jack, captured the way I felt. "You know" he said, "when you come so close, it's really hard to lose. But at the same time, if you can't lose as graciously as you had planned to win, then you shouldn't have been in the thing in the first place." I couldn't have said it better myself.[24]

The ultimate consequence of his defeat was that Ford, the only President ever to have acceded to that office from the House of Representatives, was obliged to bid farewell to Washington after twenty-eight years of residence, serving there, in sequence, as Congressman, Vice-President, and President.

Ford and his wife retired to Palm Springs, California, where they had often spent spring vacations, and where Ford enjoyed participation in golf tournaments. But it was now that Betty's prolonged bouts of illness, compounded by the tensions and pressures of being First Lady during a very difficult period of presidential politics, began to take their toll. She combined medication with alcohol, and when, during the fall of 1977, she had been invited to Moscow to narrate the Nutcracker ballet for television and was reported in the press as having given a "sloe-eyed, sleepy-tongued performance," her family took action.[25] It was because of their love for her that they insisted that she undergo medical treatment, and, in 1978, she agreed to enter the Alcohol and Drug Rehabilitation Service Center at Long Beach. Her subsequent, candid description of the entire episode, written with the positive objective of assisting other persons confronted by an identical and apparently hopeless situation, has since drawn her much praise and admiration.

Susan, who had enrolled at Mount Vernon College in the capital in 1975, had transferred to the University of Kansas in Lawrence following her father's election defeat, but then she withdrew by reason of unsatisfactory grades. She fell in love with Charles F. Vance, a Secret Service Agent assigned for duty with the ex-President in California, and they were married in 1979. Vance set up his own private security service for VIP visitors to Washington,[26] where the couple made their home, and where Susan gave birth to their two daughters, Tyne Mary, and Heather.

Ford's eldest son, Mike, completed his master's degree in theology in Massachusetts, and then, in 1981, he returned to his alma mater, Wake Forest College, Winston Salem, N.C., as a counselor and member of the faculty. There he has remained with his wife and two daughters, Sarah and Rebekah.

The two younger sons, Jack and Steve, have from time to time been victims of sensational "headlines" press coverage. During the White House days, Jack was "news" when he invited such celebrities as Chris Evert, Bianca Jagger, and (Beatle) George Harrison to the presidential residence.[27] He later expressed interest in pursuing a political career, and, in 1981, he had intentions of seeking office as a California state controller, but he later withdrew. He remained very interested in the domain of radio and television, and, for a while, was involved in the NBC radio program, "Great Outdoors."

In 1983, he was indicted and found guilty on a charge of reckless driving along Coastal Highway 101. He was fined $250 and placed on probation for two years. He resided in Leucadia, north of San Diego, where he had found employment as a consultant with a public relations firm.

Following his adventures in bronco riding, Steve, the youngest son, set out upon a career of acting, although, according to Betty, one of his first roles involved some dancing, when Steve discovered "he had two left feet, so quit."[28] He later obtained a regular role, as Andy, an easy-going bartender, on the television soap opera series, "The Young and The Restless."

In 1980, he was named in a paternity suit which was settled out of court. His continued love of outdoor life led him to participate in protests directed against the construction of the Diablo Canyon nuclear power plant in Southern California.

Jimmy Carter
(James Earl Carter, Jr.)

(1977–1981)

Jimmy Carter was the first President to use, at his own request, a familiar first name at a formal inauguration. He was a relatively unknown political personality outside his home state of Georgia where he had been Governor, 1971–1975, and, when his name was put forward as a Democratic candidate, the general response of the country was "Jimmy Who?" to which he himself supplied the response in his book, *Why Not the Best?* (1975):

> I am a Southerner and an American, I am a farmer, an engineer, a father and husband, a Christian, a politician and former governor, a planner, a businessman, a nuclear physicist, a naval officer, a canoeist, and among other things a lover of Bob Dylan's songs and Dylan Thomas's poetry.[1]

Carter's successful presidential bid in 1976 was very much a consequence of continued public dismay over the Watergate scandal. While Gerald Ford was considered an honest man, he, nevertheless, remained the personal nominee of Richard Nixon, to whom, in the eyes of very many citizens, he had granted too quickly a pardon; but yet, in the presidential election, he was still able to mobilize a substantial number of electoral votes.

Jimmy Carter was born in 1924, the eldest child of James Earl Carter, Sr., and his wife Lillian (Gordy) Carter. There were three other children: Gloria (1926), Ruth (1929), and William (Billy) Alton (1937). James Earl, Sr., was a hard-working farmer who later owned an auto service shop but came to hate the grease and grime of the business. His wife, known to the entire local community as "Mizz Lillian," was a generous, dynamic woman and a qualified nurse who gave unstinting service in her chosen professional domain to all persons in need, irrespective of their ethnic origins.

Jimmy Carter attended the local elementary and high schools. He enrolled at Georgia Southwestern Junior College, and later proceeded to Georgia Technical College, whence, in 1943, he entered the U.S. Naval Academy at Annapolis, Maryland. No sooner had he graduated than, at age 21, he married Rosalynn Smith, 18, on July 7, 1946.

Rosalynn and Jimmy Carter were both natives of Plains, Georgia. She had long been a close friend of Jimmy's sister, Ruth, but she had been passed by unnoticed for years by Jimmy himself. The latter became the focus of considerable attention when he began returning home on leave in the smart cadet uniform of the Naval Academy, and he, in turn, began to respond favorably to feminine observations in general, and to those of Rosalynn in particular. Events then moved quickly, and hardly a year elapsed between their first date and their marriage.

Carter spent his next seven years as a peripatetic career naval officer, being transferred from one base to another, and it was during this period that three sons were born to Rosalynn, all at different locations. The first was John William (Jack), who saw light of day on July 3, 1947, at Portsmouth, Virginia. Carter, sensing the opportunity for quicker promotion, had volunteered for submarine duty, and was, thereupon, sent to Hawaii as electronics officer on board the U.S.S. *Pomfret*. It was at Honolulu that Rosalynn gave birth to James Earl Carter III on April 12, 1950. Apparently, the maternity ward nurses labelled him "Chip," and that became his name ever thereafter.

Carter returned to the mainland, first to San Diego, and then to New London, Connecticut, where, on Rosalynn's 25th birthday, August 18, 1952, a third son, Donnel Jeffrey, was born. By this time Carter was a full lieutenant, and had enlisted in the atomic submarine division (headed by Admiral Hyman Rickover). There was every good reason to presume that he was destined for a highly successful naval career.

But that presumption ended in July, 1963, when his father unexpectedly died of cancer at age 58, and Carter resigned his commission to return to Plains, Georgia, to supervise the family peanut farm business.[2] Rosalynn was furious: she had come to enjoy the exhilaration of friendships and social activities associated with the naval bases, and to relish living in close contact with the sea and ocean, in place of the monotonous inland landscapes which were all she had hitherto known.

Rosalynn's father, Wilburn Edgar Smith, had been a school bus driver and an auto mechanic, and he also ran a small farm in Plains, but had died of leukemia at age 44, leaving his wife, Frances Allethea (Allie), 34, to rear their four children, the eldest of whom was Rosalynn, aged 13.[3] Determined not to seek, or depend upon charity, Allie had taken in sewing, and then obtained a position in the post office, while Rosalynn had worked part-time at the local hairdresser's. She had gone to college after graduating from high school in 1944, but never obtained a degree, since she left to marry Jimmy in 1946.

Her life had been humdrum and hard at Plains, and after seven years of marriage and of "seeing the world," it was small wonder that her opposition to her husband's decision to abandon it all was intense and sustained. It was their first real married quarrel, but Carter was adamant, determined, and impervious to all her emotional appeals. The result was the return of the family to Plains.

Rosalynn remained depressed for months, and domestic conditions were made no easier by the absence of a regular monthly income, as well as the failure of the peanut crop in 1954. But the demands of home and farm living permitted no prolonged brooding, and, in due course, she gradually became domiciled, a process which was measurably facilitated by the ever-pressent company of the extended families on both sides.

James Earl Carter, Sr., had long involved himself in local affairs, and had been elected to the Georgia State Legislature, but his political career was all-too-soon terminated by reason of his untimely death. The mealtime conversations between himself and his wife, Lillian, had almost invariably been concerned with public affairs and politics, whether parochial, national, or international; under these circumstances it appeared inevitable that Jimmy, the elder son, attentive, precocious, and inquisitive, would have had good reason to reflect frequently upon the colloquies, comments, and conclusions made by his parents, and that in time he might seek out opportunities of emulating some of his father's accomplishments and aspirations.

So it was that, upon his return to Plains, Jimmy Carter became active, first in his local Baptist church as a deacon and Sunday school teacher, and he slowly broadened his social involvements to include membership of the school board, the library board, and the Chamber of Commerce.

Rosalynn, likewise, became active in the church, the P.T.A., and the Cub Scouts, and they all made an effort to spend time with the boys at weekends on outdoor activities, such as camping and all manner of sports, while, for their annual holiday, they loved fishing and swimming in Florida, where they enjoyed the thrills of attending motor racing events at the Sebring circuit.

So as to further her participation in the family business, Rosalynn took correspondence courses in accounting and management, and she developed as an extremely efficient bookkeeper and secretary.

Jimmy's father and mother had both been strong-minded liberals, and this was a trait which Jimmy inherited. 1954 was the year of the momentous Supreme Court decision, Brown versus Topeka, when school desegregation was made mandatory, much to the fury of many Southern states, including Georgia. Jimmy voiced his support of desegregation for the Plains schools, action which aroused much bitterness in the community, where a movement was set on foot to boycott the Carter store, a threat which, however, did not materialize, but the unpleasantness remained for years.

On October 1, 1962, Carter's 38th birthday, he announced his intention of running for the State Senate, and, in a remarkable and almost unprecedented campaign, wherein the opposition was eventually found guilty of all manner of election cheating and irregularities, he was declared elected.

During the subsequent months that her husband was in Atlanta, Rosalynn lived a terrifying and fearful existence at home with the three boys, since so many threats had been directed against the family property. At night, she barricaded the doors and kept the house lights burning until late, and sleep only came after long, exhausting vigils. Fortunately, the threats remained just threats, and no direct assault was ever made against the home.[4]

Because of its advocacy of the civil rights movement, the Democratic party had made itself highly unpopular in the South. The assassination of President John F. Kennedy on November 22, 1963, brought more rejoic-

ing than sadness in many communities, including Plains, except in the
Carter household. As Rosalynn describes one incident:

> When the news was announced in Chip's classroom, the teacher
> said, "Good!" and the students applauded. Chip, who has a quick
> temper, like mine, picked up a chair and threw it at the teacher—
> and spent the next few days in the principal's office. It was not a
> proper thing for him to do, but we never blamed him.[5]

Chip, only 14, was brave enough to wear a Lyndon B. Johnson
campaign button to school at the time of the 1964 presidential election,
and for his temerity he suffered much verbal abuse, and, at times, was
even attacked physically, but, to his parents great pride, he did not waver
but "kept the faith." Likewise, so did "Mizz Lillian," who, when no one
else could be found to manage the Lyndon B. Johnson campaign office,
she volunteered to do it herself, at age 66, and, as a reward, she frequently
suffered minor vandalism to her car.[6]

In 1966, Carter had, at first, considered being a candidate for the U.S.
Senate, but he changed his plans to enter the Georgia gubernatorial race,
to no success, since he was defeated in the Democratic primary. One
month later, in December, 1966, Mizz Lillian joined the Peace Corps, and
departed to India, where she spent two years utilizing her medical training to good effect among sick and destitute villagers. She was a frail
woman, but she had a sturdy constitution, so that upon her return to the
United States, she remained in remarkably good health and spirits even
though she had lost thirty pounds in weight.[7]

In October, 1967, there occurred an unexpected happy event.
Rosalynn, at age 40, and with three boys aged 20, 17, and 15, respectively, gave birth to her one and only daughter, Amy Lynn Carter. The
family was delighted, and Rosalynn, especially, was overjoyed at being
the mother of an ever-so-longed-for baby girl. Carter was later to state:
"Her brothers are so much order that it is almost as though she has four
fathers and we have had to stand in line to spoil her."[8]

Undeterred and undismayed by defeat in his election bid in 1966,[9]
Carter campaigned so vigorously in the succeeding years that, in 1970, he
was finally elected Governor of Georgia, and the family moved into the
Governor's mansion in Atlanta. By this time, Jack, having graduated
from high school,[10] enrolled first at Georgia Tech, and then at Emory
University in Atlanta. But since most college students were exempt from
the draft, he had felt that an unfair distinction was being made between
noncollege and college students; and so, much to the concern of his
parents, he dropped out of college to join the U.S. Navy, and, in time,

saw service in the Vietnam theater of war. Upon his return, he re-enrolled at Georgia Tech, whence he graduated with a degree in physics, and went on to the University of Georgia to pursue, and complete, studies leading to a qualification in law.

Chip had the unfortunate experience of becoming overinvolved in an alcohol-drug group at Georgia Southwest College. To rid himself of negative peer group pressure, he courageously made the decision to drop out of college, and he made good his time by assisting first of all in his father's election campaign, and later in the Governor's office itself. He eventually continued his studies at Georgia State University. Jeff, the youngest son, also entered Georgia State University after graduating in 1970 from Woodward Academy, a private high school.

Rosalynn described Amy's room at the Atlanta mansion as the best in the house. It was large and spacious with a giant closet "that became a perfect toy room for a three year old."[11] With all the inevitable demands made upon both Jimmy and Rosalynn Carter in their respective official capacities, it became necessary to employ a full-time nursemaid for Amy in the absence of her parents. The person chosen was Mary Fitzpatrick, a black parolee, who, according to Carter, had been unjustly accused of manslaughter and was serving sentence at the Georgia Penitentiary near Atlanta. She proved to be a devoted friend and personal maid to Amy both in Atlanta and later in Washington. She was later granted full pardon by the State of Georgia.

Amy would, at times, be permitted to accompany her parents upon ceremonial occasions, so as to ease the trauma of feeling completely isolated from their social life. Carter would take every possible opportunity of sharing in the activities of his young daughter, and would, at Halloween, for example, take her around to neighbors' homes to "trick or treat."

While the Carters were resident in Atlanta, the two elder sons were married: Jack to Juliette Langford in November, 1971,[12] and Chip to Carol Griffin (an interior decorator) in June, 1973.[13] Entertainment at the mansion was both elaborate and expensive, and demanded of the First Lady of Georgia an extensive wardrobe. Rosalynn found herself unexpectedly blessed by the fact that she and all her new daughters-in-law as well as one of the mothers-in-law, all shared the same physical measurements so that they were able to undertake mutual exchanges of apparel, thereby appreciably reducing the overall bill for dress expenses.[14]

Carter served as Governor from 1971 and 1975, during which period the Watergate scandal had culminated in the resignation of President Nixon, and the assumption of office by Gerald Ford in August, 1974. In

December of that year, Carter announced his intention of seeking the
presidential nomination in 1976, and, beginning with the New
Hampshire primary in January, the whole family fell to campaigning
vigorously on his behalf. Jack and Judy (Juliette), Jeff and Annette, and
Chip and Carol between them visited, at least once, virtually every state
holding a primary. Carter had entered all the primaries and he eventually
won 19 of the 29 state contests. At the New York Democratic Convention of June, 1976, he was overwhelmingly confirmed as the Democratic presidential candidate.[15]

The presidential vote in November was unexpectedly close, with
incumbent President Ford receiving 240 electoral votes from 27 states
(including California with 45), and Carter 297 votes from 23 states. The
final result remained uncertain until the early hours of November 5.

After the ceremony on Inauguration Day, January 20, 1977, Carter set
the precedent of walking the one-and-a-half miles from the Capitol to the
White House, while his Vice-President, Walter Mondale, rode behind in
the bullet-proof limousine.

When the Carters moved into the White House, they were accompanied by Amy, now 4, along with Jeff and Chip and their respective
wives. Jack remained in Calhoun, Georgia, where he was at first a lawyer
in practice with his father-in-law, and then he entered the business world
as a grain elevator operator.

Jeff enrolled at George Washingon University to complete his studies.
He was a keen amateur astronomer and found the roof of the presidential
mansion to be ideal for his purpose. There, he set up observation instruments and made full use of the Dial-a-Phenomenon facilities of the
Smithsonian Institute.[16] He and his wife, Annette, represented the President at the funeral in Kenya of Jomo Kenyatta.[17] As described by Carter,
Jeff was "highly opinionated and also very well informed about current
events, (and) had inherited from his mother a habit of never losing an
argument."[18]

Chip worked for the Democratic National Committee in Washington,
and he and Carol had rooms on the White House third floor where a
nursery was set up for their young baby; unhappily, problems arose
between the couple, and they were divorced in 1978.

It was no doubt Amy who was most bewildered by the political
moves of her father, since, within the first ten years of her life, she had
resided at Plains, next Atlanta, then returning to Plains, and now she was
in Washington. Her parents enrolled her in a public desegregated school,
an event to which the media gave great publicity, much to the annoyance
of the President. She was the first child of a President to attend a public

school since the days of Theodore Roosevelt, and, since she was at all times accompanied by Secret Service agents, her very presence aroused considerable notice by and attention from the students.

Amy's greatest distress came with the necessity to straighten her teeth by wearing braces, which, at times occasioned her considerable pain. Her sole consolation came with the fact that several of her friends were likewise stricken. Rosalynn would encourage Amy to entertain some of her classmates at the White House and, when they stayed overnight, they sometimes slept in Lincoln's bed, and would spend hours in delightful terror awaiting the appearance of his ghost.

The problem of coping with unsolicited gifts, especially from opportunistic commercial enterprises, plagued the Carters as much as any other presidential family. One particularly embarrassing yet highly amusing incident occurred as the result of a misunderstanding on the part of one of Amy's friends. In casual conversation concerning their respective Christmas present wishes, Amy had mentioned that she would love a train set. Possibly by reason of a combination of a Southern accent confused by braces this was misinterpreted to mean "chain saw," and her young friend, justifiably mystified, communicated her astonishment to her other acquaintances, and before the Carters were aware of what was happening, chain saws by the dozen were being delivered at the White House. Rosalynn commented:

> We sent them all back except one that came with a card signed by everybody in the factory where it had been made. We kept that one for the Carter presidential library![19]

Rosalynn took the opportunity of having Amy attend a children's Suzuki violin group, while, for his own part, Carter himself would share with the family his particular interest in the poetry of Dylan Thomas and others, and they would listen together to records of the poet reading his own works.

In 1979, the Carters took along Amy on an official visit to Europe,[20] during the course of which they were received by Pope John Paul II at the Vatican. The event prompted a reciprocal visit to the United States by the Pope, this being the first such occasion in U.S. history.

On November 4, 1979, militants stormed the U.S. Embassy in Teheran and took 66 hostages, to be released only upon the return by the United States of the Shah of Iran who had flown to New York for treatment of cancer only two weeks earlier.[21] Carter refused to acquiesce in the demands of the militants, and thereby precipitated the crisis, which contributed appreciably to his overwhelming defeat in the 1980 presidential election,[22] and which terminated only one-half hour following his relinquishment of office at midday on January 20, 1981, when the hostages were permitted to leave Teheran by plane.

In addition to the international and national setbacks experienced by Carter, the family public image was not enhanced by the antics and activities of his younger brother, Billy, an unabashed opportunist, who sought to "cash in" upon the presidential name. He was 5 years old when Carter had left home for the navy, and was only 16 when his father died, and when Carter returned home. Upon graduating from high school two years later, Billy married his school sweetheart, Sibyl Spires, and then joined the Marines. Four years later he came back to Plains and assisted Carter in the peanut business.

Billy was very independently minded—as he himself stated: "I wasn't going to live my life under anyone else's norms," but nothing exceptional had occurred until Carter began his campaign for the presidency. Then, hordes of newspaper and media reporters descended upon Plains, and Billy

> . . . became caricatured, not unkindly, as an entertaining red-neck country bumpkin, always ready with a lively quip about government, politics, the press, or any other subject of current interest. . . . He also took advantage of the chance to present the other side of the Carter family—not so serious, full of fun and laughter. Perhaps his most famous quote was, "My mother joined the Peace Corps when she was 70, my sister, Gloria, is a motorcycle racer, my other sister, Ruth, is a Holy Roller preacher, and my brother thinks he is going to be President of the United States! I'm really the only normal one in the family."[23]

No sooner had his brother entered the White House than Billy arranged for the marketing by the Pearl Brewing Company, San Antonio, Texas, of "Billy Beer," and it was soon obvious that he was developing into an alcoholic, for which he subsequently had to undergo treatment.[24] His notoriety gained him extensive publicity, and his income was much enhanced from his acceptance of invitations for personal appearances from varied groups and associations eager to amuse their members, and willing to pay for his clowning.

Embarrassing as were these performances to the President, far more serious was Billy's involvement on the international stage. When Carter was attempting to defuse the Middle East political crises between Israel and the Arab states, it was revealed that Billy had accepted $220,000 from Libya (an arch-enemy of Israel), ostensibly to promote the sale of oil in the United States as well as to induce the President to release transport planes upon which he had placed an export embargo by reason of Khadafi's support for international terrorists.

In 1980, Billy's activities were formally investigated by Congress, and he was accused of being an unregistered foreign agent for Libya. He was subsequently cleared of any wrongdoing, but his activities reflected upon the President himself when the Senate inquiry formally concluded that Carter had shown "poor judgment" in regard to the entire affair.

Another relative who received undue negative publicity during the Carter administration was his nephew, William Carter Spann, son of Carter's sister, Gloria. She had been very much of a tomboy in her early years, and was known in Plains as a "motorcycle fiend" who tore along country roads at speeds of seventy to eighty miles per hour, regardless of danger either to herself or to others. She was two years younger than Carter, but physically more robust. In his memoirs, Carter recalls one occasion during childhood when she threw a wrench at him and, in retaliation, he peppered her butt with a BB gun, for which offense his father soundly paddled him, one of the very few occasions when James Carter, Sr., ever resorted to physical punishment of his children.

In 1945, Gloria had married Lieutenant William Everett Hardy, a Purple Heart war hero, but they were divorced in 1949. The one son of this marriage was William, and when Gloria remarried Walter G. Spann, a Plains farmer, in 1950, the latter formally adopted William and gave him his family name.

William had behavior problems throughout his childhood and was expelled by both public and private schools, and he subsequently descended into a career of petty crime. At the time of Carter's presidency he was in a California prison serving sentence following his conviction for robbing two taverns in San Francisco.[25]

Carter's final year of office produced nothing but problems. In April, 1980, an attempt to rescue the diplomat hostages proved abortive and eight members of the military mission were killed in a collision involving a helicopter and a transport plane in the Iranian desert. During that same month, the decision not to participate in the Olympic Games in Moscow (in consequence of the invasion of Afghanistan by the U.S.S.R. in December, 1979) was not universally acclaimed by all citizens of the United States. The grain embargo of Russia, likewise, because of its economic impact upon the wheat farmers of the Midwest, was yet one further hostile item compounding the mounting negative Carter image featured during the presidential campaign of the same year.

During the course of the televised campaign debates between the

President and his Republican opponent, Ronald Reagan, possibly the only part ever to be recalled by the viewing public was the nothing-short-of-malicious sarcastic interpretation by the obviously hostile media of an otherwise innocently made comment by Carter: in referring to the topic of military confrontation between the United States and the U.S.S.R. Carter mentioned that his daughter, Amy, then 13, had expressed her viewpoint that the major concern of both herself and of her own generation was that of the possibility of nuclear war and of its disastrous consequences. His comment was viciously greeted by a howl from the media which hilariously proceeded to mislead the public into the assumption that national leadership of the United States was now being conducted by a hopelessly unsophisticated teenager. It was the yellow press at its worst. The fact that Election Day, 1980, coincided with the first anniversary of the hostage takeover in Teheran on November 4, 1979, merely rubbed salt into an already politically wounded President, and the election debacle was a foregone conclusion.

By January, 1981, the Carters were back home in Plains, but the immediate family was now dispersed. Jack and Judy moved from Georgia to Illinois where Jack had found employment with the Continental Illinois Corporation as a floor manager at the Chicago Board of Trade Building. Chip, divorced in 1978, was remarried in 1982 to Ginger Hodges, an accountant. He and his wife remained in Washington, and Chip later helped in the campaign to select Walter Mondale as the Democratic nominee in the election of November, 1984. Jeff and Annette also remained in residence in the capital city, where they successfully engaged in the computer software business. Their first child, Joshua Jeffrey, was born in 1984.

Amy returned with her parents to Georgia in yet another upsetting move, and it was now decided to place her in a boarding school in Atlanta, although, in June, 1981, she returned temporarily to Washington to graduate with her classmates at the Hardy Middle School which she had attended for eighteen months. Following the completion of her senior high school studies, she enrolled at Brown University in the fall of 1985, with the intention of majoring in physics.[26]

In 1983, Carter suffered the loss through death of both his mother, "Mizz Lillian," aged 85, and of his younger sister, Ruth, 54. The latter was a Baptist evangelist who practiced faith healing and had rejected medical attention after being diagnosed as suffering from cancer of the pancreas. She had written several books including *The Gift of Inner Healing,* and *The Experience of Inner Healing,* and had established a retreat center, Hovita, where she held training sessions in faith healing.

Ruth had married Dr. Robert Stapleton, a veterinarian, and had reared four children, although she confessed in one of her books that she had found it difficult to be a warmhearted mother, and was away on lecture tours for at least half of her time.

Ruth also wrote a book about her younger brother, which she had entitled *Brother Billy,* who, at the time of her death, had long quit Plains and the peanut business. He had become a successful public relations and marketing consultant with firms engaged in the manufacture of prefabricated buildings and mobile homes.

Meanwhile, the ex-President kept himself occupied physically with his carpentry tools and equipment, a complete set of which had been donated to him by his cabinet and White House staff. His skills were applied not only to the making of furniture for his own home and for those of his relatives and friends, but also towards the rehabilitation of dilapidated residences in downtown urban areas, including New York. He was kept alert mentally partly by the monumental task of having to arrange for the cataloguing of the twenty-five million items pertaining to his presidential documents, and by the writing, first, of his memoirs, *Keeping Faith,*[27] and later of his observations on the crises in the Middle East, entitled *The Blood of Abraham.*[28]

Ronald Wilson Reagan

(1981–1989)

Herbert Hoover, the 31st President of the United States, was the first President elected from a state west of the Mississippi, but of his nine successors to date no fewer than five have either been born or had their political base west of that river. Ronald Reagan, the 40th President, though born in Tampico, Illinois, became a resident in California, and was elected state Governor in 1966.

He was born on February 6, 1911, to Nellie Clyde Wilson Reagan and her husband, John Edward Reagan, and he has lived to be the nation's oldest President at the time of his inauguration, as well as the first divorced person ever to be elected as chief executive.[1]

Ronald Reagan was the younger of two sons, his brother John Neil, being two years his senior. Both boys received nicknames, Neil being known as "Moon," and Ronald as "Dutch."[2] Their father was, among other things, a shoe salesman and store manager, but was not too successful and, as the future President once commented, "Our family didn't exactly come from the wrong side of the tracks, but we were certainly always within sound of the train whistles."[3] After several residential moves, the family finally settled in Dixon, Illinois, and it was here that the brothers went to high school.

Ronald was handicapped by nearsightedness although he did play football and, later, at Eureka College, near Peoria, he participated in track events, and was an exceptionally good swimmer. His academic record was unexceptional,[4] and, in 1932, he graduated in economics and sociology.[5]

Before entering politics, Reagan was known to the American public as a movie actor, and his entry into the film business was very much a fortuitous circumstance. He had obtained employment as a radio sports announcer at Davenport, Iowa, and he covered a variety of sports events. In 1937, he was sent to Catalina Island, off the coast of California near Los Angeles, to report upon the spring training sessions of the Chicago Cubs baseball team. Through casual contacts, he agreed to submit himself for a screen test at Hollywood, and made a successful debut into his film career as a radio announcer in a film, *Love Is on the Air*. Not long afterwards, he featured in *Brother Rat*, a satirical film farce based on a military school; it was while on this set that he met Jane Wyman, who was playing the part of the commandant's daughter involved in romantic episodes with one of the cadets (Ronald Reagan).[6]

Jane Wyman had been born in St. Joseph, Missouri, in 1914, and had been christened Sarah Jane Fulks. Her mother, Emma Reise Fulks, born in Germany, had come to the United States and had married Richard Fulks who was at one time Mayor of St. Joseph. When Sarah Jane was born, her parents had a teenage son and daughter, and when growing up, she felt very distant from both siblings as well as her parents.

Whether her mother ever performed in music halls remains uncertain, but, according to Jane herself, Emma Reise believed there was a future for her younger daughter in the developing film industry of the 1920's, and even took her to Hollywood to explore the possibility of child roles. They also went regularly together to the theater on Saturday afternoons, and these visits were eagerly anticipated and thoroughly enjoyed by young Jane.

When Richard Fulks died in 1929, Emma took Jane with her to live in Los Angeles, where both her elder children lived, the son being a qualified doctor while the daughter was a college graduate. Jane, apparently, was not of college caliber or, at least, expressed no interest in education beyond high school, but instead was talented enough to be in the chorus line of several films, her first being *The Kid from Spain*. In due course, she obtained "bit parts" and, eventually, in 1936, she was given a contract with Warner Brothers, who insisted that she change her name and it was at this time that Jane Fulks became Jane Wyman.

It was in this same year that she met Myron Futterman, a successful businessman engaged in dress manufacture. He was almost twenty years older than Jane, was divorced, with a teenage daughter. They were married in New Orleans in 1937, but the thrill and ecstasy of a whirlwind courtship faded rapidly and they soon separated. She formed a new attachment, in consequence of the film contacts in the *Brother Rat* series, with Ronald Reagan, and they were married on January 24, 1940.

Both husband and wife continued in their film careers, with Hollywood publicity now pounding out the fantasy image of their fairy tale romance, climaxed with the fairy tale birth of their daughter, Maureen, on January 4, 1941. But before the end of this year, the United States was at war, and the future direction of the film industry lay in question, and all this when Reagan's reputation was in the ascendancy. Two films, in particular, had demonstrated his talent as a gifted actor: the first was *Knute Rockne, All American* in which he played the part of George Gipp (The Gipper),[7] and the second was *King's Row*, in which he featured as Drake McHugh (who suffered amputation of both legs in the film version of Henry Bellamann's novel of the same title as the film).[8]

Because of his weak eyesight, Reagan did not serve on active military duty, but was instead assigned to a special services unit concerned with the making of training and propaganda films in Culver City, California, not too far from the new home he had built after his marriage.

Reagan and Jane Wyman were now being portrayed as the ideal mother and father "service couple"[9] with baby Maureen ("Mur-mur") becoming one of the nation's most photographed children. It is uncertain as to why in 1945, the Reagans decided to adopt a few-days-old boy whom they christened Michael Edward Reagan. Among the several conjectures advanced by the gossip columnists were those relating to reports alleging that Reagan needed his wife's salary to pay the household expenses, and that a new pregnancy would remove her from filmmaking, at a time when she was being widely acclaimed for her performances.[10] Then there was four-year-old Maureen, who, apparently, was exerting constant pressure upon her parents to provide her with a baby brother:

> Grown-up Maureen has recalled, "I wanted a baby so badly that I went to the toy department at Saks Fifth Avenue and asked if they had baby brothers—to the surprise and chagrin of my poor father, who had to stand there and listen to this." Maureen had "wanted two things in this world—a baby brother and a red scooter. And

they kept telling me that if I wanted a baby brother, I would have to save up. And one day they said I was going to get what I wanted that night. I was sort of looking for a red scooter. But sure enough, it was a baby brother, a four-day-old baby brother. And my father said, "Where is it?" And I went up the stairs. I had ninety-seven cents. So I gave the lady from the adoption agency my piggy bank.[11]

After the war, Reagan encountered difficulties in becoming re-established as a film actor, but he found himself increasingly involved in the labor-management dimension of movie making, and his interests were acknowledged by his peers who accepted him as president of the Screen Actors Guild.

Apparently, this new direction of interest did not please Jane since conversation at home or upon social occasions now seem to consist of a political monologue on the part of her husband, to such degree that, to the astonishment of the public, though not to their exclusive circle of Hollywood acquaintances, Jane announced her intention of separating from her husband.

According to Reagan, the announcement came as a complete surprise to him, and, in some strange way, he seems not to have comprehended the situation. He attributed the decision to Jane's depressed condition following upon the death of a prematurely born baby girl in June, 1947, although, as an afterthought, he expressed the view that "perhaps my seriousness about public affairs had bored Jane."[12] This has been termed the understatement of the year since by reason of the many violent union strikes, not only had Reagan been provided with a license to carry a gun (which he wore almost every day for nine months), but the police had actually stationed an armed man to patrol the Reagan home, greatly to Jane's consternation and trepidation on behalf of her husband, herself, and particularly of the children.

Reagan's political involvement, to Jane, had far overstepped the mark of discretion, and she accused him of irresponsibly jeopardizing the safety and well-being of the entire family. Yet, there were genuine efforts towards reconciliation,[13] but they all failed.

The divorce was finalized in July, 1949, when Reagan happened to be hospitalized after breaking his leg in a charity softball game. While their major differences remained irreconcilable, both parents were cooperative with respect to the welfare of their children. As Reagan has commented:

The problem hurt our children most. Maureen was born in 1941 and Michael came to us in March of 1945—closer than a son; he wasn't born unasked, we chose him. There is no easy way to break up a home, and I don't think there is any way to ease the bewildered pain of children at such times.[14]

It was while Reagan was still recuperating from his leg injury that he met Nancy Davis. She was born Anne Frances Robbins, in a New York hospital in 1921, to Edith Luckett Robbins, a professional actress, and Kenneth Robbins, a graduate of Princeton and a successful businessman, first of all in the woolen industry (in association with his father), and later as an independent car salesman. Ann Frances had always been called "Nancy," and her parents had married before Kenneth Robbins had left for overseas duty in World War I. But the marriage did not survive too long after his demobilization, and Edith had to return to the stage to support herself and Nancy. This meant a roving, living-out-of-suitcase, hotel-apartment existence, which was disastrous for the upbringing of a young child, and so Edith, reared in a family of nine children, persuaded one of her married sisters, Virginia Galbraith, to take in Nancy as part of her family. Virginia, and her husband, Audley, lived in Bethesda, Maryland, and their daughter, Charlotte, was of Nancy's age. The two children proved to be amicable companions.[15]

In 1929, Edith was remarried to Dr. Loyal Davis, a distinguished brain surgeon living in Chicago, and Nancy came to live there with her mother and stepfather. She became very fond of Davis and when, five years later, he seriously discussed with Nancy, now 14, the suggestion that he formally adopt her as his legal daughter, she readily acquiesced, and she became Nancy Davis.

In Chicago, she attended the Girls' Latin School, whence, after graduation, she proceeded to Smith College in Northampton, Massachusetts, where she became interested in dramatics. She returned to Chicago in 1943 to be with her mother while her (legal) father was serving in the armed forces.

By reason of her profession, Nancy's mother had many stage connections and, after Davis's return to Chicago, Nancy obtained her patiently awaited-for opportunity to embark on a theatrical career when, in 1946, Zazu Pitts offered her a one-line part with a touring company. It was an inauspicious start, but it was the breakthrough, and, in time, Nancy was able to evoke the anticipated responses when, at cocktail parties, she could casually remark that (through the good auspices of Spencer Tracy) she had once dated Clark Gable.[16]

In 1949, Nancy went to Hollywood, and she featured in a number of small film parts. This was at the time when the film industry was under suspicion of sheltering numerous actors, directors, producers, and other employees accused of being subversive "pinks" (Communist sympathizers). Nancy had become very concerned that her own name had appeared on a listing of "red" activists, and she immediately shared her anxieties with her director who suggested that she contact Ronald Reagan, as president of the Screen Actors Guild.

A meeting between Nancy and Reagan was arranged, and a new romance was "on," although understandably, since he was still in a very depressed mood following upon his divorce, Reagan himself proceeded very cautiously before entering upon a new commitment. Still, the friendship was maintained. In 1951, he purchased an extensive 350-acre ranch in the coastal region of the Santa Monica Mountains where he reveled in his favorite pasttime of horse-riding, and where he could entertain Nancy, along with his daughter, Maureen, and son, Michael.

Reagan's association with Nancy ripened into love and, on March 4, 1952, they were married in a simple ceremony at the Little Brown Church in the Valley in North Hollywood, at which William Holden and his wife were best man and matron of honor, respectively. The wedding night was spent at Riverside, California, whence the newlyweds drove to Phoenix, Arizona, to spend their honeymoon and to meet with Nancy's parents, who were in the area for a spring vacation.[17]

The Reagans' first child, Patricia Ann (Patty, later Patti), was born on October 21, 1952, and, while Nancy was still in the hospital, the proud father had an olive tree planted in their new home in the Pacific Palisades as a surprise homecoming gift. Patti was a premature baby, and Nancy was rushed to the hospital while attending an International Horse Show; to avoid possible complications, the doctors performed a Caesarian section.

One week after the birth of Patti, Jane Wyman went away secretly with Frederick Maxwell Karger, a handsome bandleader who was two years her junior. They were married on November 1, 1952, at the El Montecito Presbyterian Church, Santa Barbara. Karger was a divorced man with one daughter, Terry, whom he brought with him into the Jane Wyman household of her two children.

All three children were boarded in school during the week, coming home for weekends and vacations only, thus permitting Jane and Karger to continue work with minimum interruption. But problems increasingly developed as husband and wife were seldom at home together, although their respective careers brought them deserved public acclaim. Jane Wyman was nominated for an Oscar for her outstanding performance in the remake of *Magnificent Obsession* (released in 1954), but the award went to Grace Kelly (in *The Country Girl*).

Jane and Karger were separated and reunited several times but their final divorce came in December, 1955. The stresses and strains took their toll on both Jane and her two children. Possibly in a desperate effort to achieve some degree of inner emotional stability, she converted to Catholicism, and she brought Maureen and Michael with her into the Church.

While the children did spend time with their father and Nancy at the ranch, it was Jane who found herself with the major responsibilities of their rearing and disciplining. Maureen recalls

> that her mother used a tactic different from physical punishment. "Mom is a great actress, and she could make me cry on or off the screen. If I did something wrong she'd put on her wounded act and that would hurt me more than any spanking would."[18]

Michael, on the other hand, would occasionally be subjected to the use of a riding crop, "Ten times on the back of each calf,"[19] although he admitted that he probably deserved it. But his father never "spanked me in my life . . . He doesn't even yell, he tries to talk it out with you."[20] In later life, Michael was to state:

> I didn't get to know my mother and father personally until I was 25. Mom was working double time. I was more or less raised by Carrie who was Mom's cook. I would go to her with my problems and inner feelings.[21]

By the early 1950's, it had become obvious to all Hollywood that television was making substantial inroads into the entertainment world, hitherto virtually monopolized by the movie theater. Reagan had been forced to concede that his promising early career as a film actor had been terminated by the outbreak of World War II; his film roles after the war were best forgotten.

But, by good fortune, he was offered, in 1953, a position as host of the new "General Electric Theatre," which sponsored Sunday night dramas on the CBS television channel. Overnight, Reagan was reinstated as a national entertainment-world personality. For the next eight years he functioned not only as the Theatre host, but he also traveled around the country making personal appearances at all the G.E. plants, such visits being calculated to boost employee morale.

By coincidence or otherwise, Jane Wyman made her own television debut in 1954, and this, in a G.E. Theatre show hosted by her ex-husband. In the following year, she was offered the opportunity to set up her own show on the NBC television network's "Jane Wyman Presents the Fireside Theatre," a title later simplified to "The Jane Wyman Theatre."

By late 1957, Nancy, after several miscarriages, was again pregnant, and, taking no chances, her medical advisers insisted that she remain in bed for three months and have weekly hormone shots. Her second child, a son, was born on May 20, 1958, this time by a planned Caesarian section. He was christened Ronald Prescott Reagan, nicknamed by his father, "Skipper" (Skip), a sobriquet which he accepted until he entered high school, when he insisted on being called Ron.

By this time, Patti had attended a public school in Pacific Palisades, but had then been withdrawn to be enrolled in the Dye School, a private institution in Bel Air, to which Skip was also sent when he became of age.

In March, 1961, Jane Wyman remarried Fred Karger, and, in this same year, Maureen, now 20, had married John Filippone, a 32-year-old police officer. After graduating from high school she had enrolled at Marymount Junior College in Arlington, Virginia, but had left to work in several occupations in the Federal District area, including functioning as a secretary in a real estate office. The marriage lasted only a year. In 1964, she married David Sills, a Marine Corps lieutenant, who had qualified as a lawyer, but this marriage also ended in divorce three years later. Jane Wyman's marriage to Karger again ended in divorce (her fourth) in 1965.

Reagan's contract with General Electric expired in 1962. Then, through the good offices of his brother, Neil ("Moon"), he became host to, and also performed in "Death Valley Days," a show sponsored by the U.S. Borax Company. In 1964, he starred in a film presentation of Ernest Hemingway's novel, *The Killers,* and played the uncharacteristic role of a villain. It proved to be the last of his 55 feature films, since he was now increasingly involved in politics, although his allegiances were most indefinite.

He was a registered Democrat, but he had voted for Eisenhower in 1952 and 1956, and for Nixon in 1960. In 1964, he had made a nationwide television presentation on behalf of Barry Goldwater, by which date his Republicanism had attracted the party's establishment which set him up to oppose the Democratic incumbent, Pat Brown, in the California gubernatorial election of 1966. Reagan was victorious,[22] and in great elation the family moved to Sacramento, the state capital. But no sooner had the Reagans occupied the Governor's mansion than domestic problems immediately loomed up.

Nancy took an instant dislike to the building which she described as "Victorian ugly." There were no grounds around the house where the children could play outdoors in safety, and the mansion itself was a veritable firetrap without a single fire escape;[23] it had seven fireplaces but, by law, no fires could be lit.

It was an intolerable situation, and by dint of Nancy's uncompromising persistence (despite fears of adverse political comment), the Reagans moved out to another house (on the outskirts of the city) with a large backyard, which provided ample play space (along with a swimming pool) for the children, as well as opportunities for peaceful relaxation by the parents.

The move to Sacramento entailed a disruption of the children's schooling. Young Ronnie, now 8, was enrolled in Brookfield, a private elementary school, which he attended daily and returned home in the late afternoon. A decision regarding Patti's education was more complicated, and, after carefully considering several alternatives, she was sent to a girls' private boarding institution, the Orme School, in Phoenix, Arizona, which was a long distance from Sacramento, but, since she had spent an appreciable amount of vacation time in the vicinity, it was felt that she would not feel too unfamiliar with the surroundings. However, Patti's reaction was unexpected: regarding herself now freed from all home restrictions, she resorted to an overindulgent eating orgy, and became excessively corpulent, to the concern of all, including herself. She was sensible enough to recognize that she was in the process of inflicting considerable harm to herself unless she terminated her newly acquired vice, and, to her credit, she made a complete volte-face, and went on a crash diet. This was followed by a slow relaxation of the self-imposed rigid regime, and, in time, she reverted to more sensible eating habits.

Maureen, with two failed marriages before the age of 30, remained very uncertain as to a career. Possibly influenced by her father's growing political involvement, she had worked as a Republican party volunteer in Richard Nixon's presidential campaign during 1960. In due course, she left Washington for Los Angeles, where she dabbled in the entertainment world, first as a dinner theatre actress, then as a talk-show hostess, but she appeared to have found satisfaction in neither. In this occupational drift-world she was acutely aware of the concerns of both her parents; as she, herself, once expressed her feelings: "My folks were disappointed in me because I wasn't fitting into the recognized world, staying in school four years, and then graduating with honors or something."[24]

Michael's career, likewise, was erratic and seemingly bereft of purposeful direction. At high school he had been star quarterback on the varsity football team, but remained disappointed that his father never once saw him play. He had entered San Fernando Valley State College, then the University of Southern California in Los Angeles, but had dropped out successively from each. When working as a dockhand in Los Angeles, he had become fascinated with speedboats, an interest which was to give him not only great personal satisfaction, but also considerable national and international recognition, since at Lake Havasu in Arizona in 1967, at the age of 22, he gained the title of world outboard racing champion. He received multiple injuries while speedboat racing in Texas in 1969, but that did not deter him, and, following a long and painful period of physical recovery, he returned to his chosen occupation.

In 1970, Michael announced his intention of getting married to Pamela Putnam, a dental assistant, and, upon receiving the announcement, Reagan penned his son a letter in which he stated:

> . . . you know better than many what an unhappy home is and what it can do to others. Now you have a chance to make it come out the way it should. There is no greater happiness for a man than approaching a door at the end of a day knowing someone on the other side of that door is waiting for the sound of his footsteps.
> Love, Dad
> P.S. You'll never get in trouble if you say "I love you" at least once a day.[25]

His father's advice proved of no avail, and Michael's marriage lasted only one year. In 1975, he was remarried to Colleen Sterns, a college graduate in decorating, by which time he had embarked upon a new career of selling gasohol equipment to farmers.

Reagan's gubernatorial career ended in 1975 after two consecutive terms of office. He had unsuccessfully campaigned for the Republican presidential nomination in 1968, and again in 1972. He believed he could reunite the Republican party after the disastrous Watergate episodes, and set himself against President Ford in 1976, but, once more, he found himself rejected at the Republican National Convention in Kansas City.

He remained confident and undeterred and, following Ford's defeat by Jimmy Carter, Reagan emerged as the only possible Republican presidential nominee for the 1980 election. At the Republican Party Convention in Detroit, he was overwhelmingly nominated on the first ballot.[26] In the following November he was, again, a decisive victor.[27]

All members of his family had given Reagan their unequivocal support during the 1980 election campaign,[28] although the personal lifestyles of each of the children had been quite diversified, and, upon occasion, had given their parents reason for considerable concern and anxiety.

Maureen, always interested in politics, had become increasingly involved in the campaign for ratification of the Equal Rights Amendment, during the course of which she had formed a close friendship with Judy Carter, the President's daughter-in-law, who was likewise very active in the movement.

In 1980, Maureen founded a private organization entitled "Sell Overseas America" (which grew to some 2,000 corporate members) for the purpose of encouraging U.S. companies to trade in international markets. She made several overseas visits, and claimed that "the U.S. must either limit imports, which would be catastrophic, or increase exports." In April, 1981, at age 40, she married for the third time. Her husband, Dennis Revell, was twelve years her junior. Only a few weeks earlier, Reagan had suffered a chest wound in an assassination attempt and he was unable to attend the wedding. The bride was given away by Reagan's brother, Neil.

Since the tide of Republicanism was on the flow, Maureen sought to take advantage of it by entering, in 1982, the California primary elections for U.S. Senator. But her father, possibly fearing accusations of nepotism, gave her no support, neither did his brother, Neil, who actually campaigned for one of Maureen's opponents, San Diego Mayor Pete Wilson.[29] Even her mother, Jane Wyman, could not be induced to endorse her daughter, stating tersely, "I've never been political, and I don't intend to start now—or ever." Maureen was defeated, polling only five percent of the primary votes.

By the time that Reagan was re-elected in 1984, Maureen had developed as a leader among the Republican party women, and occupied a position as special consultant to the Republican National Committee on women's issues. She stated, "The fact that I have some differences with my father, especially about the Equal Rights Amendment, doesn't mean that I don't think that overall he's been a great President. And I hope he's re-elected because he deserves to be . . . . He has never asked me to temper my opinions, or not to say such-and-such in public. . . ."[30]

In July, 1985, Maureen was asked to head the 37-member U.S. delegation to Nairobi, Kenya, for the final conference of the U.N. Decade for Women which had been launched in 1975 at Mexico City in an effort to improve conditions for women around the world. The Nairobi conference was attended by over 3,000 delegates and at least 11,000 women. Maureen's performance was a most creditable one, despite criticism of the U.S. from Communist and Third World countries, as well as personal attacks from U.S. activists who objected to her presence on the grounds that she was actually representing her father, the President, who was said to lead "the most sexist, the most racist, the most warlike government in the entire history of the United States."

After his father's election in 1980, Michael continued in business with powerboats, and he was also marketing salesman with Dana Ingalls Profile Inc., an aerospace defense contract firm. It was in connection with his work for this company that he became involved in adverse publicity relating to a circular he had written and mailed to a number of military bases. The letter began, "I know that with my father's leadership in the White House, this countries (sic) armed services are going to be rebuilt and strengthened. We at Dana Ingalls Profile want to be involved in that process." Michael later recognized the foolishness of his action and publicly apologized for the embarrassment he had caused his family.[31] Unfortunately, the episode did appear to have led to a marked cooling in the relationship between himself and his father.

In a published interview in September, 1983,[32] Michael referred to some of his past family problems. He had attended boarding schools, and complained that he really only came to know his parents from television. He added that:

It's very tough to live a life being an appendage of other people, even if you love them. You're proud they're your parents, but it's awesome to live up to them . . . but it took Dad seventy years to get where he is and you're expected to be on the same pinnacle of success with a guy who's got a good thirty years or more on you. Anything you do that is questioned is front page, and people don't often print things you're doing right because that's just not news. . . .

Michael had, in fact, been "doing (some things) right" by his participation in fund-raising projects on behalf of the United States Olympic Committee. In 1982, he raced a power boat up the Mississippi from New Orleans to St. Louis, a distance of approximately 700 miles, in a little over 25 hours. The project raised half a million dollars, and a dinner commemorating the event was personally attended by President Reagan.[33]

In 1983, Michael, again on behalf of the Olympic Games funding project, raced his power boat between Chicago and Detroit, via Lakes Michigan and Huron, while, in the following year, he carried the Olympic torch for one kilometer in Orange County, California.

By 1983, Michael had two children, a son, Cameron, born in 1978, and a daughter, Ashley Marie, born in 1983. His father had not yet seen his only granddaughter, but Michael recognized that Reagan was "a busy, busy man," yet he could find time to send

Cameron and Ashley special letters about things that are not known
to the American people about what he's done in Government. He
writes them on White House stationery, signs them, "Love
Grandpa," and then puts in a dash and adds "Ronald Reagan"
because everything the President writes is history. This is his way of
giving his grandchildren a piece of Americana. Dad jokes it's also a
way of paying for their college education—if they want to sell the
letters.[34]

What actually led to the confrontation between Michael and the First
Family in November, 1984, remains obscure, but, at Thanksgiving, all
the children were assembled at the Reagan ranch in California, all, that is,
with the exception of Michael, who was spending the festival holiday
with his wife's family in Omaha, Nebraska, this being the first time for
many years.

When press reporters questioned Nancy she stated that the President
and his son, Michael, were "estranged," and she hoped that "someday it
will be resolved." This published comment took Michael completely by
surprise and, in turn, he retorted that he was both "shocked and hurt" by
Nancy's statement. He added that, "I have noticed . . . that Nancy has
not been as warm toward us," because he and Colleen had the only two
grandchildren of the President: "She would like it to have her kids have
the grandchildren of the President." When he next appeared before the
press, Michael wore a T-shirt on which was printed, in capitals: I'M
NOT THE DANCER. Somewhat rashly, perhaps, he was drawn on to
comment upon Maureen and her several marriages, which provoked the
latter to remark that Michael's outbursts might possibly by related to the
fact of his adoption, in consequence of which she made the suggestion
that "Michael should seek professional help."[35]

So it was, by this unexpected fracas, that Reagan's sweet nectar of
presidential victory became soured within weeks of the election. His
initial efforts, over the phone to Michael, to effect reconciliation were
repulsed, but he persisted, and the breach was finally healed, first in Los
Angeles, and then at the White House, where photographs were taken of
the President and his grandson, Cameron, playing together in the snow
and building a snowman. As a result, Nancy was able to say, "All is
resolved. Everybody loves each other."[36]

Michael, at age forty, now expressed a wish to become a film actor like
his parents and, in June, 1985, he held a news conference in Vancouver,
Canada, in which he disclosed the information that he had taken up
acting lessons and was in negotiation with a Canadian agent. He declared
that he was more interested in films, and television talk shows, game

shows and commercials rather than in "live plays" which, he stated, "don't excite me. . . . I wouldn't enjoy the three, four performances a day, and matinees and weekends. Weekends are very important to me. My family is more important to me than anything."[37] The press reports of the news conference referred to the complications of providing security for the son of a President since there were in attendance no fewer than eight U.S. Secret Service officers along with at least two members of the Royal Canadian Mounted Police.

Nancy's daughter, Patti, having graduated from high school in Phoenix, was uncertain as to her future. Her mother recognized the problems of children reared in political families and, in her autobiography, she commented,

> If you could pick the ideal time to go into politics, it would be when the children are grown up and settled because there's no doubt that political life is difficult for them. I think Patti was the least happy about her father's new career, but I think she realizes now he's doing what he wants to do and what he feels is important.[38]

Nancy acknowledged the many difficulties encountered by children growing up in the '60's and '70's in a sexually permissive and chemical society, but added

> . . . it's also a difficult time to be a parent. If only young people could realize how very much their parents want to insure happiness for them and how deep are their parents' heartaches. Parents aren't always right, but they try to be right and can only go by experience. I believe strongly in the family unit, and I'm disturbed by what seems to me to be a gradual erosion of it. . . .[39]

Patti entered Northwestern University, Evanston, Illinois, for a year, but left to enroll at U.S.C. in Los Angeles. She became interested in drama and she took the female lead in John Osborne's play, *Look Back in Anger.* Commenting upon her role, Patti said, "I related to Allison in a lot of ways. She had a lot of strength, but she couldn't stop loving someone who was destroying her, and I understood that. It had happened to me."[40]

Patti had dropped out of college in her senior year, and, seeking anonymity, she adopted her mother's maiden name, to become known as Patti Davis. For a while, she was quite a rebel, not merely publicly voicing her opposition to her father's political views as California Governor, but also causing her parents much concern and embarrassment by moving in to live with Bernie Leadon, a member of a rock band, The Eagles.[41]

During the course of her subsequent acting career she appeared in episodes in the television series, "Love Boat," and "Fantasy Island," in several films including *The Curse of the Pink Panther,* as well as making a successful debut on stage in *Vanities,* produced in Traverse City, Michigan.

Always informal and independent, she did consent to be more formally attired for her father's inauguration in 1981 when she wore a very expensive Dior creation, but later she wryly commented, "I didn't have very much success walking in that dress. As I remember I had masking tape on the hem by the end of the evening. I sort of walk like a baseball player. Not exactly grace in motion."[42]

The fact that her father was now President made little impression upon her. She actively campaigned against nuclear power and nuclear weapons, and when questioned about Reagan's attitude towards her activities, she admitted that he was "not happy," but that he made no attempt at restraining her.

During the Christmas season of 1983 at the White House, Patti introduced to her parents Paul Grilley, a yoga instructor at the College of India in Beverly Hills. While on a visit to Paris in the following year, Grilley proposed marriage and, since Patti had no wish for an elaborate White House wedding, the couple were wed in a private ceremony in Los Angeles in August, 1984. Patti was given away by her father,[43] her sister-in-law, Doria, was in attendance, and both Maureen and Michael were also present.

In August, 1985, Patti announced that she had completed a fictionalized account of her life, to be given the title, *Home Front,* and it was published during the early months of 1986. Press reviews appeared lukewarm in their enthusiasm for the book, and it was variously described as a "thinly veiled autobiographical novel" with no sensational revelations, or as "the sting of a resentful child."[44] The work portrays the career of a (thinly disguised) father, Robert Canfield, and his supportive wife, Harriet, with Canfield as an ambitious politician who is elected first as Governor of California and, subsequently, as President of the United States. Patti is depicted as the Canfield's daughter, Beth, misunderstood by her parents, who apparently regard both Beth and her brother, Brian (Ron), as political liabilities. As Patti described it, she wrote about a father "who's interested in his political career to the exclusion of his children and a mother who was a clothes horse and so protective of the father that she won't let the kids have their own feelings."

In a television interview[45] relating to their joint reaction to the book, Reagan and Nancy acknowledged that their immediate response had been one of hurt, anger and annoyance. Reagan had thought he "was a good father," but "maybe there were times when I should have been sterner than I was." For her part, Nancy "tried to be a good mother. I don't think anybody's perfect, but then you know, there's no perfect parent—there's no perfect child."

Ron, the youngest son, was as uncertain regarding his future career after graduating from high school as Patti had been. He was a talented young man and had been accepted at Yale, but becoming quickly disillusioned with college life, he decided upon a stage career in dancing and ballet. While attending dancing classes in Hollywood he supported himself by all manner of jobs, and then, in due course, he became a member of the Joffrey Ballet Company in New York, and made his debut at the Lincoln Center in March, 1980. Reagan and Nancy attended a gala performance in which their son appeared.

Ron was to surprise both his parents later in the same year: three weeks after Reagan's victory in the November presidential election he received an evening phone call from Ron who announced that he was getting married the next day. Ron's bride was Doria Palmieri, a philosophy graduate from California State University at Northridge, whom he had met at the dancing school in Hollywood. They had lived together for a number of months in Greenwich Village, and had finally decided upon a completely unconventional wedding free of all publicity. Ron was "dressed in jeans, red sweatshirt and running shoes," while Doria "wore a bulky crewneck sweater, blue jeans and cowboy boots."[46] A Secret Service agent served as one of the witnesses.

The abrupt nature of the wedding very much upset the White House family, and for several months the relationship between parents and son was decidedly cool. But then on March 30, 1981, there occurred the attempted assassination of the President. Ron heard the news when he was on tour in Nebraska with his ballet company; he and Doria immediately flew back to Washington to be with his mother, to whom, at this moment of crisis, he provided great support. It led to a quick thaw, and, in gratitude, on Ron's 23rd birthday (May 30, 1981) Nancy accompanied her son and daughter-in-law on a 45-minute joyful ride over the Virginia countryside in the Goodyear blimp, "The America." When asked about her change of attitude towards Ron and Doria, Nancy acknowledged that, "Your priorities are quickly rearranged" (by force of circumstance).

Ron's ballet company guaranteed employment for only 36 weeks a year, and although this was frequently extended, it did mean that the dancers were out of work for an appreciable length of time and were consequently eligible for unemployment compensation. This was the case in October, 1982, and, when news reached the media that Ron was standing in line for benefit pay, the reaction was hostile, acidic, and soaked in sarcasm. Typical comment was that of Ellen Goodman of the *Washington Post* writers group in an article headlined, "Independent first son turns to Uncle Sam." Stating that the spectacle of seeing the son (Ronboy) of the President (Rondad) claiming relief money "was not designed to warm the hearts of the American people." She went on to deride several of Reagan's declarations with respect to family self-help:

> On one occasion, Rondad said we should all look to the Mormons as our model. On another occasion he said "I made a point to count the pages of help wanted ads in this time of great unemployment. There were 24 full pages of classified ads of employers looking for employees."
> It does not appear, however, that his son pounded the pavements in his ballet shoes before heading for the unemployment lines. . . . Deputy press secretary, Larry Speakes, said, "The Reagans talked to Ron about being helpful and he expressed a desire to be independent and they respect that desire. . . ."
> What is most notable about this modest family rebellion is the course that Ronboy has taken. He has refused help from Rondad and accepted it from the government.

And all this, Goodman continued, at a time when the President was in the process of substantially reducing social welfare budgets. She concluded:

> Whatever nostalgia we have about a mythical and real past in which people took care of their own in times of trouble, we have elaborate and expensive entitlement programs partly because millions of us would rather go to a bureaucracy than to a brother-in-law.
> The elderly would rather receive a check from the government than from the children. Reagan the Son finds it easier to take $125 a week from the government than from Reagan the Father.
> For better and for worse, our independence often depends on the same government programs the president has threatened. Rondad might think about that as he watches Ronboy "making it on his own."[47]

It was later reported that Ron rejected the offer of a job selling cars during the lay-off period.

Ron's ballet career lasted only four years. To his dismay he had found that the remuneration accorded to a ballet dancer was most inadequate to support a family. With considerable reluctance he found himself forced to quit, and he embarked, instead, upon a career in free lance journalism, one of his first contributions being an article in *Newsweek* explaining why he had resigned from the Joffrey II:

> I left because I want to make a home with my wife and to one day have a child. The finances of ballet and the prospect of touring for months on end made these goals distantly attainable at best. . . . I admit my mistake (in becoming a dancer): ballet is much more and much less than I'd imagined as an eighteen-year-old.[48]

The Republican Convention at Dallas in 1984 gave Ron the opportunity to become a newspaper columnist and, in the *Dallas Morning News,* he wrote that, ideally, "a candidate and his family should appear to the nation to be as accessible as Disneyland and just as harmless" except that, as regards the Reagan family, the "irony is that we are normal people" with all the normal virtues and vices, and the normal ambitions, desires, passions and eccentricities.[49]

Ron's subsequent assignments were both novel and diverse: he conducted a series of interviews with such prominent personalities as Jimmy Stewart, Tom Wolfe, and Fred Astaire, while, in 1984, he became a regular correspondent for The Source, NBC's rock radio network, of which he said

> . . . at 25, I'm right smack in the middle (of the rock 'n roll audience). I believe this audience identification is a tremendous advantage, and I plan to reflect it in my reporting on the movies.[50]

Also, in 1984, Ron covered his father's visit to Ballyporeen, Ireland, the village whence came one line of family ancestors, while in the following year he and his wife visited Moscow for the May Day celebration, and Geneva, for the historic event of the initial meeting between President Reagan and the Soviet leader, Mikhail Gorbachev. He has subsequently guest-hosted several television shows, such as ABC's "Good Morning America," and NBC's "Saturday Night Live." In his introductory comments on the latter program, he openly admitted that he was there "because my father is President of the United States," and later, one skit showed him dancing through the White House in "shirt tails and skivvies." His parents appear to have accepted his antics as an implicit ingredient of "show biz."

When directly confronted with the accusation that he was capitalizing on family connections, Ron, in an interview reported in a national weekly magazine, expressed his concern that people might think "I'm just taking advantage of the situation and grabbing for the golden ring. But then I think: who wouldn't jump at the opportunity? I'm working hard at my job and that's what counts,"[51] a statement, probably with which the first President, himself, would concur when his successor, John Adams, fearing the charge of nepotism, sought his advice in 1797 regarding the recall of his son, John Quincy Adams, then serving as U.S. Minister to Holland.

Notes

George Washington

[1] He was the son of Franklin's daughter Sarah.

[2] NDAB vol. 13., p. 265.

[3] Marcus Cunliffe states in a biographical article on George Washington that it was addressed to George Posey. *London Times:* Feb. 20/1982, p. 9.

[4] Miller: *Scandals in the Highest Office,* p. 53.

[5] George Washington was the eldest of the six children, and he outlived all nine of his siblings and half-siblings.

[6] In whose honor Lawrence named his estate on the Potomac.

[7] At one time he wrote "Would anyone believe that with 101 cows I would still be obliged to buy butter for my family?"

[8] Some time later Washington had reason to reproach his London agent for the poor quality of the clothing received.

[9] Where two half-brothers of Washington had been educated.

[10] Not all of Jacky's activities at the Boucher school could be classified as negative. In 1772 he brought as guest to Mount Vernon the artist Charles Willson Peale, who persuaded the reluctant Washington to sit for a three-quarter-length portrait in the blue and scarlet uniform of a Virginia colonel. In addition, Peale completed three miniatures, one each of George, Martha, and Jacky.

[11] In 1775 both Jacky and Nellie had accompanied Martha to the Army H.Q. at Cambridge, Massachusetts.

[12] Lund Washington was cousin to George Washington and had been resident at Mount Vernon since 1768 when he was appointed as estate manager to relieve George of some of his many duties.

[13] Nancy, Martha's favorite sister, had married a widower, Burwell Bassett, but she had passed away a year earlier, leaving a nine-year-old daughter, Fanny Bassett, who later came to live at Mount Vernon.

[14] Jacky's widow, Eleanor (Nellie) Calvert Custis's, continued to live on at Abingdon with the two oldest children. Some time later she fell in love with a neighbor widower, Dr. David Stuart, with children as old as she was. Hesitating to remarry, she consulted Washington, who replied that he had never expected her to spend the remainder of her life as a widow, but that she should exercise care in making her decision. Lund had already warned him of the growing friendship between the two persons to which Washington replied in writing: "For my part I never did, nor do I believe I shall ever give advice to a woman who is setting out on a matrimonial voyage, First because I could never advise anyone to marry without her own consent, and second, I know it is to no purpose to advise her to refrain when she has obtained it." Nellie did remarry and raised another brood of at least a dozen children.

[15] In due course Fanny married George Augustine Washington (son of George Washington's brother Charles) who came to Mount Vernon as his uncle's estate manager.

[16] Tobias Lear had moved with them from Mount Vernon, but had less time for the children, first because he functioned as part-time secretary to the President, and second, he remarried.

[17] Martha (Patty) Custis (17) married Thomas Peter, son of the former Mayor of Georgetown, in 1795, and Eliza Custis (19) married Thomas Law, a wealthy merchant in 1796.

[18] Washington did not leave him entirely bereft and had bequeathed him a square of land in the future federal District of Columbia. Martha, likewise, in her will provided him with a share of the furnishings at Mount Vernon, while he himself later purchased, in an auction settling the estate at Mount Vernon, the bedstead upon which Washington had died.

[19] Parke Custis, in his will, had requested that, five years after his death, all his slaves be freed. When that time came, Robert E. Lee, his executor, summoned as many of them as were within his lines, provided them with their papers of manumission as well as passes to move north to freedom through the Confederate lines.

[20] In a letter to John Augustine Washington (1736–1787), father of Bushrod Washington (1762–1824), eventually chosen by George Washington as heir to the Mount Vernon estate.

[21] He died in 1793.

[22] Harriot did plead to him for a "gettar" but he was some two years before getting around to accede to her request.

John Adams

[1] 90 years and 247 days.

[2] John Adams 1735–1826, Benjamin Franklin 1706–1790; Franklin once described Adams as "always an honest man, often a wise one, but sometimes in some things absolutely out of his senses."

[3] John, 1735–1826, Peter Boylston, 1738–1823, Elihu, 1741–1776.

[4] Meade Minnigerode. *Some American Ladies,* pp. 50–51.

[5] Minnigerode. *Op. cit.,,* p. 53.

[6] *Op.cit.,* p. 54.

[7] *Op. cit.,* p. 54.

[8] Abigail was ever a prolific letter writer and her letters were eventually published in two collections by her grandson, Charles Francis Adams.

[9] Named after Colonel Johnny Quincy, his maternal great grandfather who had died that same year, actually on John Quincy's christening day.

[10] Russell, *An American Dynasty,* p. 143.

[11] Minnegerode, p. 61.

[12] Mary Ormsby Whitton, *First First Ladies,* p. 24.

[13] Whitton, *op. cit.,* p. 26.

[14] Russell, *op. cit.,* p. 81.

[15] Russell, *op. cit.,* p. 81.

[16] The Treaty of Paris was signed on September 3, 1783.

[17] Francisco Miranda (1750–1816) was a Venezuelan revolutionary who had fought under George Washington against the British in 1783, and had later gone to Europe seeking support for the liberation of the Spanish colonies. In 1805 he recruited mercenaries in New York and set out to free Venezuela on his own, but was unsuccessful.

[18] Named after Baron Von Steuben, a Prussian soldier who had fought on the side of the colonies during the Revolutionary War, and was in command of a division at Yorktown. He was granted U.S. citizenship in 1783, and helped to organize the Society of the Cincinnati, a fraternal organization of Continental Army officers, of which he later became president and was succeeded in that office by William Stephen Smith.

[19] Dorothie Bobbe, *Abigail Adams,* p. 271.

[20] Concerning his election, John Adams wrote to Abigail the oft-quoted remark: "My country has in its wisdom contrived for me the most insignificant office that ever the invention of man contrived or his imagination conceived."

[21] When John Quincy appeared hesitant in accepting the appointment, John Adams urged him to "go and see with how little wisdom this world is governed."

Thomas Jefferson

[1] Shadwell was so named after the parish in London, England, where Jane Randolph had been born in 1720.

[2] Peter Jefferson was a surveyor by profession and is credited with having drawn the first accurate map of Virginia.

[3] Some 20 years were to elapse before he ever went overseas.

[4] A daughter of the couple was later to become the wife of Jefferson's kindred cousin, but political enemy, Chief Justice John Marshall.

[5] Among whom was the mulatto family of Hemings: the mother Ursala (Queenie) dominated the kitchen; her husband was known as King George.

[6] "At his death, 44 years later, locks of hair, and other little souvenirs of his wife and each of his children, both living and dead, with words of endearment written in his own hand, were found in a secret drawer of a cabinet." (McConnell)

[7] Shadwell had belonged to Jefferson's wife Martha, and its vocabulary was reputed to have consisted of "I want a bath!" "More water!" "More towel!" "Get the oap" (It could not sound an *s*).

[8] "Isabel" was Sally Hemings.

[9] Abigail in a letter to her son, John Quincy, had written: "I have had with me a fortnight a little daughter of Mr. Jefferson's who arrived here, with a young Negro girl, her servant from Virginia. Mr. Jefferson wrote me some months ago that he expected them, and desired me to receive them. I grew so fond of her and she was so attracted to me that, when Mr. Jefferson sent for her, we were obliged to force the little creature away. I could not help shedding a tear at parting with her. She was a favorite of everyone in the house. She is a beautiful little girl."

[10] Which also included Kayenlaha, a young Iroquois Indian boy brought by the Marquis from America.

[11] A few years before his death, Jefferson suffered another fall, this time breaking his left wrist, an accident which rendered him helpless ever again to write at all.

[12] Although Jefferson very much enjoyed traveling, he appeared to have reservations as to its benefits; he once wrote (1787) to his nephew, Peter Carr: "Travelling: This makes men wiser, but less happy. When men of sober age travel, they gather knowledge which they may apply usefully for their country, but . . . they learn new habits which cannot be gratified when they return home. Young men who travel are exposed to all these inconveniences in a

higher degree . . . They carry home only the dregs, insufficient to make themselves or anybody else happy . . ."

[13] Upon her enrollment at the convent Polly had become "Mademoiselle Polie," which later she changed to "Marie," while later, upon her return to the U.S., she became "Maria," by which name she became known to all the family, and it is "Maria," and not "Mary" which is inscribed upon her tombstone.

[14] This was the reputed beauty Gabriella Harvie, whom none of the family liked. The wedding took place after Tom's marriage to Patsy in 1791 but neither of them was invited to the ceremony.

[15] Jack was the son of Francis Eppes who was married to Elizabeth Wayles, half-sister of Martha Wayles, Jefferson's wife.

[16] Martha had hair as red as that of her father.

[17] Her widowed husband, John Wayles Eppes, took Francis to live with him. He later married Martha Jones, daughter of Colonel Willie Jones, revolutionary statesman from North Carolina. From 1803 to 1811 and again from 1813–51 John Eppes served as a (Jeffersonian) Republican in Congress, while from 1816–19 he was a U.S. Senator. He died in 1823. His second wife survived him by nearly 40 years.

[18] Jefferson's wife, Martha, was the daughter of John Wayles' first wife, who had died within three weeks of Martha's birth.

[19] He was later to state he "would never see the columns of the newspaper . . . for while I would be answering one, twenty new ones would be invented."

[20] Ellen Wayles was named after a baby of similar name born in 1793 but which lived for less than a year.

[21] Jefferson kept a "garden book" with regular entries from 1776 to 1824.

[22] Meriwether Lewis, hero of the famous Lewis and Clark expedition (1803–06), was Jefferson's private secretary 1801–03. Lewis was appointed Governor of Louisiana Territory after the expedition but was then disappointed in a love affair with Theodosia, daughter of Aaron Burr. He died mysteriously, possibly by suicide in 1809.

[23] Named after the professor at William and Mary College, Williamsburg, at whose home Martha had stayed as a child.

[24] The marriage proved to be felicitous (since 13 children were born to the happy couple) as well as long-lived since it terminated only with Jane's death 56 years later.

[25] Not long after, Bankhead left the country, along with Anne, who refused to leave him. He later returned in a somewhat better mood, but his temporary reform did little for Anne's happiness since she died in February, 1826, at the age of 35, the mother of four children.

[26] He attributed much of his longevity to his practice, extending over sixty years, of regularly bathing his feet in cold water every morning. He also prided himself on possessing most, if not all of his teeth, unlike George Washington who had lost them all.

[27] George later became a prominent lawyer in Virginia and served in the Confederate Army.

[28] Jeff was also his grandfather's literary executor and he was editor of *The Life and Correspondence of Thomas Jefferson* (4 volumes) published in 1829. For over thirty years he served as a member of the Board of Visitors of the University of Virginia, and for seven years he was rector of the university. During the Civil War he was commissioned as a colonel in the Confederate Army although, due to age, he saw no active service. In 1872 he was chairman of the national Democratic convention which nominated Horace Greeley as presidential candidate. Before his death in 1875 he published one other work: *Sixty Years' Reminiscences of the Currency of the United States,* a well-written, authoritative document.

[29] It later passed into the hands of Uriah Levy whose family retained possession (except for the brief period of the Civil War when the Confederate government confiscated the property) until 1923, when it was purchased by the Thomas Jefferson Memorial Foundation.

[30] John Quincy Adams, in response to an appeal by Monroe, had awarded Trist a clerkship in the State Department to help him support his family.

[31] Almost one hundred years later, the controversy over the association of Sally Hemings and Jefferson was revived when in 1974 Fawn Brodie, professor of history at the University of California, Los Angeles, published her book *Thomas Jefferson: An Intimate History.* In it, she appeared to substantiate the allegations that Jefferson was the father of Sally's children. A novel, *Sally Hemings* (1979) by Barbara Chase-Riboud, likewise assumed that an intimate love affair had existed between the two for over a thirty-year period. An effort to refute the allegations was made by Virginius Dabner, a Pulitzer Prize-winning journalist and historian, when in 1981 his work *The Jefferson Scandals: A Rebuttal* was published.

James Madison

[1] When James Madison, Sr., died in 1801 at age 77, the house and estate passed to James Madison who once described it as "only a squirrel's jump from heaven." Eleanor continued to live on there until her death at age 98.

[2] The epithet "great" was one justly conferred upon Madison since his career to date had been prestigious: at age 29 he was the youngest delegate to the Second Continental Congress at Philadelphia (1780–83); he had served on the Virginia Legislature (1784–87), and it was he who wrote the main draft of the Constitution of the United States, in recognition of which he has ever since been known as the "Father of the Constitution."

[3] His father was Colonel Samuel Washington, brother of George Washington.

[4] Madison's sister, Nelly, had married Major Isaac Hite. Their firstborn was named James Madison Hite.

5 The lack of offspring from the marriage was to provoke a spate of malicious gossip, particularly at election time, upon the theme of "sexual infidelity in the wife of an allegedly impotent husband."

6 Anna remained with the family until 1804 when she married Congressman Richard Cutts. She was nicknamed White Eyes by reason of her very pale blue eyes and very white skin.

7 Dubourg was a West Indian of French origin who in due course was elevated to the rank of archbishop.

8 Jackson experienced several misadventures while in Washington: one a fractured skull after being assaulted in the street by hoodlums, and from the other he suffered a bullet in his hip during a duel.

9 Phoebe was the daughter of the widowed Anthony Morris, a lawyer who had served as groom at the wedding of Dolley and John Todd.

10 The English had rejected the Czar's offer of mediation and had instead proposed a meeting in London or Ghent. Gallatin was awaiting approval from the U.S.

11 Gallatin wrote to Payne: "Permit me . . . to urge the propriety of your leaving Paris where you have remained long enough for every useful purpose. . . . I would be very sorry that either your propriety should be injured or your time improperly wasted by your trip to Europe and you must ascribe my anxiety solely to my attachment to you, your mother, and Mr. Madison."

12 Both Madison and Dolley had narrow escapes from capture, and Dolley is credited with having saved from the fire the famous full-length portrait of George Washington by Gilbert Stuart. It is believed that the term "White House" came first to be applied to the mansion as the result of a decision by James Hoban, the original architect, to paint the walls of the burnt building to cover the damage by the fire.

13 Commemorating a certain man, named Todd, member of a group of explorers, the Knights of the Golden Horseshoe, who had camped on the site en route for the Shenandoah Valley in 1716.

14 Vide, *The Incomparable Dolley,* p. 284.

15 In 1892, 3,000 of Madison's letters were sold by McGuire's heirs to Marshall Field on behalf of the Chicago Historical Society. In 1910 they were finally purchased by the U.S. government.

James Monroe

1 Monroe, always conscientious and of high moral rectitude, was yet never a person gifted with eloquent expression. In a letter to Jefferson announcing his marriage he wrote: "You will be interested to learn that I have formed the most interesting connection in human life with a young lady. . . ."

2 He was later to become one of the founder members of the New York Chamber of Commerce.

[3] This was Eliza, born in December, 1786.

[4] Mme. Campan was the eldest sister of Citizen Edmond Charles Genet, the tactless Minister of France to the United States (1793) whose recall to France was requested by George Washington. Upon hearing of his likely execution upon his return to France, he requested, and was granted, asylum to remain in the United States. He subsequently married the daughter of New York Governor George Clinton.

[5] There is no recorded name for the son, and upon the headstone of his grave there are the simple initials "J.S.M."

[6] Who claimed to be a younger son of the Earl of Erroll.

[7] John Quincy's wife, Louisa, was in full accord with her husband's assessment of Eliza Hay, describing her as being "full of agreeables and disagreeables, so accomplished and ill bred, so proud and so mean," and who had such a "love for scandal that no reputation is safe in her hands." Eliza Hay was not entirely an ungenerous person, for in 1820, when she was supervising wedding arrangements, she volunteered to assist as nurse to the fatally-ill five-month-old daughter of John Calhoun (Monroe's Secretary of War), and she is said to have sat up with the child for three consecutive nights with loving devotion.

[8] Following the return to Washington of the young couple after the honeymoon, festivities were planned in their honor, the first of which was that at the home of the Decaturs, but within two days Commodore Stephen Decatur died of wounds received in a duel. This led to the cancellation of all the other receptions. The Gouverneurs' first son, James Monroe Gouverneur, was born in the White House, but, not long afterwards, it was discovered to the great sorrow of the family that the child was a deaf-mute.

[9] It was one of Samuel's descendants, Mrs. Rose Gouverneur Hoes, who initiated the collection of First Lady dresses now on exhibit in the Smithsonian Institution.

John Quincy Adams

[1] She remains the only First Lady to be born overseas.

[2] John Quincy Adams recorded that upon arrival at the Brandenburg Gate in Berlin, the lieutenant in charge demanded to know, "Where are the United States of America?"

[3] In a letter to his brother, Thomas Boylston, John Quincy Adams wrote: ". . . I know not whether upon rigorous philosophical principles it be wise to give a great and venerable name to such a lottery-ticket as a new-born infant—but my logical scruples have in this case been over-powered by my instinctive sentiments."

[4] The Johnsons returned to the United States and, after his descent into bankruptcy, Joshua was appointed Superintendent of Stamps in the new Federal District of Washington by John Adams so that the family should not become destitute.

5 His brother, Thomas Boylston, wrote of Charles: "Let silence reign forever over his tomb."

6 Many texts suggest that a substantial part of John Adams' approval of his daughter-in-law arose out of the claim that her uncle, Thomas Johnson, was one of the signatories of the Declaration of Independence. Since his name does not appear on the document, her personal charm alone must have captivated him.

7 One of John Quincy's students was Edward Everett, a renowned orator of the mid-nineteenth century, but whose two-hour-long oration at Gettysburg was completely eclipsed by the two-minute presentation of Abraham Lincoln.

8 Named Charles after John Quincy's brother, and Francis, in honor of Francis Dana, for whom John Quincy had functioned as secretary in Moscow (1781–83).

9 He was the elder son of John Quincy's sister, Abby.

10 John Quincy had considered asking Czar Alexander I to be godfather of his only daughter, but upon reconsideration, he decided it would be too monarchical for American democratic sentiment.

11 Czar Alexander I had earlier volunteered to mediate between the United States and Britain, and an American peace mission (including John Payne Todd, son of Dolley Madison) had arrived in St. Petersburg, but the British, at that time, had appeared reluctant to end the war.

12 Entitled *Narrative of a Journey from Russia to France, 1815.*

13 John had died in 1834.

14 Nancy had died in 1810, and her husband, Walter Hellen, had died in 1815. The children had moved in permanently with John Quincy and Louisa in 1818.

15 This was the first marriage of a President's son at the mansion. Mary was to become Louisa's closest friend and confidante and was to live with her for the last years of her life.

16 Mary and her two young daughters were to take up permanent residence with John Quincy and Louisa.

17 Abigail's older sister, Charlotte Gray Brooks, was married to Edward Everett, Harvard professor, U.S. Congressman, and later Governor of Massachusetts and Ambassador to Great Britain.

18 Entry for 24 April, 1827.

19 Peter Brooks had announced his intention of bestowing his daughter with a $20,000 dowry upon marriage.

20 In October, 1843, John Quincy traveled to Cincinnati to lay the cornerstone for the first observatory in the United States.

21 Brooks was to be the last occupant of the Adams' home in Quincy. After his death it was dedicated as a memorial to the Adams' family.

22 In 1877 he completed the editing of the papers of his father, John Quincy Adams.

23 For his presentation at the Court of St. James, Charles dressed in a blue coat with gold buttons, white waistcoat and knee breeches, in contrast to two of his predecessors who had worn black, a distinction which apparently led Queen Victoria to express thanks that "we shall have no more American funerals."

Andrew Jackson

[1] The small community of Waxhow straddles the boundary of North and South Carolina and historians remain uncertain as to where precisely Jackson was born. The community itself settles the problem annually according to the result of the Old Hickory Football Classic when two high schools teams (representing the North and South State counties respectively) play each other, and the winning team assumes the right to display a stoneware bust of Andrew Jackson in its county courthouse—until such time as it is defeated—when the bust is transferred to the other county courthouse.

[2] Her father was Colonel Donelson, a prosperous ironmaster of Pittsylvania County, Virginia, and a member of the House of Burgesses. In 1779, he led an expedition of settlers westwards into the region now known as Tennessee, and he was among the earliest settlers of Nashville. He was killed by Indians in 1785, and his widow then set up a boarding house, where Andrew Jackson used to stay.

[3] There were seven other sons in the Donelson family.

[4] Vincent Nolte, *Fifty Years in Both Hemispheres* (New York, 1854), p. 238.

[5] Subsequently burned in 1831, and again in 1834, the original mansion was extensively remodelled after each calamity.

[6] One of Earl's paintings of Jackson on horseback was purchased in 1821 by the City of New Orleans. Seen by John James Audubon, the famous ornithological artist, he wrote of it: "Great God forgive me if my Jugment is Erroneous—I never saw a Worst painted sign in the streets of Paris."

[7] Major Lewis was Eaton's brother-in-law by reason of Eaton's first marriage.

[8] By so doing, Van Buren earned himself the appointment as Vice-President in Jackson's second administration, and as presidential nominee to succeed Jackson in the 1836 election.

[9] At one time she was seriously courted by Abraham Van Buren; then she became engaged to a naval captain whom she jilted after the wedding date had been set, but finally she settled down to marry Lucius J. Polk in April, 1832, and returned to live in Tennessee. (Lucius was a relative of James K. Polk, eleventh President of the U.S.).

[10] Until 1833, when Hutchings attained his majority, and Jackson handed his inheritance over to him. Providing him with two hundred dollars for expenses, Jackson arranged for him to learn plantation management with General John Coffee of Tennessee. In due course, Hutchings fell in love with the General's daughter, Mary (also a grandniece of Rachel Jackson), and the couple settled down to a happy marriage.

[11] While at the White House, young Andrew was described by a writer as having a countenance which "is sweetness and innocence itself, his eyes as soft as the dewdrop."

12 As was Senator Thomas Hart Benson who wrote of her: "She has the General's own warm heart, frank manners and hospitable temper; and no two persons could have been better suited to each other, lived more happily together, or made a house more attractice to visitors."

13 Jackson wrote: "I feel deeply indebted to you and my dear Sarah. Shall I be spared it will be a great pleasure to watch over and rear up the sweet little Rachel, and make her a fair emblem of her for whom she is called."

14 But these two loyal colleagues never submitted claims for the outstanding monies.

15 Within a month of the writing of the will, Sarah gave birth to her fourth child and third son named Robert Armstrong Jackson, but he died shortly afterwards. The other two sons were to serve in the Confederate Army.

16 In 1841, Donelson had remarried another cousin, Mrs. Elizabeth Martin Randolph, and proceeded to embark upon a distinguished diplomatic and political career. In 1844, President Tyler had appointed him U.S. chargé d'affaires to the Republic of Texas with instructions to negotiate with Sam Houston a treaty of annexation. This was successfully concluded in May, 1845, to Jackson's immense relief. In 1846, President Polk appointed Donelson as Minister to Prussia and, following his return to the United States in 1851, he entered the political arena. In 1856, he was nominated as vice-presidential candidate, with Millard Fillmore as presidential candidate, but after James Buchanan's victory, Donelson retired from politics and pursued his law practice in Memphis until his death in 1871.

17 us-the firm of Blair and Rives.

Martin Van Buren

1 Abraham had married a widow, Maria Hoes Van Alen, with three children; Martin was the third of five children born to Maria in her second marriage.

2 Upon his return to the United States, Van Buren's son had bestowed upon him the sobriquet of "Prince John."

3 John had gone to London on his personal legal business, but, at the same time, he had helped to negotiate, on behalf of his father, a U.S. settlement with Great Britain relating to the irritating border dispute with Canada, known as the Aroostook affair.

4 At the first White House reception following her return she wore an incredibly beautiful dress of royal blue velvet with a skirt ten yards full, and her headdress was crowned by three feathered plumes.

5 Johnson, nominated as Vice-President, did not receive a majority of the popular vote, and his election was subsequently decided in the Senate; this made him the only Vice-President in U.S. history to be so elected.

6 The Republican party, headed by Jackson, was officially transformed into the Democratic party at the Baltimore Convention of May, 1832.

[7] Historians often attribute the failure of Van Buren to be re-elected in 1840 to the ostentious image which he radiated from the White House, in distinct contrast to that portrayed by the buck-skin Jackson. In particular, his regular use of gold spoons (acquired by Monroe but seldom used by any subsequent President) at his informal dinners attracted much unfavorable publicity. In spring 1840, Charles Ogle (Pennsylvania) embarked on a three-day tirade in Congress, an effort which became known as the "Golden Spoon Speech," in which the Congressman soundly castigated Van Buren for his hedonistic way of life in the White House.

[8] Van Buren was nicknamed the "Fox of Kinderhook"; John became known as "Young Fox."

[9] She was to be the future aunt of both William and Henry James.

[10] After leaving Martin in London, Van Buren traveled to Scotland, Ireland, and Holland, where he visited the village of Buren, whence presumably came his ancestors, although he failed to trace any direct descendants still living in Holland. Van Buren, now over 70, appeared to have inexhaustible energy, such that his travelling companion and old friend, Gouverneur Kemble, was led to remark: "I was constantly in the situation of an old bachelor who had married a young wife."

[11] Abraham, who died in 1873, gave his father assistance in writing his autobiography, but it was never completed. The work related mainly to his political career and made scant reference to members of the family. The unfinished work was not finally published until 1920.

William Henry Harrison

[1] A variant of the slogan was "Hog and Hominy" which fared little better.

[2] The Whig slogan occurred purely as a matter of chance. A Democratic newspaper in Baltimore had scornfully derided Harrison's intellectual weaknesses, and had proposed that he had best return to a log cabin with a barrel of hard cider. It was the latter phrase which a Whig propaganda genius seized upon and employed to good effect during the campaign.

[3] Anna was the first First Lady not only to attend school on a regular basis, but to successfully pursue her studies to secondary level. She was educated first at Clinton Academy, Southwold, and then at a highly reputable boarding school for young ladies, that of Mrs. Isabella Grahams, on lower Broadway in New York City.

[4] At the age of four (in 1779), she had been taken by her father, wearing a British uniform, through the enemy lines to her maternal grandparents living in Southwold, Long Island.

[5] During the campaign, Harrison was to receive the support not only of "honest" Abe Lincoln, another log cabin pioneer, but also, unaccountably, of Chang and Eng, the famous Siamese twins.

6 His "family" included the daughter of Thomas Randolph, who had been killed at Tippecanoe, as well as James Spencer, son of Captain Spier Spencer (leader of an Indian fighter volunteer group, the Yellow Jackets, who also died at Tippecanoe). Harrison assisted James to graduate at West Point.

7 Carter became a lawyer, and, in 1836, he married Mary Anne Sutherland of Hamilton, Ohio, but he died suddenly three years later.

8 He was named after Dr. Scott who journeyed all the way from Lexington, Kentucky, to attend Mrs. Harrison at the time of his birth.

9 All six children of John Scott's second marriage were boys.

10 In 1836, Anna had married her second cousin, Colonel William Henry Harrison Taylor, but, in 1845, she died at age 32. Harrison's only other living daughter at the time of his presidency was Mary Symmes, who, in 1829, had married Dr. John Henry Fitzhugh Thornton. She died in 1842, at age 33.

11 By 1846, with the death of Betsy (Short), Harrison's first child and daughter, John Scott was the family's only surviving member.

John Tyler

1 In the case of Harrison, six of his children had died before he assumed the office of President, and only one of his children was to live to an age older than the father.

2 In addition to his 15 children, Tyler had at least 32 grandchildren, one-third of whom he never saw since they were the offspring of the children of his second marriage.

3 It was John Quincy Adams who made the sarcastic comment that he feared that Tyler's nose might cast a shadow to eclipse the granite obelisk of the Bunker Hill Monument upon the occasion of the dedication ceremony of 1843.

4 McConnell, *Our First Ladies*, p. ___.

5 Named after Tyler's oldest sister, in turn named after her grandmother, Anne Contesse, the daughter of a French Huguenot doctor. Tyler's sister had married James Semple, who became professor of law at William and Mary College, and it was with them that Tyler boarded when he attended the college.

6 Vol. 1, *Letters and Times of the Tylers*, p. 389.

7 *Op.cit.*, p. 548.

8 *Op.cit.*, p. 549.

9 *Op.cit.*, p. 392.

10 *Op.cit.*, p. 428.

11 This letter was dated December 28, 1831, so that the girls were aged, respectively, Letty (Letitia) 10, Lizzie (Elizabeth) 8, and Alice 4. When Tazewell was born in December, 1830, Tyler had written to Mary: "I have not yet fixed upon a name for him and incline to drop the family names altogether. Inform me of some one which may occur to you."

12 In one of his replies to Letitia's letters, he proudly announced:

> I have just found out the way to make ice cream in the shapes: It must be frozen in another vessel, stirred with a spoon until it gets pretty thick; then emptied into the shape and set in ice. So tell your mother. A teaspoonful of flour should be sifted through muslin into it.

[Vol. 1, *op. cit.*, p. 558]

13 He had earlier recommended to John: "Have *hours* for reading, and *minutes* for playing, and you will be a clever fellow."

14 In his letters to Mary, Tyler had already made ample reference to the great English writers of the Enlightenment period, and he had implored her not to regard the reading of the classics as labor; rather should she "consider that you are conversing with those great and wise men, and learning wisdom from their lips."

15 Vol. 1, *op.cit.*, p. 530.

16 Vol. 1, *op.cit.*, p. 531.

17 Her husband was William Nevison Waller of Williamsburg, and the marriage was eventually to be blessed with four children named Mary, William Jr., John, and Robert, respectively.

18 Sadler, *America's First Ladies*, p. 69.

19 Tyler, aware of the pitfalls of office, had, early in his tenure, provided his ' several "First Ladies" with the following advice: "My daughters, you are now occupying a position of deep importance. I desire you to bear in mind three things: show no favoritism, accept no gifts, receive no seekers after office."

20 Julia was known as "The Rose of Long Island" since she had permitted a colored lithograph of herself, with that title, to be used as an advertisement for a New York store. Accompanying her picture was the statement: "I'll purchase at Bogert and Mecamly's . . . their goods are beautiful and astonishingly cheap."

21 Julia recorded the event in a letter:

> . . . He welcomed us with an urbanity which made the deepest impression upon my father, and we could not help commenting. After we left the room, upon the silvery sweetness of his voice, that seemed in just attune with the incomparable grace of his bearing, and the elegant case of his conversation . . . .

22 After signing the formal document of the annexation of Texas days before his tenure ended, Tyler gave Julia the pen he had just used, and thereafter she wore it proudly as a pendant around her neck.

23 *Letters and Life of the Tylers*, pp. 454–5.

24 Kossuth, the leader of the Hungarian patriots, visited the United States in 1851 and was accorded a hero's welcome.

25 *Letters and Life of the Tylers*, p. 534.

26 *Op.cit.*, p. 554.

27 *Op.cit.*, p. 557.

28 In his final will Tyler bequeathed to his daughter, Julia, (of his second marriage) "her choice of the negro girls under her own age as a maid servant, and I hope my wife will, upon each of our children (the boys) obtaining the age of 21 years, select for each a negro boy as his separate property."

[29] Many years earlier, at the time of the Mexican War, Robert had been instrumental in raising a regiment in Philadelphia but the government declined his services on account of the number of volunteers already in the field.

[30] The first pensions specifically accorded to presidential widows were awarded by Congress in 1882 to Lucretia Garfield and Sarah Polk, respectively. Each received $5,000 annually.

James Polk

[1] Hence, Polk's sobriquet of "Young Hickory."

[2] He wrote: "I yielded to the request of an artist named Brady of New York by sitting for my daguerrotype likeness today." Matthew Brady was later to gain fame for his Civil War photographs.

Zachary Taylor

[1] Over a hundred years later another First Lady, Mamie Eisenhower, was to comment upon her identical experience of endless camp existence after her marriage to Dwight Eisenhower.

[2] Fort Knox, itself, was named in honor of Henry Knox, general in the Revolutionary War, who followed Washington as commander of the Continental Army.

[3] Margaret Taylor always kept at the ready a loaded pistol in the pocket of her army greatcoat in the event of an attack by marauding Indians.

[4] Tyler once wrote "The rearing up [of] our children and establishing them in life so that they can sustain themselves is in my opinion the most important of our duties."

[5] Their elder son, John Taylor Wood, was the first white child to be born in Minnesota, and he later served as a Confederate naval officer.

[6] As Taylor stated to one of his colleagues: "I will be damned if another daughter of mine shall marry into the army. I know enough of the family life of officers. I scarcely know my own children or they me. I have no personal objection to Lieutenant Davis."

[7] Walter L. Fleming, *Jefferson Davis' First Marriage,* Mississippi Historical Society vol. 12, p. 25.

[8] Fleming, *op. cit.,* pp. 28–29.

[9] Fleming, *op. cit.,* pp. 31–32.

[10] Fleming, *op. cit.,* p. 32.

[11] While on the riverboat on his way to the wedding Davis accidentally encountered his former father-in-law, but the meeting was apparently a cordial one, with Taylor exhibiting no feelings of resentment. Davis was warmly appreciative of Taylor's effort at reconciliation.

12 After hearing Davis' first speech in Congress, John Quincy Adams was said to have made the comment: "That young man will make a mark in American history."

13 After his nomination at the Whig Convention of 1848, Taylor's letter of acceptance had been delayed because he had refused the postage on the mounting quantity of mail being sent to him. This was the time when prepaid postage was not the custom and Taylor had resented the cost of postage for unsolicited mail. Eventually he did reply to a duplicate letter of nomination.

14 Taylor had written to Davis in September, 1850: "I wish you to pursue that course . . . which your good sense, interest (and) honor prompt you to do . . . even if not in accordance with my views . . . it will not interrupt our personal intercourse, or my esteem and friendship for you."

15 Margaret Taylor remains the only First Lady of whom there is no portrait, engraving, or photograph.

Millard Fillmore

1 In the middle of his (vice) presidential campaign, Fillmore took time out to send his daughter a case of the finest available peaches as a reward for a good school report.

2 A news item described her as "full of vivacity, of intellect, of cordiality and of goodness."

3 On his visit to England he politely declined an honorary degree, (whose citation was written in Latin), from the University of Oxford, stating "I had not the advantage of a classical education and no man should, in my judgment accept a degree he cannot read."

4 Her husband was Ezekiel McIntosh, who acquired his fortune as builder of the Mohawk and Hudson Railroad between Albany and Schenectady.

Franklin Pierce

1 It was said that Appleton worked and prayed himself to death (in 1819). He ate sparingly to avoid having to exercise, and he allowed himself only four hours of sleep so that he could devote more time to his work. He died of consumption leaving behind a widow with six children. Jane was aged 13 at the time of her father's death, and was already tubercular.

2 From her cousin, Senator-elect Atherton.

3 The country was left without a Vice-President from 1853 until 1857, when John C. Breckinridge of Kentucky was appointed to the office by President Buchanan.

4 She was the second wife of one of Jane's uncles.

5 Charles Mason of the Patent Office wrote of it in his diary: "Everything in that mansion seems cold and cheerless. I have seen hundreds of log cabins which seemed to contain more happiness."

6 Jane Pierce always wore black, and hers is the only black dress in the Smithsonian collection of the dresses of the First Ladies.

James Buchanan

1 At the time of his departure for England, Buchanan was uncle to at least 22 nieces and nephews, and 13 grandnieces and grandnephews. He provided full financial support for at least seven of the foregoing relatives who were orphans, and he displayed concern for the well-being of most of the others. It is claimed by some biographers that Buchanan feared for the welfare of this extensive brood of relatives if he were to remarry.

2 Buchanan also brought in his nephew, Colonel Lane, to act as his private secretary.

3 Later Presidents were to add still more greenhouses until Theodore Roosevelt called a halt to the process and had them all demolished.

4 Harriet died in 1903.

Abraham Lincoln

1 In 1826 she married Aaron Grigsby, but two years later she died in childbirth (as did the baby).

2 See below, p. 222.

3 Apparently, she had, earlier, been courted by Stephen A. Douglas, Lincoln's presidential opponent in the 1860 election.

4 Lincoln jocularly remarked of the wedding that it epitomized "the long and short of it," he being taller than six feet, while Mary was at least one foot shorter. Later in the same month he concluded a letter to a friend with the comment, "Nothing new here except my marrying, which to me, is a matter of profound wonder."

5 The boy waas possibly so named because Mary's father donated $112 annually to the family until Lincoln had established himself securely in his law practice; in all, he gave them over $1,100.

6 He was named for Dr. William Wallace, husband of Mary's sister, Frances.

7 Upon being informed of his defeat, Lincoln, likening himself to the little boy who had stubbed his toe, said, "It hurt too bad to laugh, and he was too big to cry."

[8] Photographer McNulty had Lincoln pose with his beard before his final departure from Springfield, and it is this likeness of him which appears on the $10 bill.

[9] Lincoln's victory was achieved as the result of a split in the Democratic party: He polled 1.8 million votes; his opponents 1) Stephen A. Douglas (Democrat) polled 1.3 million, and 2) John C. Breckenridge (Southern Democrat) polled 0.8 million votes.

[10] Just one month earlier, at the inauguration ceremony, Robert unwittingly gave his father reason for great anxiety by mislaying the wallet containing the Inaugural Address. Fortunately, it was recovered before the presidential train arrived at Washington.

[11] Ruth Painter Randall, *Mary Lincoln*, p. 274.

[12] Randall, *op. cit.*, p. 272.

[13] Baker had been a close colleague of Lincoln's, and the latter's second son, Edward Baker Lincoln (1846–1850), had been named in his honor.

[14] Elizabeth Keckley, *Behind the Scenes*, pp. 99–100.

[15] Randall, *op. cit.*, p. 290.

[16] Emilie was again at the White House during the summer of 1864 when, destitute, she came to plead with Lincoln to permit movement of her cotton crop from the South to the North so that it could be sold. Lincoln refused. Emilie had a little daughter, Katherine, who had arguments with young Tad as to who was President of the United States, since she claimed it was Jefferson Davis. In attempting to settle the question, Lincoln set up each child on one knee saying, "Well Tad, you know who is your President, and I am your little cousin's Uncle Lincoln."

[17] Another of Mary's relatives, her half-sister, Martha White, of Selma, Alabama, had been granted permission to come North, but, according to the newspapers, she had returned with trunks full, not of her personal possessions, but of medicine of use to the Confederate Army in the treatment of its wounded.

[18] Randall, *op. cit.*, pp. 281–91.

[19] At a later date, Carl Sandburg encapsulated Mary Todd as a "cultivated wildcat" and her husband as a "slowmoving wilderness bear."

[20] Once, when Lincoln was reviewing the Union troops, Tad stood behind him waving the Confederate flag.

[21] One medium, Mrs. Nettie Colburn Maynard, later wrote a book, *Was Abraham Lincoln a Spiritualist?* (Philadelphia, 1891).

[22] Robert's unduly serious view of life very much affected his behavior while on vacation from college at the White House. He seldom tolerated Tad's innumerable pranks, and never went to the theater which Lincoln and Mary so very much enjoyed.

In February, 1863, there occurred the famous "Romance of the Dwarfs" when "General" Tom Thumb (Charles Sherwood Stratton) married Miss Lavinia Warren. They came to Washington and a hasty reception on their behalf was held at the White House. Robert refused to attend, telling his mother, "I do not propose to assist in entertaining Tom Thumb. My notions of duty perhaps are somewhat different from yours."

23 Not until 1870 did Congress provide her with a presidential widow's pension of $3,000, a sum increased to $5,000 in 1882.

24 Upon hearing of Lincoln's election as President, Mary had taken train to New York to purchase a wardrobe for her forthcoming role as First Lady, but she had not anticipated that Washington society patronized only the latest Parisian fashions, against which she could not possibly compete.

25 It is recorded that, on one spending spree, Mary purchased three evening dresses ($5,000), a lace shawl ($500), along with no fewer than 300 pairs of gloves.

26 Robert had been formally admitted to the Illinois bar in 1867.

27 Mary obtained only $800 from the sale of her belongings in New York.

28 A parody of the book appeared under the title *Behind the Seams* by Betsy Kickley.

29 Ruth Painter Randall, *Mary Lincoln*, p. 407.

30 In 1869 she had received news of a daughter born to Robert and Mary which they had named Mary Lincoln in her honor. She wrote immediately to Mary: "That blessed baby, how dearly I would love to look upon her sweet young face. . . . I do so trust that Bob will come over with you, if it is only for three months." Mary always referred to her granddaughter as 'Little Mamie."

31 Randall, *op. cit.*, p. 418.

32 In a letter dated April 5, 1882, Robert wrote:

Poor Tad was a good boy and extraordinarily affectionate & firm in his friendships . . . he studied diligently and overcame the defect in his speech. He was only 18 when he died, but he was so manly & self reliant that I had great hopes of his future. He was cut off by his death after a torturing illness."

33 Her loneliness upon arrival at New York must have been intense, since, at the dockside, tumultuous greetings were accorded Sarah Bernhardt who was traveling on the same boat. Mary Lincoln was ignored.

34 In June, 1879, Mary read a reference in the *American Register* published in Paris that Robert was being considered as a possible presidential candidate. Family pride temporarily surged to the surface of her resentment against her son and she wrote to Lewis: "Little Mamie with her charming manners and presence, in the event of success will grace the place," i.e. the White House.

35 Robert, by some coincidental quirk of fate, was close in attendance at the time of the assassination of three presidents: in 1865, he was at his father's deathbed; in 1882, he arrived at the railroad station in Washington just minutes after the shooting of Garfield; and, in 1901, he was at the Pan-American Exhibition at Buffalo, where he visited McKinley after he, too, had been shot.

36 In the *Illinois State Journal* of August 31, 1887, Robert is quoted as having stated:

As to being a candidate for the Presidency, I regret the use of my name in connection with any public office whatever. It seems difficult for the average American to understand that it is possible for anyone not to desire the Presidency, but I most certainly do not. I have seen enough of the inside of Washington official life to have lost all interest for it.

The Presidential office is but a gilded prison. Its cares and worries outweigh the honor which surrounds the position. I don't think there's any likelihood of my receiving the nomination. The men who make the ticket would hardly do so without exacting certain pledges, and those pledges I would not give. [J. J. Perling, *President's Sons,* p. 145].

[37] Abraham's body was buried in the family crypt at Springfield, but, since his father Robert was interred in Arlington, Robert's wife, Mary Harlan, had Abraham's body disinterred for reburial with his father in 1930. After her death in 1937 she, too, was buried at Arlington.

[38] Robert fervently dismissed all comparisons made between himself and his father. He brushed them aside by his simple statement, "My father was a great man. I am not."

[39] The misuse and falsification of statements innocent or otherwise by William Herndon (as well as by Elizabeth Keckley) might well have influenced Robert in this action.

[40] In 1921, Robert deposited with the Library of Congress at least 10,000 documents relating to his father's career. They were to be preserved from inspection until 21 years after his (Robert's) death. They were made available for research in 1947. Of all these documents there was only one letter preserved between father and son.

[41] The famed English dramatist, George Bernard Shaw, was cynically led to comment upon the change of venue by remarking that, a sloppily dressed statute of the Great Emancipator would have been more appropriately sited near London's Parliament, which, he alleged, housed the worst-dressed men in the whole of Britain.

[42] He had had installed at his home a well-equipped observatory.

[43] In 1897, Jessie had eloped with Warren Beckwith while they both attended Iowa Wesleyan College, where he was a football star. Their son, Robert Todd Lincoln Beckwith, was born in 1904, and became a law graduate of Georgetown University. Before his death in December, 1985, he had donated most of the remaining documents pertaining to his famous great-grandfather to the state of Illinois.

Andrew Johnson

[1] Johnson escaped conviction by only one Senate vote.
[2] His mother, Mary McDonough Johnson, was later remarried to Turner Dougherty, also of Raleigh, N.C.

[3] The master tailor, James J. Selby, published an advertisement on June 24, 1824, in the local newspapers, offering a ten-dollars reward "to any person who will deliver said apprentices to me in Raleigh, or I will give the above reward for Andrew Johnson alone." Andrew was described as being "very fleshy, freckled face, light hair, and fair complexion."

[4] Johnson married at a younger age than any other President.

[5] He was commissioned as Assistant Surgeon in the Middle Tennessee Infantry Regiment.

[6] The crucial vote, in Johnson's favor, was cast by Kansas Senator Edmund Gibson Ross. Ross was anti-Johnson in sentiment but he believed that an impeachment precedent would greatly impair presidential power. The vote cost him his political career.

[7] Sadler, *America's First Ladies*, p. 116.

[8] He was buried under the branches of a willow tree which he himself had planted, and which was alleged to have been an offshoot of a tree which overlooked the burial place of Napoleon on St. Helena. Johnson's funeral was covered by a cub-reporter of the *Louisville Courier-Journal:* he was Adolph Ochs, later to become the famous editor of the *New York Times.*

Ulysses S. Grant

[1] Her slight squint was attributed to a boating accident in her youth.

[2] His lack of success on the Pacific coast was in direct contrast to his activities during the Mexican War, when, during periods of boredom, he went into the bakery business, and later wrote in his memoirs that "in two months I made more money for the (regimental) fund than my pay amounted to during the entire war."

[3] Their second son, Ulysses S. Grant II ("Buck"), was born on July 22, 1852, but Grant did not hear of his birth until the following December, upon receipt of Julia's first letter.

[4] *In the Days of My Father, General Grant,*

[5] Grant had apparently once replied to the question as to what political office he aspired, by stating that his one and only ambition was to be Mayor of Galena, and that was only for the purpose of fixing the sidewalks, "especially the one reaching to my house." When he subsequently visited Galena in 1865, he was greeted with the prominently displayed sign: "General, the sidewalk is built." Grant was reduced to tears when he learnt also that the city had purchased his old home and was now presenting it to him in recognition of his service to the nation.

[6] Grant installed the library in the White House and it had the indirect and unexpected consequence of making his son, Fred, into a nationally recognized bibliophile, who, during the 1880's, came to acquire the most extensive collection of first editions of books and pamphlets of Dr. Samuel Johnson and

Alexander Pope in the United States. The library was inherited by Fred's brother, Buck, who took it with him to San Diego. In 1952, it was purchased by Dawson's Book Shop, who offered the volumes for sale individually.

7 Within the same decade, however, a black cadet, Henry O. Flipper, did successfully graduate from West Point (in 1877).

8 Recounting the episode with great glee upon many a subsequent occasion, Fred alleged that the Sultan's pants must have consisted of at least twenty yards of material.

9 Ida's sister, Mrs. Potter Palmer, was a prominent member of Chicago society.

10 October 21, 1874, quoted by J. J. Perling, *The Presidents' Sons,* p. 168.

11 In September, 1899, at Newport, Rhode Island, Julia married Prince Cantacuzene, a major-general in the Russian Army. She went to live in Russia and, during World War I, she served with the Russian Red Cross and was decorated for her services. After the Revolution she returned to the U.S. and took up residence in Florida. She wrote several books relating to life in Russia, and she was very active in the lecture circuit. She died in 1975.

Fred and Ida's second child, Ulysses S. Grant III, was born in 1881. He followed a military career and rose to the rank of major-general. He maintained the family interest in Grant's contribution to military history and his work, *Ulysses S. Grant: Warrior and Statesman,* was published (posthumously) in 1969. He married Edith, daughter of Elihu Root, statesman and 1912 Nobel Peace Prize recipient.

12 Ulysses III was the son of Fred and Ida.

Ulysses IV was the son of Ulysses II and Fannie.

Ulysses V was the son of Chapman Grant, the son of Jesse.

13 Wm. McFeely, *Grant,* p. 400.

14 Borie had once been Grant's Secretary of the Navy, but he had resigned in 1869 to devote himself to the task and pleasures of making a fortune, which he did.

15 Helen Todd, *A Man Named Grant,* p. 458.

16 At Cheltenham, near Philadelphia.

17 He wrote of these to his father and said, "I want to come home." Grant sent a telegram: "We want you too. Come home at once."

18 In another episode relating to Jesse, his mother recalled a visit made by Grant and the family to Detroit. Crowds gathered outside the hotel to greet the President, who, however, was reluctant to make a speech, whereupon young Jesse strode out on the balcony and promptly began a recitation of "The boy stood on the burning deck. . . ." Grant was left with no alternative, and went out to address his (and Jesse's!) admirers.

19 In 1921, members gathered for a formal 50th anniversary celebration at the Army and Navy Club in Washington, and, in that same year, one of its members, the Rev. Charles Morris D.D., published a history of the activities under the title: *Half Century of the K.F.R. Society.*

20 They did see her again a year later while she, along with her husband and his parents, was on vacation in Italy. They spent time together in Rome (where the Grants were received by the Pope), Florence, and other cities before journeying

back to Paris. It was after a visit to Venice that Grant made his oft-quoted remark that "it would be a fine city if they drained it."

21 In Egypt, Julia had bought some expensive ostrich feathers, which, upon returning to America, she found to be a perfect nuisance. In her *Memoirs* she added: "Let me give a bit of advice here. Only buy what you need. You can buy everything in New York better and cheaper than you can import it yourself."

22 On board ship, Fred read Thackeray's *Vanity Fair,* and came to the conclusion that the main character, Becky Sharp, must have been modeled upon a woman of his acquaintance in Washington.

23 Commenting on the Taj Mahal at Agra, Julia stated: "Everyone says it is the most beautiful building in the world; and I suppose it is. Only I think that everyone has not seen the Capitol in Washington."

24 He never received more than 313 votes; an absolute majority demanded 370.

25 When she had been obliged to vacate the executive mansion in March, 1877, she had wailed "Oh Ulys, I feel like a waif, like a waif on the world's wide common!" (*Memoirs,* p. 197).

26 The cancer was said to have had its origin at the time of the Civil War when Grant received hundreds of cigars from grateful admirers: he claimed he had no alternative but to smoke them. But after the supply was exhausted he continued the habit, smoking as many as 25 a day. When cancer was diagnosed, Grant stated "A verb is anything that signifies to be, to do, or to suffer. I signify all three."

27 Edition of May 10, 1884: quoted in J. J. Perling, *The Presidents' Sons,* p. 176.

28 Fred lost his savings in the Ward fiasco. Creditors repossessed his home in Morristown, N.J., so that he, his wife, and their two children were forced to move in temporarily with Grant and Julia in their New York home.

29 Thus, while he was U.S. Grant, his wife was America Grant.

30 *Letters of Henry James,* vol. 2, pp. 233–4.

31 Julia, like her husband, also wrote her *Memoirs,* and was the first First Lady to do so; but, unlike her husband, she failed to secure a publisher, and the *Memoirs* did not see the light of day until 1975.

32 When, in due course, the German Emperor was known to be seriously considering the prospect of a Berlin to Baghdad railroad the news spread convulsions throughout the foreign offices of the Western European powers.

Rutherford Hayes

1 Hayes's election as President remains one of the most controversial in U.S. history. In terms of the popular ballot he received only 4 million votes compared with 4.3 million cast for Samuel Tilden. In the electoral college, Tilden had 184 votes and Hayes 165, but 185 votes were needed. Twenty votes were in dispute, and Congress spent four months before deciding on March 2,

1877 (three days before the inauguration), that the crucial votes were to be cast in favor of Hayes.

[2] The college was the first chartered institution of higher education for women, and Lucy was the first college graduate to serve as First Lady.

[3] Hayes, *Diary*, vol. 1, p. 456.

[4] Lucy's grandfather was Isaac Cook.

[5] Hayes, *Letters*.

[6] Hayes, *Letters*. vol. 2, p. 437.

[7] Hayes, *Diary*, vol. 3, p. 257.

[8] Hayes, *Diary*, vol. 3, pp. 218–9.

[9] Hayes, *Diary*, vol. 3, p. 257.

[10] Webb was to become a manufacturer of house-building hardware in Cleveland.

[11] Hayes, *Diary*, vol. 3, p. 257 (August 13, 1874).

[12] Hayes, *Diary*, vol. 3, p. 267. (Feb. 22, 1875) Hayes approved generally of the college facilities, and advised Ruddy to buy "a few good strongchairs," but "*no* rockingchair." What he most disapproved of was the "two-in-a-bed system. It is bad." He recommended that, unless Ruddy had already done so, he had best not tell his mother "of the doubling in bed."

[13] Scott was only 4!

[14] She purchased a dinner service of almost 1,000 pieces, for which future First Ladies were no doubt most appreciative. Since she (and Hayes) refused to serve any alcohol at official receptions, she became known to posterity as "Lemonade Lucy."

[15] Of one of these parties held in March, 1880 (given by the children's dancing master), Hayes commented that "Fanny was beautiful as Martha Washington, and Scott as an orderly sergeant of the Twenty Third. Fanny copied the picture in the East Room."

[16] Initiated by Dolley Madison.

[17] It was Hayes who had installed the first telephone in the White House.

[18] Hayes, *Diary*, September 20, 1888.

[19] Hayes, *Diary*, March 19, 1892.

[20] Hayes, *Letters*, November 12, 1882.

[21] Hayes, *Letters*, January 13, 1883.

[22] Hayes, *Letters*, June 1, 1883.

[23] Hayes, *Letters*, December 11, 1883.

[24] Hayes, *Letters*, January 29, 1884.

[25] Hayes, *Letters*, January 14, 1885.

[26] Hayes, *Letters*, January 24, 1886.

[27] Hayes, *Letters*, March 6, 1887.

[28] Hayes, *Letters*, December 18, 1887.

[29] She again visited Bermuda in 1890, this time in the company of her father, and two of her brothers, Webb and Rutherford.

[30] He died on January 17, 1893, at age 70.

[31] His business eventually developed into the prestigious Union Carbide Corporation, and he amassed a substantial fortune.

[32] President McKinley and his invalid wife were inseparable, but at the time of the signing of the documents relating to the U.S. declaration of war on Spain, Mrs. McKinley was in New York. The President, feeling depressed and lonely, asked Webb to sleep at the White House in his wife's twin brass bed.

[33] Webb had also served in Mexico in 1916–17, and in Italy in 1917.

James Garfield

[1] The escapade was later exploited by Horatio Alger in his biography of Garfield entitled *From Canal Boy to President*.

[2] Eliza Ballou, and Arabella Green Mason Rudolph, respectively.

[3] Edward (Neddie) was still without a name six weeks after his birth, since his parents had expected a girl baby and, accordingly, had prepared only a list of female names. Garfield commented: "The sixth is a little harder to name than the first or second!"

[4] Ruth S-B Feis, *Mollie Garfield in the White House*.

[5] Leech and Brow, *The Garfield Orbit*, p. 189.

[6] Leech and Brown, *op.cit.*, p. 189.

[7] *Ibid*.

[8] Leech and Brown *op. cit.*, p. 190.

[9] Leech and Brown *op. cit.*, p. 190–1. He also sent the children puzzles to solve as, for instance, the following: "When I went to bed it was just 12 o'clock at night by Toledo time, but it was 12:28 by my watch, which is Washington time. Now please take a piece of paper out of the lower drawer of my desk and cipher out how many degrees west of Washington I am." (Allan Peskin, *Garfield*, p. 390.)

[10] One of the main features of the home was its library of more than 3,000 books. Both Garfield and his wife had been teachers, and they retained their love of good literature, and made every effort to transmit this love to their children by ever reading to them. Mollie's daughter, Ruth, was led to comment that the family motto might well have been taken from Tennyson's "Denone": "Self-reverance, self-knowledge, self-control; these three alone lead life to sovereign power."

[11] There was one moment of great anxiety, when Mollie's horse shied; she was unseated and thrown to the ground but with one foot caught in the stirrup. She was dragged along some distance until Jim managed to stop her horse. Fortunately, there were no lasting injuries.

[12] Jim was once described by a newspaper reporter: "as a rollicking boy. He is never known to be still unless asleep. He masters his studies almost without effort. At school he excels on the trapeze and the springboard. At home he

stands on his head, walks on his hands with his heels up, turns handsprings and somersaults, and jumps the fence in preference to opening the gate."

[13] Lucretia G. Comer, *Strands from the Weaving,* p. 20.

[14] One of his college classmates at the convention sent a telegram to Mark Hopkins: "Glory to God, glory to Williams, glory to Garfield." (Leech and Brown, *op. cit.,* pp. 208–9).

[15] Comer: *Strands from the Weaving,* p. 24.

[16] Leech and Brown *op. cit.,* p. 310.

[17] Lucretia Comer, *Strands from the Weaving,* p. 28.

[18] He was to deliver the commencement address on the occasion of the 25th anniversary of his graduation from the college.

[19] He had, that morning, entered his son's bedroom singing his favorite tune "I Mixed Those Babies Up" from Gilbert and Sullivan's *H.M.S. Pinafore.*

[20] To relieve Garfield of the anxiety concerning the future of his young family, Cyrus W. Field (promoter of the first transatlantic cable), proposed that a fund of $250,000 be raised on their behalf. The project was successful, and the amount subscribed eventually exceeded $350,000.

[21] During the course of his studies at Columbia, Harry spent one semester studying law at Oxford and Lincoln's Inn, London.

[22] Belle was the daughter of James Mason, a prominent Cleveland attorney.

[23] When World War I broke out, Harry and his family (except for his son, Mason) were in Austria, and it was with some difficulty that they made their way, first to Munich, and eventually to London, whence they left by boat in September, 1914, for home.

[24] He was survived by his wife, and four children, James, Mason, Stanton, and Lucretia. The latter (Mrs. John Preston Comer) wrote a biography of her father entitled, *Strands from the Weaving* (1959).

[25] *New York Times,* Obituary notice, March 25, 1950.

[26] Cavanah, *They Lived in the White House,* pp. 98–99.

[27] In 1897 he married Sarah Granger Williams, daughter of Edward Porter Williams, co-founder of the Sherwin-Williams Company, paint manufacturers.

Chester Arthur

[1] The state of Vermont in 1954 placed a plaque to commemorate Arthur's birth on the wall of the "new" manse, but this had been built in 1829. Arthur was named Chester, in honor of Dr. Chester Abell, the physician who attended his birth, and Alan, in honor of his paternal grandfather.

[2] Its president, Dr. Eliphalet Nott, had admitted so many boys expelled from other schools that the college became nicknamed as "Botany Bay." Union has an enduring place in U.S. college history since it was here that the first of the Greek letter fraternities was instituted.

[3] In his letter of dismissal to Arthur, President Hayes wrote: "You have made the Custom House a center of partisan political management. . . . With a deep sense of my obligation under the Constitution, I regard it my plain duty to suspend you" (Perling, p. 221).

[4] Following his election as Vice-President in 1880, it was alleged that Arthur was not a U.S. citizen but had been born in Canada, of a British father and an American mother. The "facts" were published in a pamphlet entitled *How a British Subject Became President of the United States,* authored by Arthur P. Hinman, a New York attorney.

[5] Arthur had several large greenhouses built on the White House grounds to ensure an all-the-year round supply of flowers in season.

[6] He reputedly would order 25 suits at a time and was the first President to employ a valet.

Grover Cleveland

[1] Oscar Folsom was the name of Cleveland's law partner in Buffalo, and the Democratic district leader.

[2] The *American Heritage Pictorial History of the Presidents of the United States,* vol. 2, p. 556.

[3] The "kid" was adopted by one of Cleveland's friends, who provided him with a good education, such that he was subsequently qualified as a physician. Maria Halpin latter married, but years later she wrote to Cleveland demanding money, but he did not answer any of her letters.

[4] Cleveland's brother, William, a Presbyterian minister, officiated at the ceremony.

[5] Allan Nevins, ed., *Letters of Grover Cleveland,* p. 264.

[6] After his success in being renominated in the first ballot of the Chicago Convention in June, 1892, Cleveland wrote to thank Wilson Bissell for his assistance. Bissell was also at this time a proud father and Cleveland added the comment: "I don't see how your baby got 'them teeth.' Ours could have plenty of them, I suppose if she wanted them, but she don't eat any wasted beef or things of that kind—so that's the use? . . ." (Nevins, *op. cit.,* p. 289).

[7] This was after Cleveland's operation for carcinoma of the jaw. It was one of the best-kept secrets of the century, the operation being conducted on board a ship, and it entailed removal of part of the jaw and its replacement by a rubber insert. The operation took place on July 1, and the President made such a remarkable recovery that he was able to address a meeting of Congress on August 7.

[8] Nevins, *op. cit.,* p. 335.

[9] During the campaign preceding the election of 1892, Cleveland found himself accused of abusing his wife, and Frances was obliged to make a public statement refuting all the unfounded allegations. The occasion was by no

means unique, since throughout his presidential career, Cleveland appeared to have undergone a sequential barrage of accusations involving immoral conduct, many of them by religious leaders who obviously had never forgiven him for his earlier indiscretion in allegedly fathering an illegitimate child.

10 He did play center but only in 1916.

11 Nevins, *op. cit.*, p. 488.

12 Nevins, *op. cit.*, pp. 569–70.

13 *New York Times*, March 11, 1960.

14 More than thirty years after the Clevelands had left the White House, Marion was invited to the presidential mansion by President Hoover's wife, Lou Henry. When she stepped out of the elevator she noticed "a sweet musty scent," resembling that of roses, but she saw none. Marion said "Later I asked my mother about it. She told me that when we lived in the White House she had always kept roses upstairs. The memory of their fragrance must have come back to me across the years." (Cavanah, *They Lived at the White House*, p. 115).

15 Perling, *The Presidents' Sons*, p. 230.

16 Perling, *op. cit.*, 232: "Called 'Dick' by his classmates, he was voted the 'most thorough gentleman,' the 'most respected,' and also, the student 'who did most for Princeton.' He was not included among 'those most likely to succeed,' but he was considered one of the six having the biggest drag with the Faculty!"

17 She was the daughter of Bishop Gailor, executive head of the Episcopal Church in America.

18 Perling, *op. cit.*, p. 236.

Benjamin Harrison

1 Perling, *The President's Sons*, p. 145.

2 A yet more distant ancestor had been a member of the English House of Commons in 1649 and had voted in favor of the execution of Charles I.

3 Harry J. Sievers, *Benjamin Harrison (Hoosier Statesman)*, p. 335.

4 Harry J. Sievers, *op. cit.*, p. 339.

5 Harrison subsequently appointed Robert Todd Lincoln as U.S. Minister to London, and Frederick Dent Grant to the Court in Vienna.

6 Russell was named after Russell Farnam Lord, who had married Carrie's older sister, Elizabeth.

7 Mary was always known to the family as "Mamie."

8 Perling, *op. cit.*, p. 23.

9 Sievers, *op. cit.*, p. 7.

10 Perling, *op. cit.*, p. 239.

11 The wedding ring was made of gold obtained from Russell's own mine in Montana.

12 Sievers, *op. cit.*, p. 236.
13 Carrie once said, "Ben would never allow an ungodly fiddle in the house." (Sievers, op. cit., p. 65).
14 Seviers, *op. cit.*, p. 294.
15 Seviers, *op. cit.*, p. 297.
16 Seviers, *op. cit.*, p. 309.
17 Seviers, *op. cit.*, p. 308.
18 Lizzie was taken seriously ill during her first summer at the White House, and she died in November, 1889.
19 When Marthena contracted scarlet fever, the entire White House was placed under quarantine.
20 It was during the Harrison administration that electric lighting was first installed at the White House, though the President himself appeared so terrified of receiving a shock that only with great reluctance did he ever use the light switches. The installation was performed by the Edison Electric Company, who sent Ike Hoover to do the wiring. He was persuaded to stay as an employee of the White House and remained there forty-two years. He acted as chief usher from the presidency of Taft to that of Franklin D. Roosevelt.
21 The collection was considerably extended and completed by Mamie Eisenhower during the 1950's. (Sadler, *America's First Ladies*, p. 145).
22 Neither was Carrie to know of the death of her father at the White House just one month later, on November 29, 1893. He was in his 93rd year.
23 Harry J. Sievers, *Benjamin Harrison (Hoosier President)*, p. 250.
24 They also brought with them the recalcitrant White House goat, who was joined by a burro, the gift of John Wanamaker (Sievers, *op. cit.*, p. 250).
25 Sievers, *op. cit.*, p. 256.
26 Sievers, *op. cit.*, p. 257.
27 Russell Harrison's second child, William Henry Harrison, had been born on August 10, 1896.
28 Asa Martin, *Benjamin Harrison*, p. 365.
29 Harrison canceled debts relating to loans he had made to Russell.
30 Final settlement of Harrison's estate was not made until nearly fifty years after his death, due to complicated litigation. (Asa Martin, *op. cit.*, p. 365). Because she had married Harrison after his retirement from office, she never became entitled to the $5,000 annual pension usually accorded by Congress to the widows of Presidents.
31 Perling, *op. cit.*, p. 245. Russell's daughter, Marthena (married to Harry A. Williams), was active in the Veterans' Bureau during World War II.
32 *New York Times*, December 26, 1955.

William McKinley and Theodore Roosevelt

1 The proceedings accompanying his nomination are outlined later in this chapter.

[2] Tragically, while sparring in the White House gymnasium with Dan Tyler Moore (his first wife's cousin), he lost his sight in the left eye after it had been accidentally struck. The incident was never revealed to the public.

[3] Elliot's daughter, Eleanor, was the subject of Edith (Carow) Roosevelt's sarcastic comment that as "an ugly duckling" it was still possible that she could "turn out to be a swan." It was the same Eleanor who became the bride of Franklin Delano Roosevelt in May, 1905.

[4] At one time, Bamie and Alice lived in 422 Madison Avenue in New York City, next door to the Clarence Days, the rambunctious family immortalized in *Life with Father.*

[5] Letter dated August 15, 1889. (Sylvia Jakes Morris, *Edith Kermit Roosevelt*, p. 119).

[6] Morris, *op. cit.,* p. 121.

[7] Harrison later said of Roosevelt as Commissioner that he walked as though "he wanted to put an end to all evil in the world between sunrise and sunset."

[8] Morris, *op. cit.,* pp. 132–3.

[9] Morris, *op. cit.,* p. 137.

[10] Eleanor wore a back brace for two years to correct a presumed curvature of the spine.

[11] Brough, *Princess Alice,* p. 60.

[12] What influence her Bible readings had on Alice is a matter for pure conjecture. Her spirit remained irrepressible, and she was all too wont to shock respectable visitors to the White House by her loud-voiced proposal to give birth to a monkey.

[13] Morris, *op. cit.,* p. 163.

[14] *Ibid.*

[15] Whom he once described as having "no more backbone than a chocolate eclair."

[16] Morris, op. cit., p. 168.

[17] To everyone's surprise, Bamie, at age 40, during an extended visit to England commencing in 1893, had met and eventually married (in November, 1895) Lieutenant William Sheffield Cowles, naval attache to the U.S. Embassy in London. They returned in 1897 to live in New York City.

[18] Some time later, Alice began smoking. In the hope that they would make her so sick as to force her to give up the habit, a relative gave her two cigars. Alice smoked both with delight and with no ill-effects.

[19] Morris, *op. cit.,* p. 196.

[20] Mark Hanna was the G.O.P.'s national chairman.

[21] His wife, Ida, survived her husband by five years and died in May, 1907.

[22] Upon which event Mark Hanna again commented: "Now look, that damned cowboy is President of the United States!"

[23] Morris, *op. cit.,* pp. 207–8.

[24] J. B. Bishop, ed., *Theodore Roosevelt's Letters to His Children,* p. 43.

[25] Roosevelt had directed: "Begin in June and finish by mid-November" during which time he evacuated the family to Oyster Bay.

26 When his friend, Owen Wister, enquired of Roosevelt why he did not "do something" about Alice, Roosevelt replied that he could be President of the United States *or* manage Alice, but that he could not do two such jobs at one and the same time.

27 The fact that her favorite color was blue led to the designation of a particular shade as "Alice Blue," which, in turn, led to the song, "Alice Blue Gown."

28 Alice wrote in her diary, "I pray for a fortune. I care for nothing except to amuse myself in a charmingly expensive way" (Morris, *op. cit.*, p. 274). Among her favorite companions in Washington was Marguerite Cassini, daughter of the Russian ambassador. They drove around the city together in Marguerite's red touring car, and smoked openly as a deliberate gesture to shock and defy the staid ones in Washington society. Later, in her book *The Crowded Hours,* Alice cheerfully admitted that her chief characteristic in those days was "total irresponsibility."

29 J. B. Bishop, ed., *Theodore Roosevelt's Letters to His Children*, p. 61.

30 Bishop, *op. cit.*, p. 63.

31 Bishop, *op. cit.*, p. 83.

32 Wood was his close friend of the Rough Rider days.

33 Bishop, *op. cit.*, p. 93.

34 Bishop, *op. cit.*, p. 148.

35 Roosevelt proudly proclaimed "I am no longer a political accident." He was the first Vice-President entering the White House, by reason of the death of his predecessor, to win a subsequent presidential election.

36 Alice dismissed F.D.R. as simply a "feather duster."

37 Vide, note 28.

38 It appears that Nicholas had once proposed marriage to Marguerite but that she had refused him.

39 Taft had served as Governor of the Philippines prior to his appointment as Secretary of War.

40 Morris, *op. cit.*, p. 298.

41 Later, at a private reception where the wedding cake was being cut and distributed, Alice, impatient with the knife, borrowed a sword from a military officer and demolished the cake quickly with that.

42 James Brough, *Princess Alice*, p. 184.

43 J. J. Perling, *The Presidents' Sons*, p. 254.

44 Perling, *op. cit.*, p. 255.

45 Bishop, *op. cit.*, p. 153.

46 Another gang member was Earle Looker, who was later author of the book *The White House Gang*. The cavernous attic in the White House was as much a paradise for Quentin's gang as it had been to Jesse's.

47 Bishop, *op. cit.*, p. 223.

48 Bishop, *op. cit.*, p. 217.

49 Morris, *op. cit.*, 315–16.

50 Alice was still further incensed when she understood that Helen Taft had been instrumental in vetoing the appointment of her husband, Nick Longworth, as Minister to China, because she believed that Alice's behavior might result in international embarrassment.

51 He had been awarded the Nobel Peace Prize in 1906 for his assistance in negotiating a peace treaty between Russia and Japan, signed at Portsmouth, N.H. (1905).

52 The event also led Archie Butt (the White House aide) to comment that "with Roosevelt and the Kaiser at King Edward's funeral it will be a wonder if the poor corpse gets a passing thought."

53 Morris, *op. cit.*, p. 373.

54 Roosevelt, Mrs. Theodore, Jr., *Day Before Yesterday*, p. 60–62.

55 Morris, *op. cit.*, p. 400 (December 24, 1913).

56 Archie, on April 14, married Grace Lockwood at Emmanuel Church, Boston.

57 Morris, *op. cit.*, p. 418.

58 In 1927, Kermit underwent an operation for the removal of part of his thumb which had become infected through an overdose of radium to which he had been exposed as a boy for the removal of a wart.

59 While awaiting news of embarcation in Paris, Ted and a number of his fellow officers conceived the idea of the American Legion, an organization which quickly gained wide acceptance and acclamation in the United States.

60 Ted had held stocks in the Sinclair Oil Company, which was the firm implicated in the scandal.

61 F.D.R. had run as Democratic vice-presidential candidate to James M. Cox in the 1920 presidential election, won by the Republican Harding.

62 Perling, *op. cit.*, p. 259.

63 Ted wrote several books during this period, including *All in the Family* (an account of life at Sagamore Hill) and *Rank and File* (a collection of World War I stories).

64 In January 1935, Ted's daughter, Grace, presented Edith with her first great-grandchild, a son named William McMillan, Jr.

65 He had contracted malaria in South America and, thereafter, suffered from recurrent attacks of fever.

66 Morris, *op. cit.*, p. 442.

67 Edith, who had once described F.D.R. as "nine-tenths mush and one-tenth Eleanor," had been very upset when, following F.D.R.'s nomination at the 1932 Democratic Convention in Chicago, more than 300 congratulatory messages had been delivered to the Sagamore Hill home: the American public had presumably failed to distinguish between the Theodore and Franklin factions within the Roosevelt clan. To help publicize the distinction, Edith purchased

photographs of Hoover and stuck them on envelopes containing letters to his friends and associates. (Morris, *op. cit.*, p. 476).

[68] His son, Archie Jr., was at Groton. His eldest daughter, Nancy, a firm favorite of Edith's, later wrote a memoir of her grandmother, *A Sense of Style*.

[69] Brough, *op. cit.*, p. 251.

[70] Brough, *op. cit.*, p. 268.

[71] Outward family decorum was observed by Alice with respect to, but with reservations from, the White House—hence the note she received from Eleanor: "Naturally, we are going to ask you to everything that goes on, but you mustn't feel that you have to come."

[72] His wife, Belle, established a fund in his memory, to foster "a better understanding and a closer relationship between the military forces of the U.S. and those of the U.K." by the mutual exchange of officers as lecturers at their respective military academies. (Perling, *op. cit.*, p. 268).

[73] He was awarded the Legion of Honor by the French for his services in North Africa.

[74] Lyndon Johnson underwent gallbladder surgery, and was later photographed exhibiting the abdominal scar, upon which incident Alice was quick to comment that the nation should be grateful that LBJ did not have an operation on his prostate gland.

William Howard Taft

[1] Phyllis Robbins, *Robert A. Taft*, p. 276.

[2] Ishbel Ross, *An American Family*, p. 108.

[3] He was the longest-lived President between James Buchanan (77) and Herbert Hoover (90), a consecutive span of 68 years and 14 Presidents. Taft was never averse to telling stories against himself as, for instance, in his remark: "The other day I gave up my seat in a street car and three ladies sat down."

[4] Taft's daughter, Helen, was (much later) to ask her father: "Why is it we can never go anywhere without catching something?" (Robbins, *op. cit.*, p. 39).

[5] Ross, *op. cit.*, p. 125.

[6] Mrs. William Howard Taft, *Recollections of Full Years*, p. 122.

[7] Robbins, *op. cit.*, pp. 91–2. Apparently, at this time Nellie was concerned more with Robert's clothes than with his curriculum, her main grief being that her eldest son was now quitting childhood and donning the outward accoutrement symbol of manhood—a pair of long trousers.

[8] Robbins, *op. cit.*, p. 95.

[9] Robbins, *op. cit.*, p. 97.

[10] As might be expected, some of these "outdoor activities" also included "escapades" by night, when the participants would often contrive to include Robert, hoping that, if discovered, the severity of the punishment would be appreciably alleviated by reason of the fact that the HM's nephew was with them.

11 Robbins, *op. cit.*, p. 121. The play was called *The Two Buzzards* . . . "and very funny, although I had about the least important part of the five parts, but it was lots of fun, and not so much responsibility." (Letter, 2.26, 1905).

12 Ross, *op. cit.*, p. 181.

13 Robbins, *op. cit.*, p. 126.

14 Ross, *op. cit.*, p. 192.

15 In a letter dated July 15, 1908, Roosevelt chided him: "Poor old boy! Of course, you are not enjoying the campaign. I wish you had some of my bad temper. It is at times a real aid to enjoyment." (Ross, *op. cit.*, p. 199).

16 She was to survive William's death by thirteen years.

17 His weakest marks were in Bible Study, which his father generously attributed to an "inherited trait." [Ross, *op. cit.*, p. 226.] When Charlie vacationed at Washington he found that his family was far more restrictive upon his behavior than had been the Roosevelts, a situation which led him to expostulate: "Doggone the White House anyway. It's no place for kids." [Ross, *op. cit.*, p. 242.]

18 After Taft, despite Roosevelt's opposition, had won the Republican nomination at the Chicago Convention of 1912, one observer stated: "The only question now is which corpse gets the most flowers." The November election produced the following result:

Candidate	Electoral Vote	Popular Vote
Wilson	435	6.2 M
Roosevelt	88	4.1 M
Taft	8	3.4 M

19 Upon the occasion of Taft's death, Will Rogers was led to comment: "It's great to be great, but it's greater to be human. He was our great human fellow because there was more of him to be human. We are parting with three hundred pounds of solid charity to everybody, and love and affection for all his fellow men." [Ross, *op. cit.*, p. 26.] Taft was the first President to be buried in Arlington Cemetery. He had never served in any of the armed forces, but he had been Secretary of War during Roosevelt's administration.

20 Describing the ceremony, Robert's father wrote "Bob looked trim and, when he was asked the question, answered 'I will,' as if somebody said to him, 'You won't,' his answer was so positive and sharp." [Ross, *op. cit.*, p. 290.]

21 Her justification for travelling was her humorous comment that a husband was like a furnace: "If you don't do something about them, they'll go out." [Robbins, *op. cit.*, p. 190.]

22 He was editor of the school's *Papyrus* magazine, and his uncle had him classified as belonging "to the kind who never need a vacation, and never fail to get one" (Ross, *op. cit.*, p. 278).

23 She was the daughter of the president of the Ingersoll Watch Company.

24 They were named, respectively, Sylvia, Cynthia, Rosalyn, Lucia, Seth, and Peter.

[25] Edna Colman, *White House Gossip*, p. 323–4.

[26] Ross, *op. cit.*, p. 320.

[27] Her thesis topic, "Colonial Policy in the Eighteenth Century," was researched in London.

[28] In 1925, Bryn Mawr attained headline status when Helen announced that the girls would be permitted to smoke under fixed rules. This was in the same year that the Mannings second daughter, Caroline, was born.

[29] Robert was Speaker of the House during his final year of office.

[30] Which included the Cincinnati Street Railway Company, the Baltimore and Ohio Railroad, and the Taft Cotton Oil Company.

[31] Such as the Orphan Asylum, the Symphony Orchestra, the Conservatory of Music, the Institute of Fine Arts, and the Art Museum. Robert received such firm and active support from his wife during the election campaign that one newspaper headline proclaimed, "Bob and Martha win."

[32] In the *Saturday Evening Post* edition of May 4, 1940, Alice (Roosevelt) Longworth contributed an article entitled, "Why I am for Bob Taft" in which she declared:

> I am for Bob Taft because I do not yearn and long for the man who is always on his toes, raising his voice, raring to go here, there, anywhere. I want one whose feet will be firmly on the ground, and whose mind will be upon finding solutions for the national problems rather than in becoming the shining hero of the undiscriminating masses.

[34] It is not known who Robert's vice-presidential nominee might have been, but had he selected the same person as had Eisenhower, then Richard Nixon would have assumed the office of chief executive in 1953 rather than in 1968.

[35] He based his objection upon the fact that their deeds, however infamous, were yet committed before specific international laws outlawing such behavior had been prescribed.

[36] In 1933 he wrote *The Cincinnati Experiment*.

[37] He voiced his approval of the U.S. lend-lease program at the outbreak of World War II.

[38] *New York Times*, 6.25.1983, p. 741.

Woodrow Wilson

[1] Eleanor Wilson McAdoo, *The Woodrow Wilsons*, p. 3.

[2] E. M. Alsop, *The Greatness of Woodrow Wilson*, p. 17 (26?).

[3] McAdoo, *op. cit.*, p. 20.

[4] McAdoo, *op. cit.*, p. 55.

[5] McAdoo, *op. cit.*, p. 27.

[6] Margaret Axson Elliott, p. 110.

[7] McAdoo, *op. cit.*, p. 57.

[8] *Ibid.*

[9] McAdoo, *op. cit.*, p. 44.

[10] McAdoo, *op. cit.*, p. 235.

[11] McAdoo, *op. cit.*, p. 238.

[12] Ten years later the car driver turned up at Los Angeles where Eleanor was living, and demanded payment for the cost of replacement of the wheels, since the reporters had refused reimbursement.

[13] McAdoo, *op. cit.*, p. 188. McAdoo was described by John Garraty as a "lean, rather ugly Georgian, with a long neck and a nose like a bird of prey."

[14] Eleanor McAdoo, *op. cit.*, p. 184.

[15] Eleanor McAdoo, *op. cit.*, p. 272.

[16] McAdoo, *op. cit.*, p. 182.

[17] Ike Hatch, *Edith Bolling Wilson*, p. 11.

[18] The catering arrangements for the reception were under the direction of Hector Boiardi, who later founded the Chef Boiardi Foods Company, a name which he changed to Chef Boy-ar-dee Foods.

[19] En route, in the train, Wilson is said to have danced a jig to his own whistling accompaniment of "Oh, You Beautiful Doll."

[20] *New York Times*, February 14, 1944, p. 1.

[21] Edith Bolling Wilson, *My Memoir*, p. 215–216.

[22] E. B. Wilson, *op. cit.*, p. 263.

[23] Wilson was only too well aware of McAdoo's public sobriquet, "The Crown Prince."

[24] His elevation to this high rank was in direct contrast to earlier days when, according to Ike Hoover, Sayre would wear his shoes until the rubber heels were worn down to the outside and he would then have the heels shifted around to even out the wear and tear.

[25] On December 29, 1961 (Wilson's birthday), the Woodrow Wilson bridge over the Potomac was dedicated by Francis Sayre, in place of Edith Wilson who had died only one day earlier.

[26] In 1945, Eleanor repeated in public her sister Margaret's story that, on his deathbed, Wilson had said that the United States was right in rejecting the concept of the League of Nations. By so doing, Eleanor brought down upon

herself all the wrath of Edith Wilson, her stepmother, in the same manner that the latter had responded towards Margaret twenty-one years earlier.

Warren Harding

[1] The amendment was first ratified on August 18, 1920, but then Tennessee rescinded its vote. The amendment was, however, declared ratified by the Secretary of State on August 26, 1920. Final doubts were removed when, on September 14, 1920, Connecticut cast its vote in favor.

[2] Her son was later adopted and renamed Marshall King, but he died of tuberculosis.

[3] Florence had eloped at the age of 19 to marry him.

[4] In 1927, Nan Britton authored an autobiography entitled *The President's Daughter*. The book was dedicated: "With understanding and love to all unwedded mothers and to their children whose fathers are not usually known to the world." The book was the basis of the film *Children of No Importance*, made in 1928.

[5] Nan Britton, *The President's Daughter*, pp. 32–33.

[6] Nan's sister was married to Scott Williams, a professional violinist, and in March, 1921, they formerly adopted the baby who was renamed Elizabeth Ann Willitts.

[7] Britton, *op. cit.*, p. 193.

[8] Vide, *Scandals in the Highest Office*, pp. 228–230.

[9] The letters were deposited with the Library of Congress, and will remain sealed until July 29, 2014.

Calvin Coolidge

[1] Cavanah, *They Lived in the White House*, p. 141.

[2] Cavanah, *op. cit.*, p. 141.

[3] Cavanah, *op. cit.*, p. 142.

[4] Bess Furman, *White House Profile*, p. 309.

[5] The Coolidge family enjoyed the company of their many pets, which included an Airedale, Paul Pry, so-called because of his irrepressible curiosity; a pair of white collie dogs, named Prudence Prim and Rob Roy, respectively, by Grace; a marmalade cat, with which Coolidge loved to walk around wrapped around his neck, and two dozen chickens. The latter were inadvertently housed over a former herb garden until it was discovered that, upon being served up at mealtime the main course was mint meat.

6 Calvin Coolidge, *Autobiography,* p. 190.

7 William Allen White, *A Puritan in Babylon,* p. 308.

8 Coolidge was asked why members of the arts—musicians, poets, actors—were never invited to the White House. He replied, "I knew a poet once when I was at Amherst, class poet, name of Smith . . . never heard of him since."

9 J. J. Perling, *Presidents' Sons,* p. 298.

10 Celebrating the 60th anniversary of Coolidge's inauguration, during August, 1983, the Festival Committee of Northampton, Massachusetts, included among its items, the "I do not choose to run" road race. "The Calvin Coolidge look-alike contest was dropped when it became apparent that no one in the area chose to claim the distinction of looking like the grimmest, unsmilingest man ever to occupy the White House." (*Kansas City Times,* August 1983).

11 He sent a copy of his book to another father of whom he had read that he, too, had lost a son. On the flyleaf Coolidge wrote, "To my friend, in recollection of his son and my son, who, by the grace of God, have the privilege of being boys throughout eternity."

12 It had long been believed that Coolidge had destroyed all his private papers before his death, but in 1985, it was announced that John had discovered a dozen cartons of his father's papers in the attic of his home and had donated them to the public library in Northampton. (New York Times, March 14, 1985, p. A21).

13 Cavanah, *They Lived in the White House,* p. 187.

Herbert Hoover

1 The Hoover papers are kept either at Stanford University or in Iowa.

2 He had bought out the "Sons of Gwalia" mine from some Welsh miners, and, after development, it was to yield an annual average of one million dollars worth of gold over the next fifty years.

3 Joan Hoff Wilson, *Herbert Hoover,* p. 18.

4 Eugene Lyons, *Herbert Hoover,* p. 95.

5 Hoover was to become the first person of Quaker persuasion to be elected President of the United States.

6 Coolidge was later to remark of Hoover: "That man has offered me unsolicited advice for six years, all of it bad."

7 Eugene Lyons, *Herbert Hoover,* p. 223.

8 Lyons, *op. cit.,* p. 332.

9 Lou Henry had died in January, 1944, at the age of 68. In her will she penned a note to her sons: "You have been lucky boys to have had such a father, and I am a lucky woman to have had my life's trail along the path of three such men and boys."

[10] Lyons, *op. cit.*, p. 432.

Franklin D. Roosevelt

[1] His daughter Alice succinctly commented that her father always wished to be "the bride at every wedding and the corpse at every funeral."

[2] James Roosevelt, *My Parents*, p. 17.

[3] Eleanor Roosevelt, *My Story*, p. 143.

[4] James Roosevelt, *op. cit.*, p. 36.

[5] Eleanor Roosevelt, *op. cit.*, p. 162.

[6] James Roosevelt, *Affectionately, FDR.*

[7] Eleanor Roosevelt, *This Is My Story*, p. 172.

[8] James Roosevelt, *Affectionately, FDR*, p. 41.

[9] James Roosevelt, *op. cit.*, p. 44.

[10] In 1920 Lucy Mercer married Winthrop Rutherfurd, a wealthy widower with six children.

[11] Asbell, ed., *Mother and Daughter*, p. 38.

[12] Miss Cook and Miss Dickerman had cooperated with Eleanor in a school in New York as well as in her Val-Kill Furniture Factory Project at Hyde Park.

[13] Elliott Roosevelt, *An Untold Story*, p. 272.

[14] James Roosevelt, *Affectionately, FDR*, p. 69.

[15] Asbell, *op. cit.*, p. 41.

[16] *Ibid.*

[17] James Roosevelt, *Affectionately, FDR*, p. 122. (Mt. Auburn St. was the college section where the most fashionable and expensive dormitories were located.)

[18] James Roosevelt, *Affectionately, FDR*, p. 124.

[19] James Roosevelt, *op. cit.*, p. 211.

[20] James Roosevelt, *op. cit.*, p. 118.

[21] James Roosevelt, *op. cit.*, p. 119.

[22] James Roosevelt, *op. cit.*, p. 89.

[23] James Roosevelt, *op. cit.*, p. 221.

[24] Asbell, *Mother and Daughter*, p. 55.

[25] Cavanah, *They Lived in the White House*, p. 157.

[26] This was the visit best remembered by the publicity in the press given to the picnic at Hyde Park when Roosevelt served "hot dogs" to their Majesties.

[27] James Roosevelt, *Affectionately, FDR*, p. 239.

[28] Eleanor Roosevelt, *This I Remember*, p. 11.

[29] James Roosevelt, *Affectionately, FDR*, p. 305.

[30] Elliott was later to accompany his father to Cairo and Teheran, when Roosevelt and Churchill conferred with Stalin.

31 Elliott Roosevelt, *As He Saw It*, p. 227.

32 John Boettiger had achieved his ambition to attend high-level sessions by being present, along with Elliott, at both the Cairo and the Teheran conferences of 1943.

33 Lucy Mercer Rutherfurd died on August 1, 1948, at age 57.

34 Elliott Roosevelt, *Mother R*, p. 254.

35 Elliott, *op. cit.*, p. 169.

36 James Roosevelt, *My Parents*, p. 312.

37 Ethel DuPont committed suicide in 1965.

38 Eleanor Roosevelt, *This I Remember*, p. 11.

39 Faye Emerson died in Majorca in 1983, aged 65.

Harry S Truman

1 A "judge" in this context was not expected to be legally qualified, since it referred only to a person responsible for administering the business of the county.

2 Margaret Truman, *Letters from Father*, p. 33.

3 Margaret Truman, *op. cit.*, p. 34.

4 Margaret Truman, *op. cit.*, p. 149.

5 Margaret Truman, *Souvenir*, p. 117.

6 Margaret Truman, *op. cit.*, p. 115.

7 Margaret Truman, *op. cit.*, p. 237.

8 J. B. West, *The Trumans*, pp. 89–90.

9 Harry S Truman, *Mr. Citizen*, p. 177.

10 Margaret described the bed as "bulbous, cavern, gloomy, dark, and—I'm here to tell you—lumpy!" *Souvenir*, p. 108.

11 Margaret Truman, *Letters from Father*, p. 73.

12 Margaret Truman, *op. cit.*, p. 85.

13 Margaret Truman, *op. cit.*, p. 68.

14 Margaret Truman, *Souvenir*, p. 2.

15 Clifton Daniel, *Lords, Ladies and Gentlemen*, p. 175.

16 Margaret Truman, *Souvenir*, p. 320. The identical embarrassment occurred in the same place to Mamie Eisenhower when First Lady some years later, but Mrs. Gifford (wife of the U.S. Ambassador) now experienced in such matters, knew precisely what to do!

17 Margaret Truman, *Letters from Father*, p. 71.

18 Clifton Daniel, *Lords, Ladies and Gentlemen*, p. 245.

19 Daniel commented that he married Margaret just in time to be included on p. 360 of her 365-page memoir, *Souvenir*, published in 1956.

20 While Margaret was still in the hospital after the Caesarian-section birth of her firstborn, Truman, the proudest of grandfathers, brought in a collection of sweaters which were designed for a six-year-old, not six-day-old, grandson (Margaret Truman, *Harry S. Truman*, p. 571).

21 Thomas Washington was named after his father's great uncle.

22 Clifton Daniel, *Lords, Ladies and Gentlemen,* p. 84.

23 Clifton Daniel, *op. cit.,* p. 84.

24 Clifton T. Daniel and William W. Daniel: "House was Wonderland for Grandsons." *Kansas City Star,* May 6, 1984, p. 1F

25 Clifton Daniel, *Lords, Ladies and Gentlemen,* p. 252.

26 Margaret Truman Daniel, *Bess W. Truman* (New York: Macmillan, 1986).

Dwight David Eisenhower

1 Icky was buried in Denver, alongside the graves of Mamie's two sisters, but on 1966, his coffin was transferred to the chapel at the Eisenhower Memorial Center in Abilene.

2 Lester David and Irene David, *Ike and Mamie,* p. 86.

3 John S. D. Eisenhower, *Strictly Personal,* p. 12.

4 Another First Lady, Bess Truman, was to share Mamie's love of the national game and both were staunch supporters of the Washington Senators.

5 John S. D. Eisenhower, *op. cit.,* p. 14.

6 Grandfather Eisenhower once sent a postcard to Ike in the Philippines, with just one word, "Hot." (John S. D. Eisenhower *op. cit.,* p. 14).

7 He remains as the only U.S. President to be thus qualified.

8 John S. D. Eisenhower, *Strictly Personal,* p. 40.

9 Following Pearl Harbor, Eisenhower, now a lieutenant-general, was given responsibility first for Operation Torch (the invasion of North Africa in November, 1942) and then for Operation Overlord (the invasion of France in June, 1944), for which he was promoted to the five-star rank of General of the Army.

10 Kay Summersby published a book, *Eisenhower Was My Boss,* in 1948, but in it she made no reference to intimacy. She had settled in the United States, was married in 1952, divorced in 1958, and developed cancer in the 1970's, when she wrote a second book, *Past Forgetting* (possibly designed to cover medical expenses), in which she described her sexual adventures with Eisenhower. But she died in 1975, two years before the book was published.

11 They were engaged in January, 1947, and John, having in the meantime returned to the United States, made a phone call to Ike, assuring him that Barbara had a strong foot. "Through the years Dad had said he hoped we could breed my tendency toward flat feet out of the family." [John S. D. Eisenhower, *op. cit.,* p. 128.]

12 Harry S. Truman, *Mr. Citizen,* p. 17–18.

13 Eisenhower was very interested in the progress of his grandchildren through school and he once said "I encourage good grades . . . in this way: I give them two bucks for each A, nothing for a B plus; and if they get below a B they have to give me a buck."

[14] John S. D. Eisenhower, *Strictly Personal,* p. 377.

[15] Harry S. Dent, *Cover Up: The Watergate in All of Us.* (San Bernadino, Calif.: Here's Life Publishers, 1986).

John Fitzgerald Kennedy

[1] Lee Bouvier eventually married Prince Radziwill, whose Polish family had settled in England during World War II.

Janet Lee Bouvier was remarried in 1942 to Hugh D. Auchincloss, a New York broker. John Vernon Bouvier III never remarried and died in 1957.

[2] Rose Fitzgerald Kennedy,: *Times to Remember,* p. 87.

[3] Rose Fitzgerald Kennedy, *Times to Remember,* p. 79.

[4] Rose Fitzgerald Kennedy, *Times to Remember,* p. 187.

[5] Joe Sr. encouraged his son to become familiar with noncapitalist economic doctrines, so that he would "get to know the enemy."

[6] Rose Fitzgerald Kennedy *op. cit.,* p. 350.

[7] Jack, exhausted by the campaign, had gone to relax at his parents' overseas home in the South of France, and was on the family yacht when he received news of his wife's premature, stillborn baby.

[8] Jack's hectic campaign activities took him away from home so frequently that Jacky claimed that Caroline's first spoken word was "airplane." (Martin, *A Hero For Our Time,* p. 145).

[9] J. F. K. Jr was christened in the hospital chapel. Afterwards, when asked whether his son had cried, his father replied "Not a bit—he laughed." (M. V. R. Thayer, *Jacqueline Kennedy,* p. 7).

[10] John F. Kennedy's inauguration was the first such ceremony to be attended by *both* parents of a President of the United States.

[11] As part of Caroline's morning ritual, she would come into Jack's bedroom and possibly share his breakfast; then, after he had dressed, she would formally walk him down to his office. In the evenings, she and John-John, would go to the oval office just before dinner where the President and his children would enjoy a playful romp on the floor (Martin, *A Hero for Our Time,* p. 268).

[12] After November, 1963, the school was transferred to the British Embassy, and was conducted there until the close of the school year.

[13] McConnell, *Our First Ladies.*

[14] Rose Fitzgerald Kennedy, *Times to Remember,* p. 401.

[15] M. V. R. Thayer, *Jacqueline Kennedy,* p. 229.

[16] M. V. R. Thayer *op. cit.,* p. 229.

[17] His body was reburied on December 3, 1963, in Arlington National Cemetery, alongside that of his father.

[18] Also on board was Franklin D. Roosevelt, Jr, who was criticized at home for possibly compromising relations between the Onassis shipping interests and those of the U.S. Maritime Administration, where Roosevelt held a post as Undersecretary of Commerce.

19 Rose Fitzgerald Kennedy, *Times to Remember,* p. 401.

20 In response to questions regarding her marriage, Jacky is quoted as having said that she "wanted out" of the United States, ". . . if they're killing Kennedys, my kids are number one target."

Earlier in 1968, she had phoned Bobby from Greece to tell him that Onassis had proposed marriage. Bobby, "joking weakly from the initial shock had said, 'For God's sake, Jacky, this could cost me five states' " (Collier and Horowitz, *The Kennedys,* p. 367).

21 The yacht was the epitome of luxury: "El Grecos on the walls, gold fixtures in the bathrooms, even bar stools covered in leather made from the tanned skins of whale testicles" (Collier and Horowitz, *The Kennedys,* p. 366).

22 Rose F. Kennedy, *op. cit.,* p. 470.

23 *Ibid.*

24 Rose F. Kennedy, *op. cit.,* p. 469.

25 Rose F. Kennedy, *op. cit.,* p. 472.

26 *New York Times,* July 17, 1986, p. C.10.

Lyndon Baines Johnson

1 The family had a collection of beagles, and when Johnson himself, as President, yanked one of them up by its ears, there came, in Liz Carpenter's words "a yap heard all over the world." (*Ruffles and Flourishes,* p. 102).

2 High Sidey, *A Very Personal Presidency,* p. 7. Lyndon was born on August 27, 1908.

3 Out of a total of a million cast votes, he won by only 87, and became jocularly known as Landslide Lyndon. Creekmore Fath, a Texas lawyer, said of the controversial election that "both sides were stealing and Lyndon won."

4 Booth Mooney, *LBJ,* p. 250.

5 Lady Bird Johnson, *A White House Diary,* p. 68.

6 Lyndon B. Johnson, *A Vantage Point,* pp. 129–130.

7 Sam Houston Johnson, *My Brother Lyndon,* p. 251.

8 Johnson polled 43 million votes to Barry Goldwater's 27 million, a margin of 16 million, the largest ever in U.S. presidential election history. It also helped that, during the same month of October, 1964, the Jenkins affair was replaced suddenly from press headlines by two international events of major portent: the ousting of Khrushchev as leader in the USSR; and the explosion of the first nucleur bomb by Communist China.

9 Lyndon B. Johnson, *The Vantage Point,* p. 294.

10 Lyndon B. Johnson, *op.cit.,* p. 233.

11 *Ebony* (vol. 20, no. 4), February 1965, pp. 40–46.

12 Lady Bird Johnson, *A White House Diary,* pp. 327–8.

13 Lady Bird Johnson, *op. cit.,* p. 95.

14 Lady Bird Johnson, *op. cit.,* p. 300.

15 Liz Carpenter categorically and hilariously lists them as the *Six Crises* of Luci's wedding.

[16] A hurried press release produced the delightful misprint: "Priscilla of Boston taught the bridesmaids how to sin in the car." (Carpenter, *Ruffles and Flourishes*, p. 287.)

[17] The fact that the wedding was held on the twentieth anniversary of the bombing of Hiroshima did not contribute to the happy wedding occasion, since protestors had lined up outside the church.

[18] Liz Carpenter, *op. cit.*, p. 268.

[19] When Eleanor Randolph Wilson (the President's youngest daughter) married William Gibbs McAdoo.

[20] Mooney, *LBJ*

[21] Sam Houston later (1970) wrote a biography, *My Brother Lyndon*, which resulted in a rupture in the relationship between the two brothers.

[22] Liz Carpenter, *Ruffles and Flourishes*, p. 292.

[23] Lady Bird Johnson, *A White House Diary*, p. 617.

[24] One of Johnson's ancestors, Mary Desha, was one of the three joint founders (in 1890) of the Daughters of the American Revolution (D.A.R.).

[25] *Kansas City Times*, Wednesday, April 7, 1982, p. C4.

Richard Milhous Nixon

[1] White House "Farewell Speech," August 9, 1974.

[2] Henry D. Spalding: *The Nixon Nobody Knows*, p. 28.

[3] Actually, it was a resettlement, since Frank had worked there from 1907 to 1911. Whittier was founded by a Quaker, John Greenleaf Whittier, in 1887, and one of its early settlers was Richard Nixon's great-grandfather, Joshua Milhous, whose biography in the form of a novel entitled *The Friendly Persuasion*, was written by Jessamyn Wood, Richard's cousin. In the film version of the novel, the lead role was played by Gary Cooper.

[4] "Pat" Ryan had been christened Thelma Catherine, but her Irish father had insisted on calling her Pat, because she was born on the eve of St. Patrick's Day—March 16, 1912, at Ely, Nevada. Her family had moved to California, where both her parents died. She struggled hard to gain entry into the University of Southern California where she majored in business, and, at the time of meeting Richard Nixon, she was teaching at Whittier High School.

[5] It was during this campaign that Douglas became known as the Pink Lady (because of her alleged Leftist sympathies), while Nixon himself was labeled Tricky Dick.

[6] Nixon, at 40, was the nation's second youngest Vice-President: John Cabell Breckinridge, Vice-President under James Buchanan, was 36 when he took office in 1857. After his nomination, Nixon was charged with using a slush fund of $18,000 for his personal use. He defended himself on television in the famous sentimental "Checkers" speech, Checkers being the cocker spaniel given to Julie and Tricia, and named by the latter.

[7] Julie, at age 8, once wrote her father a poem entitled "My Day," which, with all its errors, he still preserves in a frame:

Handsome and kind,
Handsome and kind,
Always on time
Loving and Good
Does things he should
Humerous, funny
Makes the day seem sunny,
Helping others to live,
Willing to give his life
For his beloved country
That's my dad.

(Lester David, *The Lonely Lady of San Clemente*, p. 13).

[8] In 1953, Nixon and Pat spent ten weeks on an official goodwill tour of the Far East, during which time, the two daughters, aged 7 and 5, respectively, were left in the care of Grandma Hannah Nixon.

[9] Spalding, *op. cit.*, p. 396.

[10] In terms of the popular vote, John F. Kennedy received 34,227,096 votes to Nixon's 34,107,646, but the electoral votes gave Kennedy 303 to Nixon's 219.

[11] He also received substantial royalties from his book, *Six Crises*, written after his retirement.

[12] Spalding, *op. cit.*, p. 426.

[13] It was Mamie Eisenhower, David's grandmother, who had originally suggested that it would be "nice" if he were to pay a visit to see the younger Nixon daughter. He did, and a casual friendship ripened into love.

[14] Just six weeks after Nixon had been elected President in a victory over Hubert Humphrey.

[15] Tricia's wedding cake was six-feet ten-inches high, and the ceremony was attended by three former White House brides: Alice Roosevelt Longworth (1906), Luci Johnson Nugent (1966), and Lynda Johnson Robb (1967). Tricia and her husband spent their honeymoon at the secluded Bahamas home of Nixon's affluent associate, Robert Abplanalp.

[16] Edmondson and Cohen, *The Women of Watergate*, p. 123.

[17] Including a presentation on the B.B.C. while on a visit to London during the summer of 1973.

[18] Edmundson and Cohen, *op. cit.*, p. 124.

[19] Edmundson and Cohen, *op. cit.*, p. 129.

According to Woodward and Bernstein, David may have harbored some sympathy for his father-in-law's predicament since, as an intelligence officer aboard the U.S.S. *Albany*, he too, had been involved in a "cover-up" involving some important missing documents which had been declared "burnt" (destroyed). (*The Final Days*, p. 244).

[20] Julie had once referred to her as the "Howard Hughes of the White House" (Edmondson and Cohen, p. 86).

21 Edmondson and Cohen, *op. cit.*, p. 83.

22 When Tricia's mother, Pat, was still in junior high school, her mother died of cancer, and Pat was forced to function as housekeeper for the father and two brothers. Perhaps it was this experience which led her to declare, in the school graduation yearbook (1929), that her intention was "To run a boarding house." (Lester David, *The Lonely Lady of San Clemente*, p. 29). Only after his re-election as Vice-President in 1956, was Nixon able to move into a spacious home situated in Wesley Heights. By sheer force of habit, Pat continued to darn and/or repair all the family clothes, as well to press her husband's pants, "an item which had long given her much publicity." (David, *op. cit.*, p. 97).

23 During the spring of 1974 Tricia wrote an essay for publication, "My Father and Watergate," alleging that the President was simply a victim of undisguised character assassination, and that, in the moment of crisis, he had been contemptibly deserted by all his former colleagues.

24 The biographies were duly published in 1986: Julie's book was entitled *Pat Nixon, The Untold Story,* while David's first volume (of his three-part biography) was entitled *Eisenhower at War, 1943–45.*

25 Melanie was described by her parents as a "curly-haired dead ringer for Mamie Eisenhower" (*Kansas City Star,* 11.6.86, p. 1c).

During the course of the same article, Julie, when asked how she planned to explain Watergate to her children, responded: "The explanation is that people make mistakes and there are political battles, and some you win and some you lose."

Gerald Rudolph Ford

1 According to the provisions of the 25th (the "Kennedy") Amendment, ratified on February 10, 1967, Congress was obliged to approve or reject a presidential nomination for Vice-President. Ford was the first Vice-President to be subjected to the procedures required by this amendment. In his seven-minute acceptance speech Ford remarked, "I'm a Ford, not a Lincoln. My addresses will never be as eloquent." His comment later became the title of a biography written by Richard Reeves.

2 Ford Jr. later changed the spelling of his middle name to Rudolph.

3 Different versions exist as to the truth of these facts. His father's name was Leslie Lynch King and he was a wool trader by occupation. He died in 1941 at Tucson, Arizona.

4 Prior to her first marriage, Betty had emerged as a dancer of appreciable talent, even teaching classes at the age of fourteen; later, she spent two years at Martha Graham's School of Dancing at New York.

5 *The Times of My Life* (1978).

6 Ford, *op. cit.*, p. 76.

7 Ford, *op. cit.*, p. 90.

8 Ford, *op. cit.*, 10.

9 Ford, op cit, p. 108.

10 These were Ford's parents. Betty's father had accidentally died of carbide monoxide poisoning when she was only 16. Her mother died not long after Betty's marriage to Ford.

11 Ford, *op. cit.*, p. 76.

12 Bud Vestal, *op. cit., Jerry Ford Up Close*, p. 22.

13 Betty Ford, *The Times of My Life*, p. 132. Susan left for private school just about the time when the Fords lost the services of Clara Powell, their housekeeper, who had given them faithful and loyal home support for 20 years. She left solely to provide for her aging parents.

14 Grandma Ford was a fine, resolute, and independent lady, who had always vowed that "she was going to die with her boots on, and she did—in church." (Betty Ford, *op. cit.*, p. 129.)

15 Betty Ford, *op. cit.*, p. 113.

16 Compounding the complicated process of Susan's adjustment to White House life was the distressing news, in September, 1974, that her mother was diagnosed as having a malignant tumor on her breast which demanded immediate attention. Betty underwent a mastectomy, which was followed by a period of painful chemotherapy, but she made a good, though slow, recovery.

It did not help, in terms of social commitments and obligations, that "Happy" Rockefeller, wife of Ford's Vice President, underwent identical surgery later on in the same year.

17 His first visit had taken place in June, 1972, following the Nixon "thaw" visit in February of that same year.

18 Betty Ford, *The Times of My Life*, pp. 167–8.

19 Betty Ford, *op. cit.*, p. 167.

20 Gerald Ford, *A Time to Heal*, p. 307.

21 *Ibid.*

22 Betty Ford, *The Times of My Life*, p. 207.

23 Following upon his renomination as presidential candidate, Ford along with Betty and Jack attended the European Security Conference (to which 35 countries had sent representatives) at Helsinki, Finland.

24 Gerald Ford, *A Time to Heal*, p. 436. When it came to the reading of the brief concession speech on November 5, Ford discovered he had lost his voice, and it was left to Betty to perform this last and final task of protocol. Just one day later, Susan underwent the agony of having all four of her wisdom teeth extracted.

25 Betty Ford, *The Times of My Life*, p. 280.

26 Since the District of Columbia is the only area in the United States which prohibits the carrying of arms by private agents, Vance has, from time to time, encountered obstacles in the promotion of his service.

27 Ford favored use of the term "presidential residence" in place of "presidential mansion."
28 Betty Ford, *The Times of My Life*, p. 112.

Jimmy Carter

1 Jimmy Carter, *Why Not the Best?*, pp. 9–10.
2 Earlier, it had always been assumed that Carter's younger brother, Billy, would inherit and manage the family business, but when the father died, Billy was only 16. After graduating from high school, he married Sibyl Spires, and went off to join the Marine Corps.
3 The others were, respectively, Gerry (11), Murray (8), and Althea (3).
4 Rosalynn Carter, *First Lady from Plains*, p. 52.
5 Rosalynn Carter, *op. cit.*, p. 54.
6 For the first time in a century, Georgia voted Republican. In the 1964 presidential election, Johnson received 486 electoral votes and Barry Goldwater only 52, of which Georgia contributed 12, the latter figure being the most from any of the six states which had supported Goldwater.
7 After the death of her husband she had become a fraternity house mother for seven years at Auburn University, Alabama. Having made the decision to go to India she had prepared herself by attending the University of Chicago to learn the Marathi and Hindi languages.
8 Jimmy Carter, *Why Not the Best?*, p. 71.
9 Despite the fact that the desegregation of schools had been strongly resisted in the South, it was achieved without violence in Plains, at least in token form, when, in 1966, two black students, accompanied by police, enrolled in the local school.
10 Where he attained high honors, having been finalist in the National Merit Scholarship competition, as well as runner-up in the Georgia Third District "Star Student" competition. He had also been selected to attend as Governor's Honors (summer) program at Wesleyan College in Macon (Betty Glad, *Jimmy Carter*, p. 72).
11 Rosalynn Carter, *First Lady from Plains*, p. 80.
12 Their first child, and the Carters' first grandchild, Jason, as born in August, 1976.
13 Jeff, the youngest son, was married in April, 1975, to Annette Jene Davis.
14 Rosalynn Carter, *First Lady from Plains*, p. 90.
15 He received 2,468½ votes, while his nearest opponent, Morris King Udall received 329½.
16 Rosalynn Carter, *First Lady from Plains*, p. 146.
17 When President Ali Ahmed Fakhruddin of India died, President Carter sent his mother, accompanied by Chip, to represent him at the funeral. "She took the opportunity of visiting Vikhroli, the village near Bombay where she had lived

for two years while serving in the Peace Corps, and received a great welcome" (Rosalynn Carter, *op. cit.*, p. 182).

18 Jimmy Carter, *Keeping Faith*, p. 34.

19 Rosalynn Carter, *op. cit.*, p. 171.

20 Presidents Carter and Brezhnev signed the Salt II Treaty in Vienna in June, 1979. Earlier, in March, Israel and Egypt signed a formal peace treaty in Washington, an accord which owed much to Carter's initiative and persistence.

21 Fourteen of the hostages were released during the earlier stages of the crisis. The remaining 52 served out the entire ordeal of 444 days.

22 Ronald Reagan received 489 votes from 44 states, and Jimmy Carter 49 votes from 6 states and the District of Columbia.

23 Jimmy Carter, *Keeping Faith*, pp. 544-5.

24 Years later he said, "History will probably remember me as a beer can, but it doesn't bother me—A lot of people don't get remembered as anything."

25 After Carter had been elected President, Gloria's husband, Walter, embarked upon a scheme to sell souvenir titles to plots of land in Plains adjoining the Carter peanut holdings. The scheme was condemned by Carter, but his publicly voiced objections did not prevent the sale of titles.

26 While in college, Amy, living in a cooperative of vegetarians, involved herself with several activist movements, as, for example, in March, 1986, when she and other students entered the office of IBM to protest the company's operations in South Africa. The students were arrested and later appeared in court on a trespass charge. Later in the same year, Amy was again arrested, this time for demonstrating at the University of Massachusetts at Amherst against recruiting on campus by the CIA.

When Amy, a natural blonde, dyed her hair black in mid-1986, her dismayed mother commented, "Why, with her pale white skin, she looks like a witch! . . . It looks as if she put black shoe polish on her head."

27

Published in 1982 by Bantam Books.

28 Published in 1985 by Houghton, Mifflin.

Ronald Wilson Reagan

1 On his inauguration day, January 20, 1981, Reagan was 69 years and 349 days old. Up until that date, the oldest President upon inauguration had been William Henry Harrison, who was 68 years and 23 days old.

2 This sobriquet was bestowed upon him by his father who, upon hearing him screaming in the arms of his mother, said, "For such a little bit of a Dutchman, he makes a lot of noise, doesn't he?" (Bill Adler, *Ronnie and Nancy*, p. 46).

3 Lee Edwards, *Ronald Reagan*, p. 20.

4 He once commented of his high school career, "I knew if I got a lot of good grades, I'd be automatically categorized as an intellectual and a teacher type. I certainly didn't want to be a teacher!" (Bill Adler, *Ronnie and Nancy*, p. 48).

[5] While at college, Reagan led a successful student strike against decisions made by the college president to cut back the faculty and thereby reduce curriculum offerings.

[6] They reteamed in the film sequel, *Brother Rat and a Baby*.

[7] George Gipp was the legendary young Notre Dame football star who died within a few weeks of his last game. In the film, George Gipp, on his deathbed, suggests to Coach Rockne that, when his team was on a losing streak, he should ask them to "Win One for the Gipper," a phrase which Reagan was subsequently to use many times in the course of his presidential campaigns.

[8] Upon awakening from the anaesthetic, McHugh cries out "Where's the Rest of Me?" This became the title of Reagan's autobiography published in 1965.

[9] Apart from making films, Jane helped to sell war bonds and entertain the troops.

[10] During the middle 1940's, two films were released in which Jane's performances were greeted with great enthusiasm by the critics: *The Lost Weekend*, when she co-starred with Ray Milland; and *The Yearling*, with Gregory Peck. In the latter film, as Ma Baxter, she had to shoot a fawn, for which "foul deed" Maureen refused to speak with her mother for days.

[11] Morella and Epstein, *Jane Wyman*, p. 78.

[12] Morella and Epstein, *op. cit.*, p. 124.

[13] In 1948, both parents featured in *It's a Great Feeling*, a film in which Maureen, now 8, made her movie debut.

[14] Ronald Reagan, *Where's the Rest of Me?*, p. 202.

[15] Nancy's father, Kenneth Robbins, later remarried, and they saw each other from time to time. But, on one occasion when Robbins said something unfavorable about her mother, Nancy became angry and replied derogatorily, which caused Robbins to lock her up in the bathroom. Recognizing that he had overreacted, he released her and apologized, but Nancy never forgave him for his action.

[16] Bill Adler, *Ronnie and Nancy*, p. 76.

[17] On March 13, 1952, nine days after the wedding, the engagement was announced of Jane Wyman to Travis Kleefeld, a building contractor and the scion of a wealthy Beverly Hills family. At the time of the engagement Jane was 38, and Kleefeld, 26, and their age discrepancy drew much adverse comment, and may have led to the further announcement, made only three weeks later, that the engagement had been broken off. (Morella and Epstein, *op. cit.*, p. 167).

[18] Morella and Epstein, *op. cit.*, p. 173.

[19] *Redbook* magazine interview, September, 1983, p. 70. Michael stated in the same interview that Jane had jokingly offered Michael's wife, Colleen, the use of the same riding crop if need be.

[20] Morella and Epstein, *op. cit.*, p. 172.

[21] Morella and Epstein, *op. cit.*, p. 189.

[22] Four years earlier, in 1962, Richard Nixon had failed in his bid to unseat Brown, a defeat which placed his political career in limbo until 1968, when he was nominated for President by the Republican party.

23 When Nancy discovered that the windows in eight-year-old Ronnie's bedroom were stuck fast, she inquired of the fire marshal what Ronnie should do in the event of a fire. His reply was, "Well, Mrs. Reagan, tell him to get a dresser drawer, hold it in front of him, run toward the window, break it, and climb out."

24 Adler, *Ronnie and Nancy*, p. 151.

25 Adler, *op. cit.*, p. 150–1.

26 Reagan received 1,939 votes. His closest rival, John Anderson of Illinois, received 37.

27 Reagan was accorded 489 electoral votes (44 states) to Carter's 49 (6 states plus the District of Columbia).

28 Michael alone made over 600 speeches in 35 states on behalf of his father.

29 Neil was quoted as having said, "I don't look well upon kids riding upon their father's coat tails." (Morella and Epstein, *op. cit.*, p. 234.) It was also at this time that Jane Wyman had embarked upon a highly successful television career, being cast as Angela Channing in the CBS production, *The Vintage Years*, later renamed *Falcon Crest*.

30 *U.S.A. Today*, March 19, 1984, p. 16.

31 Michael had also been involved in a court case relating to stock fraud, but he was completely vindicated, and was declared the victim of unscrupulous speculators.

32 *Redbook*, pp. 68–72.

33 Adler, *op cit.*, p. 199.

34 *Redbook*, p. 70.

35 Adler, *Ronnie and Nancy*, p. 213.

36 Morella and Epstein, *Jane Wyman*, p. 214.

37 *Kansas City Times*, June 22, 1985, p. A-2.

38 *Nancy*, p. 137.

39 *Nancy*, p. 139.

40 *Kansas City Star*, April 5, 1981, p. 20.

41 She wrote a song, "I Wish You Peace," which was recorded by the band. She was quoted by a California newspaper as saying that living with a boyfriend is as normal as "brushing your teeth," and that arresting people for smoking marijuana is "silly."

42 Adler, *Ronnie and Nancy*, p. 200.

43 Actually, when formally asked by the officiating minister of Bel Air Presbyterian Church as to who was giving away the bride, Reagan answered, "Her mother and I do." *Kansas City Times*, August 30, 1985.

[44] *Kansas City Star,* April 13, 1986, p. 9D.

[45] On ABC–TV, March 24, 1986.

[46] Adler, *op. cit.,* p. 165.

[47] *Kansas City Star,* October 22, 1982, p. 7A.

[48] *Newsweek,* February 14, 1984.

[49] Adler, *op. cit.,* p. 209.

[50] *Kansas City Times,* April 6, 1984, p. B8. Ron was also host of NBC's radio program, "Screen Scenes."

[51] *Newsweek,* March 10, 1986, p. 45.

Bibliography

General

Baldridge, Letitia. *Of Diamonds and Diplomats*. New York: Houghton Mifflin, 1968.

Barber, David. *The Presidential Character*. Englewood Cliffs, N.J.: Prentice-Hall, 1927.

Beard, Charles A. *Presidents in American History*. New York: Messner, 1961.

Bryant, Traphes and Frances Spatz. *Dogs Days at the White House*. New York: Macmillan, 1925.

Burke's Presidential Families of the United States of America. London: Burke's Peerage.

Calhoun, Arthur W. *A Social History of the American Family* (3 vols.). New York: Barnes & Noble, 1945.

Cavanah, Frances. *Children of the White House*. Chicago: Rand McNally, 1936.

Cavanah, Frances. *They Lived at the White House*. Philadelphia: Macrae Smith, 1959.

Coleman, Edna M. *Seventy Five Years of White House Gossip: from Washington to Lincoln*. Garden City, N.Y.: Doubleday Page, 1926.

Coleman, Edna M. *White House Gossip: from Andrew Johnson to Calvin Coolidge*. Garden City, N.Y.: Doubleday Page, 1927.

Crook, William H. (Ed.). *Memories of the White House*. Boston: Little Brown, 1911.

Dictionary of American Biography. New York: Charles Scribner's Sons, 1928.

Fields, Alonzo. *My 24 Years in the White House*. New York: Coward-McCann, 1961.

Furman, Bess. *Washington By-Line*. New York: Alfred A. Knopf, 1949.

Furman, Bess. *White House Profile*. New York: Bobbs-Merrill, 1951.

Gerlinger, Irene Hazard. *Mistresses of the White House*. New York: Samuel Frenec, 1948.

Graham, Alberta P. *Thirty Four Roads to the White House*. Camden, N.J.: T. Nelson, 1957.

Henry, Reginald Buchanan. *Genealogies of the Families of the Presidents*. Rutland, Vt: Tuttle, 1935.

Hoover, Irwin (Ike) H. *Forty Two Years in the White House*. New York: Houghton Mifflin, 1934.

Hunt, Irma. *Dearest Madame: The President's Mistresses*. New York: McGraw-Hill, 1979.

Jaffray, Elizabeth. *Secrets of the White House*. New York: Cosmopolitan Book Corporation, 1927.

Jeffries, Ona Griffin. *In and Out of the White House*. New York: Wilfred Funk Inc., 1960.

Jensen, Amy La Follette. *The White House and Its Thirty-Two Families*. New York: McGraw-Hill, 1958.

Kane, Joseph Nathan. *Facts About the Presidents*. New York: H. W. Wilson, 1981.

Langford, Laura Holloway. *The Ladies of the White House*. Philadelphia: Bradley & Co., 1881.

Logan, Logan B. *Ladies of the White House*. New York: Vantage, 1962.

Martin, Asa. *After the White House*. Pennsylvania State College, 1951.

Martin, Edward Winslow (pseudonym of James Dabney McCabe). *Behind the Scenes in Washington*. New York: Continental Publishing Co., 1873.

McConnell, Jane and Burt. *Our First Ladies*. New York: Thomas Y. Crowell. revised edition, 1969.

Means, Marianne. *The Women in the White House*. New York: Random House, 1963.

Miers, Earl S. *America and Its Presidents*. New York: Grosset, 1959.

Miller, Hope Riddings. *Scandals in the Higher Office*. New York: Random House, 1973.

Minnigerode, Meade. *Some American Ladies*. Freeport, N.Y.: Books for Libraries Press, reprinted 1919.

Moses, John and Wilbur Cross. *Presidential Courage*. New York: W. W. Norton, 1981.

Nesbitt, Victoria Henrietta. *White House Diary*. Garden City, N.Y.: Doubleday, 1948.

Parks, Lilian Rogers with Frances Spatz. *My Thirty Years Backstairs at the White House*. New York: Fleet Publishing Corp., 1961.

Pendel, Thomas F. *Thirty-Six Years in the White House: Lincoln-Roosevelt*. Washington: Neale Publishing Co., 1902.

Perling, J. J. *The Presidents' Sons* New York: Odyssey Press, 1947.

Prindeville, Kathleen. *First Ladies*. New York: Macmillan, 1964.

Randolph, Mary. *Presidents and First Ladies*. New York: D. Appleton-Century, 1936.

Ross, George E. *Know Your Presidents and Their Wives*. Chicago: Rand McNally, 1961.

Shaw, Maud. *White House Nannie*. New York: New American Library, 1965.

Smith, Margaret Bayard. *The First Forty Years of Washington Society*. New York: Gaillard Hunt, 1906.

Stevens, William Oliver. *Famous Women of America*. New York: Dodd, 1950.

Stoddard, William O. *The Lives of the Presidents*. New York: (Private Printing) 1889.

Thomas, Helen. *Dateline: White House*. New York: Macmillan, 1975.

Thompson, Charles Willis. *Presidents I've Known and Two Near Presidents*. Freeport N.Y.: Books for Libraries Press, 1970.

Upton, Harriet Taylor. *Our Early Presidents*. Boston: Lothrop, 1891.

West, J. B. *Upstairs in the White House*. New York: Coward, McCann and Geoghegan, 1973.

Whitton, Mary Ormsbee. *First First Ladies, 1789–1865*. Freeport, N.Y.: Books for Libraries Press, reprinted 1948.

Wise, John S. *Recollections of Thirteen Presidents* Freeport, N.Y.: Books for Libraries Press 1906, reprinted 1968.

Young, Klyde H. *Heirs Apparent*. New York: Prentice Hall, 1948.

George Washington

Alden, John R. *George Washington*. Baton Rouge: Louisiana State University Press, 1984.

Borden, Morton. *George Washington*. Englewood Cliffs, N.J.: Prentice-Hall, 1964.

Custis, George Washington Parke. *Recollections and Private Memoirs of Washington*. New York: Derby and Jackson, 1860.

Decatur, Stephen, Jr. *The Private Affairs of George Washington*. New York: Da Capo, 1964.

Desmond, Alice Curtis. *Martha Washington*. New York: Dodd, 1942.

Fitzpatrick, John C. (Ed.). *The Diaries of George Washington*. New York: Houghton Mifflin, 1925.

Fleming, Thomas J. (Ed.). *Affectionately Yours, George Washington*. New York: Norton, 1967.

Flexner, James Thomas. *George Washington*. Boston: Little Brown, 1970.

Freeman, Douglas Southall *George Washington*. New York: Scribner's Sons, 1968.

Hobby, Laura Aline. *Washington, the Lover*. Dallas: Southwest Press, 1932.

Irving, Washington. *Life of George Washington*. Tarrytown, N.Y.: Sleepy Hollow Restorations, 1975.

Lossing, Benson John. *Mary and Martha, the Mother and Wife of George Washington*. New York: Harper, 1886.

Moore, Charles. *The Family Life of George Washington*. Boston: Houghton Mifflin, 1926.

Nolan, Jeannette C. *The Story of Martha Washington*. New York: Grosset, 1954.

Prussing, Eugene Ernest. *George Washington in Love and Otherwise*. Chicago: P. Covici, 1925.

Rush, Richard. *Washington in Domestic Life*. Philadelphia: J. B. Lippincott, 1857.

Swiggett, Howard. *The Great Man: George Washington as a Human Being*. Garden City, N.Y.: Doubleday, 1953.

Thane, Elswyth. *The Life of Martha Washington*, Duell Meredith, 1960.

Thane, Elswyth. *Mount Vernon Family*. New York: Crowell-Collier Press, 1968.

Vance, Marguerite. *Martha, Daughter of Virginia*. New York: Dutton, 1947.

Weems, Mason L. *The Life of George Washington*. Edited by Marcus Cunliffe. Cambridge, Mass., 1962.

John Adams

Adams, Charles Francis. *Familiar Letters of John Adams and His Wife, Abigail Adams*. Boston: Houghton Mifflin, 1875.

Adams, James Truslow. *The Adams Family*. Boston: Little Brown, 1930.

Akers, Charles W. *Abigail Adams, an American Woman*. Boston: Little Brown, 1980.

Bobbé, Dorothie. *Abigail Adams*. New York: Minton, Balch and Co., 1929.

Butterfield, L. H. (Ed.). *John Adams: Diary and Autobiography*. Cambridge, Mass: Belknap Press, 1961.

Criss, Mildred. *Abigail Adams: Leading Lady*. New York: Dodd, 1952.

Kelly, Regina. *Abigail Adams: The President's Lady*. Boston: Houghton, 1962.

Kurtz, Stephen G. *The Presidency of John Adams*. Philadelphia: University of Pennsylvania Press, 1957.

Mitchell, Stewart. (Ed.). *New Letters of Abigail Adams*. Boston: Houghton Mifflin, 1947.

Russell, Francis. *An American Dynasty*. New York: American Heritage Publishing Company, 1976.

Shaw, Peter. *The Character of John Adams*. Chapel Hill:University of North Carolina Press, 1976.

Smith, Page. *John Adams*. Garden City, New York: Doubleday, 1962.

Wagoner, Jean Brown. *Abigail Adams: A Girl of Colonial Days*. Indianapolis: Bobbs, 1949.

Whitney, Janet. *Abigail Adams*. Boston: Little Brown, 1947.

Withey, Lynne. *Dearest Friend: A Life of Abigail Adams*. New York: Free Press, 1981.

Thomas Jefferson

Bear, James A., Jr. (Ed.). *Jefferson at Monticello*. Charlottesville, Va.: University Press of Virginia, 1967.

Beloff, Max. *Thomas Jefferson and American Democracy*. New York: Macmillan, 1949.

Betts, Edwin Morris and James Adams Bear. (Eds.). *The Family Letters of Thomas Jefferson*. Columbia, Mo: University of Missouri Press, 1966.

Bowers, Claude G. *The Young Jefferson*. Boston: Houghton Mifflin, 1945.

Boykin, Edward. *To the Boys and Girls, being the delightful little known letters of Thomas Jefferson to and from his children and grandchildren*. New York: Funk and Wagnall, 1964.

Brodie, Fawn. *Thomas Jefferson*. New York: W. W. Norton, 1974.

Chase, Barbara. *Sally Hemings*. Ribaud, N.Y.: Viking Press, 1979.

Criss, Mildred. *Jefferson's Daughter*. New York: Dodd, Mead & Co., 1948.

Dabney, Virginius. *The Jefferson Scandals*. New York: Dodd, Mead & Co., 1981.

Dumbauld, Edward. *Thomas Jefferson, American Tourist*. Norman, Okla.: University of Oklahoma Press, 1946.

Fleming, Thomas J. *The Man from Monticello*. New York: Morrow, 1969.

Gaines, William H., Jr. *Thomas Mann Randolph: Jefferson's Son-in-Law*. Baton Rouge, La., 1966.

Hall, Gordon Langley. *Mr. Jefferson's Ladies*. Boston: Beacon Press, 1966.

Johnstone, R. M., Jr. *Thomas Jefferson and the Presidency*. Ithaca, N.Y.: Cornell University Press, 1978.

Kuenzli, Esther Wilcox. *The Last Years of Thomas Jefferson, 1809–1826*. Hickesville, N.Y.: Exposition Press, 1974.

Mayo, Bernard. (Ed.) *Jefferson Himself*. Charlottesville, Va.: University Press of Virginia, 1970.

McAdie, Alexander. *Thomas Jefferson at Home*. Worchester, Mass., 1931.

Patton, John S. and Sallie J. Doswell. *Monticello and Its Master*. Charlottesville, Va, 1925.

Pierson, Hamilton Wilson. *Jefferson at Monticello*. Charlottesville, Va, 1967.

Randolph, Sarah N. *The Domestic Life of Thomas Jefferson*. Monticello-Charlottesville, Va.: Thomas Jefferson Memorial Foundation, 3rd ed., 1967.

Schachner, Nathan. *Thomas Jefferson*. New York: Appleton-Century, Crofts, 1951.

Smith, Page. *Jefferson: A Revealing Biography.* New York: American Heritage Pub. Co., 1976.

James Madison

Arnett, Ethel Stevens. *Mrs. James Madison.* Greensboro, N.C.: Piedmont Press, 1972.

Brandt, Irving. *The Fourth President; A Life of James Madison.* New York: Bobbs Merrill, 1970.

Cutts, Lucia B. (Ed.). *Memoirs and Letters of Dolly Madison.* New York: Houghton Mifflin Co., 1886.

Desmond, Alice Curtis. *Glamorous Dolly Madison.* New York: Dodd, 1946.

Gaillard, Hunt. *The Life of James Madison.* New York: Doubleday, Page & Co., 1902.

Gerson, Noel. *The Velvet Glove.* New York: Nelson, 1975.

Ketcham, Ralph L. *James Madison.* New York: Macmillan, 1971.

Mayer, Jane. *Dolly Madison.* New York: Random House, 1954.

Monsell, Helen Albee. *Dolly Madison: Quaker Girl.* Indianapolis: Bobbs, 1953.

Moore, Virginia. *The Madisons.* New York: McGraw Hill, 1979.

Nolan, Jeannette. *Dolley Madison.* New York: Messner, 1958.

Peterson, Merrill D. (Ed.). *James Madison.* New York: Newsweek Book Division, 1974.

Thane, Elswyth. *Dolley Madison, Her Life and Times.* New York: Crowell-Collier Press, 1970.

James Monroe

Ammon, Harry. *James Monroe.* New York: McGraw Hill, 1971.

Brown, Stuart Gerry. (Ed.). *Autobiography of James Monroe.* Syracuse, N.Y.: Syracuse University Press, 1959.

Cresson, William Penn. *James Monroe.* Chapel Hill: University of North Carolina Press, 1946.

Morgan, George. *The Life of James Monroe.* Boston, Small, Maynard & Co., 1921.

John Quincy Adams

Adams, Charles Francis. (Ed.). *Memoirs of John Quincy Adams.* Philadelphia: J. B. Lippincott, 1874–77.

Allen, David Grayson. (Ed.). *Diary of John Quincy Adams.* Cambridge, Mass.: Belknap Press, 1981.

Bobbé, Dorothie. *Mr. and Mrs. John Quincy Adams.* New York: Minton, Balch & Co., 1930.
East, Robert A. *John Quincy Adams: The Critical Years.* New York: Twayne, 1962.
Shepherd, Jack. *Cannibals of the Heart.* New York: McGraw Hill, 1980.
Hecht, Marie B. *John Quincy Adams.* New York: Macmillan, 1972.

Andrew Jackson

Bassett, John Spencer. *The Life of Andrew Jackson.* Boston, 1967.
Caldwell, Mary French. *General Jackson's Lady.* Kingsport, Tenn.: Kingsport Press, 1936.
Colyar, A. St. Clair. *The Life and Times of Andrew Jackson.* Nashville, Tenn.: Marshall and Bruce, 1936.
Coy, Harold. *Real Book About Andrew Jackson.* New York: Doubleday, 1952.
Govan, Christine. *Rachel Jackson: Tennessee Girl.* Indianapolis: Bobbs, 1955.
Johnson, Gerald W. *Andrew Jackson.* New York: Minton Balch, 1927.
Marquis, James. *The Life of Andrew Jackson.* Indianapolis: Bobbs-Merrill, 1938.
Parton, James. *Life of Andrew Jackson.* New York: Mason Brothers, 1860.
Remini, Robert V. *Andrew Jackson.* New York: Twayne Publishers, 1966.
Vance, Marguerite. *The Jacksons of Tennessee.* New York: Dutton, 1953.

Martin Van Buren

Curtis, J. C. *The Fox at Bay.* Lexington: University Press of Kentucky, 1970.
Fitzpatrick, John C. *The Autobiography of Martin Van Buren* (edited). New York: A. M. Kelley, 1969.
Lynch. *An Epoch and a Man, Martin Van Buren and His Times.* New York: H. Liveright, 1924.
Nevin, John. *Martin Van Buren.* New York: Oxford University Press, 1983.
Shepard, Edward M. *Martin Van Buren.* Boston: Houghton Mifflin, 1891.

William Henry Harrison

Cleaves, Freeman. *Old Tippecanoe, William Henry Harrison and His Time.* Port Washington, N.Y.: Kennikat Press, 1969.
Young, Stanley. *Tippecanoe and Tyler, Too!* New York: Random House, 1957.

John Tyler

Chitwood, Oliver P. *John Tyler.* New York: D. Appleton-Century, 1939.

Tyler, Lyon G. *The Letters and Times of the Tylers* (3 vols). New York: Da Capo Press, 1970 reprint.

Zachary Taylor

Dyer, Brainerd. *Zachary Taylor*. Baton Rouge, La.: Louisiana State University Press, 1946.
Hamilton, Holman. *Zachary Taylor* (2 vols). Indianapolis: Bobbs-Merrill, 1941.
McKinley, Silas Bent. *Old Rough and Ready*. New York: Vanguard Press, 1946.
Taylor, Zachary. *Letters of Zachary Taylor*. New York: Genesee Press, 1908.

Millard Fillmore

Grayson, Benson Lee. *The Unknown President*. Washington, D.C.: University Press of America, 1981.
Griffis, William E. *Millard Fillmore*. Ithaca, N.Y.: Andrus and Church, 1915.
Snyder, Charles M. *The Lady and the President (The Letters of Dorothea Dix and Millard Fillmore)*. Lexington: University Press of Kentucky, 1975.

Franklin Pierce

Hawthorne, Nathaniel. *The Life of Franklin Pierce*. New York: Garrett Press, 1970 reprint.
Nichols, Roy Franklin. *Franklin Pierce, Young Hickory of the Granite Hills*. Philadelphia: University of Pennsylvania Press, 1958.

James Buchanan

Klein, Philip Shriver. *President James Buchanan*. University Park: Pennsylvania State University Press, 1962.
Smith, Elbert. *The Presidency of James Buchanan*. Lawrence, Ks.: University Press of Kansas, 1975.

Abraham Lincoln

Angle, Paul M. *Abraham Lincoln*. Springfield, Ill.: Springfield Life Insurance Co., 1926.
Barton, William E. *The Women Lincoln Loved*. Indianapolis: Bobbs-Merrill, 1927.
Bayne, Julia (Taft). *Tad Lincoln's Father*. Boston: Little, Brown, 1931.

Carpenter, Francis Bicknell. *Six Months at the White House with Abraham Lincoln.* New York: Hurd and Houghton, 1866.

Carruthers, Olive. *Lincoln's Other Mary.* New York: Ziff-Davis, 1946.

Clark, L. P. *Lincoln: A Psycho-Biography.* New York: Charles Scribner's Sons, 1933.

Current, Richard. *The Lincoln Nobody Knows.* New York: McGraw Hill, 1958.

Curtis, William Eleroy. *The True Abraham Lincoln.* Philadelphia: J. B. Lippincott, 1903.

Evans, William A. *Mrs. Abraham Lincoln.* New York: Knopf, 1932.

Goff, John S. *Robert Todd Lincoln.* Norman: University of Oklahoma Press, 1968.

Hall, Gordon Langley. *A Rose for Mrs. Lincoln.* Boston: Beacon Press, 1970.

Helm, Katherine. *The True Story of Mary, Wife of Lincoln.* New York: Harper, 1928.

Herndon, William Henry. *Herndon's Lincoln.* New York: Belford, Clark & Co., 1889.

Keckley, Elizabeth. *Behind the Scenes—Thirty Years a Slave and Four Years in the White House.* New York: Arno Press, 1968 (reprint).

Lockridge, Ross. *Abraham Lincoln.* Yonkers-on-Hudson, N.Y.: World Book Co., 1931.

Masters, Edgar Lee. *Lincoln, the Man.* New York: Dodd, Mead, & Co., 1931.

Morgan, James. *Abraham Lincoln, the Boy and the Man.* New York: Macmillan, 1917.

Neely, Mark E. and R. Gerald McMurty. *The Insanity File: The Case of Mary Todd Lincoln.* Southern Illinois Univ., 1987.

Randall, Ruth Painter. *Mary Lincoln.* Boston: Little Brown, 1953.

Randall, Ruth Painter. *Lincoln's Sons.* Boston: Little Brown, 1955.

Ross, Isabel. *The President's Life: Mary Todd Lincoln.* New York: Putnam's, 1973.

Sandburg, Carl. *Abraham Lincoln.* New York: Harcourt Brace, 1926.

Sandburg, Carl. *Mary Lincoln, Wife and Widow.* Part I. New York: Harcourt Brace, 1932.

Stephenson, Nathaniel Wright. *Lincoln.* New York: Grosset and Dunlap, 1924.

Suppiger, Joseph E. *The Intimate Lincoln.* Lanham, Md.: University Press of America, 1985.

Tarbell, Ida Minerva. *The Life of Abraham Lincoln.* New York: McClure, Phillips, & Co., 1902.

Turner, Justin G. and Linda Levitt. *Mary Todd Lincoln.* New York: Knopf, 1972.

Wilkie, Katherine E. *Mary Todd Lincoln: Girl of the Blue Grass.* Indianapolis: Bobbs, 1954.

Andrew Johnson

Bowers, Claude G. *The Tragic Era: The Revolution After Lincoln.* 1929.

Lomask, Milton. *Andy Johnson: The Taylor Who Became President.* New York: Farrar Strauss, 1962.

McKitrick, E. L. (Ed.). *Andrew Johnson.* New York: Hill and Wang, 1969.

Stryker, Lloyd Paul. *Andrew Johnson: A Study in Courage.* New York: MacMillan, 1929.

Winston, Robert Watson. *Andrew Johnson, Plebeian and Patriot.* New York: Barnes and Noble, 1928.

Ulysses S. Grant

Badeau, Adam. *Grant in peace . . . A personal memoir.* Hartford: S. S. Scranton, 1887.

Carpenter, John A. *Ulysses S. Grant.* New York: Twayne Publishers Inc., 1970.

Cramer, Jesse Grant. (Ed.). *Letters of Ulysses S. Grant.* New York: G. P. Putnam's Sons, 1912.

Goldhurst, Richard. *Many Are the Hearts.* New York: Thomas Y. Crowell, 1975.

Grant, Jesse R. *In the Days of My Father, General Grant.* New York: Harper and Brothers, 1925.

McFeely, William S. *Grant.* New York: W. W. Norton, 1981.

Ross, Ishbel. *The General's Wife.* New York: Dodd, 1959.

Simon, John Y. (Ed.). *The Personal Memoirs of Julia Dent Grant.* New York: G. P. Putnam, 1975.

Todd, Helen. *A Man Named Grant.* Boston: Houghton Mifflin, 1940.

Woodward, W. E. *Meet General Grant.* New York: Liveright Publishing Corp., 1946.

Rutherford Hayes

Barnard, Harry. *Rutherford B. Hayes and His America.* Indianapolis: Bobbs-Merrill, 1954.

Davison, Kenneth E. *The Presidency of Rutherford B. Hayes.* Westport, Conn: Greenwood Press, 1972.

Geer, Emily A. *First Lady: The Life of Lucy Webb Hayes.* Kent, Ohio: Kent State University Press, 1984.

Williams, Charles R. *The Life of Rutherford Birchard Hayes.* Boston: Houghton Mifflin Co., 1914.

Williams, T. Harry. (Ed.). *Hayes: The Diary of a President (1875–81).* New York: David McKay C., 1964.

James A. Garfield

Alger, Horatio. *From Canal Boy to President.* New York: J. R. Anderson, 1881.

Brown, Harry James and Frederick D. Williams. (Eds.). *The Diary of James A. Garfield.* East Lansing, Mich.: Michigan State University, 1967.

Comer, Lucretia G. *Strands from the Weaving (The Story of Harry Garfield).* New York: Vantage Press, 1959.

Feis, Ruth S-B. *Molly Garfield in the White House.* New York: Rand McNally, 1963.

Leech, Margaret and Harry J. Brown. *The Garfield Orbit.* New York: Harper & Row, 1978.

Peskin, Allan. *Garfield.* Kent, Ohio: Kent State University Press, 1978.

Smith, Theodore C. *The Life and Letters of James Abram Garfield.* New Haven: Yale University Press, 1925.

Chester A. Arthur

Doenecke, Justus D. *The Presidencies of James A. Garfield and Chester A. Arthur.* Lawrence, Ks.: The Regents Press of Kansas, 1981.

Howe, George F. *Chester A. Arthur.* New York: Frederick Ungar Publishing Co., 1935 (reprint 1957).

Reeves, Thomas C. *Gentleman Boss.* New York: Alfred A. Knopf, 1975.

Benjamin Harrison

Harrison, John S. *Pioneer Life at North Bend.* Cincinnati: O. R. Clarks, 1867.

Sievers, Harry. *Benjamin Harrison: Vol. 1: Hoosier Warrior (1865)* New York: University Publishers, 1952. *Vol. 2: Hoosier Statesman (1865–1888).* New York: University Publishers, 1959. *Vol. 3: Hoosier President (1888)* Indianapolis: Bobbs-Merrill, 1968.

Grover Cleveland

Tugwell, Rexford G. *Grover Cleveland.* New York: Macmillan, 1968.

Lynch, Denis Tilden. *Grover Cleveland. A Man Four-Square.* New York: Liveright, 1932.

McElroy, Robert McNutt. *Grover Cleveland.* New York: Harper & Row, 1923.

Nevins, Allan. (Ed.). *Letters of Grover Cleveland.* New York: Houghton Mifflin, 1933.

Nevins, Allan. (Ed.). *Grover Cleveland. A Study in Courage.* New York: Dodd, Mead & Co, 1932.

Parker, George F. *Recollections of Grover Cleveland*. New York: The Century Co., 1909.

William McKinley

Corning, A. Elwood. *William McKinley: A Bibliographical Study*. New York: Broadway Publishing Co., 1907.
Leech, Margaret K. *In the Days of McKinley*. New York: Harper and Row, 1959.
Morgan, H. Wayne. *William McKinley and His America*. Syracuse, N.Y.:Syracuse University Press, 1963.
Olcott, Charles S. *The Life of William McKinley*. Boston: Houghton Mifflin Co., 1916.

Theodore Roosevelt

Abbott, Lawrence F. (Ed.). *The Letters of Archie Butt, Personal Aide to President Roosevelt*. Garden City, N.Y.: Doubleday Page, 1924.
Bishop, Joseph Bucklin. *Theodore Roosevelt's Letters to His Children*. New York: Scribner's, 1919.
Bishop, Joseph Bucklin. *Theodore Roosevelt and His Time*. New York: Scribner's, 1920.
Brough, James. *Princess Alice*. Boston: Little Brown, 1975.
Cassini, Marguerite. *Never a Dull Moment*. New York: Harper and Bros., 1956.
Cavanah, Frances. *Adventures in Courage: The Story of Theodore Roosevelt*. Chicago: Rand McNally, 1961.
Hagedorn, Hermann. *The Roosevelt Family of Sagamore Hill*. New York: Macmillan, 1954.
Lash, Joseph P. *Eleanor and Franklin*. New York: Norton, 1971.
Lewis, William Draper. *The Life of Theodore Roosevelt*. Philadelphia: Winston, 1919.
Longworth, Alice R. *Crowded Hours*. New York: Scribner's, 1933.
Looker, Earle. *The White House Gang*. New York: Fleming H. Revell, 1929.
Morris, Sylvia Jukes. *Edith Kermit Roosevelt*. New York: Coward, McCann and Geoghegan, 1980.
Pringle, Henry F. *Theodore Roosevelt*. New York: Harcourt Brace, 1956.
Putnam, Carleton. *Theodore Roosevelt: The Formative Years*. New York: Scribner's, 1958.
Rixey, Lillian. *Bamie: Theodore Roosevelt's Remarkable Sister*. David McKay, 1963.
Robinson, Corinne R. *My Brother, Theodore Roosevelt*. New York: Scribner's, 1921.
Roosevelt, Edith Kermit, *et al. Cleared for Strange Ports*. New York: Scribner's, 1924.

Roosevelt, Kermit. *The Long Trail.* New York: Review of Reviews, 1921.

Roosevelt, Kermit. (Ed.). *Quentin Roosevelt: A Sketch with Letters.* New York: Scribner's, 1921.

Roosevelt, Nicholas. *T.R.: The Man as I Knew Him.* New York: Dodd, Mead, 1967.

Roosevelt, Theodore. *Autobiography.* New York: Macmillan, 1913.

Roosevelt, Theodore and Kermit Roosevelt. *East of the Sun and West of the Moon.* New York: Scribner's, 1926.

Roosevelt, Theodore, Jr. *All in the Family.* New York: Putnam, 1929.

Roosevelt, Mrs. Theodore, Jr. *Days Before Yesterday.* Garden City, N.Y.: Doubleday, 1929.

Teague, Michael. *Mrs. L. (Conversations with Alice Roosevelt Longworth.)* London: Duckworth, 1982.

Thayer, William Roscoe. *Theodore Roosevelt: An Intimate Biography.* New York: Houghton Mifflin, 1919.

Wister, Owen. *Roosevelt, The Story of Friendship.* New York: Macmillan, 1930.

Wood, Frederick S. *Roosevelt as We Knew Him.* Philadelphia: The John Winston Co., 1927.

William H. Taft

Anderson, Judith Icke. *William Howard Taft.* New York: W. W. Norton, 1982.

Patterson, James T. *Mr. Republican: A Biography of Robert A. Taft.* Boston: Houghton Mifflin, 1972.

Pringle, Henry F. *The Life and Times of William Howard Taft.* New York: Farrar & Rhinehart Inc., 1939.

Robbins, Phyllis. *Robert A. Taft, Boy and Man.* Cambridge Mass.: Dresser, Chapman and Grimes, 1963.

Ross, Ishbel. *An American Family: The Tafts, 1678 to 1964.* Westport, Conn.: Greenwood Press, 1977.

Taft, Horace Dutton. *Memories and Opinions.* New York: Macmillan, 1942.

Taft, Mrs. William Howard. *Recollections of Full Years.* New York: Dodd, Mead & Co., 1914.

Woodrow Wilson

Alsop, Bowles. *The Greatness of Woodrow Wilson.* Port Washington, N.Y.: Kennikat Press, 1956.

Baker, Ray S. *Woodrow Wilson: Life and Letters.* New York: Doubleday, 1937.

Broesamle, John J. *William Gibbs McAdoo.* Port Washington N.Y.: Kennikat Press, 1973.

Craig, Hardin. *Woodrow Wilson at Princeton*. Norman: University of Oklahoma Press, 1960.

Daniels, Josephus. *The Life of Woodrow Wilson, 1856–1924*. Philadelphia: The John C. Winston Co., 1924.

Elliot, Margaret Axon. *My Aunt Louise and Woodrow Wilson*. Chapel Hill: University of North Carolina Press, 1944.

Freud, Sigmund, and William C. Bullett. *Thomas Woodrow Wilson: A Psychological Study*. Boston: Houghton Mifflin, 1967 (reprint).

Garraty, John A. *Woodrow Wilson*. New York: Alfred A. Knopf, 1956.

Grayson, Cary T. *Woodrow Wilson: An Intimate Memoir*. New York: Holt, Rinehart, and Winston, 1960.

Hatch, Alden. *Edith Bolling Wilson*. New York: Dodd, Mead & Co., 1961.

Hulbert, Mary Allen. *The Story of Mrs. Peck, an Autobiography*. New York: Minton, Balch & Co., 1933.

Lawrence, David. *The True Story of Woodrow Wilson*. New York, 1924.

McAdoo, Eleanor Randolph, and Margaret Y. Gaffey. *The Woodrow Wilsons*. New York: Macmillan, 1937.

McAdoo, Eleanor Wilson. *A Priceless Gift: The Love Letters of Woodrow Wilson and Ellen Axson Wilson*. New York: McGraw Hill, 1962.

McAdoo, William Gibbs. *Crowded Years*. Boston: Houghton Mifflin, 1931.

Osborn, George Coleman. *Woodrow Wilson: The Early Years*. Baton Rouge: Louisiana State University Press, 1968.

Reid, Edith Gittings. *Woodrow Wilson: The Caricature, the Myth, and the Man*. Oxford: Oxford University Press, 1934.

Ross, Ishbel. *Power with Grace*. New York: Putnam, 1975.

Saunders, Frances Wright. *Ellen Axson Wilson*. Chapel Hill: University of North Carolina Press, 1985.

Smith, Gene. *When the Cheering Stopped*. New York: Morrow, 1964.

Steinberg, Alfred. *Woodrow Wilson*. New York: G. P. Putnam, 1961.

Thompson, Charles W. *Presidents I've Known and Two Near Presidents*. Indianapolis: Bobbs-Merrill Co., 1929.

Tribble, Edwin. (Ed.). *A President in Love: The Courtship Letters of Woodrow Wilson and Edith Bolling Galt*. Boston: Houghton Mifflin, 1981.

Tumulty, Joseph P. *Woodrow Wilson as I Knew Him*. Garden City, N.Y.: Doubleday, Page & Co., 1924.

Weinstein, Edwin A. *Woodrow Wilson: A Medical and Psychological Biography*. Princeton, N.J.: Princeton University Press, 1981.

White, William Allen. *Woodrow Wilson: The Man, His Times and His Task*. Boston: Houghton Mifflin Co., 1924.

Wilson, Edith Bolling. *My Memoir*. Indianapolis: Bobbs-Merrill Co., 1939.

Warren G. Harding

Adams, Samuel Hopkins. *Incredible Era: The Life and Times of Warren Gamaliel Harding*. Boston: Capricorn Books, 1939.

Britton, Nan. *The President's Daughter.* New York: Elizabeth Ann Guild, Inc., 1927.

Britton, Nan. *Honesty or Politics.* New York: Elizabeth Ann Guild, Inc., 1932.

Daugherty, H. M. and Thomas Dixon. *The Inside Story of the Harding Tragedy.* Boston: Western Islands, 1975 (reprint).

Downs, Randolph Chandler. *The Rise of Warren Gamaliel Harding.* Columbus: Ohio State University Press, 1970.

Means, Gaston B. *The Strange Death of President Harding.* New York: Guild, 1930.

Russell, Francis. *The Shadow of Blooming Grove.* New York: McGraw Hill, 1968.

Sinclair, Andrew. *The Available Man: The Life Behind the Masks of Warren Gamaliel Harding.* New York: Macmillan, 1965.

Johnson, Willis Fletcher. *The Life of Warren Harding.* Chicago: John Winston Co., 1923.

Calvin Coolidge

Coolidge, Calvin. *The Autobiography of Calvin Coolidge.* New York: Cosmopolitan Book Corp., 1929.

Green, Horace. *Life of Calvin Coolidge.* New York: Duffield and Co., 1924.

Ross, Ishbel. *Grace Coolidge and Her Era.* New York: Dodd, 1962.

White, William Allen. *A Puritan in Babylon.* New York: Macmillan, 1931.

Woods, Robert. *The Preparation of Calvin Coolidge.* Boston: Houghton Mifflin, 1924.

McCoy, Donald R. *Calvin Coolidge; The Quiet President.* New York: Macmillan, 1967.

Herbert Clark Hoover

Corey, Herbert. *The Truth About Hoover.* New York: Houghton Mifflin, 1932.

Burner, David. *Herbert Hoover.* New York: Knopf, 1979.

Hinshaw, David. *Herbert Hoover: American Quaker.* New York: Farrar Strauss, 1950.

Hoover, Herbert. *A Boyhood in Iowa.* New York: Aventine Press, 1931.

Irwin, William H. *Herbert Hoover.* New York: The Century Co., 1928.

Lyons, Eugene. *Herbert Hoover.* Garden City, N.Y.: Doubleday and Co., 1964.

Nash, George H. *The Life of Herbert Hoover.* New York: W. W. Norton, 1983.

Pryor, Helen B. *Lou Henry Hoover: Gallant First Lady.* New York: Dodd, Mead & Co., 1969.

Wilson, Carol Green. *Herbert Hoover.* New York: Evans Publishing Co., 1968.

Wilson, Joan Hoff. *Herbert Hoover.* Boston: Little Brown & Co., 1975.

Franklin D. Roosevelt

Asbell, Bernard. (Ed.). *Mother and Daughter (The Letters of Eleanor and Anna Roosevelt)*. New York: Coward, McCann and Geoghegan, 1982.

Black, Ruby. *Eleanor Roosevelt: A Biography*. New York: Duell, Sloan and Pearce, 1940.

Boettiger, John R. *A Love in Shadow*. New York: Norton, 1978.

Burns, James MacGregor. *Roosevelt: The Lion and the Fox*. New York: Harcourt Brace, 1956.

Davis, Kenneth Sydney. *Invincible Summer: An Intimate Portrait of the Roosevelts*. New York: Atheneum, 1974.

Douglas, Helen Gahagan. *The Eleanor Roosevelt We Remember*. New York: Hill and Wang, 1963.

Eaton, Jeanette. *The Story of Eleanor Roosevelt*. New York: Morrow, 1956.

Hershan, Stella K. *A Woman of Quality*. New York: Crown Publishers, 1970.

Hickock, Lorena. *The Story of Eleanor Roosevelt*. New York: Grosset, 1959.

Josephson, Emmanuel M. *The Strange Death of Franklin D. Roosevelt*. New York: Chedney Press, 1948.

Lash, Joseph P. *A World of Love*. New York: Doubleday, 1984.

Lash, Joseph P. *Eleanor and Franklin*. New York: Morton, 1971.

Lash, Joseph P. *Love, Eleanor: Eleanor Roosevelt and Her Friends*. Garden City, N.Y.: Doubleday, 1982.

Lash, Joseph P. *Eleanor: The Years Alone*. New York: Norton, 1972.

Lash, Joseph P. *Eleanor Roosevelt*. Garden City, N.Y.: Doubleday, 1964.

Lash, Joseph P. *Life Was Meant to Be Lived*. Chicago: World Book, 1985.

Lash, Joseph P. *Without Precedent: The Life and Career of Eleanor Roosevelt*.

Nesbitt, Henrietta. *White House Diary: F.D.R.'s Housekeeper*. Garden City, N.Y.: Doubleday, 1948.

Perkins, Frances. *The Roosevelt I Knew*. New York: Viking Press, 1946.

Roosevelt, Eleanor. *Autobiography*. New York: Harper, 1961.

Roosevelt, Eleanor. *This Is My Story*. New York: Garden City Publishing Co., 1939.

Roosevelt, Eleanor. *This I Remember*. New York: Harper, 1949.

Roosevelt, Eleanor. *Tomorrow Is Now*. New York: Harper & Row, 1963.

Roosevelt, Elliott (with James Brough). *An Untold Story: The Roosevelts of Hyde Park*. New York: G. P. Putnam's Sons, 1973.

Roosevelt, Elliott (with James Brough). *A Rendezvous with Destiny*. New York: G. P. Putnam's Sons, 1975.

Roosevelt, Elliott (with James Brough). *Mother R.: Eleanor Roosevelt's Untold Story*. New York: G. P. Putnam's Sons, 1977.

Roosevelt, Elliott. *Eleanor Roosevelt: A Centenary Remembrance with Love*.

Roosevelt, Elliott. *As He Saw It*. New York: Duell, Sloan and Pearce, 1946.

Roosevelt, Elliott. (Ed.). *F.D.R.: His Personal Letters*. New York: Duell, Sloan & Pearce, 1970 reprint.

Roosevelt, James (with Sidney Shalett). *Affectionately, F.D.R.* New York: Harcourt Brace, 1959.

Roosevelt, James (with Bill Libby). *My Parents: A Differing View.* Chicago: Playboy Press, 1976.

Roosevelt, Sara. *My Boy Franklin.* New York: R. Long & R. R. Smith, 1933.

Steinberg, Alfred. *Eleanor Roosevelt.* New York: Putnam, 1959.

Stidger, William Leroy. *These Amazing Roosevelts.* New York: Macfadden Book Co., 1938.

Tully, Grace. *F.D.R.: My Boss.* New York: Scribner's, 1949.

Harry S Truman

Daniel, Clifton. *Lords, Ladies and Gentlemen.* New York: Arbor House, 1984.

Daniels, Jonathan. *The Man of Independence.* Philadelphia: J. P. Lippincott, 1950.

Ferrell, Robert H. (Ed.). *Dear Bess: The Letters of Harry to Bess Truman.* New York: W. W. Norton & Co., 1985.

Ferrell, Robert H. (Ed.). *The Autobiography of Harry S Truman.* Boulder, Col.: Colorado Associated University Press, 1980.

Ferrell, Robert H. *Truman: A Centenary Remembrance.* New York: Viking Press, 1984.

McNaughton, Frank, and Walter Hehmeyer. *This Man Truman.* New York: McGraw Hill, 1945.

Poen, Monte. (Ed.). *Strictly Personal and Confidential: The Letters Harry Truman Never Mailed.* Boston: Little Brown, 1982.

Poen, Monte. (Ed.). *Letters Home by Harry Truman.* New York: G. P. Putnam's Sons, 1984.

Steinberg, Alfred. *The Man from Missouri.* New York: G. P. Putnam's Sons, 1962.

Truman, Harry S. *Mr. Citizen.* London: Hutchinson, 1961.

Truman, Harry S. *Memoirs.* Garden City, N.Y.: Doubleday, 1955.

Truman, Margaret. *Bess W. Truman.* New York: Macmillan, 1986.

Truman, Margaret. *Harry S Truman.* New York: Wm. Morrow & Co. Inc., 1973.

Truman, Margaret. *Letters from Father.* New York: Arbor House, 1981.

Truman, Margaret (with Margaret Cousins). *Souvenir.* New York: McGraw-Hill, 1956.

Dwight David Eisenhower

David, Lester, and Irene David. *Ike and Mamie.* New York: G. P. Putnam's Sons, 1981.

Donovan, Robert J. *Eisenhower: The Inside Story.* New York: Harper & Row, 1956.

Eisenhower, Dwight D. *At Ease: Stories I Tell to Friends.* Garden City, N.Y.: Doubleday, 1957.

Eisenhower, John S. D. *Strictly Personal.* New York: Doubleday, 1974.

Eisenhower, Milton Stover. *The President Is Calling.* Garden City, N.Y.: Doubleday, 1974.

Griffith, Robert. (Ed.). *Ike's Letters to a Friend.* Lawrence, Ks.: University Press of Kansas, 1984.

Hatch, Alden. *Red Carpet for Mamie.* New York: Henry Hole & Co., 1954.

Larsen, Arthur. *Eisenhower, The President Nobody Knew.* New York: Charles Scribner's Sons, 1968.

Neal, Steve. *The Eisenhowers.* Lawrence, Ks.: University Press of Kansas, 1984.

Smith, Merriman. *A President's Odyssey.* New York: Harper and Row, 1961.

Summersby, Kay. *Eisenhower Was My Boss.*

Summersby, Kay. *Past Forgetting.* New York: Simon and Schuster, 1976.

John F. Kennedy

Birmingham, Stephen. *Jacqueline Bouvier Kennedy Onassis.* New York: Grosset and Dunlap, 1978.

Bradlee, Benjamin C. *Conversations with Kennedy.* New York: W. W. Norton, 1975.

Buck, Pearl. *The Kennedy Women.* New York: Cowles Book Co., 1970.

Clinch, Nancy Gager. *The Kennedy Neurosis.* New York: Grosset & Dunlap, 1973.

Collier, Peter, and David Horowitz. *The Kennedys, An American Drama.* New York: Summit Books, 1984.

Curtis, Charlotte. *First Lady.* New York: Pyramid, 1962.

Damore, Leo. *The Cape Cod Years of John Fitzgerald Kennedy.* Englewood Cliffs, N.J.: Prentice-Hall, 1967.

Davis, John H. *The Kennedys: Dynasty and Disaster.* New York: McGraw-Hill, 1984.

Dinneen, Joseph F. *The Kennedy Family.* Boston: Little Brown, 1959.

Gallagher, Mary Barelli. *My Life with Jacqueline Kennedy.* New York: McKay, 1968.

Goodwin, Doris Kearns. *The Fitzgeralds and the Kennedys.* New York: Simon and Schuster, 1986.

Kennedy, Rose Fitzgerald. *Times to Remember.* Garden City, N.Y.: Doubleday and Co., 1974.

Lasky, Victor. *J.F.K.: The Man and the Myth.* New York: Macmillan, 1963.

Lincoln, Evelyn. *Kennedy and Johnson.* New York: Holt, Rinehart, and Winston, 1968.

Lincoln, Evelyn. *My Twelve Years with J.F.K.* New York: McKay, 1965.

Martin, Ralph G. *A Hero For Our Time.* New York: Macmillan, 1983.

Thayer, Mary Van Rensselaer. *Jacqueline Kennedy: The White House Years.* Boston: Little Brown and Co., 1971.

Lyndon B. Johnson

Carpenter, Liz. *Ruffles and Flourishes.* Garden City, N. Y.: Doubleday & Co. Inc., 1970.

Harwood, Richard, and Haynes Johnson. *Lyndon.* New York: Praeger, 1973.

Johnson, Lady Bird. *A White House Diary.* New York: Holt, Rinehart, and Winston, 1970.

Johnson, Lyndon B. *The Vantage Point.* New York: Holt, Rinehart, and Winston, 1971.

Johnson, Sam Houston. *My Brother Lyndon.* New York: Cowles Book Co., 1970.

Kearns, Doris. *Lyndon Johnson and the American Dream.* New York: Harper and Row, 1976.

Lincoln, Evelyn. *Kennedy and Johnson.* New York: Holt, Rinehart, and Winston, 1968.

Mooney, Booth. *L.B.J.—An Irreverent Chronicle.* New York: Thomas Y. Crowell, 1976.

Rulon, Philip Reed. *The Compassionate Samaritan: The Life of Lyndon Baines Johnson.* Chicago: Nelson-Hall, 1981.

Sidey, Hugh. *A Very Personal Presidency.* New York: Atheneum, 1968.

Steinberg, Alfred. *Sam Johnson's Boy: A Close-up of the President from Texas.* New York: Macmillan, 1968.

Richard Nixon

Brodie, Fawn McKay. *Richard Nixon, The Shaping of His Character.* New York: Norton, 1981.

David, Lester. *The Lonely Lady of San Clemente.* New York: Thomas Y. Crowell, 1978.

De Toledano, Ralph. *One Man Alone: Richard Nixon.* New York: Funk and Wagnall, 1969.

Edmonson, Madeline, and Alden Duer Cohen. *The Women of Watergate.* New York: Stein and Day, 1975.

Eisenhower, Julie Nixon. *Pat Nixon, The Untold Story.* New York: Simon and Schuster, 1986.

Mankiewicz, Frank. *Perfectly Clear: Nixon from Whittier to Watergate.* New York: Quadrangle, 1973.

Spalding, Henry D. *The Nixon Nobody Knows.* Middle Village, New York: Jonathan David, 1972.

Woodward, Bob, and Carol Bernstein. *The Final Days*. New York: Simon and Schuster, 1976.

Gerald Ford

Ford, Betty (with Chris Chase). *The Times of My Life*. New York: Harper and Row, 1978.
Ford, Betty (with Chris Chase). *A Glad Awakening*. New York: Doubleday, 1987.
Ford, Gerald. *A Time to Heal*. New York: Harper and Row, 1979.
Hersey, John Richard. *The President*. New York: Knopf, 1975.
Reeves, Richard. *A Ford Not a Lincoln*. New York: Harcourt, Brace Jovanovich, 1975.
Ter Horst, Jerald F. *Gerald Ford and the Future of the Presidency*. New York: The Third Press, 1974.
Vestal, Bud. *Jerry Ford Up Close*. New York: Coward, McCann, and Geoghegan, 1974.

Jimmy Carter

Carter, Jimmy. *Why Not the Best?* Nashville, Tenn.: Broadman Press, 1975.
Carter, Jimmy. *Keeping Faith*. New York: Bantam Books, 1982.
Carter, Jimmy, and Rosalynn Carter. *Making the Most of the Rest of Your Life*. New York: Random House, 1986.
Carter, Rosalynn. *First Lady from Plains*. Boston: Houghton Mifflin Co., 1984.
De Mause, Lloyd, and Henry Ebel. (Eds.). *Jimmy Carter and an American Fantasy*. New York: Two Continents (Psychohistory Press), 1977.
Glad, Betty. *Jimmy Carter*. New York: W. W. Norton and Co., 1980.

Ronald Reagan

Adler, Bill (with Norman King). *All in the First Family*. New York: Putnam, 1982.
Adler, Bill. *Ronnie and Nancy*. New York: Crown Publishers, Inc., 1985.
Barrett, Lawrence I. *Ronald Reagan in the White House*. New York: Doubleday, 1983.
Davis, Patti (with Maureen Strange Foster). *Home Front*. New York: Crown Publishers Inc., 1986.
Edwards, Lee. *Ronald Reagan*. Houston, Texas: Nordland Publishing International, Inc., 1981.
Leamer, Lawrence. *Make Believe: The Story of Nancy and Ronald Reagan*. New York: Harper and Row, 1981.

Morella, Joe, and Edward Z. Epstein. *Jane Wyman.* New York: Delacorte Press, 1985.

Quirk, Lawrence J. *Jane Wyman: The Actress and the Woman.* 1985.

Reagan, Nancy (with Bill Libby). *Nancy.* New York: William Morrow, 1980.

Reagan, Ronald (with Richard Hubler). *Where's the Rest of Me?* New York: Duell, Sloan, and Pierce, 1965.

Index

Also by C.M. Castillo

The Pages of Adeena

www.cmcastillowriter.com

To my wife, Kris, whose humor and honest feedback always proves to be just what my story needs, and to my friend and editor, Laurie Shoulter Karall. Your friendship, humor, and wisdom will forever inspire me.

CONTENTS

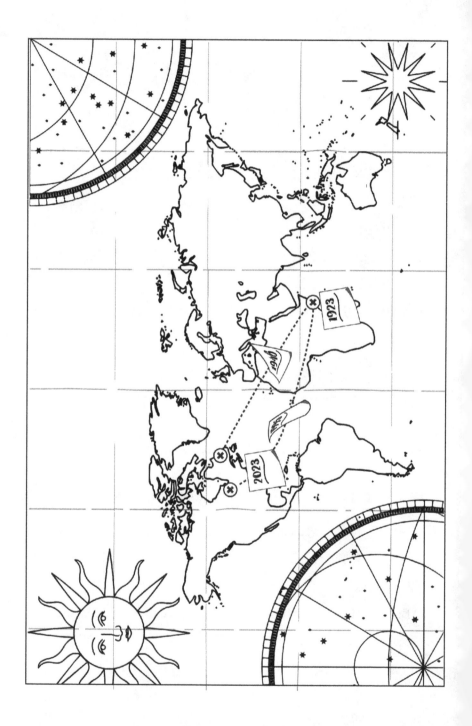

CHAPTER 1

Early Autumn, 2023

The heat, as they drove toward the consignment shop, felt unbearable to Simone. She could feel the sweat drip down her back under her sleeveless linen shirt; cringing slightly she made a mental note to never again wear linen in Florida. Only in Florida, could it be this hot and humid in September. As she reached over to turn up the car's air conditioning to its highest setting, she briefly turned toward Katherine, her future mother-in-law who sat erect and proper in her seat. Seeing pursed lips and tense brows, Simone relented, knowing that Katherine would most likely not approve. She wondered if Katherine ever perspired. At 75, Katherine maintained her striking good looks and was always impeccably dressed; her makeup was perfect, and her hair was never out of place. Next to this formidable woman, Simone, with her unruly auburn hair now up in a messy bun, lanky 5' 9" frame, and unusual golden-brown eyes, always felt awkward. No matter what she wore, or how carefully she applied her makeup or styled her hair, she still sensed that, in Katherine's view, she was merely ordinary.

Today's outing was to be a kind of reacquaintance for her and

Katherine, a new start. Michael, Katherine's only son and Simone's fiancé, had arranged the day trip after Simone had shared with him that she wasn't comfortable around his mother; she had sensed that Katherine did not approve of her. To her surprise and annoyance, Michael had simply laughed, treating her concerns as ridiculous and unfounded. To make matters even more uncomfortable, he suggested to his mother that she and Simone spend an afternoon together while they visited his family in Florida. Now, as they drove to Katherine's favorite consignment boutique for a shopping day, Simone wondered how she would ever get through this morning and the planned lunch afterward. Her stomach churned slightly from nerves and this morning's coffee. She silently thanked her good fortune that she and Michael were only in town for a few more days and would be heading back home to Chicago at the end of the week.

"Simone, would you mind turning down the air dear? I'm chilled." Snapping out of her internal diatribe, Simone quickly gave Katherine her best professional smile and obliged. "You know dear, I do appreciate you driving this morning," said Katherine, sounding slightly annoyed. "Your little economy vehicle is so much easier to maneuver through traffic than my Mercedes. Although why you and Michael chose to drive to Florida in this Lilliputian putt-putt rather than fly is beyond me." Turning to look at Katherine, Simone opened her mouth, but could not come up with a retort that sounded as smooth and effortless as Katherine's blatant dig about her compact hybrid and their decision to drive. So, instead of attempting to explain to Katherine that they drove simply for the joy of road tripping, she surrendered to the fact that Katherine, once again, had the last word.

They had been in the consignment shop for less than ten minutes when Simone concluded that The Purple Alligator was not a store she would ever wish to set foot in again. She saw it as the true definition of bourgeois Florida. Looking around at the well-displayed cocktail dresses, tennis outfits, scarves, and designer bags, Simone knew she would not be caught dead in any of these outfits. For one thing, she couldn't afford them. She simply could not believe the amount of money they were asking for consignment clothes! Glancing over the racks, she spotted Katherine in deep conversation with another woman. Realizing she must appear entirely too bored to Katherine, who periodically glanced her way, she made an effort to check out a few dresses to appear more interested. Walking over to a particularly hideous orange cocktail dress, she casually glanced at the price tag. "What the hell?!" Realizing she had spoken aloud, she quickly turned to see if Katherine had heard her shocked outburst. Luckily, her future mother-in-law was still deep in conversation. Grabbing the dress, she waved to Katherine and pointed to the dressing room. Katherine smiled, dismissed her with a flip of her manicured hand, and turned back to her conversation.

Escaping into the small dressing room, she closed the privacy curtain and sat on the stool. She hated being here with Katherine. The woman frayed her nerves. She knew the way she was feeling was partially her own insecurity around Michael's mother but dammit, she simply could not warm up to her. She was always able to read people well and she knew that Katherine only tolerated her. Reaching into her pocket, she pulled out her cell phone and punched in her best friend's number. "Answer, for fuck sakes, answer!" she whispered frantically into her cell.

"Simone? Why are you calling me? I thought you were on a shopping adventure with the Wicked Witch of South Florida?"

"Oh, real funny woman. Maggie, you are not going to believe this! Right now, I'm hiding out in the changing room of a crusty, uppity consignment shop trying to avoid Katherine's scrutiny. To make matters worse I am about to try on the most hideous cocktail dress I've ever seen, and it cost $500! It's used for Christ's sake!"

Laughing into the phone, Maggie, Simone's closest friend since the third grade, shook her head at her friend's frantic voice. When Simone finally took a breath, Maggie spoke soothingly to her friend. "Simone, hon, listen to me. Before you and Michael drove down to Florida, you promised yourself that you would do your best to get to know his mother. This week is supposed to be your bonding time with her. You know how close they are."

Exasperated and beginning to sweat in the small changing room, Simone took a deep breath. "Yes, I know…I know what the plan was Mags, but this woman's presence reduces me to a ten-year-old child. I swear I may start crying the next time she says something nasty to me." Suddenly noticing the sweat from her palms was making the dress damp, she gasped. "Oh, fuck Maggie, I'm sweating on this ugly $500 dress. I've got to go. I'll call you later." Simone clicked off her cell and did her best to smooth out the wrinkles created by her perspiring fingers. "I frigging cannot believe this! Christ!" she whispered. "Maybe if I hang it back up immediately, they won't notice." Leaving the changing room, she decided she needed to get out of The Purple Alligator as quickly as possible; she felt like a bull in a china shop. She did not want to handle another item for fear of somehow damaging it.

Seeing Katherine browsing through the racks of dresses, Simone straightened her shoulders and quietly cleared her throat. As gracefully as possible, she walked over to where Katherine stood. "Katherine, if you don't mind, I think I will wait for you outside. I noticed there are some small tables on the plaza. Please don't rush; take your time shopping. I'll just grab a coffee."

Looking up at the taller Simone as if she were a stranger asking for a hand-out, Katherine let out an exasperated sigh. "Well, yes dear," Katherine droned, "if you must." Now squinting at Simone, Katherine appeared contemplative. "I thought you'd enjoy the shop, but clearly, the prices are a bit out of your range. So, yes dear, I will meet you outside at the café once I've finished my shopping."

Cringing slightly, Simone did her best to appear unaffected by Katherine's remark. "Please take your time, Katherine, I'm not in a hurry." Giving Simone a curt nod, Katherine turned without another word to continue her browsing.

Leaving the shop, Simone felt her nerves immediately calm. She breathed in deeply, exhaled, and made her way to the plaza. "That woman makes me want to drink, but I'll settle for coffee," she said, walking the short distance to the coffee shop. After purchasing her iced latte, she spotted an empty table outside in the shade, which was protected from the sun by a colorful umbrella. "Perfect," she said. Settling in with her drink and cell phone, she dug into her bag to pull out her day planner. Smiling to herself, she knew she was considered old school by her colleagues. As a fundraiser for a non-profit healthcare organization specializing in helping low-income communities, she juggled many clients and needed the hands-on attention to detail and easy access that a day planner added. She was meticulous about every event, meeting, and call. Most of her colleagues did not use a day planner any longer; they had all their appointments and notes logged into their smartphones. Simone however, loved writing her notes longhand, noting details such as what kind of coffee clients preferred for their events, how they wanted their meetings set up, which caterers to hire, all the things that helped her clients know she was there for them 100 percent. Because of her attention to the smallest details, she was one of the top fundraisers in the business, and several new clients had asked for her by name based on the feedback from other enthusiastic philanthropists. She knew she owed her attention to detail and expertise to her brilliant mentors who had taught her that to be successful, one must care, really care, about the goals that their clients strived to achieve. She did care, and she told herself that she'd always remember that lesson. Smiling, she jotted down some notes specific to her next fundraising project, an infant vaccination awareness initiative geared to young single mothers in Chicago's low-income neighborhoods. Assuring herself that all details were in place for the next week's client meeting, she stretched out her legs and slowly drank her coffee.

Without the scrutiny of Katherine to fray her nerves, she relaxed and enjoyed the solitude, yet her mind soon moved to thoughts of the next day's dinner at Michael's parents' estate, and an introduction to his extended family. Closing her eyes, she took a deep breath and a sudden pang of sadness and melancholy enfolded her. It was a now-familiar feeling, nagging at her and becoming a constant over the past few months. Bowing her head, she allowed herself to analyze these feelings. Sitting in the heat of the Florida sun, she could not stop herself from believing that, with her engagement to Michael, she was somehow compromising the life she has always believed she was destined to live. Thinking back, she recalled that fateful day when she was twelve, looking up at the fluffy white clouds in the bluest of skies, and eating ice cream on the back stairs of her family's home. She had suddenly known that she had a special providence; she knew her destiny. In her certainty, she had looked to the sky and smiled; it was as if a kiss from the universe had touched her cheek. Her assuredness of her future had led her to her desire to help people, to a career in nonprofits, and to the belief that there was someone special with whom she would spend her life, her soul mate. What had happened to that certainty for her future?

Hearing a loud noise, Simone turned toward a sight that made her laugh in surprise. Standing in front of a small shop window, with the name Metamorphosis in bright white script elegantly displayed above the shop door, was a little man dressed as an elf. He wore a dark green jacket with silver buttons and matching hat, and even wore opaque green tights and black silver-buckled patent leather shoes. Now, struggling with a large planter, he was huffing and puffing so loudly that Simone, fearing he'd have a heart attack, felt compelled to help him. Jumping up, she threw her planner in her bag and quickly made her way over to the little man. "Excuse me, would you like a hand with that? It looks a bit heavy." Simone asked, already helping the little man by steadying the planter that appeared in danger of tipping over.

Looking up at Simone, the little man smiled broadly. "Oh! Yes, yes, please. Thank you! I must place these planters in front of the shop. Today is our grand opening, and I am already running late in preparing." Simone liked this strange little man immediately. His broad dimpled smile was genuine, and his eyes were kind and the most unnatural color green, like an ocean. With her help, they quickly moved one additional planter and placed it in front of the small shop.

Turning to the little man, she asked. "Is there anything else I can help you with?"

Looking around as if he forgot something, the little man placed his hand on his chin, appeared reflective, and then smiled. "No, no, I think that's all I need. But will you come in and see our shop? It's quite nice." Charmed by his easy manner, Simone smiled broadly and nodded as he led her inside.

Feeling a cool breeze as soon as she walked through the door, Simone smiled; it felt like a spring day inside and she breathed in the scent of fresh-cut flowers. She scanned the shop, surprised at how spacious it appeared, and how beautifully each item was displayed. Earrings, necklaces, and bracelets made of jade, amber, silver, and other metals were positioned on a canvas to showcase their intricate details. Delicate china vases in cobalt blues and deep greens were bursting with colorful lilies and irises. There were portraits in exquisite frames and an assortment of music boxes that played small snippets of baroque music, unbelievably, in sync with each other. In awe of the unusual beauty of the shop, Simone wandered slowly through the seemingly endless array of objects. Browsing the racks of clothing, she leaned over to look more closely at a woman's bomber jacket hanging on an ornate coat rack. It was a soft brown leather and had a winged insignia stitched on the shoulder. Taking the jacket from the rack, she held it up, admiring its appearance. Seeing the monogram *A.M.E.* stitched on the breast of the jacket pocket, her eyes widened in amazement. "What in the world?" she blurted out. Hearing the little man humming, she turned to see him walking toward her. "Excuse me," she said, a bit unbelievingly. "This couldn't possibly be Amelia Earhart's jacket, could it? Because that would be, well, remarkable."

Placing his hand on his chin as he had done earlier, he seemed to be thinking. Finally, looking up at Simone, he smiled. "It is a very smart jacket, is it not? Please, why don't you try it on? It seems to be your size, and I'm sure Amelia won't mind a bit," he said with a wink. Smiling, Simone slipped the jacket on and, as she thought it might, it fit perfectly. Walking over to a decorative floor-length mirror, she gasped at her reflection. Of course, it was her, however her normally auburn shoulder-length hair seemed brighter and fuller. Her bright golden-brown eyes sparkled, and she stood taller, more erect, as if she were beaming with a new confidence. She couldn't pull herself away from her reflection. "It definitely suits you," said the little man, pulling her out of her wonderment.

"Would you like to purchase it? As today is the grand opening, everything is on sale. I can sell it to you for, let's say, \$20."

Simone, returning from her complete surprise at how this jacket made her feel, turned to look at the little man in astonishment. "\$20? Did you say \$20? Are you serious? For this amazing jacket that couldn't possibly have belonged to Amelia Earhart, you want to sell it to me for \$20?"

Helping Simone remove the jacket, the little man hummed. "Why yes, no one else could do this jacket justice but you, my dear, other than Amelia, of course," he said with a smile. "Now come and look at a few more items I think you might be interested in before we ring you up." Following the little man, Simone realized that she didn't know his name.

"Excuse me, I'm Simone. Simone Adan." She smiled. "May I ask, what is your name?"

"Oh! Forgive me, my dear. I am Henry, at your service." Bowing slightly, he reached for Simone's hand, smiled, and gently shook it. "We have quite the collection of historical items toward the front, Simone." Smiling, he waved for her to follow as he started to walk toward the front of the shop. Stopping in front of an array of colorful scarves and hats, he bowed again. "I'll leave you to browse at your leisure. Just come see me if there is anything you fancy."

Simone watched in amazement as he walked toward a tall desk and hopped up onto a swivel stool. Staring, she was enthralled by the unusual sight of the little man in the elf suit holding a quill pen and humming as he twirled in his seat and concentrated on his work. Shaking her head, she looked at her watch. She had only been in the shop for fifteen minutes. Strange, it felt as if she had been there at least an hour. Regardless of the time, she knew she needed to get back to The Purple Alligator to meet Katherine or

17

there would be hell to pay if she kept her waiting. Deciding to purchase the jacket and quickly leave, she made her way toward what she assumed was the sales counter when she noticed a large steamer trunk in the corner near a window. It was perfect, she thought, to use for a coffee table. She had been half-heartedly looking for the right piece for her condo's living room for months, but nothing seemed right. She knew that this trunk would fit perfectly. It was in excellent condition too. Crouching down, she looked closely at the trunk, taking in its details. It was a deep dark yellow, subtle and not bright. It had worn dark brown leather straps with bright silver buckles. There were a few stickers plastered to it from Madrid, Peking, Buenos Aires, and Africa. Simone could picture it being loaded onto a large steamer ship. She wondered if the stickers were authentic. Looking closer, she noted faint stamp marks. "Holy shit," she whispered, "These *are* real!" She knew then, at that moment, that she had to have it; this trunk would be hers. Turning quickly, she searched out Henry. "Henry! Henry are you here?"

As if summoned by the queen, Henry appeared. "Yes, Simone, how may I be of assistance?"

Taken by surprise at his instantaneous appearance, Simone cleared her throat and smiled. "I think I may want to buy this trunk. However, I have a small compact car…"

"Oh! Not a problem, we ship all over the world. We can certainly ship this purchase to you."

Simone walked over to the trunk and reached out her hand to gently caress the leather straps. "I love this trunk." Attempting to lift it by its handle, Simone grunted at the unexpected weight. "Henry, can you please open it? There's something inside."

Looking questioningly at Simone, Henry sighed. "Oh, no, I cannot unlock it. You must purchase it as is; those are the rules." Looking curiously at Henry, but not questioning his remark,

Simone simply nodded. A few minutes later Simone had made arrangements with Henry to have the trunk shipped to her Chicago address. Saying goodbye to the little man, Simone stepped out of the shop. The sun shone brightly, and the heat felt unbearable on her skin. Turning, she was relieved to see that Katherine had just stepped out of The Purple Alligator. Thank goodness, it was perfect timing.

*   *   *

The trendy upscale bistro with its hip music and extravagant prices was out of Simone's comfort zone but she knew that Katherine was making a statement. A statement that said, "This is my life and it's Michael's life too. Can you handle it?" The servers knew her by name and waited on her as if she were royalty. Even the owner came by to greet her. Once lunch was served, no fewer than five people that Katherine knew had come over to the table to say hello. Simone was introduced by name, not as Michael's fiancée, a slight that Simone knew was meant to hurt her. "Tell me, dear, how is your job coming along? Michael tells me you work for a nonprofit charity. Honestly, that can't pay much. I understand you have an advanced degree. I have contacts in Chicago who can help you secure a position making more money than you could ever make at a nonprofit."

Looking up at Kathrine between bites of her shrimp scampi, Simone carefully formulated her reply. Katherine was obviously not a fan of Simone, but she was still Michael's mother and Simone knew she needed to be respectful. "Thank you, Katherine, I do appreciate the offer. However, I am quite happy with the organization I work for; they are gaining ground with their efforts to assist low-income families in the Chicago area. We have been very successful over the past twenty-four months, and our outlook for 2024 looks promising."

Putting down her fork, Katherine looked at Simone for a moment, then lifted her glass of wine to her lips and took a drink. Simone waited. "A word of advice dear," Katherine said, draining her glass and then snapping her fingers to get the attention of the server, whom she asked to bring another wine. "Michael will take over the Florida dealerships. We have groomed him from an early age. He will also be relocating from that Midwest ghetto you both currently live in, back to Florida. You'd best think about that before you get too cozy with your current career choice." Bending close to Simone, Katherine practically seethed. "I'll be damned if I'll allow my son to stay in that crime-plagued city that he currently calls home."

Stunned at Katherine's outburst, Simone was at a loss for words. Who was this woman? She was like a lioness protecting her cub but protecting him from what? Just as she was about to counter Katherine, their server arrived to check on them. Looking at him with an impossibly serene smile, Katherine asked for the bill and then promptly stood and walked off to powder her nose, leaving Simone with no choice but to pay for their meal.

CHAPTER 2

U nlocking the door to her condo, Simone stepped in, breathed out a long sigh, and stretched, feeling a satisfying pop in her lower back as the tension she had been experiencing was released. She was exhausted, physically and mentally, from both the long laborious drive back to Chicago and the events of the past week. Walking into her living room, she threw her purse on the couch and turned to make her way to her bedroom, trailing her suitcase behind her. Lifting it onto the bed, she began to unpack as her thoughts moved to the disaster the past week had been. She should still be in Florida. Instead, she and Michael weren't speaking, and she was certain that Katherine now held a much more negative opinion of her than she previously had. She looked down at the jumble of clothes. Exasperated, she decided to let it all go for now. All she wanted at that moment was to open a bottle of her favorite wine, sit back and not think.

Abandoning her unpacking, she made her way to her kitchen and reached for a Merlot. Uncorking the wine gave her a sense of calm. Being home alone was what she needed at this moment. She poured the wine and sipped it slowly. Taking in the tart fruity taste, she leaned against the kitchen island thinking about the disaster that she knew would end her engagement.

She and Michael had been in Florida for less than two days when things had begun to unravel. Katherine had been pushing her buttons since she had arrived. First there was the disastrous shopping day and lunch, and then the dinner party fiasco. Simone had known that Katherine had reservations regarding her and Michael's engagement, however, until recently, she had no clue of the depth of his mother's desire to see an end to their relationship.

To Katherine's utter disappointment, Michael had not chosen a woman of their own proud Cuban heritage. Instead, he chose a half-Mexican, half-Spanish American as his fiancée. The fact that Simone held two advanced degrees and was a top performer in her field offered no esteem in Katherine's view.

They were attending a dinner party at Michael's parents' home. Katherine had already had a few glasses of champagne before she and Michael arrived. Simone sensed an underlying burn in Katherine as she walked over to greet her. It had made her extremely uncomfortable, and she found herself on guard. As soon as Michael left her side to speak with his father, Katherine wasted no time sharing her true feelings.

"I'm sorry, Simone, didn't Michael explain that this evening's dinner party was cocktail attire?" Katherine wasn't the least bit sorry, and her bored and slightly drunken gaze oozed her disapproval of Simone's outfit, a pale-yellow cotton sleeveless dress, and flat tan sandals. Caught by surprise by Katherine's direct hit, Simone was temporarily at a loss for words. "Really, Simone, must you always be so average?" Turning, Katherine waved to a few newly arrived guests and walked off.

Simone watched her glide through the small group as if she were the fricking Queen of Sheba. Trying to wrap her brain around the reasons Katherine disliked her so much, she didn't notice when